PLENILUNE

PLENILUNE

JENNIFER FREITAG

Cover Design: Carlos Quevedo
Cover Stock: Katie Litchfield and Cindy Grundsten
Layout: Penoaks Publishing, http://penoaks.com

Contents

I | THE TRAIN CARRIAGE

Margaret Coventry stood on the station platform at Leeds with a rain-speckled umbrella folded in one hand and her carpetbag in the other. Her guts shook inside their panels of corseted bombazine, but whether they shook out of fear or anger she did not know. She hoped it was anger. Anger, like martial music, would stand her in good stead for the task which stretched out complicated and distasteful before her.

The train was empty. The platform, which had been bare but for the dull tramp of the inspector's boots and the noiselessly skirling puddles of rain that the wind kicked up, shook beneath Margaret's feet as people strode up and down, sorting themselves out and calling up their trunks from the baggage carriages. Her own luggage would be going into just such a car soon. She watched the station hands wheeling carts of trunks toward the rear cars...

"Want a paper, miss?"

She flinched with surprise and came round, starched skirts hissing angrily, to find a boy standing at her elbow. He was mouse-haired and old-eyed, and he regarded her kindly but frankly from beneath his uncut mane.

"I beg your pardon?" She looked down at the stack of papers he held under one elbow and the flagship paper he produced in one half-outstretched hand. Something vivid was printed on the front page, something unutterably dull about India.

He gave the paper a coaxing shake. "Would you like a paper?" The edges of his English sharpened for her benefit. "It will keep you company in the coach. There could be another shooting!" he added helpfully.

She frowned, her right heel instinctively sliding backward to break herself from contact with him. "No, I'm quite all right, thank you," she insisted, declining to point out that another assassination attempt on the queen would most certainly have pushed the news of India beneath the fold. She broke away from the boy while he favoured her with an expressive shrug.

Hefting umbrella and carpetbag, she crossed the platform like one walking off the side of a mutinous galley, chin high and lips set squarely, and came briskly down the line to an empty first-class carriage. There was no one close enough to see she was getting aboard, and she did not desire the help at present. Under her own power she orchestrated her belongings under her arms, clicked the door latch open, and, with a little jump and a breathless second or two of indecision with physics, got her long limbs up into the car.

The wooden door swung shut after her under its own weight. A kind of mausoleum gloom clapped over the compartment, sepia and greyed with the pine panelling and the rainy light of the October afternoon. She settled into the forward-facing bench, placing her bag beside her and dropping her damp umbrella on the floorboards. It was quiet, warm, scented softly with someone's perfume and the lingering tendrils of pipe-smoke from earlier passengers, and something knotted beneath her corsets unwound a little.

The noise from the engine came back to her, humming, salamander-voiced; the carriage vibrated almost imperceptibly beneath her palms.

Soon, Margaret considered, *it will all be behind me.* She turned her head and was joined by her reflection in the glass pane of the car. For a moment she regarded it, pale and long, with high cheekbones and eyes that were plunged several shades beneath their ordinary brown colour by the wallwork of the station in the background. She was young, too young to begin resembling her mother, and yet in that muted image she saw the perverse outlines of her mother's features, grim and angry, glaring back at her. An unpleasant thought stung Margaret—how alike they must have looked in those last moments before she had left home!

She remembered slamming the lid of her last trunk and jerking at its latch. She had been angry—furious in that swift, hot, smothering sort of anger that she could possess.

"I'm sorry, *Mother*." She had snapped up her bonnet and whirled, thrusting it over her coiffure and yanking at the ribbons. The woman had stood like brickwork in the doorway of her bedroom, mirroring Margaret's anger. In the teeth of her mother's squalling derision Margaret had launched back acidly, "I'm sorry that we can't all be beautiful. I'm sorry that we can't all be foreign beauties spirited off by handsome young men."

Margaret glanced down at the throat of her reflection. She had done damage to her ribbons in her thoughtless tying of the bow. With pursed lips she reached up and began readjusting the knot.

"*I'm sorry that I wasn't a boy so I could take care of this mess. But you can go on being disappointed, Mother. I don't care. You can wish I were pretty like Firethorne, and while you're at it you can be happy I wasn't loose enough to let myself be run away with and dishonour the whole family in the process!*"

And the real triumph, Margaret considered, looking back on the incident, was that her mother had not flinched as the acid was hurled into her face. There had been no regrets, no wounds inflicted to sour the memory of their last battle. She hoped it would be their last. Wherever she went, Margaret knew that face in her reflection would haunt her—judging, weighing, strangely hating. With a calm resignation Margaret knew very clearly that even if she could secure a good attachment with a man of her distant relations, as she was setting out to do, her mother would still despise her. She only wished she knew why.

Having adjusted the ribbons of her bonnet, Margaret sat back into the bench with the feeling of a better ordered mind. Out from the immediate scenery of familial strife and dissension rose the cold truth of her future. The sheer mileage which lay between her and her relatives in Naples yawned vast and cold before her, and even when she arrived, trusting that the Italian winter would be kinder than her fierce Cumbria, she must coax and finagle her way into the heart of an eligible male who would help counteract the disgrace of her cousin's elopement.

The distance was necessary. Her relatives would not have heard of Firethorne's disappearance, and Margaret's own reputation would remain untainted...

She glanced back out the window, squinting to see through her own reflection to the platform beyond.

A man had accosted the mouse-haired boy with the papers. Idly Margaret watched them converse, disproportionately sized as one towered over the other. The man carried no umbrella, and though he was sombrely dressed in black, his clothing appeared unusual. Margaret scooted toward the window and watched as the man took a paper from the boy without any money seeming to pass between them. Her reflection frowned...then started when she realized the man was coming at a long-legged, purposeful walk toward her carriage. She quickly faced forward again and rejoined her carpetbag, rearranging her skirts and wishing other passengers had joined her car. If she had been alone, at least for a leg or two of the trip, it would have been pleasant. If other female passengers could but climb aboard with her and diminish the awkwardness of her pending company—

The door latch sounded loud in the little compartment, and the carriage rocked violently as the man ducked his head and climbed up into the interior. Water gushed from his clothing as he moved, pouring over the wooden floor. With a soundless cry Margaret instinctively lifted her boots up onto their toes to avoid the deluge. In perverse contrast, the paper crackled between them, crisp and dry: the bold headlines regarding India flashed their secret mockery at Margaret as she looked up covertly from beneath the rim of her bonnet.

The man sat down on the rearward bench, giving a soft imperative sniff from the hawkish nose beneath the brim of his Aylesbury; he tipped the thing forward as he unfolded his paper and a runnel of water shot off the brim into his lap, leaving the paper untouched. Margaret stared, despite herself, but the man did not seem to notice the puddle he had dropped onto his trousers.

An uncomfortable silence fell over the carriage. With the unquestioned instinct of a small animal, Margaret sat quite still, watching the man out of the corner of her eye for any sign of movement. The muffled rumble of feet on the platform and the scarlet chuffing of the engine droned in the background, but within the compartment the silence was as crisp and dry as the paper.

The man's mouth twitched, as if humoured. Margaret's senses jumped to the alert: *A young jaw-line: angular, but young. I would feel better if he were an older man.*

A whistle screamed ahead. Beneath Margaret's rigid body she felt the wheels grind, the engine throw momentum into the whole body of the train, and in a moment she was instinctively slamming her hand round on the front of her carpetbag to keep it from hurling headfirst off the carriage seat and onto the wet floor. The lethargic chunking of the train punctuated the air and the light began to grow, silvered and cold, as the engine slid out from under the station's overhang into the bleak elements.

The movement seemed to unlock something. The man turned over a page in the paper—coincidentally sending a new puddle of water oozing from the tails of his outlandish jacket—and with that same sniff he remarked lazily,

"It is very rude to stare, you know."

Margaret coloured slightly. "Good afternoon," she returned stiffly. She could think of no apology to make for her fascination with his persistent dampness, nor did she dare mention, now that it was too late to change cars, how uncomfortable she felt in his singular presence.

He lifted the paper as if to block out the pale glare coming in the window, and the movement allowed her a look at his profile. It was as angular as his nose and jaw-line had suggested, with a pair of almost colourless blue eyes so sharp and aware that the sleepy droop of his lids could not stop a shudder from running through her body.

"Good afternoon," he purred. Then, stirring swiftly, he snapped the folds of the paper shut and let it fall precipitately out of his hand onto the bench beside him; the puddle seeped through it and spread like the mark of a disease. His head was up, regarding her with those uncanny silver eyes, and she knew that she could no longer escape his notice. "Rupert. Rupert de la Mare. I beg your pardon," he added. His voice was as sleepy as his lids, but not deceived by either façade. "The news is very interesting."

At a sweeping glance, with his voice still tenderly brushing back the tendrils of hair from her ears, she took him for a foreigner. His dress she could not place, and he spoke English as if he were master of it, and not it master of him.

"Margaret Coventry. How do you do...?" She kept her hands in her lap and tried to keep the defensiveness out of her voice. "And—indeed, is it?" Her eye fell on the paper and her blood chilled. "I had not read anything today."

It would not do to risk provoking him by admitting that she took no interest in the affairs of state, enormous and perplexing as their entanglements became, no more than she took interest in the equally treacherous waters of ladies' societies and social interaction.

He looked down critically at the paper, the corner of his mouth still smiling faintly. It was a cruel kind of look. "You have a very young queen, I mind," he said. "I wonder if you have not had better queens in the past."

Margaret coloured again with formless outrage, but before she could say anything reprehensible, Rupert de la Mare was looking at her again, something soft and something cutting in his face.

"You yourself might be a better queen."

Before she could stop herself, panicked humour and cumulative stress overtook her, and she broke out in a sharp, ringing laugh over some swift, bizarrely distorted image of herself as Her Majesty—Her Majesty Queen Margaret! "Perhaps," she heard her own voice saying—coming, it seemed to her, from a long way off and a little too highly pitched—"perhaps if I were Danish, but I would have to be—*oh!*"

She gave a great leap as the man, without warning, sprang up from his bench and clapped a hand over her mouth. Mingled rage and panic surged through her veins, but he had one hand firmly on her mouth, the other on her shoulder with the power of a solid bar of iron, and his feet seemed to be pinning down the voluminous hem of her skirt so that she could not worm out from under him.

The Aylesbury had come off. The face above her was sharp and bare like a sabre, and seemed to hover coldly against her skin.

She could feel her pulse banging in the hollow of her shoulder beneath his grip.

Her nostrils flared: she drew no air. A smothered whimper of terror beat like a dying bird in her throat.

"No need for that, darling."

He was *laughing* at her. The realization made her heart pound a little faster, but her anger was extinguishing: she did not have enough air to fuel it.

One hand moved to her throat. She could still feel the barred pressure of his fingers on her mouth but knew, dimly, in the airless chambers of her brain, that he had uncovered her mouth but that she could not drag it open to take a breath. He slipped his other arm round her body and lifted her, with her starched skirts and her hand-bag trailing from her wrist, off the wooden bench.

The carriage rocked steadily to its own movement beneath them.

What are you doing to me! Where are you taking me! Who do you think you are? Let me go!

She imagined that she was resisting, as one tries to resist in a dream, but her limbs lifted with his arms and her head fell useless upon his black, damp shoulder. The last ordinary English image she had before she squeezed her eyes shut was her carpetbag, jigging slightly to the train's rhythm, warm and prosaic on the wooden bench...

"When you are ready," said the gentleman—and did not seem to be speaking to her.

In the next instant there was a sensation of things rushing over her, things like feathers and thin bits of chicken-skin that made her own skin crawl. The air was ripped from around her, punching her ears with the thunder of a sudden vacuum. If she had her eyes open, she could not tell. The darkness around her was profound and hollow and lifeless. Was the man there too? She tried to move her body against the nauseating sensation which lifted her stomach from her middle into her throat. As one in a dream she saw without vision: black feathers, darkness, teeth, a sense of longing after blood—

Then mercifully the darkness snapped away into shreds and she saw a confused, faded image of sunlight and something like green lawn. Naples...?

She fainted.

II | THE ENGLISHWOMAN

When Margaret awoke, her first instinct was to call for Amy to help her dress. Then she remembered that she was on her way to Newhaven to embark for Naples, and that she had left her maidservant in Aylesward—but that that was all wrong too. Images of a man's beautiful, angular face returned, images of blue eyes so pale they were almost silver, images of a nightmare and a sensation of being strangled without hands. As though surfacing out of a pond of molasses, Margaret forced herself out of bed.

She was in a wide suite that was plunged into shadow. The curtains were pulled across the windows, but she saw enough light peeking around the edges to surmise that it was full daylight outside. If she listened carefully through the ringing in her ears, she could hear birdsong. The bed she occupied was spacious, luxurious; the room was no less opulent. Everything purred in a kind of half-sleeping splendour around her. Her hand gripped the blanket and touched silk. Her cheek remembered the press of velvet pillows.

"Where am I?" she asked aloud, slipping off the side of the bed. Then, just to hear the sound of her voice, "*Where am I?*" She padded on bare feet to the window and pulled a curtain back a fraction.

She was looking down on the vine-twisted roof of a garden walk, a roof full of huge green leaves and massive clusters of rich red grapes. On either hand spread lawns and walkways, gardens and paddocks, swallowed up in the distance by a wood. She shivered and felt ill. How long had she been asleep? Where had the monster taken her? Where, she wondered, glancing at the door behind her, was the monster now? She touched the foreign nightgown that draped from her shoulders and wished for something more substantial. With another look out the window she saw the sun was shining brilliantly, more brilliantly than she could ever remember it shining before. The air outside looked crisper and cleaner than any air she could remember breathing. The colours, too, were sharper and deeper.

She made the mistake of glancing upward to the colourless sky, and there she had her greatest shock. Hanging high above the horizon, huge and colourful, the only colourful thing in that empty sky, was the earth.

With a despairing cry Margaret crumpled, kneeling on the floor, her fingers digging into the casement of the window as she stared unblinkingly at that blue-and-white disk in the sky. How could it—how *dare* it! As if to wrench it back under her feet she shook the casement, rattling the pane in its track. But it did no good, and for a long while Margaret sat on the cool floor, trying to regain her breath, forcing herself to gaze unwaveringly at the hideous thing above her. She stared like a cat, and it stared back, and slowly, slowly, her heart began to beat its normal tune.

"Rather beautiful, isn't it?"

The staring contest broken, she looked round to find the monster from her dream in the doorway, his rich black tunic and trousers pushing the limits of outlandishness, as though Hamlet had somehow stepped off his stage into her life. He carried a pair of hawking gloves in one hand.

"Be a gentleman," said Margaret shakily, "and go away."

He strode into the room. "Let's have none of this bashfulness, my dear."

Gathering herself up, she ground out, "I am in my nightgown!" and she swung backhanded at his shins.

In a single fluid gesture he was down on one knee, her arm firmly in his iron grasp, her eye fixed in his. His hand hurt like claws—and it burned. "I know," he said softly. Once again there was that dangerous laughter in his eye which she knew she could not fight. She relaxed and he let her go.

He got back to his feet and gazed out the window, eyes narrowed against the glare. With her arm tucked up to her chest Margaret pulled herself together, sitting with her back ramrod straight, her eyes averted.

"You looked up," he said presently. "Did you look out at the garden? They are very beautiful, my gardens. You will like them."

I shan't, she thought venomously.

He turned. "What was that?"

She sniffed. "I said, I shan't."

"Of course not." He resumed his perusal of the gardens from the window. "Not yet, but presently you will. You do not yet know what my grounds look like, nor my power, nor my offer."

Her gut spasmed with the same broken, panicked laugh. "I'm sorry, was there an offer?"

"No," he purred thoughtfully. "No, of course not. I find that if you want a woman, leaving the choice up to her doesn't prove satisfactory."

"That is very efficient of you, I'm sure."

His voice was flat. "I should have known not to pick an Englishwoman." He bent down and forced his hand under her chin, drawing it up. "I'll be back, my sweet. Feel free to explore your new realm." And he planted a stinging kiss on her lips before she could wrench back out of his grasp. With an angry gasp, head reeling, she fell against the wall and sat there in a furious daze, listening to the echo of the shut door and the receding sound of his boots.

Presently, with some effort, Margaret pushed off the wall and used it to support herself as she got to her feet. Her nightgown was far too thin for comfort and she wanted a heavier dress. There was no Amy. Who did one call for in a place like this? She hesitated, then decided with defiance that she would dress herself, God help her, just to spite the horrid man.

An adjoining room was a bath and closet, both very spacious and lavishly outfitted. Perversely, Margaret chose a black gown, though it made her skin look deathly pale. A mourning dress was certainly the most applicable attire she could wear at such a time as this. She washed her face and tended to her thick, unruly brown hair, and with her teeth gritted and her stomach clenched, wrestled bodily into the dress. It was a fight, but at last she stood before the mirror with hot cheeks and a gown that made her look ghastly, and she could honestly say that she was satisfied.

She would have stayed in the room, too, to spite de la Mare further, but hunger drove her at last out of her suite on the wide upper hallway. She looked over the railing at the atrium a story below. There was a pool and a fountain, tinkling softly away to themselves, skirted by plants and beds of rose quartz and the figures of the servants that were going to and fro. With a rush of black taffeta Margaret backed away from the rail, careful to keep out of sight as she tiptoed down the hallway toward the stairs. If she took the main stairs and kept in the shadows—de la Mare seemed to be lavish with his shadows—there was a good chance the servants, using the servants' passageways and stairs, would overlook her. She glided along easily, quiet but for the sound of her skirts and the occasional rumble of her belly. She was not sure how she was supposed to get any food if she was bent on avoiding the servants, but she would rather try her luck alone first and give in to unwanted company later when she had run out of options.

The stairs took her down, not to the atrium, but to a round vaulted entryway. Through the fractalled front windows she could see twisted images of the landscape outside, green and white and dark farther off; but she did not look long, for the threat of the looming earth in the sky still murmured on the periphery of her consciousness. Glancing several ways to be sure she was alone, she took a doorway past the atrium, pushed between two rich hangings that served as doors, and slid into a dim-lit dining room. The room was built for many, sporting a long, beautiful table of polished wood and numerous chairs of matching make with feet of lions' paws and padding of striped gold and green. She moved through, past the head of the table and the biggest, grandest chair which must have been de la Mare's, past the sideboard and the china cabinet full of the most glorious-looking drinks and chinaware, and on through a low wooden door at the other end of the room.

Skulking through this doorway, feeling at once like a child on holiday and a prisoner trying to escape, she found herself in a narrow hallway of white with countless doors on either hand. Sound suddenly broke over her: the rattle of pots, the bang of pans, the clatter of silverware and dishes stacked on dishes. Hot scents of cooking and washing bloomed in her nose. With a start of panic Margaret realized she had made the wrong turn and plunged herself into the kitchen hallway. There was nowhere to hide: she was black against the clean white tile surfaces around her. Pure stubbornness forbade her from going back, so when she heard the opening creak of a door down the hall she impulsively seized the handle of a door by her elbow and pushed it open, lunging through and hoping to find it empty.

With a little gasp she pushed the door shut with infinite care and leaned against it, listening to the footsteps passing. The room around her was small and dark, bereft of any gleam of light. The door fit snugly in its frame: not even a thread of light seeped through. The footsteps died away and Margaret stood a moment longer, listening now for sound of anyone or anything within.

The only sound she could hear was the soft rush of plumbing overhead and to her right.

He had given her leave to explore his realm—her new realm, he had called it—but she wondered if he had meant this little room. Perhaps it was only the boiler room. She put out her hand and felt for heat, but a constant damp coolness washed against her skin. "Brr!" she said, and let go of the doorknob. With a rather delicious sense of doing what she was not supposed to, she took a few tentative steps forward, her hand brushing the wall to ensure her balance. It was bone-chillingly cold; beads of slick damp stood on the stones. With one careful foot set in front of the other, keeping vigilant purchase on the stones and eyes wide open for any hope of light, Margaret came to the head of a stair. She stood for quite some time on the top step, imagining what she would look like dashed at the bottom after missing her step in the dark. She could not be sure anyone would find her, and even if de la Mare did find her, she was not sure she would appreciate his support even then.

Thank goodness I am English, she thought sourly, and put her foot on the next step down. Gingerly, painfully, with the utmost care, she climbed down the stairs in the dark. She ran against a wall once, which thoroughly confused her, until she found she was on a landing and had to turn off and continue the downward plunge. She ran into three landings until she found no more, and there were no more stairs, and she was standing in a room of inky blackness whose dimensions she could not make out, not though she strained until her head pounded. She almost called out, just to hear the sound of her voice, but she touched her tongue to her dry lips and made herself move on, both hands out to catch herself in case she ran against anything.

It seemed like all of earth's autumn must have gone by while she walked in that lightless place. Once, with a calm clarity, she thought to herself, *This must be the valley of the shadow of death. This must be the last road of all.* It was strange how muffled all her senses were—her sense of fear, her sense of direction, her sense even of hunger and loneliness. The only sense that was keen was a heady, formless sense of standing with each step on the edge of a cliff, waiting for the empty step, waiting for the fall, and not minding it very much.

A sudden light winked out at her from her left, down amidst the well of the dark. She paused, perplexed, and bent down to stare at it. It took her some time to realize that she was standing at the head of another stairway, and she was gazing down the stairs at a little glow of light. She put her foot on the top step—then stopped.

This would be a nasty place to meet de la Mare. If she had thought the train car difficult, what about now, seemingly miles beneath the ground, cut off from civilization? Her lips burned. She might have hated herself in the kitchen hallway if she had gone back, but some things were not worth the risk run. She turned back, retraced her steps along the endless hallway, and tripped back up the slippery stairs.

At the head of the stairs she stood leaning against the wall, breathing heavily, drowning out the sound of plumbing. "Well, Mother!" she gasped, and shoved away from the wall as she had shoved away from her bedroom in Aylesward. "I hope you're happy!"

Dizzy with fatigue and hunger, cold, damp, and feeling dirty, Margaret stepped back out into the kitchen hallway, looking both ways, and managed to retrace her way back through the dining room and up into the first story hallway without being spotted. She almost lost herself, having forgot to mark which door was hers. She stepped in on a library and another bedroom before finally opening her own door. She locked it behind herself and fell into a chair, exhausted.

For a while she stared up at the vaulted ceiling, breathing unevenly, listening to the blood drum in her ears. In a few moments she would have to rouse enough energy to step into the bath, but for now she stared unblinkingly upward, breathing, being alive, and thinking. Her body felt beaten and somehow distant, which made thinking easier.

I must not forget earth, she told herself. *I must get back home somehow. Even Mother and no husband and my cousin running off with some n'er-do-well is not as bad as this. And above all, I will not marry Rupert de la Mare, not even if my queen and country depends upon it. The queen can ask someone else, if it comes to that. And he will not be allowed to kiss me again.* She pulled her arms up, pushed away from the chair with great effort, and limped to the bath.

She had shut and locked the bedroom door; she shut and locked the bathroom door too. Something about de la Mare made her doubt locked doors would prove any difficulty to him, which was discomforting, but she did not know what else to do. She found a robe and put it on while the water ran, pipes shaking and booming and rattling, and heated in the bath. She sat down in the single chair by the tub to wait, breathing in the scent of steam and lavender and something like muffins. At last the bath was ready. She cast a wary glance at the doorway. Giving in to her sense of paranoia she tiptoed over and peeked out. The bedroom was empty. She shut the door again and locked it, and, slipping off the robe, eased her body into the bath.

The hot water, the smell of lavender, were all familiar to her. She lay back, cupped in the buoyant hand of the water, feeling the heat crawl into her tightness and quietly work it loose. Her mind sorted itself as she relaxed. When she was done, she resolved to go down and get something to eat, even if she had to talk to all the servants in the house. She would survive, she would thwart de la Mare, she would get back home. She would not let her resolve waver over a trivial fact such as her inability to conjure up dragons to translate her back to earth. She would find a way, somehow.

Overheated and shaky, Margaret slowly made her way back down from her bath to the dining room. A little bell stood by de la Mare's chair on the table, and with daring she leaned across and struck it sharp, listening to the sweet peal of it ring through the ground floor rooms.

There was a momentary pause, then the door to the kitchen hallway clicked open and a man stepped through, looking subservient but also surprised. When he saw her he checked, but asked with distant politeness, "May I help you?"

"Please prepare something for me," said Margaret. "I will take a light meal."

"Will you take it here?"

She glanced around the room. It was dark and depressing, but she could think of no other place in which to eat. "Yes, I'll take it here."

The man nodded and retreated through the door, leaving her to find a seat and wait the agonizing length of time until he returned. She found a pleasant place near the window which overlooked the park. She had nearly forgot about the thing in the sky, but now it was a little less grotesque to her and she could look at it from time to time without flinching. Now that she beheld it at a distance, she realized that it was rather beautiful as a whole, and shone with a silvery-blue radiance in the light of the sun. It was beginning to lose its eastern edges to the turn of night; it was strange to see the empty sky slowly eating up the edges of her planet. And while it was night down there—or was it up there?—it would still be daylight here. How many people were gazing up at her now—or was it down?—not knowing at all what they looked at? How many times had she looked and not known? How many times had she not even looked?

The man appeared at her side without a sound and slipped a tray of coffee, tomato soup, and two wedges of bread and cheese before her. She nodded her gratitude and began to eat once he had gone away. The food was excellent: the bread and cheese filled her, the soup warmed a hollow place in her that was more than her stomach, and the coffee she held close until it was cool. She was more accustomed to drinking cocoa than coffee, and until she took her first sip she had mistaken it for the former. So she held it until it was cool and then put it away on the tray.

There was a sudden gust of wind and a door banged somewhere. She jumped, undone by the suddenness of the sound, and only just recovered before the tall, black, stalking figure came striding into the dining room, head erect, his pale blue eyes searching for her. He came over, stripping off his hawking gloves as he did so. She could see that he was spattered with mud. But when he bent down, presumably to try for another of his impulsive kisses, she jerked her head away.

She could feel how motionless he had gone beside her, still inclined with his cheek at her ear; she could feel his breath against her neck. She could feel, above all, the dark, shifting thundercloud that was brooding inside him. She wondered if her resolve might cost her life: he seemed the sort of man who could kill.

With a rather pale face, but a steady voice, she asked, "Did you have a nice ride?"

"How domestic a question," he purred, and released himself, drawing back upright. "As a matter of fact, I did. The game was swift, but I gave chase, and I got it in the end. I always do."

His words sent a shiver to her soul. "Tell me," she said, turning round and staring him squarely in the eye. "If you always get your quarry in the end, what count am I?"

He smiled mirthlessly down at her. "I hunt many things, both of wood and water and air, but you are the first of your kind for my chasing."

"Then how can you be sure you will get it?"

"I always catch my quarry," he said simply, and she found herself believing his words.

Through their reflections in the glass, she gazed across the lawn. The first forerunners of darkness were falling across the grass: a haze of shadow, a purple hue in the air. Looking up she could see the high sun swallowing up her earth in a blaze of white light. The feather-silver planet was blinking out of that colourless sky and the colourless sky was swiftly fading into a sudden night.

"An eclipse," she said, mostly to herself. Then, with a harsh laugh, "I never thought I would see it from here."

"A rare, fine sight," said de la Mare.

She refocused and took in his reflection. He, too, was gazing upward, reflection pale in the glass, his eyes even paler, his dark hair lost in the hawk-plunging dusk of the sky. In a few minutes he would be swallowed up in the twilight of the room, save for his skin which, like her own, was ghastly pale against black clothing. Strangely disembodied by earth-shadow, he seemed even more a figure of dark magic. An uneasy energy hummed in the air.

When she looked again, the darkness outside was complete.

De la Mare let out a long-held breath and turned into the room. With a double snap of his fingers the room sprang alight: every candle in every holder flashed and flared and stretched up its flame to throw its light around the room. A sudden warmth burned away the swift evening chill. "I am sorry you have just eaten," he said, casting a look at her over his shoulder. "I was hoping you would dine with me tonight."

"I am sure you were," said Margaret. She was disquieted by his figure, fair to see and slender as a racehorse, pacing down the room toward the sideboard. He had a strange, compelling handsomeness about him which she loathed.

"You have not touched your coffee." He unstoppered a flask of gleaming amber-coloured liquid and turned a tumbler out from among its fellows, meticulously filling it. "Would you like something stronger?"

Margaret folded her hands in her lap with a little bird-wing rustle. "I think it would be unwise to trust your vintage."

He laughed, high and bright. Swinging round with the flask in one hand, the tumbler in the other, the candlelight playing in the depths of both, he said, "What a careful creature you are. I like that." He shook his head. "There were many pretty girls, but then there was you. *You* will do well. You have wit and gut and cunning, and hell knows I need that by me."

"Hell would know what you need," agreed Margaret.

De la Mare set the flask down and leaned back against the sideboard, supporting himself with his legs crossed at the ankles. The light glittered in his glass, swaying a little to his almost imperceptible movement. For a long while he gazed at her, silent, his face inscrutable behind a cool little smile. She felt uncomfortably that his pallid eyes could see right through to her skin and she held up under that gaze only through sheer power of will. She could not bear the thought of caving to him. He wanted her to, and she could not do it.

In time he broke off to take a drink and move away from the sideboard to the wall where there were several hangings. Margaret had not noticed them in detail before, but de la Mare drew up before one and gestured toward it with his glass. "Come here, my dear," he said. "I want to show you something."

With a weary incuriousness Margaret got up, smoothed out her skirts, and rustled down to join him before a large faded print. It was a map, framed in heavy wood, supported by wires from the head moulding. The light from the candles cast sharp shadows from it; the pale yellow light danced across its pane. She moved away from the glare and saw the boundary lines on the map, unfamiliar with their unfamiliar names of cities and towns, mountains and valleys, rivers and seas. For a while she gazed at the map, feeling de la Mare's eyes on her, but saw only the unfamiliarity of a strange place. She shook her head and turned away.

"Very pretty. Did you draw it up yourself?"

"No," he said lightly. He leaned in, touching her shoulder with two fingers extended while he still clasped the tumbler, his free hand pointing to a mark on the map. "We are here, in Marenové, and this—" he swung his finger over a wide area in which Marenové occupied the western corner "—is Mare." He took a step back. His fingers still rested on her shoulder. "It is a poor example of power, a tract of land, as if power were somehow measured in acres, a potentate judged by how straight his oxen plough the furrow. There is some truth to that," he admitted, dropping a heavy gaze on her, "but we strive for better things, you and I."

"You might at least *try* to be a gentleman," said Margaret hotly. She jerked away from his touch. Her cheeks burned.

"Might!" said de la Mare in a low, terrible voice which somehow stopped her in her tracks. "Come here, Margaret. I am not finished yet."

She loathed the man, but turned back and stood rigidly beside him, fixing her unwilling gaze on the hateful piece of map.

He spread his hand over the territory of Mare, encompassing it between thumb and index finger. To the southeast of his palm was what she understood to be ocean. Under the fan of his fingers, north, northeast, and northwest of his thumb and index finger were other territories whose names she leaned in to read: Capys, Thrasymene, Orzelon-gang. Below his palm were the names of Hol and Darkling. She read them and they were senseless to her, and with each word a pang of homesickness, even for her mother, wrenched in her gut. She wanted Leeds and London, Aylesward and the Avon. She wanted the bleak prospect of the Channel running riot under an October sky. This uncanny darkness that pressed against the windows of de la Mare's house made her ill.

His signet ring, a thick band of engraved gold clasping a fiery topaz, clinked softly against the side of his glass. "Margaret, do you know why I have brought you here?"

She continued to stare at the map, unwilling to meet his gaze. More so than she had felt under her mother's hand, she felt like a pawn, a piece to be moved about by de la Mare's hand, a piece to gain power. Her eye roved over the territories with their strange names. And how, precisely, did she fit into this chess game? He wanted her to marry him—to what purpose? To fix for himself an heir? She shuddered.

"I think that I have an inkling why," she replied.

He said warmly, "That is my girl. Margaret," he mused, and frowned thoughtfully to himself. "It is a good name—a strong name, respectable, well-fitted to a Queen of the Mares." He was quiet for a while, presumably listening to his own thoughts which stayed hidden behind the motionlessness of his eyes. Presently he said, in a tone altogether different, "They have set me at a foolish wager, but I will play the game. They cannot be without their Overlord for long, and they will soon see reason. You," he turned to her, "will help them see reason."

"Who is this that I am enlightening?" asked Margaret delicately.

His fingers snapped against the map again. The candlelight danced wildly on the glass as the picture rocked under the force of his blow. "Capys my cousin and Darkling, ever bedfellows in their schemes, Thrasymene and her triumvirate sisters—I might have picked a wife from one of them, the cows!—the Lord of Orzelon-gang and all his countless provinces. All their territories, provinces, duchies, estates and all their petty lords—you will show them reason. You, my dear, for there is a woman's cunning which no man can play at." He smiled a devil's smile. "They wanted me to play their game, not knowing what pieces I brought to the table."

If she looked at that map another minute Margaret thought she would hit the bottom of de la Mare's glass and dash the contents up into his face. She turned away, content with the image of his fine face drenched in brandy. She tried to breathe evenly and pace out her thoughts as she walked the length of the room. De la Mare remained by the picture as if knowing she needed to think. It worried her that he did not follow: she felt as if she were still walking into his hand.

Passing another picture she glanced up, catching a glimpse of de la Mare's distant reflection in it. He was leaning against the table, glass in hand, gazing at the map with a grim countenance. *He is being elusive. Get the truth out of him, even if it takes you all night. How long,* she wondered, looking to the window, *will this moon-dusk last?*

"De la Mare," she said, turning.

"Rupert."

She pursed her lips. "Rupert, what is the game that you are playing? What is at stake? What are you after? What stands in your way? I will do nothing until I know."

"Hmm!" he purred, pushing off from the table. His thin-set lips had curled into a smile. With a little sidewise gesture he slid himself onto the corner of the table, perched an inch or two above the floor, foot swinging idly. "The stakes are these: that one must be Overlord of Plenilune. And the game is that I will be he."

She watched his glass resting on his knee, swinging to his motion, casting wild amber light.

"I am best suited to the task. The Overlords have time out of mind come down out of the House of Marenové; we are bred to it, raised with the shadow of its mantle across our shoulders. Now on the eve of my taking office Capys would dare to sow dissension among the ranks and declare me unfit by my arts to rule—as if they did not know that the men of Marenové have always tossed magic

from their fingertips as a child might toss away so many pebbles."
His voice grew hard and hateful. "Capys adjourned the gathering,
and when they returned had made up their minds that I must fix for
myself a wife, and prove that I had some humanity to my soul
before I could rule."

Margaret laughed softly, bitterly. "You are fit to be a king,"
she said, lifting her eyes to meet his gaze. "But you would be a
tyrant."

His face was an unsmiling mask.

Unable to long hold that wretched gaze she went back to the
window and sat looking out across the lawn. It was lit very dimly by
the aura of light shining from the disk of earth's rim. In the
distance she could see the edge of the park and the lift of hills,
covered over in trees. Which way did she look? Without earth she
had no sense of direction. The taste of nightmare rose in her
mouth.

Where was true north?

There were stars, more stars than she had ever seen before.
The skies of Aylesward had become murky of late, competing with
the overspill of smoke from neighbouring mill towns. English skies
were changeful, and she had never been inclined to look at the
night sky when it had been clear. Sometimes in the summer, when
the nights of northern England were long twilights lingering into
twilights, she had lain awake at night watching the purple play on
the horizon, but had never thought to look for stars. And now she
did; each star was a perfect glowing pearl fixed above her head,
ringing round the haloed earth, distant and distinctly mocking. She
suppressed another bitter laugh. They mocked her and she loved
them.

She looked back at Rupert. He had finished his brandy and
was putting up the flask, setting aside the soiled tumbler for
someone to fetch and clean. It struck her that he had not eaten yet.
This sudden night made everything feel as if a full day had come to
a close. What time was it, really?

"De—Rupert."

"Yes?" He slid a flask back into the cabinet and shut the
glass door with a little click.

She got up with a voluminous rustle. "I am going to bed. I am not used to this eclipse and I want to sleep while it is dark."

"Pull the curtains well shut. They are thick, and made to keep out the light." He turned back to her. "I will be in my room next door, should you need anything."

She narrowed her eyes at him. "My door will be locked, should you need anything."

With rampant brows and a short little laugh he stood at the dining room door and let it open for her, nodding deferentially to her as she went past. She met two servants by the stair and another in the upstairs hallway; she could feel them all looking over their shoulders at her as she went by. She soared up the stairs and down the hallway with grim determination and they all got quickly out of the way, but once inside her own bedroom her grimness faded. She leaned against the door, listening to the soft footsteps and hushed voices of the servants without, her hand gripping the lock until her knuckles turned white. Unbidden and unwanted, their unfamiliar faces and searching glances conjured up in her the notion, *You are all alone.*

It was strange how hollow those words echoed in her soul. She had always been alone, even before the train at Leeds. Her whole life she had stood alone, trying to be something better, never quite attaining this goal. She remembered her mother's face, she remembered her sisters' faces—so very like to her mother's, it was no struggle to call them up. She looked on them as they fell under her mind's eye, looked on them as from a great height, raised above and apart so that a gulf seemed to open up between them. She had always been alone among people who disliked and used her, and she had borne it like a queen; only in those parting moments when she had hurled her mother's visceral emotion back in her face had she descended to their level.

"I would be fit to be queen," she murmured—her voice caught and broke, and she hated herself for that. "But I would be cold."

Empty, but with her head held high, Margaret turned from the door and entered the room, going patiently and methodically through the motions of undressing and getting into bed. They were small, bright, familiar things that she clung to fervently. As she lay under the warm blankets, staring up at the darkened ceiling, she almost said the old familiar childhood prayers solely for the sake of their being old and familiar, but somehow they were too earth-like, too far away, too unattainable and, somehow, hopeless. She thrust them aside and turned over, hiding a face which was suddenly damp in a velvet pillow.

It was still dark, though that meant nothing to her, when Margaret was brought up with a start out of a twisted dream. She had been standing on the Leeds train station platform, watching a dragon-coloured train coming in with the rain falling all around. Instead of her carpet-bag she carried a falcon, and it kept turning about and digging its claws into her arm while she struggled to keep the umbrella over it. The train came in, shrieking and growling and howling until her ears throbbed. Then, with a jerk, the howling separated from the dream and pulled her to waking.

The pictures on the walls were rattling as though a real train were coming through. Something was howling, the howl echoing round and round the house until the whole building seemed to shake. Margaret clapped her hands to her ears and stumbled out of bed, staggering against the moonquake-shudder of the floor. It was like a cannon going off, off and off and never ending. The roar went on until her head seemed ready to split with the noise. Reeling through the dark she crashed against the door and fumbled with the lock, one hand over her ear, the other ear pressed into the upward crook of her shoulder.

She had got the door unlocked when she hesitated. It was still dark, she was in her nightgown, and God knew what that howling was. Did she really dare to go out and investigate? For all she knew it could be Rupert himself. For all she knew it was some hell-hound he kept in his possession with which to go hunting.

Margaret wrenched the lock back into place and stumbled into bed. The blankets welcomed her with their residual warmth and there she lay for some time, ears blocked but still hearing the tide-rising surge of howling. The sounds roved about the house like ghosts looking for something, desolate, anxious, lost. She knew that feeling, and though she loathed the unknown, wretched noises, they called up something deep within her, and she knew that feeling.

At last the howling died away, a door slammed far off, and she managed to go back to sleep.

III | SKANDER RIME

She ventured into the garden the next day. The sun was shining and the ever-present earth loomed gleaming overhead. There was a flutter in her chest as she stepped off the rear threshold and stood under that vast naked sky. It was so clear that she felt nothing was stopping the earth from plummeting and crushing her out of life forever. But the earth did not plummet, a bird struck up a pretty tune from somewhere down the path, and Margaret walked out across the porphyry gravel with a slight wind tugging at the thin white fabric she had draped over her head. Ginger-coloured flowers danced in the beds, stoked up to a fierce burning by the wind and sunlight so that she felt she could warm her hands at them. She followed their glow down the path and into the long grape-vine arbour where the wind was chill and the shadows were deep. She moved among them as one of them, dressed in another black gown.

In one place the arbour crossed a stream by way of a bridge, and there she paused, looking out through the leaves at the estate of Marenové. She could see the hills and their fur of trees; she could see the gentle slope of the land as it made a shallow valley for the stream; she could see what appeared to be farms in the distance. *I must be looking east*, she told herself. *Marenové is in the extreme west of Mare.*

She lingered only a while longer, noting the muted blues in the distance and the way the farthest horizon was limned with orange as if it were a cat's eye, catching the light and throwing it back in fantastic angel-hues. She went on until she reached the end of the arbour, and there stood at the head of a little timber stair, looking down on a long perpendicular avenue of grass bordered on its far side by the long, high slope of hill and its trees. She had come to the end of the garden and almost turned back, ready to explore the rest, when she drew up, hearing on the wind the familiar throb of hooves on turf. She listened for the sound of hounds and pulled herself back within the vine-shadows as she did so, but she picked out only a single horse's feet, drumming lightly, swiftly, but catching once or twice as if the mount were laboured. Brow furrowed, she looked out between the fanning leaves and spied a horse coming into sight, swinging down out of the woodshore to turn up the grassy aisle.

To her surprise, it was not Rupert. She almost mistook the one for the other, but realized as the rider approached that he had a stockier build under his sullen red cloak and, though he wore hawking gloves and bore a discontented, flapping hawk on one fist, he was not Rupert. A hawking hunter yes, but this was not Rupert. The face was too open even in its grimness.

The hunter loped by her, foam dripping from its lips, turf-clods flying from its hooves. Margaret flinched, avoiding one such clod as it flew past her. Tail uplifted, splayed in the wind under the cloak, the horse went on past her. She watched it go, perplexed, noting the tired but strong form of the mount. But at the turn its rider suddenly reined it in, jerking round to cast a look over his shoulder. Margaret froze, her foot halfway out into the path. She could not imagine he had seen her; was it possible he had felt her looking at him? She held perfectly still, inexplicably afraid.

The rider turned the hunter about and came back slowly. Unflappable, the horse shuffled big-boned along, snuffling softly to itself while the falcon, perturbed in the extreme, squealed and bated on the man's fist. Margaret could see the man's lips moving, speaking quietly to the bird in an effort to calm it while he peered among the hedge and trees and grape foliage, clearly suspicious. He was bare-headed, dark-haired, but his eyes, too, were dark, which ruined the look that was so similar to Rupert's. The ride had cast his cloak askew, revealing a mud-spattered jerkin of leather beneath. The man was dressed for travel, but there was something in his look and bearing which was not messenger or soldier.

His eyes slid past her, stopped, and jerked back to her face, narrowing against the sun's glare and the shiver of shadows in the wind. Only a moment, only a heartbeat, and she saw that he was sure. With a little sharp laugh that was completely mirthless he reined in at the foot of the stairs, looking up at her.

"Madam!" he said, clearly surprised. "I did not realize Rupert had visitors. I might have come in better state."

"We will overlook it, just this once," she said, feigning a supercilious air. "I don't believe I know you."

"I don't believe I know you, either." The man switched his reins to his hawking hand and leaned forward, free hand outstretched. With the briefest of hesitations, she leaned down and took it. It was a rough paw that closed over her long, lean one. "Skander Rime." His tone was one of hesitant warmth.

"Margaret Coventry... Have you come to see Rupert?" She let go of his hand and straightened.

"After a fashion," said Skander, which Margaret thought was an odd and unsatisfactory answer. The man was looking at her scrutinously. It dawned on her with a little jolt that this must be Capys, Skander Rime of Capys, who had dared his cousin to find a wife, if he could win one, and prove thereby that he was human enough to take the overlordship of Plenilune—whatever that might be. No wonder she kept seeing Rupert in his face. For a moment she was at a loss, her wits shattered. Did he loathe her as much as she loathed Rupert? Was he surprised and hopeful for his cousin? How on earth—no. She winced inwardly. How did she address him?

She managed a little bob of a curtsey. "I am sorry, correct me if I am wrong. You must be Skander of Capys. Am I right?"

An uncertain smile flickered around his mouth. "You are correct. Now you must forgive me, and correct me if I am wrong."

Margaret looked up from under her brows as she hung at the curtsey's lowest point. Her heart was in her throat.

"Are you with Rupert?"

She emerged from the curtsey with cheeks burning, head held high. From the head of the stair she was able to look down on Skander. "After a fashion."

This took Skander by surprise, and for a few minutes the two regarded each other in silence. The horse champed placidly at its bit. The falcon scowled to itself. Finally it seemed neither of them could stand the silence, and Margaret herself was glad when Skander looked away and said, clearing his throat, "I am afraid I must go on and put up my horse. It was a pleasure to make your acquaintance, madam."

"And yours."

"Until next time."

Margaret wondered how much Skander Rime was lying as he turned his hunter about and trotted up the avenue, disappearing from sight. She wondered how much *she* was lying. For a moment longer she lingered at the head of the stairs, listening as the drum of the hunter's hooves died away. She could not be quick to make an ally of Skander Rime until she was certain of his character, but if he disliked his cousin enough to throw roadblocks in his way to power, she approved of that.

Gathering up her skirts, she hastened back along the arbour to the house. It was time to get out of this cold air. Glad for her change of dress, which was linen and not taffeta, she scuttled across the porphyry gravel, up the back steps, and entered noiselessly into the rear hall. A servant was tending to some houseplants under the windows, but otherwise she was alone at the rear of the house. With casual care she made her way to the atrium and stood in the shadows of a doorway, looking around and upward. There was as yet no sign of either Skander or Rupert.

She had nearly put her foot out of hiding, when she snatched it back again, hearing voices. The building took the sounds and threw them about deceptively. She kept perfectly still, biting her lip, waiting to see who was coming and from where.

The two of them came into view, climbing the curving stair to the upper hall. "You seem unusually jocund about it, who are so often as dour as the backside of the moon." Skander pointed wide, his wrist bereft now of his accompanying bird. "Does this change of spirit have anything to do with the little mouse I saw on the back lawn?"

Mouse? Margaret frowned and liked Skander Rime less.

De la Mare said lightly, carelessly, "Oh, she has gone that far, has she? Precocious little chit! What do you think of her?"

They had nearly reached the head of the stair. If they looked back they would see her. She held more still than death itself, not breathing, not blinking, hoping Skander could not feel her gaze and turn, giving her away.

"I would not call her a precocious little chit," said Capys. "I would call her a force to be reckoned with."

De la Mare turned at the head of the stair and looked soothingly at his cousin. Margaret's heart stopped in her chest. "You didn't really believe that I would take you at your word, did you, sir?"

"For the love of heaven, Rupert—" burst out Skander.

But Rupert cut him off with a swiftly upraised finger held almost to the other's lips. "For the love of what?"

Skander remained silent.

Rupert dropped his hand and crossed the upper hall to the library door. His figure was shrouded in the gloom of the hallway, and his own shadow, mingling with the others against the panelled wood and dark print of the wall, reared up like a monster above his head. "By Ivy-tide," he went on in that same careless sort of tone, "she should be fit to come out in a social gathering like Lookinglass." He laughed. "Black Malkin will hate her."

"Black Malkin hates every woman: they are not man enough for her," replied Skander dryly, and the two of them stepped out of sight into the library. The door shut behind them.

Margaret let out a heavy gasp, slumping against the column. First she was a pawn and now she was a mouse. With a shaky hand pressed to her forehead, she rallied her mind, pulling herself together. The door to the servants' stair was nearby; fixing it with a flagging gaze she finally went to it, listened, and drew it open. There was no one on the stair that she could see. She started up, round and round, setting her feet down with care not to make a noise, until at last she came out on the first story hallway.

The library door stood directly opposite her, the expanse of open atrium in between. She wrapped the shadows around herself and moved quickly around the perimeter, feeling much like the hare in the open, anxiously hoping the hawk would not spot her.

Through the deep blue shadows she stole until she stood near the library door, her heart in her throat. She had to swallow twice to get it down properly before she could hear anything above the drum of blood in her ears. She stood at the door, fingers pressed against the wood frame to support herself, and listened with painfully straining ears to the communications inside.

"Are you thirsty?"

"Water will do to get the dust out of my throat."

There was a distant clink and clatter of glassware. From another part of the room came the heavy thump of a book being tossed down.

"Water for you," came Rupert's voice, mild and sleepily panther-like in a way that made Margaret's skin crawl. "If it is all the same to you, I'll take a stronger draught."

"By all means, don't let me hamper your tastes."

If she shut her eyes, leaning lightly, gingerly, against the doorframe, Margaret could almost see the way Rupert turned aside to look curiously at his cousin, a cool gleam playing in his eyes. *Hamper them, you idiot!* she thought violently. *His tastes are me!* But if Skander Rime caught the look, he did not speak.

A leather chair crackled as someone sank into it. One of them began talking again, but at that moment a servant shut a door down the hall and Margaret jumped, pressing herself as small as she could into the shadows as the maid padded by. She went away toward the servants' stair and Margaret breathed again, returning to the door.

"—surprised me," concluded Skander with a little indifferent sniff. "Bloodburn will be gratified."

"Bloodburn," said Rupert, "is a man who can weigh another for what he is worth and not hit far from the mark. He held by me, and I'll not forget that. He is a good man, Bloodburn."

Ice rattled in an emptying glass. "Ah, yes, he is a shrewd one, Lord Hol. For shrewdness I warrant he has no equal except— did I tell you the date of the gala?"

"No, only that it was Ivy-tide," purred Rupert.

"A month from now, on the New Ivy. News are always quiet, and if I can't have a quiet house I want a quiet countryside."

"Poor Skander. You never liked balls and galas much, did you?"

The leather chair gave a restless creak. "They have their purpose—"

"But this one, I think, is not to your liking?"

"—but winter closes in and I am poor company in the Hollow Moons. Better I am at hunting among the hawks and hounds, or better yet beyond Murklestrath among the Carmarthen, who have a way of pestering my borders and giving me leave to keep my sword sharp."

Rupert's voice turned oddly hard when he answered. "Time enough for sharp swords and bright spears when the cherries put on their gala gowns. Winter is an hour of high fires and warm company."

Margaret discovered that if she knelt, arranging her skirts with the utmost care, she could peep through the key-hole. She looked in on a white-lit scene, the two—Rupert seated and Skander having risen—framed in black the bright casement of the window. It was Skander, now, who turned a pointed look his cousin's way and asked in a low tone, so low that she barely: "Warm company?"

Rupert's image was all sleepy power, and there was a light laugh in his voice when he replied. "I know full well where I stand in your heart, Skander. Did you not throw down this obstacle of a wife in front of me because of it? But though you may dislike me, take me not for a blackguard."

"I'll take you as you are," said Skander coldly.

De la Mare rose up in a tower of dark splendour, looking his cousin squarely in the eye, his square jaw lifted a fraction, nostrils swelling faintly as if drawing in with a relish the scent of his cousin's dislike. "We look forward to the gala at Lookinglass on the New Ivy. Until then, you might do well to fetch yourself your own chit. It is poor hosting to greet your guests alone."

Skander Rime laughed mirthlessly. "Only you complain, and I know where I stand in *your* heart."

"Perhaps," said Rupert. "My man must still be tending to your horse. I will show you to your room."

Skander waved a hand. "I know the way."

But Rupert stopped him. "Do you? But you'll find it occupied already. I fear I must put you up in some other place."

She did not get to see Skander's reaction to this news. She gathered her voluminous skirts and retreated to the disputed chamber, shutting and locking the door behind her. She listened to the heavy tread of the two men going by, then, on an impulse, unlocked the door again and peeped out. The two men, almost identical in height and bearing, though Skander was the broader of the two, stalked along the hallway, the blue shadows breaking up and slipping in behind them like mist. She shivered at the sight. They passed through another door and out of sight altogether; the sound of their feet fell into silence.

Margaret let out a heavy breath, finding that she had forgot to breathe. Despite the butterflies jerking and fluttering in her stomach, she felt better for having someone else under Marenové's roof whom she could rely on, someone else who disliked Rupert perhaps as much as she. Skander Rime was a man in a position to know how to handle Rupert de la Mare. She wondered—though she hardly dared yet to hope—if he might be persuaded to release her.

Is this what they mean by a Godsend?

She left the door and sat at her dressing table behind the folding partition of beaten brass and silver, cut in the images of peacocks. It gave her an eerie feeling, running her eyes over the little chests and draws of veils and jewellery that littered the table. Rupert had been anticipating her, for she could not imagine such things would stand in the room while it had been Skander Rime's especial chamber. How long had he known about her? How had he found her? Until this moment, as her eye fell on a cluster of beautiful smoky pearls, she had always thought Rupert had chosen her at random on the train. But now...now she was not so certain.

A cold shudder ran through her. She looked at the clock just as it chimed the three-quarter: it would be time for dinner soon. She could count on Rupert and Skander Rime having it together, and both of them expecting her company. She slid her first two fingers around the ivory knob of a tiny drawer and slid it silently open, digging into its depths for a comb.

I feel like a bone being pulled at by two dogs. She turned in the chair, watching her reflection as she drew the comb through her brown hair. What little light filtered in around the partition played golden on individual strands. *Curse it.* She put the comb down with deliberation. *I am pretty. Why—why did I have to be even a little pretty? Why did I have to have wit or intelligence? What on earth—no.* She set her fist down heavily on the tabletop. *What did providence mean by giving me any of this?*

For a long while she sat staring blindly at her reflection, willing the framing images—the cherry-wood panelling, the dark green wall-print, a silver trail of gauzy scarf—to be the images of her own bedroom in Aylesward. The clock ticked loudly in the silence. Once, across the front park, she heard a lapwing warble and yap, and another answer it faintly from far up in the fellsides. At last, slowly, she reached out and picked up the comb and pulled it through her hair again. The reflection picked up its comb and began tidying its hair too, long brown, full hair framing a face that was cold and pale.

Tick-whirrr!—clong! clong! clong! clong! clong! clong! clong! clong! clong! clong! clong! clong! The clock went off in strident measure. With inhuman punctuality, as the last *clong!* died away, there was a knock at the door. Margaret hesitated before calling.

The door cracked ajar and a maid stuck her head inside, fetching a glance about the room before falling on Margaret where she sat at the dressing table. "It is dinner-time, my lady. Are you ready or do you need any assistance?"

"I am not ready," said Margaret, "but neither do I need any assistance. Tell de la Mare and Skander Rime that I will join them presently..."

"In the solarium," offered the maid.

A quick frown pulled at Margaret's brows, but she resisted the momentary urge to ask the way. "In the solarium. Thank you."

"Ring if you need anything," said the maid. She dropped a curtsey with one hand extended, and withdrew.

Margaret let out a frustrated breath as the maid's soft footsteps were swallowed up in the heavy silence of the house. She pulled the comb violently through her hair one last time, parted it, and began rolling it up behind her head, pinning it in place. Her arms, not accustomed to such work, were sore by the time she achieved her desired effect. With a lack of hats to hand, she chose the silver gauzy scarf off the peg of the dressing table and pinned it into place over her curls. Her appearance, when she frowned into the mirror, was more suggestive of Athena than of Her Majesty the Queen, but though Rupert had prepared for her arrival, he had not afforded her the latest fashions—or even the fashions of the past few centuries. She rose with a soft rustle of black velvet, choosing at the last instant to add the smoky pearls to her neck.

I will regret this touch of vanity, she told herself, *but I needn't appear surly for Skander Rime.*

She was a full half-hour late to dinner. She clipped down the marble staircase, having forgot to replace her walking boots with something softer and more formal, and, after a moment's hesitation, made for what seemed most likely to be southward, where she thought any sensible building planner would put a solarium.

The only sounds in the building were those of her boots as she walked the tiled floor and the distant rattle of cookingware in the kitchen. The tilleul light of noon came breaking in through the tall arched windows. She passed through the south peristyle; a great wind bore down on her and sent her skirts and veil whirling. She followed the walk alongside the dancing heads of hazel-bushes with their nuts abob in the wind, alongside the bryony which was trying valiantly to take over the azalea shrubs, and alongside the roses which had shut themselves up and curled dragonwise and thorny in their beds.

At the far end of the peristyle the solarium reared its glassy head above the walled garden. As she approached the door Margaret could spy the shadowy shapes of both men seated among the hot-house plants within, the one in a folding chair of wicker-work, the other in an armchair of deep yellow velvet that was beginning to grow worn. A lamp hung from the ceiling flickered over them, drenching them in a pool of golden light while the shadows raced around them, shadows of the walls and shadows of the clouds that the high winds were scuttling across the brilliant disk of the sun.

The brass latch was cold under her hand when she turned it and stepped inside. The wind tore in past her, blowing the light wildly about and bringing round the two men to look at her. With some effort Margaret shut the door again and stood in the uneasy quiet before the door, returning their stares.

Rupert was the first to move. Skander Rime, uncertain, shifted a little in his seat, but Rupert rose up out of the massive velvet-covered armchair and stepped forward, gesturing back to it as he did so.

"So you did come," he said lightly. "Lilith said you would, but I was not certain..."

"I was not certain either," said Margaret in a tone to match the velvet chair. She stepped past him and took it, feeling it swell around her like warm gold sand.

Rupert took a dark-stained, high-backed wooden chair, which was rigid and unmoving as he, and rested his hands on his knees. In contrast, the easy bulk of his cousin rested in a low folding camp chair, and out of it he leaned just then to offer Margaret a glass of wine. She hesitated at first, but finding herself thirsty, and guessing Skander had already partaken, she took it gratefully, careful not to meet Rupert's eye.

"Do you like Marenové, Miss Coventry?" asked Skander, his tongue wrapping around the word with some slight difficulty.

She took the plate of tarts he offered and chose her words and her finger-food with care. "The grounds are very prettily laid out. The house is a kind of strange combination of close and open. I am not sure what it thinks it means to be."

Skander tossed a mocking glance at his cousin and laughed heartily. "No? You have an eye for architecture. The garden there—" he pointed to the peristyle "—is the oldest part of the building. The family built up the rooms around the garden, and as the family grew larger over the years, continued to build off in wings from that. Three generations ago the massive bulk of the house was built at the height of an Overlord's rule." His laughter flickered away like a salamander around a stone wall, and Margaret noticed he also took care not to meet Rupert's eye. He looked up through the light and plants and glass at the tall mass of building towering over the smoking chimneys of the kitchen wing, and his look held a dark and far-away aspect.

At last he went on. "It was built primarily to host a ball. A peace had been made with Hol, which was a thing not easily to be attained. It was a splendid gala, more splendid than the one I am scheduled to throw, but that was the last one this house has seen. Three generations ago."

"That is a long time," murmured she, "to not hold a ball."

He smiled at her sidelong. "Yes, ma'am. Quite a long time."

The long, iron-black figure of Rupert finally spoke. "You pressure me unadvisedly. Marenové's meads are ill adjusted to many folk, and not so grand and old-fashionedly splendid as Lookinglass. And, too," he trained a level, cold gaze on Margaret, "I had no one before to entertain with me."

In that light, Rupert's eyes were so pale as to have no colour at all.

With a kind of cold iron in her own soul, Margaret forced herself to look back into that hateful gaze. "You owe it to your cousin, then, for bettering your circumstances."

"Saddle me a hunter," he replied, "but I am the one who gives chase."

"Rupert," said Skander in a chilly tone. Then he turned back to Margaret with a pleasant countenance. "How long have you been in Marenové?"

"Only since yesterday." Only since yesterday? She felt as if a lifetime had elapsed since she had stood on the station platform at Leeds. It felt like a lifetime, and yet her family would not even begin to guess her whereabouts. They would not begin to guess for...for months. She was a poor letter-writer, and she knew her mother would not expect to hear from her. She had been going to surprise her relatives in Naples; even they would not know where she was. No one would think to worry. No one would miss her.

I have always been alone.

If Skander was surprised, he did not show it. His smile, all warmth and confidence, reached across the distance to her. "You will have hardly seen anything, then! Do you ride at all?"

"Oh, yes. That is one of the few things that I do well."

"You do many things well," said Rupert.

With a conscious effort not to touch her tongue to her dry lips, she went on. "Did you have a ride in mind?"

"Well, yes. I thought we might go on a ramble through the countryside tomorrow morning. These autumn mornings are so fine, it seems a crime to coop oneself up when the scent lies low on the mists and there is good sport to be had."

From a scroll-worked pewter plate Margaret took a small sandwich and began to politely work, it bite by bite, into her mouth. Between bites, to keep the conversation going which threatened to peter out under Rupert's silence, she admitted to Skander, "I have never been hunting before. Is it very dangerous?"

This news seemed to take Skander by surprise. The thoughts flickered swallow-shadowed across his brow. "Well, that depends," he replied slowly. "The most dangerous hunting I have done is boar, but that is done in winter and I would never dream of taking a lady along. The little red deer of the fells are good to chase, and not too dangerous unless you corner a buck. And there are hare and fox, too."

Margaret reached for another sandwich, but Rupert was reaching for one at just that moment and his fingertips brushed her knuckles. She closed her hand, feeling his eyes on her, but managed not to jerk away. "Are there no wolves?" she asked carefully, recalling the awful noise that had awoken her in the night.

It was Rupert who answered. He slid his right leg over his left and leaned sidewise in his chair, elbow poised on the arm of it, sandwich between his fingers, yet somehow still remaining rigid. "There are few wolves in this part of Plenilune. They keep mostly to the wastes. Even boar are scarce, though you can find them in the woods at the See's watershed. For the most part, when we hunt, we hunt deer and hare—and fox; I enjoy fox-hunting. So there is precious little sizeable enough in these parts to harm you on a hunt, my dear."

She felt a flutter of apprehension at the thought of meeting a wild boar or a wolf and she was not wholly sure how she felt about hunting even a hare. But the sun was peeling back the yellow glow of the lamp and burning the place with a fierce silver colour that somehow stuck in her heart—and perhaps, she thought, a little in her eyes—and she flashed back at him scornfully, "I am sure I would comport myself with honour whatever the quarry."

After that even Skander seemed to give up keeping a velvet cloth on the tension in the room. They ate in silence, making noise only with the ancient pewter-ware and the fine travertine. The clouds had burned off from the sky as Rupert finished his last glass and set it down, rising. "I need to fetch down a book from my library," he said. "Skander, would you take Margaret through to the withdrawing room? I will be there in a moment."

Skander got up and stepped out of the way of the table and chairs. Margaret waited for him to come around to her side. "Of course, of course. Would you fetch down Songmartin's *Commentaries* while you are at it?"

Rupert drew up, looking over his shoulder at his cousin. In the same moment, as if waiting for it, Skander, too, had stopped and watched Rupert. Margaret watched the inexplicable tension run like threads of lightning between them before Rupert, still as motionless as ever, said in a low, regretful tone, "I'm afraid I have misplaced that particular collection."

And Skander, in just the same voice, said, "That is a shame. I'll find something in the withdrawing room, then." And he stepped up to Margaret's side.

The wind rushed into their faces as Rupert left the solarium. Margaret, holding onto Skander's proffered hand, squeezed her eyes narrowly into the knife-slice of that wind, watching the tall, lean figure of her kidnapper vanish within the darker shadows of the colonnade and kitchen wing. She thought she ought to have been glad to have him go, but the feeling of his eyes on her only intensified in his absence. Whatever strong genius he possessed seemed to pervade every inch of Marenové House. She thought of her bath, and shivered.

"He is a charmer, isn't he?" asked Skander in a wry tone.

She cast him a look askance. *He* could take it blithely, if he liked. *He* was not being courted against his will.

He saw her face and fell grave once more. As they stepped out into the wild blowing of the peristyle, the wind catching Margaret's veil and whipping it up like a wing behind her head, he said apologetically, "I am truly sorry. You don't like him at all, do you?"

"Would *you?*" she retorted.

His eyes fell a moment to a patch of stone in the middle distance of the floor, but whatever he was thinking in the face of her blistering words, he did not reply. Margaret looked away, balling her fists and feeling suddenly, unaccountably wretched.

After a moment he made a small gesture toward the door and she moved mechanically with him, allowing him to lead her wordlessly to the northeast wing of the house into a fairly square, high room lined with full bookshelves and two tall windows looking out on the back lawn, and fitted overhead with an exquisitely-carved, dark-stained tray ceiling. An instrument, appearing to be an enormous harp laid flat and on legs, stood under one window. Into the south wall was set a great fireplace which was not made up, and around it clustered sofas and chairs and little end-tables that sported their age in gnawed legs and water-winged surfaces. The whole place was chilly and gold-shot and smelled of old books, and to Margaret, though she knew Rupert would be hard on their heels in a moment, it reminded her of her own drawing room back home, and it seemed almost comforting.

Skander kindly took Margaret to a sofa and made sure she was settled before strolling about, perusing the literary selection. With her hands folded in her lap, back straight, feet tucked together ankle to ankle, she watched him somewhat blandly. He was a fine figure, tall and strapping, with a touch of unconscious swagger that she found appealing. He was cheerful and pleasant, and though cheerfulness and pleasantries were not to Margaret's taste at present, she found she could not resent him. He seemed honest, and her soul ached for honesty.

There was a step and knock at the door, and the maid which Margaret had seen before leaned into the room. "I beg your pardon," she said. "The master has been detained. He said to bring down this book for the lady to look at."

Margaret, quizzical, held out her hand as Skander took the book from the maid and gave it to her. She turned it over, but it seemed to have no title.

"Thank you, Lilith. Mind you, would you send in someone to build up a fire in here?"

"Yes, of course, sir."

Lilith shut the door behind herself. Over the edge of the book Margaret saw Skander's boots come up, and the whole sofa shifted ominously as he perched beside her, leaning in to get a look at the book as well. "What is it?"

"I don't know." She turned back the first few pages, and started. "Why, they are dress designs. Whatever does he mean by this?"

"Oh, ha!" said Skander, laughingly. He took the book from her and began thumbing through its pages. Gaily-coloured images flashed by, beautiful gowns and smart men's wear, all fine and foreign to Margaret. "He means for you to pick out a style. You will have a new gown for the ball I am going to throw."

"A ball?" asked Margaret, carefully keeping her gaze on the book.

He returned it to her hand. "Oh yes, I did mention that, didn't I? I'm to give a ball at Lookinglass next month. That was really why I came down today, to tell Rupert about it. All the lords and ladies of Plenilune should be there." He leaned down and smiled, catching her eye encouragingly. "So, of course you must come."

To her dismay, she found herself colouring at the cheeks. She wished that the manservant might come in to make up the fire and cause a distraction, but for a long, agonizing moment the awkward silence lay unbroken between them. In a bid to take control, Margaret pointed out a dress.

"This is rather ghastly," she said. "There is no form to the dress."

"It isn't very flattering, no," he admitted. He turned a page and a rather splendid gown in red sprang out. She made a note of it but did not call his attention to it. But though he continued to turn the pages and other gowns flickered across her vision—high-waisted gowns in deep blue, floor-length tunics in whites and off-whites and saffron, gowns that left the back bare and gowns that came wildly off the shoulders—the scarlet dress lingered in her memory. It was rich and full, sitting becomingly close and riding against the collar-bones in a way that could, with the right poise, be cold and uninviting.

Their perusal and her assessment were interrupted by Rupert's arrival. She was careful not to look up at him, but a strip of mirror inserted between the fireplace and the mantle allowed her an inconspicuous view of his person. He stepped in with a mottled book, pencil, and ruler under one arm, a compass thrust into the breast-pocket of his tunic.

"Is that your star-work?" asked Skander. He deposited the gown book in Margaret's lap and rose. With a little sniff he folded his arms impassively.

"You might call it that," Rupert said.

The two of them drifted apart with Margaret uncomfortably in between. Rupert stationed himself in a chair with an end-table drawn close to support his things; Skander wandered back to the shelves to look at books. Margaret, with nothing else to do, continued to idly turn the pages of her book, looking but barely seeing what passed before her eyes.

The clock over the mantle showed a quarter to two when at last a big black fellow, dressed trimly in white, emerged from a small second door in the south wall and began wordlessly to build up a fire in the grate. Margaret cast him only a cursory glance before automatically returning to her book, but Rupert broke her concentration by asking in a low, strangely gentle tone,

"Did you see anything that you liked?"

Rather perversely she saw, not the red dress, but Rupert's water-logged travelling outfit leaking on the train-car seat. She kept her countenance with the perfection of an Englishwoman and did not reply.

Skander banged a book on the shelf and whistled to himself under his breath.

"Hmm," said Rupert after a while. He picked up his pencil and began sketching on a paper—she could see him in the mirror—and with a little painful jerk of his brows added, "They are only suggestions. The patterns can be altered and made in any colour and fabric that you like."

With a round, mare-ish gesture she lifted her head and regarded him briskly, snapping out the book with it open to the page she wanted. "Since you are being so generous, I will take this dress."

She felt Skander turn at the window behind her, but he did not come forward. Rupert put down his pencil and squinted faintly, for the light was in his face, running his eyes over the image. There was a little of the dubious in his tone as he asked, "You are sure this is what you want?"

"I am sure."

He raised his eyes to hers. His pupils had shrunk almost to nothing and, once more, the pale blue was nearly washed out to white. "Well, then. I'll have Rhea begin at once. You can work on measurements after tea. Livy."

He caught the eye of the big black man who nodded without a sound and, having made the fire, came across and took the book from Margaret. The long, powerful dark fingers reaching toward her, powerful enough to snap her neck in half if they liked, made something clench inside her, but she willed herself to offer the book with icy politeness. Big black Livy folded the book shut, his finger among the pages, and withdrew from the room.

After that the silence that settled was aching. Margaret stared, unseeing, into the new fire, trapped in an odd stillness that was not calming. Why did all the silences of this place sound like the silence before a scream? Why did the stillness of this house feel like the stillness before a storm?

"Miss Coventry." Skander slid a book off the shelf, turned it over, and approached her with it. "Here is something you might like. Do you know *The Tempest?*"

With a little startled breath she turned, reaching a hand for the book. "*The Tempest?* By William Shakespeare? Of course I know it!" He placed the book in her hands and she pressed it in her palms, gazing down at the fine, straight, cloth-bound spine. "He is one of our own."

She could hear the smile in Skander's voice. "There! I thought that might bring a smile to your face. I've always liked that book. I read it as a boy, and looked at the pictures before I could read."

When she looked into the mirror, Margaret caught a swift, dark look on Rupert's face. It was almost the look of murder, but mirrors could be tricky, and she thought she could be mistaken. She hoped she could be mistaken. She dropped her eyes to the book and began turning back the pages. There was a bit of scrawl on the frontispiece but she could not make out the signature. She turned to the title page and the *dramatis personae*, with each page pulling in the alluring scent of old book. She had never read *The Tempest*—truth to tell, she admitted to herself, she was not fond of plays. But it was Shakespeare: it was as English as English could be, and she clutched it desperately for the sake of sheer familiarity. It was touching of Skander to fetch it for her; with a feeling of gratitude mingled with self-loathing, she realized her homesickness must be apparent.

True to Skander's word, the book was beautifully illumined. The margins, like the more ancient texts that Britain had produced, were crammed full of fishes and sea-birds, thunder-blasted pines and the narrow trickle of water down sea-worn rocks. The prow of a foundered ship wedged itself in a margin, showing its shivered stern on the opposite. Men in ragged garments knelt on a shore. A man with one arm around a maiden raised his other arm as if to plead with the heavens. But the shackled spirit himself had his own full page. In body he was strangely featureless, but in genius masculine, tall, beautiful, standing legs apart and with his back to her, turned to give her his profile. There must have been a wind in his face for his hair stood wildly on end, and there was a smile on his face that was meek, pleasant, but somehow unnerving. He had about himself more magic than mere ink could bestow. She gazed on his serene, god-like face and felt a strange thrill: Rupert, splendid as a racehorse, might have been like this once. Only the light flicker in the ink eyes was not to be found in the cool, deadly depths of Rupert's.

Then she remembered that Skander was hovering nearby and that she was looking at a naked spirit. She hastily turned the page. And for a thankful while the book kept her occupied. She looked at all the marginal illustrations and, that done, returned to the beginning and began to read. The fire rose up in the grate, building as time passed and as Skander threw to it an idle log as one might throw a dog a bone, and she felt it warming her shins through her skirts. The soft scratching and shifting of pages from Rupert's quarter went on, broken only at intervals by the deep chiming of a clock somewhere in the house. Skander had sunk himself into a chair and was deep into a book. She glanced up at him once to see his eyelids had fallen shut, though he still held the book upright; she smiled a little secret smile.

But when she glanced round again she saw Rupert looking at her through the fireplace mirror and she felt a sudden stab of guilt, though for what she did not know. With an effort she held that gaze, arching a brow inquisitively, but because it was like looking at a painting, she did not think to speak. He stared and stared, and she made herself stare back, far longer than was polite, far longer than was reasonable, with the firelight dancing on their faces and the light of daring in their eyes. At last—it made Margaret thrill a little with a red sense of victory—Rupert broke his gaze off and returned to his star-work.

For a long while after that the only sounds were those of Skander's book falling to his lap and he was quite asleep and the tinselly rustle of the fire that was slowly putting Margaret to sleep as well. The characters on the pages swam beneath her vision—warm, yellow-coloured pages that were veined with darkness like a kind of marble. A dark, despairing kind of weariness that faded her vision to grey at the edges was slowly overcoming her, but she did not like the thought of sleeping with Rupert about. She fought off the sleepiness, trying to pull each word bodily out of the page and understand what the playwright was trying to say. She had to stay awake...

IV | THE DEVIL'S HUNTING GROUNDS

"Did you rest well?"

Margaret unfolded her napkin on her lap, careful not to meet Rupert's gaze. She and her captor and his cousin were seated in the dining room over late tea, grouped about one end of the table where the cluster of lit candles sent little koi-coloured flecks of light across the polished tabletop. In the cracks between the closed curtains she could occasionally see the silver gleam of light in the sky that was the earth; all else was quenched in night's dark.

"I did," said Margaret, "well enough," and passed on the soup tureen.

With a little sniff that she was coming to know of him, Skander unfurled his own napkin with a violent flick and said, "I was reading Dante's first instalment of his *Comedy*. I don't advise doing so before a nap. It gives one the most curious dreams."

Margaret, who had never read but had heard of the *Inferno*, canted her head politely and opened her mouth to ask about the dreams, when Rupert interrupted.

"I don't know why you read such rubbish." His voice, though low, was rather cutting. With a deft flick he had the ladle out and was curling a bit of soup round-wise into the curve of his own bowl. "I don't know why I still have it. It's so full of lies."

The air crackled between the cousins. The light, amiable nature that hung so well about Skander's big shoulders seemed to slip away like a cloak: the man sat heavily, broodingly in his chair, spooning out his own soup, but watching Rupert sidewise from under his brows. Rupert was busy making his own cup of tea with a bit of brandy to stiffen it, but he took the time to raise a daring look at his cousin, a look that was to Margaret like a rapier, so light it was, so cold and bladed.

Livy took the soup tureen from Skander and set it down on the table, making the little fish-mottled patches of light dance.

"Why," said Skander, picking up his teaspoon and putting it back down for his soup spoon, "do you say it is all lies?"

The rapier darted away, put back in its sheath for now. Rupert closed up the brandy bottle and, by way of Livy, offered it to Margaret. She declined. The bottle was put back up on the sideboard where it cast its own little shards of light, gold and amber-coloured, jinking from the movement of Livy's hand. She watched it in that long silence that Rupert made, her head turned from the two of them, but she did not see what lay under her eye. She was waiting for his answer.

"Is it that you must get rid of everything?" Skander demanded in a low thrusting tone.

She looked back at them. Rupert had begun to drink his soup in a thoughtful sort of way, but even she caught the smile that was playing at one corner of his mouth. She hoped a bit of soup slid out of that smile, just for the indignity of it. But no soup did.

"When your father died, you made changes to Lookinglass. It is not that I 'get rid' of things. This is my house, and it is mine to do with as I please. Also, it is my own opinion that Dante was a liar, and that, too, is an opinion which I am free to hold."

"Then hold it!" Skander said, rocking back in his chair. "And don't pass it off on me."

For a moment, a heartbeat, the time it takes a candle to flicker just one way, the blade was in Rupert's eyes again. And then, just as quickly, it was gone.

With a sigh very like exasperation, Skander turned to Margaret. In that moment she was achingly grateful for his presence. Without him the meal would have been unbearable.

"Do you have riding things for tomorrow, Miss Coventry?"

She scooped up some soup and set the spoon to her lips. "I believe so. My closet seems to be quite large. I am sure to find something suitable inside it."

"Excellent. And remember, we leave early, and it is bound to be chilly and fog-some. Dress warmly. We can't have you catching cold."

"No..." mused Rupert.

Skander kept her busy, detailing her with facts about his harriers and alaunts, and particularly about his falcon Thairm who was kept upstairs on her perch, but would be coming with them in the morning. He surprised her by relating the story of a big doe the falcon had taken down once, her talons and beak in the poor brute's eyes. Margaret would never have thought such a small creature could fell something so much larger than itself.

"We have always been good hunters, we Capys men," he added. "When you come to Lookinglass, I will show you the ballroom floor that is tiled in the pattern of our falcon displayed. It is really quite pretty, and very well done, though I say so myself—it was put down generations ago, so I can't very well take much credit for it."

"That's really very remarkable," said Margaret a little bewilderedly, "about Thairm. How did you teach her?"

"*I* didn't, my falconer did. She is a gyrfalcon, a rather rare bird, caught on a migratory flight four years ago. She was quite the haggard at first, but she has done well and I rather trust her. She has the sweetest way of purring after you feed her, though she is pure devil beforehand."

It was stirring to listen to the warm, round pride that shimmered beneath Skander's tones as he spoke of his falcon, making her sound more like a pet than a creature to put food on the table or a fury bred to kill. Margaret saw her again, bating madly on Skander's fist—and she saw Skander hushing her softly, gently, lovingly. Something twisted in Margaret's gut and the smile on her lips became forced.

She was glad when the meal was over and she could fall back on social habits. She took her leave of them—both gentlemen rose as she left her seat—and, thanking Skander for his conversation, took herself back up to her room. It was a relief, in many ways, to get away.

To her surprise the maid Rhea was waiting for her when she arrived. She had forgot about the dress and about the measurements that needed to be taken. She stood in the doorway to her room, staring at the sewing box and the coil of measuring tape laid out beside her dressing table, and felt a swift jerk of rebellion in her chest. She could tell the maid to go...but that fight had been fought and Rupert had won it—much as it galled her to admit. She stepped into the room and shut the door with a meaningful thump.

Rhea emerged from behind the brass and silver changing partition. She was a little thing, put together rather finely but strongly, and it struck Margaret how tall-seeming she was, though she reached only to Margaret's shoulder. There was something smooth and quiet and uncanny about the girl's dark eyes, like a pool in a forest, a pool whose depths she could not guess.

"If my lady is ready," said Rhea, "we will do something with her hair first, and then we will see to the measurements."

"Your lady is not ready," Margaret replied archly, breezing past the maid. "But that does not much matter in this case, does it?"

Rhea said nothing, though in the reflection on the mirror's face her eyes seemed darker still and still more secret, and for a long while there was nothing but silence between lady and maid as the maid unpinned the lady's hair and began to brush and braid it. Margaret thought that if she shut her eyes she might be able to pretend it was Amy brushing her hair, and not this strange, witching maid at all—but then the thought seemed inexplicably treacherous, and she did not shut her eyes.

Rhea finished and took a step back, hands at her sides. "If my lady is ready," she said, still in that same low, husky tone which was like the warmth of earth, "we will take the measurements now."

Margaret was not ready, but this time she did not say so. She undressed and stood rigidly on an ottoman, moving when told to move, holding still when told to hold still, staring ever straight before her with the constant movement of her heartbeat just on the rim of her vision. It was most pounding when Rhea stepped around and looped the measuring thread around her bust and pulled it tight, tight like a noose, and it was something of a struggle not to throw both off. There was one last hesitating moment as Rhea took the measurement, then the thread fell away and the maid stepped back, saying,

"Small wonder that the master took a fancy to you. You have an excellent figure."

Margaret looked down and around at the cool, dark eyes of the maid. "Is it resentment that I hear?" she asked daringly, cuttingly. "And was your figure to his fancy too?"

The eyes flashed back at her with a dark, mirthless laughter. "No...but it might have, had it been in my mind to make it so." She broke off her gaze to turn to the table and begin wrapping up the contents of her sewing kit. "But I am my lord's maid, and it is well enough to me that you are fit in his eyes." And suddenly she turned back on Margaret with a look like anger. "Mind that you are sure you do not disappoint him."

She was tall-seeming still, for all that Margaret stood on an ottoman and was some ten inches her superior already. A dark chill crept over Margaret, and not merely because she stood in a room that was feeling autumn in its shadows: there was a likeness between Rhea's look and that which Rupert gave slywise to Skander: a dark, half-murderous look that ill-bore reproach and hindrance. But Rhea was only a maid, so Margaret said scornfully, "Well, I am not your lord's maid, and as fit as I may be in his eyes he is not fit in mine."

The young woman seemed to retreat back into the earthy dark of her own eyes; it was as though a veil were dropped between the two of them, and Rhea was suddenly some distance off, though she stood just below Margaret. "Mayhap it is," she said coolly, "that you are blind."

The hot colour flushed in Margaret's cheeks. Not even in a neighbour's house had she ever suffered such insolence from a maid. But the Norman in her, which had long ago mingled with her Saxon Coventry blood, forbade her from rising to the blow. She withdrew into herself, giving back look for look, and watched the maid pack up her kit and retire to the door.

At the door she turned, head up, eyes hooded like a merlin's. "Will my lady be needing any more assistance tonight?"

"Your lady will not."

Rhea smiled mirthlessly. "I did not think so."

"Stay a moment," Margaret said suddenly.

Rhea, her hand upon the latch, stayed obediently, but there was no light of obedience in her eyes.

Margaret sought her words carefully, and all the while made herself to appear careless. "I am going hunting tomorrow. Are you native to this country?"

"I am."

"Tell me, are there wolves in these parts?"

"There are fox and red deer," said the maid, slowly, consideringly, "but no wolves have yet got wind of the sheep we pasture on these slopes. Good-night, my lady." The door clicked softly shut.

Margaret stood on the ottoman with her hands clenched at her sides, cold but ignoring the cold for the low smoulder of velvet-soft anger that kept her warm inside. She had hated before—her mother and her sisters, and even her cousin in a small, shapeless kind of way—but never before had she hated like this, with a warm and passionate hatred, a hatred that like dragon-fire kept her alive inside.

She slipped off the ottoman and stalked back to her vanity. It was a good face that stared darkly back at her, far different and fiercer than the face she had reflected on that noon before dinner. Anger had touched her cheeks with colour, anger had made the low golden flecks of her eyes stand out with a sparking snap.

Well, Mother, she thought, *I hope you are very happy now!*

The clock on the bureau read five to ten. Heaving up the mantle of a dressing gown about her shoulders, Margaret folded up in an armchair with *The Tempest*, for with her own temper up she did not feel at all tired. The room withdrew into itself, a little shell of gold candlelight around her where she sat, and she let the tiring word-figures dance across her vision to charm her into sleep.

Under the quiet of the house there woke a sudden thunder-murmur of sound and she stopped reading, sitting up to listen. With a jewel-vividness she recalled the heart-wrenching howls of last night and the desolation with which she had answered the call. She sat poised on the edge of her seat, expecting to hear it again, her eyes fixed on the pictures around the walls. But nothing began to rattle, and the surf-murmur of angry sound rose and fell in muffled tones but never became the train-roar of last night. It was somehow less frightening thus and without turning back Margaret rose from the chair and crossed to the door, unlatching and opening it to look out on the dark hallway.

It was no hell-hound crooning. From the direction of the library came the sound of men's voices, men's voices raised in a heated discussion. On carefully planted bare feet, Margaret left her room and stole closer, her eyes ever on the shadows of the hallway lest a servant step out and take her by surprise.

She could hear Skander Rime's words before she had reached the door.

"She does not care for you, Rupert! There is not even a spark of affection in her for you."

And Rupert's voice, low and panther-like: "I know what you are doing, Skander, and you had better stop it. I am a jealous man and I do not take kindly to people tampering with my things."

"Ah—!" Skander's voice was momentarily choked off by his own incredulity. "She is not *your* thing—she is not your *thing*! You see, this is exactly the sort of behaviour I was talking about. You look on her as though she were some kind of pawn: something for you to own, to move about to your own ends."

Rupert's voice did not change, which made it somehow more terrible. "You do me very little credit, Skander. That's very uncharitable of you."

"Charity!" There came a scornful snort. "What do you know of charity?"

Unwilling to hear more, Margaret retraced her steps to her room and shut the door behind her, leaning against it, feeling at once sickly cold and furiously hot. With her head back against the roughness of her door, she stared unseeingly at the barred earth-light that came in through the cracks of her curtains. In the glow of her candles, the earth-light was very like the white claw-marks of a tiger on the floor.

"*I would not call her a precocious little chit. I would call her a force to be reckoned with.*"

She let out a shaky, uneasy breath. Her fingers, questing along the wood, found the cold iron protuberance of the lock and twisted it until it clicked sweetly into place. A door slammed somewhere in the house. A dale wind boomed suddenly round the house, rattling the shutters, then all dropped back into that familiar eerie silence.

"*...a force to the reckoned with.*"

She switched her gaze to the clock. Six past eleven. If she was to go hunting in the morning—and she hoped Rupert owned no hell-hounds to accompany them—she had better get to bed at once. She slipped the figure that Rhea had called excellent out of her dressing gown and approached her bed, but with her clustered the ghosts of looks and words and something like the way light played bright and dark within Rupert's brandy. Pawn and mouse! mouse and pawn! She flung back the covers with a vicious flick and crawled in under them, pulling them up close as if to shut off thereby the thoughts that jostled about her head. But she was no longer a child, and the coverlet did not shut off the thoughts that jostled about her head. She lay in the darkness of the lowering candles and stared up at her thoughts that shifted like dark water on her vision. She knew only two things with certainty: firstly that she hated Rupert, and secondly that she was glad for Skander's words in her defence, for without them she would not have felt like a force to be reckoned with at all, but a pawn and a mouse between Rupert's hands.

She turned on her side and closed her eyes against the ghostly sights. She would teach his panther-smugness! Her cheek lay against one of the many velvet pillows and her fingers traced the embroidery of a fine white rose. *I am English*, she thought with a similar white fierceness. *I am English, and I will not be moved by him.*

In the pearly dark of the morning, clad in a riding habit of scarlet which seemed to shout out through the mists, Margaret stood in the great semicircle of the stable yard, adjusting her gloves while the stable hands brought out the horses. Rupert, too, wore scarlet: a fine coat of it with tails like a cardinal's fluttering behind his legs. He stood at some distance from her, fondling the ears of an enormous chequered alaunt and talking in low undertones to Skander. Skander seemed oddly sullen-quiet, and stood stooped a little over his own bulky frame, wrapped up birdwise in his sullen red cloak, Thairm perched and hooded on his fist. Rupert was incongruously in a good mood, which worried Margaret.

Through the stable doors stepped the first of the horses. It was the Master of Marenové's, as was fitting: a beautiful amber champagne creature with loose white feathering about the fetlocks and the soft mizzle striking white sparks off the copperiness of its hair. It shouldered in and stood by quietly as Rupert swung up, suddenly very high and very far away, etched in darkness and scarlet against the mucky sky.

Next came Margaret's own horse, a darcy-coloured grey palfrey that seemed, emerging from the dark interior of the building, to emerge from the otherworld itself. It was unnerving at first, but as her fingers closed about the familiar roughness of the reins and the stable-hand was holding the stirrup-cup steady for her, the solid mortality of the creature warmed her with reassurance. She heaved herself up and settled her skirts as Skander's hunter was brought out.

When all was ready the three horses and the alaunt, joined by a shaggy, lithe grey creature that melted into the mists as much as Margaret's horse did, struck out through the stable yard gates and turned down the lane, moving at an easy lope under the dripping autumn boughs of the damson trees. And Margaret, quite against her will, found it enjoyable. The warm body of the palfrey pulsed under her, rocking with the curious but water-smooth gait of its breed; the shuffing of its breath boomed quietly around her, mingling with the knife-edged whistle of the wind through which they moved. And all around her was a jinking silveriness of grey early morning, a cool clear waking in the nearly bare trees and lawns. In the east the horizon began to pale, and from time to time as they rode, breaking off from the lane and following a cow-path up the side of the fell, the sunlight would break through a crack in the clouds and set a patch of grass and trees ablaze with gold. The light came through more and more the higher they went, and the higher they went the thinner and more hawk-piercing became the air. At last, Margaret in the rear, they skirted a downward curl of blackthorn, scrambled up a broken slope, and stood at the first shelving of the steep fellside just as the sun was burning around the ceiling of cloud.

Rupert paused on the overlook and Margaret's mare, perversely, chose to pause as well, though Skander's hunter clattered on along the slope with the alaunt and the greyhound behind him.

They had come up very high, higher than she had thought; Margaret found herself looking out over a stupendous drop. The fellside rolled steep and far down to the dale where the river lay, a tangled web of silver water on the valley floor. She narrowed her eyes against the sun's sidewise level rays. Harvest was in full swing; the crab-apples were in their last days. The paddocks, meads, orchards and ploughlands mingled together in motley greens and ruddy tawnies and rolled together westward into a smoky-blue where the great sharp-edged arm of the far fell sloped to an abrupt halt.

"Those are the Marius Hills," said Rupert idly, as though he spoke to himself; "and that river is the See, which joins the Glass south of my meads." Then he pointed south and west across the See to where a farm-mead lay around a long hall. Even at that distance Margaret could see the thorn-hedge around the garth and the rolling rows of pear trees that backed up the last foothill of the Marius Hills. "That was my Manor," he went on. "For three years I held it, and these two years past Malbrey has held it for me while I sit at Marenové House."

Behind them on the sidewise-blowing wind came the sound of Skander's hunter and the two dogs coming back to them; with them on the wind came the thin, high scent of late-blooming heather. Down there in that garth that two years ago and for three years had been Rupert de la Mare's Manor, thought Margaret with a sudden and inexplicable touch of sadness, they would be making perry out of the little brown half-rotten pears of the little brown half-wild pear trees.

"Who did you hold the Manor for?" she asked, not looking round.

But Rupert, the heavy bit clanking in his hunter's mouth, took up the reins and called, "*Sa sa cy avaunt*, Talbot! *So ho*, Curoi!— it's time you found a scent for us, you fools."

Neither dog barked, though it took Curoi, the alaunt, some time to be broken off the scent of a polecat and placed back alongside the greyhound. Margaret lingered a moment on the overlook, looking down toward that farm-stead in the lee of the Marius Hills. It was strangely beautiful, with antiquity and durability running through the thorn-hedge veins of it; and she felt herself hating it, because unlike all other things she knew it was beautiful as a thing ought to be beautiful, and it was an impossible distance away.

"Margaret!" Rupert's voice was tell-tale sharp.

"Step up!" she snapped to the horse, and turned its head about on the bit. It gave a little furious squeal and plunged into the fellside wood after the champagne.

Presently they settled down to a gentle walk, letting the dogs cast about, moving steadily through the woods that were flung down the slopes and valley of Seescardale. Sometimes, when they moved up higher and the trees thinned a little, Margaret could look back and see Marenové House beneath them, a splendid block of house and rambling garth couched in its bezel of green. It was mid-October, the air thin and chill and the colours of the landscape brilliant on Margaret's vision. They rode through thickets of hawthorn and hazel, all entwined together with berry-laden bryony. The squirrels were at the hazelnuts, their little russet-grey bodies flickering in and out of sunlight and shadows, anxiously trying to strip off the half-green nuts. It was with some difficulty that Curoi was kept off hunting them.

For the most part, rather incongruously, Skander led the way. Once or twice he seemed to hang on the bit as if meaning to let his mount drop back alongside Margaret, but Rupert rode tenaciously on her near side, never straying out of hearing. No matter what they rode through, wood or stream, Rupert was always there; she could feel him watching her constantly, paying only half-mind to the dogs, and his gaze was like a cold shadow gone widdershins around her, always touching her skin. He took all the splendour out of the morning, all the light out of the sun, and she hated him for that, too, because otherwise she might truly have enjoyed herself. She could feel his eyes as strongly as if they were a hand clamped over her arm.

Strangely, it was a relief when he spoke. They slipped into a narrow glen, fighting with blackthorn and hawthorn and sudden purl of water all the way. As they began mounting the other side, riding up through the tangled red embrace of mountain ash, he slipped in closer and murmured,

"It is an ill thing for me that you look so like the Huntress—unless I be Orion."

The palfrey heaved itself up onto the turf-and-rocky level and for a moment Margaret was looking down with a rampant brow on Rupert. "Orion died."

The beautiful russet-and-grey bulk of the hunter heaved up after her, skittering, churning, throwing its head around against the tightness with which Rupert held it. Shadows and the shadows of shadows flickered swiftly across the man's face and it was more than just the October air that chilled Margaret's skin. But then a wind brushed up the boughs overhead and a shaft of light came though, and it seemed to dissipate the tempest on Rupert's brow. "Then mayhap we will rewrite the story, you and I," he said, "and Orion will not die."

She pursed her lips, thinking it unlikely, but she knew better than to tell him so. With hooded eyes she looked away, urging her mount on after Skander Rime.

The land was almost always sloping, but after another half-hour of riding it began to level out a little, and it was then that Curoi first caught the scent of something worthwhile. His great whiplash tail stuck out straight behind him as he stepped stiffly through the curling ferns, Talbot's lean, shaggy body thrust in beside him. Skander's falcon began to bate wildly again, bells jingling thinly and clearly in the woodland quiet.

"Best let her go," said Rupert, hastily adjusting reins and stirrups. "*Swef, swef,* you fool Curoi!"

With another more vicious jingle, Skander pulled aside and uncovered the magnificent hawk. One fierce golden eye flashed out, looking like murder; the dark wings beat, the thrush-speckled breast lifted with fury. She hung so for a moment, then Skander cast her off, up into the air, wings thrashing, silent but for the frantic tinkling of her bells. She grabbed at the air and gained a height above the trees. There she began circling slowly, upward and upward, while on the forest floor the two dogs were still following the scent.

Margaret watched the hawk, a hand shielding her eyes, and wished that she could fly as well.

They began to move again, following hounds and hawk, moving at a low loping pace through the steadily widening aisles of hornbeam and oak. The grass here was patchy and short, the ground firm and level—excellent country for riding. The steady drum-throb of hoofbeats rolled around them as they turned down light-and-shadow alleys of trees, one eye on the falcon, one eye on the dogs. With the smothered thunder-sound of the horses' hooves rose the drum of Margaret's heart, for it was coming home to her that this was a hunt, a reckless chase through scrub and open to catch and kill a creature. She did not much mind the death, but as her palfrey took a liquid leap over a fallen oak-bough and she had to keep her seat, she began to be a little afraid of this pace.

But the pace was nothing to that which they set when, without warning, Thairm suddenly tucked in her wings and plummeted. Skander, in the lead and his cloak a snapping red flame behind him, rose up in the stirrups, doubled over his hunter's neck, and cried encouragement to the hounds. Rupert burst in beside him and the three horses and the two hounds were eating up the ground, hurling headlong through the wood. The high, throaty, blood-curdling cry of a hound on the scent suddenly issued from Curoi's mouth.

"*Avaunt! avaunt! Sa cy avaunt!*"

It was hard to breathe, moving at that reckless pace, whipping up through a sudden lift of land, crashing through low-hanging hornbeam, plunging through blackthorn, skirting sudden mucky streams. Margaret's hair pulled itself out of the neatness into which Rhea had tamed it; her cheeks were flushed, her hands sweaty in her gloves. Through snatches of stinging boughs she was thankful for the palfrey, whose gait was otherwise gentle, even at this swiftness.

It was in a dog-leg of glen that she first spotted the quarry. They tore round a wooded bend, the drum of hooves dulled by a thick blanket of grass, and between the low-hanging, thick bodies of yew she caught sight of a ruddy flash, like light in amber, broken up by the wing-beat of speckled brown that was Thairm. They swung about and came up the glen, the hounds in the lead, and Margaret saw the quarry.

It was a fox, large and leggy with the colour of flames in its coat. Thairm had backed it into the bottleneck of the rock-sided glen where it was fighting for its life, springing and dashing and snapping at the big bird that dropped on it like a brick, slashing with talons and beak. Scarlet mingled with the fire-colour of its fur.

"Harry!" cried Rupert in an awful voice. "Harry him! Harry him!"

Margaret yanked on the reins, bringing her palfrey to a sitting halt. If there was an unruly thickness in Curoi's head, he at least understood his master's last command. Thairm broke away with a jingle of bells and an angry shriek as the enormous dog hurtled in, its sharkish mouth open like the mouth to hell. She saw the fox turn in that single, bright, feather-hanging moment; she saw the look that passed across its snarling face as it saw its mottled black-and-white death coming.

"*Harry him...!*"

Curoi hit the fox with a thump. There was a squeal, a snap, a jerking, writhing movement, and the fox hung from the alaunt's mouth, its head at a painful, lifeless angle. But the alaunt, in its own animal rage, began worrying the body of the fox this way and that, a sick, high whine of joy coming through its nose. Talbot lunged in, lips curled back, snapping at the hind legs of the fox. Suddenly it was a fight, the fox's body in between. The beautiful flame-coloured coat was torn, bloodied, useless.

And Margaret saw, as she looked hard and coldly up into Rupert's face, saw as Skander did not see—who was tending to Thairm—the swift soft expression of satisfaction pass over the young man's face.

When the fight was beginning to turn ugly, Rupert broke in, thrashing at both until they backed snarling off the fox's carcase.

While he was busy with them, Skander found a moment in which to sidle close, Thairm once more leashed and hooded on his fist.

"Are you unwell?" he asked in a gentle undertone.

She would not look at him, for his gentleness rankled and she could not quite bring herself to be as cross with him as she presently felt. "No, I am not unwell."

Out of the corner of her eye she saw him turn and look toward the dead fox, and she realized he was as sorry as she was, if less angry.

"Is he always like this?" she demanded of a sudden.

He looked back at her, sharply, and hung a moment as if in thought. She could not meet his gaze; she suffered not knowing what particular look was on his face. But Rupert was finishing with the hounds and would be back soon, so Skander said, in an oddly desperate, quiet voice, "I would be lying if I said yes."

She looked then at him, and he looked back, his expression as pitying and tender as hers was cold and hard. Her gaze did not waver, but she saw, too, the brown-shadow figure of Thairm on his hand. *If you could unhood me, and take off my leashes, I would fly too.*

I wonder—whence would I fly?

With a darkly jovial spirit Rupert plunged back in among them, driving his horse up between theirs. With the red collar of his jacket turned up and the wind having got in his hair, he was like some giddy cardinal-bird. There was a fierce and laughing smile on his face which reminded Margaret more than ever of some type of devil.

"Not bad, Curoi," he said warmly, bending down to rough the alaunt's ears. "Not bad, you old fool!"

The hounds pressed in close around Rupert, fawning around him, and she and Skander were driven apart. They did not speak again until they had broken their casual hunting expedition and were coming down the long low slopes toward the House. The sun was high in the afternoon quarter, and the earth's enormous sliver was but a seraph's feather in the sky above them as they skirted a little stream and crossed it, coming down into the stable paddock. The high sun and thin air made Margaret warm under her scarlet habit and she was heartily glad to leave behind the bee skeps on the slopes and wind through the elm-shaded lawn of the paddock. The robins were in the elms, twittering their notes as thin as the dale air—as thin and as electrum-coloured—and from somewhere back toward the more unruly woods came the liquid notes of a single thrush.

Skander put down the hurdle at the mouth of the stable yard and let them through, closing it after them. It was strange how different the yard looked, bathed in yellow sunshine, when that dim morning it had been an otherworldly hollow of mists and cold. The sounds of the horses' shoes, which had sounded as hollow and as lifeless that morning, rang out sweetly on the cobbles.

The stableboys and one particularly wizened old stable-hand came to fetch their horses. Margaret unhitched her leg from the fixed pommel and dismounted a little gracelessly under her own power—but she could not bear to have Rupert help her, and she did not dare to let Skander step in lest he make Rupert angry. Rupert, if he caught her gesture of defiance, did not mention it, but stood back from his own mount as the boy took the reins and gave its gold-flaming hindquarters a hearty slap in passing.

"It conjures up an appetite, doesn't it," he asked her, "being out on the chase all morning?"

It was uncanny how the shadows of the stable door made the amber champagne's coat flare to foxy colour as it passed through.

"Yes," said Margaret, and it was only half a lie for she was hungry and put off at the same time.

He stripped off one glove and, before she could resist, grabbed her hand in his free one with such a crushing grip that she could not pull away, though her instinct was to jerk back. He was smiling, so that at a distance he looked pleasant, but thrusting a sharp, hateful glance at him Margaret saw the tell-tale hardness that lay like a veil behind his eyes.

"You're a game girl," he said. "Now let's go get you washed up, you little vixen."

"I may be game," she said in an undertone as he pulled her away from the stable yard, "but I am *not* a vixen."

"No?" A quizzical smile played on his face. "You have fangs enough."

Yes, and she wanted to bite him, and for a moment the sullen Saxon blood nearly overpowered the cooler Norman judgment. But only for a moment, and then she said quietly as they passed through the long north corridor toward the atrium, with a cutting that she relished, "That may be, but it is an ill thing for me if I am a vixen for I have seen how you deal with the fox."

He stopped her then and there, his hand suddenly gone to her upper arm—she could feel the powerful thumb pressing, pressing, pressing into the tender softness of her vein—and there was a high, dark, horrible power in his face as he stared at her. She could almost feel the tingling rasp of their iron gazes sliding against each other like blades.

"Yes," he murmured, half-laughing, wholly in earnest. "And the vixen would do well to remember that."

Margaret slowly clenched a length of her skirt in one hand, dissipating through it the pain in her arm and the unnerving shiver caused by the realization that Rupert's face, divided sharply by shadow and light, crowned by a raven's darkness, was more handsome than any face she had ever seen. Angular, powerful, keen—like a hawk.

"It's very rude to stare, you know," she said.

A mirthless smile flashed up on his features. With a cruelly painful jerk he turned her about, thrusting her on before him. Her toe skimmed the floor, barely missing tripping her up, but somehow she held her head high and kept her shoulders square though the pressure of Rupert's fingers was like talons and the sudden twisting movement, added to the morning of riding, sent screams of pain up and down her back.

Once they were in the entryway, she shook him off, warning him with the pricking of her glare to keep away. He put his hands on his hips and watched her out of the paleness and darkness of his eyes—she could feel his gaze on the back of her neck as she climbed the stairs, even after she had passed out of sight. When she had reached the relative safety of her room, and locked it against Rhea's unwanted help, she stood staring out the window on the bright front lawn and, with a mingled wave of heart-sick weariness and rebellion, thought perhaps she would not go down to tea.

Skander left Marenové House early the next morning. Wrapped up in tartan wool against the mizzling dampness of the dawn, Margaret stood on the stable yard steps watching the brown hunter brought out. The single enormous hornbeam, which looked as though it had been left behind when all other hornbeams had been cleared for the building of the house, stood by the door, dropping now and then its wets leaves to splatter on the cobbles and make odd, sad, fish-scale patterns there. She felt the odd, sad, fish-scale pattern on her soul, but she did not want to admit it. A part of her raged against Skander for ever coming. She might have met this long, horrible stay at Marenové House with equanimity had it not been for his friendly advances upsetting the otherwise austere atmosphere of the place.

As the old walnut stable-hand moved to adjust the horse's accoutrements, Skander sauntered over, donning his hawking gloves as he did so. His face was crumpled slightly against the soft rain, but there was also a kind of confused tenderness there which Margaret was suddenly and keenly afraid of.

"I won't see you until New Ivy," said Skander as he stood by her under the hornbeam. She felt him looking at her, uncertain, searching for words to say. But there was nothing to say, and after a long pause he put up his hand and said, "Good-bye, Miss Coventry."

She put a hand in his and let him kiss it, and she knew she said something appropriate, but her words felt smothered by the misty rain. He went off, spurs sparking light in the gloom, the sound of his boots and his horse's shod hooves ringing on the cobbles. The mists curled around him as he mounted, he and his great gyrfalcon etched and smudged dark-grey against the grey steel sky, framed by the old timber ramparts of the yard walls. He turned and turned about, settled in, and left with one last wave of his hand through the yard gate. The soft drub of the hunter's hooves on the damp turf of the paddock rolled back to her, softly, softly...until it, too, faded into the grey of the October morning.

Someone breathed out deeply beside her. "It's good to have one's house to oneself again," said Rupert from where he stood at her elbow in the doorway, arms folded comfortably across his chest.

Margaret gathered up her black skirts and moved off the step. "Almost," she said, turning to blink up through the rain at him. His eye fell on her: a horrible gaze from a god's horrible height. "I am still here."

He said nothing, though even through the greyness of the air she could see the barb had stung. In a moment he stirred, leaned forward a fraction, and touched her cheek with one outstretched finger. She felt the warm pressure of it against her chilled skin, but though all her sullen pride yearned to jerk away, she made herself suffer under it until, apparently satisfied, Rupert withdrew his hand. Without a word, without another glance, Margaret turned and left him on the doorstep.

It was quiet and warm-smelling in the barn. The building ran the length of the north stable yard wall and had a big door cut into the middle of its south face; on either end the haying doors were cut into the stable yard walls, and these were open too. Standing in the dark blue-amber interior of the barn, Margaret looked from side to side, catching the square misty images of the paddock outside. The muffled, sleepy sound of horses came to her through the many partitions.

There was something comforting in the simple, brute presence of the animals. She left the doorway and moved along the rows of stalls, peering through the gloom at the many name-plates by the boxes. She caught a glimpse of her own palfrey but the horse was half-dozing and she did not stop to wake it. With her tartan pulled over her head, she left the stable overhang and emerged into the paddock where the wind was blowing in fitful gusts and the scent of winter was strong.

She was looking out and over the gentle swell of the paddock; the bodies of those horses at grass shifted in and out of the mists and once, from far off, she heard one give a kind of liberated whinny that rang hollow in the dale. The border-hedges of blackthorn, holly, and barberry were mingled in the distance into a dark, spiked wall that cut off the paddock from the road and from the neighbouring fields. Through a gap in the low-growing, tangled trees she could see a grey glimpse of the river valley, very pale as though seen through an aged mirror; and on the far side of that lifted the Marius Hills, detached from everything and looking down iron-sombre over all. It occurred to her that she could hear only the horse and the wind and the swish of the wind in the grass: those hills looked down on no mill towns or shrieking, puffing trains. A great hush was all around her, the quiet of a spacious and unbroken farmland. This quiet, at least, did not feel as if it were about to erupt into a scream at any moment.

A new sound startled her. The rasp of iron over stone broke her concentration and she looked round to see the old walnut stable-hand, his gnarled body bent double, working with a hoe in a messy patch of garden. He had an enormous wheel-barrow parked outside the little wattle fence, a wheel-barrow Margaret was not sure the old man could possibly lift, let alone push, and it was filled to the brim with dead leaves. As she watched, the old man stuck his hoe into the earth and turned aside, picked up an armful of the damp, smelly leaves, and threw it broad-cast over the garden plot, all the while grunting and grumbling to himself like a pig that is truffle-hunting.

Margaret moved closer, watching with detached interest as the man worked. If he noticed her standing outside the wattle fence he did not let on, but continued to throw down dead leaves—leaves of oak and hazel, hornbeam, red flame-shaped leaves of alder, hawthorn and blackthorn—and stamp them thick and close as if his life depended on it.

"Why do you do that?" she asked at last.

The old man breathed deeply and straightened, and she realized that he must have been rather tall in his youth, and big of build; but time, and hard work, and the sun had wrinkled and shrivelled and burnt him into the little walnut thing he was now. He looked at her out of his wrinkled, brown, walnut face, his eyes like sloe-berries, and he seemed not cross, as she would have expected, but slow and patient and cheerfully grumbling—which, being English, was a thing she could understand.

"Every year, nigh on fifty years, I knowed this plot o' garden," he said in a voice that had been rich once, but had been wrinkled walnut-wise along with the rest of him, "I covered it up in leaves for winter." He tapped the ground with one beaten leather boot. "Keeps 'em warm, hmm?"

She looked dubiously at the ugly wet leaves. "My father's gardener never did such to *our* gardens."

The old, wrinkled, walnut face turned up in a patient, contemptuous smile. " 'Tain't for *me* to interfere," he said in his slow walnut drawl, "but if ye have mind to see that man again—tush! cain't call 'im a gardener!—ye might tell 'im otherwise."

"Perhaps I will."

He picked up his hoe and leaned on it, though she had a feeling he did not need to, and regarded her placidly for a few minutes, seemingly unhurried to return to his work. She lifted one brow artfully and gazed back at him. She had been taught, as all good, well-born girls are taught, to stand with perfect stillness and attention, and to look well while doing it; but this old wrinkled stable-hand, gardener, farm-worker, labourer stood with perfect stillness too—and upon one leg, she realized after a few moments, like a heron, with only the sloe-berry darkness of his eyes winking back and forth as he looked at her face. The gesture was somehow less unnerving than she thought it ought to be.

"Nah, then," he said broadly, and sniffed in an oddly deferential kind of way, "ye's mus' be the new lass young Mus Rupert has brought home. En' beg all pardon, but I allus reckoned transplantin' so foreign never was good for the plant."

Margaret quirked a mirthless smile. "On that score I would have to agree with you, Master Gardener."

"Ol' Hobden!" he said, waving one hand. And then he shook his head. "Nigh on sixty years I knowed Marenové 'Ouse, an' my father afore that, and 'im father afore *that*, but never a badder business any of us knowed than young Mus Rupert. 'E don't take to soil," he said passionately, as if Margaret would understand. "Got too much acid in 'is veins an' Lord love ye if ye can get a touch o' lime into 'is soul. Never a badder business—never a badder business." He continued to shake his head. "I knowed 'em since they was two, an' Lord knows why he took t'one and not t'other."

It was rainy-silent for a few moments. The horse called again, hollow in the quiet.

"I beg your pardon?"

"Hur!" said old Hobden, quizzically.

Margaret leaned forward slightly from the waist. "I beg your pardon. You knew who?"

The man bustled about like a little old bird. He shoved his hoe against the wattle fence and began digging his arms into the earthy mass of leaves that was still in the wheel-barrow. " 'Tain't for *me* to interfere, if 'e ain't told ye. Dunnos as 'e would, though. Them was allus the light an' dark sides o' the moon." He quirked one grizzled brow and sloe-berry eye at her. "Them was the two of 'em, young Mus Lords of Marenové, nigh over a year apart in age. Funny odd thing how's close they'd be, an' how's allus at hammer an' tongs with t'other. I allus say, Lord hadn't taken t'older o' the two, 'e done right by Marenové 'Ouse."

Margaret looked up, squinting against the mizzle that was quickly turning to full rain. The strange bulk of the north tower, alone-seeming among all the rest of the house's architectural shapes, loomed brooding and forbidding over her. "How did he die?"

"Not as I knowed anythin'," said Hobden, "an' tha's more than I knowed. All I knowed was they brought 'im 'ome one day like a fish what's been gutted. Boar, mus likely." He fell into a soft kind of quiet after his harsh and descriptive explanation, and added a moment later, "Them roses n'er did bloom rightly after that, I swear to ye. Don't rightly knowed if 'twas for 'im they un-bloomed or for the sadness in me own fingers."

She brought her eyes down from the squat, stupendous bulk of the tower and followed the line of his waved gesture. The roses, rather splendid, thick, full roses whose age she did not dare to guess, had flung themselves over the stable yard wall and clung to it in a thick mass, dark reddish-green in the gloom, fish-scale shining in the rain—but bud-less and barren. What colour would they be, she wondered, if they were to bloom again? A dormant spark of imagination thought their last bloom ought to have been crimson, and any resurrecting bloom ought to be white as York.

With a shiver of cold she shook off the notion and turned back to old walnut Hobden. "You seem to have the way about you with plants," she said, and meant it genuinely.

He smiled grimly, his mouth a long gash in his wrinkled face. "Sixty-some years'll teach a body to be plant-wise—and other things, iffen ye listen."

Margaret looked on him as a kind of Indian conjuror who mingled a familiar slowness of body and speech that she found comforting. He was no more than a labourer, and an old one at that, but she found herself wandering out to him in the following days, wrapped up in tartans and furs, to sit and read or merely to sit. As beneath her as he was, his quiet, truffle-hunting presence was far more agreeable than Rupert's. She followed him about the grounds, and came to know the grounds passing well, and listened patiently if uncomprehendingly to the times when Hobden sought to invest her with some knowledge. But for the most part they were silent with each other, withdrawn even when they were together—for even Hobden, old and revered as he was, took off his cap to her and was gruffly polite, and Margaret, ever conscious of protocol, let him do so.

One night Rupert broke the silence which reigned so supreme and chilly over their suppers by setting down his glass and saying with a marked touch of regret in his tone, "This weather will not last. Soon you will have to give up your walks."

The hour was late; Rupert had gone down to his tenant Malbrey's manor that afternoon and had not got back until dusk. He had come back up the Marenové track, the wild cardinal-coloured clouds of evening rampant and upraised behind him, the shadows turning his horse into a dark ruddy creature that pranced and shivered beneath him as the sparse leaves of the damson trees pranced and shivered in the wind. It was strange how at ease Margaret had felt when he had been away; watching him in his red fury of colour riding up the lane, something in her stomach had clenched again.

Margaret busied herself with her own wine glass, tipping the liquid gently onto the fore of her tongue to take the delicate, rich taste of the drink. The lights on the glass, in the wine, and on her tiny chain bracelet, dazzled her eyes for a moment.

Rupert went on. "I am glad to see that you are adjusting well. I suppose that is the English in you."

She looked up over the rim of her glass and caught the half-disdaining sneer that lifted his lips from his dog-teeth for a moment.

"And if you do not have the walks to keep you busy presently, there is the gala that Skander Rime is throwing to occupy your mind...though it is in my mind that you are not a woman to care overmuch for such frivolities."

The fractalled images of a party glanced across her mind. Gowns, tunics, ceremonial swords, the distant scream of carriage-horses and the distant trill of music, all bound up in a web of golden light... She set down her glass with a deliberate click. "No?"

"No. But you will go anyway."

His eyes were the paleness of a knife when she looked into them, the paleness and coldness of a knife held almost to her throat. He had given her a great deal of freedom in her walks and rambles about Marenové House, he had removed himself to a distance and given her room to grow accustomed to her new surroundings. Looking back on the past two weeks since Skander had gone back to Lookinglass, she realized what a cool, masterful ploy it had been of Rupert's to let her wander. Now she had reached the end of her leash, and he was letting her feel the pull of the collar.

Her eyes narrowed at him.

"How poorly you have sketched my nature!" she said with a flippant and caustic tone. "I have no objection to balls and parties. What is the point of shining if there is no sky to shine in?"

There was a warmth in his smile, though the knife was in it as well. "That is my girl." He got up, not waiting for her to do likewise, and began to walk the length of the room toward the windows, his supper finished, his wine-glass in hand. At such a vantage he appeared well physically, framed between two lit candelabra, dark, tall, clad in a deep moth-wing grey tunic. She might have hated him less had he been homely or a hunchback, but her heart blistered with the heat of her hatred for him because he was chiselled and handsome, like a god of war, and he knew it.

I despise you, she mouthed the words. Aloud she said, in an altogether new tone, "I have one objection, though."

He turned his hawkish profile on her, one brow rampant.

"I do not think it is appropriate that we should go to any ball in these circumstances."

He swung about, the light flashing wildly and redly in his glass. "My dear Margaret," he said softly, the way a cat purrs. "My dear Margaret—these circumstances? You hold the power to change them in your hand."

Impulsively her left hand, which lay in her lap, closed until the nails bit into her palm.

The cat's purr, the cat's smile, the cat's little flicker of enjoyment in the eyes all played about Rupert. "If you think it is inappropriate for us to appear officially in public until we are married, only say the word."

She did not recall getting to her feet. She did not recall throwing down her napkin. She only knew that she was leaving the room, skirts rustling anxiously around her, and she could hear Rupert's mocking laughter in her mind. He was not laughing, but she could hear it. She could hear it as plainly as if he stood beside her.

I despise you. I despise you! The words beat to the cadence of her feet on the stairs upward. *I despise you all!*

Once in her own room she shut the door and went directly to the window, throwing back the curtains to let in the strong electrum light of the earth. It was in waning gibbous, if she could call it such, and its light was powerful, flooding over the lawn and paddock, fields and dale. Far away the Marius Hills were a bulk of dragon's shoulder lifted against the terrestrial glare, silhouetted and black as the mother of all shadows. She stared up past them, up past the oak that grew on the lawn, past the pale tendrils of cloud that had been torn by high winds across the sky, up at the earth.

It no longer rattled her as it had that first night. She did not often look it squarely on, if she could help it, but she did so now for no reason she could put into words. She gripped the casement in a light but steady hand and stared into the half-pearl eye of mottled white and blue.

She was caught between two evils. Which did she choose, since she had to choose—Rupert, or her own family? At her back breathed the threat of her suitor's proposal, before her loomed the impossible distance of space and the dislike of her own kind.

"A little more than kin and less than kind," she murmured. Her breath fogged on the cold pane, and for a moment the glaring light was diffused through a mothy web of silver, and it was almost beautiful. Then, with a painful unchanciness, her mind jerked aside to Skander. Was he a way out? Was he the *tertium quid* she hardly dared believe she could have?

No. That thought was dashed almost the moment it came into her mind, leaving her pained and empty inside like a fly that has been a spider's dinner. She knew Rupert little—she wanted to know him little—but she understood him well enough to know he would not stay his hand should anyone or anything come between him and his ambition. Nothing would be spared, not even the life of his own cousin. She could not put Skander in a position to suffer such a fate.

From the northern head of the dale came the muffled sound of autumn thunder.

With a gusty sigh Margaret folded her arms across her chest, rubbing her hands viciously on her upper arms in an attempt to warm them, for the air seeping through the pane was very cold. She wore a gown of cambric and the fabric made the softest, most whispering noises under her absentminded hand.

At last she turned away from the window. She cast a quick eye about the dark room and saw that everything was in order. Rhea might or might not return to see if she needed anything. It would be well for both of them, thought Margaret, if the maid chose to surreptitiously forget her evening duties to her mistress. As she turned her back on the glare of earth-light, her own shadow long and looming dark across the floor, she knew there was only one answer. Earth was too far away for her to reach, her family too ignorant and uncaring to reach out to her. She was caught between Rupert's thumb and first finger, a pawn in his hand, and she could only do his bidding.

Her eye lighted on the door. He would not have gone to his chamber yet. He might still be in the dining room, standing at the window, looking out on the lawn even as she had—but across at the hills and down into the valley, which were his, and not up at the oblong gash of planet that was hers. If she went now she would find him and tell him she would accept his proposal. What else was to be done? She had no other way out, and he was handsome and rich and attentive, if sometimes cruel and dark, like the dark side of the moon. She stirred, half-heartedly, like a bird in its feathers...

But she did not move forward. Perhaps it was mere apathy that held her back, or the single spark of pride in her that Rupert had not found and stamped out. She reached behind herself and began to earnestly tug at the buttons of her gown, dismantling it and casting it heedlessly on the back of a chair. She hastened into her lawn night-gown, which was even cooler than the air of her bedroom, all the while telling herself with renewed vigour that though it was only a week to the gala she would go with her head held high and unshackled. Skander had called her a force to be reckoned with, well—let Rupert reckon with her. She climbed into bed and turned her face into the full glory of the earth's light. She could not reach it, but its unwilling ambassador to Plenilune would make it proud.

She lay back, staring up at the canopy of her bed with her arms tucked behind her head and pillow. Everything was broken up in ebony and white; from within the pool of earth-light she could not distinguish the shapes of her own bedroom. But she knew that in one corner, underneath a cloth, was the red dress that she was to wear to the gala. It was very nearly done; it did not need a whole week to complete it.

The light began to hurt and she shut her eyes. Far away, but rolling and angry and long as the length of a dragon, growled the thunder.

The red looked well on her. It brought out the subtle red tones of her hair and made her cool eyes flash, and even if she looked to herself totally foreign, she had to admit that it became her. She smiled, coolly and a little scornfully, at the thought of her mother's long monologues on what a girl could do to look beautiful.

I am English, she thought, rolling over and pulling the blankets close to her chin, *and we have no beauty but in our tempers.*

V | EXILE

The storm broke over Seescardale and Marenové House in the cobwebby-grey of the early morning, and kept the world wrapped in cobweb-grey to the threshold of the New Ivy Moon. The bad weather kept both Margaret and Rupert indoors, and as vast as the house was, she could not quite avoid him. She felt at times that he was deliberately following her, or deliberately preceding her; once she stepped into the long upper hall above the kitchen wing and found him standing at the bank of windows, looking out westward into the rolling surge of the storm, his body bound up in a cloak so deeply purple it was almost black. There was the briefest flicker of worry between his brows in that single instant, then he caught sight of her out of the corner of his eye and turned to look directly at her. It was strange, but in the jab of his eyes—a jab that hurt her breastbone—she felt as if the storm were all her fault.

She picked up her skirts and left him without a word.

It was with a vindictive sense of satisfaction that Margaret rose from her bed on the morning of New Ivy Eve and, turning back the curtains, found the world drenched in a blinding clear gold. The storm was gone: the freshness, the brightness, the crispness of Plenilune autumn burned across the landscape as Margaret had never seen an autumn burn before. The lawn and lane were covered in a fish-scale coat of brown and red leaves—and gold in places, where the half-wild maples had thrown down their mantles. The horses were in the paddock, leaving tracks in the dew where they went. At the end of the kitchen wing she could just see old Hobden splitting firewood.

Inexplicably she pulled back, letting the curtains drop in place again. She felt now as she had when she had looked down on Rupert's old Manor: a mingled sense of beauty and of pain, and everything that was worth anything seemed as far away from her as earth.

Rupert was not at breakfast. When she went down, Margaret found a neatly-cut card on her plate which read:

"I have gone up-See to fetch one last touch for your gown. I will be back by dinner. Take care of yourself, my dear—Rupert."

It was brisk, touching, caring, and Margaret tossed the card away with a flick of her wrist. It fluttered feather-wise on the tabletop, sliding on the smooth surface, and hid itself under the edge of a silver candelabra. She let it lie, out of sight and out of mind, and ate her breakfast in solitude.

It was her first clear day in almost a week. There was no time to dawdle. She put on a frock of fawn-coloured corduroy and stepped out of doors, following the sound of the slow, incessant chopping.

It surprised her how very much old Hobden looked just as she had left him. His bent, wrinkled, nut-brown body was encased in the same cotton shirt, the same tattered leather vest, the same corduroy trousers and boots. He made the same soft, irritated grumbles as he always did. For no reason she could explain, she thought he ought to have changed; for no reason she could explain, she was glad he had not.

"Good morning," she said graciously, finding a seat on a giant block of wood. Her fingers dug into the hard, sun-warmed bark and she felt the rough rings of the tree's heart under her palms. In this little southern corner of the House, the sun of late autumn, the sun of early morning, dreamed of being warm.

With a slow, circular, ambling movement Hobden swung the axe down and away and gave a little salute, tugging with thumb and forefinger on his forward tuft of hair. "G'moornin'," he rejoined in that rich, raspy, walnut tone of his. He squinted northward and added, "Mus Rupert's gone away for the day, hmm?"

Margaret nodded.

Hobden turned away and fumbled with his handle on the axe-haft, grumbling under his breath like a badger all the while. " 'Tain't for *me* to say, but I knowed Marenové took a breath of relief when 'e passed beyond t'intake."

"Marenové and I both," murmured Margaret, with her head turned away so that Hobden would not hear.

Old walnut Hobden went back to his work, swinging slowly away at the wood while the wood fell away beneath his blows, sheering off in even twos so that he was presently surrounded by a pile of large, split, almond-looking pieces of wood. He did not seem to tire, but went on with all the steadiness of an engine. Margaret watched him absentmindedly for some time, wrapped up in her tartan against the November chill; but presently, as he showed no signs of stopping, she began to grow tired of the monotony. She got up, skirting him carefully, and began to wander along the southward arm of the home-meads which were less cultivated and bore the stamp of the wild encroaching fells more clearly than the other gardens.

Broom and furze, whose flowers had long since fallen, and bramble, whose berries had long since been picked, made a kind of wild hedge at the end of the low slope that took and channelled the little stream. It seemed to be the oldest piece of garden; there was no foot-bridge over the stream, which Margaret would have expected to find elsewhere on the grounds, but a mere loose collection of flat stones rising out of the stream-bed. She took the stones without another thought, crossed a bit of grassy, unkempt soft turf that might have been a flower-plot once, and squeezed gingerly through the thorny gap in the intake hedge.

After that there was a thin, short wood of alder that did its best to sink its roots into the stream. She climbed through it and out, with the suddenness of stepping from one world into another, upon the tawny shoulder of the fell. The wind was all around her as it had not been in the low hollow of the House grounds: it boomed and galloped, thundering, brushing, lunging and kicking like a stampede of horses round her shoulders. It was a golden wind, golden and bronze like the wings of an eagle, and the bright colour of it swelled around her with a potency like water. She moved through it, borne and buffeted by it, with the House falling away behind her like a bad dream.

A narrow goat-path, a mere thrush-coloured thread in the tawny turf, stretched upward before her, skirting the steep side of the fell, but always stretching upward, upward and around and out of sight behind the distant shoulder of the fell. Without a thought she struck out on it, climbing upward with the swell of the air all around her. It became a bother to wrestle her wrap around her shoulders and she let it go, holding onto it with only one hand so that it flew out before her like a multicoloured banner of primitive war, fierce and free, its snapping and billowing the very laughter of its genius. She felt it stirring something in her blood.

After a quarter-hour of walking, the wind had slackened into a soft constant rush, and she paused on the goat-path to look back. She had come far and high; Marenové House lay below her, the view of it unobstructed by trees—if she strained she could just make out the tiny toy-figure of Hobden still at work. If she was careful, if she stood perfectly still, with one hand up to shove her wayward hair out of her eyes, she could almost imagine she was not wearing Rupert's collar and leash.

It was a cruel trick, she thought, to be trapped in a land that seemed so high and wild and free.

With prim deliberation she gathered up her wrap and skirts and continued on. She rounded the swell of the hillside and found herself above a flock of sheep, quite a large flock, overseen by two squat calico dogs. They ranged all down the slope and into the finger of a green stream valley. To Margaret, walking along to the tune of their thin bell-notes, they looked like a spray of blackthorn blossom flung across the fell's slope. Quaint and picturesque, pastoral, uninhibited by the torments and cares of the young woman poised above them, they went on grazing—and would go on grazing, she thought with a pang of strange longing, time out of mind as they had always done, no matter who sat at Marenové House.

And suddenly, from somewhere high in the folds of the fell's flank, high up above the flock of sheep that was like the blowy white blossom-fleece of a blackthorn, high and clear there came to Margaret the sound of a panpipe playing. The sound stopped her in her tracks, frozen like a bird, and she listened to that sound as she had never listened to a sound before: and it seemed to her, as she listened, to be the very calling of a soul. It spoke across the dale, silver and thin, but full-bodied like wine, crying and self-satisfied, alien and remote. A pianoforte and its notes, a harp and its notes, were all separate things, but to Margaret the panpipe and its song were living and eerie, as though it were, not the voice of an instrument a man had made, but the soul's-voice of the fell itself.

Just as quickly as the song had come, she ached as she had not let herself ache in weeks. It was not for home, it was not for her family. She did not know what it was for. She only knew that she had to get away from that free, melancholy voice among the fells— which was the very voice of the fells themselves—before it crushed her.

The music of the panpipe came after her for a distance until, with a struggle between the wind's upward rushing, it gave way to the intermittent gurgle of a plover. Without haste, but without hesitation, Margaret moved into the face of the wind, fighting for each step downward. She was glad for the fight: it gave her something to occupy her mind with and it lessened, a little, the ache that had sprung up like a candle's flame beneath her breastbone. It was with relief that she finally came down the last stretch of slope and saw the alder-hanger and the thorn hedge, though it was not with relief that she saw the looming bulk of the House.

She stopped inside the gap and looked around, feeling oddly more out of place than ever. Hobden must have finished his work: there was no sound of axe barking on wood. The plover still gurgled somewhere on the fellside; from the thickest tangle of alder a chiffchaff was singing *Ode to Joy* and, from farther off, a blackcap was shrieking something about freedom. She cast a baleful glance backward and began up the garden, keeping to the rear path.

It would be the dinner hour soon, and Rupert would be returning. Beyond the thorn hedge she left her walk of freedom; ahead she anticipated Rupert's questions. Was her walk refreshing? Did she enjoy herself? And all the while as she strode up the path she could just see the faint mockery that flickered in the backs of

Rupert's eyes. But what appalled her most was that she could find no answer. Her walk abroad beyond the home-meads, where things went on with the rhythm of the land, had pained her almost as much as the familiar routine of a manor house.

She stopped by a massive rose-bush, bereft of buds but still adorned in green-flame leaves. As she knew it would, the inexplicable pang returned as soon as she ceased motion, but this time she understood its meaning. It was not for home, it was not for family—it was for belonging. The thought lay in her mind like a feather lying in her palm, quivering, anticipating with every heartbeat a wind to come whisk it away.

The only belonging she had was her own entrenched determination. She gave a little gesture, as if to toss away the thought, and moved on. There was no other belonging for her to be had anywhere save, by a mocking twist of providence, in the company of one wrinkled old labourer, and even then Margaret could not fool herself into believing that was anything like belonging.

She was roused from her thoughts as she rounded the kitchen wing by a sudden splash of colour against the shadows. In the narrow darkness was growing a straggling but defiant little broom bush, its limbs petrified by the night colds, but still holding, even at this late quarter of the year, a handful of golden sparks in bloom. They seemed to call out to Margaret, not with the crushing beauty of the panpipe, nor the distant homeliness of Rupert's old Manor, but with a small warmth like a fire. Instinctively she went over to it, pulling her wrap close as she bent into the shadow by the building, and looked intently at the blossoms.

They were quite old, and rather browned, clinging to their mother plant only because it grew in a sheltered part of the grounds where the wind could not rattle it. Even the week's storm had not managed to denude the bush of its early summer flowers.

I know how you feel, she thought pityingly, straightening once more. *But at least you have shelter. We may cling to ourselves, but I am always in the wind here.*

With a delicate finger she touched one outstretched blossom of crumpled, browned, flaming saffron-colour, and watched as a single petal broke off and floated down on a soft gust of wind.

"Oh!" she said, starting as if stung. With a complaint of fabric she strode forward and crouched down, putting one hand out to the object on which the broom-petal had fallen.

She had missed it in the shadows, for it was almost the exact colour of the shadows themselves. A little ashen heap the smudged colour of a titmouse, ringed in scorched grass, lay at her feet, broken up only by the single thumbnail of yellow petal and, where a touch of light came in, the glitter of what looked like lettering. Curious, Margaret shoved up her sleeves and, gently replacing the petal on the grass, eased and levered the charred object out of the pile. Ash fell away, hissing upward and spiralling outward like imitation smoke; she got her hands horribly dirty carefully brushing off the flat face of the object.

It was the back cover of a volume, illustrated in simple design by a gold Chi-Rho; its spine was still attached, but frayed and burnt beyond repair. She put it down and began questing for the front. Her resting heart-rate was strangely low at this moment: she felt the numbness and at once the sharpened awareness of being in a dream. She found two other backs and handfuls of burnt book-leaves which were ruined, too, beyond repair. At last, near the heart of the pile, she unearthed a front piece that, though it had been divorced by fire from the rest of its body, was legible and otherwise intact.

She had a strange sensation, kneeling there, staring at it, that she had been there and stared at it before.

In neat gold print, as gold as the broom-petal, she read off the author and title: Songmartin's *Commentaries*, Philippians, Volume XI. She held the thing lightly so that it would not break, but her hands had gone suddenly tense. As keenly as she could hear his laughter, as keenly as she could see his mocking glance, in her mind's eye Margaret heard Rupert's words to his cousin, low and regretful.

"I'm afraid I have misplaced that particular collection."

Misplaced... Misplaced! She stared with a sense of horror at the burnt bodies of the ecclesiastical books and felt the sharp blade of rage cutting open all her veins inside. She saw broken images, scraps of words—the war-banner of her tartan cloak, the blackcap singing, the sullen scarlet of leaves on a garden plot, Skander's voice saying, "For the love of heaven!"—little things: little things that somehow mattered.

Gently she laid the book back down among its dead fellows and rose, turning to the broom bush. With one hand cupped beneath, one hand running tightly up the branches, she shaved off curls of bright yellow bloom until her hand was full of them. With all the silence of ceremony she stood over the ash pile and let them fall, scattering in a sidewise cascade of flower-sparks. The last petal fell, drifting clockwise, spinning like a top, and rested on the Chi-Rho. For a moment Margaret expected it to catch and leap alight, and for the whole thing to burn up into nothing.

Her heart had forgotten to beat. She was not sure how she lived without the blood-thrum of it going through her. Detached but determined, she followed the porphyry gravel path to the rear door and let herself in. With the clearness of one walking in a dream, she was glad her heart was not beating: she might not have been able to walk so knowingly into the throat of the dragon otherwise—a dragon that, python-like, had its coils round and round Marenové House and was quietly cutting off the life of it. But Marenové knew, and Hobden knew, and now, with a clarity that hurt, Margaret knew.

One of the chamber maids met her at the stairs and came forward to take her wrap away, saying something about dinner being laid and what had she done to her hands? Brow arched, body numb and spirit detached from everything, Margaret stared at the girl coldly, blankly. Whatever the maid saw in her mistress's face made her own go pale, and with a deferential bob the girl murmured something and turned away.

With measured step Margaret climbed the stair. The silence, which she always felt was about to scream, the stillness, which she always felt was about to break into a storm, both seemed suffocating now. She moved through them, still with the numbness and intensity of feeling as in a dream. Even in her room she knew there was no sanctuary—was there sanctuary to be found anywhere?—but at least there she might cut off the dark flow of Rupert's genius so that she might sit and think.

Once within her room, quite alone save for the little maid who was sweeping out the fireplace, she pulled her armchair close to the window and sat in the pale cold sunlight, her chin in her hand, staring out unseeingly across the lawn.

There was not much to think. The first blaze of rage had died out into a low firedrake smoulder. It was the only thing that kept back the sense of wickedness that haunted the halls of this House. When Margaret had thought she was an ambassador for Earth, she had not realized that she was representing her to Hell.

A sharp wind blew outside—the hollow echo of it hummed inside the room—and the movement of the damson trees drew the young woman's attention. And suddenly it seemed to her that she could have been standing at the west window of her house in Aylesward, looking outward and upward at her familiar Cumbrian fells. As far back as she could remember there had always been the stark rise of the fells around her, tawny in summer and ribbed with snow and cold like the sides of some great animal in winter. Had she ever not lived here?

Had she ever not lived in Hell?

Margaret had not been aware of the maid leaving until suddenly she returned, bobbing respectfully and said, in a low, ginger murmur, "The master is waiting for you at dinner, my lady..."

Margaret tore her eyes and thoughts from the damson trees. "Yes, thank you... Send my regrets, and say that I overtaxed myself in my walks this morning. I will see Rupert at supper."

"Very good, my lady," said the maid in a tone that belied her doubts that it was. She bowed again and withdrew, and as Margaret took her eyes from the door they slid across the upright figure of her ball gown in the corner. For a moment she stared at it, little sparks of anger hissing just behind her heart, and wishing she could have the satisfaction of taking the hateful thing in her hands and tearing it, tearing it long and slowly in two from top to bottom as God must have had the satisfaction of tearing the temple veil.

She was afraid that Rupert would come for her and that she would have to face him before she was ready. But he did not come, and as the hours dragged by in agony she almost wished he had, so that the ordeal would have been finished. She felt like a prisoner waiting for her execution, trapped within her own room, going over and over again the words that she meant to say. She had been right, there was a third option, another way out.

She stopped once before the mirror. *Never mind, Margaret. You were never pretty anyhow—never very witty, never much, hardly missed.*

The hours crawled by. She could not bring herself to read, to sleep, to do anything of worth. Her only companions were the screaming sense, the storming sense, that lay over the whole house, and the sputtering, smouldering fire of her own determination.

Yet it was with an odd calm that she heard the clock downstairs chime six. She rose, put off her frock and replaced it with her black taffeta, and stepped out onto the landing.

The evenings were coming swift now. The glass dome of the atrium was darkened to bluestone and flint, speckled with stars. The lights in their sconces were lit; she moved through the tendrils of their smoke and the pools of their glow, quite alone, as alone as she had ever felt before. They were beautiful, the lights: they looked each like broom-blossoms to Margaret, perfect and saffron, burning away against the gloom.

The Rupert that Margaret found waiting for her in the dining room was the same cool, mocking thing she remembered. But her senses, sharpened by her dream-like horror of him, made him stand out doubly real against the shadowy dark panelling of the room. Tall, powerful, wrought out of iron, he turned toward her as she entered and she felt a shudder of despair go through her body.

"Margaret, my sweet," he purred, and, going over to her, took her hand but did not kiss it, only showed her to her chair. She could feel his eyes on her, peeling back her skin. "Sioned told me you were unwell this afternoon. Did you rest well?"

"I kept to my room," said Margaret, unwilling to lie. "It is quiet there."

It was uncanny how he kept an eye on her all throughout the meal. She ate mechanically, though with perfect poise, but was preoccupied both with his constant gaze and how she was to tell him...

At last she could stand the silence no longer. With an introductory sniff, raising her eyes from her plate, she asked in a half-interested, detached tone, "Your letter said you went north this morning. How was the ride?"

One dog-tooth showed out of his crooked smile. "Not altogether bad," he replied. He gave her the platter of mutton roast.

"The northerly tracks are little more than cow-paths and wretched after a rain. Witching Hour is in need of a wash, but he is indefatigable. A little rotten track doesn't deter him."

Margaret gave a painful, forced smile and ate her mutton. The watchful silence continued a few minutes more, then, stirred to breaking it once more, still with that odd calm, Margaret said,

"Rupert?"

He looked at her directly but did not say a word.

It was worse that he was silent. Her words seemed to fall into the quiet like drops of glass, drops that shattered on the ear. "Rupert, I'm not going with you tomorrow."

There was no sound, it seemed, in all that screaming, storming, silent house but for the enormously hollow, unbearably mocking rhythm of the clock in the entryway. Margaret felt swallowed up in Rupert's gaze. His pale eyes did not waver—his whole face did not change from its careful, attentive lightness—but she knew the mocking glint was gone from behind them. She did not know how long that horrible moment lasted, but she was glad for one thing: Rupert did not press her. He had sketched her nature well enough to know she was in earnest.

"Margaret, my dear," he said at last, gently, as much in earnest as she was, "go to bed."

The calm was gone. The clarity was gone. In total numbness, like an enchanted doll, Margaret rose from the table, put aside her napkin, and left the room. She was almost to the top of the stairs when a sconce, overfilling, dropped hot wax on the back of her hand and sent a jagged crimson streak of pain into her brain, clearing it for one moment. She had been certain he would kill her. He was not one to let anything stand in the way of his ambition. She stopped at the head of the stair and looked back down into the well of darkness.

Does he mean to murder me in my sleep?

Rupert was a killer if he had to be, she knew that, but she did not know what *kind* of killer, and that made it worse. Completely mazed she went to her room, found herself alone there, and began pacing, trying to rally her wits.

She had not expected to live out the interview. That had been her *tertium quid*, her way out—and Rupert had not given it to her. She passed a stiff, shaking hand across her forehead, feeling her nails drag at her skin, as if to rip the cobwebs from her brain. What was to be done? She had thrown the dice back in the devil's face and the devil had not flinched. Horribly, acutely, through all the numbness of shock and despair and uncertainty, she felt she was in Rupert's hand still, playing along with his little game, helpless to break free.

She had the strong desire to cross the dimly lit room, ball up her fist, and put it through a pane of glass.

Instead she passed into the washroom and began undressing once more, mechanically, drawing a bath for herself. Sitting on the cold edge of the tub, watching the water fill it—watching the water shake and roil with its own movement and the lights darting fish-like in it—she thought suddenly of the Channel, and of the Tyrrhenian Sea. She ought to have long been in Naples by now. The sun would still be warm, and Rupert would not be there... One hand slipped into the water and, as it flowed around her, the water-sensation, the silvery voice, of the wind and the panpipe came to her. A headache was coming on, and the thoughts of her earth seas and Naples and the beauty of the fells, all thoughts of places that shut her off and would not let her share their beauty, only added to her agony.

What is wit? she thought. *What is cunning, what is beauty, what are love's pleas and hate's rages? They all come to dust, and the devil is by far a better player at them than I.*

She got into the bath presently and sank up to her neck in the water, feeling it close her in its warm embrace, and she thought that never in the history of mankind had any convert to Christianity felt so keenly the water's symbol of being buried in the earth.

There were still two hours until a reasonable retiring time when Margaret finished her bath. Her body was clean but the ache of straining was still present. She needed to sleep, and sleep a sleep of death, before the hard knots of anxiety unwound in her muscles. But it was far too early to retire, so she sat in her nightgown and robe of velvet Tyrian purple and put herself to an idle game of chess with the little white and crimson morse-ivory chess-pieces on their board of obsidian and mother-of-pearl.

A storm had come up during her bath, an idle storm, as idle as the game she played, and it filled her room with a gentle, melancholy music that seemed to speak her mind better than her own words. She moved her pieces, and moved Rupert's—Rupert was red, devil-red, and unaccountably winning though she moved his pieces for him—with the light and the shadows chasing each other in smudges across the board.

She jumped and cursed as much as she knew how when a sudden knock disturbed her. Picking up her castle where it had fallen and reasserting its threat on Rupert's knight, she turned in her chair and called out.

It was Rhea who entered, sweeping in, Margaret noticed, without the marked deference that a maid should give to a lady of Margaret's potential station. The lack of gesture stung.

"I've come to take the ball gown," said Rhea, "and give it the last touches for tomorrow. I will have it boxed for the journey."

"That will not be necessary," said Margaret icily.

Nothing changed in the maid's face—she was as careful as her master—but behind that pool-dark, pool-deep pair of eyes Margaret felt a hostile spirit. "Nevertheless, I will take the gown."

"Do," said Margaret. *And burn it behind the kitchen wing.*

Rhea dropped her eyelids and moved to take the dress away. Some of the over-sheet slipped off as the maid moved it, and Margaret saw again the startling crimson of the gown. Crimson. She, dressed in crimson like one of the crimson pawns on the chess board—one of Rupert's pawns. Her stomach twisted.

Rhea departed, gown in her arms, and with the door shut once more the room was filled with the tinselly rustle of the rain and, when Margaret roused herself to think, the harsh click of a chess-piece set down. She played with a strangely renewed vigour, as if to beat Rupert by means of proxy, as if the genius of the chess game on this stormy night that was the threshold of winter, the threshold of a new moon, might cast its power over them and let— oh, God, might *let*—Margaret win.

But something went awry. The stars were wrong, or providence unhappy, for as the clock began chiming downstairs that it was time to turn in, that the hour was late, she found herself looking down on a helpless stalemate. Their pieces were useless, unarmed but for little daggers, circling each other like dogs. A confused rage welled up in her, blinding her. Her throat tightened and her eyes were blurred suddenly by unreasoning tears. Heedless, she jerked out her arm, sending the pieces flying with a choked cry of anger. They fell somewhere, far away, thumping with white and crimson noises across the carpet.

The blow was strangely relieving. She leaned on the table, panting, crushing her eyes shut to kill the tears, and somehow found herself again. When her vision cleared she saw, not white and crimson, but darkness and a few small points of sullen golden candlelight. How dark everything had grown! She straightened, staring blankly about her. The last notes of the clock died away. The storm broke against the windowpanes. The curtains were drawn, but the racing, fitful silver light of earth still made it through the storm-clouds and chinks in the fabric; in desolate patterns the light showed up on the floor, broken by the windward leaves that plastered against the glass and stuck there, forlorn. She laughed softly, genuinely, and like a madman. This was something the fells could share with her: this was something she understood. She put aside her heavy robe and stood in the middle of the floor in her nightgown, the strings of the neck draped in her transfixed hands, watching the way the light played on the glass and the floor, the way the wind bore the rushing shadows of the leaves around her. The nightmare taste of white and crimson was clearing away. She breathed deeply, shakily, and breathed in the far-off mountain thunder. It echoed inside her, loud and empty, and she distilled some strength from it.

The thunder was hushing away, the storm dropping to a blowing rustle that was more wind than rain, and she was just turning to the knowledge that she must sleep when of a sudden her bedroom door flung open and harsh yellow light split the darkness. With a cry Margaret started back and recovered, blinking through the broken gleam to see Rupert's face.

For a moment he was a mere wild silhouette, framed in the black doorway and fierce yellow light, his head up, his hand gripping the knob as if to strangle it. Then she saw he was in his shirtsleeves, dishevelled and disreputable, hair racked upward into disarray. He was clearly drunk. Her stomach clenched within her.

"You are coming, Margaret," he ground out low and dangerous. "You are going to come at my biding and do what I say. There is an end to it."

She swallowed. Her dry throat caught on the taste of crimson. "Go back to bed, Rupert," she said in as soothing a tone as she could muster with her heart beating wildly in her chest. "You are drunk."

He swung into the room, steady and fast on his feet, and had her by the wrist before she could pull away. She knew better than to struggle in that grasp. She had tried it before to no avail. She held still as death, staring up into the storm-lashed paleness of those wide, furious eyes.

"I am sober when I am drunk," he hissed. The scent of his breath was scarlet. "All other times I am beset by this strange sense of conscience." His eyes lowered, fixed, unfocused. His hand loosened a little on her arm and the fingers gently worked the skin as if to atone for the pain they had inflicted. His body shuddered. "There is a dark art at work inside me." His eyes lifted to hers. "Will you release me?"

She met those eyes, those hateful, pale blue, beautiful eyes. That odd, unreasoning calm in the face of terror, a calm that was oddly white, washed over her. Her voice came as if from a long way off. "What you call darkness and I call darkness, Rupert, are two completely different things."

The eyes hardened into glass. The lips parted, revealing the teeth on edge as if they were fangs. The hand on her arm remained light. She did not see it coming, for he had the knack of hiding his thoughts behind the glassiness of his eyes: of a sudden he snapped her forward, his free hand behind her head, and bit her lip with the violence of his kiss. She gave a muffled shriek of pain and kicked, hurting herself more than she hurt him. She forgot that it was no use to fight. Instinct to protect herself clawed at her mind and she clawed at him, writhing in his unforgiving grasp. The long angry whine of tearing fabric filled the air. Renewed thunder boomed overhead. Lightning lashed across them, lashed across Rupert's down-turned face, turning it into a snarling mask. She tasted blood. She tasted her own blood. The sweet scents of wine and blood and tears mingled and, with an upsurge of rage, Margaret somehow found his hand and she bit it to repay him. She bit as deeply as her jaw would allow and revelled high and viciously in the cry of pain he gave.

He picked her up around the waist and hurled her through the air with surprising force. She fell with a shriek, her fall cushioned by the mattress of her bed. Something was in her mouth. She spat it out. It was too dark to see what it was. She pulled herself together lest Rupert should come after her.

He stood his ground. He clutched his bleeding hand to his chest and watched her coldly, rigidly. His worst anger, his cold anger, rested on his brow. The thunder growled and fell away. The light flickered and broke up around him. Only the sound of her heavy breathing filled the room.

"Good night, Margaret," he said quietly, and with a silent tread he left the room, shutting the door with a little click behind him.

"*Oh!*" cried Margaret, bursting into heedless, furious tears. "Oh, you worthless, p-pitiless, filthy creature! I despise you! I d-d-despise you! *I despise you!*" Her raging words fell into sobbing—furious, terrified sobbing. She crumpled into the bed-sheets and sobbed mingled tears and blood; with every hysterical gasp she smelled her own blood, tasted it, felt the cut agony of her own broken lip. She held the torn neck of her nightgown close in a grip that even Rupert could not have pried loose. Through the broken, jagged images of pain and his face, the horror lashed her with the thought: what if he had? He was a man who could kill, a man who would get his own way. The sound of tearing fabric screamed and screamed in her memory, the heat of his touch seared her arms. If he truly wanted her, as he said he did, what was stopping him? The thread that she had taken for granted which held Rupert back seemed suddenly horribly thin.

In the last raging throes of agony she reared back, strangling the bed-sheets in her hands, and let loose one long agonized scream, wrenching it out of the depths of her soul. In her own ears it was blood-curdling. She screamed that single scream until she no longer had breath, and then she fell, like a bird which has suddenly lost all wind, plummeted into a pit where even the shadows seethed. Her body was cold. She knelt in her thin gown in the fireless, cheerless, empty room, listening to the silence and her own sobbing breath, shivering as with a fever.

No one came at the sound of her scream. She knelt and waited, expecting someone to come to her, but no one came. She felt like a child lost in the dark, woken by nightmares that no one cared to chase away.

You have always been alone...

...You have always been alone...

...You have always been alone.

The echo of her scream died away into the empty depths of her soul. The house, mockingly, was silent—pressing silent, like a pillow smothering her. She knew he would not come back, but that knowledge did not serve to comfort her. Did she dare sleep? Did she dare close her eyes? Her hand fumbled on the coverlet and her mind, child-like, pitiful, fumbled into her past.

"Now I lay me down to sleep, I pray the Lord my soul to keep. If I should—if I should—"

With shuddering breath and shaking body, Margaret stole from the bed and crept corpse-cold across the floor. Her hand slid against the wood of her door, found the cold knob, and closed tightly over it. With infinite care, trying desperately not to make the latch rattle in her own shaking hand, she worked the knob over and eased the door open.

There was a single light in the hall, just at the head of the stair. Otherwise the hall was empty and silent, and if she took the greatest possible care, she thought she could steal past Rupert's door without him hearing her. After the scare he had given her, he would not expect her to be walking the halls at this hour. But Skander had called her a force to be reckoned with, and though in her tortured, flogged, horrified brain she felt no spark of heroic defiance, she reeled blindly on.

A thin bar of marigold light showed from beneath the master's door, and that gave her some weak measure of comfort. He would be in there, locked up in his own brooding, too busy to anticipate her.

Like a whipped dog, cold, bent double, Margaret stole painfully down the stairs and padded barefoot across the entryway floor and through the dining room, taking each step with care lest she run up against something in the dark. Everything seemed impossibly long and far away, as though the House, like a dog in its sleep, stretched out in the night and was twice as big again as it ought to be. At last she reached the long kitchen hallway and her hands, sweeping along the wall, found and caught hold of the doorknob that led down into the damp cellars below.

She had nearly forgot about the stair. Having turned back the first time she had put it from her mind, content that she would not think nor need to think of it again. It was hardly the sort of place a woman ought to go, no matter how curious she might be. But now, for all its dampness, for all its loathsomeness, it seemed apart from Rupert's hand, as though that earthy pit were too small, too unimportant for him—so to it and to its dampness she went, knowing full well that a night spent in such quarters would deliver a dolorous blow to her health.

She was too shaken to take comfort even in that.

It was like going back into time, walking down those stairs. The slimy damp, the noisome air, the almost physical pressure of dark, felt like the tomb of ages, and she was walking down its throat. She went down and around, from landing to landing, until at the fourth landing she knew she was almost to the bottom—and then she was at the bottom of the stairs, small in the long dimensionless room. Miles beneath the ground, ages from the present, walking in a dead stupor that was broken only by involuntary sobs she continued on, dragging herself across the floor. The cold had got into her bones and they ached, ached with a pain she had not known before. Every step was agony, but she kept doggedly on.

It was strange, she thought, how fear found strength the body never knew about before.

At last she reached the head of the untraversed stair. The light still burned down there: it jiggled and flashed and played on her bruised vision. Like a moth to a flame she went on, drawn by it, walking as if in a dream. She felt inexplicably safe now, so far away from Rupert and the world and everything that might do her harm. She walked among the dead down here. They would not hurt her. This was where she belonged.

It was a straight stair, carved into the rock around her, a stair of some dozen steps. A pleasant warmth wafted up from below.

Margaret stepped down the last few steps, ducking to avoid the low header, and stood with her feet pressed into a hard dirt floor, blinking her eyes in the sudden glare of yellow light.

"Rhea!" a voice barked suddenly, startling her before she could see or get her bearings. "And here I thought you weren't coming. Are you trying to starve me?"

Rigid as a bird, hands clutching the torn neck of her gown, she stood her ground and squinted into the light as a figure came around a pile of old wine crates and into view. Her heart, which had been misplaced already, lodged in her throat.

The fox stood as dead still in its tracks as Margaret stood, staring back at her with its ears forward, its mouth a little open. For a few heartbeats the two stood frozen, staring at each other, then the fox's mouth began to move, soundlessly at first, then with bursts of half-finished thoughts until it finally blurted out,

"He *hasn't*! Who the devil are you!"

She had not thought, when she had imagined this was a kind of valley of death, that she had been right. Skin crawling, she stared at the ruddy-furred ghost of the fox whose body Curoi and Talbot had worried into a bloody mess. "Y-you died!" she stammered. It took supreme will to hold her ground, but she managed it. And suddenly she was angry. Was it not enough that Rupert haunted her? What right did the fox have to haunt her as well? "You died! I watched them tear you apart!"

The fox looked startled. "I died, madam? When? How so? I think I ought to remember my own death."

She stood a moment in thoughtful silence, looking carefully over the fox. Foxes all looked so alike, perhaps it was not the same one. It could be only the poor lighting, but she thought perhaps this fox's fur was not so vibrantly red as the other's had been.

"Oh," she said, relaxing slightly. "I beg your pardon. I think I mistook you for someone else."

"Rum luck on his part," said the fox, and he sat down, drawing his bushy tail around his forepaws. "Now, as I was saying— would you be so kind as to tell me who you are and how the devil you got here? Because you oughtn't be."

"Don't think I don't know that," said Margaret snappishly, more than ever convinced that she had wandered into a dream. "The devil brought me here to make me marry him."

The fox jumped up, letting loose a single derisive bark. "Hark! He did, did he?" Then he resumed his seat, carefully arranging his leggy limbs and long brush. "Well," he said in a more gentle tone, "that's rum luck on *your* part. Rum luck seems to be positively flowing in these parts."

"I am Margaret Coventry," she said for the sake of saying something familiar. "Who are you—and—how do you talk?"

"I am heartily sorry to meet you, Miss Coventry." The fox gave a little imperial sniff and held out a paw, which Margaret came forward and took, feeling very surreal as she did so. It was warm and furry and the pads were deliciously smooth under her fingers. "I'm a sort of jester," he went on, "but a poor fox can only think of so many jokes and Rupert, who will not laugh at anything worth laughing at, put me down here."

"Are you enchanted?" she asked.

"Yes, an enchanted talking fox. The wonders you see these days! Like young women trekking about in nightgowns in the middle of the—hang yourself," he broke off, lunging forward to peer up into her face. "What happened to you? You're bleeding! Did Rupert hurt you?"

Her hand flew to her lip and came away sticky and red and tasting like iron.

"You look positively awful, if I may say so," the fox went on, getting up and turning in a worried circle about her. "Have a seat. No, no, just sit. There are no seats."

Stiffly Margaret folded up on the dirt floor and the fox sat beside her, ears perked, head canted, peering attentively into her face.

"Did Rupert hurt you?" the fox asked again when she had settled. His voice was thin, but imperious, and thrust at Margaret like a knife.

Pride struggled for a moment with Margaret's vacant sense of horror. It was ridiculous, it was dream-like, to be conversing with a fox—but it was her only way out and in the end, reluctantly, hating herself for it, she pushed away her pride.

"Yes."

The fox wiggled himself into a more comfortable position. He seemed to be waiting; she knew he was waiting for her to go on, but the brutalized blankness of her mind resisted her attempts to begin.

"I—I don't know..."

"Never mind," he said gently. "Just start at the beginning."

The beginning. The grey-rimed image of the Leeds train station jerked and squealed into her mind. She began, and once she had begun it came out in a rush, as though she were vomiting out her story. "I was going to Naples. My sisters are all idiots and my cousin ran away with an architect, and I was the only one left to recover the family name. My mother had me sent to Naples to stay with some relatives and catch a husband. My relatives didn't know. It was going to be a surprise. I would have gone cheerfully, but my mother *pushed* me. She pushed me so hard. I hate being pushed. I would have gone. I would have been happy. She needn't have *pushed* me. But Rupert was on the train and he kidnapped me and brought me here. I've been here since mid-October. He tells me that he will have me marry him so that he can be Overlord of Plenilune. His cousin made him a wager, that if he could woo a woman he could win the throne—or whatever it is they call it here—so he kidnapped me. But he hasn't won me yet." She laughed, shakily, sickly. "He woos with iron! How does he expect to win a woman with iron?

"I've hated my time here. Everything is so different—so half-familiar, and so different. I don't know anyone. No one can help me. I don't even know if I want to go home anymore. That's why I came down here: to die."

Out of the corner of her eye she saw the fox give a little angry start of surprise.

"I thought—I have nowhere to go. My family does not care for me. Rupert is impossible. I'm caught... I was supposed to go with Rupert tomorrow to Lookinglass; his cousin is throwing a gala, and I'm to come out so everyone can get to know me. Only, I feel I can't do it, living with Rupert as I am and not married to him. It sounds horrid when I say it like that—how much more horrid will it sound to others who don't know my situation? I can't open myself up to that kind of censure. This is precisely what I was going to Naples to avoid!"

There was a lamp set on the wine-crate, a hurricane lamp that was burning brightly and valiantly with the colour of broom and amber. She stared into it until her eyes smarted, and wondered if there was a world in which broom and amber really burned like that, where flames were flowers, where flowers were flames...

"I wonder if Heaven laughs," she added quietly, "to do this thing to me."

The black-tipped ears of the dog-fox twisted backward, thoughtful, but he remained silent.

She breathed a deep, shaking breath, rustling a little, finding herself again. After that first tumultuous explanation she felt spent, beaten and wrung like a piece of washing. The nightmare quality of her life, which had seeped through her fingers as she had cast up these events out of her belly for the fox to hear, was quickly rising again as, like a vivid spectre, the horror of the past hour loomed over her. She began again, but this time in a carefully detached monotone, as if thereby to avoid the sting of terror.

"Rupert had told Skander that he had lost his commentaries by...by Songmartin. He said he had misplaced them. I didn't think anything of it at the time, but this morning I found them behind the kitchen wing, deliberately burnt beyond repair. And then I knew—or maybe I had always known it—but I knew clearly then that Rupert was evil—*evil*. He is wicked. I can taste it in my mouth. He is *wicked—wicked!* And I could not go with him or marry him because of that. And...and I told him so."

Her courage faltered and dissipated like smoke. She could still taste her own blood on her lip and it made her sick.

The fox, with his voice the thinness and softness of a feather, and somehow as comforting, said, "You told him so, and it was that he took the telling hardly."

She shook her head. "He took it...strangely. He said nothing, but sent me away to my room where I would be alone, I thought, for good. I was alone for hours, but just as I was preparing for bed he came—" She set her hand to her aching forehead. "He was drunk. He set on me and fr—fr—*frightened* me. He told me I would come because he said so, and that would be the end of it. I thought—I thought he was—because he was so drunk—"

The fox laid a paw on her forearm. "There, now. Forget about that. Rupert is a devil, but I can say that he won't take an unwilling partner. It's one of the few things that can be said for him."

She caught her trembling lip between her teeth and crushed it until it stung like fire. Her wrist still hurt where Rupert had gripped it, hurt enough to bruise, though in this dim yellow light she could not see it well enough to tell what it was doing. And the fox, as if following the line of her thoughts, leaned forward with a little sidewise, hesitant movement, and drew his tongue along the veined hollow of her wrist. His tongue was warm, her skin cold, and it was strangely and ridiculously strengthening.

"I don't know what to do," she admitted.

The fox lay down and put his head on his paws, got up again to shake himself, and lay down once more. "I'm not advocating any marriages," he began with a condescending sniff, "but I think you ought to go. It won't be as bad as all that."

"No?" Her tone rose with a surge of scorn. "It is easy for you to say—you are just a fox!"

He turned his head on his paws and grinned, all his perfect white fangs showing. "So? So! But does it really matter what people think? You have yourself to think about, and though I think it unlikely that Rupert would press himself against your will, I would not put beatings past him." He groaned and stretched out one back leg so that he looked more like a heeler lounging at the side of a shepherd's fire than a fox. "As honourable jester and fool, I've had my own beatings from his hand."

She gazed down at him frowningly, and he gazed back, still, with that perfect stillness that animals can have, the light making a crescent moon on the edge of his eyes, the inside of his eyes deeply and darkly blue. He was without a doubt the most irreverent fox she could ever think to meet, and the most unamusing jester she had thought to know. If this was a dream, it was the most vivid, poignant, uncomfortable dream she had ever had—yet somehow, as with the sea, as with the rolling upward tawny of the fells, she felt safe in that powerful discomfort, even as it crushed her.

She almost reached out to stroke the fur behind his ears, but caught herself at the last moment and looked away.

"I can manage to be in the same house as Rupert," she protested stiffly, hotly, "but to be in a carriage for an entire day's ride, to be that close to—to such an *evil* man... He is *evil*."

"Then best we not provoke the devil," said the fox gently. "The wall is too high to jump at present, Miss Coventry. Let's run along it for a while to see if there are any gaps in it further on."

She shut her eyes and shook her head, confused, furious, crushed, tired, ridiculously comforted by the presence of a fox. "Please call me Margaret. It is absurd that you call me 'Miss Coventry.'"

The fox grinned. "As it pleases you! Does this mean I can expect more interviews in the future?" He looked around at the cellar, his eyes taking the yellow light of the lamp and flashing like the watered scales of a fish. "It gets so damnably lonesome down here. No one ever comes down except for Rhea, and even then she takes it upon herself to forget."

While he was looking away, Margaret cast an eye over the lean body of the fox. He was underfed, which made him seem taller and lankier, and behind the faint mockery of his friendly wall eyes she thought she saw a haunted look. "Of course I will try. I will not promise, in case I cannot keep the promise. I don't know how long I will be away at Lookinglass."

"No, of course, I understand. Take care of yourself and dress warmly." He looked at her quizzically. "You wouldn't happen to have a switchblade about you, would you?"

She looked blearily at him, askance. "A switchblade? Of course not."

He sniffed. "No, I didn't think so. Well, do attempt to enjoy yourself. I hear Rupert's relative is a passing good chap."

"You mean Skander Rime?" She saw the young man's face again, so like Rupert, suspicious but at the same time open and friendly. He was a kindly, sporting figure. "He isn't so bad. But Rupert hates him. I'm afraid to give too much attention to him lest Rupert think of something particularly nasty to do to his cousin. I w-wouldn't put it past him."

"No, nor I." The fox heaved a great sigh, flanks expanding, and climbed to his feet. His great red brush of a tail swept the ground behind him and he carried himself, for all that he was a fox, rather royally and, for all that he was a fox, with a rather supercilious air about the tilt of his nose. "Now we have settled it. You must go with Rupert tomorrow to Lookinglass and be a good girl and take care of yourself, and be the prettiest girl at the gala. It is late now, and far past time for any more talking. You had better get yourself to bed. It is hardly an appropriate hour," he added, pausing to sit down and give his left ear a brutal clawing with a hind foot, "for young ladies to be out of bed and walking about." He sniffed prodigiously and shook his head as if to put his ear back in place, and remained seated, looking up at her in a cocky, attentive manner.

With the obedience of blind weariness Margaret got stiffly to her feet. She was still shaking, but from cold now more than from terror. There was a moment in which the world blurred and shifted dangerously to the side, each blinking image like single pearls sliding off a string...but then the warm pressure of the fox's flank against her calf steadied her.

"Will you be all right up the stair?" he was asking as her vision cleared. "Take it one step at a time. What were you thinking, coming all the way down here in your nightgown...?"

He fussed gently around her as she walked toward the stair, making the occasional jest which she felt vaguely guilty for not hearing clearly and not laughing at. But she stopped, wide awake with a pang of terror, when she realized that he left her several paces from the stair and was not coming with her any farther.

He sat primly on the dirt floor, his flaming bush of a tail wrapped up before himself with the fluffy white tip of it mingling with the fluffy white of his waistcoat. The lamp diffused its light around his head, making for him a kind of hero's aureole.

"Aren't you coming?" she asked, thrusting the words at him like a knife.

His whiskers twitched wryly. "Well, no. I would, but I'm afraid I can't."

She stared at him. He was small, coloured like fire and darkness and the plume of blackthorn, with all the vivacity and gallantry of the three. Yet he did not come. In her crushed weariness her reason deserted her, and in its place her intuition felt that he was the sort of person who, when flint struck steel, would prove to be a coward.

You are always alone, Margaret.

"Good-night, fox," she said.

His teeth flashed in an apologetic smile. "Good-night, Margaret. Be careful."

VI | LOOKINGLASS HOUSE

The evening was washed in a warm rose light damson as Margaret's palfrey, following after Rupert's, came up the last stretch of the metalled road through a beech-wood, crossed the stone bridge that spanned the chasm, and came in sight at last of Lookinglass. The light, diffusing over everything—the turf, the numerous sprawling tangles of blackthorn and furze, the steeply descending pine-woods, the cascade in the chasm—hardened along the skyline with the furnace-colour of a flame, but the air cut like cold iron in Margaret's lungs.

Rupert had not said a word about her lip. When she had risen in the morning, stiff and hardly rested, she had looked in the mirror and found her lip conspicuously swollen and broken inside. There was no time to do anything about it, and nothing that could be done. She had suffered with cool dignity the dark, almost sadistic, mirthless smile that had been in Rhea's eyes while she dressed and packed and, as the sun was just rising, met Rupert in the stable yard. The lip had stung so dreadfully for several hours that it took much of Margaret's will to keep her mind off the pain, but by noon the crisp November air had numbed it, as well as all the other features of her face. Between the cold of the air and the cold of Rupert, who had not tried much to make conversation with her, she had retreated back within herself to a warm place that was, perversely, the fiery colour of a fox's coat.

As if waking from his thoughts, Rupert stirred in the saddle. The rings in the reins jinked brightly in the late autumn air as he shifted them, raising his hand to indicate the rocky cliff face ahead.

"There you are," he said, almost as if he were presenting it to her. "There is Lookinglass. Don't mind the precarious visage: she is as sturdy a manor as Marenové House."

Through her frosty crust and the swimming golden air Margaret stared up—*up*—at Lookinglass. Even in that yellow light the walls and buildings, climbing like a square-boned dragon up the steeply sloping fellside, were a hue of pale blue stone. The level rays of the sun struck off dozens—hundreds—of windows, flashing them all back at her with a power that Margaret thought was enough to reach Earth. It stabbed at her as the shepherd's panpipe had, only more war-like, as if the monstrously delicate construction, growing, it seemed, out of the soil of the fells, was the tip of a spear ready to be dropped from on high. She looked up past its many courts and terraces to the topmost tower, a single octagonal tower rising above everything to etch its powerful figure against the molten November sky. She wished with a strong longing to be up there, and to look out on a landscape hammered out of bronze.

They left the bridge behind. The roar of the cascade made the air tremble all around them and the spray of it gathered on Margaret's bare cheeks and turned them pale. The road became gravel and stone corduroys raised out of the floor of the lower terrace; it took them up a gentle slope, past the clusters of limed timber houses, horse-sheds, long-barns, the smithy and the glass-blower and the slight, ever-present reek of the butcher's to the first gate of Lookinglass. It stood open, and she and Rupert passed through unhindered. The guards on duty must have known Rupert by sight for they straightened at once, grim, eyes level-set, and did not speak a word as their little cavalcade passed by.

They never turned, but Margaret could feel their eyes on the back of her neck.

The light seemed to grow stronger the higher they went. Though she kept herself properly still and never turned her head, Margaret was looking all about as they went up through the levels, past the baths and the church and the common meeting hall, through the exquisite court of horses, a block given over entirely to Skander's mounts. The single tower at the top of all which stabbed upward still and made the heavens bleed a deepening blue, reeled like a compass-point to the pole-star above them, its angle sharper and sharper the closer they came. Margaret was careful not to look at it much now: the sheer stupendous height of the thing made her head swim.

After all its curtain walls, Margaret had almost expected the House itself to look somewhat small and ridiculous—a small thing couched defensively behind a mind-numbing tonnage of stone. So she caught her breath in spite of herself when they passed up through the last gate—guarded by watchtowers and garlanded in hoarwithy—and came under the light-spangled shadow of the House.

The late light, caught up here like yellow wine in a glass, struck off the House's numerous windows and scattered it brokenly all over the courtyard. Here the gold air was embroidered with silver. The House itself was loftier-built than Marenové, which was squat and somewhat sullen of appearance: it had the delicacy and liveability of a working cathedral with its soaring gables and pinnacles, its ramparts decorated in verdigris copper. The front doors were double and immense, the porch semi-circular and spacious. It struck Margaret that, though Skander Rime was unaccustomed to, and did not enjoy, entertaining, he had a happily situated home in which to host his guests.

As they entered the courtyard there was a fine stir from the low private stable wing; of a sudden it seemed a hundred dogs began to bark from somewhere behind a long colonnade and a row of yews. From out of the stable wing came half a dozen hands, all of them smartly clad in black with polished rubbers on their feet. Crows, dozens of crows, erupted from a garden and scattered dark across the sky. The noise, the commotion, broke on Margaret with a startling violence and she sat rigid in the saddle, by all appearances waiting to be helped down—in reality, waiting for the world to stop reeling.

Between Livy and the stable hands, the palfreys and Rupert's champagne were quickly arranged and preparations were swiftly going forward to accommodate the expected guests. Rhea, in her quiet way, busied herself with arranging Margaret's things. It was Rupert who came for Margaret.

She had always known he would. He swung off his palfrey, delivered it over to the care of a stable hand, and swung round, fetching a glance over the crowd until he saw her nearby. Like a black heron he stalked through the cheerfully chaotic mess, the only seemingly solid thing about her small, surreal world, and with a cool half-smile reached up to lift her down. Margaret felt her insides crawl and shrink in on themselves as his hands closed around her waist. It was by instinct that she put her hands on his shoulders to keep her own balance; everything else was crawling away from him.

The late light glinted in his eye as he looked slantwise at her. "There, here we are," he said in a low tone under the shriek and clatter of horses and the call of men—and she understood him to mean, not merely "Here we are," but "Here we are, and you will play your part to my satisfaction."

She could not have spoken had she wanted to. Her throat was cold and constricted. With a stiff movement she broke her gaze and looked away from him, wearing her chin high.

Rupert's hand moved to her wrist and tightened, warningly.

"Rhea," she called, a little sharply for his hand hurt.

The maid straightened from seeing to the latches on a trunk and regarded her, coolly, quietly, the dark hostility just lingering behind her eyes.

"Rhea, I will want my brown muslin for this evening's supper. Have it laid out for me."

The maid nodded wordlessly and turned away with her characteristically fluid motion which was at once beautiful and insolent.

It was strange how quiet rage could so compose a spirit. The constant, unspoken insolence of the maid roused the old rage in Margaret, subsuming the fear of Rupert's presence. It still pulsed inside her, quietly, far down at the base of her being, but for now she thought she could move on in spite of it. With an effort that was almost visible, she composed herself.

A familiar, disconsolate shriek turned her attention to the House steps. Skander Rime stood on the threshold, hanging for an instant supreme and detached above them, Thairm bating on his wrist. Even at that distance she saw the swift cool look of displeasure lash across his eyes when he saw his cousin, but then his eye fell on her and he smiled—a real, warm smile. With a practiced movement he turned aside to his manservant—who seemed in his big blue tunic to be rather like a massive blue-jay—and passed the gyrfalcon off on him, then descended the steps toward them.

He looked a lot more solid and imposing here under the shadow of his own tower than he had in the shadows of Marenové House. His friendly bulk swung toward them, and Margaret noticed for the first time that he showed signs of becoming bow-legged in the future. No matter—she smiled shyly—he would sit a horse to the end of his days and be happy.

Provided she was careful his days were not cut short.

"Lady Margaret!" He took her free hand and raised it to his lips. "So, you have come. It is a pleasure to have you."

As she made her reply, she could see behind the veil of his eyes that he had not been certain she would come. She wondered if he would rather she had not. "But of course," she said with affected gaiety, dipping low. "I had no choice." Rising, she added to soften the blow, "Who would miss a gala thrown by you?"

But both Rupert and Skander had caught the jab. The former's pressure on her arm increased a fraction; the latter's eyes lit up with a serious, mocking light that fetched in Rupert with their glance.

"Do not count the chickens before they have hatched, Miss Coventry. You are the first to arrive and the punch has yet to be sampled."

"Well, if there is one skill that I have, it is sampling punch—and goodness knows I need *some* thing to wash the dust of the road out of my throat. My lungs are near frozen, too."

Skander appeared uncertain what to do with her. He made a little gesture, as if he meant to take her arm, then caught himself and tucked his arms awkwardly at his sides again. "It is a long ride up from Marenové for a lady, especially at this time of year," he admitted sympathetically. "And now the sun is going down, it will be twice as chilly. I oughtn't keep you out talking in the wind. Come along inside and tell me if I have made the place cheery enough."

But Rupert, in his iron-dark, level tone, protested, "Lady Margaret is in need of a little time to herself to wash and dress for supper. I will go with you."

"Will you?" laughed Skander, rather bitingly. "Then we are certain of cheer." He gestured to Margaret as they began walking toward the doors. "Of course you will want to wash and dress. Only say the word: all I have is at your disposal."

"You are very kind," Margaret replied, with genuine gratitude.

They went indoors, into a long, lofty hallway like the nave of a cathedral, well-lit and golden. It was lightly but lavishly furnished to allow for traffic. The low side-tables, the columns, the arcades all sported wreaths and garlands of cranberry and bright mistletoe; a sweet scent of cedar-wood burning filled the air.

"Why," said Margaret, turning from the servant who took her wrap, "I had no idea you lived in church."

Skander's smile, quick and pleasant, was oddly mirthless. "You think so? Perhaps you're right. I had always thought it the other way around... Just this way."

He took them down the nave, past the groups of servants putting last-minute touches to the garlands, dusting, adjusting, seeing to the perfect angles of the carpet. Carried along on Rupert's arm, Margaret felt a twinge of embarrassment: it seemed they had arrived early.

As they approached the foot of a swooping staircase, far grander than Marenové's and positioned so as to give to any viewers below a perfect image of anyone poised above them, Skander called a maid over and said to Margaret, "I believe your maid has already gone up. Is that so?"

Rupert nodded wordlessly.

"Excellent. Aikaterine will show you the way, then. I look forward to your presence at supper."

Skander nodded deferentially and took a meaningful step backward away from her. Rupert, on the other hand, set his palm into the small of her back—a very informal gesture—and, bending to her ear, murmured, "I will see you soon, my dear. You should have every comfort. Only ask if you need anything."

She resisted shying away. With a curt nod she disengaged herself from the pressure of his hand against her back and glided away with the maid in tow, feeling her heart thumping in her throat with each step and the eyes of both young men burning into the skin on the back of her neck. And she had to walk with that feeling on her up the massive steps and across the walkway that spanned the width of the nave. Then, as she was passing through the arched doorway, she heard the click of boots behind her and Skander, his voice muffled by the distance, say,

"Well, coz—would you care for a drink?"

With a smooth motion the maid Aikaterine slipped in front of her and beckoned her on with a jerk of her chin. Margaret was too tired and too cold and too preoccupied to offer even the most gracious comment to the maid; she followed after the girl in the white gown that was more like a nurse's outfit than a maid's attire, down the carpeted, well-lit hall, turned a few corners, went up a short stair, and stepped off of another short hallway into a little vaulted room.

Aikaterine stood aside for Margaret to stoop through the doorway and straighten. She found herself in a not unpleasant place, simple but adequately furnished, high enough for the late light to stream through the single window—the lead lattice made diamond-patterns on the east wall around the little dressing table. Her travelling trunks were arranged on the floor and her fawn-coloured gown, which she had requested, was already laid out on the bed.

From the second chair in the room, set in the corner, rose Rhea upon her entrance. She broke up the light as she stood, and the sun's rays made an angry, glorious halo of amber around her hair. For a moment it seemed to Margaret that the careful veil which Rhea kept behind her eyes was pulled back and there was but only one maid in the room. She could not see those eyes through the silhouette's darkness, but she could feel the genius of the woman more clearly than ever before.

"Rhea... Thank you for laying out the dress. Now you may go. I am sure you are as tired as I am: I give you leave of the evening's duties. Aikaterine will see to my needs."

With a war-like fierceness, Margaret watched the sting sink into Rhea. That careful expression never flinched, but she felt the barb hit true. Nevertheless, with perfect poise, the maid said, "Of course. As my master's lady wishes."

Without a further glance Margaret turned into the room and stepped up to the bed, looking over the gown prepared for her. She heard, rather than saw, Aikaterine step aside for Rhea to pick up her wrap and depart. She heard, rather than saw, Aikaterine press the door gently shut.

For several minutes complete silence reigned over the little room. No, not complete—from far off and rather far below came the rhythmic bell-tang notes of a blacksmith working late. Those notes were the only sound around them, and they came to Margaret's ears thinly, making the room seem hollow. The softness of the gown's fabric between her fingers felt like a link between her and the real world: a surreal, sleepy emptiness lay in between.

At last, with a heavy intake of breath, she broke away from the dress and shot a forced smile at the white-clad maid. She spread out her arms and the maid dutifully stepped forward, dismantling her cloak and coat, and working at the buttons of her habit. She was cold, but the cold only increased as the heavy layers of her travelling gear were taken away and laid across the back of the room's second chair.

As though it were the room of a little inn, everything seemed low to Margaret; she looked sidewise in the mirror but could only see her hip and abdomen, and the late light breaking up in the windowpanes beyond. It struck her how thin she had grown in the past month. Breakfasts, dinners, suppers came back to her, all the ones she had taken with Rupert, all lacking appetite, all hollow and the hollowness full of a straining against Rupert's dark presence. The wholesomeness and richness of his table had done no justice to her figure.

There is a moral in that, I suppose, she thought grimly. *Vegetable dishes in peace rather than lavish meals where there is strife, or something like that.*

Even Aikaterine noticed. The maid had a friendly look to her eye, if she was politely silent, but after she had taken off

Margaret's boots and began removing the last layer of her dress, the maid said in a swift, soft, husky tone,

"Lord love you, madam. And here I thought you wore a corset."

Margaret put herself quickly into the dressing gown Aikaterine held for her, sliding the warm inside of rabbit-fur over her skin, tucking the outsides of pale blue satin close and tying it off. "Did you so?" she asked, seating herself before the mirror. How haunted and pale her face looked! "I was just thinking much the same thing about myself."

"You sound regretful, madam." Aikaterine began unpinning Margaret's hair. "I've handled dozens of women in their corsets trying to reach a figure like yours. And you come natural."

Margaret resisted informing the maid that she suspected her figure was unhealthy.

Long, waving strands of hair fell out of their braids across her shoulders. Aikaterine drew them through the comb with precise gentleness, her fingers working with perfect deftness to keep the body in the hair. With each loosed strand Margaret could smell the scent of wind and pine-woods.

"You are having supper with only the master, I think. I will keep the style casual, if it pleases you."

"Yes, of course." Margaret turned her head and held still as Aikaterine caught up a length of hair. Moved to be polite, she added, "You are very good at this. Have you been long a lady's maid?"

"Oh, long and long... My mother was lady's maid to my Lord Skander's mother and I tend to my lord when it befits the occasion. But I got the knack of it from my mother, and I've always been blessed with a good constitution, if I may be so bold to say. I've never had a chance to regret being lady's maid so early." There was a brief pause. A single hair, straying from the rest, tickled Margaret's nose unbearably for a moment. "Have you a maid of your own, madam?"

It was a bold question, almost unforgivably bold, but as the dart of rage ran up into Margaret's chest she remembered how swiftly news spreads among servants, and guessed that Aikaterine already knew she was a foreigner and only lately come to Plenilune. She breathed low to find her temper again.

"Not as such," she said briskly. "Lord Rupert's handmaid sees to most of my needs, but I don't have a maid of my own."

"That's a shame," purred Aikaterine soothingly. "And *she* has the Evil Eye."

Margaret burst out in a peal of honest laughter. "Doesn't she, though?" And suddenly the laughter, which was completely unexpected and relieving, broke and threatened to turn into something else. At the last minute she caught herself and resumed her still position before the mirror while Aikaterine drew a damp cloth over her hands and neck and gently applied perfume. A low, golden, elusive scent of roses threaded through the air as she left the table to put on her gown.

It was a pretty but simple gown, the sort of simple prettiness she thought best suited her English complexion: it was a fawn-brown colour, pale and unassertive—and, like a fawn's coat, it had paler speckles of varying size ascending from the hem which, on closer inspection, proved to be dog-wood blossoms. It went on over a long white under-gown, and a simple string of pearls was added to the ensemble. In a few moments Margaret was bending to look into the mirror and take in the effect of it before heading down to supper.

"It becomes you very well," Aikaterine remarked. "Your shoes, madam, and I will take you to join my master."

Margaret sat a moment with her feet on a little ottoman while the maid put soft indoor shoes of doeskin on her. Then, somewhat stiffly for the room was chilly and, after a long ride, the time sitting had turned her muscles to unresponsive iron, she got up and followed white Aikaterine out of the room. They went back down the hallway and across the high width of the nave, down the impressive staircase and along the nave aisle toward the east end. There they passed through a stone-capped archway, through a high atrium, and, ducking into a low doorway in one corner, began to ascend a heady flight of stairs. They passed a number of doors on their way up, and numerous narrow windows all sporting a stained-glass falcon in red at the top. Neither lady nor maid said anything about the climb, but Margaret's limbs were screaming in agony by the time they were halfway up, and Aikaterine mercifully went at a leisurely pace.

Pausing for a fraction of a second to rest, Margaret chanced a look out of one of windows. It was a good pane, unwrinkled by time, and she was afforded an eagle's view of the countryside. Lookinglass was perched on the brow of a cliff, and this tower in whose bowels she climbed rose higher even than that: the mighty fells were below her now, drenched in Tyrian purple and darker greens than jade or emerald could ever be. The horizon in the south distance was a mingled pale sea-colour where it seemed Plenilune faded into the fabric of the sky; in the high quiet of the tower, Margaret could hear the uncanny surf-sound of the wind murmuring all around them.

At last they reached the top of the stairs, the very last landing, the very last door. It broke on Margaret then that she was going to supper, again, with Rupert—that all interludes of peace without him were but passing and brief. She balked at the last moment and felt her already chilly veins go frozen-cold.

Aikaterine knocked pre-emptively and, with a little bang, pushed down the old latch. She open the door and announced,

"Lady Margaret Coventry, my lords."

It was pure instinct that pushed Margaret into the doorway. It was pure pride, a moment later, that found her cool, proper mask and allowed her to look around the enclosure.

It was a low, round room with all its narrow windows shuttered; the floor was of dark-stained wood, the limed walls were white. In the light of the candelabras and braziers, Margaret felt as though she stood in that curious circle-place where light and dark divided. Likewise, the room gave her an impression of paradoxical Spartan features and rich comfort. A small circular table, obviously meant for private meals, stood in the middle of the room, attended by a number of richly carved, straight-backed chairs, each with a red velvet cushion on its seat. Along one side of the room was set up a sideboard; against the opposite curve of the room were two braziers, sparking warmth, and two low Roman couches. It was simple, yet comfortable.

Margaret allowed herself the time to take in the room before letting her eye fall, unfocused and dilated, on the two young men at the table. Her heart was pounding horribly in her chest, especially at the light, scrutinous gaze Rupert was giving her new gown, but she dared not show emotion. She wanted, above all, to sit down.

There was a brief scuffle among the two men which, in her tired, uncertain state, made her almost sadistically amused. Skander, as the host, half-rose in his chair to assist her, but at the same time Rupert, lancing a deadly look across the table at him, stopped him mid-rise. Rupert slid gracefully out of his chair and came toward her, his right by being escort. She turned her head away to one side as he took her arm.

"Did you find all you needed?" he asked, drawing her forward. She saw him glance over his shoulder at Aikaterine, who still stood waiting at the door.

"I did."

"Aikaterine," said Skander—he crooked a finger.

The white-clad maid swept in on silent feet, skirting Rupert, sailing over to the table to arrange Margaret's place at the table. There was a sparkle of pewter-ware and tiger-striped travertine, the flash of a crisp white napkin, and the languid glimmer of wine as it was poured into a cup. More deliberately Rupert took her over, his hand a little heavy on hers, though otherwise perfectly attentive, and lowered her into her seat. She found herself breathless and hoped that the mellow light of the room was enough to obscure the hot spots on her cheeks.

She smiled at Skander as Rupert resumed his seat on her left. "Thank you for giving me Aikaterine for the evening. I've never known a better maid."

The young man turned in his chair to regard the maid frankly, a smile on his lips. "Really, do you think? I think so too. I could not get on without her—or Tabby. I dare swear they are my two hands together."

Aikaterine quite properly said nothing, but stealing a coy glance at her, Margaret saw the flush of pride on her cheeks.

Rupert reached out as languidly as the flow of wine and slid his hand around the neck of his glass. Margaret watched his hand, long, powerful, the gem of his ring sparking fire with his movement. It gave her an inexplicably uneasy feeling. "Anyone can find a servant," he purred, "not everyone can find a good one. They are indispensable, and something to be thankful for."

His eyes were on his glass, his voice purring and pensive, as if he were talking to himself. Skander opened his mouth as if to speak, seemed to think better of it, and shut his mouth again. The brief quiet that followed was only saved from being awkward by Aikaterine setting the dish of venison before Skander and handing him the carving utensils. Margaret had never had venison before; she watched curious as the warm ruddy meat curled away beneath the even movement of Skander's knife. The heady scent of the meat filled the room and made her mouth water.

When he laid a few slabs on her plate, she said, to make conversation, "This is a very well situated room here. I like what you have done with it." She glanced around. "It is very cosy and unpretentious. It is very *you*."

"Do you think so?" he said, this time with a grim, self-deprecating kind of cheer. "This is my hide-away where I will not be bothered. You can see it would be not at all advantageous to stuff a great many people in here. I like it that way."

Margaret stole one last look around. *I wish I had a hide-away like this. The most I have is a cold cellar and a coward fox—and not even that, now.*

In the two heartbeats that followed, while they picked up their utensils to begin on the food, Margaret caught Skander throwing her an unveiled look of iron, scrutinizing her in that bare instant before asking, with all pleasance of tone, "I haven't seen you in a month, Miss Margaret. How have you—two—been? Are you finding Plenilune to your liking?"

She knew Rupert was watching her, and that made it only worse. It was a hard question Skander put to her, and for a moment she stared with a thoughtful darkness between her brows, searching for an answer among the raw tempest of her soul. "I—" she began, stopped, and tried again. "When it has not been rainy, Rupert has been b-busy and I have been about the grounds. Plenilune—Marenové—is very lovely," she admitted, then added regretfully, "but it is nearly winter now."

The young lord of Capys nodded sympathetically. "We had a head of sleet-storm through here just last night."

"Truth to tell?" interposed Rupert, glancing up under his brows. He shifted his forearm forward on the edge of the table, hand poised with his forefinger in the small of his fork's back. "We had fair weather down our way." He looked into the fire as one might look at a clock. "I dare say they will be finishing the last of the day's slaughter down there about now."

Skander opened his mouth to speak, seemed to think better of it yet again, and shut it once more. Instead he rounded back on Margaret and said gaily, "I promised you a look at the ballroom and our acclaimed falcon. Would you care to trot around that way after supper?"

With warm, wholesome food going into her empty belly and the braziers throwing up mellow light and a close, smoky atmosphere, Margaret wanted chiefly to retire to bed and sleep. But she could not very well say that, and poor Skander was doing a magnificent job being civil—she hated to leave his gesture unrequited. She struck a coy pose with her head. "Just you show me this falcon of yours. Every way I turn Plenilune has some new outlandish feature."

Skander looked surprised. "Do you not have falcons where—where you come from?"

Rupert laughed, short and scornful. "Of course they have falcons. Go the whole world over and you will find a falcon peering at you on the wing."

"True," said Margaret, slowly, easing herself into the waters of memory so that it would not hurt too much. "Even in town, though we lived on the outskirts of it, we would see the occasional falcon. They are very magnificent creatures," she added, glancing sideways at Rupert.

Skander leaned back in his chair, glass poised in his hand. "Dodgy and temperamental, forsooth," he protested. "And I should know. Oh, I like them, and if you can win one's heart she will stand by you as my Thairm does; but birds of prey are calculating, cold-blooded things. They make themselves ill allies."

For no reason she could apprehend, Margaret looked up at that moment and caught Aikaterine's eye. The maid's face was white, her cheeks two spots of colour... But two agonizing heartbeats later Rupert, too, stretched languidly in his chair and said,

"I wonder that you keep them. Hounds are so much more temperate."

Skander said gently, "To learn one's enemy, I suspect."

Margaret got through the courses of the meal by habit and instinct, going through the motions in a daze, a daze that became sharp where Rupert and Skander sat, or wherever their words fell.

The fire had gone down to the colour of red morse-ivory, and the room had become a hollow of tinselly quiet broken only by the chink of silverware and glass when Margaret, starting violently at the movement, realized that Rupert was climbing to his feet. "Aikaterine," Skander said at the same instant, also getting to his feet, "we are ready for the pudding. We will take it along with us now."

With a deftness and quietness of motion which Aikaterine shared with Rhea, the maid turned aside into the shadows and fetched three platters from the sideboard. She distributed them and Skander said meaningly, "Thank you, Aikaterine," and the maid took three steps back, hands folded before her, head up at attention. In the red light of the braziers she reminded Margaret of the watercolours of Japanese cranes.

Skander held out his hand. "If you'll come along now," he said, "I will show you the ballroom."

Margaret could think of nothing to say so she nodded, and with Skander before her and Rupert behind, one hand holding her pudding and the other pressed against the chill stone wall, she found herself descending the stair-well. She knew now why it was called a stair-well, her house in Aylesward having no such: the steps went down and down in a rigid spiral, down into the inky black. She had to remind herself with force that she was on the top of a fell, not descending into the lowest heart of the earth.

She imaged the heart of the earth would be a bit warmer.

With a relieved, shaky breath she came out of the door at the bottom, blinking in the sudden light of torches. Skander snatched a look at her over his shoulder before continuing on. She felt dizzy but kept on doggedly. Halfway across the atrium Rupert stepped up alongside her and slid his hand under her elbow, sending a thrill of horror down her spine. She wished to shake him off but she did not dare.

They left the atrium and turned into the north transept. They went across a series of galleries, walked the length of one, and at last approached two tall, narrow, panelled doors of white and gilding. The Lord of Capys, with another quick look over his shoulders, depressed the two knobs and gave the doors a sharp thrust, swinging them open together.

With an effort to steady her hand and keep her spoon from rattling in the cup, Margaret lifted her saucer like a lamp and stepped forward into the thick cold black of the room. A single bar of light pierced in with them through the doorway, but it barely drove back the immense gloom that surrounded them. She could feel that it was a large room, long and high, perhaps as much so as the nave, but her eyes were so tired and the darkness so complete that she could discern nothing.

"It is very dark in here," purred Rupert. His voice seemed one with the dark. After a moment's expectant pause he said, "Let's have a little light, then, for the lady." And with a harsh snap as of two fingers together, there sprang out from above them and along the walls hundreds of points of light. Margaret drew in a sharp take of breath but managed to hold her ground.

Skander pulled on the front of his tunic. "A pretty trick," he sniffed wryly.

"Yes." Rupert put his hands into his pockets and turned about, looking at the chandeliers which were now blazing with light. "Prometheus started that one. There is nothing to it."

While Rupert's back was turned, Margaret caught the wary, searching look his cousin gave him, but as soon as Skander's eye fell on her face his features unfurled into a genial smile. "You wanted to see our falcon. Well, there it is."

He gestured expansively across the length of the ballroom and she, following his gesture, saw, with a step back to take in the immensity of it, the Byzantine-work of an enormous falcon under their feet. It was done in shards of polished marble, travertine, and glass, each piece coloured and matched to perfection so that, from a height, it must have looked like a painting and not a construction of tiny, individual parts. She had expected it to be heraldic, like the glass falcons in the windows, but this one was depicted at an angle, hanging in that single moment when the bird turns from the climb into the killing dive, wings tucking, beak half-open, eye gleaming with the scent of its triumph. It was so life-like, so terrible, so fierce and proud and enormous, that Margaret feared Rupert's foot upon it, lest by his dark arts he somehow bring the thing to life.

They were standing now at the south end of the ballroom, just on the talons—beautiful gilt talons that took the candlelight and burned with the fury of the war-god star. To their right was the beak: a larger kind of talon and also gilt-angry. The jet and vermilion eye seemed almost to follow Margaret as she moved, hesitantly, across the floor. Everywhere the barred and tabbied feathers of the bird chinked with light; she kept expecting it to move, or the semi-precious stones of the feathers to lift and rustle with the sound of the high wind outside.

Skander's voice was warm and muffled with pride. "Is she not very fair? She is easier to see, so, without a hundred skirts obscuring her."

"She is very fair," Margaret agreed. "And so very smooth! I would not be even a little afraid of tripping on it."

The young man smiled and looked at the stones beneath his feet. His trim, bulky figure seemed a little withdrawn, pleasantly so, almost coy—but in the heraldic figure of his House there was no such coyness: under Margaret's feet was a picture of the pureness of his prowess, the sheer splendour of his thinly veiled power.

If only I could stay here! she thought longingly. *I would do well in this place. But no, only over Rupert's dead body, and such an eventuality seems unlikely.*

She turned away from her thoughts so quickly that she nearly lost her spoon from her cup. Rupert, who seemed to have been watching her all this while, raised an inquiring but not unfriendly brow. The sight of him sent a chill through her veins.

"This room is very well lit," she went on, listening to the hollow sound of her own voice, "for being so large. And we will be in here tomorrow?"

"And all over the House between whiles," replied Skander with a cheerful wryness.

She smiled apologetically. "Will there be many people coming?"

He drew his hands from his pockets and seemed to consider his fingers, as if counting. "Quite a number. I have not roused myself to memorize the guest-list. I know most of them by face, anyway, and that suffices, most times."

"Hol will be here?" inquired Rupert.

Skander flung up his head, gazing past Margaret at his cousin. A sleepy, cool light flashed in the young man's eyes. "In all likelihood..." he said slowly. He seemed about to add more when a chime from a long way off disturbed him, and he amended himself: "There, that is the clock in the Red Gallery. I have kept you long enough." Bending, he reached out and took Margaret's hand. "I trust you will sleep well. If you have need of anything only call Aikaterine. I put her at your disposal."

As if summoned by magic, there was a soft clearing of the throat in the doorway and the maid herself was standing there, ready to take Margaret away. She looked from the maid to the master.

"Good New Ivy, Miss Coventry." Skander smiled downward at her.

Catching her skirts in one hand, Margaret bobbed politely. "Good New Ivy to you, sir. Thank you for everything." She turned, fetched another look at Rupert to be sure he was not following, and at the last moment attempted: "G-g-*good* night, Rupert."

She walked away, purposing not to move hastily, her cheeks burning but her head held high, feeling the two men looking after her—or the one looking after her, and the other looking at the one.

Aikaterine's face was carefully closed when Margaret came abreast of her. With a small deferential movement and gesture, the maid led the way again back through the galleries toward the central nave of the House and from there up, up the stairs and along the passages to Margaret's bedroom. The hallways had grown darker and more in-drawn since she had passed. Though there were no windows in the halls, she could feel the high night pressing in all around them. The air outside must be thin indeed, she thought, treading lightly behind the soft-footed servant, for the genius of night to wrap so close about their garrets.

"Here we are, my lady," said Aikaterine at the door of the bedroom, as much to hear her own voice, Margaret thought, as to reintroduce her room. "Will I see you to bed?"

Stopping in the middle of the room and seeming to come to herself, Margaret looked around on the sparse, close, pale-walled room and felt a sudden stab of desolation. Her heart, floundering under the blow, jerked and spasmed in her breast. Breathing hurt. "No," she said gently, "I think I will manage tonight, thank you. Only take away the pudding cup and leave the light, and I will be fine."

Aikaterine's face, uplit by the lamp as she bent to set it on the dressing-table, opened for a single moment, searching, comprehending. She knew Margaret was not well, but with no more than a little curl of an understanding smile, she took the pudding cup and withdrew, murmuring only, "Good night, Lady Coventry. Sleep well."

Lady Coventry. Tall-standing in the middle of the room, Margaret stared blindly at the shut door, listening to the silence of the maid's footsteps in the hall. Lady Coventry. To her desolate pain was added a twist of ruthless irony. Her mother had always wanted her to be something, to make a name for the family. Here she was at last, miles, thoughts, dreams from home, an alien on the moon—and here at last she was a lady.

Her long white hands slowly clenched. *I hope you are proud of me, Mother.*

With a deliberate gesture, Margaret pulled the pins from her hair and dropped them on the dressing-table-top, and with some four steps crossed the room to stand by the little window, looking out on the swimming star-shot dark of the dale country below. Overhead was the bulk of earth, dark in its massiveness, the crest of it ablaze with blue light like some enormous frightened cat on All Hallows' Eve, stiffened and hackled in the heavens. And beyond earth's arched figure, beyond the long rays of light that broke off its back, stair-stepped the stars of heaven—upward and deeper—so that to Margaret, who had not bothered before to look beyond the inner ring of earth, it was like looking into a pool that went on infinitely until the end of time where eternity hung its veil so that little people like herself might not look in and die. Looking at earth, she had always felt small and angry and defensive. Looking at the stars beyond it she felt small again, but somehow right in her smallness.

Her cheeks cooled, the tempest of her soul stilled to a soft feathering, Margaret turned at last from the window and sat on the edge of the bed to undress. She could still see a little of the landscape through the window: a pale, ghostly thumbnail of a picture, a gash of upland cut level and coloured like the impassive face of a diamond. The wind moaned desolately, and seemed to get in through the chinks in her skin and blow about desolately in her soul. Down in the dale an owl hooted, which, as her fingers fumbled in the weak light of her lamp with her dress, reminded her of the hunt, and subsequently of the fox in Rupert's cellar. He would be sitting in a light much like this one, alone much like she was, looking out at the dark like herself. Was the little red-coated coward thinking of her as she thought of him?

She slipped off her shoes and put them aside at the foot of the bed.

Before she had been angry at him for being a coward, but now she pitied him. Who was she to despise him? She knew what it was like to be an alien, alone, lost, chained to a place which was not her own, unable to go where she belonged. She had heard the mockery of the panpipes playing the song of captivity. Who was she, unlovely Margaret, to despise the little brute?

Passing a hand across her forehead, she thought, *I have just enough hatred for Rupert. I cannot hate everything without breaking myself, no matter that everything hates me.*

Feeling small and cold and strangely calm, she climbed into the narrow bed and lay in the dark and silver of the Lookinglass night, listening to the Lookinglass owls, waiting for the Lookinglass morning that would bring countless strangers to her and to Lookinglass House.

VII | THE NAMES OF THE GREAT ONES

The following day was a world apart from anything Margaret had witnessed yet on Plenilune. Life at Marenové House, though every moment taut with stress, was quiet compared to the fluttering, wild, uprushing flight of activity that greeted Margaret in Lookinglass House. She ate breakfast in her room, dressed, and dismissed both Rhea and Aikaterine so that she might have the morning alone. Rupert did not come for her, so she wandered through the House, down the hallways she knew and several that were new to her, careful not to be buffeted by the many servants that were coming and going and getting things ready for the arrival of the guests, guests that were too many for their host to count. She moved among everyone like a fawn-coloured leaf on a sun-white stream, quiet and unheeded, until she washed up at last on the front porch of the House in the open wind of a clear, cold November morning.

She was the only one on the foreporch, alone and uplifted with the wind swelling white-embroidered all around her so that the ends of her shawl lifted like wings, and the colourful movement of the House and its terraced levels spread below her. She had not seen it from this vantage point; she had been too full of fear and pain yesterday evening to look back—*Like a coward*—at the twilit view she might have spied from such a height. But now she looked, alone and struck-still to her core by the sheer clear beauty of Capys. The fells were amber-crowned, the Earth above them faded to a feather in the sky. Far away over the pine-woods hung a single star and from the woods, as she looked their way, sprang the gurgling, spangled notes of a cowbird. She spread her fingers and grasped the ends of her shawl to keep it from being torn away by the wind, and it seemed to her as if the whole of Plenilune was knit together by the silver of that wind. Small wonder it seemed to her that Plenilune looked so silver from Earth.

How peacefully I am killed by you, she told the landscape. *How quietly you break me into pieces.*

Aikaterine had thought it best that she wear her fawn-coloured dress and her boots for the day, which would be better wear for wandering, and change in the evening when it was time to come out for the gala. The clicking of her boots was a hollow noise in Margaret's ear as she descended the stairs, hollow and reserved from the rush of wind and the organic throb of the courtyard.

The sounds of activity in the young lord's personal stables had been going on since before daybreak. The head groom seemed to be ordering the horses all over again to make room for the horses of important heads of Honours. As Margaret stepped into the courtyard and to one side, Skander's courser—a big-boned blue dun with a mind of its own—was being brought out of its stall and was making a fuss about its handler and the presence of a lean yellow dog. The dog began to bark, the blue dun went up in a twisting rear on its hindquarters—nearly wrenching free of the stableboy's hand—and there was an enormous flutter of bodies as people ran to put out the fire that was about to blaze up between the horse, the dog, and the boy. Margaret watched from a distance, twisting her shoulders to avoid the press of people rushing past her, feeling detached from everything, aloof and empty and, somewhere in the back of her mind, wishing for the horse's freedom.

From a rampart high on the House came three bull-blasting notes on a trumpet, as if it were a call to order, belling over the shouting and squealing and barking. Margaret started and looked up, but could not see the trumpeter. The notes alone were enough, tearing through the chaos, calling out a warning. The warning was put into words when she heard the head groom call out,

"Just put him back, just put him back! It's too late, the guests are arriving already. Mark Roy is just going to have to put his brute up someplace else. And get that dog out of here before it gets a hoof through its skull." The head groom, looking thunderous and preoccupied, turned and walked past her, muttering to himself, "Though it would serve it bloody well right..."

He did not notice her, nor, it seemed, did anyone else. He was busy, they were busy. Everyone was busy. Everything swirled around her like the upland wind, and everything seemed to have meaning and purpose save herself. With a kind of bitter, self-deprecating melancholy she stood alone and out of the way. She watched the horse fought with and put away; she watched the dog shooed away, slinking off with its yellow tail between its yellow hind legs. She stood in the sun but the air was cold, and she shivered, drawing up and in on herself as if to withdraw completely from the bright, clear-edged scene before her.

Of a sudden she saw a movement on the periphery of her vision, and she turned with a fresh jolt of flurried blood to find someone at her shoulder: a young man in a loose blue shirt and long jay-wing sleeves. After a disconcerted moment she recognized him as Skander Rime's man. He was tall and thin, taller even than she, and had to bend a little to speak to her, his hands clasped behind his back so that more than ever he had the look of a blue-jay.

"Your lord and mine are busy," he said, not offering to introduce himself with anything more than a musing sort of smile, "and there will not be time enough for it later, but if my lady will come up with me on the guardhouse parapet I will name to her the names of the great ones as they pass by."

She frowned slantwise up at him. His eyes, of a hazel colour, were owlish in the shadow that was cast by his bent head and forelock of thick fair hair. "Did Skander Rime send you?"

He grinned coyly.

With a forgiving sigh Margaret gathered up her shawl, and with a little hand-spread gesture let him lead her onward. With a smooth heron-like stride he towed her after him across the teeming courtyard—the working folk seemed to part like water around him—under the long shadow of the curtain wall, and up a flight of alarmingly narrow stone stairs to the rampart above. There, more than ever, Margaret felt as though she was on top of the world with alarmingly little between her and the sky, and a great deal of a fall between her and the ground below. Her stomach clenched and her spirit, detaching itself from her instinctive fear of heights, soared at the prospect.

She could see much of the dale below, its river and streams and ploughlands empty after the harvest. She could see the pine-woods in their green abundance and the smoky trail of blue that was rising out of its heart where a wood-cutter must live. Wind and sounds on the wind rolled up to her, buffeting her with their mingled confusion and clarity.

"Indeed!" she said loudly over the wind. "I can see why your master lives here. He is a man who loves the falcon, and the falcon must love a place like this."

The blue-jay man was looking over the wall, his head up and his eyes steadfast on the distance, but he smiled acknowledgingly and seemed to share her sentiments.

The top of the parapet was cold under Margaret's hand, so cold it almost felt damp, but she clung on with one hand, the other holding onto her shawl and held up to keep the wind-teased tendrils of hair out of her eyes, as she followed the line of the manservant's gaze. She tried not to look down too directly because, once she did, she could no longer feel the grip in which she held the stone wall and her vision would blur.

"From the tower," the blue-jay man said presently without seeming to raise his voice, "they will be able to see for miles, and have given us good warning. In a minute or two now we will see them, there, coming out of the beech that grows beyond the fall."

The direction, thankfully, was southerly, and facing a little westward. Margaret had only to switch her shawl to her left hand and hold it up beside her cheek, gripping the parapet with her right, to shield her eyes from the fringes of the level east-rising sun. Between the snapping tassels of the shawl's end she watched the beeches for any sign of movement. Her heart began to beat uncomfortably strong in her chest and she was not sure why.

The blue-jay man raised his arm and pointed wordlessly at the same instant Margaret caught the first flicker of movement down among the bare trees. At first it was formless, a mere suggestion of moving shadows that were dun and grey coloured, and then the sun hit a piece of metal and flashed like a shout, and after it came a backwash of purple hue, like the shadow that follows after a single harp-note. She saw a horse come out, a big chestnut with a long, easy stride, caparisoned in purple and gold with an almost savage head-dress obscuring much of its face. She almost mistook it for some kind of elk, for the head-dress was adorned with a pair of gold antlers, a scarlet tassel on the end of every tine; but as it emerged from the beech-woods and came toward the bridge and the thunder of the fall, it danced wildly to one side, bounding on all fours, jerking at the bit in a way that was wholly equine. Its rider, whom she took to be a man, gentled it back under control and steered it toward the bridge, his train, no less gaily arrayed, following after.

The blue-jay man's mellow tone held obvious amusement. "Blue-bottle Glass has the victory today, it would seem. He may keep his box stall, and Mark Roy's Altai-tek must needs find a lowlier board—and he is one of the finest horses in Plenilune, too."

"Mark Roy." Margaret ran the name off her tongue. "Where is he from?"

"He holds the Honour of Orzelon-gang, sitting southerly of Carmarthe." He sniffed and shifted his weight from foot to foot, bird-like. "Consequently that is where he got his horse. They breed long-legged, barbaric horses on the steppes of Carmarthe."

Recalling Skander's mention of these people, and feeling suddenly smaller than ever in a strange place, she asked, "Have you been there, to the steppes where Mark Roy's horse comes from?"

The blue-jay man jerked his head up higher, looking at her almost as one might look down on a child, smilingly. "In spring, when the Murklestrath is in full spate and the nomadic blood of the Carmarthen is too, then perhaps I go with my lord when my lord goes out to defend our borders. I am my lord's man, and I go with him wherever he goes."

She said, "They are over the bridge now."

In silence they watched the head of the long cavalcade make its way over the bridge and pass out of sight among the lower levels of Lookinglass. The cavalcade continued trailing out of the beech-woods and over the bridge. Margaret saw one horse shy wildly as a gust of wind, wedged down hard along the side of the fell, sent a long spray of water out from the fall across the arm of bridge stonework. She held her breath but the rider got his mount under control, nothing was upset, and no one was sent over the edge.

"It will take more than water to wash Gro FitzDraco off a horse's back," said the blue-jay man. "Three riders there are in all Plenilune no other man born of woman can match—"

Flicking a look upward, Margaret found the blue-jay man gazing down at her again, as though she were a child, as though he were at any moment expecting her to give back the answer to some question he had asked.

"—Lord Gro FitzDraco of Orzelon-gang, my own Lord Skander Rime, and Dammerung War-wolf."

Something swift and bright and awful passed across the manservant's face, something which at once chilled her and fired her blood. "Will we meet the third here come this evening?" she asked.

The look passed—clouded by thought or shadow, she could not tell—as the blue-jay man turned away. "Nay, my lady, unless you have passage through the gates of horn." He was silent a moment longer, while she stared bewilderedly at him. "The War-wolf has run his last. He runs no longer."

And it did seem as if a shadow had passed over them, for the fire went out of her blood and the wind seemed chill, chillier than ever; she pulled her shawl close, but what good was a shawl when one's spirit was suddenly benighted?

With an upward flutter, as if to rouse her and himself from gloomy thoughts, the blue-jay man raised both arms, one out to nearly rest a hand on her shoulder, the other pointing away over the garden and lower curtain walls.

"I see a neighbour of yours. Sure as I am that is Malbrey."

Margaret leaned over the wall. "He, there? The one on the cream-gold horse?"

The blue-jay man nodded.

She watched the distant individual that was coming out of the beech-wood and following after Mark Roy's train across the bridge. From that height and distance she could not possibly discern his face, nor make out much of the features of his clothing save that he seemed to be wearing armour, but she had a vested interest in him ever since Rupert had mentioned his old Manor. She had liked the Manor with a liking that hated, and while the liking-hatred still wrestled inside her she wanted the man who held the place to be a good sort of man. She felt intuitively that the odds were not in the Manor's favour.

"Is it that you know the man?"

She jerked back from the edge, realizing how close she was to the drop. Skander's manservant was looking at her expectantly.

"No?" he queried gently. "It is just the wind, then, that brings the angry colour to your cheeks."

"Yes," she murmured, turning away. "It is only the wind."

Malbrey passed out of sight and after him came two other neighbours, landowners from the south of Marenové House whom Margaret had never heard of before, and whose names she promptly forgot. But she was interested when a rider in red livery came through, quite fast, and the blue-jay man grew disdainfully quiet for a few moments, watching him. Margaret watched him too, as he skirted the metalled road and tore past the other caravans, plunged in through a flock of sheep, and disappeared out of sight in the lowest terrace.

"He must think very well of himself," she remarked.

The blue-jay man laughed mirthlessly. "Oh, he does. And come not long I will have to long-suffer his well-thinking of himself. That is Lord Bloodburn's man, riding as the vanguard to make sure we know he is coming."

"Lord Bloodburn?" She turned sharply upon him, frowning.

Even his smile was mirthless. "*That* is a name you know, by the look of your face. Lord Bloodburn is a close friend of my lady's lord. Hol is beyond the Marius Hills—some dales beyond. Likely as not he came up with Darkling; we should see them presently. There," he added, "is Hol himself."

In a tunic of red and a cloak of sullen thunder-colour Lord Bloodburn emerged from the beech-wood. He had a woman beside him on a grey palfrey, but Margaret could not distinguish any features, only that she was blonde and wrapped up in some kind of grey fur so that she appeared to be attached bodily to the horse. The man himself sat like a rock in the saddle, the horse moved with trained precision, and the whole image gave Margaret a strange prickling feeling along the bare parts of her skin.

"It is an ill name," she remarked with a carefully flippant air.

"It is an ill face," rejoined the blue-jay man.

With a sudden abandon she threw back her head, giving a soundless laugh at the manservant's frank improprietous comment. "For shame," she said.

He folded his blue wings behind his back. "Is it? Sure as I am it is true—and my Lord Skander made me promise to get a laugh or two from you, for your health's sake."

She nodded. "And that is very considerate of your master, I am sure. Who is this now—Darkling?"

A gentleman-looking fellow in aquiline gold and brown rolled at a canter from the woods, standard-bearers flanking him sporting smart yellow and green pennants. The wind of their going made the pennants look like the flame-work of leaves in spring.

"Centurion of Darkling-law," said the blue-jay man, leaning close, "politely behind Bloodburn though he has rights enough to be first. He is a good man, Centurion, and a seasoned warrior."

"Is that the measure of a man?" asked Margaret with a faint edge in her voice. She watched the figure of the neighbouring lord drawing closer. A numbness, a disinterestedness, was stealing over her.

The blue-jay man, having straightened with his arms still tucked behind the small of his back, said nothing, though his brows looked askance, and for some time he seemed to respect the distance to which she had withdrawn inside herself.

You would be a queen, she thought, *and you would be cold.*

She stood on the open parapet, the wind making a flurrying brown-and-tawny figure of herself, watching from aloft as the broken trails of horses and their dusty riders made their way across the bridge and through the levels of Lookinglass. Already Mark Roy was entering the gate on the terrace below them, his train much smaller than before, having shed at various levels his retainers which would not be honoured with entrance to the House itself. His purple and gold, splintered by the bare boughs of the garden trees, flickered peacock-like back at Margaret from below. His horse, a masked creature, leggy and of great height, pranced up the garden path; the *ta-ta-tock ta-ta-tock* of its hooves on the cobbles was a warm, persistent sound in an atmosphere which trembled with chaotic noise. Once out of the overhang of trees Margaret saw it give its head a mighty shake, antlers and tassels flying, caparison snapping like purple wings, and it belled furiously as only a stallion can bell.

From within the courtyard came the answering scream of another horse, tell-tale defiant, and the blue-jay man laughed as if he knew the joke in the horse-language.

"Unhappy Altai-tek," he said, grinning down at Margaret as they turned to watch Mark Roy enter the yard.

Even Skander Rime's horse, she mused, was inhospitable. Now the sun was in her eyes and she had to cup her hands over her brow to see. Below them the train was filing in, unusually tidy, each rider pulling his or her horse up in three smart lines before dismounting. In all Margaret counted nine: Mark Roy, someone who appeared to be his wife, their manservant and maid, and five men of soldierly bearing she guessed held land for the Lord of Orzelon-gang.

She pulled her shawl tight cross-wise over her chest and wore her chin high, wishing keenly that she were a mere falcon on the blue-jay man's fist. Sketched against the skyline, it would take nothing for one of those below to turn and see her—and know her. More than anything, save Rupert, she dreaded their censure. Unlike the fox she could not so lightly pass off the opinion of others. She was here for the express purpose of impressing them. She felt small and paper-thin on the parapet, as if the gilt-edged knife of the wind cutting out her figure against the sky might at any moment slip and slice right through her. With everything that weighed on her shoulders it took some effort to keep them rigid.

The blue-jay man's sleeves fluttered a little with his sudden bird-like movement: his master had come out of the House, stumping good-naturedly down the steps to greet his guests. He was dressed simply this morning, as though he had just been round to the mews and kennels and had not stopped to put on something more formal: the only elaborate piece of clothing he wore was a saffron-coloured cloak, which the wind took and made into an angry leaping flame behind him.

And Rupert? Margaret looked upward at the bulk of House, wondering where he was, and whether or not he was the shadow cast by Skander's flaming cloak, or the shadow which the flaming cloak drove back. But he was not to be seen.

There was a soft thunder-splutter of talk in the yard. Skander she could hear clearly, but most of the communication was lost in the bustle of horse-boys and horses. Her eye fell on one horse, a grand, skittish thing of dun-colour, a bold stripe of black down its spine, and recognized its rider as one of the three best riders in Plenilune. He was talking in a low tone to one of the horse-boys, so low his voice was completely drowned in the surf-sound of the others, but Margaret could see his gentle, condescending face in profile. He even looked horse-ish, his complexion long and grey and brown-freckled beneath his dark forelock of hair. It seemed the conclusion of the matter was that he would put his mount up himself, though the horse-boy appeared, at the end of the conversation, not at all sure what to do with himself.

The boy was just turning away, and Lord Gro FitzDraco was just attending to his dun, when suddenly he looked up and around. Margaret's heart contracted in her chest. She did not have time to look away: he knew she had been watching him. He saw her, full in the sunlight, standing overhead on the guardhouse parapet, watching him. His grim horse-ish face showed little emotion, but it did not seem particularly unfriendly. She endured that light, emotionless gaze for almost longer than she could bear before Lord Gro nodded, just once, as though some communication had passed between them, and turned away to lead his horse off.

Why, she wondered, *do I always feel as though I were in the middle of a conversation between people, a conversation which I can neither hear nor understand, but people seem to assume that I can?*

Mark Roy's attendance was all but squared away by the time Malbrey and his retainer, clattered through the gate. Drawing back against the parapet lest she have another silent interview with a newcomer, Margaret got a good look at the man's face. He was big, built like a bear, and had a thick beard which was brindled like a badger's coat. Contrary to his appearance, Malbrey was quiet-spoken: she could not hear what words were exchanged between him and his host when they greeted each other. Contrary to his appearance, he moved dextrously across the yard after dismounting, the *jinkeh-jink* of his metal accoutrements a sweet sound in the hoof-churned air.

Malbrey had barely made it to the foot of the House stairs when Lord Bloodburn's man came tearing in, dropping his horse to such a halt that it nearly sat down with a startled squeal and grunt, to spring up again, shaking its head as if with embarrassment at such an entrance.

The blue-jay man turned aside to Margaret, hands spread as if to catch up the whole scene within them. "If my lady would excuse me, I think I must tend to this matter."

She gestured him off and stood alone on the parapet, listening to the soft scuffling of his boots on the narrow stairs, watching his tall, thin, blue apparition blow across the yard toward the hot-faced manservant from Hol. Even among that press he strode like a heron cutting back the water around his legs: everything seemed to give way for him and wash back together again bewilderedly in his wake.

Alone on the parapet, Margaret turned from the milling scene in the yard to the wind-swept prospect of the garden. Though the light and the colour of the fells were autumnal, winter had nearly got its hold on the garden. The holly trees were in red regalia and the elms, which had been splendid, were bare save for a single blackbird that was trying to sing above the noise. Abruptly it broke off, falling through the air with the military-red cap on its shoulder blurring with a sudden sullen thunder-red of movement on the level just below. Margaret remembered in time that it was Bloodburn; she moved instinctively into the shadow of the guardhouse.

The singsong dog-snarl of the lord's red clothing trembled through the garden as he came in by the lower gateway and passed at a collected trot up the path. She could not get a clear sight of his face until he was nearly beneath her—his horse seemed to hang a moment in hesitation at the upper gateway—and then she could see as clearly as if they were on level ground, face to face, what sort of face he had. It was a fleeting moment, one in which he was not on guard, and she saw him nearly perfectly as he was. His hair was thin and pale grey, cropped close, his brows thick but pale grey too; his features were all heavily hung, and yet strangely empty, as if they had been big and full once, but time had sucked the life from them and left them cobweb-bare. Scarred, grey, wrinkled and haggard, but with a cold and ruthless spark in his eyes that would make Rupert look warm and rustic, Margaret thought that if Julius Caesar had lived a long life, he would have looked like this.

The inspection passed in a moment, as fast as the sidewise dart of a swallow. No sooner had she seen Bloodburn then Margaret moved on to the grey-shrouded figure at his side. The woman was entirely swathed in wolfskin and no features other than a fine-boned, ivory-coloured face and two long plaits of golden hair showed through. She was beautiful, but in her beauty she seemed oddly lifeless. Margaret, aloft on the parapet, cool and collected, felt a spark of pity in her own cold heart for that cold, lifeless woman.

Lord Bloodburn and his lady passed through and, not a moment later, as Margaret was just turning away, the flickering gold and brown of Darkling's representative showed at the lower gateway and she looked back to see him riding in alone, unattended. Centurion, who was a good man and a seasoned warrior, came clipping lightly up the path, the face-guard of his helm thrust back, a fair and cheerful face revealed beneath. He struck up whistling as he came, idly, pleasantly, some pretty song that Margaret liked the sound of, and a second later he spotted her. He flung back his head, still whistling, face-guard clanging, and gave her a raised hand in salute. Almost instinctively she replied, stretching out a level, silent hand—and flushed afterward with embarrassment: as if *she* were in a position to welcome anybody to Lookinglass!

She felt it was time to go down, but before she went to the stair she looked once more at the bridge and beech-wood to know if any more comers were in sight. All was still, hazed with the sidewise blowing of someone's fire-smoke, and turning light-saturated as the sun rose higher and morning wore on. Still she hesitated, lingering on the far horizon, wishing in vain that she did not have to go down, knowing that in a moment she would have to. The cowbird called again, liquidly and beautiful, and the song stung her cruelly.

"Margaret!"

She did not think she showed it, but she felt a jump of shock inside as the voice snapped on her senses. She shut her eyes tightly, recovering for two heartbeats, then turned and with deliberate movements made her way down the stairs. Rupert was waiting for her, having materialized as darkly and as persistently shadow, and was standing by Lord Bloodburn. Bloodburn had turned away and was busy with other things; she thought that for the moment she might avoid making his acquaintance.

She said nothing to Rupert, nor did he speak again to her, but she felt his high, cold gaze following her as she stood at his side and turned to watch the newcomers, felt the icy paleness like an almost unbearable pressure on her senses. But she bore it because she had to, and because she was English.

With a flutter of brown and a bound Centurion sprang off his mount, leaving it in the hand of a stable-boy. After a moment's bewildered look about, he spotted her with Rupert and came striding over, a hesitant but sincere smile on his face. On foot he proved to be tall and lean—rather like leather, Margaret thought—but he had a cultured look in his eye and, as he came up to her, acquitted himself by bowing largely, as sincerely as his smile. The sun flashed with a violent whiteness off his helm as he straightened, blinding her with its fierce pure colour, and it seemed that, in the faintly downward gaze he gave her, warm and supercilious—was there anyone in Plenilune who was not supercilious?—that same fierce pure white was in his eye as well.

"A good morrow to you, my lady!" he said in a warm, husky voice which made her think of autumn nut-gathering. He looked to her feet and back to her face, eyebrows rampant under the embossed rim of his helm. "And sure I know all the pretty faces of Plenilune, but here is a fair one I have not seen—passing fair, I think. Is there a price on your face, stranger, that you hide it from the other girls and have not come out till now?"

It was with supreme effort that Margaret kept from thoroughly blushing, though she felt the colour creep into her cheeks and the chill go out of the edge of the wind. She did not quite know what to say so, holding out her hand, she said truthfully,

"I am but lately come to Marenové, and Skander Rime was kind enough to extend an invitation to his gala to me."

For the flicker of an instant something dark and suspicious winged across the Lord of Darkling's face and his eyes, swifter still, darted to Rupert's. It was barely a moment, and so coolly done that if Margaret herself had not been so keenly conscious of the matter she might have missed it. But there it was, and when Centurion returned his gaze to her she felt he understood. He understood perfectly. Yet the warmth in his countenance did not diminish.

"Is there any possibility," he asked in a gentle tone, "of procuring a dance with this lady?"

He spoke with a sort of high pity and boyish earnestness, as if it were only he and she, quite alone. But even if he could ignore, for the present, Rupert's iron-dark figure, she could not: the figure made the pink cut on her lip sting anew, and the cut got in between her words and jostled them. "There m-might be. I'll beg your pardon in advance for I am new to these steps."

Centurion's brown eyes winged with a violent stab of smile. "And I!—used to making four legs dance, not two. We will be quite the couple on Rime's dance floor, you and I."

With that he bowed again, still lower, still more flashingly, and took a polite leave of her. She noticed that he gave Rupert no other glance. She watched, without turning her head, the retreating brown-and-gold flutter of his cloak across the courtyard.

"I wish you had not accepted his invitation to dance," said Rupert morosely.

"Why?"

De la Mare, too, was watching the Lord of Darkling, his eyes narrowed so that either the sun could not get in or the fullness of his displeasure could not get out. "His gallantry has too much of the feel of illusion. He gives himself too readily. I do not trust him with the ladies."

"And you trust yourself?" she asked back before she had thought about her words.

The barb had stung. The eyelids flickered open on the pale, hypnotic eyes and they looked at her, into her, with the pain of one driving in a surgeon's knife. She shuddered.

"*You*," he said coldly, "get to your room. And do not come out until it is time to be introduced for the gala."

"Oh, you do a wonderful job at winning a woman!" Margaret wanted to retort—but she did not dare. Smarting, furious, and not wanting to admit just how terrified she felt, she picked up her skirts and dodged him, carefully masking her face so that no one would know the rage and torment that was crushing all the organs in her chest.

"And don't you dismiss Rhea!" Rupert called after her.

A sob nearly escaped. Hurriedly she climbed the stairs and plunged into the busy traffic of the nave, losing herself in it, anonymous in the crowd. She bumped against someone, felt someone catch her elbow to steady her, but she moved on at such a pace that she tore herself from the person's grasp, only hoping that, whoever it was, her face had not been seen.

I despise you. I despise you!

In a blind rage she mounted the stairs, lost her way once along the corridors, and finally found her little high room. It was empty, for which she was glad. She knew she would have dismissed Rhea just to be alone, despite Rupert, despite everything. She locked the door with a quiet, deliberate thrust and threw herself into the corner chair. It rocked with a bang on its legs under her force, then the silence of the room was like a leaden sheet dropped over her. The only noise was her hot breathing, and even that seemed smothered.

Presently her breathing evened, though she still gripped the arms of her chair in a strangle-hold, staring intently at the gap under the door. Now, very quiet, like the pulsing rush of the ocean, she could hear the bustle outside and below. In a flash she remembered herself as a little girl sitting in her room on a summer's afternoon, alone, her door locked. She could not remember what she had done—she felt she had deserved the punishment—but she could remember the sounds of the other children outside, shrieking and playing and enjoying themselves while she, like some German fairy princess, was trapped in her high tower.

Eyes stinging from dryness, Margaret clamped them shut, straining her hold and slowly relaxing again. It seemed the height of unfairness, the bitterest of twists, that her only hope of a hero was

Rupert. She did not think even Skander would cross him decisively enough to help her.

With a start she came aware of a presence in her room and looked round, seeing her room as if for the first time. It was her dress, the only real bit of colour in that lime-washed place, set up on a manikin at the head of the bed, defiantly scarlet, defiantly real.

VIII | THE NEW IVY GALA

Candlelight splintered off countless rubies and the rushy red contours of her gown. It was like wearing fire, fierce and sullen fire. Pale blues and crystal whites mingled and glinted off the gem-facets on her breast and hip whenever she moved, striding at a conqueror's pace across the high nave corridor. Yellow light seemed to well up around her like an ocean. Sounds, cheer, the clink of mercury-glass and silver, and a warmth like wine overwhelmed her on either hand. Her shadow, an immense shadow such as live only in the farthest corners of a nightmare, was Rupert, and she linked to that shadow with a hand on his arm. She did not seem linked to her heart anymore. She could feel it pounding, but only as one might feel the reverberations of a hammer: a dull calm like that of horror lay on her.

They turned at the head of the stair together and paused by the blue-jay figure of Skander's manservant. Margaret looked down past the poppy-glitter and ember-rose of her own image, past the dull horror, to the multicoloured, shifting sun-field below her. There were countless people, all of them gaily decked in richness and candlelight, in gems and velvet and the easy pomp of station.

"Rupert de la Mare, Lord of Marenové, and Lady Margaret Coventry!"

He did not seem to raise his voice, yet the blue-jay man was heard all across that thunder-seethe of noise. Faces turned and looked. They were all familiar with Rupert but they did not know her. Margaret felt the collective surge of their curiosity rise up the stairs. She felt, through the numbness, something like a hand gripping her throat. Breathing was impossible so, to save herself, she went beyond it to a light, fierce, shining kind of feeling that was in some confused way much like the falcon on Skander's ballroom floor.

With a red flutter she descended the stair on Rupert's arm and began picking out faces in the crowd. She saw the familiar harsh gold and auburn figure of Darkling's war-lord: a tall, laughing figure which seemed carefree and distant. He was speaking with a laughing kind of condescension to Bloodburn and Bloodburn was taking it with light patience. At a farther distance Margaret saw Mark Roy and a woman who seemed to belong to him, standing close side by side, conversing in a friendly way with someone she did not recognize but who wore a garment of holly-green and golden trim and a jaunty mask to match. She looked away and around, colours blurring on her vision, countless strange faces shifting all around her. More than ever she felt like an alien in a strange place.

With a looming suddenness, completely silent in that thunder-roaring room, Malbrey appeared in front of them. Margaret halted with a shock: the man was enormous, like a bear. His badger-coloured beard was curly as a ram's fleece and bristled with emotion—whether from impatience or pleasure she could not tell for the beard obscured his features.

"Here you are," said Rupert quietly. He let go of Margaret and reached out a hand for the other man, who took it in a great paw and squeezed.

"I came up this morning." Malbrey's voice was soft, almost perversely pleasant. "I made an attempt to find you. Where have you been hiding?"

Rupert smiled with regret. "I was working in my room. Frezen went out last night and it seemed ill to my mind."

Puzzled, Margaret flicked a glance to the big man's face. He seemed surprised, almost unsettled. "Frezen has gone out? Out? Gone?"

"Gone, man," replied Rupert tersely.

Malbrey looked away but whatever he was seeing, Margaret thought, it was not the pressing crowd around him. "It seems strange, almost impossible, that it should have gone. To think that every generation has always looked up and seen Frezen and the Sparrow—and now Frezen is gone and the Sparrow lacks its brightest star, and our children, our children's children, will never see it."

De la Mare nodded but the sentiments did not seem to move him so much as they did Malbrey.

Malbrey laughed mirthlessly: a beautiful, spine-tingling sound that was almost like the laugh of a woman. "Does a sparrow fall out of heaven and you don't notice, de la Mare? Does it still seem ill to your mind?"

"I don't think so, but we will see." Then, as she knew he would eventually, he turned aside and placed his hand under her elbow, drawing her forward a step. "I would like to introduce you to Lady Margaret Coventry. Margaret, this is Baron Malbrey. You have heard me speak of him."

She heard herself saying politely, "I have," while her eyes were fixed on Malbrey's eyes as a bird is fixed under the serpent's glare. She felt with a horrid tingle the feeling of her hand slipping into his. His hand was rough like leather cool and living, and she wished strongly to step away and to avoid looking at him further.

"Enchanted," said Malbrey.

"Likewise," Margaret said in a careful voice. Then, "I did not realize you were a baron. Rupert has told me you hold the manor for him beneath the Marius Hills."

Malbrey beamed expansively, the badger on his face shaking and spreading ominously. "You speak our language already!"

Margaret smiled back with patient coldness. "Your language is not too unlike my own."

The baron nearly went on when, with a note of bemused surprise, Rupert said, "Why, physic! I had not expected your little pony-trap to make this journey,"—and both Margaret and the baron looked round to see a little wizened bird of a man striding carefully by them. The little man shook constantly and he did not seem able to help it: even the force of Rupert's voice, taking him by surprise, seemed enough to topple him over, but he managed at the last moment to regain his balance. He squinted pale, watery eyes up past them to the ceiling. The white wings of his hair were ruffled and perturbed. He held out one claw of a hand as if expecting Margaret to take it. Disturbed, she pretended not to notice.

"I left everything in his care," the ancient physic wheezed. "He minds how everything works. He minds how everything works. He minds... I left everything in his care. I put my faith in him." His hand still outstretched, he turned away, eyes on the ceiling. "I wonder where he's got off to..."

The man shuffled away and the crowd closed him off from sight.

"Who was that?" Margaret asked.

Rupert, who had before seemed almost to laugh with surprise at the little man's expense, now appeared troubled. It took him a moment to reply. "That was Melchior, the oldest physic in civilised Plenilune." He seemed to pull himself together and threw a laugh at Malbrey. "What an old bird! I had not expected him to be well enough to make it this year."

Malbrey hefted his massive shoulders. "For my part, I had not thought of him since last Wolf Moon. I like not his eyes."

Rupert smiled indulgently. "Do they see too much of you?"

"There is enough of you to see." The words were out of Margaret's mouth before she could stop them.

The baron frowned at her under his bushy brows. Her suitor, suddenly diverted, gave a swift, mocking laugh that was like a growl. He stepped out, setting a hand on Malbrey's shoulder and shoving him back good-naturedly. "So ho, Malbrey! She is a match and more for *you*."

The girlish lightness in Malbrey which Margaret had marked before became a girlish sullenness which, in that enormous frame and war-like bent of mind, made it all the more terrible. "And for you, de la Mare?" he asked softly.

The Master of Marenové seemed to have had enough of his friend's company and, taking Margaret's hand, was about to draw away. But at the last moment he turned back, a flash of dark daring in his eyes. "Hush!" he said swiftly, dangerously, all the while laughing mockingly. "And ever you loved me, Malbrey, you will not doubt me, and you will keep your mouth shut."

She kept her head high and her eyes averted from faces as they passed through the crowd. She could not tell if Rupert was angry with her for insulting his friend and was for now hiding it, or if he had been genuinely amused by her. She was not sure, either, which she preferred. Before Rupert could broach the subject they skirted a heavy table of mercury-glass, stopped as the way was blocked by several young ladies, and were overtaken in his silent, rushy way by the blue-jay man.

Erect, with his head to one side so that he looked bird-like at Rupert out of one eye, the manservant said purringly, "My master has need of you, sir de la Mare. If you would oblige me—" and he gestured meaningfully to the east end of the nave.

Rupert looked darkly from the man to the top of the room, but he said nothing. Putting away Margaret's hand, he told her, "I will be right back. Do not wander." And he went, though he begrudged it in the sharp lines of his shoulders and back.

Margaret breathed deeply as he disappeared. Though he left her alone in a crowd of strangers, she felt less uneasy in his absence. He, who marked her out for his own and likely made her abhorrent to many of these people, could no longer make her uncomfortable now that his branding presence was removed. She felt free. With a mirthless breath of laughter she looked about herself, taking things in with more interest than before.

Her way was still blocked by the table on one side, a pillar on the other, and before her by the cluster of ladies. They were talking among themselves and did not seem to have noticed her, nor to be disposed toward doing so soon. She found she did not mind. She set herself against the pillar and looked up and around, noting the way the light seemed to diffuse into the very air so that she seemed to breathe it, and the way the colours around her seemed to melt into each other and come out again, like a bold flutter of tapestry which the wind picks up and dashes about. The room was lightning-warm and full of thunder and she, like Andromeda, stood against the pillar alone, waiting quietly for her demise.

To her surprise and disquietude, out of the miasma of bright colour she saw a figure of Puritan-grey, and she hid an involuntary start when she realized Lord Gro FitzDraco was coming over, looking grim and almost disobliging, but clearly intent on talking with her. For no reason she could determine, he worried her more than Baron Malbrey, but she had caught his eye again and, as before, she could not look away. His long, freckled, horse-ish face seemed to hold her under a spell as he approached, growing taller and taller with each step.

Before, he had been accompanied by his horse, and he was not alone now. Someone stepped aside and gave him room, and her gaze, momentarily freed from his, looked down to see an enormous dog at his side. Its size made her shudder: never in her life had she seen such a dog of such a size, so tall the gentleman could rest his elbow on its back as one might rest an elbow on a tabletop. It was leggy and bushy-tailed, its fur, though brushed, long and wayward; its ears, which were moving this way and that with some annoyance, were each as big as her hand. Its heavy brow, wide cheeks, and long nose all spoke of the wild canine to her.

She dragged her eyes off the thing to meet Lord Gro's as he stopped before her. At this proximity she realized, with some surprise, that among the harsh brown hairs about the man's temples were some grey ones, and that in the man's cool eyes there was the marked weariness of one who is older than he ought to be.

"My lady." He bowed from the waist, no line of him bending save that which was supposed to. He retreated to an upright position. "I was unable to meet you properly earlier. Allow me to do so now."

"Sir." Margaret, feeling inexplicably flattered, held out a hand to him. She wished he would not take it, but he did, and she braced because she was not sure how the touch of such a man would feel. It did not hurt, but nor did it feel at all pleasant. The man's long, strong hand was cool and able, but as emotionless as his voice. "Forgive me for staring earlier. I h-heard you were something of a horseman and I marked your attention to your animal."

At her own words her eyes went involuntarily to the dog who was still standing uncomfortably near. She could see now that it had a thick collar of scarlet leather about its neck, studded with little silver balls. Against its grizzled grey fur it looked rather well.

"Do not mind Snati," Lord Gro said in his curious detached tone when he noticed the inclination of her gaze. "He is perfectly behaved."

Still she looked with veiled apprehension on the beast. Its size was almost beyond bearing, its body ominously strong and well-proportioned; it had an intelligent look in its savage eyes and she would not have been surprised, she thought, if it could actually speak. But it did not seem able to speak. Its disinterest in her was apparent: it turned its head away and began idly panting, watching the movements of the other people around them with the almost conscious flicker and blink of its eyes.

"Is it very wolf?" she asked. "I was told there were no wolves here."

Lord Gro set his hand companionably on Snati's hoary forehead. "Mostly, but not wholly. His sire was a waste-wolf, but his dam slept by my fire since she was a pup—and not a better-tempered bitch have I known."

She found she had to take his word for it, for though his voice was not unpleasant it did not belie any movement of the soul.

He stared at her passively for a few minutes and she, feeling awkward and desperate for some kind of conversation, dared to reach a hand out toward the dog. It did not notice her, not even when her fingers brushed its ear. The fur was soft as velvet, and mottled black and grey as though it had been through soot. She drew her hand away, rubbing her fingers as if to remove the soot, and felt puzzled when she found they were clean.

"He—he is a very big dog," she prompted. Why could she not think of something sensible to say! She wished Lord Gro were of a bad disposition: at least then her courage would rise to the occasion.

"Quite," he said.

She looked away, muffling a sense of fury. The rubies and flame-colour of her dress seemed suddenly much too warm. If only Skander would come! But Skander was doubtless busy as the host, not having—as Rupert had pointed out—a woman to help share the burden.

Lord Gro shifted a fraction from foot to foot, as a horse will do that has stood long and idle in the traces, and she realized that he meant to stand by her indefinitely. She could not think why, and she did not know how she felt about his presence. He was certainly not a vicious person, but he was not wholly pleasant either.

His silence baffled her, his gaze discomforted her, and his strange horsy air, though completely unaffected, rendered her unsure whether to speak or to whinny to him.

A woman brushed by them, forcing her to step back into Snati's muzzle. The dog grumbled and the man, in a swift, soft undertone, calmed it. Margaret watched the sky-blue gown flicker in among the other garments and get lost again, and something—either in the man's voice or the paleness of the blue—sent a lash of self-deprecating laughter across her chest. *How disagreeable he must find you! You are a pickle-wrinkled, sour, wretched thing, Margaret. Be pleasant. You are English, after all.*

But the chance was lost. As she turned with a genuine smile to ask him if he meant to dance that evening, a young buck broke out of the press and accosted Lord Gro by the shoulder. There was a blunt-faced signet-ring on his finger and, against the dull grey of Lord Gro's jacket, the jewel seemed to flash out like a star at twilight.

"Here you are!" said the young man in an exasperated undertone. His eyes flickered to Margaret—two straight black brows clenched together for half a moment, then sprang apart again. "My father asks for you."

Lord Gro turned his head quizzically toward the young man, looked at him for a moment under his brows, then detached himself from the hand. In a single fluid motion he bowed to Margaret, slipping his hand through the collar of his dog as he did so. She went down gracefully, too, expectedly sorry to have him go. When she looked up she saw the young man bowing too, though he had not even been introduced to her; as he straightened she thought she saw that same dark flicker of distrust in his eyes that had been present at the first moment of their meeting. They went away through the press, and just before it swallowed the young man up—for he was shorter than Lord Gro and bulkier of build—she saw him turn sharply to the other and seem to ask a question. Then they were too far away for her to discern anything clearly and she was alone again.

And yet... And yet, they had not gone. She knew Skander, though he was not present, and the blue-jay man, though he, too, was not about; and now she had met Lord Gro FitzDraco, one of the three best riders in all of Plenilune. She could not tell from his countenance what he thought, but he seemed not to dislike her, and the knowledge that she had met someone of his standing and won a sort of acquaintance with him fortified her against the loneliness that was never far off. She lifted her chin a fraction and looked with hooded eyes over the gathering, listening first to the tinkle of glass and silverware, then to the thunder of boots and voices, and then, still further removed, to the low purring sound of luxurious cranberry-wreaths and bright mistletoe.

She smiled vindictively. *What would Mother think of me now? What would she think of these people?*

A wind-rustle of movement went through the whole nave of Lookinglass. Margaret, looking up from attending to her skirt, caught the sidewise bluster of it and looked up the length of the room to determine its import. There was a flicker of pale golden movement, soon lost in the movement of the crowd, and then the black figure of Rupert appeared wraith-like at her side. He looked almost jocund.

"You stayed," he remarked. "How submissive."

She turned aside so that he could not see her face.

He went on in a politer tone, adjusting his gloves as he spoke. "I am sorry I was gone so long. There was some debate over who would lead off the dance."

"It is to be you and me, isn't it?" she asked blandly.

Rupert was not able to answer. At that moment a horn blared from the upper end of the nave, yelling out through the whole room like some golden-throated bird from a summerland of giants. The whole room answered in a quick forward rush and check, a gem-coloured sea of wild movement, and a cheer as if the Wild Hunt itself were about to set off at that moment. Raised above them stood Skander Rime, the host of the gala; it was he who wore the pale, almost buff-coloured gold coat trimmed with rougher golds and silvers. It was a handsome outfit, but on that blunt, big, friendly frame Margaret thought it did none so well.

"My lords and ladies, gentlefolk of Plenilune." Skander put his hands comfortably on his hips and stood over the room, looking this way and that. The candlelight played in the stark bare brown of his hair and made it almost beautiful. "Last year at this time we all met in the house of our friend Mark Roy of Orzelon-gang—I well remember Romage's punch." He looked faintly wistful. "There is not a better punch in all of Plenilune. But this year I am pleased to have the honour of hosting the New Ivy gala and of welcoming you into my home. Be it not the punch—I hope that it be something else that you remember come next year, when the New Ivy fires are lit again to herald in the Hollow Moons: something bright, something beautiful, something small upon which worlds turn." With an upward rush of his arms, a ring somewhere among his fingers glinting like starfire, his voice became like thunder, like power, and it stung Margaret horribly. "Welcome the Hollow Moons, my friends! Welcome the Hollow Moons!"

And the room gave back the cry, "God rest the Hollow Moons! God rest the year!"

Skander stepped down and was instantly lost in the crowd. The chaotic noise started up again. It seemed irreverent to Margaret, when reflective quiet would have been appropriate. The Lord of Capys' words banged inside her chest like hammers, chipping away at—something. The fierce sting of unbelonging made holes in her heart and she felt herself bleeding.

"For being flagrantly unsociable," mused Rupert, "he can deliver a stirring speech when the occasion requires it."

She grabbed her heart and squeezed it to plug up the holes. "Wha-what would you know?" she snapped back. "N-no one will rest your Hollow Moons."

He looked at her sharply, the pale steel of his eyes snaking along her face so that the look was almost physical—she nearly felt it cutting her skin. But he said nothing. He held out his arm to her and made her take it, and began pulling her through the general movement of the crowd toward the north wing of Lookinglass and the ballroom with the falcon displayed.

Already music could be heard playing, a little roughly, as though the band in the ballroom was just tuning up. It grew harder and harder with each step to manage the panic that was putting itself vise-like around her heart, and with each step Margaret suspected her countenance, too, grew harder. They went through the galleries and she could hear the thunder of talk being replaced by the thunder of blood in her ears. The galleries were ill-lit, or rather, lit like the mysterious insides of ceremonial caverns in the hollow primeval days, slumbering dark and glinting with point on point of gold and silver and rich humane red. And like motley, happy, reverent worshippers the elite of Plenilune passed through, Margaret among them as a detached alien creature and feeling much like the sacrificial victim who was to go beyond the rich darkness and flare of candlelight, beyond to where the worshippers themselves could not go.

For no reason she could discern, the panpipe sound came to her just then, not among the instruments calling from the ballroom, but from the high memory of the fellside. As the two enormous doors loomed before her she felt as though she, Margaret Coventry, would pass through alone and come face to face with Plenilune itself.

The doors were opened—she did not see by whom—and like a colourful wave the whole crowd went through, laughing and taking hands and partners, wading through the sudden surf of light. Cold air gushed out with the light, making Margaret flinch, but before she could resist or do anything rash, she was pulled in by Rupert and they were striding out into the middle of the room while the crowd and music whirled like compass-needles around them. And in that moment Rupert was very handsome, handsome and terrible, with a high laughing light in his eyes, his head up, his hand upraised, the aurora of Apollo splintering behind his head. She saw one of his eyes trained on her, dilated and fiercely blue. There was a brief check in the music, three distinct heart-beats that Margaret felt like drums, and then, like a bird, like an angel, like a god, he stepped in and the music and the dance and the whole terrible power of it rushed in with him, in and up and thundered like unthinkable wings over her. She had expected the dance to be stately and demure; instead he whirled her, and she whirled with him, in a kind of red-and-black crane-dance, as earnest as it was wild—and the fierceness of it helped to rouse the iron in her will. Let her mother, she thought as she spun in the midst of her flaming-poppy skirts, see her now! Light and scarlet flew from her, defying the empty black figure that danced across from her. Music grabbed at her feet and hands—she stamped and clapped, not like an Englishwoman, but a Tartar's girl.

She did not know if it was the magic of the music or the witchcraft of the warlock, but it seemed almost wrong to think of herself now as an Englishwoman. The terrible dance into which she was swept, more wild and alive than any dance she had stepped through before, seemed more akin to the pounding of the life-blood in her ears than anything else and, by virtue of that, more true. Here the stars were closer, the colours brighter, the goods and evils starker, than they were on earth. She could not remember England very well, though that might have been because her vision was running riot with whirling colours, peacocks' feathers, light, movement, and music. All she could remember was a broken sense of hoary discontentment, a sense of living drudgery, of fighting against small, insignificant shadows of things—when here in Plenilune lived and walked the sharp-edged things of a higher plane: the gods and demons in their palaces, dancing together on the eve of winter.

With an executioner's abruptness, the first dance had ended and she was curtsying diagonally to someone by Rupert, he bowing to a lady by her. She was panting, her blood was up, her ears were ringing with exertion and the crashing echo of the orchestra. The aching hollow of noiselessness lasted only a few moments before it was punctuated by a gentle albeit persistent thrumming jerk of a violin's strings. There seemed to be a rearrangement of bodies, quickly and lightly as if they were only leaves that an autumn wind was picking up and kicking about. Rupert snatched a glance at her before he was replaced by Centurion.

Margaret had almost forgot he meant to dance with her. For the moment she was more ill at ease with him than she was with Rupert. But his brown eyes were dancing even before their feet started, and he was smiling at her with the utter abandon of the utmost encouragement. The orchestra began a high, whining song in a minor key, an eerie tune, and the two bowed languidly to one another before stepping in side by side, right hand to right hand at shoulder height, moving counter-clockwise with the other couples. He had changed his brown travelling gear for a coat of thick velvet-work, a ruddy-colour slashed and picked out with gold and beige and subtle points of red like a grouse's coat. In his wild plumage he looked very well.

"My lady!" he said in a laughing, accusatory tone, "I think you told a falsehood. You danced very well just now."

She was too flushed with the dance to blush at his words. "Perhaps!" she gasped a little laughingly, a little mockingly. "But it seems like a fever, which one catches quickly and loses one's mind to. I did not know what my feet were doing—" she passed round him in a skipping gesture, imitating the movements of the other women with their partners "—half the time."

He laughed, shiningly, soundlessly. Yet as she snatched a glance over and upward at his face, there was something that was not laughing and not shining, and not quite soundless about his face. But he said aloud, "I heard second-hand and round-aboutly that your name is Lady Margaret."

"Coventry," she corrected him. "Margaret Coventry. *Lady* was given to me out of politeness, I think. And you are Centurion—" she took his hand, fingers interlocked, and backstepped clockwise "—of Darkling-law, I am told."

The young man passed out of the orbital movement and clapped twice with the other men before taking her hand once more. "Your knowledge is better than mine, then. You say it so assuredly, as if you have always known, whereas I wake up every morning, look about me, and say, 'Well, old boy, I suppose you really are master of this dene!'"

"It is odd, isn't it," she replied, "how for granted and as infallible we take the word of textbooks?"

Centurion barely missed treading on her skirt, and looked apologetic. "And how quickly we doubt our own natural reason, though perhaps we have good cause to."

"Perhaps."

For several minutes more there was silence and music between them, and she was sure he was as painfully conscious of getting through the dance gracefully as she was. She caught sight once of Rupert, and once of Mark Roy—though it took her a moment to place him—but the fact of the matter was that Centurion, though by far more agreeable, was much less splendid than the prince of the Mares, and she was caught up, not in the shining splendour of the movements, but in the individual steps that she must make without tripping or falling behind. She was just feeling as if she had got into the rhythm of the thing when, to her surprise, it was over. She was bowing, and so was Centurion, and she felt hotter than ever.

Instinctively the man reached out to take her hand, but seemed almost to hesitate in the after-act. Her eyes flickered to his but there was no look of hesitation in his face.

"Very well footed," he said warmly. He blew out, cheeks swollen, and glanced about the room as if looking for something. "Do you have a partner for this next dance?"

A wave of weariness blinded her for a moment. After the heat of the dance the weariness was cold as fainting in her brain. "Not to my knowledge," she replied honestly. "If it is all the same to everyone, I think I will sit this next dance out."

The grip on her hand became stronger. With a jagged stab of apprehension in her breast she looked to the gloved hand holding hers. "Of course!" she heard Darkling say. "Allow me to escort you to a chair."

With a flamboyant, bird-like rustle he tucked her at his side and threaded the way through the milling press toward the inner side of the room. With a backward glance, she wished she could have sat under the windows where it was more likely to be cool and the fell-land dark, like a black sea which had overwhelmed the citadel of Lookinglass, was washing purple and indigo against the pale fractalled panes. But it was under the gilt peacock panels of the east wall that Centurion placed her, having walked a distance in search of an empty chair and, failing that, having ousted a younger fellow from his repose.

Centurion put her down and straightened; from her low seat, Margaret looked up into the blinding aura of his face, framed in amber and gold by the high light of a chandelier. She could not see his features. His voice, when he spoke, was eerily detached and grimmer than she had known it before.

"You will be well enough on your own, madam? May I get you any refreshment?"

He did not mean to, but the erasure of his face and the alien nature of his accent cut fiercely into her. "No," she said, more harshly than she meant. "No, I thank you. I am well here alone."

Again he hesitated, and this time she was sure he hesitated to a purpose. But whatever he weighed in his mind, whatever he thought, she never knew for he did not speak again, but bowed fluidly and withdrew, leaving her alone in a room full of people.

At least the worst was over. Another gentle song began, thrumming from the upper end of the room. Colour like an edenic sea washed back and forth across Margaret's weary, disinterested vision. The hollow dark of the galleries, which had been like walking down something's throat, seemed a long time gone now, a long way off. Sitting on the other side of it, she felt as hollow as the dark and fragile at the edges, like a shell.

You are tired, that is all. You are fighting all the time. You are just tired. You can rest for a minute now. Dear God in heaven—she let her eyes fold shut—*let me rest for a minute.*

It was a minute, she reflected later, a perfect minute, after which she was joined at her right hand by another woman who had left the dance. Margaret did not recognize her; underneath the plumage of white feathering and chiffon and masque of black velvet and swan's-down, she did not think she would have recognized the woman if she had been her own mother. She swooped close, paused a moment like a bird stalling in mid-flight, and finally alighted soundlessly in the next chair. Two pale gold, owlish eyes blinked at her out of the masque. Margaret's face felt naked under that stare without a masque of its own.

"I don't believe we've met," said the woman in a cool but not unfriendly voice. It was the sort of voice, Margaret thought, the most perfect mother would have.

"No, madam," she replied, uncertain whether to be cool herself and not unfriendly, or to hold the stranger at a distance. "I don't believe so either."

The woman turned her head inward: the light caught her eye and made it spark yellow. In the shadow cast by the black velvet, the spark was very uncanny indeed.

"Comitissa Woodbird, of Thrasymene."

"Thrasymene." Margaret smiled lightly, triumphantly. "I have heard of you."

The owlish eyes flickered over her. "I see, yes. You are chatelaine of Marenové, I think."

Like a pigeon struck out of the sky by the brute force of the peregrine's dive, Margaret's smile took the cold blow. For one moment she almost lied, for one moment she almost said nothing, but she knew more strongly than anything that she would have loathed herself afterward if she had. "I do not have the keys."

The comitissa moved her head in a kind of mirthless amusement. Perhaps the blow was not meant, for her voice was friendly as ever, if ever as cool. "I see, yes... I did not attend to your name when you were announced."

With some effort she recovered her faintly mocking smile. "It is Margaret Coventry. Is it as strange to you," she dared to add in a surge of reckless testing, "as your name is to me?"

Up went the swan's head. Fiercely flashed the owlish eye. But the lips, which struck Margaret then as being deeply red, smiled genuinely. "Maybe it is and maybe it is not. It has the sound of the moon-witch about it. Is it that you are a moon-witch?"

"I do not think I am any sort of witch."

The smile twinkled on the comitissa's lips.

With a heavy sigh, Margaret said, "What is it about my name, Comitissa, that makes you think of a witch—whether of the moon or of anything else?"

But the other only shook her head. "I could tell you if you could come in and see the dreams of my mind's eye. It is not an image for which there are any words."

A month ago Margaret knew she would have laughed cuttingly and had some biting remark for a reply. Instead, at this moment on the near side of a month gone by, she passed her hand through the air as if to dismiss something and said, "Yes. I know those sorts of thoughts."

"Hm!" said Comitissa Woodbird in such a tone that made Margaret start, and she looked up to see the lady had left off her thoughts altogether and was rising, rather quickly, as if to get away. At that instant Margaret started again, more violently, when a familiar voice said,

"Why, Comitissa Woodbird! I do not scare you off, do I?"

Margaret stood in a hurry as Rupert joined them, such a look on his face as of a man who is being amused by being cruel. Out of the white feathering and black velvet of the masque, Comitissa Woodbird glared at him, the lights like cat's-fire in her eyes.

"Hm!" she said again, which, Margaret thought, was the safest answer to Rupert. "Your cousin had promised me a dance. Do you know where he is, Lord Marenové?"

"Am I my cousin's keeper?" rejoined Rupert laughingly. He waved a hand in the direction of the orchestra. "You might try him over there. And was that all he promised you?"

Confused, Margaret looked to the comitissa's face and saw some kind of barb had stung there. With an odd breathy, hissing sort of sound the woman pushed Rupert's words aside with one hand and retorted, "No, I think not, if you could not be your brother's."

What light, laughing atmosphere had lain over Rupert was gone upon the instant and what dark titan remained might have, if his necromancy had allowed him, set the swan-white woman alight on the spot. Wordlessly Rupert bowed her stiffly off, and the comitissa had nothing more to say and left.

How Margaret hated that woman in that moment for making Rupert so angry!

For a long moment he said nothing. For a long moment Margaret stared at the floor, her hands clasped before her, waiting for the inevitable break in his thoughts that would bring him back to her. She could not hear them, but she could feel the pressure, the fury of his thoughts. Finally he breathed out gustily through his nose, pushed his coattails back, and shoved his hands violently into his pockets.

"The cow!" he growled derisively as the comitissa withdrew, white feathers mingling with the colourful crowd. "The cow would think to jump the moon!"

"Let her b-be," said Margaret. A rush of panic and a sensation of taking her life in her own hands nearly blinded her. "What is she to you?"

Rupert looked at her sharply, and let the sharpness of his eyes linger like a blade against her throat for an unbearably long time. At last his shoulders relaxed. "So... The little vixen speaks sooth. What is she to me?" Then, as the music was beginning the introduction to another dance, he slid his hand down her arm and took hold of her—her skin tingled in revulsion—and said gently, "One last dance, I think, for you and me tonight."

She swallowed the panic and weariness down her throat. "Yes, Rupert. One last dance."

It was a smooth, slow dance into which he led her, like the slow swing of stars—and it was the one she hated most of all. Its unhurried but inexorable steps seemed all too akin to the persistent pull of Rupert's will. Bound up in his arms, moving to his steps, Margaret felt more than ever that she was moving through a nightmare. She once saw Skander close at hand, warped by her weariness into a pale stag-like figure, dancing with an enormous, graceful swan. She met eyes with him for a fraction of an instant and struggled with a fresh surge of panic not to let the weariness and huntedness show in her face. She forced a smile. He, she thought, forced one in return, and the couples swung apart again.

How long that dance lasted she did not know. They seemed to dance down the corridors of time, from the first sung dawn to the world's last night. Civilisations rose and fell beneath their feet. Stars bloomed and shed their petals overhead. In her muffled state the only clear feeling was her lip, which was stinging worse tonight. She wondered in a detached way if the rouge might not be harmful to it. More and more Rupert had to support her through the movements until, at last—she gave a half-checked sob of relief—he stopped completely and the dance was over.

"What is this?" he murmured. She was not sure if his tone was one of concern or condescension. "Lift up your chin, my dear. You are born to this."

Another sob welled up in her throat but she forced it down in time. In a spurt of rage she wanted to strike his hand and face away, but she only turned her face from him and said, "I would like to sit down again. I have not danced like this in too long. My feet are weary."

He turned her about, supporting her without seeming to, and she managed to glide gracefully toward the perimeter of the room where a new chair waited for her. It was a heavy, plush, winged thing of white wood and gold satin cushions, and a sweet smell wafted from it when she sank down, doing her best not to look as tired as she felt.

Rupert leaned close and let the back of his hand brush her hot cheek. "I will fetch you something cool to drink. Sit quietly and do not stir."

"For myself or for you?" she asked with a flicker of annoyance.

He quirked a smile. "For both, I imagine."

She leaned her head back against the chair when she was left alone, as she had been left alone before, but this time relief did not come to her. Her hair-piece—a jewelled butterfly of rubies and shards of amber—got in the way of her comfort, as did the knowledge that soon Rupert would be coming back. The room, which had been cool when it had been empty, was full and hot now. There was a pressure building behind her eyes which was only faintly alleviated by shutting them.

A familiar voice began speaking beyond the darkness of her closed lids. "It is my understanding that the dancing is going to be cut a bit short by a solo piece by your wife."

She recognized the voice as Darkling's, but it was a new voice which replied.

"Romage is to play her harp. Capys so greatly enjoyed her performance last year that nothing, he said, would satisfy him until she had played this year."

Centurion gave his shivery, silvery laugh that was nearly inaudible. "It is a great compliment to her, sir. No one plays the harp so well as the Carmarthen folk, and among them no one so well as she."

The second speaker said nothing but the silence was not disapproving. *He is a good gentleman*, Margaret thought with a touch of a smile, *to not milk Centurion for more praise of his wife than comes willingly*. The silence was brief, however, for with a new tone of warning the second gentleman said, "Hie to your wit. There goes Baron Malbrey."

Her eyelids fluttered involuntarily but she kept them down. The silence that lingered between Darkling and his neighbour was long and hot, broken at last by the former musing,

"I smell a rat."

"Indeed?" replied his neighbour.

"Oh, aye!" She risked cracking one lid open and saw Centurion turn, his head up, gazing at his shorter companion with a supercilious air. "*He* sold his soul to the devil and lives on the devil's land. Moreover, he and the devil are friends."

It was Mark Roy who was Lord Darkling's companion. He turned his head away and looked after the baron, his own face clouded by thoughts, the muffled sound of thunder in the lift of his shoulders and the gold-traced dragons that were depicted there. "I do not like de la Mare's baron," he admitted carefully. "There is an air about him which I do not like—*moreover* there is some dispute between him and my man FitzDraco which puts him not in my graces."

"Really?" Centurion raised a brow. "The game moves on apace. What cause?"

Mark Roy only shrugged, the dragons soaring and falling and rustling as with wings. "FitzDraco has never told me, and much as I stake my life upon him, he is not a man I would pry for information. I let him keep it to himself on the condition that it not upset affairs of state."

"And does he mind that it would?"

For a long while Mark Roy looked after the baron, who had long since disappeared, and there was an uncertainty in his dark, noble face which chilled Margaret's blood. "Not him, I think, never Lord Gro. Lord Gro is among the best of men. And I think that, for all his chanticleer pride, Baron Malbrey would not strike a blow of any sort for anything. He would not risk himself like that." Mark Roy looked to his companion. "He has not the power. But de la Mare, on the other hand..."

Centurion said in a soft, serious voice, "But de la Mare, on the other hand, throws the equation of power against us."

Mark Roy shivered involuntarily, as if someone had trod on his grave, and he crossed his arms tightly over his chest with a great murmur of scarlet velvet. "Ill I like him!" he whispered vehemently. "Ill I like him..."

But the moment of seriousness had slid from Centurion and he gave a breathy but genuine laugh. "Our host tried—worthy man! But it seems the gates of hell prevail yet."

With a spark of premonition, just in time, Margaret looked away before Mark Roy turned a furtive gaze to her. "Truth to tell, I thought Capys a little mad to go running his head into such a lion's mouth. But what is bravery and what is madness, and is there such a difference between them? Capys tried—and he is a worthy man—but de la Mare is a man who will dare all things." And again he shivered, nostrils flaring, and again Centurion said with a light air,

"Despair not, sir. God works in mysterious ways."

"Fair mysterious," grunted Mark Roy. "I would like a light in the dark all the same."

Lord Darkling put his hand on his friend's shoulder and gave him a little turn-about. "You never know, sir, but there might be. You never know, sir..." His gaze slid, as he and his friend began to move off, over Margaret and lingered there, eye linked with eye, and for the briefest moment she felt pierced by him, plumbed by him... She was not sure what he read in her face, or her eyes, or her soul, but at the last instant he smiled and his gaze passed on from her.

Margaret turned her lip between her teeth and then let it go at once, wincing at the pain. With a heavy sigh she shifted in her chair, uncomfortable, uncertain. No—she gave a mirthless breath of laughter—*wishing* she were uncertain. She knew what Centurion meant by his look, no matter what he read in *hers*. He, far from despising her, hoped her to be a friend within those alleged gates. Little did he know, she considered with her elbow on the arm of the chair, her chin in her hand, and a small, mocking smile on her face, little did he know that there could be no friends within those gates, no matter how much she might wish otherwise.

IX | THE RED PAWN

"Ah, my jailer," she wanted to say aloud when she saw Rupert returning. The glass which he placed in her hands was cool, made of cut crystal, and he seemed to have poured light into it for her to drink.

"You look better," he remarked. "I was gone so long for this." He held out a fan to her, spread open, distorted images of fieldmice on it in beige and ecru.

She took the fan. "Never mind. I have been quite content to sit here on my own."

He smiled like steel. "I'm sure you have."

For a few minutes they kept their own silence. Margaret drank the cool wine, which tasted as much of sunshine as it looked, and fanned herself until the tendrils of hair around her brow danced wildly and her wrist began to hurt. Rupert stood by her, looking to her from time to time, but not speaking. If he had found his temper after losing it over the Comitissa Woodbird, he did not mention it. Meanwhile the last dance was coming to a close and there was some movement among the servants which, catching it out of the corner of her eye, Margaret thought must mean the end of dancing altogether and the preparations for the performance Lord Darkling had spoken of. She was just rousing herself to mention it when Rupert said,

"Ah, I seem to have tarried not long enough. The pigeon is going to warble for us."

So, she thought, pursing her lips, he had not found his temper.

With a sigh Rupert held out his hand. "Come along, vixen. We must find ourselves a good seat."

"I think this one will do," she snapped, sore on the pigeon's behalf. With an uprush of scarlet she rose, skirts in hand, and waited while he hefted the chair over one shoulder. He beckoned her on before him and she went, weaving her way among the others while chairs were set up and the orchestra was rearranging itself to accommodate the solo performance. In the dark wings of the north end of the ballroom the players sat, tiered on their benches, like a jury of angels. They were all in warm, dark colours and seemed to melt into the shadows, illumined only by their single candles. It was a strange, eerie thing to sit below them, looking up into their shadows, while it seemed the candles, not their fingers, played the light upon the strings. It was a strange, eerie note they played, a minor key which seemed to conjure the formless, painful longing in her soul and give it a kind of voice. Margaret sat in her seat, her hands gripping the arms of it until her knuckles turned white, and suffered the mournful song to wash out of the high dark down over her. Rupert sat stiff and sidewise in his chair by her side, and if the music affected him as it did her, she was not sure: she only knew that his eyes were hooded with bare displeasure and his lips were pressed into a thin, iron line.

Someone spoke. Margaret did not know who or where they stood. The voice seemed to come out of the dim dark, as if Plenilune itself were introducing the harp-player.

"I am honoured to give to you tonight a song by none other than Queen Romage of Orzelon-gang. Please—"

As if the voice had drawn back a veil, Margaret noticed the woman at last. She sat foremost among those in the orchestra, on a level with the audience and not far from Margaret herself. And in her pomp and quiet, smothering splendour, Margaret knew she was only gracing the orchestra's ensemble: *she* belonged among the lords and ladies. Her hair was caught up with pins of blue amber—which the candlelight behind her was making into a furious cluster of fractalled flame—but if it had been let down it would have been long and tawny-striped like honey and a tiger's coat, and Margaret almost hated her for the beauty of it. She was in a gown of peacock-blue, the same colour as the drenched night outside the windows, and her gown was chased over heavily by gold threads as if the golden harp-strings of her instrument were tied to her, and she to it—and when she glanced up across the audience from attending to her harp and the light of the chandeliers illumined the look in her eyes, Margaret was certain of it.

There was no more introduction. The lady smiled in a small, bewitching way, and her fingers began to work the strings. The lights ran up and down the strings, pale as her fingernails, red as her lips.

> *Fear no more the heat o' the sun,*
> *Nor the furious winter's rages;*
> *Thou thy worldly task hast done,*
> *Home art gone, and ta'en thy wages.*
> *Golden lads and girls all must,*
> *As chimney-sweepers, come to dust.*

Her voice and the harp's were matched to perfection, and both of them golden, so that it seemed to Margaret as if they had but one voice between them and spoke at once two languages, though their words were the same.

> *Fear no more the frown o' the great,*
> *Thou art past the tyrant's stroke;*
> *Care no more to clothe and eat;*
> *To thee the reed is as the oak:*
> *The sceptre, learning, physic, must*
> *All follow this and come to dust.*

> *Fear no more the lightning-flash,*
> *Nor th' all-dreaded thunder-stone;*
> *Fear not slander, censure rash;*
> *Thou hast finisht joy and moan:*
> *All lovers young, all lovers must,*

Consign to thee and come to dust.

Their voices, harp's and woman's together, rose up hauntingly toward the arched rafters of the ballroom hall and hung there as if on golden wings, hovering, tremulous, and seemed to draw all the light out of the room so that it was dark to Margaret, dark and hollow and golden with singular song. Slowly her hands unclenched.

No exorciser harm thee!
Nor no witchcraft charm thee!
Ghost unlaid forbear thee!
Nothing ill come near thee!
Quiet consummation have;
And renowned be thy grave!

With this potent benediction the queen's voice fell away from the harp's into the silence, and still the harp played on softly, softly under her hands, until it, too, hushed into the quiet dark. Margaret's eyes were fixed on her and could not look away, for her song, like the panpipe's, bore a power she had never known music to possess. The queen sat with her head bowed by the instrument, the flat of her hands upon the still strings...and then she turned her head slowly, turned up her amber-coloured eyes, and looked back at Margaret as if they were the only people in the room. As with Lord Gro she felt something run between them, but what she did not know, only that it sent shivers along the backs of her arms.

The gaze turned away and the queen smiled to her audience. Someone began clapping and the rest followed. She rose, curtsied, and Skander stepped forward to thank her and help with the harp.

Rupert leaned in, his hand on Margaret's arm. "It is in my mind," he whispered, "that you hate Plenilune a little less now."

She flung a hot look at him, all the splendour of Queen Romage's song whistling down the wind. "Plenilune, perhaps," she retorted. "But not you."

His brows flickered betrayingly, but he only took her by the arm and raised her up; cold now, cold from the eerie song and Rupert's persistent attacks at her will, she laid her fan down on the seat cushion as she left. It was one less thing to carry about with her, one less thing of his to be concerned with.

"What do we do now?" she asked dispassionately. The orchestra seemed to be retiring for an interim and there was a definite flutter of apprehensive expectation in the air.

Rupert took a firmer hold on her arm. "We go to light the fires—which is a thing *your* people have not done in many generations. How faithless you all are!" His tone was one of mockery and triumph.

But his blow fell wide of Margaret. Far from attending to his words, she had caught sight at that moment of Skander on the east side of the room. He was talking with a lady in a great swan's dress and his figure was one of contradiction. Even at that distance she could see the idle, genial softness in his countenance—but when her eyes travelled to his hands, which hung at his sides, she saw they were clenched to white. He seemed on the verge of leaving politely, the woman intent on holding him back—for *her* figure was one of rigid constraint. Whatever she spoke to him, Margaret thought it could not be pleasant.

Well, I shan't stick my neck out for you again, the young woman thought savagely.

Abruptly Skander bowed and stepped away. With a snap and muffled thunder of feathers the woman opened a fan and whirled away like a cloud driven by an angry wind.

Margaret lost sight of him. The crowd came between, moving out of the ballroom and down a long, high, dark passage which was full of draughts. Margaret shivered and wished for a wrap, but there did not seem time to get one and she would not have asked Rupert. She went with him until they reached a high beaten copper door, tabbied with red glint and verdigris, and were let out into the dark, windy garden. The wind rushed at Margaret, sending her red skirts dancing, and she clenched her fists to keep from recoiling or being carried off on the gale. What a wild night on which to light bonfires!

The crowd fanned out naturally, making room, and as she looked about she found they were on a wide, level place of short grass bordered by a thick, square hedge of ilex. Other than three dark lump-shaped objects in the middle of the lawn, there was no other feature in the square. The emptiness of the sky reigned supreme, despite its stars, and seemed closer and deeper than ever before, and made Margaret seem small indeed.

Skander reappeared at their side momentarily, looking, Margaret noticed, somewhat overrun and trying not to show it. "How are you enjoying yourself, Margaret?" he asked in a preoccupied tone.

"Well," she replied, then added, fearing she had been rude, "it is very Good King Whenceitwas."

"Hmm?" Skander was already looking away as if for something that should be there and was not, not fully attending to her. Margaret, cold, blind weary, and not at all sure, now that she thought about it, that she had got it right, chose to let it pass without further attempt at explanation. Skander muttered something, shot her a hurried glance and smile, and melted off with a mixture of reluctance and haste which puzzled her.

Her stomach growled in the low murmuring quiet of people moving and talking. She pulled it in and clenched her fists. "Will we eat after this?" she asked.

"Yes, afterward," said Rupert. He, too, sounded preoccupied, but not flustered, and when she looked at him she saw a low, slumbering pleasure in his darkened face. He drew in an immense breath, as though he were breathing in the crowd, the lumps, the ilex, the turf, the dark, the hill, the sky, the stars, the night itself, all down into his lungs, his veins, his soul. But all he said was, "There will be snow tomorrow."

The tall octagonal tower cut off the view to the north; all clear views of the sky showed up bee-black and star-spangled. Margaret tried pulling in a deep breath to get the tell-tale scent of snow, but she tasted nothing. The cold wind cut deeply into her lungs, nothing more. Colder still and hungry now, in addition to being weary, she huddled bewilderedly next to Rupert's unbending figure, waiting for someone to light the fires.

Someone brushed by her in the dark. Shying into Rupert's elbow, she peered into the deep-green gloom—a gloom slashed with velvet black and studded with silver stars—and saw that it was Mark Roy, backlit by the light from the House, accompanied by two young men. The smaller of the two, the one most like Mark Roy, was one she recognized: he had called Lord Gro away earlier, and had given her a disapproving look. The second was taller, thinner, and in the dim light of the House Margaret saw his mane of hair was streaked with red. It reminded her of someone, or perhaps of several people, but she did not quite know who.

As if feeling her glance, the tall young man with the red-lined hair flung a look back at her. Her own face was hidden in shadow, but she saw a bemused flicker of geniality pass over the other's features.

"Who was that?" she asked when they had passed on.

Rupert was looking off another way. His voice came muffledly: "You know Mark Roy. Those were Aikin Ironside and Brand, his sons. Aikin is much like Centurion in temperament—I do not trust him, though his blade is quick to bite deep. Brand—" Rupert looked round and peered, too, into the gloom after them to where they stood in the ring that was forming round the piles of wood. "Brand has high sentiment and a short temper. He knows how to be violent. He may make a good friend."

She could almost see Rupert's malicious will undermining the three standing in the dark distance. "And what if I don't like him as a friend?"

"You will not much like any of my friends."

"No," she said helplessly, after a brief and futile struggle with something in herself. "No, I suppose not."

Aikin Ironside. She said the name to herself several times until she had looked and felt all round it. *Aikin Ironside. A strong name. Him I should like to be my friend.*

It was odd how something so simple—the name of a stranger—could remind her with a debilitating pang that she was only a young lady, little more than a girl.

From the other side of the lawn, leftward along a long line of spectators, Margaret's eye caught the feeble leap and splutter of a newly-lit torch. Her attention was drawn to it, off Mark Roy and Aikin Ironside, Brand and Rupert: the light took and strengthened, and seemed to send its flame walking down the line with a flick of a fiery wrist, pulling out from among the crowd a jink of gold here, an upsweep of blue plume there, the darkness of a cloak in another place into which the light ran and hid and put itself out. All down the line figures haloed in thin angry lines of candlelight from the House windows had a sudden light and shadow on their faces. How terrible they all looked, Margaret thought with a shudder. How awful, like transfixed gods the world thought it had killed long ago. Like Puck, with a gleeful prancing, the light came out from among them, casting a chancy glow every which way on the grass. Margaret never saw who held the torch; the curious thing was, the person did not seem to matter. The light was going out to wake them, to thrust a fire back into the heart of them, and this great ring of silent, wax-work gods would soon spring to life again.

The ballroom, the dancing, the heat and noise, seemed far behind them.

As though playing coy, the torchlight cavorted round all three wood-piles, then dodged in and out between them, leaving a corkscrew of blue smoke on the air behind it. The wind stirred the blue, fanning it out, feathering it softly; the rich scent of it woke something in Margaret which scared her.

"And—now!" breathed Rupert quickly. With an upthrust of his hand, like a magician conjuring, he made a sudden gesture that made her start, and the smudge and sharp outline of fire in the dark darted into the farthest of the pyres. The light sank like a gigantic newly-lit candle, wondered if it meant to be serious or not, and in a few heartbeats the light sprang aloft, roaring richly with the scent of cedar and pine through the timber tangle. Margaret's stomach tightened as the fire crawled and jumped upward, etching clear-cut silhouettes of branches against the ilex darkness, branches that looked like fingers trying to drag heaven down to a burning end.

Bee-bright the torch zoomed to the middle pyre and stung its heap: the air was roaring with burning and the light hurt Margaret's eyes. By the time the last pyre was lit, and the crowd of wax-work gods came to life with a joyous explosion of cheers and applause, she had to turn her head away from the brightness, though instinctively she clapped with the crowd.

But Margaret could not help feeling that she had missed the import of the bonfires. The firelit ring of faces, all laughing easily, breaking bronze with skin and ivory with flashing teeth, those features seemed to understand, she thought, looking round on them all. They understood it instinctively as a thing they had been raised with. To them the bonfires meant something, something perhaps symbolic and sacral, something ancient and comfortable that honoured time. But as Rupert moved away to talk with someone, Margaret lingered behind, once again feeling adrift from the colourful menagerie of people. She lingered because the awful crawling feeling had not dissipated, but had worsened, because the bonfires flung open an inner door to her and lost their happy, comfortable feeling. As an outsider, which she felt keenly, they could never have that feeling for her: instead they turned her a frank, open, honest face, and they told her what they really were. Was it primeval? She hurried on from the thought of pagan, because she did not like it and she knew it did not fit. She did not know what the fires said—their language was starkly different from her own—but she knew it was awful and real and Plenilune.

Yes, it was Plenilune.

"Margaret?"

She jumped violently at Skander's voice in her ear. She had been staring narrowly into the fire and her eyes came away sparking red, smudging his down-turned face. If he looked concerned—which he sounded—she could not see him clearly enough to tell. "I thought you had gone away to be busy," she said, blinking hard and trying to be light-hearted.

"I am sorry I have been too busy to attend to you." He held out an arm and pulled her in Rupert's direction. "I know there are few familiar faces in this crowd."

There, I have offended him! In an attempt to smooth her rough words over, she purred casually, "Oh no, nothing of the sort. People have been very friendly, if they are strangers." She peered at the bonfires again: the pillars of fire were high now, throwing up sparks into the empty gash of night, but the heat was low and the wind that stirred the ilex was biting cold. Almost she dared to mention the comitissa—the words were on her lips—when she killed them hastily and gave instead a little choked noise that she tried to cover up by saying, "This cold makes one hungry!"

"Doesn't it? We will go in, presently, and have a bite to eat. Ah, here is my cousin..."

He said they would "have a bite to eat," and Margaret had rather crestfallenly expected titbits and finger-foods such as she had eaten all her life at tea-parties and fine social gatherings. She had not expected the banquet wing which awaited them, nor the tables groaning with their burdens of food. Such a mixture of spices, colours, sweets and savouries mingled in the air as to baffle her senses. For the first fifteen minutes of the meal, positioned—not unlike the sardines in front of her—between Rupert de la Mare and the enormous Earl of the Ritts of Trammel, she was too overwhelmed to have any appetite. But as the sights and sounds and smells settled and became distinct, like a moth about a flame, and her weariness resurfaced along with her gnawing hunger, she gingerly began to feast with the rest.

It was a culinary experience to rival any she had ever witnessed, full of all the pomp of red royal feasting, but it would have been dull for her had it not been for one small, disturbing instance. Rupert was talking with someone down the table just out of her reach, someone she did not recognize, and her enormous neighbour was so busy making delicate cuts in a titanic pork loin that she was cut off from him, too, and felt awkward trying to strike up a conversation with his agonized face. The two women across the table seemed suspiciously careful not to catch her eye. But she had wanted to eat, she told herself, wrestling with grim disappointment and fury at the snub, so she was here to eat.

It was the drabness that caught her eye. To her left, on the extreme corner of her vision so that it was almost like catching a glimpse of an old dream rather than seeing anything real, she became aware of an anomaly in this rich tapestry of colour. With another start she looked its way and lost it a moment among a yellow plume and a slashed burgundy sleeve. Had she dreamed—no, there it was, breaking out of the press. It was a small, stooped figure, with the frailness and colouring of a withered apple-leaf. At that distance Margaret was not sure if it was a man or a woman, but it was not supposed to be there, of that she was certain. It looked round slowly on the crowd, but it did not have the wide-eyed startled attitude of the very old. Quite the opposite: it seemed to be horribly deliberate, like death, casting lingeringly over the crowd until it chose its victim.

"Ru—" Margaret began, then choked herself off. Her curiosity overwon her formless fear. She had some confused notion, too, that she was breaking faith with something if she spoke up against the withered apple-leaf figure. She felt that strongly, though she had no idea why, so she was not surprised when the slow swing of the figure's perusal came to light and fixed upon Rupert beside her.

"*Ah-h-h!*"

The screech of discovery it gave knocked the bell of happy sound from the atmosphere: Margaret saw it shatter on the floor of their consciousness as every head whipped round, every mouth open either for food or speech, every mouth empty, every face full of surprise—every face save her own. She felt like a spectator watching a play.

"*Ah-h!*" The crone—it was a woman—stepped forward with her hand upraised toward Rupert. Her movements were fluid for one so old, her voice blue-veined and thin, but certain. "Thou marks it, young man, and 'twas a death-knell in thy soul for omen! Thou marks the star Frezen blinked out, like a snuffer put on thy hope! Let not Hell hope! Let not Hell hope! Aye! aye!" she laughed with both hands clutching the air before her, as if shaking something in their faces. " 'Tis an omen! 'Tis an omen! It may yet go ill with the evil lords! He is the God not of the dead but of the living! Aye, thy omening star goes out and he sits in Heaven and laughs at thee! Uncovered are thy wickednesses! Unhappy are thy auguries! Ill will it go with thee! Treble confusion on thee! The death of thy enemies is wormwood and gall in thy bowels!"

Margaret did not remember rising. She stood at the side of the table, twisted round to stare at the old apple-leaf woman, her hand whitely clutching her napkin. They were all staring, some having risen, some still seated. For some time not one of them moved, though Margaret was aware of Rupert's hand, which had been very tense upon the stem of his wineglass, slowly relaxing its hold and flushing with blood once more. But before he could do anything, if he was meaning to, Skander broke away from the rest and came gently toward the softly laughing old woman.

"Come you away, old mother," he said kindly. "It is cold: warm yourself in my kitchens."

She deftly avoided his hand, though her iron-coloured, sparking eyes laughed kindly back up into his face. "Let me be, young man, or I'll vanish before thy eyes."

"Well I believe it." Skander's tone was somewhere between laughter and vexation. Somehow he turned the old apple-leaf woman over into the care of two askance men and one of the head maids of the banquet hall, and with a lack of ceremony which troubled Margaret, the four passed from the room.

There was a breathless silence, a rush of taffeta and a sigh, and then the low, subdued murmur of talk and clinking of glasses. Rupert's face, when Margaret dared to look at it, was oddly light and distant, as if he were careful to let the whole nightmarish matter slip from his shoulders like an old cloak. But she knew him better than that and was shocked to realize that he was quite shaken. He carefully finished his wine and carefully replaced the glass exactly upon the table, and under the hum of talk said to her,

"There has been enough excitement for *you*. I think it would be best if you retired to bed."

"And if I am not tired?" she asked, arching a brow. She kept her head primly cocked to one side, so that if anyone looked their way she would appear aloof and no one would know how her heart pounded. "What then?"

"But you are, so do you go." And the smile he turned to her, shocked out of its granite mockery, was actually soft and genuine when it lighted on her face. "I danced you hard tonight, and you did me justice. Go to bed now, Margaret."

With all eyes on them, as she knew they were, she thought it best not to test him and risk ruining his good humour. She put her napkin in a tell-tale gesture on the table, hesitated, and, clenching her stomach, leaned close by Rupert's cheek as though to peck it. No one could see: only he and she knew she did not actually touch him. He was laughing at her softly, coldly, when she drew away and rose. It was a light, awful, piercing sort of laughter. Walking away from the table and the soft surf-sound of talk, walking in the swish and swirl of her red dress, she felt like a red pawn on his chessboard.

Oh yes, she had played very well for him tonight.

Wave after wave of weariness broke over her as she mounted the stairs and made her way to her room. Her red dress and the knowledge of it seemed to grow heavier with each step she took. And there was no relief for her when she reached the high little garret for Rhea was there, rising silently from turning back the bedcover. Margaret stopped in the doorway and stared coldly and blearily, almost blindly, at the maid; the maid stared back, but Margaret was too tired and bewildered by formless thoughts to mind the look on the other's face.

"Where is Aikaterine?" she asked bluntly.

"Does my lady's lady know?" replied Rhea.

Margaret's temper flared, clearing away the haze for a moment. "Ring for her," she snapped. "And then lay out my nightgown. Aikaterine will dress me."

Rhea's face was closed and careful as she crossed the room and pulled the bell. While the maid opened the trunk at the foot of the bed to fetch out the nightgown, Margaret sat down before the mirror and began removing her jewellery. She kept a close eye on Rhea's reflection, but she suspected that the maid was aware of that: her face never unfolded from its cool, careful expression.

There was a soft knock on the door and Margaret called to admit Aikaterine. The maid was dressed in white still, but there was a thin silver chain with a single diamond pendant around her neck, and a small clear gemstone in either ear. If she had not known that she was a maidservant, Margaret would have called her beautiful.

There was a brief moment when Aikaterine looked wide and saw Rhea, and Rhea saw her, but the looks were exchanged almost too fast for Margaret to mark them. "You called?" Aikaterine purred, and turned from Rhea without another glance.

"Yes." Margaret rose and stepped away from the dressing table.

Gently the scarlet gown was peeled off and put over the manikin in the corner. Balling her fists to stave off her shivering, Margaret swam into the folds of her nightgown and stood with her chin up and her head to one side as Aikaterine deftly buttoned the clasps at the throat. Margaret kept an eye on Rhea, who was placing hot water-bottles in the bedsheets, to make sure the maid did not puncture them: but even Margaret thought such a joke rather below Rhea.

"Is there anything more that you need?" asked Aikaterine.

Margaret looked around on the sparse, clean room. In her weary state she was past thinking. She almost asked Aikaterine if she could inquire after the curious old crone—but even that was becoming distant, as though it had happened only in a dream, as though she had wandered into one of Rupert's nightmares and watched what happened there. "No-o..." she replied slowly. She blinked hard. "No, I think that will be all. You may leave me, and tell Rupert I have gone to bed."

Aikaterine looked at Rhea, as if to pass this duty off on her, and then moved to the doorway. Margaret saw that Aikaterine was careful to let Rhea go first. With a shudder, Margaret thought of having that evil-eyed cat stalking through the dark after her. Then they were gone, silently, taking one of the lamps with them so that her room was lit by only a low fat candle on the bedside table.

Margaret bent wearily over the flame and snuffed it out before climbing into bed. The sheets were stiff with cold but her feet were soon toasty from wrapping themselves around the water-bottles. She lay in the dark and the musty scent of blown-out candle, shivering from the cold, listening to the moan of the wind around the castle. The wind was loud tonight, loud and desolate, and it kept her awake when she should have fallen instantly asleep. Too soon the water-bottles went cool, and then cold, and she kicked them out from under the covers and fell to shivering, mournfully alone in her cold sheets. Her nightgown seemed too thin, her blankets inadequate, to keep her warm. For a quarter of an hour she told herself she ought to get up and put on the red dress for warmth—surely the red colour would be warming—and in a fitful, dozing state dreamed over and over that she had done so, only to reawaken and realize that she was still in her white nightgown, and still cold.

If I married Rupert, she thought once, *I would not be cold. I wonder—do they keep separate rooms here in Plenilune or do couples sleep together?*

In the morning she knew she would scoff at such a mercenary idea, but in the high garret among the roar of the wind, anything to get warm seemed permissible.

There was nothing to mark the time. Not the earth's light, for the night was growing thickly overcast, nor even the distant chime of a hall clock; so Margaret did not know how late it was when it finally occurred to her that she had left her fan behind in the ballroom. She sighed and tried once more to find a warm, comfortable position in which to rest her aching, cold limbs, but she knew she would not be able to rest until she had gone down and fetched it. She could always yank the bell-pull to have a servant fetch it for her, but if she went downstairs herself, where there had been warmth and even some jollification—which was not to be found up here—she might feel better. Surely it was late enough that everyone had gone to bed: it did not seem likely that she would run into anyone worse than a servant.

Stiffly, her limbs frozen with weariness and cold, she crawled out of bed and felt in the dark for her matches. She burnt herself with the first match and accidentally extinguished it before she could reach the wick. The second match took and a warm yellow pall of light spread slowly over the room. By its light she slung on her dressing-gown and did up its toggles. Then she took the lamp from her table and stole out on bare feet into the long empty corridor. Her feet made no noise on the carpet: she glided mutely forward in a pool of candlelight, mingling now and then with other pools and passing on again through darkness. Sounds came, now and then, from behind the doors she passed: sleepy, creaky sounds of guests getting into bed and the old four-posters groaning in complaint, or someone, once—it startled her with its suddenness—stabbing at the remains of a fire in a grate. The night-witchery made the Lookinglass House seem long, as it had made Marenové House seem long, but Lookinglass was warm and Margaret was oddly not a whit afraid. She knew it was the sleepiness and light which dazed her, but she was nevertheless humoured by the sense of being a fairy passing through the dreams of others, always on the outskirts, always moving on.

The dark and sleepiness turned her about. She missed the turn for the nave overpass; she found herself blinking at the head of a new stair, a narrow one—probably a back way used by servants—with a panel of lattice as its right wall. Through the lattice shone diamonds of light, which turned the stairway into a freckled grouse's wing, and up from the bottom of the stairway came the murmur of many voices. Margaret glided on, roused by curiosity. She took care to pass so quietly down the stair as to be taken, if seen, for a shadow, with the candle hid under her sleeve. Through the lattice she got a view of a narrow hallway, and across the hall, by which the stair ran parallel, she saw a door ajar through which came the voices. In the stairwell she stopped, bare feet chilled by the hardwoods, and stopped to listen, if she could, without exposing herself in the hall.

At first the voices were muffled and indistinct, seemingly from far away on the other side of the room within the door, then a voice nearer said, laughingly,

"Why, what about her?"

A muffled voice repeated its query.

That is Centurion, thought Margaret. *I recognize that laugh of his: like rain when the sun is shining.*

"Oh!" said a woman's voice, jumping to reply. Margaret did not know this voice. "I don't know. I hardly met her, myself. She has a pleasant, husky voice, I think, and almost handsome."

Someone asked, "Where did she come from?"

"Under a rock, for all I know," retorted a man.

Margaret began to blush angrily. Of course they would speak of her. It was just what she feared, just what she expected, but she could not tear herself away. For a moment the fan was forgotten: she had to know what they thought.

The man who sounded angry went on. "This is a rum turn of luck, if I dare swear before you on it. We *had* hoped—"

"We had," laughed Centurion. "Some of us still do."

Several people bubbled at him like pipits, trying to get a better answer, but he only laughed and seemed to step away: a shadow passed over the crack in the door.

The woman held to her first assessment and tried to advance it. "Her voice is pleasant. I think she sounds almost as pleasant as Romage. Do you suppose she could sing? I wonder if they could perform a duet."

A young man spoke up—hardly more than a boy, Margaret thought, perhaps in his late 'teens. "Your Grace, forgive me for saying so, but I should not like having that siren sing for my ears. I would not trust my soul with her."

For one wild, blazing moment, Margaret considered coming forward and showing herself to them. Oh, to see their faces when she pushed the door wide, candle aloft, and looked round on them with all the knowledge of their words in her face! Her foot slid forward...

But then she remembered that she was in her dressing-gown, her hair undone. She hesitated: the moment was lost. All that was left was an awful sense of shame.

Then, unexpectedly, she heard the familiar dry, cool voice of Lord Gro FitzDraco say, "She may wear his hood and jesses, but she is a haggard on his fist."

There was an empty silence full of thoughts which Margaret could feel, one by one, as if they were each cold rain-drops falling on her hot skin. A long, tingling silence filled her with something like smugness, but kindlier, and she turned away with her lips pursed against a smile, liking Lord Gro better now than she had before.

After that she wandered oddly, composed of two or more parts and the feelings of colours: a part of her, an ashen-coloured part, was still weary as if it had been beaten. And it had, had it not? Dreamy, sometimes nightmarish images of the evening's festivities sprang through her mind as she wandered down the empty passageways of Lookinglass. Each one struck at her like Rupert's hand. Another part of her was cool and golden, sleepy-fierce and defiant—was it only the candlelight, or was it something greater? Yet another part of her, a far, back part which seemed to tag after her like a shadow, and seemed at other times to spring on ahead and look back at her from beyond the rim of candlelight, was the colour of a fox's coat.

The ballroom was empty when she arrived. The servants had cleaned and gone their ways. The smarting scent of freshly extinguished candles gripped at Margaret's throat. Tiny, ashen, and defiant at once, she pressed in between the huge doors and hesitated on the edge of that vast emptiness. The room was deathly quiet: from a distance she heard the wolf-howl of the wind running long-wise with the building. Where the orchestra had sat among its candles all was dark; the falcon in the floor was swallowed up in shadow. Only her spitting candle cast any glow and it seemed, small as it was, to make the dark around her deeper.

There is a moral in that, she thought, looking back over her shoulder, *I shouldn't wonder*.

No one was behind her, she could not imagine anyone could be before her, so she strode across the ballroom floor alone, candle lifted high. The light of it jinked elusively off the tall panelled windows—the dark outside seemed to turn and look in at her out of horrible eyes. She went on, discovering the first bank of chairs, then the one beyond it, and so on until at last she got to the first row and found her fan exactly as she had left it. It was not until she picked it up that a new part of her began talking: not ashen or golden, but frankly starched white and black, like a nurse's outfit, and it told her that she had been ridiculous to come down alone in her dressing-gown. If anyone stumbled upon her, what would they think? As much as she was grateful to him, she did not imagine Lord Gro to be the sort to win men's hearts over by eloquence and sound reasoning.

Regardless, Margaret told the starch, *if I had not come down I would not have heard him—I would not have heard all of them—and I did want to know. Now I do, and I know where I stand in the game.*

With a wiggle and shove she stowed the fan away in her dressing-gown pocket and retraced her steps to the hallway. There she deliberated and chose to continue southward through the building in the hopes that one of these passages emptied out onto the nave. She thought she could find her way back to her room from there.

It was uncanny how quiet the house was. The wind was the only sound she heard as she walked, and it was a from-time-to-time sound, like the surf, or a dream: she did not like it, for it bled the black into the white and turned things ashen again—she tasted ash in her mouth—and took away all charade of stability which Lookinglass imposed upon her attention. She was an exile: this wind was the wind of exile.

Sleep, sleep, my baby.

So, she and the wind were not the only ones awake. On the threshold of the nave Margaret turned back, hearing a sweet, light voice singing wanderingly behind one of the many doorways she had passed.

Sleep, sleep, my baby.
And when you wake
I'll give you a little black pony—

Overcome by curiosity once more, Margaret stole back and set her hand upon the door from which came the singing. Even as she pushed, her better sense braced her for whatever might befall. The door swung open easily.

—With a coat of night
And eyes of dragon-fire.
Sleep, sleep, my baby.
Sleep, sleep, my baby...

As the last notes were coming out of the singer's mouth the singer looked up. Margaret found the woman as her intuition had expected: a fine-boned, tall woman, with demurely plaited hair that shone in the lamplight, soft grey eyes with a little fierceness in the depths of them, and a puzzled smile about the lips. There was a pregnant silence for a few minutes—neither woman moved—and in that time Margaret was able to place her as the fur-enshrouded woman who had ridden up that morning with Lord Bloodburn from Hol. How different the two were! Brother and sister or man and wife, whichever they were, she could not have imagined them more different. The fierceness in the woman's eyes was tiny, like a single spark, and was there only because of the small bundle of a thing which she held in her arms. All else had been quenched.

There sit I should Rupert ever conquer me.

"Why do you sit here in the dark, madam?" asked Margaret, lifting higher her candle to see better. "It is well past the child's bedtime."

She schooled her voice to be gentle and watched with satisfaction as the face before her remained open and hesitantly friendly. "The dark is peaceful," the woman replied.

"And the bedtime?" Margaret was not sure why she persisted, since it was none of her business, but the quiet horror of the woman kept her from saying good-night and turning away.

The woman turned her head to the babe—one heavy plait slid over her mantled shoulder and encircled the thing. One tiny hand reached out and grasped it energetically. "The cub sleeps poorly—and consequently so do I—but likes rather to play. So I sit in the dark and shush him."

Margaret took three steps forward and positioned herself by the woman so that she could look down into the child's face. The light did not seem to dazzle it: it played with the braid with its chubby, useless little fingers that seemed more like an octopus's limbs than a human's. The thing was pale and golden and white, and did not look at all disposed to falling asleep. Margaret's mother, disagreeable in most things, unaccountably held that babies were adorable, while Margaret, despite her attempts in the past to be temperate and sociable, had always felt that babies were rather ugly. This baby, she found, was not exactly ugly, but nor was it beautiful. It was a blunt-faced, determined little thing, trying to eat with the teeth it did not have the braid which its mother was working to dislodge from its grasp.

"The cub made a long morning journey and is in a strange place. Why does he not sleep, like a sensible baby, or at least cry?"

She had guessed at the outset that the child was the pride of the mother's heart, and possibly her only thing worth living for. Now the woman proved it. With a flash of her eyes she looked up into Margaret's face, a grim smile yanking at her mouth. "The cub is a great cub, and does not cry at silly things. True, he tries me, but then all babes are trying. Nevertheless, he is a great cub."

"So." Margaret sank stiffly down into an adjacent chair and set the candle on the table with a small deliberate click. "The cub is great, and he will look after his mother in her old age, I'm sure. Out of gratitude."

The eyes lost their fierceness and darted almost guiltily down to the child's face. "Yes," she said quietly, but she did not sound sincere.

Margaret waited in the ensuing silence for the woman to say something more on her own account, but the normal space of silence passed on unbroken and stretched into awkwardness—though, she noted, neither of them showed it—and one after the other Margaret picked up and discarded things she could say. Ought she to mention the strange old woman from the meal hall? Ought she to say good-night, having so deliberately come in, and go back to bed? Ought she ask if the pale, golden-haired woman had a pleasant evening? No, not that—her brows pulled together a moment. It would be insulting to mention pleasantries with *this* woman. She debated strongly and rather desperately with the suggestion of taking the child herself to give the poor mother a moment's rest, but in the end, deciding her courage was not up to that, she said, simply and quietly,

"I am Margaret, by the way."

The blue-grey eyes like sapphires that had been crushed out under someone's heel flickered up into her own and hung there a moment in a face that had an unfathomable look. "Yes," she said at last. "I did know that... I am Kinloss, Bloodburn's wife."

Margaret jerked a smile across her face with conscious effort. "And I knew that, though no one told me your name. I saw you come up with your husband this morning—or yesterday morning. Is it a very long way from Hol?"

She had hoped Kinloss would be mildly pleased that she had a passing familiarity with the names of their places, but the woman's face registered little beyond acute pain as the cub burbled and moved at that moment. Margaret's hands shifted first forward and then back as she fought with her fear of the tiny thing and her concern for the mother.

"It took us three days and this morning—yesterday morning—to reach Lookinglass," replied Kinloss when she could. "But I don't mind," she went on with an unexpected flush of personality after Margaret had thought she would fall silent again. "I don't mind. It is peaceful here."

Margaret stared blankly at the beautiful, thin, quenched woman and did not know quite what she felt. Pity and horror were foremost, confusion not far behind and, aft of that, a fox-coloured, clear-cut, dreadful understanding. With little effort she let the horror take charge. The yellow-lit picture of Kinloss and her baby, alone in the dark which was their only friend, was a picture that was beginning to look more and more like a nightmare. How familiar nightmare pictures were becoming!

Margaret put out one knee and bent both, head inclined demurely though she felt as though she moved and spoke in a dream. "I must go. Good-night, my lady. It was a pleasure meeting you."

Kinloss said nothing. Margaret retreated to the door and had a last fleeting image of a long face looking at her from a distance, lips parted as if a moment from speaking. But too much time passed between them and it seemed Kinloss had begun to think again—for reason, Margaret knew, is the great murderer of blind courage—and Kinloss remained silent. The door clicked softly shut between them.

When she found it, the nave was rather awful to face alone. It was huge and lightless—she had left her candle with Kinloss—and the sound of the wind outside made the room hum ominously around her. Moving through the cotton darkness, moving between the black bulks of pillars and the smaller black bodies of tables and chairs, she found the stairs and took comfort in the familiar, thoughtless rhythm of mounting them. She stopped once to look back over her shoulder, down into the swimming dark below, and wondered if she had heard something else move behind her. Was it Kinloss come after her, or the old woman from supper, or—worst of all, far worse than going mad—was it Rupert? In brief breathlessness, all her insides held in the tight grip of her stomach muscles, she listened with her lip caught painfully between her teeth. But either she was going mad or it had been only the wind, for no one came. The motionless dark remained unmoved and she passed on up the stair and down the rarely-lit passages trying to find her own room.

She had found the head of her own corridor only to hear a new noise hard by, just behind the nearest door. A familiar voice was speaking: having eavesdropped once already she moved closer without a second thought. She reflected with a grim sort of humour that she was getting rather experienced in leaning against closed doors without being detected.

"—never had to solicit your opinions," said a rough, panther-coloured voice.

"Oh, you've done very well with her." Skander's tone was both sincere and bitingly caustic. "She looked beautiful this evening—charming, assured—in that red gown she looked like a goddess." There was a brief, hot silence and swift step on the floor. "But you can't hide that look in her eye, Rupert. She looks *hunted*. And don't think I was the only one to notice! FitzDraco, who does not go out of his way to say anything, marked to me her countenance."

"Truly?" came Rupert's voice turned languid again: that dark, sleepy, velvet tone which made Margaret's skin crawl with cold loathing. "I wasn't aware FitzDraco was wont to mark any woman."

The tension of the following silence was so great that Margaret could almost see Skander's face, white with choked rage. At last he said, in a tone low and awful, "I do not know what you mean to do, Rupert, but I swear if you hurt her—I swear you will regret it. Don't be a fool. I *swear* you will regret it."

Her lungs spasmed. The breath she took was an involuntary, hiccupping one which sounded like the crack of a hunter's gun in the quiet. She clapped her hand over her mouth and kept perfectly still.

There was a long silence, still longer than before, then a swift sound of movement somewhere as of someone rising, and Rupert's voice, changed from roughness to softness to a horrible tone of evil, replied,

"No one provokes me with impunity. Look well that you do not cross paths with me, or it will be the last thing you do."

She knew Skander was coming. Any minute now he would break away from that stark murderer's glare and stalk away—it took a brave man to put that face behind him—and come through the door. She had to turn away. But the fire which FitzDraco had struck in her had gone pitifully out. She had to leave but she could not move. The wind had been knocked out of her. She knew that if Rupert caught her he would be in a mood to kill her, quickly, with his hands on either side of her head and a quick snap around.

Skander was surely coming now.

Move, Margaret! Don't be a fool!

It was not until there was an actual creak on the floor inside the room that she was able to move. The sound seemed to release her; running on bare feet, hands gathering her gown around her knees, she fled down the hall in a breathless rush of fabric and hid in the corner of her doorframe, not daring to open it lest it squeak on its hinges.

Skander stepped out into the hallway. Without a backward glance—what an effort that must have took!—he shut the door behind him. She expected him to go on quickly, anxious to get away from that horrible man who was his cousin, but he stayed a moment, took a step toward her room, and then stood still again. She dared not breathe. Crouched in the shadow of her door she stared back at him, lit only slightly by the thin line of light from under Rupert's door. She knew what was happening. He, too, had taken the time to think, to reason, and on cue he turned away, the window for rashness shut perhaps forever.

When all was empty and silent again she breathed out and let herself into her room. Curiously she stood in the middle of the space, looking round on the black enclosure, and almost laughed—to keep from crying—over the insane trouble a simple fan caused. Yet her lungs turned treacherous just at the crucial moment: she hiccupped again, lost her handle on her mirth, and fell across her bed in an agony of angry sobbing. She throttled the blankets who stood proxy for Rupert and hated—hated—*hated* the immensity of everything. Most of all she hated herself. She, the victim, had been thrown into this world of crowns as a bone to be squabbled over, a pawn to be moved, a woman to be coddled, a slave to be prodded, a curse to be averted, a fate to be thwarted.

X | A FLICKER-FLAME OF A PARTY

"Aikaterine, be so kind as to find a journal and pencil for me."

Rather lost in the mothy-coloured corner of the garret, the maid straightened and peered back at her for a moment, quizzical. "I understand the journal to be blank."

"H'ip!" Rhea had pulled savagely on the lacings of her undergarments. Margaret glared the witching maid's reflection in the mirror. "Yes, I would like the journal to be blank. Thank you, Aikaterine."

Aikaterine obediently left and, as it was a long way down to anywhere from her room, Margaret expected to be alone with Rhea for some time. She found the only thing that kept her from worrying seriously about Rhea doing her bodily harm was the fact that Rupert had not told her to. She tried to keep her thoughts centred on her request for a journal and off the movements of the maid behind her.

Rhea interrupted her thoughts. "There was talk last night of hunting, and I am told the huntsman left before dawn this morning to quest for a reasonable beast. I think therefore," she turned from the depths of the clothes-trunk, "you had better go down in your riding habit."

Margaret looked hard at Rhea and wondered if the girl was telling the truth and whether or not it would be ridiculous to be caught walking about in a riding habit if no one intended to go riding. But as there was nothing truthful or devilish to be read in those eyes, Margaret finally put out her hand and said bluntly,

"Let's have it, then."

The day had dawned with a low sky over all like a grey lid, windless and chilly, though not bitingly cold. Looking down from her window Margaret had seen that snow had fallen during the night: only a light dusting, but enough to make the grounds and pine-woods turn black and foreign. The walls of Lookinglass appeared cold and bloodless under that colourless sky. As she put on her scarlet habit and sat while Rhea put up her hair, she could see her reflection in the mirror as brilliant against the pallor of the November morning.

"In that red gown she looked like a goddess."

Having laid the preliminary bun, Rhea pulled the forefront hair from out of Margaret's eyes, divided and twisted it, and curled it into a neat, sprigy body at the back. It was annoying, thought Margaret, but considerably neater and more becoming than anything she had managed for herself. She pressed her lips in a thin line and shot a withering glance at the door as it said, "Thump! thump!"

"Here you are," said Aikaterine, coming at Margaret's call with the book and pencil. She straightened and stood by as though waiting for orders. Ignoring them both, Margaret set the pencil in her lap and opened up the leather-bound book. It was plain, painfully plain, with rough-cut edges and a spine that had not been opened before. It would take some breaking in, but then Margaret felt desperately in need of something to break. Aikaterine was speaking.

"It is a very good style. Hair is something I have never quite mastered."

The praise came stiffly, but sincerely. Rhea replied cuttingly, "No, you wouldn't have." Then, just as Margaret was getting ready to turn around and tell her to speak civilly, the maid added, "But I don't see why you shouldn't. Neither of our households is very abundant with women."

Aikaterine wisely said nothing else. Feeling dismally hungry and rather lively for having cried things out last night and having risen to a stark white morning, Margaret got up and put the writing things away on the dressing table, and stepped from the mirror toward the door.

"Are we to dine all together, Aikaterine?"

The maid nodded. "A buffet has been laid out in the ballroom." She watched with faintly veiled suspicion as Rhea stepped forward. "Have you further need of me?"

"No," Margaret admitted reluctantly. She loathed having Rhea tag like a shadow at her back, but it would not do to start Rupert off with a disagreeable attitude first thing in the morning. "R-Rhea is with me. Thank you, Aikaterine."

It would have been better, Margaret reflected, if Aikaterine could have taken her down. She would have felt more at ease going in alone: with Rhea she felt strangely naked and exposed, as if all the while the maid was making some joke of her behind her back that everyone but herself could see. She could feel the gaze of wicked, jealous scorn on the back of her neck. She wished she could understand it. She wished, above all, that she could blot it out.

A high white light was shining in the ballroom when she arrived. The winter lighting made a difference in the room: all colours were softer and paler, colder and more subdued. A pleasantly sleepy atmosphere lay over the humming room. There was no real order to things: people were standing about or sitting down, refilling their plates or lounging with a cup of coffee while having a quiet chat with friends. The pale light helped, a little, to make the crowd of them less intimidating.

Margaret caught sight of Skander. It was hard to miss him, even in that cluster of well-proportioned, handsome men. He was standing by the coffee table, one hand on the tabletop to support himself, and was deep in conversation with Woodbird Swan-neck. The conversation seemed to be going gingerly if the quirk and pull of Skander's brow was anything to judge by, and at that moment he caught sight of her and made a sideways movement, as if he meant to break politely away from Woodbird and come greet her. But at the same moment, perhaps out of instinct or a sense of self-preservation, he looked out for Rupert and stopped himself, for at that moment Rupert, too, had caught sight of her, and was coming to her side.

Margaret's spine shivered as Rupert stepped between two men and came toward her. He was dressed for a day outdoors, in leather and furs, and there was a dusting of snow on his boots and shoulders which suggested he had been out already. He bent deliberately for her cheek—her stomach clenched—and the cold scent of pine emanated from him. His lips, however, were warm.

"Good morning. You slept well?"

"I slept deeply."

He searched her face and it was all she could do not to show the fear and rage she had felt last night when she had heard him speak to Skander. But he did not seem to see. He took her arm, gently but firmly, and smiled to her as he led her toward the breakfast table. "I see you got the word that we are to go hunting today. I am glad you have had a little taste of that already: you will know now what to expect."

She marked with relief that he was in a good mood this morning. After last night she would not have gambled on his attitude being so gentle and agreeable—she wondered if it was a good mask, but did not have the courage to attempt pulling it off to see.

She caught sight of her reflection in a mirror: a sudden, startling reflection of a tall, fine-boned woman done up in red, burning bright against the mellow silver backdrop of the winter-lit room. Acute regret twisted in her middle.

I wish I were not to wear red all the time. What must they think of me! I look like—

"Is something the matter?" Rupert murmured.

"N-no," she lied. Her eye accidentally met with Skander's as they passed and she offered him an instinctive, forced smile. "I am ravenous."

They stopped at the buffet and Rupert stood by while Margaret mechanically began filling a plate. "Winter does that," he added gustily. Seeing the snow on his shoulders he began dusting it off. "It gets the blood up, and the appetite too."

She felt his gaze slide back to her and knew that if she gave him a chance he would push her again. She could be sure he would push gently this morning, but he would push firmly, testing her mettle set square against his. It made her angry, and the weariness she felt when she realized what he was about to do frightened her. Swiftly she turned away, narrowly missing the neck of a fluted glass: but this time she was aware of turning hastily away from herself, not merely from him.

Don't be a coward. She dodged his hand and went on before him to a low table and chair. *Don't lose your head nor let him get to you... But I wish he would give it a rest! It is too early to have to fight him already.*

He settled down in a chair across the table from her, one leg flung over the opposite knee, and twisted to watch the others in the room. It was uncanny to know that, though he was turned from her, he was still watching her, too. Every now and then, as she ate, Margaret looked up to see his proud dark head flung back, wall eyes squinted against the light. The hand resting lightly on his supported heel was moving unconsciously, the thumb rubbing fore and middle-finger round and round and round...as if some back part of his mind was gradually grinding down the people he watched even as he was grinding down herself.

Would there be anything left of them when he was done?

He turned his head abruptly, spotting something behind her. Turning too, she saw the blue-jay man approach Skander. Skander deftly extricated himself from Woodbird and the two men exchanged a brief word.

"It seems Gabriel has found something," said Rupert. He put up his hand on the table; his signet flashed in the light. "I would finish that, if I were you," he added, nodding to her plate. "Skander likes to get on the scent as soon as possible—and he likes wily game."

"Does it run in the family?" she asked cuttingly.

He was much amused. "Very likely, wench." He got up, fiddled a moment with a button on his jacket, and looked significantly at her. She got up in a rushy noise of scarlet cloth, paled to the colour of a hibiscus blossom in the fanned winter light, and walked with him across the room to join Skander.

Skander had just sent the blue-jay man off again and was standing with his arms folded impressively across his chest, shoulders slumped, lips twisted into a fighting gesture. He turned his head as they approached.

"Good morning," he said gingerly.

Rupert returned lightly: "What bee has got in your bonnet?"

"Not a bee—a boar."

Rupert made an instinctive gesture toward Margaret as if he had meant to put her behind him; it was swift and thoughtless and almost instantly quelled, but she had seen it. Furthermore, so had Skander. He dropped his eyes a moment to where Rupert's hand had fallen back at his side. His thoughts had visibly shifted, but a heartbeat later he drew them back.

"Gabriel found a rich one," he went on slowly, suspiciously, "between Ryland and Cheshunt. That cuts the participants nearly in twain."

"We will come," Rupert said firmly. Skander looked hard at him, lips pressed tightly. Margaret watched the almost overwhelming desire to speak catch and strangle in the young man's throat, but somehow he held his peace. Having recovered from his start, Rupert smiled mockingly. "We are in need of a little sport, Margaret and I. She has seen not but fox-hunting since she has come here. Boars have no use for dodging and cunning play as the fox and hart have. If she sees naught else she is like to think us mealy folk in the chase."

"Not like," she heard herself say quietly.

Skander sidestepped the remark deftly and rushed on before Rupert could say anything else. With an outward flick of his hand, as though to indicate her—his ring glinting in the sunlight—he added, "Woodbird Swan-neck, I hear, comes also. So then Margaret will not be the only lady in our train."

"Nay, but I protest she is." Rupert's tone was soft, but laced with that quiet, almost inaudible laughter which, when mocking, hurts the most.

Skander flung up his head, nostrils widened like an insulted stallion. His face, so often amiable, was stark-pale with rage and a quick sense of fury lashed out from him, only a moment from being clenched in both fists and made kinetic by a blow to Rupert's cheek. They stood a moment so, both gone pale—Rupert's left fist closed very, very slowly—and Margaret waited tensely, her heart in her throat, expecting after each throb for one of them to raise a hand. But neither moved, and after half a minute Skander said tersely,

"I go down now to the stables. You'll find your horses there."

He turned and stalked away. At that moment the blue-jay man had reentered, coming to fetch him, and stopped, turning in his tracks to fall into step with the young man's angry pace. Margaret would have watched them until they disappeared, acutely sorry for the insult, when a swift blur of white movement caught her eye and she saw Woodbird come abreast of them a little distance off. The sharp, owlish eyes looked after Skander, cut to Rupert's face with a swift, scared, accusing look...then the woman hurried on, going out after Skander and the blue-jay man.

"And you wonder," said Margaret, when they were alone, "that people do not like you!"

"I never asked for them to like me," Rupert said. "Liking is a small, dear door out which you pass in the night, unseen—but should any see you go out by it, anyone desirous of seizing your house knows by which little secret postern to come in and catch you unawares. I never asked for them to like me. I like, as to that, none of them."

She looked hard into his cool, unblinking eyes. "Really? Not even Malbrey? not even Bloodburn?"

"Them less than most, because they will do what I ask—and yet for that very reason I strangely loathe them." He pulled down his brows and his smile, which had been bitter and mirthless, ran from his face as he turned to look about him at the people in the room. "They are all little to me, silver and sanguine-coloured, petty in their finery like chanticleers in their barnyard runs. They have little thought for aught else. They have their pride. They have their stubborn self-wills which I will break—"

"But you will loathe them all the more because they break," Margaret finished, finding, with a curious mingled horror and pity, that she understood.

"Yes," he said, a sudden melancholy catching at his brows. "I will loathe them because of that."

They went down then to the stables to fetch their horses. Margaret was quenched and quieted, but the early winter wind caught at her sharply and, blowing her skirts sideways, stung the colour into her cheeks. The yard was busy. Almost all of the men were turned out, seeing to their horses, checking a bit of sheeny spur-ring on a heel or hauling on a girth-strap there, the wind and pale, level winter light blowing all around them, catching up their cloaks and smiles and the high, daring light in their eyes. And though Margaret was afraid of the hunt she was suddenly glad—hard and fiercely glad—that she was riding out among them.

But then a little thing happened that destroyed her momentary pity of Rupert. She was standing at her mare Hanging Tree's side, fiddling with the length of the stirrup, when a man in his thirties, honey-haired and pleasant looking, came up behind her to where Skander stood at his horse, a yard and a half from her elbow, and hailed him warmly.

"Why, Periot!" Skander cried. He struck the man on the shoulder and drew him close. "So word got through to you, after all. I had hoped you might come."

"Gabriel dropped in on us on his way back in from scouting," the man Periot explained. "So I came along."

"But not Ely?"

"Nay, it is Ely's rotation to the pulpit tomorrow. He wanted a quiet day to prepare."

The smile, which Rupert had stamped on earlier, flashed up on Skander's face again. "Is it that time already? How the time flies! But of course he will need today to study, and never mind that we'll miss him keenly."

Periot tugged at the buttons of his great coat and fished among the inner pockets. "I did remember to bring up that book you wanted, by the bye. It lies somewhere in these black holes..." And he drew out a dark-bound book, small and well-used with the coffee-pale inner skin showing where the binding had been worn off, and handed it over to Skander. Margaret looked over her shoulder just then, overcome by curiosity, and saw, clearly, the lettering flash up on the cover like a knife into her chest.

Songmartin.

The catch of her breath was too small for anyone to hear, but it shook her whole body as the images of the books, the man's words, the man's life and his beliefs, flashed mutilated and burned into her mind, whipping away any pity she had felt a few moments ago for the man who held her captive. Something rose in her, something wretched and red-coloured, a ringing warning feeling, and she almost reached out to snatch the book from Skander's hand before Rupert, who was standing only a few horses away, turned and saw the book himself. But the colder Norman part of her held her back, sure that a grab like that would draw more attention, would make her look like an unreasoning fool, and would make Rupert angry with her.

She turned her back on the exchange, the snap of blood in her ears drowning out the men's conversation. With hot cheeks and unsteady breath she fumbled with the stirrup-straps, rubbing the old cracked leather hard between her thumbs and forefingers before, with an effort, she could force herself to tip the world right-side up again and go mechanically through the motions of preparing the saddle and mounting for the ride.

"Shee hee!" Skander whistled, his mood restored, ignorant of the blush of fear on Margaret's face. "Come by, Twiti! Come by, Latimer!"

They went out by the curtain-wall gate north along the wooded fellside, dropping single-file by way of a narrow walking-path into the thick pine-woods. The land below was swimming in silvered mist: every now and then the stark bare black of orchards swaths of snowy pasture showed through, looking, at that distance, like the swells of the sea. It was beautiful, clean, and clear with a light dusting of snow everywhere, and Margaret's spirits could not help being lifted on a tenuous upward draught of pleasure. They were a merry, handsome group in a fiercely bright, handsome land: a flicker-flame of a party, trimmed in gold and ermine, riding among the snow-laden pine-boughs, dressed in scarlets and greens, and blues as clear as Lord Gro's aquamarine ring.

Margaret's dark-dappled mare was frisky this morning and took the sloping path downward at a hard, jogging trot, vying for space with Witching Hour on her left and, she found, Periot Survance's horse on her right. The horses' breath steamed in the shadowy air. She took the reins firmly in hand, giving her mare little head to fight with. White breath streamed backward over her, pearling on her cheek and once, as her mare shook loose from a low pine-branch, she got a dusting of snow on her lashes.

The second time Hanging Tree bumped into Survance's horse he said, "We seem to have lost the hunting line, haven't we?" and pulled his horse back alongside her mare's flank.

"We do seem to have bunched up a bit," Margaret admitted. She swung sideways in the saddle and bent to avoid another branch—and to see what look was brooding on Rupert's face to gauge his attitude. His mount had pulled ahead and she could see only his shoulder and the back of his head. "I am sorry: Hanging Tree is fidgety this morning."

"No need to apologize. We all have fidgety mounts some mornings... Have we met before? I don't believe we have."

Margaret had been dreading the question, knowing when he had spoken out that it was only seconds away. She had wanted to like him, and had wanted him to like her—that was about to be over, now. "You haven't." She twisted and reached out, putting her hand in his. "I'm Margaret Coventry, from the Mares."

"Ah!" said Periot. A smile, almost hard with sincerity, flashed across his face. "Is this your first time to Ryland—I mean, to Lookinglass? I don't suppose you would come up this way just to see Ryland."

"Yes, it is my first time to Lookinglass. Where is Ryland?"

"Just there." Periot pointed to their left and downward. Through the ragged pine-tops Margaret could see the homely red roofs of buildings emerge from the mist. "I am Periot Survance. I am one of the shepherds there."

"I can see that it is in the shadow of Lookinglass," Margaret admitted, "but it looks pleasant from here." She almost added that it must be good to have a home, no matter what grander shadow it was in, but she bit it back just in time. "I did hear your name when you spoke to Skander in the yard. You have a friend, I understand, who could not make it?"

The man—he must have been fifteen years her senior—put down his heels and leaned back to dodge another low-hanging branch. "Oh yes, Ely—I just finished my rotation in the pulpit and Ely begins tomorrow, so he stayed home to study. He will be sorry he was not able to meet you. He is fond of new people."

"Well, perhaps another time," Margaret heard herself saying. At that, Rupert turned his head and she could see his brow uplifted, the faintest, softest feather of a smile touching the corner of his mouth.

They passed over Ryland and left the track altogether, following Skander Rime and his huntsman Gabriel into the thick, scrubby ground of the wood itself, riding fetlock-deep in snow and leaf-muck, crashing over fallen logs after the leashed hounds, following the pock-marks that Gabriel had made going and coming back from locating the boar. They fell back into single-file. The wood afforded bare space for one horse to walk comfortably, and the ground was rough, more so than when she and Rupert and Skander had gone on their flurry of a fox-hunt. They went through clear wood for awhile, passing between empty maples and birch, but soon left those to fight with holly and heavy, ancient pine where the new morning light, which had been mounting in the air, was nearly strangled by the thick evergreen growth. Though the difficult ground made her uneasy, Margaret found herself enjoying it more than she had the fox-hunt, for though they went largely in silence, they were gaily-spirited and pleasant, even Gro—who rode in the unenviable position before Rupert, with Rupert's eyes on the back of his neck.

Were it not for the bulk of fell which ran roughly north and south, Margaret would have lost sense of direction. They wandered at a walk and breaking trot after the hounds for the better part of an hour, worming and weaving through the harsh winter wood, keeping much together though, after awhile, the string broke up into a staggered pattern around her that worked into a crescent-shape. They pushed on northward and a little westerly, always going down a bit of slope so that the constant motion of leaning back and swaying from side to side began to make Margaret ache. The sun had got clear of Glassfell and was shining beautifully down between cloud-streamers and the crazy, pin-wheeling pine-branches, stabbing down into the snow and scrub and scouting hounds so that the images of them all showed up brightly and clearly on Margaret's vision and seemed painfully, wildly dear—

The foremost hound raised his head and gave a strange exultant wail, like a howl and a scream at once, and quick as thought the others took it up, clustering, bunching in around the leader, straining their leashes almost to the breaking point. Imperiously Gabriel's horn blared, shattering the crystalline beauty of the quiet wood—sending up a pair of partridges out of a thicket in a flurry of tawny wings—and the dog-boys stooped as one to let loose their charges. The motley crew of dogs, all big-boned, fierce beasts like Curoi, heavily-limbed and swift in motion, broke from the clustering group of horses. Yanking in their leashes the dog-boys ran after them, dodging Gabriel on his horse, trying not to be crushed underfoot as the huntsman kept flying pace with his hounds. His encouraging shouts and staccato horn-notes beat back on Margaret's ears as she, too, lurched into the chase. It was just as before, only more dangerous with the uneven, half-hidden ground underfoot and a sudden rocky bed of a stream opening up before them, steep and cold as horror on her skin; one horse, a new-looking, lanky bay, gave a scream of shock as it went in and grumbled and squealed as its rider urged it up the opposite bank after the disappearing tail of one of the biggest of the dogs. Margaret clung on only because she had to; her mare did most of the footwork for her, following after Rupert and answering, as if it knew the language, to the call of the horn.

They turned uphill once and came into a roughly shallow piece of fellside that might have once been a cirque, but was now as wooded as the rest of the ride, and came flying up a damp, empty bit of streambed to what must have once, after the cirque, been a kind of pool at the foot of a low waterfall. There was a big, swift movement of black on the background which, in the confusion, Margaret understood intuitively to be the boar. In the flurrying motion she did not get a clear view of it.

The horn screamed again. The dogs all gave tongue, closing into a tight ring at the mouth of the dead stream to keep the boar from escaping. Most of the men, and even Woodbird, had flung themselves off their horses and were forming the tight, hesitant ring around the beast. Feeling somehow unsafe on the back of her hunter, though it stood patiently beneath her, Margaret unhooked her leg and foot from the saddle and slid to the ground, hanging back with a clear view of the fight. Against all better reason she did not want Rupert to think she was a coward.

The saddle had afforded her the best view of the boar, but even from the lower sloping ground of the old damp streambed she could see it clearly enough between the bunched ring of the hounds and the group of men. It was backed up against a low rocky fall which, in spring, would be gushing with snow-water, but now was littered with dead leaves and rattling pebbles. Plant-growth and dirt shunted upward in a brown spray around the boar as it dug its forehooves in, sheeny back bristled, its gargoyle face leering at them as it swung about slowly, this way and that, to take them all in. It was a wily beast. Even at that distance, and with no foreknowledge of the animal, Margaret knew it was awful and cunning, far more horrible than that thoughtless half-moment with the fox in the wood; this was a thing of brute and bloody strength, and her own blood ran chill in her veins to look at it. She tore her eyes from its gaze: there was something bewitching about its flickering red eyes that would be her death, she thought, if she met it and let it hold her.

"Hy! hy my!" someone cried, and as if the cry were an archer letting loose his fingers, three alaunts sprang forward at once, hurling their heavy bodies at the boar. Three of them was significant weight and fang to throw against anything, but the boar was waiting for them. Transfixed, Margaret watched the boar swivel its thick, craggy body like a corkscrew—it seemed not to be on the ground at all. A dog screamed, another snapped and howled; one got a good mouthful of bristling boar-hide before it was shaken off, with a hind leg torn wide open, to stumble across the bodies of its fellows. Margaret had come to know from watching Curoi that alaunts have little sense save blood-lust, and this one, like Curoi, clung to the fight as long as it could. It tried to regain purchase on the ground, slipping and sliding on the muck and its game leg, but the boar was too much for it. Like a wall falling on a crippled beggar it ran the dog down, crushed it, broke open its skull with its tusks, and trampled clean over it, racing for the break in the ring of dogs and hunters.

It was all over in a moment. Margaret saw it happen clearly, everything etched with sharp edges in red: the brief struggle between the dogs and the boar, the boar's triumph, and the boar's enraged burst for freedom through the ranks. Then everything went odd to

Margaret, as if things were longer than they ought to have been, and shorter by half at once. She was aware of the two lymers, Latimer and Twiti, jumping up beside her, eager to join in the fight, and she, possibly out of her mind, letting go of her horse in a panic to grab a collar in each hand.

"No!" she cried above the clamour of boar and dogs and huntsmen. "No, you idiots—you fools! Let it to the bigger dogs!"

She dug the heels of her riding boots into the muck and clung on; she was hauled forward a step, but thankfully Skander's hounds seemed better trained than Rupert's Curoi. They stopped obediently, but nothing else did. When she could look up again Margaret saw the boar coming through the last line of hounds, hurling a hunting-boy aside with something spitting and nasty where his knee should have been, and come charging. The distance between her and it seemed impossibly long. It was more like looking down time than looking down several yards of old streambed. But at the same time it seemed the boar was only a moment from her. It did not occur to her that it was bearing straight for her—for boars, Rupert had said, have no use for dodging and foxy play as harts do—she only knew it instinctively, as if she had always known it, as if it were a dream, as if this were the perfectly natural way of things.

Her hands sprang open. What happened to the dogs after that, she did not know. There was a horse beside her which belonged to she knew not whom, and she reached for the first thing among its tack which looked serviceable. It was the *fourchée*, as long as any spear, and hooked like the devil's fork. There was a scream which she thought was her own as she turned and braced her feet into the gravel and mud—it was only the scared horse—and almost at the same instant the boar was on her. The world became brute force, the sense of being knocked off the edge of Plenilune into the empty black, the rot-reek of boar breath, a squeal of rage and a savage cry. The jar nearly wrenched the *fourchée* out of her hands but somehow she clung on, which was stupid, she realized later. But what saved her by a hair's breath was Aikin Ironside, who had sprung in with his own boar-spear. His was the savage, wordless cry of brute force to match the boar's. His was the weight which threw the boar's off just a fraction—just enough to save Margaret's chest from being gouged open by the beast's fangs.

The whole scene dived off the end of Plenilune into the black, turned on end over Margaret's head, and seemed to fall on without her. The world stopped whirling and she found herself on her side with her face raw and the raw places filled with gravel. Her hands were blistered and torn, and stung as she pressed them into the leaves to heft herself up. She had bit her lip again, just where it had been broken before: through the confusion and swimming feeling in her head, that was what she noticed chiefly, and it annoyed her.

People rushed to her side. Aikin, who was closest, was there first, with an experienced but bloodied hand under her elbow to hold her until she found her balance. The world swam a moment with brown and tawny and pale light until it became a November wood again, and she looked down and over to see the huge body of the boar scrabbling and heaving, still alive, but only barely, with her make-shift weapon and Aikin Ironside's spear in its chest.

"Someone kill it, please," a man called, half-laughing in an uncertain, shaky way. "She's all right, only tumbled a bit."

Through the ringing in her ears Margaret realized it was Aikin Ironside himself who was speaking, his dark auburn hair a mess with leaves and his face rather pale so that, looking up, she realized he had two stark brown freckles on his left cheekbone. But the tawny of his eyes was laughing, and his smile flashed white with a companionable triumph which made Margaret warm where the boar's tusk would have hit her.

Rupert was there on her other side, then, slipping an arm around her hourglass to support her—her legs did not feel certain just then—and Skander was looking from her to the boar's killing and back again, seeming bemused. "I take it back, Rupert," he said slowly. "You were right."

"Someone see to Charlock's cub!" someone yelled. "It took a chunk out of his knee!"

Margaret was momentarily forgotten as several people scrambled to help the silent, pale-faced boy sitting in a crevice on the ground, holding onto his own leg and trying gamely—and doing well—not to cry. Rupert took her out of the way and quietly put her on a log with his own cloak about her shoulders and a flask of brandy to sip from clasped whitely in her hands.

"Sit there quietly," he told her. His fingers brushed her cheek. In a still more gentle voice he added, "You have done better than all, brave heart."

His words came to her through an odd, muffling blanket of emotion and it was not until he had gone away himself to help with the task of unmaking the boar that she really heard him. She shuddered at the memory of his touch. It was uncanny and wretched how that was the clearest feeling of all: not the cuts on her hands or the roughness of her cheek, or even the sickening backwash of fear, but the warm, gentle, rough touch of his hand on her face. Impulsively she shoved the back of her hand across her cheek and took a sip of the brandy to drown the shock.

The unmaking was a smelly, disgusting business. The boar was killed thoroughly and turned over to be systematically, almost ceremoniously, taken apart. No one said much to her, but the odd thing was that their faces were rather different now: they were much more open and accepting whenever they happened to drop their gaze on her sitting alone with Twiti, who had slunk fawningly up, lounging on her feet. As the shock began to wear off, she could not quite think why. It was Aikin Ironside who had really done it. If it had not been for his thrust she would have been maimed, if not killed, and she had a cold, sober appreciation for the young man's skill and quick thinking.

"Put your head between your knees," a voice said above and behind her. "It will get the blood back into your brain."

She looked round to find Lord Gro had joined her, quietly though the ground was strewn with sticks and pebbles. His appearance had not changed since she had last spoken with him, but after the first awkward moment of finding him looming over her, Margaret thought she caught the merest glimmer of respect in his frank, cold eyes. She remembered what he had said to the others behind the closed lattice—and remembered also that he did not know she had overheard. Unavoidably she coloured and looked hurriedly away.

"I am all right, thank you," she said, trying not to sound too blunt, and failing, for her voice was not quite certain in her throat.

It seemed to her less lady-like to stick one's head between one's knees than it was to have met a boar head-on with an oversized fork.

The wind gusted and tugged at their cloaks. Margaret huddled deeper into hers while Lord Gro's danced wildly about his shoulders. Ears blowing in the wind, Twiti scrambled to his feet and wedged himself in the folds of Margaret's skirt between her knees. Risking one hand to venture out into the cold, she fondled the dog's ears, drawing the purling softness through her fingers. The fleshy underside of the ear was warm and pulsed faintly beneath her pressure: she held onto it as onto a life-line, for the stark reality of her close shave was as cold as the wind to her belly, and as biting sharp. She watched, blindly, from a distance as Periot Survance squatted at the dog-boy's feet and began poking gently at the wound. The boy lay with his head in Woodbird's lap and did not say a word, but stared in a fixed, horrified way at the wood canopy, face as white as fainting. Margaret took a deep, shaking breath and pulled herself together.

"To think," she remarked in her old familiar, steady voice, "I was concerned that there might be wolf-hunts in these parts."

There was a soft cracking sound behind her. Glancing surreptitiously over her shoulder, Margaret found Lord Gro had drawn his lips in a wide thin line which seemed to be his best pantomime of a smile.

The light began to blow around them as the high fell winds tossed the trees about. Light raced across Margaret's face and hands and made tawny-coloured Twiti turn gold. Gro's cloak caught the wind and bellied out like raven's wings. His hand slipped out, the hand with the pale aquamarine ring, and clasped one end of the fabric to keep it from being snatched away altogether.

"We do not often have fatalities, even in boar-hunts," Gro said presently, having wrestled the cloak under control. Surprised, Margaret turned in her seat and looked up into his face. She had not expected him to offer conversation, but after the first moment's surprise she heard old Hobden's voice:

"All I knowed was they brought 'im 'ome one day like a fish what's been gutted. Boar, mus likely."

And she shivered again in her middle in the wake of a wretched cold wave of fear.

Gro saw the look on her face. "So." His iron-grey brows flickered and a strange softness superimposed itself over the hardness of his face. "You have been told. You are one, I suppose, to know that we are not all mask and gala here. I am sorry."

She put her arms around herself and rose—he was still taller than she—and turned to watch with him as Brand and Gabriel began digging a fire-pit. He had not liked her, Mark Roy's youngest son, but then it had been his right to mistrust her. Now his fair young face, roughened by the winter wind, shining in the light, turned up and caught her eye. He frowned a moment—then suddenly smiled, his teeth showing with a strange kind of companionable fierceness. Beside her, Gro made a dismissive gesture with one hand and, mimicking it, Brand returned to his work.

"Yes," said Margaret quietly. "I am sorry too."

The boy was not allowed to stay. Survance made mention of taking him back up to Lookinglass and having Melchior look at him, but Skander rose up in a flurry of tawny buckskin and ermine and hushed him up, sending the blue-jay man instead with the boy slung at an awkward angle on the horse's rump.

"You cannot go," said Skander roundly, hands on his hips, "when you have only just come. The leg will mend and the cub will get about with naught but a fledgling limp and a pretty scar. Let Tabby take him. Sit down, Periot."

Periot sat down hurriedly next to Bloodburn and the matter was put aside. Margaret watched from her side of the ring about the fire as the blue-jay man disappeared into the cold wood, the low noon sun blending his hair into the golden mists. The last crackle of the horse fighting with the undergrowth died away. Skander returned from seeing his man off and, stamping the snow from his boots, sat down on his own up-turned log between Periot and Aikin, and an awkward silence fell over the group. All eyes wandered to the rump roast sizzling over the fire. It was a rich, heavy piece of meat that would take some time to cook. The dogs lay on the outskirts of the ring, quieted now into soft worrying snarls as they finished their own meal of boar-blood and bread. The horses shifted; Witching Hour, getting too close to another horse, squealed and swung away on his lead. Margaret stole a careful look around the circle. What was it that hung over them, that kept their eyes carefully on the centre of things and away from other faces? Brand had a slight, impatient smile on his face which might have been for the food or might have been annoyance toward another quarter. Margaret did not know. Aikin turned aside once to Woodbird, who was his left-hand neighbour, and murmured something; she shook her head quickly. Almost at the same instant Skander leaned forward and turned the roast, and said aloud,

"Well, we are all here. Is it too solemn a thing to discuss now and shall we save it for after the pudding?"

Brand looked squarely at Margaret, a little of the old dislike in his eye; she felt her skin turn cold. But Rupert, folding his arms across his chest and leaning back against the black split trunk of a pine, replied, "I think it would curdle your food either way, coz. Best leave it?"

"I think it had better wait," said Mark Roy peaceably, and glanced from Margaret to Woodbird meaningfully.

Periot shifted forward on his log, hitched up his trousers at the knees, and turned his head to Skander. "I beg your grace, my lord. Is there aught I should be abreast of?"

Everyone's head was up and all eyes were on Skander and poor Periot, save Rupert's—he lounged panther-like on his log, staring into the heart of the fire: a smile slunk across his face. She did not know why she did it—the blood rang so loudly in her ears that she could barely hear herself and she had the feeling of being disconnected from herself by a sharp blade of terror. Before Skander could answer—he had his mouth open—she said,

"It is for the Overlordship. It seems Rupert de la Mare has met the requirements imposed."

Now all eyes were on her—save Rupert again, who only turned his head to look at her hands clasped whitely on her knees. The faces of Malbrey and Bloodburn she could not read; Skander looked angry; Mark Roy and his sons seemed half-quizzical, half-wary, as if trying to scent where her allegiance really lay in her remark. Lord Gro, among all of them, looked sorry.

Periot's face was careful, a polite, meaningless smile on his lips. "Ah yes," he said softly. "I must have missed that, as it was not to be found in the history books in which I habitually bury my nose. Thank you."

Quite quickly the colour rushed back into her cheeks; she forced a smile and looked away, suddenly overwhelmingly sick in her stomach. *For once, can the world hold a little steady and let me get my bearings? So this is what my foot tastes like!* But Rupert did not seem displeased; on the contrary, he seemed well amused, and that made her feel sicker than ever to think she had played into his whims even as she had meant, in a confused way, to put him on the spot. *Why did I ever pity you, when you are so hateful to us all?*

As the conversation could grow no more awkward, it broke up into shards of talk between twos and threes. Margaret felt sorry for herself and Woodbird, who carried the awkwardness on beyond the men. Periot leaned forward, arms on his knees, and fell into a discussion with Lord Gro; Mark Roy and Malbrey talked amicably, if gingerly, while Brand listened in. Aikin, with unnatural deftness, had to play at mediator between Skander and Woodbird—and Woodbird clearly did not appreciate his efforts—and Margaret was trapped between Rupert and Bloodburn.

"How are things in Hol?" Rupert began politely.

"I saw the slaughtering beginning as we came out and I will go back, finding it done, and all things prepared for winter."

"By then, too," added Rupert, "there will be more things done with than the harvest."

"That, too, is in my mind."

Margaret watched Bloodburn's hands interlock themselves: long, old, vein-raised hands that were mottled by the sun, hands that were silver with scars and still strong. She shivered and wished she did not have to sit next to him, nor with her back to the open wood.

Rupert went on. "I am told by my folk that it will be a mild winter, and so an early spring, and I think that bodes well for us."

Bloodburn looked sidelong from under his grizzled brows. "Malbrey was telling me about the star you saw. And sure that we are friends, but I do not put much stock in stars."

"Do you think I quell at a mere blink of light?"

"No... But then, is it not a mere blink of light? Yet Malbrey was insistent upon your trepidation."

Rupert's face was sharp and scornful, upreared, the lips pulled off the teeth in an unconscious snarl. "Trust me, or trust nothing, to know what I am about. When the time comes, can I so count on you?"

Bloodburn turned his head away and there was in his voice a careful gentleness which belied a sullenness beneath. "The Overlord knows that he can count on me."

"Yes," Rupert said more kindly after a moment. "The Overlord knows."

When the meat was finally cooked they ate, much more relaxed with warm food before them, under a clear faience-blue noon sky with the wind in the tops of the pine-trees and the sound of water falling somewhere far off, echoing in the quiet. To Margaret it was a strange, shining experience, at once awful and enjoyable, for the cold sharpened her senses and the quick, flashing wit of her companions, like kingfishers, darted by her and seemed to weave the circle of their hunting party with brilliance. At times she hated, keenly, why she was there—and the boar-meat, cooked fresh and unsalted, was gamey to her taste—but beneath the prickling hatred she knew, very clearly, that she would have given anything, *anything*—even the familiarity of her own home in Aylesward—to be sitting among these people on this snowy November day. Whatever else came, she knew she would remember the hunting party for the rest of her life.

But Plenilune was not done surprising her. As with Songmartin's suddenness, flashing out of nowhere and startling her with a quick scene of beauty and truth and goodness, as with the shepherd's panpipe playing in the windy clearness of the fells, Plenilune flung round silver balls of shocking splendour at her again. The little party was getting up to go—someone was packing up what was left of the boar-meat and someone else was kicking snow over the fire—when they realized that Twiti the lymer had gone missing.

"So like him to go wandering," said Skander. "He got all the wanderlust of the litter. *Shee hee!* here, boy!"

They broke up, leaving some to close up the camp while others moved through the wood, calling for the errant dog. Having nothing better to do, Margaret flung the heavy length of her skirts over one arm and waded through the snow and bracken with them, Latimer tagging along behind her. She felt oddly responsible for the dog, a strange kinship for the moment when it had tried to save her life from the boar.

He cannot have gone far, she reasoned as she slid ungracefully over a log and dropped into a deep, ugly, messy depression in the earth. Latimer fell in after her. *And we are not so far from home that he can be in danger. But what a naughty dog! that he does not come when we are all calling for him.*

"Margaret!" Rupert's voice carried faintly through the woods. Stopping a moment, she frowned, elected against going back, and pushed on, as much now to get away for a few minutes as to find the lymer.

A bit of cloud had scuttled away from the low winter sun when she came stumblingly through a low hawthorn thicket, pushing aside branches and stepping on twigs as she went. Latimer whined softly. Margaret had a brief, confused sense of coming out into a small clearing before the world became a riot of gold and jewel-black and an upward rush of white and surf-sound. Goldfinches burst upward from the uncut turf in a whirling cloud, circling and chittering, filling the air with a thin, fine filigree of splendour. They finally settled in the trees just as Margaret was getting her breath back, and she got a clear view of the white thing that had lain in their midst.

Even as she stared at it, her hand clenched white about Latimer's collar, and it stared back at her, she could not quite believe her eyes. It was a unicorn, full grown but only the size of a colt, with grey on its muzzle and ears and knees. It did not look much like the horses she was used to: it seemed to have wandered out of an old orient, far off in time. Its eyes were larger and longer than most equines Margaret had seen, its ears longer too, and it wore Pharaoh's beard on its chin with such a supercilious nature that she could feel herself suddenly blushing with fear.

For a long breathless moment she and the beautiful, weird thing watched each other unblinkingly—she realized that it had enormously long, black lashes—while the goldfinches flickered by overhead. Neither of them seemed to know what to do. Margaret was not sure if she could leave quietly and respectfully, or if she did not dare move; she could see the unicorn was trying to decide if she was a threat or an annoyance. It swivelled its ears and turned its head—the light sang sharply on its horn-point—and then, suddenly, with a sighing heave of its flanks, it turned away, disinterested, high-stepping through the sodden grass with the late dew gleaming on its hide. Its soft, grey-plumed tail was the last thing she saw, glinting among the black pines, swallowed up by trees and undergrowth and the sharp pale winter sunlight.

The goldfinches swept up in a gold cloud and flew away south.

When the silence descended again—thick, smothering silence—Margaret put out her hand against the nearest tree-trunk to support herself for a moment. Then, "Come along, Latimer," she said, and turned back the way she had come.

They had found Twiti, who had wandered off with another dog, by the time she returned. No one save Rupert seemed to have noticed that Margaret had wandered off too—Skander glanced her way once from scolding Twiti, but she could not read his expression. Latimer broke away from her and ran to join his fellow lymer, and Rupert, disengaging himself from Malbrey's company, came to fetch her. With a swift upward rush of panic she schooled her face, inexplicably afraid that he would see in her eyes the thing she had seen, and that seemed to her, though she could not explain it, a breach of faith with something greater and more solemn and more brittle than herself.

"So. You have not run off, then," said Rupert quietly.

She said with tired mockery, for it had been a long day, "To whom should I go? Winter woods are unforgiving companions."

"Has the snow got into your boots?"

"No."

It was only after noon by two hours and already the light was looking westerly, the sun swinging in a low arc on the fell horizon, striking on the southern crown of Seescarfell and breaking up on the lower wooded slopes that touched Marenové's back door. Waiting as Rupert brought up her horse, Margaret felt that they stood on the threshold of winter, that autumn was a mere blink of fire-colour behind them; and squinting up the long level afternoon rays, she felt the winter would be long, long and empty with Rupert for company, and something in her middle wrenched with strong self-pity.

They were a rambling party on the homeward journey. No one kept to single file and everyone talked as much as he liked, though quietly, pleasantly. Riding along behind Rupert, the wood flooded with tarnished gold light, Margaret watched the strong, ephemeral images of her companions—Woodbird in a silvery, feathery splendour; Aikin Ironside with a rich, reddish aurora about him—and after the self-pity, as she always felt after self-pity, she knew again that she was glad she had come. The afternoon light held back the bleak prospect of the lonely winter in Marenové for a while longer and she held the pine-wood close, the company closer, knowing all the while that they looked at her askance as one might look at a hangman's noose. But she knew that if she thought too hard about the closed and closeted winter she would despair. She could not think of that.

A jewel-blink caught her eye. Skander's roan sidled close, his hand flicked out, eyes soft alight, and he saluted her privately, admiringly; and suddenly she smiled, sharply, so keenly that it hurt.

Sleepily, gladly spent by the day's exertions, with the rich, clean splendour of the golden light running in their veins, they wound back up above Ryland and passed through the curtain walls into Lookinglass. Margaret was sore and cold and glad to be helped down, even by Rupert, and to wade through the milling pack of warm hound-bodies. She flung the reins of her mare over its head and passed them off on a stable-boy.

"Well, vixen?" asked Rupert. "Did you, after all, enjoy yourself? You did very well."

She rubbed her chilled arms. "At times. I am not yet used to Plenilune. It is very alien and—dangerous. I do not know that I *enjoy* anything. I am always on my toes."

He looked over his shoulder at her from where he saw to the loosening of his horse's bridle. "You and I. We need not speak of it now, but I am very proud of you for the thing you did."

"You ought not to be," she replied tersely. "I did not do it for *you*."

The dogs began barking happily as they were led off to their kennels round the back of the stables. Blue-bottle Glass, rid of his mount and clipped with a lead, was prancing and kicking across the yard as if he had not just been taken out on a boar-hunt: his piercing squeal rang down through the terraces. She heard Skander calling out, "Take care, Periot! I'll see you on the morrow. Give my best to Ely!"

"Thank you, sir, I will—God keep you!"

"And you, sir!"

Their voices faded off into the thin winter twilight, drowned in the bustle and murmur and animal noises of the dispersing party. Feeling detached, Margaret turned from Rupert to watch the distant figure of the shepherd stalking down the damp stone stairs to the foot of the kitchen garden where he would rejoin the walking path and descend to his own village. He was a sturdy, friendly image, and Margaret liked him with an empty, desperate liking that felt like the hatred of despair. She said, without looking round,

"Would it be futile to ask you if I might go to church tomorrow too?"

She heard the chink as Rupert, having cinched the straps, let the stirrup fall to its length.

"It would."

She turned to him then, eyes reddened from the cold and stinging so that she had to squint them, and all she could see was his lean, handsome, hawkish face looking past her shoulder with a cold stare at the back of the receding shepherd. The look in his own narrow eyes was angry and hungry.

"You are spiteful."

He switched his gaze quickly to her. "Maybe—but are you not, also? But I am a disciple of verities, and I will not submit you to the womanish tradition of their assemblies and their council of lies. They wallow in their lies—returning every seven days to the same falsehoods, washing themselves in the same filth of their minds, and all the while believing they are coming clean. It is unmanly. It is despicable. Cast it from your mind at once."

"And if I will not?" she challenged in a small, hard voice. Like adamant, the pounding blows of his words only drove her into a smaller, harder, more brightly-furious lump, and she dared defy him for one moment, for Skander's sake and for Periot's, and for

Ely Jacland's, and for one small shard of a child's prayer that she had clung to in her most tormented moments.

He said finally, "You will submit and be obedient—for your own good. Furthermore, I will have you be a good example to the other women. I won't have you acting like those Thrasymene wenches who are lordless and think they can carry themselves about like men."

"Would you have me be like Kinloss, then?"

They stepped aside, his hand under her elbow, as the stableboys took away their horses. Turning together, they walked side by side into the bare garden and began mounting the hard-cut, narrow steps. "Kinloss," Rupert mused regretfully. They came above the level of the curtain wall and the late sun struck them in the back, making a dark-copper glory of his hair which the high, cold wind took and blew wildly about on its ends. "Bloodburn has a heart of steel and is passing loyal, but he is a domestic brute, that I will not deny."

Margaret had put up her hand to shove her loose hair from her face and had opened her mouth to thrust back with, "And you are not?" when she shut it again, realizing that she was inviting trouble. But Rupert had heard her abbreviated intake of breath and had paused, foot lifted to the next step, to look quizzically at her, and he had seen it in her face. His eyes dropped to her lip—the stinging was gone, but she could still feel the little break in it—and he almost lifted his hand, a spasm of regret pulling at the corner of his own mouth...but there were people in the yard and they were in the open, and his hand dropped at his side again.

"We will go home tomorrow. Malbrey is coming with us to stay a few days, and anyway, three days with family is always enough and more than enough."

He must know that she wanted dearly to stay longer with Skander Rime, and he must know that she loathed the thought of going back to Marenové in the company of Malbrey of Talus Perey. Would that he fell in a river and drowned! But she said nothing, and they went up together toward the porch and the promise of warmth within the house.

But on the top step Rupert suddenly stopped and swung round, as if stung. Margaret, too, hesitated and looked back. For a moment there was nothing unusual about the late afternoon bustle of the yard and garden, but then, on the fringes of it all, not far from where Periot had disappeared down the path, she saw the withered figure of the old woman who had interrupted their dinner last night.

It was too great a distance for either of them to see each other's faces clearly, but Margaret felt that did not matter to Rupert and the old woman. The plum-coloured rush of shadow and wind blew over them, lifting the dark hair from his forehead; his hands flickered—a swift black-and-blue electric prickle ran in the air. But even as Margaret braced herself, unsure of what would follow, it drained away with the wind. The broken shadows of the woodshore slashed back and forth and the old woman, slipping out of their gaze, disappeared among them.

XI | THE OVERLORD

That evening after supper Margaret sat alone in her room, grateful for the windy quiet and solitude, her muscles aching, her nerves raw, and lost herself in filling the blank pages of her little book with notes on the past three days. Her hand had begun to ache along with the rest of her, her eyes were beginning to smart, and she had put her pen down, thinking she was finished, when another image darted into her mind, silky red and sinuous, like the dragons on Mark Roy's robe. She picked up her pen again.

I spoke with Mark Roy this evening before coming up to my room. Somehow he got out of me, in one of those moments in which politeness must disarm my tongue, that I am leaving tomorrow, and I was surprised to see that he seemed genuinely sorry. Perhaps he believes Centurion and Lord Gro. Perhaps my episode in the woods has helped prove to him that I am not willingly Rupert's pawn, that I should wish better things for them—as if wishing had any weight. He was sorry, and urged me to visit them in Orzelon-gang's capital some day. Of course I told him that I would—what else could I have said?—and he began to tell me of its beauty, a little like a man who is homesick, and the strange thing was that I felt he was painting a portrait of his wife as he spoke. He talked of the black marble that is native to Plenilune, with which his home is made, and of the many little streams and pools that run all through it, making music in the background, and the great red and gold fish that they keep which flicker like flames in the watery dark. *He spoke of the golden dragons which are the doorposts of the* *house, of the lotus gardens that make the grounds look as if the sky has come* *down among them when the plants are all in bloom.* *I thought of strange,* *beautiful Romage and her harp-music, of the red-and-gold thread of her hair* *and song, and the huge orchestral dark behind her, and wondered if Mark* *Roy thought of that too when he spoke of his home, and if that was why he* *sounded homesick.*

To be homesick for such a place! *My heart ached so deeply as he* *spoke to me and though I did my best not to be rude, I fear I must have been* *because I have no place like that, and I know it, and I had to come away as* *quickly as I could for fear I should cry in front of him like a little girl.* *At* *least Romage, when she left her home among her own people, had a lovely* *place like that to go to.* *Mark Roy clearly loves her, and though I am not* *sure what I think of Brand, I do like Aikin: she must be very proud of him.* *I wish—I wish I had that kind of luck.* *Or grace.* *Or providence.* *I do not* *know what to call it, only I know I do not have it, and I wish so badly—* *badly enough to break this pen with the force of it—I wish so badly I had it* *too.*

There was a rustle, louder than the silken rustle of her candle-flame, and a soft knock at the door. Broken from her grey, sorrowful reverie, Margaret put down her pen and set aside the book in the shadow where the ink ran with the darkness and could not be read.

"Come in."

It was Aikaterine who entered, lamp aloft, the light rushing sharply and swiftly against her cheeks. "It is nearly ten-thirty," she murmured. "I have come up to get you ready for bed."

The weariness which Margaret had blindly been holding in check suddenly washed over her, warm and smothering, and she relaxed into her chair, bending at the small of her back. "Of course. I had lost track of the time."

They said no more for a space. The cold winter quiet, full of the murmur of the wind outside the window, fell over them. Aikaterine shut the door and set the lamp next to the candle on the dressing table and began taking down Margaret's hair. The clean, clear scent of pine fell with it and it was a sweet, bitter-sweet perfume. While the girl worked, Margaret looked down at her hands and felt with the flats of her thumbs the raw, sore places on her palms where she had fallen in the stream-bed gravel. That nightmare seemed impossible and far away. She wished she could believe it had never happened; thinking about it made her shiver with the closeness of its danger. How flippantly she had taken it at the time! She had been sick, and cold, and numb, but now, in the sea-shell hollow of her turret room, the horrible clearness of it brushed aside her hair and whispered at her ear and her heart quickened with the fear of it.

"Your dress," said Aikaterine.

She got up, turned in the light, and let the maid take apart the heavily embroidered white silk gown she wore; fold on fold of golden etching twinkled in the yellow light as it was drawn off her pale, chill-crawling skin. *It is a beautiful gown. I will wear it back home and show it to the fox, and perhaps he will like it, and it will cheer him a little.*

As if recoiling from a nasty taste of medicine, she turned her head from herself, realizing belatedly that she had called it *home*.

Aikaterine straightened from putting away the gown and looked over the room. Margaret, seated on the edge of the bed, finished tying the neck of her sleeping gown and looked back at the maid, quizzical. "I think that if you have no more need of me I will go," the other said. "My lord is meeting with the other great ones and he may need my service."

Margaret sat back, seeing, not Aikaterine, but the swiftly checked ring of men around the hunting fire, the thing that had almost come above the surface held just out of sight. It had been narrowly avoided then: it was coming into the open tonight. Aikaterine, seeing whatever look was on her face—she was not conscious of making a face—looked quizzical in turn. "Skander Rime meets with the others tonight?" Margaret echoed. Then, more cautiously, "What for?"

The other seemed to hesitate, her almond-coloured eyes sliding away and fixing for a moment on something in the distance. "For us, Lady Margaret," she said at last, huskily. "They meet for us and to know what our fate is."

Margaret did not remember getting to her feet. At one moment she was seated on the edge of the bed, turned sidewise to see Aikaterine, and the next she was standing before the maid, looking just a little downward into the other's face, with her forefingers resting heavily on the white-clad shoulders. She could feel the collar bone sharp beneath her fingertips and, at odd, punctuated moments, the soft throb of blood beneath the skin. But it was the eyes she looked into, the almond-coloured, dark-spangled eyes that looked back demurely into her own. There was no fear in them, but there was, perhaps, little hope, too.

Hardly aware of what she did, hardly knowing what she would say, Margaret took her hands away and stepped back. "C-come to me again within half an hour, Aikaterine."

And Aikaterine herself said nothing, but turned down her lashes over her eyes and broke away. Margaret did not see her go—she was looking out the round window on the sea of darkness below—but she heard the latch click behind her.

It came to her clearly in the long silence afterward that she was being a fool, but even as the knowledge came to her she knew as certainly that she did not care. Careful not to think about it much, she slowly went through the motions of drying her book page and putting it safely away. She had finished and was sitting up in bed with time to spare when, as she knew would happen, there was a brisk knock at the door and Rhea, without waiting to be called upon, stepped in.

The two looked at each other coolly. Margaret was afraid that the maid's witching eyes would see past her own careful mask of annoyance, but if she did, she did not say so.

"I see that my lady is to bed. Is there anything she needs else?"

Margaret broke her gaze and moved a pillow to a more comfortable position. "No, though you may dust the room and wash the floor, if you like. I am tired enough, I would not hear you bang about."

"The dusting and washing can wait until tomorrow," Rhea replied dryly. "I will go, then, it please us both."

"No doubt it will."

"Shall I take the lamp?"

For a moment Margaret cast wildly for an excuse to keep the lamp which would not raise the suspicions of the wildcat Rhea. She knew an excuse should come. If heaven loved her at all, an excuse should come...but none came, so she said with a jerk of her shoulders, "You can if you like. I would as soon put it out anyway."

With noiseless tread, the light hardly penetrating her well-like eyes, Rhea came in and took the lamp away, pausing only once at the door to look back over the latch like a nursemaid being sure her ward was going to sleep. It was at least the truth that Margaret was bone-tired, every length of muscle raw and sore and every nerve threadbare, and as Rhea shut the door the young woman half wished Aikaterine would forget and not come back, because the bed was soft and the blankets were warm, and she was so very tired...

It seemed Rhea had only just gone when the door opened again and a slim figure slipped in, shutting it again almost at once. Margaret sat up in bed, squinting against the blue-steel dark. The figure was not dressed in white. It *was* Aikaterine, was it not?

"Your pardon, my lady," came Aikaterine's voice. "I thought it best that I not knock nor make any noise."

"You thought well." Margaret pushed back the covers and swung out into the cold air. "I need my slippers and a dressing gown—a heavy one, for it is cold."

Even as she was saying it Aikaterine was across the room and kneeling on the balls of her feet before the trunk, the lid flung back, hauling out the wine-dark gown, ringstreaked with angry fire-colour, rich with brown marten fur that would be warm and soft against her skin. Margaret shoved her feet into the slippers and held out her arms for the gown—it settled heavily, almost ominously, about her thin body—and then she beckoned for Aikaterine to lead the way.

They went without a light. Margaret had to feel her way by the sound of Aikaterine's feet, but the girl was so light-footed and swift and sure that it was alarmingly easy to lose her in the dark. Several times as they stole down the passageway she felt Aikaterine reach back and touch her hand to reassure her, to give her her bearings. They came to the steps, and that was easier, for the steps were evenly spaced and she had gone up and down steps all her life so that it was as natural as breathing to go down them. After that it was hard, though they passed through one hallway that bore lamps, and the lamplight played furiously in the orange of Margaret's gown and silver on the fur, and she got turned about and lost all sense of direction by the time they slipped through the kitchen, down a little wine-smelling passage, and tiptoed down an old wooden stair toward a distant yellow light and a distant yellow sound of voices.

Aikaterine gestured to her lips. Margaret nodded, peeved that the other thought she had to be told to keep quiet. Hand upon the banister she slid soundlessly down after Aikaterine, each calf aching as she placed all her weight with care on the balls of her feet, and finally stood in a low, narrow, stone-walled hallway that smelled powerfully and richly of wine and hops and, elusively, of earth. There was lattice-work in the hallway-wall of the little room from which came the voices; if they stood too tall or moved too quickly, the people within would be able to see the light breaking up in flickering diamond patterns on their faces. Bending low out of the light, Margaret followed Aikaterine to the far side of the door and propped herself up against the wall so that she could get a wide view of the room within without being seen herself.

A man stooped and tossed a log into the fireplace with a bang and tinselly crash. It was cold in the hallway; Margaret wished she could huddle in front of that fire which was flinging its waving bars of light up the man's face—it was Aikin, looking stern, his fine lips set in a firm, uncompromising line. He looked blood-coloured now in the orange light, not pale, as he turned back to the others arranged about the room. Margaret could see many of them sitting at a rough wooden table on benches. Brand was backed up against a wall beam, arms crossed and pulled tight, looking out from under his brows with fierce, animal-wary eyes. Centurion was pacing, a swinging prance in his step, like a horse before it is led to the gate and the racetrack. Mark Roy sat placidly at the table, Lord Gro and Skander beside him, both looking withdrawn and grim. Rupert, sitting on Brand's side of the fire with his face toward the door and the firelight on his face, was a smooth, lounging, easy figure who seemed to hold the whole room with a dark power, lightly, in the hollow of his hand.

"And now we will speak of it, that thing which we could not speak of before, as if it were too sharp for tender ears?" Malbrey mocked. Margaret strained but could not see him from where she stood.

"In the ears of many of us," returned Mark Roy smoothly, " 'tis very sharp."

Rupert turned his head toward them. He was graceful, easy, polite—biding his time, Margaret thought, because he held the mouse in his teeth already. Under languid, drooping lids he regarded them, a faint smile catching at his mouth. "Have I faithfully met your strictures, gentlemen? Have I not done all you asked of me and bowed my neck beneath your yoke?"

I am a yoke then, am I? Margaret's face heated with disdain.

"Time runs into the well at the world's end, gentlemen," he went on. "We cannot keep Plenilune from her overlord forever."

There was a swift tension in the room—Margaret had the image of a great bird of prey sucking in its breath and fluffing out its feathers defensively—but for a long moment it seemed no one had anything to say against Rupert. Finally it was Skander, looking at the hand in which he clasped his ale-stein, who said quietly,

"But have you, coz?"

The firelight glinted redly in Rupert's eye as he looked toward the gentle, probing, daring voice—glinted redly on his teeth as he lifted his lips in a cool smile. "I am playing the long game. But the game has gone on too long with Plenilune, and that is the true heart of this matter."

They liked her, all in their own way, but she felt herself sliding out of their care as they were faced with the matter of the fate of their own country. She was only a single girl, a foreigner: and it was odd, but she found herself in that moment caring more about what they did for Plenilune than for what they did with her.

Mark Roy said, without a trace of reluctance in his regal voice, "There are no other candidates. It is only you, de la Mare."

Almost he shifted forward, but checked himself. "So are you resolved, gentlemen, to do what we all know must be done?"

"What must be done!"

The image of the room turned suddenly ugly. Brand had, until now, been totally silent, leaning, almost curled sullenly, against the wall beam at the back of the room in shadow and quiet and growing rage. Now he seemed to have lost a hold on himself and came forward swiftly—Aikin leapt to his feet to stop him—and stood over Rupert—who did not move—with a naked knife in his fist.

"What must be done!" the young man repeated. "Well I think we know it all, but none of us have the guts to it!"

"Brand!" his brother hissed, catching hard at the other's wrist. They locked, shook a moment, and held still. Aikin looked into his brother's face; Brand's gaze did not waver from Rupert's. "Is it that you would kill us all?" Aikin asked in a low voice.

Brand said bitterly, "I think it a better end to die than to submit to *his* overlordship!"

Aikin shook the wrist again. "If that is in your own heart, fine—but let others decide if they want to die or not: it is not your place to count the cost for them!"

And Rupert, who had not moved at all under the Hammer's burning eye, smiled—the way that made Margaret's flesh crawl—and asked gently, "And you have the guts to it?"

Brand seemed to be weighing his brother's words and de la Mare's, and though it was a tough struggle, he seemed suddenly to choose his brother over Rupert. "Adder's tongue," he said, stepping away. "I'll heed the pack of them before I heed whatever comes out of your mouth."

Aikin let him go, though he watched him warily; Brand slunk wolf-like into the deeper shadows until Margaret could not see him anymore. Aikin turned to Rupert and looked as if it was in his mind to say something, but Rupert was carefully looking levelly at his cousin and Aikin could not draw his eye. With a lift of his shoulders, Mark Roy's son turned away.

Skander must have felt Rupert's eye but he did not look up. He only said, grimly, through his teeth, "Let's put it to the vote."

There was a hesitation. For 'nay' no one moved, though the will to move was strong; for 'yea' Bloodburn's and Malbrey's hands were up first, followed reluctantly by the rest. In form it was unanimous. Aikaterine—Margaret had almost forgot about her—slid her hand to her mouth and turned her head away.

"And there you have it, gentlemen."

Rupert got up, stretched, and leaned his elbow on the mantle. His body obscured the firelight, plunging much of the room into total shadow. The chill of the cellar hallway passed over Margaret as if it were his shadow falling over all Plenilune in that moment. "Should we hold the installation at the full of the Rowan Moon? At least then Centurion, who is most far afield, will be in the neighbourhood, as he will be taking the two White Ones to the University around Christmas."

Centurion's face flashed round into the light. "And how are you knowing that," he demanded, "as it is a private matter?"

Rupert smiled coolly. "The same way I am knowing many things."

Centurion shivered—from rage or cold or a cold sense of dread, Margaret did not know—and lingered a moment looking from eye to eye on Rupert's face, weighing something, but finally he let it go, still suspicious, and took a seat at the table. Skander, perhaps feeling that there had been too many close shaves, pushed away and rose, saying,

"I am going to see to the carafe. I'll only be a moment."

He took the light, empty beer-carafe off the table and wove his way through the warm, dark press. With a catch of her breath Aikaterine stood up, grabbing Margaret's hand, but it was too late. The latch shot back and Skander flung open the door, stepping into the hallway.

He froze on the instant, seeing them at an angle with the faintest orange light on their cheeks. His face was in darkness; Margaret could not see what he was doing, or what he was thinking in his eyes. But before he had paused too long, before Rupert could look his way, curious, he thrust the doors shut and plunged the hallway and their eyes into darkness. His big, black form moved against the background. He made no noise save the dull, deep thud of his boots on the stonework, but Margaret felt Aikaterine tugging her forward after him. Her feet struck the stone risers and she had to catch herself and walk blindly up the stairs, groping for the railing, groping for some light.

Skander struck a light in the kitchen and spun round on her.

"What are you doing?" he asked Aikaterine in a low, growling voice.

"I made her take me down," Margaret defended the maid, though her heart was in her throat and she was suddenly afraid of the rugged, light-shot, masculine face bending toward her.

"No one makes my people do anything other than my will. Go back to bed, both of you. We will all be in trouble if Rupert discovers you were here."

Margaret looked back at the yawning mouth of the cellar doorway. Aikaterine murmured something to Skander; Skander, relaxing his shoulders, murmured something back. What if Rupert should come up now, through that awful dark? Did it really go to the cellar, she wondered, or if she went back down now would she find it went down to hell?

"I will go," she said. "I found out what I wanted to know, anyway."

Skander's face softened toward her. "I think we knew it all along, you and I... I am sorry."

She nodded. A thick, strangling feeling was beginning in her throat, a painful stabbing of tears behind her eyes. She pitied herself, she pitied Plenilune, but she also pitied Skander for he must be thinking poignantly that he was responsible for what was to become of her. For his sake she tried valiantly to fight past the coarseness in her throat.

"Good-night, Skander. Don't forget the beer. And..." Her eyes fell on the rigid, silent maid. "Be merciful. No one else will be."

His hand dropped gently on Aikaterine's shoulder. Her lashes trembled but she did not look up. It seemed the touch was word enough for her, and Skander turned back to Margaret. "I will be. And remember, Lady Margaret: you will always have a friend here at Lookinglass."

XII | KEYHOLES OF HEAVEN AND HELL

Margaret never got to say good-bye to Skander. They left early in the morning under a pale golden sky, amid the morning bustle of the yard. She heard his voice as she was mounting up, calling up from the garden, but she did not see him.

"Nay, the book Periot gave me yesterday—I put it on my desk yesterday evening. You did not move it? Fie! I am so hare-brained! We will look for it after luncheon."

With Malbrey ahead riding alongside Rupert, Rhea and Margaret behind, they went out through the highest curtain wall and descended the levels to the rough, cleared road and the icy bridge. Yesterday morning had been snow-still and even warm in places; today the winds were up again, purling sloe-coloured clouds along the horizon, diffusing the sheeny clear gold light over the sky. The chiff-chaffs, the late birds of the aging year, were rocketing in a thin webbing of wings from the forest, their shrill whispering piercing through the low rumble of the waterfall. Margaret squinted against the fanning light, watching them go, getting the heavy mass of her hair in her eyes—she had to let loose the reins with one hand and lock her fingers in her hair, shoving the mass back, to keep it from stinging her face. She had not had time to put it up after washing it, and the damp coldness of it took the wind and felt like ice on her neck. She sniffed: behind a curl of wood-smoke was the scent of winter.

Malbrey's horse, a heavy-set old palomino he called Chrysostom, was beginning to stoop in front of her, starting the sharp, winding descent toward Glassdale. Her own leggy grey, moving like an ill-omened shadow among the uncertain pine-light, felt like a rock under her: every jump and jar and skitter on the steep road, barely cushioned by saddle and muscle, made her pelvic bones jangle as if she had dropped them on a shingly shoreline. She took down her hand as they plunged into the wood and gripped the horse, wondering how many hours it would be before the level road of the dale stretched before them. Rupert and Malbrey chatted quietly together, easy in each other's company; the maid and manservant retained a stony silence. Feeling more than ever alone, cold in the wide freedom of Capys' steep fell country that seemed to mock her fiercely like the flash of the fox's white teeth, Margaret tugged her surcoat close at the throat and turned her face toward the overlook where, through the pine trunks, through the heavy silver mists and latent banks of snow, through the flicker of crow-wing, she could see Glassdale below. For a moment she became confused, her mare jostling her thoughts out of order: as if she were stumbling out of waking into a brief dream she thought she was seeing, not Glassdale, but a fresh waking view of the Cumbrian fells that knelt their knees down to the earth by Aylesward in England.

Mother... Father...

Then a blue-jay screamed overhead and the dream ripped away like cobwebs and it was Glassdale again. The memory of England was darkened by the ugly shadow of dissension and strife that still hung around her memory of her family. Glassdale, bright as an emerald and crystal-fire, was the thing that left her aching under her breastbone.

Would it not be a fine thing to have a box of paints and to paint that?

The thought reminded her of her notebook. She veered gladly away from England—appalled, and trying not to feel appalled, to find that she was glad not to think of England—toward the notes she had made. She had made very little, she was surprised to find.

With the enormity of everything that had been thrown at her, she had expected to find, when she could pull out her notebook and looked at it, that she had written much more. She had little more than a list of names and rough, scratched out, re-written places to which the names belonged, a sketch of the boar-hunt, and Mark Roy's beautiful account of his home which still made her ache to read it.

If I am not too tired this evening, she thought, folding the book back up into her coat, *I will write some more down and show it to the fox when I have a chance. Perhaps he can help me make sense of things.*

She was drawn out of her reverie by an arrest in the downward train. Rupert's horse squealed and skidded, nearly bumping into the golden horse who stumbled to the side before it could be recovered. In the gap between the horses, at the end of the lane where the road took a sharp turn downward, mingling with the shadows, stood the old withered woman.

As before, it seemed to Margaret, when they had all calmed their mounts, that for Rupert and the old woman there was no one else in the world who mattered. There was an aching, trembling silence like white-iron harp-thread that has been plucked and will not be still. The shrivelled face was bent down, the sloe-berry eyes quick with life glittering up at Rupert coyly, slyly, savagely. Rupert, etched as with stone, head upflung, put back his lips and showed her his teeth as if he could feel her between them and, like a wild animal, was savouring the moment before he ground her in his jaws.

"Get out of my way, woman," he said presently, softly. There was no real pleasure in the panther's voice now, only the low growl of a threat. "You know I will put you out of it if you will not get out yourself."

An old apple-leaf hand flickered at the downward road. "I be not in thy way. Thy way—as thou hast always made it—be clear to thee."

"Art in my way!" Rupert barked. "Play no black marble, dragon games with me, old mother, for I am in no mood to be gentle."

For a moment the sloe-berry eyes jumped, lightly, but meaningfully to Margaret's face. The woman had never looked at her before: it felt strangely like a physical touch and Margaret's stomach recoiled, her shoulders flinched, unsure at first if it was a kindly touch or an unwelcome one. Almost at once the woman looked to Rupert again.

" 'Tis a game of black marble and dragon riddles itself that thou callest me old mother, that it be sharp in thy mouth as it is sweet in the mouths of all others. Thy eyes are all twisted in thy head. But I have one word left to give thee, old as thy fears and the very shadow of them."

Witching Hour screamed and jerked his head.

"What is the secret that lies at the heart of the dark star?" asked the woman, her hands unfolding as if she held something awful and powerful between them. "What has no voice but is screaming to be heard? When will hope wander out of the barrow? When will death come to us all?"

Her words filled Margaret with dread and a rush of blood like the scent of the last victory. She was not aware that she was not breathing. She was aware of Rupert's face, cold, white, fixed, as close to a kind of horror as he would let himself appear with Malbrey beside him. He parted his lips—he had clenched them—then tucked them together again, resisting the urge to touch his tongue to them. His hand lifted from the reins and stole out, silently, purposefully. The thing in his face, in his eyes, surfacing like a nightmare Margaret had pressed beneath pillows and suffocated, was clear and awful and chilling. But the woman was unmoved. She looked back into that face and smiled, an odd, dark softness in her ancient eyes. For a moment, wrapped in shadow and sunlight and a cloak flecked with the colours of a grouse's wing, she looked purely beautiful.

Rupert dropped his hand at his side. "You are beneath me," he said scornfully. "Your blood is not worth mixing in the mortar of my walls."

"And is hers?" The hand came out from the grouse's wing, sure, thin, veins standing clear in the mottled skin. It, too, seemed to touch Margaret across the distance.

"You would do well to leave her out of it."

"She cannot be left out of it. She is heart and soul with it," the woman replied, scorn in her own voice now. "It seems, therefore, that her blood is pertinent."

Rupert jigged the reins, gathering up their slack. His calves tightened and Witching Hour, uneasy but responsive, began to shrug forward. "I am done with you. Do not let me—ever—see your face again."

Either by design or by animal impulse Witching Hour suddenly sprang forward, kicking out with his hind legs. The woman did not seem to mind. She stood placidly on the edge of wood and lane, wrapped and bent in her gold-flecked clothes, watching them ride by. Margaret, riding two abreast in the lane beside Rhea, had to brush right past the old woman. She looked down, conscious that it would have been rude not to, feeling the eerie prickling all along her arms even as she made herself do so, and touched gazes with her. She felt a ripple of power reach out from the woman, a sense of presence superior to her apple-withered frame, but the strange thing was that it felt like a salute. In a horrible rush Centurion's half-laughing words came back to her, and at the woman's salute a weight she did not want, but a weight she knew someone must carry, settled on her shoulders.

She was almost glad to arrive home that evening. The plum-coloured dusk was thick around them, rich with the sounds of cold rushing water and the rattle of the wind in the bare trees. The horses shuffled at an iron-shod trot up the drive, whickering to themselves contentedly as the numerous golden lights shone out at them from the house windows. Margaret felt the expectation of warmth on her skin. In the yard they left their horses with the crooked, shadowy figure of old Hobden, who grunted and said nothing, and with the maid and manservant carrying their luggage they crowded into the candlelit hallway that opened on the yard. Margaret could feel the blue smell of wood-smoke richly, warmly in her nose. Something in her middle relaxed.

That worried her.

Rupert turned to her. "The baron and I have things to discuss. I will have your supper sent up to your room. Doubtless," he added quietly, mockingly, "you would prefer it that way."

Malbrey exchanged places with Livy and loomed up behind him them, dark in the shadows and flecked gold with the light where his hair and beard were silver-coloured. Feeling him so close, so huge, Margaret's tired senses jangled with panic. She stepped away, then remembered to say good-night—Malbrey rumbled something equally polite—trying like a blind juggler to show neither her panic nor how glad she felt to be rid of them. Stiff from riding, her book clutched in her hand, she retraced the familiar yet surreal hallways and staircase until the knob of her own door, cold from the winter and disuse, sent a single silver bar of consciousness into her mind.

She clicked the latch back and went into her room. The lights were burning; someone had set a fire in the hearth and it was blazing merrily, casting a hollow, dancing glow of red over the long room. She felt it play like feathers on her face, and it was a kind, welcoming, relieving sort of feeling. The long three days at Lookinglass were behind her, much as she liked Lookinglass, and she was alone again without a need to smile and say the right thing or prove herself to anyone. Aching and hollow and brittle as the fire, she put her book down on a table full in the light, fetched a pen, and sat down before the open pages.

She was busily writing when Rhea came in with her bags. The maid said something coolly, reservedly, and Margaret promptly dismissed her without bothering to look up. After a few minutes the room was as it had been, empty but for the darkness and thin light, silent but for the crackle of the fire and the scratch of the scroll-worked iron nib across the page. She wrote with a chill running up the backs of her arms, for she wrote about the old woman.

When it was done and her mind had been emptied onto the page, she sat back with a heavy sigh, holding her right wrist, rubbing it between her fingers, staring into the deep blue heart of the fire until her eyes stung and she had to look away. She looked at the clock but it was too deeply in shadow for her to see. Surely it was late. She would dress and go down to the fox and sleep away the lost hours in the morning—for who would need her tomorrow? She pulled her stiffened body out of the chair and crossed to her bags.

It is Sunday, she thought as her hands yanked at the buckles, *and I got no rest today.*

She reached in for her heavy dressing robe, plunging past folded articles of clothing, and jarred her fingers violently against something long and flat and hard as her bruised bones. With a backward start she drew out her hand, hesitating, looking warily into the black depths of her bag. Her heart knocked hard at her ribcage. Then, in a single fluid motion, driven by curiosity, she swept up a candle from the table and knelt back down, holding the light aloft, driving the dark deeper, smaller, into the bottom of the bag. The light awoke gems from twisted hemlines and the flush of velvet from crumpled fabric—and the rose-red glint of leather binding. Even as she reached to pull it out, she heard Skander's voice in her mind and she knew what it was.

The title flashed out in gold, sweeping, flowing with the red light of the candle. But it was the author's name, though worn, glimmering only here and there in the embossing with gold, that pulled like magic at Margaret's eye: Songmartin. The blood shocked back to her heart. Strangely she saw Skander's face, the old woman's, Centurion's—stranger still, Brand's, fierce and tawny in the brown shadows and yellow firelight, played wildly across with the glint of light off a blade... Carefully she put it back in the bag, thrusting it to the bottom, and pulled out her dressing robe. Then, slinging the bag under her bed and slinging the robe around her shoulders, she took up her notebook, paused at the door to listen and, hearing nothing, passed out into the dark hallway.

It was a different woman who went down the hall and stairs and moved silently through the dining room toward the kitchen passageway. There was no fierce, defiant tempest, no will to die. But was there will to live? she wondered. A vaguely disquieting peace hounded her footsteps: the peace, she knew, of despair. Before her in the dark was a little fox-coloured flame, blue at its search-light heart, but the flame gave her no hope. It was a pleasant little blaze, confined as she was, at which she could warm her hands, but she had few illusions that it would do her any good. The long shadow of Rupert's game fell across even that and quenched it without mercy.

The lamp was burning, just as she remembered it. At the sound of her slipper-clad foot on the floor there was a flurry of red in the shadows, and the fox uncurled, springing up from his bed. The light shattered yellow on his eyes a moment, filling his face with an ominous glow, before he jogged forward and put the lamp behind him.

"Ding dong dell, kitty's in the well!" he cried. He came close and stood, tail swaying from side to side. A light awkwardness settled for a moment as they stared at one another—Margaret no longer knew quite what to say to the mocking coward at her feet—when the fox at last prompted, "So, you haven't forgotten me, after all... Was it as bad as you had anticipated?"

"No," she admitted. Then, after a struggle of emotions, she added, "And yes."

The sable-tipped ears twitched backward as a man might twitch a brow. "And yes? A'come: what went amiss for the belle of the ball?"

She sat down on an upturned crate, gathering her robe and the shadow of despair around her. The fox, too, sat. She met his gaze levelly, quietly, feeling the yawning hole of despair open wider in her soul—its edges were sharp, its darkness soft and inviting—but the despair seemed oddly easier to face down here with the white feather of a fox than it ever was up above. The fox might be a coward, a perfect dastard, but at least he understood misery. He could not do anything about it, but at least he understood. Even Skander could not do that.

"Everything went amiss. I feel dirty, and for Plenilune—they m-made up their minds about Rupert. There was nothing I could do."

The fox looked toward the cellar steps but he did not seem to be seeing anything. "Were they kind to you?" he asked at length.

"They." She laughed shortly, mirthlessly. "There were so many of them, like glass angels in church windows... They did not hate me as I thought they would, but neither did they really like me. I—I overheard them talking the first evening, talking about me. I shouldn't have eavesdropped, but I had to know what they thought."

The fox, having turned his head to her, looked quizzical.

"I suppose it was as I expected. Some of them were pitying, some of them were disquieted. One or two of them outright distrusted me."

"Do you trust you?"

To Margaret's surprise she went looking for the mockery in his tone and could not find it. "There was a man called Lord Gro

FitzDraco," she went stumblingly on after an awkward interval. "He was kind, I think. It...it was hard to tell *what* he was."

The fox barked merrily, a vicious, playful twinkle in his eye. "Gro? He sallied out of Gemeren for such a societal occasion as the New Ivy gala? Well, he would do it—for Capys' sake. He's got good marrow in his uncompromising bones, Lord Gro." The fox settled comfortably into a red loaf of body on the cellar floor. "He was kind to you?"

"I suppose so. He unnerved me a little. I could have managed him better had he been a bad man. I faced up to Malbrey tolerably, but only because I don't like him. Lord Gro was all manner of contradictory. He never wanted to talk, but he would always stand so close that conversation could not be avoided. I have a dreadful feeling he singled me out on several occasions because—because—because I look hunted."

She had not known what to expect from the fox when she made the confession—it galled her to say it—but she had certainly not expected the angry pale flash of the eyes nor the black backward curl of lips from the small, sharp teeth. What she found most frightening was that she saw in his face her own helpless anger, spiteful and sudden, lashing out against powers neither of them could hope to sway.

"I did not hear him say so," she hurried on before the fox could say anything in her defence. She did not want a coward coming to her defence just then. "I overheard Skander Rime telling it to Rupert. Lord Gro had spoken to Skander about me."

The fox skimmed over this remarkable outspokenness on the taciturn nobleman's part and noticed instead: "You seem to have done an awful lot of eavesdropping."

"There was a lot to drop eaves on," Margaret retorted. "I don't understand the problem with eavesdropping, anyway. If people don't want others to be offended, they oughtn't say cruel things at all."

"True," said the fox. "When you find a place like that, I'll go there too." A little more considerately he asked, "Was it very difficult, having everyone looking at you and talking about you?"

"Sometimes. Some people were kind: a few people I could converse with and not remember that I am from Earth and that I have come here under discomforting circumstances. Some people were genuinely kind. Lord Gro, in his way, was one of those. I am not used to him yet, but I think I begin to like him a little."

"And others?"

Mentioning Lord Gro dredged up the memory of the cold log in the wood and the strangely sweet, sharp-edged moment of companionship she had shared and the awful confused ache for things she could neither envision nor understand. She felt dirty and cold and lonesome, and knew she would never again share such a moment with another soul, so clean and level, so simple: merely two souls bound together in a moment of melancholy. *It is the melancholy of this place which calls out to me,* she thought, *for that is what binds us all in this life.*

When the fox repeated himself she came back out of her miserable thoughts with a start. "The others? I hardly know. I did not really get to *know* any of them. I did not like any of Rupert's friends, but then, I never expected to."

The fox looked interested. "Who was there? Do you remember?"

Margaret unfolded and picked up her notebook. "I kept a list here. Malbrey from Talus Perey was there. He is here now, actually; he came back with us on his way to his home."

"Malbrey is here? I thought I smelled a rat."

"Yes... And that awful Lord Bloodburn from Hol was there as well."

"By the twelve houses!" the fox cried, getting impulsively to his feet. "You met Bloodburn? Would that I had been there. I am sorry you met him alone."

There was no mockery in his tone, nor even cowardice, and it made Margaret's brief inclination to self-pity even harder to fight against. The face of Bloodburn returned to her, pale, weathered, scarred, and grey, like stone, like Caesar: a thrill of cold horror raced along her skin. Compared to that wretched Hol, Lord Gro looked beatific. With a desperate diving motion of the mind she swerved away. "You know Bloodburn?"

"Yes, I've seen him." Realizing he had risen, the fox bewilderedly found his seat again. "I have probably seen almost everyone you met at the gala. Name to me some others. Test my memory."

Margaret turned her book to the light, in which her fine script flashed up spidery-jet on the warm crisp pages. "To the best of my knowledge I have put them together by county—or House. I think you call them Houses here."

"Nay, Honours," the fox corrected her. "The Houses are the families which oversee them. You call them 'Counties' in your world?"

"Oh—well—perhaps—not quite." Margaret coloured with confusion and rushed on from the compromising subject of England. "I have grouped people according to their Honours. Of course there was Skander Rime." She peered at the script: the lamp was not very adequate. "FitzDraco was there, and Malbrey from Marenové—I mean, the Mares. Bloodburn and his wife and their son came up from Hol-land, and Centurion was there from Darkling-law. I am sure I have misspelled this name: Orzelon-gang. Mark Roy and Romage and their sons Aikin and Brand were there. From Thrasymene were Black Malkin—I like not *her* looks: she curdles my stomach—and Grane and Woodbird. Woodbird was...interesting."

The fox had looked attentive all the while, nodding at each name as though marking them off in his memory. "Oh?" he queried. "How so, interesting?"

For a moment Margaret looked away into the middle distance, re-conjuring the image of the youngest of the Thrasymene women—a woman not much older than herself. Across distance and time the picture seemed fantastic, too fantastic to be true: an upward rush of white feather, a brief golden glance, a piercing of eyes and a scornful, half-sharing jest. It seemed unreal. It seemed like a dream.

"She reminds me of a fairy-tale, of a gypsy-princess enchanted into a swan."

The fox was smiling when she looked at him. "You have the makings of a Fool yourself," he remarked. "I don't clearly recall the last time I laid my eyes on Woodbird Swan-neck. I don't remember her being very promising, but then people do change... So she is a gypsy-princess now? I wonder if she was jealous of you."

"Of *me*?" She was taken violently aback. For a moment she did not know whether to be outraged or to laugh. A laugh escaped, harsh and derisive. "Whyever should Woodbird be jealous of *me*? Is there aught between her and Skander? I thought I caught something."

"Did you think so? People do change... I recall there was something between them, and might have come to something save that there is bad blood between the generations just past of Capys and Thrasymene. Skander Rime and Woodbird Swan-neck might have lief forgot the bad blood, but it is in my mind that the lady's older sisters were not so ready."

The pretty script that formed Woodbird's full name shone in the lamplight, magical, running silver in places when the light flowed against it. "Ah. Then I am sorry. Skander, I thought, is still trying. I am not sure about Woodbird. She seems...conflicted."

"A commonplace malady among Plenilune ladies, it seems." The fox sat up, throwing out his fluffy white waistcoat. "You don't think much of Skander Rime?"

Another derisive laugh escaped, this time by way of Margaret's nose. "I think well of him. If I dared I would marry him to spite Rupert. But I wouldn't dare. I know what Rupert would do." How curious it was that marriage continued to be a means of spiting someone else. A horrible ache twisted Margaret's gut—only for an instant, but the pain was almost unbearable.

The brow-whiskers jigged meaningfully upward. "We do like our women gypsy-wise. I am willing to bet my cosy pillow-bed that there were quite a few bucks at the gala who would have made an eye at you, but didn't dare for Rupert."

His words, perfectly sincere beneath their veneer of mockery, warmed Margaret greatly and took the edge off her profound ache. "Do you think so, in spite of all they said?"

"I never said we weren't suspicious of outsiders, especially outsiders who are lining men up to take the Overlordship. But yes, I rather think so. Why?" He peered up into her face. "Are you afflicted with that feminine disease which causes you to think yourself unfavourable?"

The blush was growing out of hand. "I could hardly help that," she replied sharply. "And I sometimes wish I wasn't—

favourable. I'm afraid Rupert begins to think me more and more beautiful to his eye, as well as having what he calls 'wit.' I was never considered very beautiful at home—"

"What a rummy place you must come from."

"Fox—"

"You *do* have the gypsy-beauty."

Lips pursed, thoughts conflicting, Margaret stared down at him, and he stared back, sincerity and mockery warring in his wall-eyes and white teeth. At first she had been pleased and thought that he was flattering her in a friendly, genuine way, but his persistence was making her more and more self-conscious and uneasy, especially on Rupert's account. For a long moment she struggled with being helplessly angry at the fox. Then it struck her that he was being friendly, quite friendly, as a friend would be: not a mere acquaintance, but a friend. He was being honest.

"What would a fox know of such things?" she asked warily.

He gave her such a look that she wondered if he guessed the half of her thoughts "Not being well acquainted with the specie in general, I couldn't say—but this fox is generally considered knowledgeable in many things."

She rubbed at her eye with a knuckle and placed her arms around her knees. She wondered if it would do to tell him that gypsies were not considered beautiful in her world; she decided that it would not do, and she knew without deliberately admitting it that she was glad that he had called her any sort of beautiful. He was only a fox, but he said it without wanting to get anything out of it for himself, as Rupert did, or because he was jealous—he was only a fox—as some other woman might. In the wake of realizing that with the fox she could be her own unmasked person, she caught herself once again on the brink of reaching out to stroke him.

But it was he who reached, gently, with his voice. "You look tired."

She shut her eyes. "I nearly died yesterday."

There was hollow quiet beyond her black lids. Then, "Did you indeed?"

She opened her eyes and the book and showed him the place where she had begun the account of the boar-hunt. It was too surreal and at once too painful to tell him aloud. She let him read it as one might read a piece of fiction. Her weary hand held the book tremblingly open, his flashed across the dark script, black brows drawn in thought as the scenes, not the words, played behind the flickering wall-colour. "Well," he breathed at last, and looked beyond the book into her face, lingering as if to read there what was hidden between the lines on the page.

"They liked me better for it," Margaret said with hard, cold iron in her voice, "but I think they would have liked it better still if Aikin had not been just in time to save me."

"Too bad then that Aikin was just in time—but when they know you better still I think they will have still better cause to thank him for his quick thinking."

"I do not want them to know me better. I am here because of Rupert, and because of me they have had to give him what he asked for."

But the fox shook his head. "Don't overburden your shoulders with responsibility—they are too pretty for that weight. They would have given Rupert what he asked for regardless. Who—" a fierce, cutting, angry bitterness came inexplicably into his voice "—who can deny him when he puts out his hand to take a thing?"

"Why," Margaret asked, "do you keep the light burning down here? Don't you ever sleep?"

He looked at the lamp as if seeing it for the first time. Then he smiled, the soft mockery diffusing in his voice again. "Perhaps I am afraid of the dark."

She sighed and rubbed at her weary face again. Her soul was heavy; her eyelids were heavy. "The old woman did."

"Pardon?"

With an almost physical effort she drew up the will to speak. "The old woman denied him. I have never seen Rupert so frightened by anyone before. I have denied him—no, I have defied him, but I suppose I have always given in one way or another." Bitterness, wry, angry bitterness twisted in her gut. "But *she* denied him. She flung back all his pride and power in his face and did not even flinch. She laughed at him as none of us could laugh at him."

"The old among us are free to laugh when life becomes thin and pale under our touch," the fox observed. "You say she frightened him?"

Margaret smiled wistfully at the memory. It was bitter-sweet in her mouth. "It was like a parable or a story from the Bible. Thrice they met, and each time I felt him winning over his fear with sound anger. The last time it was a struggle for him, for she scared him very badly."

"And what did she say?"

She took up her book and turned to the hastily scribbled lines, but this time she read them aloud to feel the painful sweetness of the words in her own mouth.

"What is the secret that lies at the heart of the dark star? What has no voice but is screaming to be heard? When will hope wander out of the barrow? When will death come to us all?"

The puzzle had much the same effect on the fox as it had on Rupert. He rose swiftly and backstepped as if from a viper that had been dropped suddenly in his path. It frightened Margaret to see his face unguarded—she had not known how guarded it had been before—and to know she carried a strange power in those riddling words not know what that power could do.

The fox cast about for a thing he could not see, bearings he could not get. She could see his compass-needle swinging wildly. "It is late," he said finally, roughly. "You should go. It is late and you are tired. Go to bed, Margaret."

She opened her mouth to speak but no words came. Then, through the blind grey a swift, red-coloured rage crashed over her and she rose, quickly, and turned to go. Her throat was too tight for words; her eyes smarted with hurt tears. Blindly, clutching her book as if she could strangle it, she strode toward the steps.

"Wait!" the fox barked. She stopped. "Wait—no, come back. I am sorry."

"It is late," she replied flatly. "I need to get to bed. I've had a long day."

"Get back here and don't be such a woman," the fox snapped. "You will only cry yourself to sleep and I—I will know it."

Margaret turned to look at him. He stood on the rim of the light, small, wearing the fire pricked on each whisker-tip. Had he been Rupert, she thought clearly, he would have come after her and yanked her back by the arm. But he stood still, rigid, the uncanny back-light from the lamp turning his eyes into glowing saucers.

"What do you care?" she asked ungraciously.

"Does anybody else?" he retorted.

She went back, slowly. She had known the moment she stopped at the sound of his imperious voice that she would go back, but she went back slowly, suddenly very tired and very cold and very lonely. As a gesture almost of peace, the fox sat down on the wine crate beside her, touched her knee once, and settled into a brooding silence. She felt that neither of them were thinking about the riddle, but carefully steering away from the words that were upsetting every mind they fell upon, like a ship's prow churning up the sea. Finally, as the silence drew out and her staying began to seem ridiculous, she tried to redeem it with blind, tired ignorance.

"Fox?"

"Yes?"

"I don't understand. What is all this—this discontent—about the Overlord? Is he a sort of king, then? And if they do not like Rupert, why can't they choose someone else?"

"Would that they could!" the fox laughed harshly. "No one wants Rupert, but it isn't as though anyone actually dares say 'no' to him on the matter."

She recalled the dark, flashing looks that could spring at the least provocation into the man's eyes, the looks of murder, the looks which reckoned nothing of the worth of human life, only power, only himself. No, no one would want him, but no one would dare say nay. Only she had dared, in her small, petty, ineffectual way: and he had shown her up quick enough and made her obedient.

But the fox had not finished. He seemed to deliberate for a few moments, looking away with the lamplight glassy in his eyes, as if to find the right words. His countenance was unusually doleful. "The Overlord," he began at last, consideringly, "is more than just a man with a title. He is more than a king or a mere strategist or a high judge presiding over quarrels." He looked round at her, light breaking up against and throwing itself off the quicksilver mirror of his eyes. His voice was low and urgent, with a shiningness about it that made Margaret's heart quicken.

"The Overlord is Plenilune itself. He is its heart, he is its soul: he is the dark lodestone that lies at the core of everything."

"A dark lodestone indeed," said Margaret after a brief, heavy quiet, "would Rupert be."

The fox grinned up at her, all his little white teeth showing. "A dark lodestone indeed, which cannot find true north. It is a good joke," he added, his body jigging to the quickness of his foxy breathing, "don't you think?"

But the joke rang hollow with Margaret. With renewed vigour the inexplicable pangs in her chest returned, twisting upward into her brain images of the fells and the snow-hushed pine-woods, the glimpses of deep black lakes round the spurs of the hills. She saw the mews full of hawks and the kennels full of hounds. She heard the echo of proud Blue-bottle Glass declaring his power to the world. No, no one would want Rupert. Not even Plenilune.

And her heart ached because of that.

"No," he said musingly, half to himself. "I see it is no more humorous to you than it is to me." Suddenly his voice rasped like a sword being drawn. "If only I—the bastard— ...Forgive me."

She put her forehead in her palm. "For what? It is only what I say to myself a thousand times a day. I am n-not myself anymore. My country and its ways have no place among these people. I must find my own way—or learn theirs, as the case seems to be. I do not think I will ever see home again. I do not—I d-do not—I do not know if I *want* to."

The cool pad of a paw touched her knee again, cold through her gown where the robe had slipped off and the fabric was thin. "I think we have talked too long," said her companion, "and we are too young to find the humorous transience in things. You had better go to bed or we will be opening one of these bottles and drowning our enormous sorrows and all the sorrows of the Honours together, you and I. I can't imagine drunkenness becomes you."

"So we will drown things in sleep?"

He smiled. "For now, and later—did I not say?—we will look for a break in the wall." He slipped off the crate and walked forward, pulling her after him through the pool of lamplight toward the base of the cellar stair where the dark flowed down and faded away. "You remembered and you came, and I think you will remember and come again. I—" he flashed her an apologetic look over his shoulder. "I get lonesome down here."

"And I," she heard herself saying. "I get lonesome up there."

"It is a rummy world."

She had hoped, a little, that he would go up with her, but her hope had no real foundation and broke up quickly when he sat down, as he had before, on the dirt floor to watch her go. Somehow that did not matter so much now, nor did she hate him so desperately for his cowardice. She let sleeping foxes lie and went on alone. But at the foot of the stair she turned back for one thing more.

"You know, I think I asked God for comfort. I asked it badly, because I know God badly, but he was the only one to ask. I was not sure he would answer, but I never expected him to send it in the form of a fox."

The fox shifted forward as if pulled by her words, but he did not rise. "Mayhap you are asleep," he coaxed sibilantly, "and I am but a dream from beyond the gates of horn... Good night, Margaret."

"Good night, fox."

XIII | THE WHITE ONES

The morning was bright and cold. There had been no snow in Seescardale: the land lay jewel-cut and clear beneath a fair winter sky and the winds, sharp and incessant, blew down from the north between the fells and burned Margaret's face as she stepped out of the house into the mocking sunlight. The thin, pale sunlight which promised warmth and gave none, and the silvery, rushing winds were more companionable to her than the two men she had slipped away from. She had left them in the withdrawing room, talking quietly and animatedly to each other about things that eluded her hearing. Restless and bored and disliking the company of them both, Margaret had got away at the earliest possible moment.

With one hand on her shawl wrapped about her head, her other gathering her skirts about her ankles, she ran across the yard and ducked out into the face of the wind. The roses bunching and climbing up the yard walls were roaring like a storm-tossed sea of silver and green. The windbreak across the pasture was struggling at its job: the wind was in everything, roaring, thundering, buffeting, drowning out everything but the water-droplet notes of a blackbird who was perched in one elm, high up, where the wind was tossing it about with reckless abandon.

She found old Hobden planting bulbs. She had not realized that she had been looking for him until her scattered wandering with and against the wind brought her to the end of a bit of low, sloping earthwork and she found him on his knees, hands almost black with loam, digging holes for the plants. She watched him for a moment, waiting for him to look round. When he kept on silently working and did not seem to notice even her racing shadow, she folded up and sat down in the sunlit lee of the earthwork, the wind finally cut off and the light finally feeling warm on her skin.

"Tha's back," said old Hobden, glancing up once from under his badger brows.

"I'm back."

He went back to working. His gnarled, walnut-coloured hands with their blunt fingernails encrusted with dirt worked deftly at the pale bulbs, and carried each one tenderly as if it were a baby. Margaret, with her head back against the slope of earthwork, watched him blindly for a few minutes. A weariness pulled at her body—and no wonder. She had slept through odd hours and well into midmorning, and the past three days from which she had emerged had taxed her more than she had at first realized. In the sun-warmed lee of the earthworks with the wind rushing overhead, the gentle slope of Marenové and the whole of Seescardale spread out before her under a curl of earth, and old Hobden grumbling good-naturedly over his bulbs beside her, Margaret sat back and revelled in her weariness. The sun felt good; the open air blew cleanly through her veins.

She tucked her skirts around her legs and drew her knees up. From the depths of her pocket she withdrew Skander's book, the faintest twinge of guilt quickly flickering away with the rushing light. She felt the darkened leather cover and pale inner lining with the soft of her thumb. It was curiously lovely for being such an old, battered thing—clearly it had been restitched at least once—but as her hand fell flat upon the cover of it, she felt intuitively that it was the loveliness of souls that made the little, simple thing shine out with a beauty that frightened her. And it did frighten her: what was in this innocuous little book that had prompted a reckless, wrinkled old woman to steal it from a respectable land-owner and hide it for Margaret in her own bag?

She supposed she was about to find out, but as she twisted her hand, sliding it under the cover to turn it back, she stopped, frozen, knowing in that moment that she was at a cross-roads. If she turned back that cover and began reading, she would never be able to unlearn what she had read, nor would she have a choice to not act on whatever she learned. For a moment the world was devoid of Rupert and Skander, of crowns and sceptres, of bitterness and strife. It was only Plenilune and herself and Songmartin's little book. She stood upon a strange brink with them, knowing the choice lay before her, knowing she had already made it.

She turned back the cover. The wind, changing course, roared up the earthwork and fluttered the pages under her hand. Old Hobden grumbled beside her but she hardly heard him. Under a flurry of sunlight and soft flecks of dirt, Margaret began scanning through the pages, idly, reading pieces here and there as they flashed out at her. She buried deeper into the side of the earthwork, surrounded by the clean smell of winter air, the rich, dark scent of overturned dirt, and the smell, like no other, of old pages.

"*It is a mistake to suppose,*" said Songmartin in one paragraph, "*that mankind, though lost, has little to no understanding of virtue. On the contrary, he understands it almost better than the elect, for he feels the empty shape of it in his soul, the place where it ought to be; he feels the coldness of its receding shadow, knowing that no other thing can warm him as it can—and knowing that, if he could, he would be glad to be cold in its company than warm in the embrace of vice. Few men love vice: they fill the void inside them with their own pleasures, their own vices, and lie to themselves, calling these things virtues, though even they do not believe their own fantasies. They long for virtue as a man longs for his lover's face, knowing they will never grasp it back. They are encompassed by its shadow as the Great Blind Dragon encompasses Plenilune with its power—*"

Margaret started back and read the words again. Other words, *despair, restlessness of the soul, groping after God*, jostled on her vision, but the nonchalant and incredible words *the Great Blind Dragon* leapt off the yellowed page at her. What on earth—she pressed the heel of her hand to her temple as the treacherous phrase escaped again. Who was this, what was this impossible creature and this impossible power? She looked up, blinking through the smudge of black on her vision, pulling Seescardale into focus once more. In this weird but forward world, surely no one believed in dragons. There were no such things as dragons.

But then, there were also no such things as talking foxes.

The landscape turned alien under her eye; the grass under her hand burned cold. Even old Hobden, the most mundane and familiar of all images, twisted and looked strange. *Do not touch him,* she fought against her first impulse. *If he does not vanish, he may bite you.*

Slowly she got up, her fingers digging into the grass on the curve of earthwork to keep the wind from tearing her away. She meant to leave quietly, stealing away like the mystical thing she had seen in the Glassdale wood, but old Hobden caught her movement and looked up, rocking back on the balls of his feet, shoving the dirt out of his eyes with the back of his hand.

"I was never for book-learnin' neither," he said moodily. "Not one to sit tidy and muddle over words. Best be gettin' about and workin'. Good for the blood. Too much book-learnin' makes the blood go sour."

"I suppose so," said Margaret in a white voice. Then, to herself, *I want my horse. I want to ride away, just to get away. Why am I so terrified? What has changed? Why does that woman scare us all like this?*

What is this weird providence?

She found herself walking instead, leaving old Hobden behind, caught up in the full power of the wind as she went down the grassy slopes toward the road and the pastureland beyond. The Marenové trees were almost all bare, grey-brown, tossing images over a tawny turf. She was exposed in that open ground, but the power of the wind was the only thing greater than her inexplicable fear and she walked out in it, putting the house at her back, heedless of her own weariness and the inadequacy of her shoes. She walked to the lane, careful not to think, and made her way down the sodden path under the whirling branches until the lane met the road. There she turned southward, walking in and out of patchy sunlight, listening to the gurgle of a blackbird, the distant whistle of a shepherd, and the answering bark of a sheepdog. Autumn lay like beaten copper over the land, beaten by the wind, enamelled by the faience-blue sky. She walked the narrow edge of a blade of wind and wondered what was holding this curious world together. She had never asked, no more than she had asked about earth. There had been the reality of

Plenilune to deal with at first, and after that she had managed to take things in stride. Now, through a few black bars of lettering, a dead theologian from an alien world had managed to thrust her awareness down, like a spade into dark loam, into a deeper world where things could be felt but not touched, believed but never seen.

She stopped at the end of the bend of the road and looked back, up the howl of wind, up the roaring avenue of scarlet barberry. The empty hole of conscience, a dragon, a man who could do magic, a fox that could talk... They all seemed strangely thin and pale in the face of that wind, no more than a few tossing red leaves, small under her eye, and she smiled self-deprecatingly as they blew past her, into her, and settled in the stillness of her mind.

I will ask Rupert to let Centurion and his siblings stop here on their way to the University. I must learn some kind of hospitality, and Centurion...he was kind. Though God knows I loath kindness just now.

She retraced her steps and blew in at the front door of the house, wind-swept and wild-looking. She caught a glimpse of herself in the hall clock, moon-coloured, her hair like a falcon's fury. Then her gaze shifted and she saw the clock-hands: it was past noon. Her stomach called out to the clock. Putting her book into her pocket she strode to the dining room doorway and looked in.

Rupert was alone. He was sitting back with an empty plate pushed away, soiled utensils on the side of it, surrounded by a collection of papers that were covered in curious lettering, circles, and squares. He was holding a book in one hand, deep into its contents, but he looked up as she appeared.

"You missed Malbrey," he said without preamble. "He just left."

Margaret almost said, "I thought the air smelled cleaner," but she caught herself. Rupert had dropped his gaze back to his book and did not see her jerk at her mouth as she bit off the words before they could make a sound. "Did I miss luncheon?"

"No." Without looking up he put out his hand and struck a little bell on the table. There was a pause, then the slowly advancing noise of footsteps in the kitchen hallway, and presently one of the maids came through with her food. Margaret sat down, spread her napkin on her lap, and for awhile there was no sound in the room but the clink of silverware and the occasional rustle of paper.

Rupert seemed withdrawn, quietly occupied, but putting a finger on the pulse of his mood Margaret felt he was almost pleased. She did not know what breed of omen that might be. On occasion there was a chancy look on his face which she was sure he was unaware of, but with the merest flicker of an eyelid, down-turned toward another piece of writing, it would vanish again. Full of food and warm with wine, oddly detached as if the wind had dislodged her from her own body—though the odd pound of her heart still beat through into her mind—she reached out with a question, feeling as if she reached out to touch a wild animal.

"Who, or what," she asked, "is the Great Blind Dragon?"

The wild animal stiffened as if an electric charge had been run through him, then he leapt from his chair and slashed his hand to the side. Papers whirled and shredded from the force of the gesture. Margaret felt as if all the air had been ripped from her lungs. She staggered forward across the table, choking, lungs spasming, burning, her brain's light wavering for want of breath. Her chair crashed over sideways—she hit the floor with a dull, jarring thud. The world was going grey at the edges. She could not *breathe!*

Suddenly Rupert was there, kneeling at her side, and the weight seemed to wrench off her chest. She hauled in breath after breath, each breath clawing her throat like a knife. Her skull was burning. Pain throbbed behind her eyes. She could feel him touching her, trying to help her, but the panic which had filled her mouth came out in a sharp, angry cry and she pushed him away. Sliding, blind, she fell against the upturned wreck of the chair and hung on its arm, gasping, blinking until the world stopped swimming and the burning and throbbing had dulled. Through the sharp lights and greyed blurring on her vision she could see him crouched next to her, arms draped over his knees, fists clenched, jaw thrust out angrily.

"I'm sorry I lost my temper," he said gruffly. "You made me angry without warning."

"Don't apologize!" she snapped. The words were dry and hurt in her throat. "You should have thought of that before!" But she knew it was her own fault: she had known, instinctively, that she was asking an impossible question and that he would not like it. All the same, his unguarded fury had given her the answer she had been looking for.

It filled her with an odd sense of victory.

With an angry sigh he pushed upward, got an arm under her, and deposited her back into the righted chair. He sat down beside her, withdrawn and quiet. She did not like what she saw in his face. She wanted to leave, to go back to her room or to find the fox, but she dared to do neither.

"They say the road to hell," he began at length, "is smooth and trod with ease. That is a lie. It is set at every turn with outposts of the enemy—turn but a stone, and start a wing!—" he laughed harshly, almost self-deprecatingly. "It is only by sheer luck that the small-minded people do not know how close they come to heaven's doors and yet slip by, by the skin of their teeth. I am not so lucky. I know the war I am in. I know the danger of the road ahead. I have long since counted the cost. It is not an easy road." His eyes flickered to hers, focused on something beyond them, and flickered away again. Their passing left her skin crawling cold. "Everywhere they lay their traps. Everywhere they wreck my way—in law, in council, in men like Skander and—" he broke off hotly and repositioned himself in the chair as if he sat on a burning coal and must get off it "—in the very soul of me! They have cut me to the quick at times and they are knowing it. Lief I am to throw them off and put them behind me, but a part of me is afraid."

She turned her head, quizzical in spite of herself.

His eyes fell upon her glass, full of liquid golden light: a tiny, beautiful thing all alone on the table. "I am afraid to put them behind me. Better it would be to have them ever before me, and to take the kingdom by storm, than to throw them back and, in thinking they are gone, be caught up unawares from behind. The harder road is the road that I must take. But I fear for my soul while I take it."

"Almost I pity you," Margaret said, strained and cold, "for you are greatly deluded."

Without looking at her he reached out, set his palm against her cheek, and turned her head away.

She tightened her jaw under the cold pressure of his fingers. "While I am asking you questions that you hate, I might as well ask this: I want Centurion and his siblings to stop here on their way to the University. It is only polite."

"Is that a question?" Rupert growled.

She turned against the force of his hand. "No. Because I know you will not let me have my way if I ask nicely. And in this I want my way."

He sighed and seemed suddenly weary, worn out, a huge, sharp-angled shadow: his profile was the grim sketch of all great men. "I forget that you are English."

She could leave then. Swallowing back the rawness that was still in her throat, she said, "Then I will write a letter, and you will post it: I do not know your addresses here."

She wrote the letter that afternoon, seated in the dining room where the late light fell in through the western window and flooded her little desk so that it seemed she wrote, not with atrament, but with gold. She made it out to Centurion, and felt almost at once the sense of ignorance hemming her in. Who was he really? What were his titles? She hoped he would forgive her for not knowing; she did not feel brave enough anymore to ask Rupert, though he sat on the other side of the room doing his 'star-work,' as Skander had called it. Odd, she thought, how getting one's way could be so empty in the end. She wrote with delicate politeness, but made it clear that she was serious: this was more than a formality and was not meant to be gently brushed off, refused, and returned. At the end she signed it, which was the hardest thing of all. A horrible confusion welled up at her out of the characters. Her own surname seemed meaningless, detached from herself; she did not want the title 'de la Mare,' or even 'of the Mares.' To belong to Plenilune was a thing she did not dare assume, nor was she at all sure, even now, if she wanted such a place. She stuck with her thin, brittle English name, whose Saxon overtones and history meant nothing now—but it was all she had.

"Well, no, I don't really know anything about them, save that they are called the White Ones. Centurion was never very loquacious about them."

Margaret supposed that was the best she could expect from a fox, but she had been hoping for more. Doggedly, she asked, "Why are they called the White Ones?"

Having finished the scraps of pork-rib and goose-liver which she had managed to sneak down to him, the fox curled up lazily on the floor, shivering as if with a kind of private, sleepy delight. "Presumably because they are. Art not content to wait and see with your own eyes? They will be here soon."

"No," retorted Margaret. "I like to know what to expect. I almost did not think Centurion would accept the invitation, though I put my best prose into the letter. Rupert had been very untoward about it at Lookinglass. He talked about them as if they were an embarrassment, and Centurion—well, he wasn't very loquacious about it, but I had not seen someone get so under his skin as Rupert did."

The wall-eyes flicked sideways, flashing in the lamplight. "Rupert, I think, makes a special study of getting under people's skin."

Listening to what lay between the fox's words, Margaret's own skin ran suddenly cold. The fox, too, seemed to hear the shadows of his words and went on quickly.

"I get the impression that a lot of people think the White Ones unlucky in some way, though I've never heard of any unluck that came to anyone in conjunction with them. Darkling is still rich and prosperous, last word trickled down to me. Still, I understand that Centurion keeps them well out of people's way. I am surprised that he is sending them to the University."

"I don't believe in luck. But the odd thing is, through the weird, half-shaped images I get of them, I feel akin to them in some way." She looked into the fox's eyes and saw a kind of understanding there, as she knew she would: she would never have dared say it to anyone but him. "I suppose that is why I want to meet them. I know what it is like to be thought unlucky, to be shut up and belong nowhere and to no one."

The sheeny black nostrils flared. "It is in my mind that heaven is fond of those who don't belong."

"Then I should be heaven's favourite!" returned Margaret with helpless agitation.

"Perhaps."

With a sigh she put her book down on the floor beside her. She had meant to ask the fox about the dragon, but remembering how disturbed he had been by the old woman's riddle, just as Rupert had, she decided at the last moment not to chance it. She did not think she could bear being hurt by him again. She did not think she could bear hurting him. She said instead,

"It smells like the last of autumn up there. Bonfires, the bare ploughland, geese flying toward Darkling... The barberry is beautiful."

He nodded, staring blindly at her feet as if he saw, instead of her shoes, the images she conjured up. "Sometimes I smell it, even down here. And I feel it in my bones. Most things grow restless when spring pulls the sap up the trees: I grow restless when the dogwoods curl their leaves with scarlet."

"You would," Margaret said impulsively.

The fox looked up at her, quizzical.

"I walked in the autumn wind the other day, all the way down the lane to the road, and it seemed the earth—the landscape—was beaten out of copper like your fur. I thought of you in the back of my mind, as if thinking of the wind and the landscape and the smell of autumn were the same as thinking of you."

He smiled and looked away. "Funny odd thing, that," he murmured wistfully.

She realized, too late, that she had hurt him again.

With the softness in his voice that was like gentling a wound or bruise, he said, "When next Centurion comes this way they will be holding the ceremony for the Overlord, won't they?"

Margaret nodded. His voice, aimless and careful, gentle as though he did not want to jar his own soul, opened a gaping wound in her. She heard Rupert's words again—"*I am playing the long game*"—and she saw his face, the face of a great man hell-bent upon his purpose. And she knew, keenly, clearly, that no sooner had he got the Overlordship than he would turn with all his force upon the conquest of her heart. She knew, too, just as clearly, that he would crush it before he would win it, but crush it most assuredly he would.

The fox's voice lay lightly on her ear. "Autumn makes one melancholy, doesn't it?"

She forced a smile for him. "Yes, I think it must. Though I cannot think why! It is so beautiful."

The luminescent eyes gazed up at her, softly, mockingly: they seemed to see right into her. "Why, that is the very answer to your riddle. The sharpness of the sharpest beauty lies in the law that such things do not last long. This world quenches them too quickly: we all know that, and that is why they hurt us."

His words did not help. They sat in silence for several minutes while the melancholy built inside of Margaret until she thought she would break with it. Finding something to lash out at, to alleviate some of the pain, she said fiercely, "I wish it would not happen!"

As a man might put his arms about himself and clench them tight, crushing an inner agony, the fox clenched his little sides, all their bones showing through the fur. She had expected him to offer some comfort, but he said nothing.

"I should go," she said at last, flatly, aware of the bitterness like silt and brine washing in her words. "We are expecting Centurion tomorrow. I should be ready for this one last triumph of mine."

"The only one," the fox murmured before he could think.

She stared at him, furious, but mute because she knew it was the truth. He, too, seemed to hang horrified on his words, though nothing showed in his face. Finally he scrubbed at his muzzle with one forepaw, hard, digging the claws in, and said roughly, "Goodnight, Margaret. Thank you for the food. Rhea seems to have forgot that I eat. Again."

But she seemed rooted to the old upturned wine crate as if the combined, shapeless, immense weight of their sorrow had come down on her shoulders and held her there. To her horror his thoughtless words, all the truer for their thoughtlessness, stung tears at the back of her eyes. She saw Kinloss again—a hateful premonition—and her brief victory over Rupert in the matter of Centurion and the White Ones showed itself to be a mere shadow. No, more worthless than a shadow, for where there are shadows there is light, and Margaret saw no promise of light anywhere. For a long while she sat in the fox's silence, looking for a way out, looking for a break in the wall, stumbling blindly down the lines of black between the stars, stumbling into nothing but the black.

What good is virtue, she wondered, *to those who are perishing?*

She whispered, "Promise me you will tell me the truth."

Out of the corner of her eye she saw him turn toward her, hang a moment on the last frayed edge of silence. "Have I ever told you anything else?" he asked.

She broke her blind staring and looked hard into his face, summoning a swift wave of rage to bring the blood back into her voice. "Promise me."

She felt his eyes digging into her, picking at her thoughts like fingers picking at harp-strings. "I promise."

Once more she was at the cross-roads, knowing that once she turned the words over on her tongue and let them loose, once the fox had held good to his word, there would be no turning back, no unlearning what he told her. And yet, she had to know.

"Has Rupert ever had a woman before?"

Surprise, so quick it was hardly there, glinted in the fox's eyes. He made a move as if to get up, as if he were uneasy, but seemed to catch himself before he did and quelled the motion. The movement made her wonder, in a detached way, if he had not grown a little in size, or if it was only a trick of the light cast by the lamp. He said presently, warily, as if stepping gently on all his words lest he break them, "I never saw or heard any evidence that would support suspicion of a liaison. I don't believe anyone ever roused his interest. He is not exactly," he lifted one paw rhetorically, "what one would call a philanthropist... Why do you ask?"

She bit back a wince. She knew he would ask but had hoped desperately that he would not. Every inch of her felt exposed and every nerve felt raw and her stomach was a mass of knots and sickness. She almost refused but she knew that somehow he would get it out of her, gently or not, so she threw herself blindly into it. "I just thought that—as if I had a choice—it would be easier knowing that—that I was the first—that I was the *only*—"

"By all the stars—" he cut her off in a choked voice. He looked horrified, far more horrified than even she felt. "Margaret, you can't—you can't actually be thinking of marrying him!"

"I don't know!" she cried. But she did know. She hid her face in her hands to get away from those cold pale eyes. They were like looking into a mirror of her own terror. "I—I am just so tired of fighting him. Nothing I can say or do makes any difference. You said yourself it does no good. Every time I defy him I feel as though I am dashing against a rock. He takes it and does not move, and I am the only one who gets hurt. I thought that if I fought him he would give up on me and let me go home." She struck her fist on her knee so strongly she felt it bruise. "I do not even know if I *want* to go home. I am confused and tired and...and I cannot bear it any longer."

She had expected the fox to lash back instantly, full of sharp sentiment against the man who had locked him down in a dark cellar, but her words fell into a hollow, stinging quiet. When she looked at him, the fox was staring off into his own thoughts with the look of one gazing at a nightmare, and when at last he spoke, still staring unblinkingly, his voice was hard but quiet. "You know that if you do it you will regret it every day for the rest of your life."

She knew that. It was the only thing clear to her, but it made the sickness in her middle worsen to hear him put it to her so frankly.

When she said nothing he looked at her sharply, half-angry and half-afraid. "Margaret," he said in a husky voice that cut her to the quick. "Please don't."

Everything was falling away. Everything was breaking into shards. She knew that if she held that gaze or let that tone hang in her ears she would lose her dark certainty. With a sob she pressed her palms to her eyes and cried hysterically, "I'm just so *tired*, fox! I can't bear it anymore!"

He laid his paw upon her knee. "Then let me bear it for you."

His touch was like the fire-glow of the autumn wind, cold, personal, searching in a horrible, painful way, wearing at her defences so that, even as she knew it was hopeless, she wanted desperately to loose herself from earth and fling herself into the grip of that crimson gale.

But how could she, when the creature asking to carry her cross would not even crawl out of his own prison?

"Fox," she whispered, "I must go."

"Margaret—" he began softly, then seemed to choke himself off again. "Good-night, Margaret. Come again soon?" It sounded in her ears, as she broke apart her fingers and lowered her hands, like a question, as though he was unsure if he had overstepped the bounds and barred her from him. His voice was gentle, touching her hesitantly as though she, and not he, were the wild animal on the brink of shying away. "It gets damned lonely down here..."

"Good-night, fox."

She rose and left him, left the golden circle of light, and walked back, alone, into the darkness and into a quiet, quenched despair, the image of Kinloss' face clear before her tear-blind eyes.

She passed Rupert in the hall on the way to her room. He was stepping into his chambers, the light kindling on the curve of his face as on the upraised blade of the executioner's axe. He stopped and watched her approach. She felt numb to his silvery, searching eye, piercing as the fox's could be piercing, peeling back her skin and seeing the soft beating heart of her. *Let him. The pit he will find there is of his own making.*

"Are you ready for tomorrow?" he asked.

She could not fathom his tone. Shaking herself out of her thoughts, she looked back on the day's preparations. The guest rooms had been furnished. The room which had become Skander's now that she had taken up residence in his, would be given to Centurion. The White Ones would be put up in rooms in the north wing. Margaret had seen that the fireplaces were well stocked, as the north face of the house was chilly with bleak shadow in the low light of winter.

"Yes, I think everything is ready." A sudden panic of responsibility trembled at her heart.

Rupert sighed and brushed at his face as if the curious circles and squares of his work still clung like cobwebs to his eyes. "Much as I dislike the man, I am glad for you, now that I think about it. It is good practice for you. Also he will know, and others presently will know, that you are a woman of standing and can hold your own in society."

His smile was almost kindly, but when she looked past it to his eyes she saw again the uncanny paleness like silver and the possessiveness of the jet-black pupil, and the smile, though sincere, lost its charm.

"Must everything be a fight?" she asked through her teeth.

His voice lay soft and sharp upon her breast. "No."

No. She looked away into the shadows, into the cloud-shredded spangles of earth-light falling in through the glass-topped atrium. Through the darkness came some confused sense of light— not a glimpse of it, but a sense of it—and through the crowding blaze and shadow of Plenilune, she remembered that somewhere in her veins was English blood: and if there was one thing her people were good at, it was defying fate to its own face and holding out a sense of hope against the impossible. So she hid a tiny, fragmented sense of hope, too small to feel and broken like a gem someone had smashed under his heel, in the smallest corner of her heart.

The corner was fox-coloured and glowed like a little lamp.

She left Rupert without another word. In her room she disrobed, alone, and climbed wearily into bed. The woman who had forgot to feed the fox had remembered to put bottles of hot water at the foot of her bed; she curled her bare toes around them while her knees froze and her chest went numb from the grip of despair that seemed to bind as with dark magic all her vital organs.

Father God in heaven, she groaned, *if you have the least scrap of mercy for me in the entirety of your being, do not make me marry Rupert. Anyone—anyone but Rupert.*

In the shifting dark, the muted flurry of cloud-shadows and earth-light, she saw her mother's face, thick-set and haggard, unmerciful, lined with grey. It seemed far away, looking down disapprovingly at Margaret—did she lie in a grave? The images slipped out of conscious thought into shallow dream, from shallow dream to deeper, and all night she shivered in and out of dark dreams that featured her mother and Rupert and the local church at Aylesward. She seemed caught in the middle of a strange ceremony, half-wedding, half-coronation, but it was always broken up by the news of a death somewhere that inexplicably frightened her, a boar appearing suddenly on the church threshold, and the fox's voice beside her ear saying, very clearly,

"Damn."

She opened her eyes to a wide, fox-coloured light. The window-panes were overlaid with spider-fine frost, the patterns cast on the floor by the light coming through the frost looked like footprints left by seraphic visitors. For the first time it felt, not like autumn, but like Christmas.

Margaret crawled out of bed and stood shivering in her shift while the frozen light played on her skin. She peered across the lawn at the thin, argent sky, listening to the creak and coo of the wild agrarian birds. Geese were calling somewhere, hurrying toward Darkling where winter was warmer. They would pass Centurion on the way, she thought.

Rupert was out on the lawn with Talbot and Livy; the two men were watching the dog romp in the hoarfrost, the breath of all three of them smoking in the air. They were too far away for Margaret to hear even the murmur of their voices. Round the end of the stable-wing old Hobden emerged, toting a full bucket of slops in either hand. His ancient, gnarled frame barely seemed to notice the weight and strain put upon it.

I hate this place. Yet I want to belong, desperately. The life of this place calls out to me and I do not know why. Maybe old Hobden is right. Maybe it would have been better if the other man had not died. But I am always losing to Rupert: what could I do for Marenové's sake even if I should stay?

She pressed her hand against the glass. The cold burned her skin.

What do you want from me?

She turned away from the srcying-glass scene and went into her closet. For a long while she stared at the clothes by the light of a lamp, wondering what would be both warm enough for the bitingly clear winter day, dignified and beautiful, but understated enough not to frighten the shy-sounding White Ones. She found herself thinking of them as little horned creatures the like of which she had seen at Lookinglass.

In the end she chose a gown of pigeon-coloured velvet that purled back in places to let out the silky sheen of the ocean at sunset. With the muted flame of colour she moved across the barred light of the room, paused only to thrust her hair up and hold it in place with pins and sky-fire gems, before stepping out of her room as one stepping out onto a battlefield that has already been lost.

From day to day, Margaret had noticed that Rupert tended to go about his own routine, presumably as he had before he brought her to Marenové House. Only on occasion would he look in on her, drifting by as he went from one place to another. Accustomed to her father living a life separate from the feminine, domestic life she and her mother and sisters had lived, Margaret had not thought much of it. She had been glad to be left alone. But today Rupert seemed to hover closer than usual. When he realized she had emerged from her room he seemed always close by, just in the next room or, when she found a moment to sit down, in an armchair near her reading one of his dolphin-skinned books. She had just finished a battle with Rhea over the silverware she wanted to use and the placement of people at the supper table, and had collapsed on a sofa in the sitting room only to hear a soft expletive muttered nearby and looked round to see Rupert, again, leaning over his work with his elbow on the table, slashing out lines of writing on a page.

"What, you too?"

He looked up, but did not look round at her. "Was Rhea giving you trouble?" he evaded.

He never speaks of that work of his. Margaret sighed and pressed her fingertips against her forehead. As the hours went by she was growing more and more restless and nervous, her temper shorter and shorter. "I sorted it out. Have you given notice to the stable-hands?"

He frowned into his work again. "I hadn't. When I am done here I will go take care of that." He did look up then, swinging round suddenly on her, and hung a moment with a curious, searching look in his eye. "You look very well," he remarked. Was that a note of surprise in his voice? "That dress becomes you."

Her stomach clenched. With an effort she rose. "It is certainly more understated than scarlet."

"The scarlet," he pointed out, "was your idea."

She looked down into his pale, hateful eyes. "True. I will see to the stable-hands."

"Margaret—"

She had turned away. Her heart stopped at the tone of his voice, gripped in emotion. She knew without looking what his countenance would be. *Don't say it. Don't say it. Don't you dare say it.*

The silence drew out, falling like snow upon his emotions. At last he seemed to break away, repelled by the stiffness of her shoulders; she heard the nib of his pen scratching softly at the page again. Trembling she walked away, realizing that she had fully expected him to get up and grab her by the arm—or the throat. The fox's reassurance of his character seemed far away in that moment.

Her nervousness mounted almost to madness by the time evening dropped down Seescarfell and turned the eastern flanks of the Marius Hills to wine-coloured darkness. A low, cold wind moaned in the hawthorn. The stars, shaken out of the folds of the sky, reminded Margaret of Lookinglass, which reminded her of freedom. She had stepped out into the last flicker of dusk on the front stoop to listen for the tell-tale, wind-blown splutter of hooves coming from the road. There was no sound but the wind, and she lingered on the step and watched the stars break out of a ragged dark sky shredded and coloured like an old war-banner, and she found solace in the sight.

She was turning to go back inside when a dog barked down the lane and the wind, changing direction for a moment, brought through the gloam the soft drub of hooves on turf and dirt. There was a momentary jink of light down the hill between hawthorn and wind-swept barberry. It was only for a moment, then it was lost again in the curve of the pasture; but it would reappear shortly at the end of the lane and come steadily toward her, horses emerging like wraiths from the night tide, travel-worn faces awash with the moth-shuttered lantern-light. Margaret waited, feeling the moments ebb away her anxiety little by little so that, by the time the string of muddy, tired horses shambled into the ring of light cast beside the great front doors of Marenové House, she felt perfectly at ease.

"Centurion," she said, vaguely surprised by the warmth in her own voice. "Surely this is a case of there and back again. How was your journey?"

The man, wrapped up in a wine-coloured cloak ring-streaked with shadow and mud, swung stiffly down from his leggy chestnut mount and retreated toward one of the horses behind him to help a deeply-muffled figure down. His face flashed in the light for a moment as he flung a smile toward Margaret.

"Cold and tiring!" he said. "But it did not rain as I thought it might. I could smell something suspicious coming over the Marius Hills and the sky looked threatening, but nothing came of it."

Margaret watched the shrouded figure slip into the light, joined by another much its height and almost as thoroughly wrapped. She could not see any faces. "No, that was only the goose that was roasting for supper."

Centurion laughed heartily, but wearily. As he turned the horses over to the hands of the stable servants and stepped into the full glare of the light, his hood falling back off the crown of his head, she saw the long road up from Darkling-law had left him tired. As his eyes slid past her to Rupert, who had appeared with a soft breath of warm air from inside, she saw in his face the unmistakable look of a man too tired to fight.

"I must thank you again for inviting us. It is better boarding than a way-house, and no mistake."

Margaret stepped back, gesturing into the hall. "Do not thank me yet until you have tasted the goose and felt the beds. Do come in. Do come in!" she gently urged the two shy creatures that hung about Centurion's flanks. "Your luggage will be taken up and you will have time to wash and change. Supper is in half an hour. The servants will bring you down." She shot a warning look at Rhea, who had been placed in charge of Centurion. The maid did not meet her gaze, though Margaret was sure her look had been seen. "Make yourselves at home."

"Again, thank you." Centurion shook Rupert's hand in a weary, obligatory way, then, greetings past, he turned to the two creatures behind him. "Go with the servants. I'll see you at supper."

Between the curves of brindled fur Margaret caught sight of a white cheek and a deeply scarlet mouth, but otherwise the two seemed to avert their faces from all eyes with a practiced dexterity.

She felt Centurion would have liked to have said more to them, to reassure them out of their shyness, but Rupert's presence seemed to quench him. They all went wearily after the servants, Centurion treading heavily, the other two slipping soundlessly up the stairs.

"Well!" Margaret breathed.

"I like them even less than Centurion," said Rupert darkly. He shivered and crossed his arms. "*Shuh!* They smell of uncanny magic."

Margaret had to admit that they left her feeling uneasy, but she did not say it. Feeling oddly defensive of them, she turned wordlessly away and went into the dining room to wait.

Her anxiety was warring with her again by the time Centurion reappeared. She started from her seat, seeing again the Centurion she knew, polished and fair of face, his mood sturdily restored along with his self-confidence. The servant announced him and he strode into the dining room, flinging a look round to get his bearings before fixing his gaze on her. "Lady Margaret! Please—let me introduce you to my brother and sister. This is Julius and Julianna."

The two shy, white creatures slipped in behind him. They were stripped now of their fur and seemed to blaze out bare like candles. The girl was dressed in a gown of fire-coloured tabby silk, the boy was dressed in a suit of chocolate-brown corduroy. But what took Margaret by surprise, though she realized it should not have, was that they were both *white*. They were pale, almost translucent, in their whiteness. The boy's hair was cropped close like his brother's, but it was silvery white, throwing back the mellow candlelight with subtle hues of pink. The girl's hair, white as swan's down, was braided and coiled expertly in a fashion she was coming to recognize as common to the Honours, but surely, Margaret thought, even her cousin's outlandish hair could be no whiter than this. The lashes on both of them were dyed dark, which made their orchid-coloured eyes stand out in their soft, lean faces with an almost appalling beauty.

No wonder people thought them unlucky!

But then the shock was swept away and Margaret was smiling sincerely, caught by the undiluted beauty of the two young people before her. It felt viciously good, too, to not be the only strange one in the world.

"Julius. Julianna. I am so glad you could come." She found herself dipping politely, withdrawing just a fraction so that her greeting might not frighten the shy things.

The boy's pale face coloured and, stiffly, he bowed, looking at Centurion as he did so. The girl folded her hands upon her breast and, like Margaret, plunged in a froth of fiery silk toward the floor, her curtsy graceful and deliberate as someone flinging down a torch. Jewels yelled in the light from her throat and ears—but no jewel was as poignant as her uplifted, piercing eyes.

Rupert and Margaret took the ends of the table. Livy placed Centurion on Margaret's right with Julianna across from him directly on Margaret's left, her brother beside her to Rupert's right. Julianna's hand flickered beside her, as if searching for Margaret's, but, catching her older brother's eye, she put it back down in her lap.

She thought we were going to say grace, Margaret thought with a wince. *If only we were! We need it.*

"I heard the weather was clear for you coming over the Sound," began Rupert as they plunged into the goose.

Centurion looked up. "Remarkably pleasant, to tell the truth. It was very cold in the hills but we had clear skies nearly all the way. I thought the clouds might turn to something, but they never did. It has been a mild winter thus far."

"They do not get very stormy around here until after the New Year."

Centurion quietly peeled meat away from bone, but Margaret saw the half-laughing, half-hopeless look on the lord's face. He, too, would be bracing for the wretched change in the weather that was to come at the turn of the year...

Rupert's knife flashed, sending a scale of light over his cheek. "Our weather moves from east to west; if it did not break on you as you were coming over, it probably broke behind you and moved on. Incidentally, you should have fair skies for your journey tomorrow."

"How long is the ride down?"

Rupert thought a moment. *How polite he is being!* Margaret realized with a pang of worry. She wondered how long it would last. "If you take the Branhoch and don't turn off at Shirling, but keep going south through the junction at Crown, it will take you three days. If you mention my name at the Blue Royal, you will get a better room and a better price. They are none so bad a way-house as some."

Centurion quenched a look of surprise. With a tell-tale sweep over Julius and Julianna he said, "Thank you. I am...heartily grateful."

Rupert set his mouth in a hard, thin line, and for awhile it was up to Margaret to make conversation.

She turned slowly to Julianna. "I saw you have a dappled grey horse. Is that yours?"

The girl raised her head and looked steadily, wide-eyed, into Margaret's face. The dark lips were parted in surprise—and Margaret was seeing, again, the horned creature in the woods, and saw Julianna weighing whether to be spooked or at ease with her voice. Out of the corner of her eye she saw Centurion looking across the table at his sister's face, breath bated, willing her with an almost physical power to calm herself.

The jet-black lashes flickered over the eyes. The tension eased. "Yes, that is Bridget. She is my mare. Splendour of God is Julius' horse."

Margaret smiled in spite of herself. "I can think of no better mount to bear you than the splendour of God."

Rupert drew in an audible breath; the sound of it seemed to jab at Margaret under the breastbone. Grey flickered on the edge of her vision.

"Mine," Margaret went on through the tightness in her lungs, "is Hanging Tree. It is not as pretty a name as yours, but my mare looks so much like yours, I could not help marking your mare when you came." She floundered for another question, if only for the sake of hearing that sweet, lyrical voice again. "Did you raise her yourself?"

"No." The brows twitched. "Centurion—he breeds the horses. Chanticleer Down is his horse. My family has raised Down horses for generations. They are the most famous family of horses in the Honours."

Margaret looked to Centurion. "You must be very proud."

"Horses are very important to us," Centurion explained. "They are a symbol of wealth and power, a kind of magic, and often very keen friends. And," the falcon-coloured eyes laughed, "in a pinch they can get you from place to place."

Laughing back into those friendly eyes, Margaret was surprised by the thought—

Could I ask him *about the dragon?*

Julianna spread her hands in a sudden fit of confusion, for her napkin had slid off her silken lap onto the carpet. Spurred into motion, Livy brought a fresh one and held it mutely out to her. Julianna took it, but Margaret saw the shiver of the jewel in her ear as she trembled in the presence of the huge dark manservant. Seeming to catch her distress, Julius reached out, just beneath the edge of the table—Margaret could see his shoulder move—and touched Julianna. The simple gesture seemed to settle and reassure her, the roosting softness in the boy's eyes seemed to transfer instantly into Julianna's face as though by some half-magical link between them.

No wonder people thought them unlucky!

"There is chess and rummy in the withdrawing room," said Rupert when supper was finished. He added to Livy, "We will take coffee and dessert there."

"And sure we ought not stay up late," said Centurion, rising and twisting back his shoulders, stretching contentedly, "but I will play you in a game of chess."

They descended on the withdrawing room with its roaring fire and windows curtained by night. Rupert and Centurion, each a little wary of the other and each deftly not showing it, sat down on either side of the chess-board. Rupert had the red, Centurion had the white: Centurion opened. Left to entertain the White Ones, Margaret drew up a few chairs to the coffee table and began shuffling the deck of cards.

"Have you played rummy before?" she asked, assuming that they had and hearing, not her own voice, but the fox's mockingly in her head.

Julius, in a low, rich voice, said, "No, madam."

She came back with a start. "Oh. Well, I will teach it to you."

She felt she taught it badly, especially since neither twin said a word as she explained, but when they began to play she realized they had taken in every word she had said—and, what was more, they played expertly. She could not tell if they got any pleasure out of the game, for their faces were concentrated. They ate their dessert and drank their coffee almost mechanically, which disturbed her.

She lost every time they played and as the soft, triumphant word "Checkmate," was spoken in Rupert's baritone, she leaned back on her sofa and smiled pathetically. "Through no skill of mine you have both played tremendously. Of course, I have always been a bad player," she added ruefully.

Julianna seemed to latch onto her brother's face with her eyes. "It is but mathematics," said Julius patiently. "You have only to acquaint yourself with the number of cards in the deck and the placement of them. Then it is a simple matter of probability and logic."

Margaret put her chin in her hand, head shaking so that her earrings swung. "If I were half so well educated as you I might know what you mean. You must be very excited to be going to the University."

They both smiled and looked down at their laps. How curious—they were perhaps only four years younger than she and yet their shyness, despite their obvious intelligence, was tangible. To Margaret, it seemed only to add to their unique charm. She found herself regretting that they would be going away in the morning. She caught Centurion's eye across the room and smiled at him. A little perplexed, he smiled back.

They finished their coffee and rose—Rupert pinched out a light by the chess-table. "It is five past ten," he said.

"Yes, we should turn in." Centurion bowed to Margaret again. "My compliments. It has been a most enjoyable evening."

"I will take Julius and Julianna to their rooms," Margaret said, hoping, since Centurion's chamber lay only a few rooms beyond hers, that it would ease Rupert's temper to have her diverted to another part of the house until Centurion was well ensconced in his chambers.

The lord of Darkling took a sounding of his siblings' emotions. Neither appeared unduly distressed by this news. Julianna even moved a little closer to Margaret's side, drawing her twin brother after her.

"Shoo!" Centurion turned over his anxiety to her. "That seems fine. Good-night, you two. I'll see you in the morning. Good-night, Lady Margaret, Rupert."

Rupert strode toward the door. "Good-night, Centurion. Good-night, Margaret."

His last words to her drew Centurion up short with surprise. Completely unguarded, the young man flung a look at her over his shoulder, frowning, and with a hot rush of shame Margaret realized that he had assumed, and had politely ignored, that she and Rupert shared a bed. Their eyes met: Margaret felt hers go glassy and cold. Centurion, realizing his mistake and how plainly it had showed on his face, swung away and left without a word, swallowed up by the thick shadows that were gathering about the house.

Her heart was beating loudly in her ears. She felt someone touch her arm and found Julianna looking at her with her deep, impersonal, purple eyes. There was some uncanny shape about the mouth that made Margaret wonder if the girl understood. She heard herself saying something about how early a start they would have in the morning and that she had better get them to their rooms, and then she was walking through the dark with the White Ones behind her. It was almost eerie how silent they were—it would have been eerie but for the thunder of blood in her ears that seemed loud enough to drown out Curoi, had he been barking at that hour. It was not until she reached the narrow hall and stood between their doors that her heart began to quiet.

"I will see you in the morning before you leave," she told the two creatures shining out of the mothy darkness. "I hope you rest well."

But the White Ones, who had been so shy before, seemed to suddenly waken to the loneliness of the north wing and the creaking drowsiness of the old wood underfoot. Julius made a curious little gesture with both hands, spinning his palms counter clockwise over each other, and the gesture seemed meant for Julianna. She reached toward Margaret as if to stay her.

"Wait," she said imperiously.

Wait? Speechless, bewildered, Margaret stood rooted to the darkness and the ancient floorboards, feeling the hugeness of the dark creep up at her back with only the whiteness of Julius before her to light the way as Julianna, on silent feet, slipped into her room and disappeared. She fully expected the old apple-leaf woman to re-emerge with the girl, when Julianna, with no more noise than a sunbeam shaking loose in a glade of pine, slipped back into the hallway with a book pressed between her hands.

Without meeting Margaret's eye the girl said, "It was in our minds that you should have this. We do not know why. We were meant to use it for our studies at the University. We will miss it, we are sure. They will ask and we will have to think of something... But Julius and I agreed: when we saw you, it *sounded* like you."

Margaret looked at the unassuming little book. What was it with these people and their books? "It *sounded* like me?" she parroted.

Julianna held it out. Margaret's fingers responded, brushing it, but she could not quite take it. "Yes, madam. The sound it makes—the sound you make—the notes went together to us. It is part of your pattern. Please take it," she added almost desperately.

Margaret took the book, then, but she took Julianna's hand as well, hard in the grip of her long fingers. "I will take it, but I will not let you go until you tell me what you mean. Too often people have slipped by me, leaving me without answers. Not this time."

She expected Julianna to spook and bolt, and for a moment the girl looked abashed by the powerful fingers locking over her wrist. Julius, linked to his sister, also started, drawing in a swift breath of surprise or pain. But Margaret held the beautiful things and would not let them go, no matter how frightened they looked, no matter how beautiful. Finally Julius moved toward his sister, his hands going out gingerly, steadily, toward the captured hand.

"Everything makes a sound," he said patiently, as if he were speaking to a wild animal. "And all sound makes a pattern. Did God not speak, and did not his voice make the form of things? The sound of your soul and the sound of the soul of this book make a pattern together." His fingertips touched the back of her hand, cold, pressing, begging her to let Julianna go. "So we know that you are meant to go together."

"You can see that?" Margaret whispered. She was not sure if she believed him or not.

Black-spangled, flushed with lilac-colour, Julius' eyes turned to her. The fingers worked around hers. "No, but we can feel it. We can't often hear it, but we can often feel it. Madam—" His voice grew audibly pained, and Margaret suddenly let fly her fingers, letting go of the brittle wrist.

Margaret took a step back, feeling the wings of the darkness fold about her shoulders. Concerned, shy, pale-lit things, the twins watched her from the doorways of their bedrooms.

"My world is flat," she said at last. "My world is flat like a pan overtop of hell. We don't believe such things."

"You are only blind," said Julianna, as if that was a comfort. "Those who have eyes to see can see."

Where had she heard those words before...? "But I am not blind. I keep waiting for the rim of your world, but it keeps curving on toward the sunrise and I do not know if I can take the roundness of it. You live in an awful world," she said huskily. "How can you bear the spice of it?"

"It runs in our veins," said Julius simply. Then he added, "Yours will empty into ours."

She stared at him, almost beyond wanting to understand, yet that tenacious germ of human spirit drove her inexorably on, on toward the blinding sunrise. "I think yours must empty into mine, young sir, but either way I will die."

He smiled shyly, dropping his eyes, curiously abashed by her fixed gaze. Julianna laid her hand over his arm. In the dark, in the confusion, as the webs of her whirling thoughts closed over her eyes, they seemed to Margaret to be one thing, a shining light just out of reach. But they were a cold, dispassionate light. Keenly, like a child, she wanted the warm red light of the fox.

"Thank you for the book," she said huskily, as if a few moments before she had not spoken her own doom. "I will read it— and find the pattern, if I can. Good-night, both of you."

The pale candlefire parted and darkened in the doorways. Margaret swept past the shards of light, down the throat of the dark hall, listening, as if from far off, to the creak of floorboards under her shoes.

She almost looked at the book before she went to bed. All was silent in the house. Centurion had gone to bed and only a faint flicker of light leaked from under Rupert's door. It was late, night was settling on its haunches around the house. It was the eerie witching hour when anything might happen, so Margaret turned deliberately away from the book and left it on top of Songmartin, hid in a drawer of her dressing table where Rhea would not find it. She shut the curtains on another day, another bloodied battlefield of hopes and lost causes, shut out the wedding-favour streamers of cloud that licked round the arm of earth, shut out the green glow that washed the northern night sky, shut out the cold, star-flecked blue, and shut in the empty black.

Her sleep was plagued again by dreams, curious, detached dreams that tried to make sense of her curious, detached life. Skander had been arguing with her mother about Woodbird, who had mysteriously disappeared. The fox had been reading her books, complaining shrilly and ruthlessly about the syntax and the belief in the existence of dragons. She had woken from all her dreams with a start, frightened out of sleep by Rupert throttling her for the splendour of God.

XIV | THE THINGS THAT CANNOT BE AND THAT ARE

She surfaced quietly, her heart in her throat. Once again morning was breaking through the kinks in her curtains with a blazing winter clarity: once again it felt like Christmas. But Margaret did not care. She felt cold and tired and, above all things, old. In the broken light she pushed up from her pillows and pulled her hair into her hands. It was still brown, dishevelled and sleep-tossed, but brown. It came as a surprise to her that it had not been blasted grey.

Her mind slid to the White Ones. They were leaving this morning and she was meant to see them off. In a flurry, seeming to leave her blood behind, she launched herself from the bed, cursing Rhea out loud for not having woke her at an earlier hour. Rhea seemed to have a knack for forgetting duties she did not like for people she despised. Margaret had left her grey velvet dress on a chair and, as it was not badly wrinkled, and smelled of wind-blown barberry and woodsmoke, she swept back into it, jewelled herself, and plunged back out into the house.

Everyone was at breakfast when she arrived. Julius and Julianna were seated in a window, facing each other over a little table of coffees and steaming morning pasties. Centurion was at the table on the end nearest them, his face to the doorway. He was the first to see her enter. Putting down his utensils he rose, flung aside his napkin, and bowed handsomely to her. She saw the memory of his mistake from the previous evening in all the wryness of his smile.

"Lady Margaret," he said warmly. "Good morning. I trust you slept well."

It was untrue that she had, and it was the sort of thing that brought Rupert's eyes hard and suspicious over the top of his morning book to fix like a hawk's on Centurion's face. Centurion did not seem to notice. Margaret brushed it aside with a genuine smile.

"I slept passing fair. 'Tis cold these nights! To think," she diverted his attention, "it is almost Christmas."

Rupert returned to his reading. She realized, belatedly, that Christmas would annoy him too. She could count on him throttling her awake tomorrow morning for mentioning it.

Pulling out a chair for her, Centurion mused, "This year has seemed to drag by. I thought Christmas would never come. Now I almost—" he caught himself, looking up at Rupert; Rupert did not return the glance. Margaret finished Centurion's thought:

Now we almost wish the new year would linger out of reach forever. But it won't. Time is inexorable and heartless that way.

She took the proffered chair and breakfast plate, wishing she could ask him about the Honours' customs surrounding Christmas, but the stony, impersonal face of her suitor prevented her. Centurion, she quickly noticed, was polite but sought to avoid her eye. If she liked him less she might have been resentful for last night's mistake, but she did like him and she could hardly blame him: was it not what everyone thought of her? The sore muscles of her stomach clenched—angry, grieved—and crushed the breakfast she was trying to put in it. A dull ache, the sort which promised to stay with her all day, began in her middle. As she dug her knife into the steamy, peppery sausages, willing herself to put it into her mouth, she wished keenly that she might slip away and stay with the fox. At least in the cellar, cut off from the world, she might be alone to the company of her misery. But there was no chance for it.

There was not a chance for it at all that day. After breakfast the horses were sent for, the pack-beasts loaded up, and Margaret bade a fond and shy farewell to Centurion and the White Ones.

Rupert was coldly polite, Centurion no less so. She watched them on the front stoop, emblazoned by a clear sun and hard wind, shake hands and hold the grip a moment longer than necessary, their eyes meeting in a kind of silent challenge.

"Until next time," said Centurion quietly.

Rupert nodded and stepped back up on the threshold, his hand settling heavily on Margaret's shoulder. The young lord of Darkling did not miss the possessive gesture, but he swung away without expression in his eyes to help his sister onto her mare. The wind had not let up. It flung their cloaks about and caught Julianna's hair, which was undone, and spread it out like a swan's wing against the shimmering thin blue sky. Margaret felt the tug in her heart to be off with them, wherever they were going, only to get away from Rupert...

...But Rupert's hand lay warm and heavy on her shoulder and she knew there was no chance of escape. Wherever she might go, he would come for her. There was no hole deep enough, no heaven high enough, that would hide her from his pursuit.

They may have to live with him as Overlord, she considered, *but they do not have to live with him for a husband. They are the lucky ones. And yet, I pity them...*

No more words were exchanged. With an upward flutter of cloth and heave of leather and shadow, a glint of sunny steel, Centurion sprang aloft onto his horse. Under his sudden movement, the animal churned forward with a squeal, champing its bit for the open road. With a backwards twist the young lord of Darkling looked round, meeting Margaret's eye, and saluted her, swiftly, smartly, with the wind in his face and in his eyes a look of apology, of understanding, which seemed to reach across the distance and lie on her other shoulder with a more familiar, friendly touch. Her stomach tightened. Her hands, clenched in her skirts, remained at her sides.

They left in a flurrying canter, plume-tails floating on the wind, the drum of hooves rolling back to Margaret like the staccato beat of life itself. For as long as she could hear the hoofbeats her desire to run after them mounted, churned, spurned the earth—it was almost unbearable by the time the wind snatched the sounds away entirely and left her and Rupert in a hollow shell of booming wind-surf noise, watching the dwindling horses and their riders swing on to the road and disappear among the barberry.

Always I am left. There is no one to come to my rescue, as happens in the stories. No one for me, no one for Plenilune.

She turned and looked at Rupert's profile, etched darkly against the backdrop of the roiling rose-wall of the stable-yard, against the lift of the north pasture, against the mirror-curve of the winter sky. She hated that face, those eyes that seemed to look beyond the barberry and were watching Centurion still, but at the same time she felt an awful pity for him, which she hated, too. If it had not been for the books and the little broom flowers, she considered, she might have learned to love him one day, when they had come to understand each other. But the ashen books were an imprint of his heart, the crumbled broom-blossoms a figure of her own, and she knew they must both go down together, ashen and unloved, into a ruin of perdition.

There was a hollow lull in the wind of a sudden, and a sudden bloom of warmth in the sunshine that surprised Margaret into squinting up at it.

"Now I am of a purpose," said Rupert darkly. "Are you," he added presently, "resolved to yours?"

"Have I any choice?"

There was a pang in his face when he looked at her, but only for a moment: the look was swift, glancing at her eyes and off again as if he had touched on a pain he would rather avoid.

So you, too, have a heart that bleeds.

"I must needs you come and look at dress designs again," he continued after a moment. The wind had picked back up again, howling over the softly rolling valley of Seescardale, yet they both seemed reluctant to go back inside. "The new year is fast approaching."

"The red dress is not good enough for your ordination?"

He looked her levelly in the face, a slight smile tugging at his features. He seemed to watch the ecclesiastical word hang on her lips a moment with amusement. "You have blood blue-coloured enough to know that you cannot wear the same dress twice."

So she had no chance to go down to see the fox, though as the hours went by and turned into days, the wind grew colder and

Rupert's presence ever more enfolding about her. The doom of everything loomed more solid on the horizon, and she found herself wishing stronger and stronger to steal away even for half an hour to sit on the rough upturned wine-crate in the cold light of the lamp to have the little rummy creature mock her gently in her distress. One day, looking up from her needle-work on her elaborate New Year dress, the longing caught her powerfully by the throat and she wondered why. *Why.* Why did she so desperately want to sit with the oddest creature in God's creation, who could do her no good, who had a white feather where his heart ought to be? The strength of her longing surprised her, the feeling of being cast adrift when she looked over the familiar dining room in its wash of pale winter light alarmed her. Light glinted off the glasses on the sideboard: she saw the fox's eyes uplifted to hers, reserved, guarded, gently mocking. Her elbow pressing into her knee reminded her of the fox's hesitant touch, as of one reaching across a great distance to something that might turn upon him in an instant. She wanted that familiar fear, that comradeship of misery, the shared, unspoken friendship of exiles.

It was something of a relief when Livy entered, bowed to her, and announced that Skander Rime had just arrived.

He came breezing in, stripping off his massive gloves, the ruddy colour of cold riding in his cheeks. Margaret rose to receive him, flustered and at once gladdened by his appearance. But she was taken aback when, bending a little, he kissed her on the cheek by way of greeting.

"Good afternoon, Margaret!" he said gustily, rubbing his chilly hands together. "What—what do you do there?" He looked at the enormous pile of electrum-coloured fabric that lay all about her chair.

"Good afternoon! I had not expected you." Glancing beyond Skander to the kitchen doorway she spied Rhea, who seemed to have just stepped out and had seen the greeting exchanged. There was a look of thunder in the maid's eyes which alarmed Margaret. "Rhea, mulled wine for his lordship."

The maid hesitated a moment, her head lowered like a horse's which has no intention of obeying and is weighing the moment to break...but at last she dipped her knees and vanished back the way she had come.

"Mulled wine is just the thing I am wanting," Skander approved with an easy attempt at cheeriness.

"It is the dress—" Turning, Margaret stooped and began bundling the massive lengths of cloth back up into something like a tidy heap. A spool of golden thread took a tumble off her chair and a cup of tiny glass buttons began sliding down a trough of cloth, but the latter Skander managed, with a kingfisher-like plunge, to catch before it sprayed everywhere.

"This is the dress...for the ceremony?" he queried, looking quizzically into the little cup.

She took it from him and set it on the table out of elbow-range. "Yes, that dress. I have been working through the days on it, from cock-light to sun-down, in order to get it done on time." She turned her head away lest he see the involuntary grimace of her mouth, as if she had bit into something sour. "Rhea has been helping, but it was more than she could manage in the amount of time we have so I, too, have been stabbing my fingers with needles."

"I'm sorry to hear that."

His voice, coming from behind her, was low and genuine. She remembered him as she had last seen him, earnest in the lamplight of his kitchen, regretful and yet incapable of reaching across the impossible distance to help her, though he stood but an arm's length away.

She smiled at him and gestured to a chair, seating herself as she did so. "What brings you down?" she asked politely. "You are a little early."

He folded himself up in the chair, making it look small and unwieldy; she had a sudden fear that it might break under him. Folding his arms across his chest, fluttering his shoulders, he said simply, "Cooped-up-ness! I've been to see Survance and Jacland—you remember Survance?—but we've had a flurry of snow in Glassdale, particularly down from Thrasymene—they always give us the damndest weather—and truth to tell, my own fireside was feeling a little bare. Aikaterine does what she can. She's a good girl. But honestly I just got lonely."

Margaret fingered the rich, smooth folds of her half-made gown. "You must be very desperate for company," she mused, "to come all the way down here for it."

"Yes, I must be... But winter is an hour of high fires and warm company, isn't it?"

Her eyes flicked to his a moment and she almost—*almost*—betrayed the memory which she had stolen from them. She was saved by Rhea's re-emergence from the kitchen hall bearing a steaming chalice for Skander. He took it gladly and, as was his disposition's demand, looked to Rhea's face to thank her; but his countenance fell a moment, clouded by some inner doubt, and he hastily looked away.

Yes. She does that to people.

The maid padded soundlessly toward the kitchen again, but stopped a moment in the doorway to look back, not at them, but at the outer door. Following her gaze, Margaret's blood jumped in her veins to find Rupert there, as if he had always been there, disapprobation in his handsome face.

Over the rim of his cup Skander saw her face—she felt it drain of blood—and he turned around to see his cousin. "Ah, speak of the devil," he said without mirth. "Where were you?"

"In the north tower." Rupert's voice seemed carved of those very stones. "Did you just come?"

"Just now. I have barely warmed the seat."

De la Mare unfolded. "I thought I felt a draught. What is the occasion for this visit?"

"I am masochistic," murmured Skander.

Rupert turned his ear. "I cry you mercy."

"No occasion," Skander said more loudly. "I felt like getting the fidgets out of my feet and found myself wandering down this way—to which place, don't you think, we must all gravitate before long?"

Rupert's eyes moved straightly from his cousin's face to Margaret's and back again, like a sword-blade cutting through the air. Her blood slowly crawled back into her heart. " 'Tis a long way to get out the fidgets."

"Some people have gambled longer," replied his cousin caustically, "and against greater odds."

"There is mulled wine in the kitchen," Margaret interrupted softly. "Do you not have a fire in the tower, Rupert? Your fingers are blue."

Skander seemed perplexed at being cut off by her. Rupert, putting up his hands as if he had forgot he had them, rubbed his thumbs against his fingertips and said, "It is only lapis lazuli. But the mulled wine, I think, sounds agreeable."

Livy, who had stood all the while at the back of the room, motionless as the sideboard, slipped out of the shadows and disappeared down the kitchen hallway.

Skander gave an awkward cough and put away his cup. He seemed a little pained, but settled himself back in his chair and said, by way of peacemaking, "You may go on with the dress, Margaret. I am sure you will need all the time you have to finish it."

At an abbreviated nod from Rupert, Margaret took up her sewing again—though goodness knew she was wishing for a longer break from the monotony of stitching tiny glass beads onto the minute golden stems that covered the voluminous skirts. She was fast beginning to hate the sight of the gorgeous thing and, no matter how pretty Rupert or the fox might think her—no matter how pretty she might think herself—the beautiful gown seemed overwhelmingly ostentatious, even for something as grand as the Overlord ceremony.

I will look a pale, gaudy little thing, she considered vehemently, jerking at the golden thread until it threatened to snap. She grabbed hold of a spray of golden stems and glass chinaberry beads and hauled the slipping fabric back into her lap. *Even amid all their flurry of feathers and embroidered dragons.*

Dragons...

Rupert was perched on the corner of the table, one leg swinging idly in the air, his hand cupped over a steaming chalice of mulled wine. Coming back out of her thoughts, Margaret felt chilled and wished for a cup of her own. But her hands were full, and she did not dare put a drink near her dress.

"Darkling was here a week ago," Rupert was saying casually. "He brought those two young siblings of his."

Skander coughed into his fist. "Yes, I remember he was taking them to the University." Again he coughed and shifted in his chair. "I have never met them. How were they?"

"Like two dog-teeth," de la Mare replied, showing his own, "in the mouth of a dog whose show of friendliness you do not trust."

Margaret looked up, expecting Skander's puzzled expression, but was startled to find the man had gone white and seemed to be struggling to draw breath for another cough. Rupert got down off the table—his cup clinked on the wood—and said,

"To hell with you, man—what is the matter?"

Skander shook his head, still struggling for breath. He hauled in one, a long, ragged gasp that cut Margaret's nerves like a serrated knife. His lips were turning grey.

"Don't just stand there, Rupert!" she cried, flinging down the dress, beads and all. She grabbed hold of Skander's hand: it was icy cold. "Send for a doctor! He's sick!"

Rupert pried Skander's free hand away from his throat and put his own thumb and forefinger against the soft of his cousin's jaw. "There isn't one," he growled. "He went down to Bendingwood and isn't due back until Tuesday week."

His words were meaningless to her. Rigid under her hand, obviously trying to keep a handle on his mounting panic, the young lord of Capys was struggling to draw breath. She was struggling to draw breath. She felt only two things clearly: that, if Skander died, she would never forgive Rupert, and that she loved the lord of Capys more dearly than anyone she had ever loved before.

"*Don't* just stand there!" she shrieked at Rupert. "Get him to his room! Prop him up and let him breathe!"

Mutely, stone-facedly, Rupert put his shoulder under his cousin and bore him up while Margaret, sobbing and hardly realizing she was sobbing, ran on ahead screaming, "Lilith! *Lilith!* I need you at once! *At once!*"

She burst open the door to the guest chamber, stirring a flurry of chicory-coloured drapery, and ran across to the bed, hauling back the coverlet while the sunlight, streaming in through a skylight, sparkled on the heavy embroidery of the cloth.

Lilith appeared in the doorway, flustered and concerned.

"I want black horehound and tansy! I want it hot and I want it five minutes ago! *Hurry, girl!*"

Lilith vanished. As Margaret worked feverishly at the bedclothes and then flung herself upon the little private fireplace to make an attempt at a blaze, she heard a sharp scream in the hall. She heard Rupert's voice, raised and abrasive. The matches snapped in her shaking hands.

Focus, woman. Focus!

Another match snapped.

"D-damn," she swore, and was too panicked to feel a pang of guilt as she launched, a second later, into a heart-wrung prayer that, regardless of herself, God might have some compassion on the faithful soul that was hanging in the mortal balance across Rupert's shoulders.

The kindling had taken the blaze when the man lurched into the doorway with his cousin half-slung across his back. Margaret started up, dropping the match on the hearth.

Have a heart of compassion! For the sake of us all, don't let him die!

With an unusual mark of tenderness Rupert laid Skander on the bed and stripped off his cousin's heavy winter wear. He was saying something to himself, muffled and furious, but he would not meet Margaret's eye. Skander's face, gashed in half by light and shadow, was a wretched kind of death-mask, already sunken and turned grey; there was a purl of white at one corner of his mouth.

"What is it? What is it?" Seated on the edge of the bed, Margaret worked Skander's collar loose. His hands were cold; the skin under his collar was coal-hot. "What is it, Skander? Was it the ride?"

Rupert's hand closed over her wrist and tugged her hard off the bed. With an angry, cattish scream she fell, catching herself only in time to stumble after him out the door.

"Let me go! Let me go, you brute! Skander needs me!"

He jerked her away from the door. "Skander needs to get his soul right with his God, that is what he needs."

She had known from the grimness of Skander's face that the situation was dire, but looking into Rupert's level, black-splintered eyes, the lids drooping as if to hide the truth from her, something in her chest died. Rupert's face said that it was beyond hope.

Of a sudden, her spirit rose up like a Japanese wave and rebelled. "No!" She wrenched her hand out of his. "I am sending for horehound and tansy. He needs to breathe. I need to bring the fever down. He won't have a chance if we do nothing! I don't even know what is wrong with him—*oh!*"

He gripped her by the jaw; she could feel every finger digging deeply into the little hollows between her bones. A roiling mix of hatred and regret warred in his face. "Margaret, stop listening to the screaming in your head and attend to me: the thing is beyond me. There is nothing we any of us can do."

He let her go with a jolt—she felt it shock down into the darkest part of her soul.

What happened? What is going on? He was so cheerful. He was sitting there with me. He gave me a kiss on the cheek. He came down here because he was lonely. What happened?

She breathed in desperation with one hideous sob. "How can you live with yourself!" she screamed at him. He was turning away, walking away, leaving shadows behind him. A wretched, red-tinged rage welled up inside her and she ran after him. With all her force she grabbed his arm and yanked him back. Her voice was still a wrangled scream. "He is your kinsman! With all your magic tricks—with all your wizardry, is there nothing you can do?"

He looked for a long moment at her white hand gripping his sleeve—very white it looked against the black cloth, each nail a perfect fleck of red—and slowly his eyes climbed like iron, like the tip of a sword, to rest between her brows. She was staring up the naked blade of cold, calculating rage. Something held it in check, something the blade itself, perhaps, did not understand; and it was that knowledge only which kept Margaret from breaking under that gaze. His voice, dropping each word into the quiet like little glass beads, was sharpened with bitterness.

"I do not possess the healing power."

Her breath shuddered out of her lungs. He unlatched her hand, dropping it, and turned away. In numbness she watched him go, choking on an airless rage, gagging on the disbelief. His figure, rigid in spine, carried in an untouched, dark sort of splendour, held not a single gentling curve of sympathy or familial charity. Did he care? Did somewhere behind those chilling pale eyes lurk a fierce pain for the loss of kin?

There was a blur of shadow on the floor, a mixing of black and gold as birds rocketed by the window, stirring up the sunlight. Margaret was seeing the yellow sparks of bloom and charred remains of books, feeling again the sharpness of little things, sharp as the nails digging into her palms. Skander deserved better. He was twice the man his cousin would ever be, a better man than Margaret had ever known. He deserved to be fought for, tooth and nail, until nothing else could be done. He deserved everything she could give him. For spite and splendour and the sake of all good things in Plenilune, she had to do something.

She plunged down the hall. She brushed past Livy with the horehound and tansy on the stair, saying, "Get out of my way!" without a second thought, and ran down into the dining room. If he followed her she did not care: she would reckon with that later. But there was no following tread on the stair. She was graciously alone as she yanked open the kitchen hallway door and, two seconds later, yanked open the door to the cellar. The hollow dark stared back at her but she hurtled into it without check, hoping she would not miss her foot in the dark and break her neck in the fall.

"Fox!" she called as she tumbled down the short stairs into the wine cellar. "Fox, quick! I need your help! Skander is—"

She stopped in horror, staring at the spectacle before her. It was not the fox—yet it was the fox. She felt somehow that the enormous rush of black body which uncurled and leapt to its feet had the same soul. But the image was all wrong. He was as big as a horse with a thick wolf's mane and bushy wolf's tail, and the paleness of his eyes was aflame with blue fire. She gave a strangled scream but stood her ground.

"Margaret!" he cried guiltily, his voice altered from the depth of his chest. "I thought you would come sooner—what is it?" He took two huge strides forward. The wine-crate beside him trembled. "By the twelve houses, woman—what is it! You spoke of Skander—"

She gulped back the nausea of surrealism. "He's dying," she choked out. "He's cold and discoloured and he can't breathe and

Rupert will do nothing or can do nothing and he doesn't have much time and *please* can't you do *something!*"

The fox's big wolf body seemed to swell as the words came tumbling out of her. Every hair on his spine lifted into a boarback ridge. The air crackled with electric energy. "Here's a fey time to be dying!" he roared with a kind of savage ecstasy. "Go to the first floor, to my Lady's chamber, the last door on the right. It will be in the southwest corner. Find the long box under the bed with the horn in it. Fill the horn with water and give it to Skander. I will put my back into the work. Go, woman! Hitch your skirts up! Go!"

His hulking shoulders arched, green sparks flaked off his rippling fur. Margaret stood a moment longer, benumbed by the awful sight of him, then she grabbed her skirts in one hand and stumbled at a blind run back through the dark, reckoning nothing of Livy or Rupert or anything that might get in her way. The air seemed to shear behind her as if blue-fire claws were being raked through it: a howl rose up in a welling wave of sound like thunder. China rattled in the cupboards as she staggered through the dining room. Painting frames chattered on the walls as she raced up the stairs. She remembered that howl but did not know how or when she had heard it before. It seemed to her like the cry of every broken heart and every cheated love and every lost soul and every righteous fury that man had ever felt. There was power in it, a raging, thrashing, sobbing, terrible power. The hairs on her arms stood on end and prickled like cold needles.

She tore past Rupert's door, past her own, past Skander's without looking. *The last door on the right. The last door on the right.* She tore past other doors, past doors that were closed and doors that were open, letting in bars of perry-coloured light. *The last door on the right*—she met the end of the hall and turned to the last door, the last door on the right. She grasped the oblong handle and tried to turn it, but it would not give. With an enraged cry she heaved on the knob, swearing again in a choking, sobbing way while the angry electricity of the fox's 'putting his back to it' crawled up her skin. *I don't have time for this!* With all she had she flung herself backward, both hands around the knob: with a jar that nearly tore her arms from her shoulders she jerked to a stop, then felt the wood give way.

She crashed down at the foot of the opposite door with the handle lost somewhere among her skirts, the carpet under her feet littered with splinters. She was able to scramble up and get one hand through the ragged hole in the door to push the latch back and swing the door open.

Another howl rocked the building.

Margaret had first a confused glory of late light as an impression, then she saw the bed, which she was looking for, in much the same position as her own. She ran to it, flung back the skirt, and dug down underneath it. She pulled out hat boxes and wicker boxes, a strong box that gave a loud pearly rattle, and wood and bamboo boxes of all sizes. They were all dusty. She pulled out one long wooden box with dark mother-of-pearl inlay which she thought must be the one, but the lid opened up only on a thick collection of what looked like letters written in a foreign language. She dug through them and cast them aside in disgust, heedless, in her panic, of the mess she made.

At last she found it: a two-foot long box of almost black velvet walnut with scarlet scoring on its panels. It was a beautiful piece of work, but Margaret nearly broke the latch in her haste to get it open. Later she remembered rich blue velvet, pearly grey and brown flecking, but almost before she had accepted that the horn was there she had grabbed it and was running back toward Skander's room.

There was no one else present when she entered save the awful sentience of death. She could not call to Skander or even sob for her own sake: the sentient dark choked off all sound. She moved across the room, through the fractured light and bars of shadow, to the dark-stained bedside table on which stood the full mug of horehound and tansy and the cut-crystal carafe of water that was glowing as with a light of its own. The next crescendo of animal-noise seemed to blossom in the splintered light as if, by way of anchoring itself, it had fixed itself in the watery shine.

Skander lay alone among the pillows and the light and shadows and the shadow of death. His skin was pale, his hair blackened with sweat; his breathing was painfully audible and irregular, and something white glistened on his lips. Margaret steeled her stomach and reached for the carafe. She let the stream of water run into the narrow neck of the freckled, fluted horn, watching the way the light played in the dance of water, then put the crystal away while the light jinked hard back and forth against Skander's cheek.

"Skander?" She touched his shoulder gingerly. "Skander, can you wake?"

His breathing sharpened and two fingers fluttered, that was all—but that was enough. Margaret climbed up on the edge of the high four-poster and got one hand behind Skander's head. He was heavy and cold and damp, and the air smelled strongly of almonds and death, but she forced herself to put the horn to his soiled lips. Water dribbled over his lips and through his teeth. She watched his throat but it did not move.

"Come on," she begged him, and hitched hard at her skirts to lean forward so she could get her fingers into the soft of his jaw. "Blast you, Skander Rime—swallow it!" She got some water to leak in through his teeth, but when nothing more happened she flung down the horn in a spray of silver water and pushed hard at his throat with both thumbs. She pushed harder than she thought was good for him, but at last, with a panicked, involuntary intake of breath Skander gasped, gagged, swallowed—she felt the thick muscles convulse under her palms—and began coughing violently. She thought she had killed him but he continued to cough and heave heartily for several minutes, turning red in the face, before he finally dropped off into hard breathing.

His eyelids fluttered and dragged themselves open. They looked like fractured amber, vague in the light, and roved against a confusion of pain for a moment before they seemed to fix on Margaret's face. His lips moved. No sound came out.

"If you can hear me," she told him, "better be hushed. You've had a close shave—and given us a nasty shock."

His face twisted; his brows gathered as if in an attempt to drag his battered thoughts together. Finally he whispered, "I'm— quite thir—"

"Thirsty? Do you want some water?"

A lively disapprobation flashed in his eyes. Chastened, Margaret climbed off the bed and went to the cupboard by the fire— which had eaten up its kindling and since gone out—and pulled out the little spare bottle of brandy that was kept for guests. But when she gave him a tumbler-full, he was almost too flogged to drink it and his consciousness kept slipping under her grasp. With a patience worn thin by panic, she continued to slide the brandy down his throat piecemeal until he had swallowed it all, and then she watched him drift away into a sombre sleep. She listened to his breathing and found it even. His hands, which had been curled and contracted in agony, had loosened and lay flat on the coverlet: the heavy signet ring glinted with a tiny sleeping spasm, but otherwise they were still.

With a despairing sigh Margaret left him to build up the fire again. The clanging of the logs on the fender did not wake him. She moved mechanically, numbed by the hours that had thrashed her without mercy. It still seemed surreal, too fast and too horrible to have really happened. The house had dropped into a lull of windy quiet; the howling had stopped. No doors banged, no steps tread on the hall floors. Skander's breathing was too even and low for her to hear over the crackle of the fire.

After awhile—she did not know how long a while—she came back out of her blindly wandering thoughts to find herself standing by the fire with the poker in her hand, staring at Skander's dexter hand. *I think he should be safe now*, she thought with a sudden flinching of restlessness. *I should go down—I should go down to see him.*

Deliberately she put the poker away and went round to bend back over Skander's face, searching it carefully one last time. She saw no discomfort in him, but what she saw discomforted *her*. She saw the regal, uncompromising lines of the de la Mare line, the aquiline nose, the proud, aristocratic mouth and brows.

It has been a long time since the men of my world looked like this. So casually handsome, so easily born to rule. But then, we have grown more peaceful too, I think. I wonder if that is better.

Satisfied that he would sleep and that he was in no danger of remission, she stole out of the room and locked the door behind her, putting the key in her own pocket. She was startled, upon turning around, to find the light still pattered through the windows and open doorways into the hall, that the atrium was still blooming with the sepia evening light. Had not hours passed, she wondered, and the world shifted drastically under her feet? Feeling oddly as if she had wandered into someone else's dream, she brushed her hand across her eyes and continued on.

She met Rhea, of all people, coming out of the library. The maid halted in the doorway and flung up her head, a sharpened, secret hope of anger showing for a moment in her eyes. Margaret stopped and met the gaze, hung a moment on it, and suddenly she understood. She understood in a whole but formless sort of way—the greeting kiss, the black, upturned eyes, the mulled wine... She did not think, nor did she feel anything until she was staggering forward, her fist smarting from the blow, and Rhea's face twisted into a mask of fury and surprise with a broken, bloodied left eyelid.

"You little witch!" Margaret cried, and struck again. Rhea was small and quick, but Margaret was beside herself. "Nay, you will not run like a coward! I am sick of your face—here, let me make it better pleasing!"

She hit like a man, and Rhea hit back, fighting like a cat in a bag, but Margaret had the odd clarity of fury burning away the clinging dross on her vision. She beat the maid down into the library and finished her with one last parting blow to the face, dropping her with an abbreviated thump onto a low coffee table. Only then did she hear the ringing of blood in her own ears and feel the sweat prickling on her skin. Rhea looked up at her through her fingers and one good eye, her teeth on edge, the breath whistling through her nose.

"Don't you say a word," Margaret warned her, "for I am about to be finished, and if you rouse me again I'll rub your mockery in your face for good. Old Hobden is a good hand with shovels. You would hardly make a lump in the earth."

Rhea said nothing; through her busted lip, Margaret was not sure she could. But as she went back to the library door, rage singing high and sweetly in her brain, she stopped once and turned back. The maid seemed to be waiting, staring up through fingers and dishevelled hair. There was murder in the eye.

"You have always mocked me," said Margaret. "You had better never mock me again."

Rhea touched her tongue to her bloodied lip, as if she meant to say something, but she hesitated and the moment was lost. Without a backward glance Margaret left her, though the feeling of daggers in her back followed her all down the hall and into the atrium downstairs until, having got lost in her own anxiety and anger, she found herself in the rear entryway and had to double back for the kitchen hall.

There was a flustered noise of talking coming from the kitchen but there was no one in the hall or the peristyle that she could see. Silently she slipped down the cellar stair, back through the ebbing tide of green-feeling electric pulse, against the feeling of someone who was not there watching her closely, until she found herself walking down the short stair into the wine-cellar and found the fox waiting for her.

For a long while the two of them were silent. The room had seemed big before, receding into the setter-brown shadows of the underground; but the fox's sharp-etched, wolfish body, drenched with the darkest India-ink colour, seemed to dwarf even her fathomless numbness as it loomed over her, resting on its lean haunches, cupped ears like shields pricked and bent as if to catch the sounds of her thoughts. One after the other things to say blew like dry leaves through her mind, but she could decide on no one to pick up and her tongue, for the moment, was tied.

She noted that he had a single bloom of white in the centre of his chest.

"Is this the first time," he asked in his new baritone, "you have broken your knuckles open on someone?"

She put up her hand and found blood streaming down the contours of her veins. It had not hurt until she saw it: a blue-fire pain began at once and she winced. "Yes. It felt curiously good at the time, though," she added.

The fox smiled. "Were that *I* a woman! I would have done that to her long ago. Alas, I—well, I'm not." There was a brief silence, then, more quietly: "Why did you not kill her?"

She found she had been asking herself that since she had dropped Rhea on the coffee table and pulled back, not giving her a blow to the nose that would have splintered in her brain-pan.

"He did not die," she said simply.

And the fox, far from protesting, smiled more widely and rose off his haunches to his enormous equine height. "Now you taste how awful justice is in the mouths of them that speak it. How is our blithesome Lord of Capys?"

Margaret managed a small smile in return. "Something less blithesome now, but I have locked the door on him and he sleeps."

"And you did not mind the horn?"

Fixing upon the lamp she saw again the wild wind-break of goldfinches and the startled, upward lunge of a dainty white woodland animal whose disinterest in her had been, in retrospect, perhaps the most grievous insult she could remember receiving in her life. "No, I did not mind it. I had seen a live one at Lookinglass."

The fox sat back down. "Oh, really? You did not tell me that."

"Nor did you tell me," her tone sharpened, "that you grow like Chinese bamboo and turn as black as Livy."

He, too, looked into the lamp as if to hide his own thoughts among the melting yellow light. She watched his black, jewel-cut muzzle, flushed into a copper hue, eyes glazed with an icy film of light, and listened to the sound of his breathing until he found his thoughts again.

One lip curled self-deprecatingly, revealing a terrible line of enormous sharp white teeth. "The first time we met and you went away again, back into the upper graves of Rupert's company, and I did not come with you, you hated me. I felt that you did."

It would have been lying to deny it. he could not lie to him.

His eyes flung down their glassy overlay as he looked back at her. "I am sorry—but I could not come. It is not a lock on doors and a lack of thumbs that keeps me down here. Rupert has his little Fool tied up by greater powers than that. I cannot mount those stairs any more than you can scale the glaciers of Fang."

"You mean his star-work. His little squares and circles and funny mathematics." Rage burned in the back of her throat. "He can lock you down here but he could not even save his own cousin?"

Sympathy pricked at the fox's brows. "You put that to him? What a smart that must have made. I am surprised it is Rhea's eye that is black and not yours."

She frowned, her lip remembering the break which it had only recently healed. The fox, seeming to realize what he had said, turned away.

"I grow smaller and weaker in the shadowing of the moon," he said presently, quietly, his voice muffled by the fur on his shoulder. "But when it waxes I grow stronger, and I fight against my bonds, and Rupert prays to his infernal god that I do not break them."

In a small voice, into the hollow quiet, Margaret murmured, "I am sorry I hated you."

He flashed her a smile, quick and kingfisherly, and rather irreverent of her remorse. "I think you have not hated me for a while now. I have held that close and warmed my heart with it on cold, empty nights."

He was the only person whom she would let mock her, whose mockery she could take with equanimity, because his mockery held no biting edge of hatred. She sat down on the wine-crate and pulled her feet off the cold dirt floor.

"I will go grey," she said in a pitiful, half-laughing voice. The laughter was unsteady and threatened to get the better of her.

"Maybe we had better open one of those bottles after all," said the fox sympathetically.

"Maybe we better had." Margaret brushed the back of her hand over her eyes. "I got a glass of brandy for Skander, but didn't think to pour any for myself. That was an oversight." Again they were quiet, rather shy of each other, Margaret thought. She still felt chills just looking at him and he, seeming aware of that, had curled up on the floor in an attempt to make himself look smaller. The blue blaze and green-flaking fire had gone out of him. Had she been daft, she would have thought he was no more than a huge black dog.

But she was not daft.

"What was it that you did?" she asked at last.

He had been looking elsewhere—the shadow of his head turned and loomed on the wall as he moved to meet her uncertain gaze. "Have you ever heard of the Danse Macabre?" he countered.

The chill, as if in mimicry, skittered on her flesh. "Yes. It is a gruesome piece of artistry."

"Oh, is it art now...? I got in its way as it was going upstairs and messed up its footwork, that is all."

She frowned. "You make so light of it."

"To laugh," he replied, "is the blithest weapon of those who live in the dark."

She picked a shard of masonry off the floor and began to roll its roughness between her thumb and forefinger. "He came down because he was lonely. Poor thing, up there in Lookinglass all by himself. So he comes down here, to the last place in Plenilune he would really *want* to go, to just sit and talk with me—and *this* happens."

"Do you fancy him?"

"*Fancy* has nothing to do with it," she replied, her voice sharpening. "He is a good sort of man, and good sort of men don't do well in this house. It quenches them..."

The hollow quiet stretched and grew until it became almost painful; then the fox broke it of a sudden, rushing to his feet and turning away with a heavy intake of breath. The light and shadow licked around his enormous body as he paced away and, turning at the end of his prison, came pacing back. Margaret watched him sadly, recognizing, though she was sure he did not, the gesture of a caged animal.

"You are lucky down here," she said impulsively.

He swung round and stared at her; his wall-eyes wavered with an eerie blue light.

"You are lucky down here," she repeated. "There is no sun and there is no air, but at least there is no Rupert and there is no Rhea and there is no—there is no—" Her voice cracked.

The fox said grimly, "The dead in Sheol are silent of the praise of the Lord."

"I want to go to the back of the wind." She put her head in her hand. Her forehead throbbed, and against her pressed eyelids she saw the scenes of Skander in his death-throes, struggling even to the last to maintain his dignity. "I want a lee to hide in. I do not know how much of this madness I can take." She looked into his face, which had turned soft under her words. "Your shoulders can spark green fire and hold off death, but whose shoulders can bear up the huge cross I see being put up for Plenilune?"

"But I think that you know the answer to that."

"I know. I *know*. But he is otherwise silent while we all cry out for the sake of Plenilune. You have said yourself that no one is equal to contending with Rupert. Must we be our own heroes?"

The fox was silent for awhile, as if listening to the sound of God's own silence and weighing it. But whatever he thought of it, if he had any hope or any despair, his face did not belie it.

"Who knows, Margaret? But I have often observed that it is out of people like you that heroes are made."

She stood up. "Then God help the heroes," she replied definitely. After a pause she added, "I wish God would hear me in this place. It would be a joke on Rupert worthy of even you, fox."

He smiled a little.

"I should go back up to Skander now. I locked the door to keep anyone out and I am the only one with a key."

The fox got up and walked with her to the foot of the stairs. Standing so close to him, Margaret could feel the dark ripple of power shimmering around him. His huge shadow plunged the wine-cellar into a deeper gloom and, for just a moment, it seemed to her to be the dark mantle of death trailing after him, trailing after him and touching her...

He was speaking to her. "Try to mind yourself. Every time you come down here some new awful thing has happened. I can only do so much," he added apologetically.

Why did she feel as if this were their last meeting? All at once she wanted to reach across and touch him, though everything in her recoiled at the thought, just to prove to herself that the nightmarish feeling was a fraud. "Don't be so serious. If you are serious I cannot bear life. *You* must laugh, or I have no hope at all."

He smiled, but the smile was mirthless. "Better go now." He looked up and away as if to hide his inscrutable face. "Skander will be waiting—how we all wait for your step at the door...! I may be smaller when next you can come."

"Yes. I thought of that."

He looked at her. "You do not mind?"

She did mind, because it unnerved her, but for the same reason she kept coming down to the cellar, for the same reason she wanted to reach across and grab him as the only security in her life, she did not mind too much. She left him in the big black splendour of death's shadow, blue eyes shining like two gashes of heaven, and she did not mind too much.

Skander was still asleep when she looked in on him. He had shifted, flung an arm over his head, and turned a little to one side. Margaret smiled kindly on the natural pose, wishing, like some magician, she could conjure up Aikaterine, who would best know Skander's habits, likes, and dislikes. She fetched her books, Songmartin's and the little atlas Julianna had given her, and sat down in a chair drawn close to Skander's head. It occurred to her as she settled that she ought to have fetched her dress but she felt too emotionally flogged to entertain for more than one flinching instant the idea of bending back over that accursed gown. In the mystical half-light and shadows of Skander's room, the stitching of that gown seemed like the methodical movement of time toward Rupert's installation as Overlord. She could not bear to bring it closer.

One leg crossed over the other, settled in the chair, she picked up the atlas and opened to the beginning. She was startled to see the brown plates, not of Earth, but of Plenilune; but the surprise was momentary, and then she was seeing names she recognized—Talus Perry in the west of the Mares, the road through Glassdale up to Lookinglass—and as she fanned through the pages in the soft silence of the rustling fire, the formlessness of Plenilune began to take shape. She saw where the seas were, where the rivers ran, how small was Thrasymene and how vast the steppes. Darkling in the south, bordered by the swirls of warm moving sea-water, seemed a kind of sepia-toned paradise—she caught a note about rich wine-country there, and smiled.

She lingered unwillingly, out of a perverse sense of curiosity, over a detailed map of the Mares. The roads, woods, and lot-lines were clearly demarcated; she saw the ancient estates with their beautiful, foreign names—Marenové House set among them like the crown jewel of a diadem—and her heart hurt.

Over all this I might be a kind of queen, and if it were not for Rupert I should not mind it.

Her eyesight blurred. For a moment she sat in total silence, seeing nothing but a confusion of images inside her mind—her mother, her suitor, Skander, the fox, old Hobden who seemed like the steadiness of the ground he toiled over—then, with an effort, she came back to herself as an illustration alongside the Marius Hills drew her attention.

It was a dragon.

XV | NIGHTMARE

Skander was reserved when he woke. Margaret saw from the clearness of his eyes that he was master of himself once more, but he looked at her wordlessly, and wordlessly looked away, a slumbering anger between his brows. The thing which had happened lay unspoken between them, but he was thinking on it, keenly, furiously, in full awareness of what had become of him after the witching maid had brought his drink. He had felt the knife in the dark skim too close between his shoulder-blades. That was apt to change a man, and all at once Margaret was afraid of him.

He broke the silence at last, looking away into the fire. "Where are my things?"

"They are here." She got up in a rustle of taffeta—the light worried on the fabric, sending flickers into the shadows—and moved to the end of the bed where she had put his pack. "Do you think to rise? You are well enough."

If he did, he did not tell her. He lay awhile longer staring into the fire, looking at his own tempestuous thoughts.

"Rupert was in to see you," she offered by way of peacemaking, "but you were asleep. He was a little relieved to know you would not die, but sorry," she added truthfully, "that I kept watch for you."

Skander looked at her then, the fierceness of his mother's line shaping his face with hard edges. "You stayed? Methought it was Aikaterine sometimes, but then I was confused with sleep."

"No, it was me." Margaret returned to the chair, though now she felt unwelcome. She fidgeted, but the heaviness of her skirts complained and she bid herself sit still lest Skander become aware of her awkwardness.

His hand clenched the counterpane. "He need not fear anything from me," he said gruffly.

She tightened her own hands into fists.

Of a sudden he looked at her, the silk of his pillows rustling like the fire with his movement. "You are sorry, I think, that Rupert has nothing to worry about from my quarter."

Hang the man!—tears smarted behind her eyes and it was almost all she could do to control them. "It is no matter."

"It is a matter," he sighed, and put up one hand over his face. "I wish I could be sorry—truly I do—"

Anger overcame her wretched sorrow. "By the twelve houses, your heart lies elsewhere and I get on—we all get on. Please do me a courtesy and spare me no pity. I cannot abide pity."

He seemed to forget himself and the knife in the dark and the long fight against poison, and stared at her, surprise and confusion and respect warring in his face. At last, with some effort, he put them away and settled back. "It is that obvious," he asked, "even to you?"

"What, Woodbird?" She, too, settled back. She was still angry, formlessly, helplessly, but she did her best to master herself. "I have no occupation but to observe. I observed a lot—as you well know." She smiled grimly.

He, too, was remembering the night in the cellar and he, too, smiled. They were silent for some time, staring each at their own thoughts. Margaret, listening to the crackle of the fire, found her mind wandering to the dress—the thought was never far away—and realized how alarmingly close it was to being done, how alarmingly close the day was on which Rupert would bring down the top-stone on the Honours' tomb. There was a bit of thunder in the air, and the muffled sound of it made her start.

Skander began speaking again. At the sound of his voice Margaret turned toward him: he was staring off into the middle distance, unblinking, detached. "I forget that you are not native to the Honours. You say no pity, and I hear a woman of the Honours speaking—one of the old line: valiant, hard as adamant, unbending..."

Margaret gently drew him back. "It is a harsh portrait you paint. I fear I, like the images of the women of old, have lost the skill of love."

He shook his head but did not break his staring gaze. "Nay, 'tis but a harder, more enduring kind of love, is all. You say no pity, but 'tis a pity we have lost the knack of that sort of charity. I knew a man who had that knack. I do not know him, now."

Again the chill, the sense of foreboding brushing the cold up the backs of her arms.

"Would any of us die," Skander mused, his face darkened by an inner thought, "to keep what looms before us from happening?"

Would any of us die?

Before she could speak, before she could break past the awful dare that seemed, though he had not meant it, to be levelled at *her*, he shifted and pushed himself upward, letting loose a breath like a swimmer breaking the surface. "How we are poets and idealists! and have been for too long. I will get up and have a bit of breakfast. I think I should go before I overstay my welcome any further."

Margaret got up, shying away from the macabre thought. "I will personally see to your breakfast."

He looked up at her as he swung his legs over the side of the bed, brown eyes standing out sharply in a bar of firelight. Thunder rumbled in the distance. "Yes... I would be obliged if you did that for me."

Margaret took that wary, secretive look with her when she left. As she passed through the dining room and into the kitchen hall, she paused involuntarily by the cellar door. Her hand almost touched the knob, her mind going ahead down the stairs to the big black creature who, as the days passed, would be growing smaller and ruddier as his invisible chains tightened about him... A clatter from the kitchen disturbed her thoughts and she went on, blushing inexplicably. She told Livy, who she thought could be trusted, to make ready Skander's hunter, and was glad to see that Rhea was nowhere in sight near the kitchen. She oversaw Skander's meal in peace and had her own brought in with his to the dining room.

"Any sign of Rupert this morning?" he asked as he joined her.

His face, she noted when she looked up, had changed and was more haggard; the liveliness had gone out of his form also, and that discouraged her. But she roused her spirits as best she could. Even if he was incapable of helping her, he would always be a friend to her—though no one, she thought with some faint curiosity, would be a friend to her as the fox was.

She turned toward the window. Sunlight clinked off the swinging amber drops hanging from her ears. "He is on the lawn. He takes Curoi and Talbot out of a morning when the weather is not too thick."

Skander crossed to the window and stood by her, looking out on the scene. Through the heavy grey light and wind-surf noise came back the sound of dogs barking. The hawthorns were bare, the barberry wind-stripped; clouds lay thick in the lower parts of Seescardale and obscured the view within a few miles.

"It is thick enough this morning. Is that thunder I hear? There will be a storm in Glassdale for sure."

Margaret looked at her hands clenched in her lap. "It would be useless, I suppose, and cruel to ask if you would stay another day."

He did not turn. The hollow winter light paled his face; the gleam of the windowpanes chilled his eyes. "I cannot stay another day. I am sorry."

"Better eat your eggs," she told him with an attempt at glibness. "There is nothing so distasteful to the civilised world as cold eggs."

Rupert came in presently, his shoulders sheeny with mizzle. He saw Margaret first and his face brightened; then he saw his cousin and something checked, closed and quenched, crept into his features.

"Good morning. I see that you are back on your feet."

Leaning back, Skander hitched his ankle up over his opposite knee, his cup of coffee steaming in his hand. He, too, had a wariness in his face, weighing his cousin's mind in the tension of the air. "We are men to bound back quickly. What does the weather do?"

As Rupert sat down Livy entered and poured his master his own cup of coffee. "It will rain here but the main of it has come over Seescarfell already. It should pass on by tonight and leave us with bonny skies." There was a pause, thoughtful on both sides, then Rupert added, " 'Tis but a bare fortnight."

Skander nodded. "Not even—just shy of." His gaze, for a moment, slid to Margaret before passing on to the window again; and it was all Margaret could do in that moment to suppress the quick, raging twist of panic that began beneath her breastbone.

The odd thing was that Rupert and Skander parted in a kind of quietness, not at all friendly, but as two men who have a mutual respect, though given grudgingly, silently acknowledged. Margaret could not help but feel, as she stood on the stable yard threshold wrapped against the cold, that the parting gestures they gave each other were like two men saluting with duelling swords. But when Skander went away and Rupert rejoined her, she felt he was angry.

Was it her imagination, or did his eyes, brushing past her face, seem to say, "You are next"?

"The gown?" he asked as they went back into the atrium.

"It is nearly finished. As are we all, it would seem."

He shot her a burning look, eyes flint-coloured in the muted light. She felt the anger turn into something else, something that frightened her with its surge of possessive rage, but she stood her ground and the tide ebbed. Rupert wrestled himself under a pretence of patience again. "Yes, the time is nearly upon us. It is truly time for Plenilune to be taken up and shaken by the four corners. It has grown old and dusty and set in its shackled ways."

"I saw it quite otherwise," Margaret protested. "It seemed to me the very heart of a fire in its blaze; never more alive a people have I seen before."

He smiled condescendingly. "Would that you had seen her in the old days, when our blood ran with gold and the blood of our enemies ran like wine. Men were men in those days and walked the hills like giants. I long to cast back upon those days."

His face grew thoughtful, introspective, and he seemed far off. She did not know why she drew him back, but she found herself saying gently, as much to herself as to him, "Could anyone, no matter his power, turn back the inexorable flow of time?"

Instead of taking his hand off the rein of his anger—as she had expected him to—and giving it its head, he smiled a little as if to himself and, turning, set his hand against her cheek. His palm was cold. "Like stones in the ploughland you set yourself crosswise with me, and like stones I pull you up and make a border of you about me. Could a man, no matter his power, turn back the flow of time...? He could not. You and I know that. But, for all that, he might try for the sake of all he holds dear, to make a stand and to make a difference. For would we find those olden days so very golden if we were allowed to go back to them?"

Margaret moved out of his embrace. "Probably not," she replied flatly. "Only have a care, Rupert—I have said it before: what you and I hold dear set us crosswise against each other."

Again the flint, striking sparks against the iron of her words, gleamed in his eye. He set his hand on her shoulder—it was a heavy hand—and turned her about, saying, "Go finish that dress. We will see, presently, about the other things."

She put in her heels and resisted him until he went away without a backward glance; his footsteps on the stairs receded, passing to the north wing of the house, fading into wooden silence. Just this once she did not feel the chill of the open threat, nor the looming shadow of fate. She went quietly, numbly, back to her sewing. She had only an hour's worth of chinaberry clusters left to sew—not much, when she looked the whole thing over and spread it grandly out on her knee, not much at all.

It was a fine dress after all, very grand but also very beautiful. As she threaded her needle and bent her back to the work—the familiar ache beginning in her neck—Margaret wished she could model it for the fox. He would like it in his frank way of appreciating beauty, and tell her just how outrageous it was. She stopped her work to stretch her back, looking up through the frosted windowpanes. It was hard enough to sneak down any day, let alone in a full-blown gala gown. He would have to be content with a description.

Margaret leaned back over the skirt.

It would be a very detailed description.

The night she tried on the gown, it was only three days until the new year. The thought was alarming, but not so alarming as being twisted and thrust and fitted into the gown in the cold of her room, flood-lit in firelight and the backlash of jewel-glitter. It was Lilith who attended her: she had seen Rhea on the outskirts from day to day, a sullen, silent figure, oddly cowed into obedience, but she had never crossed paths with Margaret again. Margaret was glad, especially at this moment in which she was sure she would have slung another punch at the maid's face, torn out of the dress, and fled to the companionable misery of the cellar. Rupert would have had to drag her from the fox's dungeon or lock her up there with him. As it was, being pulled on all sides until the few pounds she had gained seemed to squeeze out of her again, it was all she could do to keep a handle on her simmering panic.

It helped when Rupert came to inspect. He came in silently; she did not know he was there until she saw his reflection beside hers in the mirror looking, not at her reflection, but at her real self. There was a sincere tenderness in his face at that one unguarded moment that made her hate him even more, for it was a look that should have conjured pity. She felt a pang of guilt pinch hard at the right side of her heart—she could feel it bleeding—but the hate won over. Hate was a strong weapon, she found, stronger even than his love—

And she was glad it had won over, for the moment his eyes sprang off her figure to the mock figure in the mirror, there was a hardness to his eyes, a preoccupied darkness that bespoke him elsewhere turning the pieces of the world to his own design as a man might turn the pieces on a chessboard.

Lilith finished the last adjustment to the torso and drew back, hands folded, head bowed. "Well?" Margaret asked Rupert's reflection. She did not bother to conceal the blade in her voice. "Does it suit its p-purpose?"

He smiled—she did not like the smile. "In retrospect I fear we have outdone ourselves. What will we do for a wedding gown?"

"Nothing."

He laughed, short and hard. "Suitable, but unfitting if we mean to have guests attendant."

Margaret schooled her anger—a task which required all her strength. She turned her shoulders as Lilith stepped back in to begin the long unbuttoning of the bodice at her back. She was raised on an ottoman and had to look down into Rupert's absent, angry eyes. "I think as far as many see," she remarked, "the wedding would be a moot point."

"You mean that little mistake of Darkling's?" Scorn sharpened the black spindles of his eyes. "They are all quick to think so—they like to be mean-spirited." He added in a low, musing tone, "They would not be wrong, had you unbent a little."

"I do not unbend. I must be broken."

It was gratifying to see the look of pain pull like hard wine at the corner of his jaw. The moment stretched like a violin-hair, waiting to be played upon...but they did not play upon it. Rupert nodded curtly, almost by way of a salute, and went out, throwing a shadow up the wall in a huge, unconscious parting gesture.

The shadow was cold on her soul.

It was ten o'clock when Margaret was finally alone, rid of the gown, rid of Lilith—Rupert's door had banged shut and not cracked open again—and, staring unseeingly at the clock face, she felt now was her chance to see the fox again. He would be the fox again by now. The moon's face would be small, as small as the little lick of firelight reflecting in the glass front of the timepiece. *Go now. Go now: don't think that this is the last time you will see him as you are, buffeted and caged, but free at heart. Don't think about three days hence. Don't think that in three days you will be as chained as he. Just go.*

The house was quiet as she stole through it. She had learned by now to walk with confidence, knew which stairs creaked and where the chairs and tables were put so that she would not bump against them. The door to the kitchen hall had an oddly placed handle, higher than most, but she had learned just where to reach for it. Outside the world was deathly silent: the first real snow, huge and soft, was coming down. As happens in snow-weather, she did not notice the cold. She slipped silently down the cellar stairs, and because of her silence she heard, long before she reached the wine-cellar, the sound of men talking down below. She stopped once in surprise, her heart suddenly in her throat. The voices were indistinct. She stole onward, carefully, the voices becoming clearer, sharper, cut even on every edge like diamonds, until she stood against the wall at the head of the wine-cellar stairs.

" 'Twas none of my design!" Rupert's voice surged like an oily black sea, growling, heaving with all his pent-up anger. "You would be the fool to think I was so short-sighted as to that. But the danger is past, thanks to you. Does it gall you to know you saved me by a hair's breadth from censure on all sides? Does it gall you?"

"Does not gall me that a good man was spared an early grave!" The fox's voice was high and mocking and cut like a knife. "You know that at Plenilune I am at my strongest. *You* were a fool—a *fool*—" the word came out spittingly "to think I would sit by—canst even twiddle thumbs!—while a man's life is in the balance and I at the height of my power! You set your hand once to my thigh and broke me. I guard it better now."

Margaret leaned around the corner but the lintel of the stairway blocked her view. She hid again, low in the dark corner of the wall, not knowing if she ought to come out or stay where she was and listen. She could hear Rupert pacing; his heavy tread crossed the width of the wine-cellar, measured and awful, and she knew he was furious beyond all bounds of fury. The fox probably knew it, too, but he was in a reckless, blazing mood and would not be quenched.

"And Rhea?" asked the fox. "How is she? Black-eyed and frothing at the mouth? I'd keep that chit on a leash if I were you— you're so damned good at making them. Her mistaken sense of loyalty nearly ruined everything for you."

Rupert growled, "I wouldn't talk about a woman that way if I were you."

"Says the man who bites them!" the fox barked back viciously.

There was a hissing noise and a thump. The fox gave an abbreviated squeal from the other side of the cellar. Margaret started up in horror and only just held herself back.

"Ah!" The fox groaned. "That's right, kick a fellow while he's down! That's sporting of you."

"Do you know your fault?" retorted Rupert. His voice was growing farther away and Margaret could hear a scamper of paws as the fox attempted to dodge him. He was not quick enough: there came another thump and squeal. She clapped a hand over her mouth to keep from sobbing. "Do you? You always were a prattling fool. You *talk!* And by my Lord Adam, I am sick of your talking! I will break your jaw to quiet you!"

It sounded as if Rupert had succeeded. There was a crack, a blur of shadow against the stairs, and the fox let out a single choked cry of agony. There was another blow—a crate went over.

"Where is your mockery now, red worm?"

Another blow.

Grace of our Lord Jesus Christ, make him stop!

"If I cannot kill you, I will yet take you past the brink of desire for it!" *Thump! thump! thump!* He was hammering the little thing. Margaret's stomach heaved. "You would wrestle with angels?" *Thump! crack! crash!* "Guard against corporeal blows, half-wit!" There was a pause, a panting breath, a low canine moan. "Well, physician? Can you heal yourself?"

For a long time the fox could not answer. With a silent shrieking that nearly tore her apart, Margaret begged him to answer, to be able to say something. *God, for the love of charity—!*

A rattling gasp—half a laugh choked off by pain. "Give me a moment. I'll...conjure...bit of bandage..."

"Shuh!" replied Rupert scornfully. There was a flicker of shadow on the stair again and Margaret was afraid he was coming back, but it seemed he had only bent over or stood up. "Lie there awhile in the ruin of your own making. You know me for a patient man, but I will hold grudges until hell frosts and my patience is not everlasting. And between the throbs of your headache mind this: I *will* brew a drink of death for you, no matter how hard you struggle against the chalice."

"You would...miss me if you did," said the fox with a touch of his old languid humour.

The shadow wavered. "As soon miss a thorn in my foot."

He was coming back. Nearly tripping over her skirts Margaret retreated into the darkness, huddled down into as small and black a shape as possible. Her stomach was heaving and twisting and trying desperately to squeeze up through her hands, but she did not dare let it. She did not dare breathe. The lamplight broke up into a man's figure and Rupert emerged from the head of the stairwell, bent with fury, his fists clenched at his sides. She was horribly afraid that his uncanny sensing would find her, but he seemed too distracted to take stock of the dark chamber. He went on at once, melting into the darkness; she listened to the rattle of his footsteps up the stone stair and heard, with a sickening sense of relief, the door at the top crash shut.

With a hiccupping gag she lurched to her feet, caught her skirt under her shoe and stumbled, sobbing, reeling against the wall. "Oh God, oh fox—" Half falling she made it to the head of the stair and ran down, blinking through a blur of tears and a blur of nausea. "Fox!" she called. "Oh, fox! I'm here!"

There was a bit of white movement behind an overturned crate. She ran toward it. Blindly she hauled wine-crates aside, shedding broken hunks of bottles and spraying wine about the floor.

"Oh—oh dear God—no," choked the fox when he stared up through black-rimmed eyes to see her. "Go away. Rupert will look for you—"

"You idiot!" she cried, kneeling in the wreckage of wood and wine and pulling the battered head into her lap. She was sobbing so hard that her words came out in a broken rush. "You idiot! You stupid—st-stupid idiot! How could you have done this? You are all I have! Are you broken? Oh God, you're bleeding!"

He was trying desperately to worm out of her hold and she was desperately trying to hold him. He kept gasping out that she needed to go and she, in full hysteria, kept crying at him to hold still and to be hushed and to lie quietly and how *could* he have provoked Rupert so horribly? At last he seemed to decide that the only way to calm her and keep her sobs from bringing Rupert back down on them was to oblige her by lying, like a baby, on his back in the cradle of her arms. His face was drawn in agony, all his little teeth showing through a fixed snarl of pain, but he kept still. After awhile Margaret could look at his busted brow and bleeding gums without feeling heaves.

"You idiot," she hiccupped. "Oh, I hate you! Is anything broken?"

"I always make mistakes with Rupert," he replied in a voice of shadow. "I always—ah!—I always lose my mind... A few ribs, maybe. It doesn't matter. I can't see." A drop of blood ran into his right eye and he shuddered at the sting of it, squinting to get it out.

Manoeuvring him carefully Margaret wrenched at the lace collar of her nightgown and tore off a heavy piece. "Oh!—ah!" he protested as she sponged at his eye. "Wait, you need—grr!" His black lips curled off his teeth as she bound the bloodied strip around his head. A stain of red continued to spread across it—lace was not meant to soak up blood—but it kept the blood out of his eyes.

"Please lie still." She put her arms around him and wormed her way over to his pile of blankets and propped herself against the wall. He was larger than she had expected him to be: his body was as long as a beagle's and his limbs, slender and lengthy, did not seem to have any comfortable place to be put. With extreme delicacy he curled his back legs in and turned his tail up over the white flash of his belly. He did not seem able to move his forelegs: they hung down his length in a listless fashion, twitching now and then with pain. She managed to keep one arm under his hindquarters and one arm under his head and shoulders and let his body rest on her narrow lap. She shifted him closer, carefully, trying to get him comfortable.

"You really oughtn't—it isn't—" He kept trying to speak but every time he opened his mouth a trickle of blood leaked out.

"You're a fine one to tell me oughtn't and isn't," she replied cuttingly. She found she was not quite done crying. A tear dashed onto his fur and hung there, a bead of diamond-blaze against the stained darkness of his coat. "Now please lie q-quietly."

He turned his head against her forearm and stared silently out through a swollen slit of eye. He looked mournful and pensive, but he did not look angry anymore. The fight seemed to have gone out of him. She sat on the uneven bedding with his long weight in her arms. She wanted to rock him, gently, because that seemed natural. He was big and soft and warm and in pain, and it was all she could do to keep from moving him gently back and forth in a rhythmic pattern to try to soothe him. If she did she was sure it would hurt him, and if it did not make his bones grind and his torn muscles scream, it would hurt his pride. He looked a little hurt now.

"H-h—" He licked his bloodied teeth. "How long are...are you staying?" he asked after a long quiet.

Her arms were falling asleep and one foot was already past hope, but she made no move.

He turned his head quickly, staring up at her out of one barely serviceable eye. "You can't stay here all night. I forbid it."

"I can and I will," she snapped.

He tried moving, but to no avail. The long space in stillness had cast his limbs in iron. "I can't have you holding me all night like a baby. You must go. By the twelve houses, woman, I'm not accustomed to not getting my way!"

"Pity for you!"

"Margaret!—ah!"

He choked off in mingled fury and pain and stared woundedly up at her. It was rather awful how pointed his glare could be even when it was coming out of only one eye. But he was right: she could not hold him that way all night long. She gingerly picked him off her lap, her limbs screaming in protest, and carefully laid him down on the bedding. She found a bit of blanket and put it over him, found another bit of blanket and wrapped herself up in it, and tried to get comfortable on the uneven pile beside him. It was unbelievable how painful a bit of rolled-up blanket could be: a length was cutting into her hip and no amount of shifting would right it.

The fox tried to move to his feet, got tangled in his own blanket, seemed to swim against a wave of nausea, and crashed down again, panting, defeated. He gave no more protest. He lay with his head on his forelegs, eyes shut tight against the throbbing, his little flanks heaving under the blanket.

"May I get you some water?" asked Margaret, feeling helpless.

He shook his head.

Without thinking she reached out and began stroking his head. The fur was smooth and warm; the long ears pulsed with blood as she drew them gently through her fingers. He stiffened and moved his mouth as if to say something, but gave it up. His brows relaxed. His ears bent easily under the passing of her hand. His breathing was still laboured, but the lines of his body seemed to have given in to the dark pressure of exhaustion. If only he would go to sleep, she thought, at least then he would be free of the pain.

A little brokenly, a little shyly, she recalled Lady Kinloss' lullaby. It had been a long time since she had seen the golden-shell woman, alone in the dark which was her only friend, vainly trying to sing her baby to sleep. Her own mother seemed petty now, like the minor annoyance of a small lap-dog after one has met the unfettered fury of a stallion. Her hand rose and fell over the fox's lean skull. Was there no peace anywhere? Was there no comfort or goodness or justice? Must they all be crushed, she under her mother's jibes and Rupert's steady pressure, the fox by blow, Lady Kinloss by neglect? How many souls cried out like the bare rosebushes of Marenové? How many...

Sleep, sleep, my baby.

The fox's right ear twitched. Her hand rose and fell over it, bringing the faint white hairs to light.

Sleep, sleep, my baby.
And when you wake
I'll give you a little black pony
With a coat of night
And eyes of dragon-fire.

Sleep, sleep, my baby.
Sleep, sleep, my baby...

She sang it twice through, dropping a register halfway and fighting two stammers which came inexplicably out of her dry, unsteady mouth. The fox's breathing slowly evened and her eyesight slowly blurred. She did not remember dropping off to sleep. Her hand grew heavier and slower and his breathing grew softer and quieter. Confused images of picking the fox up and running away played in Margaret's mind until she thought she was doing so until she lost the dreams in one high wave of sleep that bore her off beyond imagination.

XVI | THE MANY-SPLENDOURED THING

A warm touch on her cheek roused her from a stiff, black sleep. She came unwillingly awake, confused by pain and soreness, confused by the darkness of the room until her eyes focused on the fox and she remembered with a jolt what had happened. She sat up, scrubbing at her eyes with the heel of her hand.

The fox was sitting up, washed, carrying himself gingerly, a little subdued in his demeanour, but otherwise he seemed much his usual self. "There now," he said. "Birds have their nests and the foxes have their dens, but a wine-cellar is no place for a lady's bunk. Did you sleep at all?"

"I slept. So did you." Once her eyes had cleared she looked him over. Blood still crusted his flaming cheek-fur and spattered on his white waistcoat; one eye was still drooping. "You seem better for it."

"I mend quickly. *You* look ghastly. Margaret, what possessed you—"

She pressed her lips into a thin, uncompromising line; he saw the look and cut himself off. He shook his head pensively and winced when the movement reminded him that Rupert had nearly kicked his skull in. "Even a Fool," he said, "who has nothing to do but look and listen, forgets the sheer bull-headedness of a woman in a rage. I cry you mercy. Thank you for staying. It was nice to wake up in the wee hours when the lamp had sunk and hear someone else's breathing in the dark. One forgets those little things that make life beautiful: someone else breathing, blue sky overhead, a cheeky little robin in the lane..."

She pulled her legs up under her. The wine-cellar was bitingly cold. What hour was it? "Are you sure you are mended, just like that? I think Rupert kicked you harder than you realize."

The eyelid drooped; the shadows swam over the mirror-eye. "Nay, 'tis not the hardest he has kicked me ever. I mend."

Margaret felt her finger had fallen upon a sore and she was suddenly loathe to rough it. "Should I bring you a cheeky robin to keep you company?" she asked, not really listening to her own words.

But he heard her, and seemed to withdraw further into himself. "I would not wish this on the gloomiest of robins."

Looking at him, he seemed a world away. It hurt how far away he seemed to be, further down than a wine-cellar, cut off by more than servants and stairs and doors. He seemed cut off by stones and death. She wanted to reach out to him again, but the moment for that had passed. She blushed to think how she had stroked him last night, like a child, like a pet. His distance hurt, and yet she was tired of going away hurt. It was he who was hurt, perhaps more than she: caged, battered, bleeding on the inside and perhaps wondering, as she did, if the shrouds by which Rupert held them held in their prayers as well.

"Will you be all right if I go now?" she asked, touching him gently with her voice to bring him back.

He came back slowly, surfacing out of some black inner misery that was unlike him. Did he carry this with him always, and laugh to spite it so that she would never know? She stared into his wall-coloured eyes but it was like staring at her own reflection: she could not see into him. Suddenly he smiled, white and fanged, in lieu of laughter. "Do not pity me, Margaret. I mend. Not everyone can boast of that. Go on, before Rupert comes down to see the wreck of me and finds you here. I give you my word upon his confused honour—I dare not vouch for his temper."

She hesitated, half-gathered to rise, loathe to leave him; but she saw the guardedness had come back into his face, the edge of mockery at the corner of his eye, and she knew that, for now, he would manage on his own. He had managed before her.

But what of Rupert's threat? Margaret knew him well enough to know that it was not empty. Rupert was a man who would get what he wanted, reckoning nothing of the cost. The fox stared back along the blade of her unblinking gaze—he looked puzzled as the moment drew out. Was she willing to defy Rupert as the old apple-leaf woman had?

Was she willing to die?

"I'll come again, fox," she murmured, "as soon as I can."

He smiled, but there was in his smile a distant sadness—of premonition or memory, she did not know—and she knew he did not believe her.

Livy found her with some surprise in the dining room. She went up quietly, moving in a cold greyness, a careful thoughtlessness, for thinking hurt like walking on shards of glass. She came to herself when Livy entered and turned from the window at the sound of his step.

"My Lady Margaret?"

She saw a flush of red in his dark cheeks and jewel-dark spots on the shoulders of his jacket. He had been out of doors and there had been rain. Odd—she looked back out the window, feeling she had been staring out it for some moments—odd that she had not noticed it was raining.

She asked without turning back round, "Where is your master?"

"He has gone across to Talus Perey. If my lady will come away from the window, I will send for Lilith to attend her."

Do not think. There is not time for thinking. God, what a window! Don't look. Don't count the cost. There is not time. We have dared. Now we must do.

"Livy, do not trouble her. She has duties elsewhere and I am in no humour nor inclination for assistance. You may," she added in the wake of the manservant's displeased demeanour, "ring her to a light breakfast for me."

"To be taken here, my lady?"

"To be taken here. Meanwhile saddle Hanging Tree."

"It is raining, my lady."

"Sooth, and I am English."

He did not look as though he understood her, but neither did he appear inclined to argue. He moved toward the kitchen hallway and she, waiting until the door swung shut behind him, forced herself to run upstairs in a sudden flurry of panic with the full weight of what she was about to do racing to overtake her. She locked her door behind her as if to lock the terror out. In haste she dressed, hauling on the heavy riding gown and dressing her hair and shoulders in a tartan against the wet. The tartan was curiously real among all the heavy things she pulled on: its stripes of red sang out against the grey morning and seemed to her like slender threads of hope or sanity.

What gave the morning a dimension of pain, which the heavy fog had managed to block out until now, was the moment when Margaret, swathed against the cold, pulled the little atlas out from amongst her private things and turned it open. There again, leaping up in coffee-colour and atrament, were Marenové and the Marius Hills—and Lookinglass a kind of embattled star to the east on the edge of a long dragon-back of hills. She saw Darkling and Orzelon-gang, the steppes, the narrow, misshapen Honour of Thrasymene; but all this passed by her in a kind of fitful blur, like a fly that is angrily swatted away. What she did see was the small, intricate, almost life-like figure of a dragon hard by the east side of the Marius Hills, pointing west into the lift of the fells as if to mark a path. With her heart uncomfortably where her throat should be, she lifted the corner of the page and slid her hand underneath it.

"God forgive me," she murmured, and tore the page from the book.

The agony of terror settled in the pit of her stomach, singing a warning tune that threatened to heave back up the light breakfast she fought to swallow. The feeling did not begin to ebb until she was well out of the home meads and jigging up the sodden north road, Marenové House lost in the mist at her back. Then she was alone with the cold and the long road before her, and it was easier not to think about what she was doing. She did not feel much madness; she felt the constant but diminished flutter of fear at being met—a lady alone upon the road—and felt keenly the stinging wet knife of the wind, but over that there grew another feeling, a feeling akin to the marshlight country around her and the shepherd's panpipe on the fells, something altogether of Plenilune, which sang out of her heart like the hawk let loose on the wing. It was speckled gold like a grouse's wing and dipped itself in the blood that was still coming out of her soul. It was an awful, beautiful feeling.

She met no one on the road. Once she heard the lumber of a cart to one side, muffled as though by a bank or a thick hedge, and once she heard voices and the complaint of a cow, but otherwise she was alone, moving at alternate speeds up the damp stone causeway, moving through the roiling mists and sudden flurries of snow, the pound of her heart and the sweet ring of shod hooves the only sounds in her world. They only silenced once when she squeezed under the low-hanging branches of a cedar, plunged into a sudden eclipse of darkness, and fumbled with ice-numb hands at the crumpled paper of her map. In the gloom she studied it, struck by the sudden rational fear that she might miss the turn in the thick winter weather.

There is no room for mistakes. I will not miss the turn.

She brushed aside the cedar, flinging rain-droplets everywhere, and kicked Hanging Tree back onto the road.

For hours she moved at the palfrey's swinging lope, too numb with cold and full of determination to feel the creeping ache of being in the saddle. The sun was obscured behind an oppressive sky: she had no notion what the hour was. She felt no sense of hunger or saw any change in the light to assure her she had not passed into the lowlands of hell where time, like a cruel mockery of eternity, drew out in interminable moments of monotony. Weariness, mistaken for the fog until she found herself jerking upright again, swept over her from time to time; in time it became so severe that she reached desperately for a means of keeping her mind sharp against the elements. In low tones, pitched to the ring of iron on stone, she sang the few bars she knew of Kinloss' lullaby. It seemed oddly fitting, considering what she went to do and on what darcy-coloured mount she went to do it.

It seemed very fitting.

In time the Marius Hills loomed beside her, closer and closer, an unbroken darkness against the seething grey. It had been snowing for the past hour in idle flakes that seemed to hang upon the air and never settle; her horse, flecked in black and white, seemed a creature born of the shifting winter weather. Her weariness expected it to melt away beneath her. But it kept going, wearier than she, huffing, shoes scuffing on the causeway and dirt track onto which she led it; its pace had noticeably slackened.

"Not long now," Margaret urged it, giving it a pat on the neck. Out of the mist before her its ears swivelled back at the sound of her voice. "Not long now, girl. Step up. Step up..."

It was another thirty minutes and, by the sudden plunge of the light, well into the evening by the time the palfrey was tripping up a broken, disused road, wading through dead weeds and fallen branches, the stark rise of the hillside hanging almost over their heads. Margaret felt a new apprehension: not of being followed, but of being met.

For some time Hanging Tree fought the path, stumbling often, once nearly throwing Margaret. Her cry of surprise rang out over a seemingly empty land, bounding off rocks, startling a crow out of its barren tree. She recovered, breathless, and watched the dark bird disappear among the thickening clouds. A chill crawled over her flesh. She forced herself to go on, climbing down from her mare and tying it to a pine where it might have some shelter. Having only her skirts and the map to fight with, she struck out up the steep path, wholly alone now, with the feeling of having left the world of the living behind.

She nearly missed the opening in the dark. There was no denying the early winter night had come. Working with a sodden skirt in one hand and her other hand against the rock face of the hill, she slipped on the opening and stumbled, but picked herself back up and meant to go on when, checking, she turned into the deeper darkness. Every primal sense of the evil of the dark welled up in her throat, straining at a whimper. The force of terror was physical: she felt herself moving her feet slowly against it as one struggles to move in a dream. Her only clear thought was that she had to go on. The only feeling she felt was the almost overpowering instinct to turn and run.

Time went on and the dark became thin, less tangible with atmosphere, and warmer. She had only just really grown used to it, and even come to suppress her fear of it, when the unutterable black was broken by three faint spars of white-fire colour, fanning like a swan's wing. Round the bend and downward she saw a precise end to the dark tunnel and an opening into the light.

This time she did not stop, as she had stopped when she had held the books in her hands for the first time, though she felt even more keenly the sense of going forward and never being able to go back. But she had reckoned of that hours before. What was there for her to go back to? She forced herself to go onward into the underground unknown. She did not feel courageous, of that she was clearly, bluntly aware: she felt only a sense of desperation, a reckless desperation, which kept her not only from turning back but from halting in paralyzing fear. It was not hard to loathe herself for the thought of turning back: it took the sheer sickening taste of desperation in her mouth to put one foot in front of the other.

She stopped in the archway only because she knew she must.

There was an enormous chamber beyond, faced in black marble and supported by black marble columns, and it was lit—she did not see how—by an eerie pale blue light that seemed naggingly familiar. She could not recall where she had seen a light like that before. But her eye was drawn almost instantly to the figure in the middle ground. It was alarmingly close and huge, perfectly still, a long, thick serpentine body coiled round and round and over itself suspended by seemingly nothing in the centre of the room. It had no wings. She could not see any legs. It seemed to lie by its own necromancy on the air. It was beautiful, startlingly beautiful, but the impossibility and hugeness of it made it hideous to Margaret in that first horrible moment.

The head was facing the archway. It was resting on the topmost coil of its body, as if it had been sleeping, but it was wide awake and watchful, and it had seen her the moment she had stepped into sight. It looked at her out of a great half-moon hazel eye long and scrutinously; she could see her reflection in the precious green-gold mirror: she stared back with a combined horror and awe. Its eye was deep and quick and cunning, and it looked at her as if she had just done—and was still doing—something wretchedly wicked.

With a supreme effort Margaret detached herself from that basilisk stare and bent her knees, trembling but determined, shutting her own eyes just long enough to conjure afresh in her memory the image of the fox lying battered in her arms, his breath coming in painful, shuddering gasps—

That was what was wrong. With a body that enormous the dragon's breathing ought to be audible. The room was completely silent.

Why dost thou bow to me, asked the dragon, *when thou art a Lady among men and tread the worlds under thy feet?*

Its mouth never moved. It watched her with its unblinking eye while a wind which she could not feel gently stirred its long roan-blue mane and made its blurred, coiled reflection in the dark marble shift like moonlight on water.

That was what it was. The pale light was moonlight. But it had been so long since Margaret had seen the moon hanging in the sky that she had forgotten, and she felt, when she realized it, that she was remembering an old folktale that had long ago been proven wrong and was nothing more than a story for children.

"Forgive m-my intrusion." Her voiced sounded small in her own ears and full of the blood of her own veins and the air of her own lungs. "I am come for help."

Why?

She looked into its inhuman eye and wondered if it could understand. She was not sure if *she* wholly understood. She tightened her fists and swallowed back the sudden taste of angry, helpless tears. "I am come for help because there is no one else to whom we can turn. No one will dare stand up to Rupert de la Mare and if I do not find help he will kill my only friend and—" But what did she matter? It was of no importance now that she would have to marry Rupert. The fox was all that mattered. "He will kill my friend," she finished in a hard voice. "He will kill my friend."

The eye flickered over her for a long, silent moment, then the dragon lifted its head off its pillowing body and turned it round so that she could see up its muzzle to the poll between its fine thin horns and forelock—and she saw, too, that its left eye, which had been turned away from her, was clouded silver and the brow was cloven and scarred.

It is of great import to thee that, though the world groans under oppression and fears de la Mare's future rule, thy single friend should lose his life?

It did not sound condemning: it sounded oddly curious. Margaret suddenly felt that *she* was the strange one, and that the dragon was peering at her with the great, reserved, intense curiosity of the long-lived and mighty.

"It is," she admitted. "It is of the utmost import to me. Is there, then, something you can do?"

It was silent for a moment. The intangible wind continued to stir its mane. Its neck, reared back, its head, flame-shaped and perfect save for the one deformed eye, was a gorgeous mixture of calm and quizzicality. The fear ran away between Margaret's fingers. She wanted to touch it, as she had wanted to touch the fox, to feel the living warmth of it beneath her palm, to feel all that power under her hand. An electric prickle of excitement ran along the backs of her arms.

Dost know, Lady, how I came by this blindness?

Politely, she shook her head.

It rolled its head to the left; its good eye grew distant, introspective. *There are things and there are things which we hold dear in our beings. They come into the soul of thee and become thy life-thing—without which thou couldst not live. Even so for me, once—as it is for thee each day of thy life—my life-thing was in jeopardy, the glory of my being and the apple of mine eye at risk of damage. And so I fought for it. Is life not cheap when all life-things are taken away? I fought for it, and flung out from amidst me a lord who could, like unto thyself, pass in the guise of manlike beauty. I flung him out for anger, but at a price: the price of my own eye.*

"But you did not mind, I think," Margaret said quietly, "having to give it up."

The dragon smiled. *Well I would have given up the other with it, if that was what was needful.*

She wondered then if she would ever see Aylesward again, the long drive up to the door and the high front passage swimming with grey rainy light; she wondered if she would ever see the cellar of Marenové House and the warm gold lamplight on the fox's wall eyes. But even as she wondered it, she knew it did not matter. With a little gesture, almost of offering sacrifice, she raised both hands, palms upward, and dropped them again. "Was it Plenilune for which you gave up your eye?" she asked.

Nay. 'Twas Heaven.

Thou wouldst, then, outdeuce the devil.

Her knees had foresworn her and she had buckled to the ground. With one hand on the black marble, splayed, ready by extreme will to push herself back up, Margaret met the terrible eye. "Will you help us? There is no one else to help us and we are all wandering in God's silence."

With a breathless rustle the dragon lifted its head and shook it from side to side, pensively. *I can do the thing that is in thy mind to do. What must be done, though thou dost not know it— that power lies elsewhere, O Lady. Now, I will give to thee a spell-breaking spell—for the stricture to all spells is that they can be broken—and send thee back quicker than thou camest. Hast lost, I feel, some handle on thy timely element!*

She did not understand the dragon, but her heart lifted with a wild surmise like panic when it struck her that she was going back, alive, to see the fox and set him free. With an effort she got back to her feet and stood, feeling at once small and made of wood, fists clenched, and the blood running like fire in her veins.

An answering flame leapt in the dragon's eye. *Here now are the words of the spell-breaking spell: the dark star has paled with the morning, a voice in the silence is heard; faith will have its fulfilment now that the tomb is endured.*

It seemed to rise and gather, to draw into itself all the genius of its awful pearly light. Margaret found she had not known the glory of terror until that moment. It seemed to reach out with the power of its mind and fix upon a place—as one fixes a hand upon the handle of a door—and pull, pull with a mighty sense, and she felt the genius loci of that place come rushing up behind her. She braced, expecting it to hit her and sure that it would hurt; but the Great Blind Dragon, with its one good eye a disk of fire, opened up its airless mouth and seemed to roar, whiskers flying, knocking Margaret over backward—

Determinas loco—come home to me!
Determinas loco—far from the sea!
O hunter, come home from the hill!

—and she found herself falling hard on her back in the wine-cellar of Marenové House, the last white shred of light whisking away from her vision, replaced by the stark staring face of the fox.

For once he had been struck dumb. He came running forward, paw outstretched as if to touch her hand, but he seemed to hesitate—nothing was clear to Margaret in that moment. She tried to rise but the world seemed to tip up under her and fling her back down again with a crushing blow. Her damp, heavy skirts hampered her and suddenly she lost her temper. She wrenched them away from her feet, hearing in the back of her mind the whine of tearing cloth, and struggled upward.

"There is no time," she gasped. Before he could dodge her she swooped, gathering him into her arms.

"Margaret, are you out of your—"

"I said there is no time!" Blindly, driven by a panic she did not realize she was feeling, she ran toward the steps, all the while saying, as the fox tensed in her arms, the spell-breaking spell of the dragon.

It worked. As her foot touched the tread of the lowest step she saw the air splinter like broken glass; something wrenched at her and the thing in her arms. The fox groaned and shuddered, but then they were through and she was running in the dark, fighting panic and her skirts and the weight of the fox. He was thankfully silent and, after that first startled moment, did not fight her. She slipped once on the stone stairs and fell on her shin rather than crush him, but though she let out a helpless grunt of pain he did not make a sound.

Breathless, wary, they slipped into the kitchen hall. Margaret listened: the house was deadly quiet. That worried her in a way she could not explain.

"The solarium," she murmured. "It is the shortest way."

Then the fox spoke. "No, wait, Margaret—"

Before he could warn her the danger was upon them. The hall suddenly blazed with light, blinding them both. and when Margaret could look again there was Rupert in the dining room doorway.

There was murder in his face.

Margaret turned at once and ran, knowing that if she hesitated half a heartbeat all would be lost in that man's basilisk stare. But she swung right into Livy's arms and suddenly the fight was for the fox as the manservant tried at once to throw her off and wrench the fox out of her grasp. The fox fought along with her. He snapped and snarled, black lips pulled back into a singsong snarl. Once he bit down on Livy's hand so deeply that the bone showed.

"Hold her! *Hold her!*" someone was shouting. There were other hands now, faces she recognized from the grounds, all trying to detach her and the fox from each other. In a panic she doubled over, shielding him with her body, but it was no use. She felt the hand that closed over the back of her neck, hard like a vise; it pulled her back and nearly lifted her off her feet. Exposed, screaming in pain—she did not know she was screaming—she was open to the many hands that wrenched the fox out of her arms. In a spar of light she saw Rupert's face, sideways and blurred with terror and agony, but sharpened around the eyes with cold and around the mouth with a flash of bared white teeth.

"No! *no!*" The fox was fighting Livy, slipping in the manservant's blood. "Let her go, Rupert! Let her go! This was none of her doing! *Let her go!*"

Was it fear that made her hallucinate? Margaret had the sudden vivid image, so clear she thought she could reach out and touch it, of Rupert holding a chess-piece in one hand, a mere pawn of red: he closed his fingers on it and crushed it into powder. "It is not for nothing you are a fox," he said coldly. His arm went round Margaret and squeezed her ribs until she could hear them creaking low under the shudder of her uneven breathing. He was going to crush her. Crush her like the pawn. "Nothing to do with it, then, when the scent of magic thickens the air and I find you out of spells and her skulking about at night, you in her arms."

The fox twisted and shot a smile at Rupert. "It's not a place you are likely to find yourself."

Margaret heard the swift dark intake of breath in the barrel of chest beside her. She heard it—and heard the eerie quiet that dropped on them afterward which was like the lull that drops before the storm. Everything froze on the scene, caught sharp and pale in the light. She heard the creak of her ribs, she saw the light glint off Rupert's eye, she saw the flare of the fox's nostrils as it smelled the scent of death.

With a pained cry Margaret broke the scene. Slouching forward in an attempt to ease the agony in her side she gasped, "Let him go! I'll do anything you want. Only let him go. He's only a fox!"

Rupert's laugh was hard and mirthless, oddly choking in his own throat. With a cruel jerk he put both arms around her breasts and pulled her back a few paces, lengthening the distance between her and the fox. She could see the wild spangling white in the other's eyes as he stared at her being dragged bodily away. "Only a fox!" he mocked. "Only a thorn in my side, only the gall in my drink. As for *you*—"

She sobbed, gagging, blinded by the jagged purple lightning of pain.

"—clearly I cannot trust you anymore, and I have come to the end of my patience with your foolishness, your ungrateful, unteachable spirit, and now this—!" His arms grew tighter around her ribcage with each word. She could not see clearly anymore. Everything was swimming in blue and purple and white. "I cannot trust you, I—have no further use for you. Better I was rid of you."

Though his words were cold and there was stark murder in them, his voice tore at the end on the razor of regret. But his voice was quickly drowned out in the fox's shrill barking.

"No, you fool, you idiot, you bastard! If ever you feared me, you will not lay a hand on her!"

Pain and despair and the sense of indrawn power confused Margaret still further. But she knew that the game was up, that she and the fox were but little, worthless things to be crushed under Rupert's thumb—and that Rupert loved his purpose still more than he loved her. For a moment the grip on her loosened. She was beyond feeling pain now. Shock numbed her. She saw a narrow tunnel of light and at the end of it the flame-colour of the fox, sparking with rage. He would be the last thing she would see. Her body came out of Rupert's arms, though something far off hurt like hell. She moved forward across the distance; the surf-sound of all their voices beat against her. The fox saw her coming and gave one last twist like a dolphin slipping out of the grasp of the sea; he pushed against the servant's chest and nearly got free, but not quite. A flicker of white despair lashed across his eyes. From far off in that place that hurt, Margaret whispered, *Good-bye*, and she wrapped her arms around the fox's great ruff of ruddy mane. His nose was cold and damp against her lips and tasted of salt. His eyes, wide and wild and pale in the light, met hers with a kind of horror.

Good-bye.

Rupert had her by the throat. The servants were shouting. Someone's lantern crashed to the floor. It splintered open. Sparks went up in blinding yellow. Her fingers scraped on the stones: she was being hauled away again, almost faster than she could see in the whirling mayhem, but through the last closing gap of sight she could still see the fox, rigid in his captor's arms, mouth open so that his little teeth shone, a mingled mask of pain and horror on his face.

"Margaret!" he gasped in a reproachful tone. "Oh, damn."

Of a sudden Livy dropped him. Everyone lunged in to grab him again while the manservant cried, "He's gone cold as ice and heavy as lead!" Margaret watched, half-seated on the floor, held in Rupert's grasp. De la Mare watched in a kind of transfixed quiet, not stirring to move, as a man might meet his inevitable death.

The fox struck the floor on his belly, yelping, trying to gather his legs beneath him. Everyone tried to grab him but wrenched away again, clutching smarting hands. With an agonized cry the fox clawed at the floor, trying to drag himself forward as he grew larger and larger, and longer and longer, and his red fur was being burnt up in the glow cast by the ragged shards of light. The cry became a roar, the roar became an almost human scream. One paw swung out to claw at the stone flags: the paw became a hand. A shoulder twisted forward in a spasm of agony: the shoulder was a man's. Almost before she knew what was happening, Margaret was staring at the sweating wreck of a young man, naked as birth, crouched on the stone floor with his breath shuddering in and out of his lungs as might a warhorse after a day-long fight.

There was a splintering shriek of steel being pulled. She turned and saw Rupert drawing a knife and pulling it back. His hand took hold of a great mass of her hair and wrenched back her head. Pain cracked like lightning up her back and neck, clawing into her brain. If she screamed she did not remember, nor hear it over the roar of panic. Out of the lowest curve of her eye she saw the young man look up, hang for a moment immobile, and then gather himself to spring. The knife sparked in the air. Rupert twisted in an attempt to shield his work from the impact of the young man, but the other's hand struck his wrist, sending the blow wide. Margaret felt it graze her forehead. She dropped to the ground and rolled away, only distantly aware of the scuffle overhead. She did not see what happened, she only knew that someone was grabbing her and roaring in her ear, "RUN!" and she was doing so.

Through the long looming shadows and flickering earth-light the two of them ran, her hand in his. Desperation drove them on through the peristyle and solarium, diving into the shadows and out again fast as kingfishers, until they had hurled themselves out onto the back lawn. Cold air shivered Margaret's lungs in bloody rags but she kept doggedly on, driven by the terror of Rupert's pale, grim face that, in her pain, was nightmarishly changing places with a knife so that the two seemed to be one and the same. The long fine hand in hers was hot with sweat and slippery; she gripped it until she could feel the pain of her hold through the terror.

They ran along the gravel walk and dove into the deep shadows of the bare grape arbour. Somewhere, somewhere too close, a dog began to bark. Margaret caught a swift image of a pale face beside her, hesitating to look behind them for a single instant before plunging on. Down the arbour they raced, down the arbour for the opening beyond and the safety of the woods. A door slammed: the sound of it echoed across the yard. The barking of the dog was sharp and clear and nearly on their heels.

Without check they flung themselves down the stairs and into the grass aisle beyond. Earth-light, cold and betraying, burst around them. Only a moment later they were into the woods, thrashing their way through thick scrub and bramble. Thorns dragged at Margaret's arms and legs and face. She shut her eyes and ran on.

The sound of the fox's breathing was her constant companion. She could not hear her own—she was not sure she was breathing anymore. The roar of her own pain drowned out any other sound in her body. But she heard, as they crashed down the side of a narrow glen, grasping at every root and branch to arrest their fall, she heard the fox's breathing catch and change, and heard when he gasped out, "Can you spell while we run?"

She let go of his hand only long enough to grab an alder root to save herself from pitching headlong into the dark rushy water below. He placed an arm around her waist and steadied her on.

"Margaret!"

They hit a wet rock and slithered to a halt, up to their ankles in a stream. The high walls of the glen rose all around them, the trees higher than that and, farther up and wholly out of reach, there shone the crescent of earth, gleaming fitful silver and blue, shedding light on their upturned faces.

A dog gave tongue in the distance.

"Here," gasped Margaret. Her hands fumbled with her brooch; after stabbing her own fingers she managed to haul off her tartan. The fox bent shakily and helped her fling it around his shoulders. Then she plunged her arms around his cold thin body, wrenched the mazing pain in two from her brain, and called up the dragon's spell.

Determinas loco—come home to me—determinas loco—far from the sea. Oh, hunter, come home from the hill!

There was a howl of wind and the flapping of the cloak all around them. The ground was torn from their feet. The breath was torn from their lungs. Into the rage of a roaring airless tunnel they were thrown. In the space of a heartbeat Margaret hung in the balance, feeling nothing but the sense of falling, falling, falling in a dream.

She hit the ground sidelong, thinking all the while that she would fall on her feet. Pain, like a thousand Guy Fawkes fires, splintered through her body. Panic, like some black ravening bird just stretching its wings to fly, reared up inside her. She could not breathe, she could not see. The world beneath her was heaving. She wanted to call out for the fox.

Struggling against the pain and panic, she groped forward. There was a fire in her body as though someone were taking each rib and sharpening it on a grinding stone. Finally her fingers closed over fabric; they brushed against skin. The fox was there, somewhere, beyond the red-spangled black that throttled her vision.

"Rupert?" She heard a voice from far away and far up. Steps like shod hooves rattled against her ears. "Rupert? *Dammerung!*"

"I'm—hale enough. Look—look to the lady. I'm afraid he crushed her rather badly. Careful, you thumbs-all!"

Margaret choked on a scream as someone tried to put arms around her. Someone was cursing, soft and low and beautifully; someone was whispering in her ear, "Best go to sleep now. It will be better that way."

The blurred outline of a man's face appeared above her in the fluttering, feathered light of a lantern. Odd thing, that: he always seemed to manage a halo of light, always in that careless, unaffected manner. He always had that shining about him. Odd, that...

A long, fine hand pressed over her forehead. "Go to sleep."

As though driven in by lunar tides, washing swift and gentle through her brain, a deep and painless sleep overcame her.

XVII | THE HOLLOW QUIET

On the other side of the sleep Margaret expected pain. She surfaced—it was like surfacing from the bottom of a lake—with her limbs braced against the hot impact, and she was surprised some moments later to find that no pain came. A long shudder ran through her, and to her disgust she realized through the lightness in her head that she was shivering from fear. With an effort she pried her eyes open, squinting against the stab of white light, and tried to see where she was and to remember, between the stabbing light and sick taste of fear, what had happened.

She was in a Lookinglass bed. Not her own bed in the high, narrow garret overlooking the south-west grounds, but a lower room, lit by the morning sun, spacious and well furnished. Everything was light and delicate. To her eyes, still gummed with sleep, there was the impression of being in a birch wood with the wind carrying the light rushing and roaring overhead. And there was a wind, and light, for they were blowing in through some opening, fluttering the white hangings about her bed until they sparked with silver.

After getting her bearings Margaret noticed, among the light and racing, a great winged shadow on the floor and, looking up with rather less interest than usual at the body that cast it, got her first clear view, since that night of flurrying horror, of the fox.

He was standing in the open balcony doorway where the cold wind and frozen light were coming in, moth-wing grey with the light at his shoulders and velvet bee-black in the small of his back where the shadow was deepest. He was clad in a black tunic with fantastically long sleeves and trousers which fit tightly but were too long, the cuffs rumpled and bunched about the tops of his bare feet.

No doubt he felt her gaze, for presently he turned on one bare heel, very smoothly and like a dancer, and caught her eyes with his—the hypnotic sort, she thought with another panicked flutter where her heart was: so pale blue they were nearly silver. For a moment his face was only eyes, those witching-blue, hypnotic eyes, and then, suddenly, he smiled—a gash of a smile across the lower part of his face, that was like a spate of rain and a spate of sun at once, a mirthless sort of humour. About his eyes, when she looked back at them, there were thin, deep wing-lines that were like grief and laughter both at once, so that she could not decide if the light look of mockery was in earnest or only from long habit.

For some time they looked at each other, he smiling in his faintly mocking way which was the same with a fox's face or a man's, and she with rather less interest than usual, but at last he, with a little upward tilt of his head, broke the silence saying,

"There are many and various dull things one says to a patient newly awake. Perhaps you have heard them all by now. So I will say rather that I think I owe you the truth, which I withheld from you before."

"You mean that you—" her tongue was oddly heavy and not quite its right size in her mouth "—are Dammerung, and that Dammerung never did die in a hunting accident?"

His brows fluttered rampant, but otherwise he seemed unmoved. "No, it was not Dammerung who died in a hunting accident..." Then his light gaze became heavy on her, searching the way Rhea used to search down into her inside self. "Did you know that I am Dammerung when you went to get the Blind Dragon's spell to set me free, or was it mere womanish whim?"

She attempted a mirthless, brittle smile. "It was mere womanish whim. I knew you because—because when you turned there was the likeness of Rupert in your face."

"And there the likeness ends?" His tone and rhetoric seemed unoffended, and almost absentminded. He came a little stiffly to the side of the bed and sat in a walnut-wood chair, his legs with a bare foot on the end of each tucked up under the seat. Leaning forward, he put a hand on Margaret's temple and felt a moment for heat, and for pulse at her throat. His hand was as long and fine and sure as she remembered the fox's paws being, but even that did not seem of much interest to her.

"How do you feel?"

She thought about that carefully, for she found she had to think about it carefully or it slipped in the wake of a sense of panic out of her mind altogether. "I do not seem to feel much of anything," she admitted at length.

"Indeed?" He put his hand once more to her forehead. "That is well, then. You will not eat just yet, for I think you are not hungry and hunger will come soon enough later. Though heaven knows you are thin enough—" his tone became condescending "—you should not fast long before you waste away."

"Truly?" She looked at him witheringly. "I mistook you for your shadow when I first saw you, you are so thin."

His smile, a gash at the right side of his face, had no laughter in it. "I am going away now to eat, as to that, so that Skander does not worry more about me than he already has. What a hen that bulk can be! And you will go back to sleep presently as all good patients do—or so I am told."

She did feel sleepy and not at all clear in the head on several scores, and she had an odd, muffled sense of detachment. She watched Dammerung rise and put away the chair, looking very like Hamlet but with his hair dark and trimmed—he must have had it cut since coming to Lookinglass, for she had some vague impression of it having been longer before.

But that was on the other side of the long sleep and she could not remember that time very well...

Dammerung paused in the act of turning away. A frown pulled at his brows, a shadow dropped for a moment over his eyes. "We have sent down to Melchior our physic to come up from Cheshunt so that he may look over you. He should be here before sundown."

She stared at him bluntly. Melchior? The physic? She had a confused recollection of a watery-eyed old man shaking with age, a man so old his years had mazed him. "Why does he come?" she asked, appalled to find that she had to speak carefully to keep her voice from breaking.

Dammerung smiled, but again the laughter was not in it, though companionship was. "He comes because I bid him come, and there are yet men who come when I whistle for them. Do you bide quietly now and we will all come up again to see you this evening and fuss and make much of you. Sleep, now."

His last words had no mockery in them, but a low sort of desperation, and with a nod of deference that seemed more of habit than conscious courtesy he withdrew, shutting the door behind him without another look back.

The room was strangely more empty than his going should have made it. The blowing light seemed hollow, the white and paleness of the colours unfriendly, and there was nothing to stand between Margaret and the loathsome panic in her middle. She lay rigidly under the blankets, staring up at the ceiling where the light was making dancing spear-head patterns on the stucco. She was glad, in a small, deep part of her that could still feel a sense of gladness, that Dammerung had gone: she did not want him to see her trembling as she was trembling with a formless horror of the numbness and disinterestedness which swaddled her. She could move her toes and she could move her fingers. She was not paralyzed. Yet there was something definitely wrong and it made her afraid, horribly afraid, and she was glad Dammerung had not stayed to see it.

That day was the worst Margaret could remember. It had been morning when she had awoken—she could tell by the weight and colour of the light, and, without thinking of it, by how the wind smelled just a certain way. Dammerung said she would sleep presently, as all good patients were wont to sleep, but for a long time she lay awake, crawling through the minutes, pulling herself each moment from the brink of utter panic. Self-loathing helped a little, for she loathed herself badly during those long hours, and some sense of Providence helped a little more, but the times when she managed to doze helped the most. The blurred sense of dreaming, which was never far off, mingled with the light and birchleaf-shaped patterns on the ceiling: when she dozed and really dreamed, she seemed adrift on a green north sea with the roar of the sea in her ears and the cream of foam the coolness of the wind on her skin. It might have been a pleasant sort of dreaming, and at times it almost was, but whenever she surfaced near waking, the wolf-crouched figure of fear loomed just on the periphery of her mind like something in the dark water below her, or behind her, always circling her and waiting until she should be too tired to struggle...

At length Margaret became aware of the foam against her arms being cold—more like ice than foam now, and the green sea had turned dark. With an effort she pushed upward to waking once more, past the numbness, past the fear, past the thing-in-the-dark which waited for her and, blinking, found that the light had turned to deep amber-colour and the corners of the room were thick with shadows. The balcony doors were still open, and though the grounds below were drenched in the shadow cast by the bulk of the building, the sky upward and beyond was a pale flaming hue, yellow like wine and as thin, with curdled pink clouds scuttling across its face. It was evening at last. It took a full minute for it to occur to her, and with that thought, oddly enough, went the terror. A sense of quiet resignation took its place.

Some time afterward she heard a growing noise of feet in a corridor outside her door. She did not know whether to look asleep or remain alert, but she did not have time to choose for the knob clicked and the door swung open, letting in Skander and Dammerung, and then the blue-jay man with the little shaky figure of the physic. Margaret was dimly aware of Aikaterine being there as well, but the room seemed overfull to her now, and it was hard to focus.

With extreme and unruffled care the blue-jay man guided the ancient physic to the bedside and then, being sure the man would not lose his balance, withdrew a respectable distance into the background where the shadows had thickened. Looking up through the scant light at the physic's face, Margaret saw he had not changed. He still trembled, his bird-thin bones all seeming to rattle together under the sheer weight of his years, and his pale, watery eyes were still trained upward as if he expected any moment to see the sky rent back by Heaven's coming. There was a moment, as he stretched out one claw of a hand for Margaret's forehead, when the singsong whine of terror began crawling up her throat again—somehow she kept it in—and when the palm touched her skin it was not as bad as she had expected. The skin of the physic's hand was light, like a dried autumn leaf, yet there was a sense of being spoken to through it, soothingly, comfortingly, all the while searchingly, which stopped up Margaret's whine with surprise. Strangely enough, the hand did not shake once it had touched her. With both hands he felt her, and seemed to talk to her, and soothed her in a way which afterward she could never quite describe.

Finally Melchior let out a rattling sigh and withdrew his hands. "Some lamplight, I think," he said to the ceiling. "She would like some light. Children are afraid of the dark."

In the darkness of the background Skander gestured, and with a soft flutter of blue stained indigo by the shadows, the blue-jay man went away to fetch a light.

Melchior nodded shudderingly at the ceiling. "When we have a light for her I will take a look and see what damage has been done."

Almost Margaret touched her tongue to her dry lips, but she caught herself. Between the white hangings of the bed—which were grey now in their troughs and pink where the sky-light touched them—and the darkness beyond she saw Dammerung's face looking down to her own, and thought with a sense of puzzlement that there was something drawn and pinched about his mouth.

Skander's man returned with the light and soon a candelabra was lit, shedding a fan of warm yellow light through the room. The balcony doors were shut, cutting off the cold air and, with a nod from Melchior, Aikaterine turned back the coverlet.

"Should we go?" asked Skander. His voice was big and bold-sounding in the hollow silence of the room.

The physic put up both hands, shaking them vigorously. "Nay, I do not need ye to take off her sleeping gown for me to see. I can see well enough. Now, lass, little babe," he turned to Margaret, and for the first time she saw that his eyes, looking directly at her, were the soft colour of chicory-bloom. "This may hurt ye a trifle."

Before she could brace, Dammerung cut in quietly, levelly. "It will not hurt her, Master Doctor. I have seen to that."

They all looked to him, starkly cut in golden light and black shadow, his face like the face of new-chiselled stone, but no one spoke another word. The trembling, blue-veined hands that spoke without words fumbled and grew sure against Margaret's torso, and the numbness, rather than withdrawing like a sea-anemone when it is touched, grew only deeper. She began to have a curious feeling of floating, or being dispossessed of her body, and she thought that if she was not careful she might begin to laugh. She kept her eyes on Dammerung's face, though he did not look back at her, and somehow the stark grimness of his countenance helped.

At length Melchior finished his searching and drew back, and a sigh ran through the room—it was only then that Margaret realized none of them had been breathing. "Ye were right," the physic wheezed to Dammerung. His hands were trembling again. "Two of her ribs are broken on her left side, cleanly and not wholly, and all of them are bruised."

"What—can you do?" asked Skander, rather quickly as if he did not trust his own voice anymore.

Melchior turned to him, tottered, and regained his balance. "Why, nothing! If she bides quietly they will fain heal themselves. Naught to be done for broken ribs but let them lie and let the healing come in its time."

"But will she be fain to lie quietly?" retorted Skander, and Margaret felt sorry for the ancient bird-like physic who was taking the brunt of Skander's helpless thrust of words.

"She will have to!" Dammerung, in a new, lighter tone, took hold of the white hangings—which were gold now, and no longer white, with the glow of the candelabra—and pulled them down the length of the bed to make a sort of wall on her right hand. He padded delicately past the end of her bed and joined his cousin and the physic. "There is nothing more the Healing Hands can do. Her ribs are in her own hands now."

He had said that there were still men who would come when he whistled, but it did not seem to Margaret that he whistled at all. Of course, she was working hard at not thinking just then, and so was not much aware of what he did, only that somehow he swept the others out, talking all the while about what Aikaterine must bring up, and where Skander could find him, and generally making much of the ancient bird-like physic. Then they were gone and the door was shut, and Dammerung was coming back to the bedside with his curious careful padding as if walking too hard hurt him. He drew the chair close to the one open side of the bed and sat in it, and for a long moment they looked at each other with oddly open faces, saying nothing at all.

Finally he prompted, jerking his head upward a little, "Did you know what it was when I left you this morning?"

Now she could touch her tongue to her lips, but now her tongue had gone dry as well. "No. I knew that it was bad, but I did not know what it was." She almost added that had made the circumstances worse, but for the same reason she had been glad that Dammerung had not been there to see her shiver, she did not say it. Instead she said, "I don't understand. I feel nothing, yet I thought broken ribs hurt a great deal."

"So they do!" Dammerung's laughter was barking and harsh. Then he quieted, for laughter and grimness seemed like light and shadow blowing on the fellsides with him, chasing each other. He seemed uncertain, and made as if to speak, then with an impatient gesture pushed the words away. "Nay, it is nothing. You will mend, that is all."

"That is not all," snapped Margaret—snapped, for she was beginning to feel afraid again. "And it is something. What is wrong with me that I cannot feel my own pain!"

His eyes were uncanny and terrible in the yellow light, for they lost all of their blue colour and became pale gold like flecks of tansy-blossom, pale gold like an eagle's eye. "There is nothing wrong with you," he said in a gentle tone. Then, with an edge aimed for himself, he added, "There is something wrong with me, for...for I am taking the pain for you."

It was some moments afterward that Margaret realized she was gaping at him, and then she shut her mouth slowly, opened it again in another attempt to dampen her lips, and then pressed her lips shut once more. He was not lying, for though he did not always tell her the whole truth, he did not lie. She saw the truth in the greyness at the corners of his mouth and the way he had both hands clenched on the arms of his chair. He was in agony, but when she looked with incredulity—not really stopping to wonder how he did it—into his eyes, she saw the dancing mockery there which was the same as ever, and she knew that he did not mind.

"How long will I take to heal?" she asked quietly.

"Too long for either of us. The time it takes the earth to flick its shadow over the Blind Dragon's back and away again, I think."

"It will be a long month."

"Aye..."

For some time they were silent, and the only sound in the room was the fizzle and splat of hot wax dripping from the candelabra in the corner. There was almost always a sound of wind in the background, rushing this way or that against a corner of the house. Margaret hardly noticed it, having become used to it, but now it broke through the chinks in her careful not-thinking; but instead of being long and hollow and desolate, as she was afraid when she first became aware of it that it would be, the wind seemed rather to make the room more comfortable and less like a prison. It put the blowy, dark, unfriendly world outside, and the face of friendliness on the candlelit room within.

At last she broke the silence. "It feels late. Will you be going soon?"

He jigged his head as he had done in the days on the other side of the long sleep. "No, I do not think so. You stayed with me, you see, when Rupert had kicked me into a mazelin on the cellar floor. Now Rupert has broken two of your ribs, and bruised the others, and I will stay with you."

She stared at him carefully between the light-laced edge of the curtain and the amber-coloured background of the room, stared into his harlequin face, half in light, half in shadow...and somehow she knew that it was not merely to settle a score that he chose to stay. She had stayed then because they had both been something like exiles, and so something like friends, and now that the exiling was over the friendship had remained. So he stayed, and she knew why, and without another word, but deliberate care, she turned her head on the pillow and dropped asleep.

Margaret slept often during the first fortnight in Lookinglass: a thick, heavy sleep in which there were no dreams and hardly even a recollection of herself. But there was always a sense that she was not alone, and when she woke blearily, briefly, she would always see Dammerung nearby. Sometimes he, too, would be asleep. Skander would often be there too, but she saw him less, or cared less. After three weeks—not quite a full month—Dammerung said he was fit enough, and she was out of pain enough, for him to finish the job himself. His hands had not shaken as Melchior's had done—nor had Melchior's, like Dammerung's, seemed to flash with a sense of indrawn light as they hovered a second over Margaret's ribs. She had tensed, but there had been nothing to fear: the pressure was steady, almost pleasant, as one pressing a sore muscle, and the fingers working their way over each uneasy rib felt to her like a hand passing over the back of a great bird, soft brown and stroking smooth, putting each worried feather back into place. And that had been all. The thing had been done.

For a moment unguarded, cast up in the stark light of an evening lamp, Dammerung's face had looked pleased.

Though she was well enough to get up and even walk about if she chose, after the first failed attempt she fell back on her elbow, out of breath and shaking, fighting waves of black as they washed over her vision. A dark sleep clawed at her brain.

"I can't—I can't seem to—" The sudden danger of vomiting cut off her words.

Dammerung's hands found her in her dark. "No fuss. You have been abed too long, that is all. We will patch you back together. But come, we must go down and sit an hour with Skander or else I am liable to go out of my head. Take my arm."

Margaret obediently took his arm—a lean, hard-corded thing that was like holding warm amber—and soon found herself taken to a shuttered sitting room that was full of the warm yellow light of a huge fire. She was almost passing out of consciousness from the mere effort of coming down—had she dressed? what did she wear?— so Dammerung put her down before the blaze on a thick sheepskin, leaving her to her own sleepy devices, while he and his cousin, seated in the background, cast huge brown falcon-shadows on the walls.

Margaret lay with her face pressed into the warm, animal-smelling skin, watching the feuillemort colour of the fire weaving mysterious patterns inside itself. She had begun to feel again and care again, and in the pleasant seashell quiet she listened to the music that the fire was making and wondered, as one wonders back over many, many years, how Julius and Julianna were getting on at the University.

Skander's voice drew her attention. In a quiet, hesitant tone, as though he had not dared to ask before, he demanded of Dammerung to know what had happened.

"You have been dead," he added, by way of justification, "for two years."

The falcon-shadow made a blurred movement on the wall. A range of mercury-glass dishes on the sideboard, huge and beautiful, flashed out in light and were quenched. Margaret was aware of an acute pain that lay like an abyss, like the cut of a knife, across something, somewhere, or someone, but that seemed a long way off to her... Finally Dammerung said,

"Do you remember the winter we went to take Brand boar-hunting with us?"

"Well I remember it. It was on that hunt that you—I remember it."

"We were on our way to pick up Brand and had spotted a sow in the woods. We thought it would make a fair gift for Mark Roy and Romage—she was a big brute, none too lean for winter, either—so we went out of our way to track her down and kill her. We took her on the edge of Thrasymene territory and stopped an hour to unmake her."

Dammerung's voice trailed away into the abyss again. Margaret had shut her eyes; from behind her closed lids she searched for his voice. Both men were silent. The gaping wound's edges grew sharper and more painful.

"You remember Spencer?" the War-wolf said at last, softly so that his words were nearly lost in the black.

Skander laughed shortly, huskily. "Of course. You were nearly inseparable. A better sword-brother I could never hope to—look here," he finished sharply.

The shadow, when she opened her eyes to it, had folded in its wings and become small. Dammerung's voice was muffled. "I did not see it coming. I felt nothing in the wind. I was coming up the bank to the meadow again, having—I had just washed the boar-blood off my hands. It was as though I was in a dream, a dream of looking up and seeing Rupert on one side of the meadow and Spencer on the other, and feeling too late the murder in the air. Spencer must have felt it. He started up and turned around to Rupert and—and the look on his face I'll never forget. It was as if he had known, had always known, and had only been waiting for it to happen. The next thing I knew there was a cracking sound like thunder, but no lightning, and Spencer—Spencer—" The voice was growing confused and strangled-sounding, as if the tears at the back of Dammerung's throat were choking him. "He was flung forward like a rag-doll, insides on the outside. He was dead instantly."

Margaret wanted desperately to get up. She was staring into the heart of the fire, the heat of it smarting in her eyes, the crawling, serrated agony cutting in her chest. She wanted to get up and go to Dammerung, and put her hand upon his shoulder and say, "You took my pain. Let me take yours." But she knew as clear as the light on the mercury-glass that this was a pain no one but Dammerung himself could bear.

"At least he did not suffer," said Skander quietly—and he meant it.

Dammerung's voice hardened bitterly. "Yes. I tell myself that too." There was another long stretch of quiet. Something warm and wet fell in Margaret's ear; she could faintly smell salt. "I almost died that day. Rupert meant for me to die that day. A part of me did, I think, with Spencer, with the House of Marenové."

"It is a true saying that our hope died that day, and the light of Plenilune went out."

"I am not in the mood for dragon-riddles."

"I do not riddle you. I said I speak the truth."

Dammerung sighed heavily. "I know, and I cry you mercy. My temper seems short at present, for two years is not long and my memory is yet all too clear."

Skander turned the subject as one might turn a chess-piece on the board. "Why did you not die that day? Had it been me, I might have. Can a man live without his heart and soul?"

"And I had mine torn out and flung on the ground like a rag-doll," said Dammerung bitterly. "Spencer was my heart and soul, my Jonathan. I bare remember a time without him... But I did not die because...because of the look on Spencer's face. But how do I describe it? It was a thing between him and me which has no words."

"Nay, but I think I understand. The winning would have been Rupert's else—that was the surface of it."

"That was the surface of it... The rest I thought of later, when I was of a sounder mind, and it was simply that the instinct in me to live was very great—far greater than even I had ever imagined. And somehow that tasted of cowardice to me."

"Taste as it would," Skander replied heavily, frankly, "I have never known the merest shadow of cowardice in your character."

Margaret heard the quiet, mocking smile in Dammerung's voice. "What would you know of me?"

There was a long and easy silence between them. She could hear them both thinking melancholy thoughts until at last Dammerung broke the quiet, picking up his story again. There was a clink as of a wine-glass on a tabletop.

"Rupert meant to kill me and he tried, but while ever he had to study the old arts, they came naturally to me. And I was ever quicker on my feet than he, so that I had those two advantages over him. He cast a killing spell—it tasted of all the bitterness of vinegar, as my Lord would know the taste!—and I caught it on the rim of me before it could sink deep and I turned it into a transformation spell. So rather than a corpse I became a fox."

"A fox?"

The smile broke through the words. "It seemed a fitting form. Poor Rupert!" added Dammerung. "I was somewhat mazed by what had happened and what I had done, so catching me was no great difficulty. But killing spells are hard to break, even if you have intent to break them—and he did not at the time he cast it—nor had he, or I, any notion of what strictures were needed to break the transformation. He could not further try to kill me without undoing the other spells, else he should bring his own spell down upon his own head. So for the past two years he has been stuck with me, trying by the books of art to find a way to undo our mess."

Skander's shadow mounted on the wall. "For the past two years? All this time we have thought you dead and you were there all along—"

"Right under your noses, I'm afraid. There is a certain delicious irony in it..."

"Seen from *this* side of things, perhaps."

"Oh, by the stars, we're hardly out of the woods yet, sir."

Glass sang against the wood. "Sooth. And now? How is that you are here, and man again, and not a fox locked up at Marenové House?"

Dammerung's chair creaked. The shadow wavered. Margaret felt a hand on her white doeskin coverlet, pulling it to arrange it over her shoulders. A sudden deep contentment washed over her.

"Margaret came. Could you have known, when you dared Rupert to find a woman to be his wife, that he would find, instead, his match not in marriage but in temper and intent. She was as keen to have me live as he was keen to have me die. And so she, who has no art nor inclination to art, nor any blood-tie to this land, found a spell that set me free. And nearly," his voice turned, as a knife turns and catches the light and shows its blade, "and nearly lost her own life doing it."

Skander said gently, "You inspire that in people."

"I would fain be an inspiring spirit for Plenilune but we are not yet out of the woods, and now that I am back there is an awkward decision ahead of us still."

"I should like to be there—" Skander's voice broke with groaning and his shadow grew taller and taller "—when you make it."

"Going?"

"I am not a nursemaid, not by trade. I have other duties attendant on me. I'll come back presently, if you have not wandered off."

"We will be here, Margaret and I. We are dependable that way."

When the door shut behind the young Lord of Capys, Dammerung got stiffly out of his chair and folded up on the sheepskin beside Margaret. She rolled sleepily over until she could see Dammerung's face. She hardly knew why she asked, but the words were out of her mouth before she could stop them.

"Did you ever tell him that you saved his life?"

"No!" Dammerung shook his head hastily. " 'Twould be an awkward admission."

"Yes, that is what I thought too."

They were both silent for a moment; then, on an impulse, he reached across her into the fire and drew some of the flame out into his hand. Startled, but curious, Margaret watched him suspend it in his palm above her, the light full on his hard-cut, aristocratic face. Then, idly, he began drawing the flame through his fingers as one might draw the notes of a song through one's mind, and he smiled. The smile gave to his face a softness it had lacked. He continued to pull it through, strand after shimmering strand, each changing colour from scarlet to pearl-white—something in Margaret began to sing to its tune, keenly, painfully—until he seemed to tire of it and began to braid the strands, scarlets and blues and whites all together, until it shone like a sunbeam at golden hour.

To ease the pain in her heart Margaret remarked, "You do that as well as a girl."

Poised forward, seated tailor-fashion, Dammerung looked up from his work, jerking a smile from one corner of his mouth. "My mother taught me. I used to braid her hair."

Until then she realized that she had never thought of Rupert having a mother. It seemed still stranger to think of Dammerung having one. And to think that woman was mother to them both! What did the two men bear of her stamp, of hard pride or sudden soft, smiling beauty, as unexpected as it was pleasant? Margaret looked hard into Dammerung's face, picking out the likeness of his brother and his cousin, of the de la Mare breed. What of that other breed, that stock from whence his mother came, was there in that concentrated, down-turned face?

He looked at her from his work again, caught her frown, and frowned back. "Is something amiss?"

She shook off the search. "I was merely thinking how strange it seems that you should have a mother."

The pale blue of his eyes looked into the firelight and turned to mercury-glass. "I did not come out from under a wine-crate. I am sorry you could not have met her. She was as fair to mock the fairness of Romage of Orzelon-gang, who is accounted the most beautiful woman in the Honours. By some."

"Indeed?" A pleasant regret filled the aching place inside Margaret's heart. "I am sorry I could not have known her. What was she like?"

"She was mad."

The moment, crushed, lay scattered in little bright pieces among the sheepskin. Dammerung continued to braid the fire, turning it deftly between his fingers, while the warmth and firelight played on his cheeks and the backs of her hands, shining off her nails, shining off the smoothness of the doeskin... Finally he sighed and grew tired of his work. Closing it up into a little ball in one hand, he blew on it, sending the sparks of it back into the grate. "Now, then, it wasn't as bad as that." He smiled wistfully into some memory. "My mother was a pale, honey-coloured beauty, and very strong beneath her long, fine limbs. She was a bit more austere in her beauty than most of our women—a bit like you, but even you have the gypsy prettiness about you. But the poor thing didn't get the acclaim of the Honours for long. When I was ten years old she contracted brain fever and never quite recovered. She was mostly harmless, and always perfectly serious in her silliness. She thought she was a bird—usually a different bird from one day to the next, depending on the weather: in fine weather she was often a mockingbird, and would keep to the gardens and sing in her beautiful, unmarred voice. On wet days she would keep in and think she was a wood-pigeon, and would coo quietly to me while we went about our work. She was still breathtakingly beautiful, if a little silly, and I was still magnificently proud of her. I was, after all, only ten years old, and much too young to realize what other adults must think of her."

He fell broodingly silent for a space of time, a little wry smile at one corner of his mouth. What songs, what pretty poses and fair, far-off images must he be reliving? At length he went on. "But she was not always harmless. On very bad days, which were rare, she would fly into a passion and think she was a hawk, and come at me and my brother so that our menservants would have to rush us away and my father would have to shut my mother up until the spell passed. I always came to her afterward and found her crying, and would do my best to make her sing mockingbird songs again, which always cheered her. Poor thing. And she was so beautiful."

"I *am* sorry." Margaret was quite subdued and not a little awkward, rather wishing, despite the madness, that she could have met the woman. The irrevocable madness of the mother seemed to explain, a little, the casual madness of the son. "They say time heals wounds, but I have never believed them."

"Nor I."

Turning gingerly back upon her side, face to the fire, she thought of all the other people she had met who bore long scars and open wounds that had never healed. She thought of the long scar over Plenilune that the death of a young lord of the Mares had left, the taste of hopelessness, the shadow of a headstone at a grave. "More than ever," she mused, half to herself, "the people I have known here have been in pain, like a people walking in darkness with no hope of light or betterment."

Dammerung's voice was quiet and grim. "All people are in pain, and many walk in the dark. That is the purpose of the Overlord, that someone, somewhere, might be brave enough to light a candle, to bear the pain, to jar a pulse into the life-weary body. What is strength but the will to go on? What is bravery but a hatred for that which defies you? What is courage but a love for that which you defend?"

"And that," she said, "is why you did not die that day, though you did not feel like telling Skander so."

There was a pause, a heavy quiet. Then she heard him smile. "I did not feel like telling Skander so, and that is why I did not die that day. But—God—it was like dying!"

"Yes... But we found a break in the wall, you and I." She turned her head and looked up at him, smiling half-heartedly and hoping that it did not look half-hearted. "We'll get out of the woods somehow."

His smile, too, was half-hearted. "I had thought you had dozed off for that... I do not know, Margaret. I am not a man of sums—I can do them, but sure I have never *liked* them—but the equation under my pen has no pretty answer. I know I must balance it, but the R variable has but one other variable with which to cancel it out."

She saw half-formed memories which did not belong to her against the pearl-pink wash of firelight, images of honour and betrayal and a crescent moon adrift in a gold cloud-spun sky. "He tried to balance it."

Dammerung's smile widened with a jerk, winging mocking laughter at the corners of his eyes, but the corners of his mouth were telltale bitter. "He tried—he was ever a quiet, studious boy—but I fudge all mathematics, and I fudged his as well."

"But for now—what?"

"For now—" he arranged the doeskin where it had slipped from her shoulders, and rose in a single fluid motion to his feet, uplit by the fire, bent over her with his palm on the mantelpiece. "Now we grow better, you and I, and we grow stronger, and Rupert and I stand well off from each other to watch and see what the other might do. The playing field is set in a new shape, and perhaps neither of us fully knows how the game will go forward."

He said it blithely, with the light of his blitheness casting a great shadow behind all his stark words, but Margaret saw in the shadow a sense of expectancy in the young man, as though he knew, though he decried his skill with mathematics, how this game between him and his great brother would go forward. Looking up into his face she saw every inch of him was of the red-blooded Marenové stock: grim and, caught in stillness, almost impersonal, every bit of him a match for Rupert. Though she had learned that Dammerung could laugh and be gentle, and Rupert never had quite got the skill of that, Margaret knew in that moment that Dammerung could be as terrible as Rupert if he chose to, that beneath the sleet-storm eyes was a mind so keen it had to sheath itself in laughter lest it cut unwittingly the souls around it. The awfulness touched her, stroking cold down her spine. She shivered but could not look away.

But he saw she had shivered, and smiled companionably. "Also it is winter," he added in an off-hand manner, "and it is too cold to do anything. The only sensible thing is to stay put and wiggle our toes before the fire."

"Pad away for some chestnuts," said Margaret, recovering with some effort. "I missed Christmas and I want it to feel like the holidays again."

"I promised Skander I would not wander off. This place is somewhat bigger than a cellar."

Margaret pulled the doeskin close and rolled toward the fire's beckoning flames. "Ring a bell," she told him, "or whistle. Someone is sure to come if you whistle."

There was a pregnant silence above and behind her. The fire crackled softly. The wind, pressing its back against the castle walls, hummed a low, sea-surf tune. Dammerung caught his breath a moment, then, before he could say whatever was first on his mind, amended aloud, "But no, I don't need to ask you that."

Odd how he conjured up the old Bible narratives and gave them a flesh they never had before. Laughing softly, self-deprecatingly, more comfortable and at peace and at a loss than ever before, Margaret murmured, "To whom *would* I go...?" And she fell asleep before there could be any chestnuts at all.

XVIII | "SHE MIGHT NOT HAVE KNOWN"

When she woke the next morning, feeling stronger and more alive, Margaret was startled to find herself alone. There had been a snow in the night, but the sun was already well into the morning house of heaven and the air outside her window was full of a smoky golden light as the sun on the snow burned it back into the sky. But Dammerung's chair was empty, and the weather did not matter so long as Dammerung's chair was full.

After some fighting Margaret got herself disentangled from her bedsheets and put herself out in the cold, leaning haphazardly on the mattress to keep herself from falling. A sick singing began in her ears.

Maybe—she shook her head to clear it—*maybe he has gone to breakfast. But he always has his breakfast here.*

She was just pulling herself together to walk to the door when, to her relief, Aikaterine stepped in. The quiet white-clad maid had come and gone in the three weeks Margaret had been at Lookinglass, but she had never truly noticed the maid until now. It was such a relief to see the maid, and to realize that in Aikaterine she could place her perfect trust and be at ease, that the singing in her ears stopped at once.

"Oh my—" said Aikaterine when she saw Margaret out of bed. "What curious verities of my Lord of the Mares."

"Where is Dammerung?" Margaret demanded. "And what verities?"

The maid shut the door and went directly to the wardrobe. "I had just brought in their breakfast when my Lord's cousin sent me up to you, telling me—and I quote—'the horse would be trying to get out the barn doors' if I was not speedy."

"I have been called a vixen, a m-mouse, and a precocious chit," gingerly, on shaky foal-like legs, Margaret followed the maid toward the dressing table, "but never a horse."

Aikaterine soothed her fingers through Margaret's hair and smiled at the reflection in the mirror. "There are worse things to be called."

Margaret sat and Aikaterine worked awhile in silence. It had been a long time since a comb had been coaxed through Margaret's tangled hair, a long time since she had had a proper soak in a tub, or had slid with any kind of independence into a clean, starched set of clothes. It felt oddly like being reborn. Her body and feelings were no less tremulous when, groomed and clothed, she went out on Aikaterine's arm to join the gentlemen for breakfast. The morning sun was splitting in shear white splendour all over the Lookinglass halls, breaking up on glass and marble and diving this way and that in a confusion of brilliance. She could not remember the place looking so like its namesake, and wondered—had Dammerung done this?

She had never been in to Skander's study. It was spacious and well-furnished, full of light and books and a cheery fire in the fireplace. Skander, she saw as soon as she was led in, was seated behind his desk—an old, worn, formidable battlement of wood and iron—and Dammerung was ensconced in a sofa by the fire, entrenched in a mountain of books, searching, seemingly in vain, for something to arrest his interest. He was in the act of passing a book off on another precarious stack, having been jilted by its uninteresting contents, when he caught sight of her standing in the doorway.

"Margaret!" Skander had seen her at the same moment and was rising from his chair. He was in the middle of breakfast and was at a momentary loss as to how to dispose of his napkin.

"Oh, don't stir out of your toast," she implored him before he could put the napkin down. "I am so ravenous myself, my good-mornings would be weak-hearted."

He put the napkin down all the same and emerged from behind the desk; his boots, she saw, were damp and a little muddy. "You haven't eaten a decent meal since you came. Can you manage toast?"

Margaret left Aikaterine and slipped her arm in Skander's. It was better still to be able to lean upon such a strength and not worry that she might pull her partner down. "Toast," she agreed—the word brought the soft warm water to her mouth, "and eggs, though sausages or bacon might be a little much."

"Make room!" said Dammerung, and pushed over an entire stack of books, clearing the little table between the couches. As Skander deposited her onto the second sofa the War-wolf disentangled himself from his own, shrugged off his enormous black cloak which could have passed for a blanket over a bed of two, and bundled it around her shoulders. His feet, she saw, were bare, but blue-tinted and grimy, with the veins carved like marble down the crest of each lean appendage.

"You have been out," she noted as the black cocoon encased her.

Dammerung shifted and turned over one foot like a pigeon. "They are a bit grubby, aren't they...? Skander hauled me out into the mews this morning. It is warmer there," he added, turning with the poker to the fireplace, "than it is in here."

Aikaterine came back with a fresh tray of breakfast for Margaret. Skander took it from her and placed it on the little table, sending a pretty pattern of silver light jigging across the wood. "Your coffee is in no danger of freezing over. If you would put on stockings and a pair of boots your blood might be less chilly."

Dammerung flung the poker back into its bucket with a clang and folded back up on the couch, wooing a steaming cup of coffee with a beatific smile. "La, ice-water runs in our veins. A pair of stockings seems unlikely to change that. And anyway, I did try a pair of your horseshoes, but apparently your father comes from draught stock and they were too big for me. Also, I have got so used to padding about on my paws that, fit or no fit, I simply didn't like it."

Skander picked up the poker and brandished it like a baton. "And we are all thankful," he said condescendingly upon his cousin, "that you found clothing was still to your taste."

"You wouldn't say that..."

Skander turned away to soothe the fire and Dammerung, after watching the bright, broken network of sparks going up in the grate, turned back to Margaret, leaning forward to pour her a cup of tea.

"Are you sure you do not want something stronger? There is still a bit of white peakiness about your cheeks."

She took the cup and listened, alarmed, to the rattle it made in its saucer. "Oh, no, no. I am so tired, you could knock me over with a feather. Brandy would put me to sleep at once."

Dammerung stretched himself out toward the blaze—was it her imagination or did the fire leap at his advance?—and tucked his hands comfortably under his arms. "It is a cosy day. An' sure I like this better than a wine-cellar."

Skander had gone back to his desk but he had not yet sat down. Looking up from shuffling papers he asked bluntly, "Do you intend to go back to Marenové House?"

Margaret was in the act of raising the cup to her lips. She stopped—the sheeny liquid trembled in the light—and looked at Dammerung. The War-wolf had turned his head slowly toward his cousin, the mockery and lightheartedness for a moment pulled back, and the long dark wrestling with thought and sentiment and circumstance stark on the lean de la Mare face. But only for a moment, and then it was gone again, and Dammerung was laughing.

"What a shuffling of cards there would be. Rupert to Talus Perey again—it is too small for him, and he feels the pinch. Malbrey to—he is a little better than a hovel. I could give him an outlying tower from the days when our borders were a little less certain. But I should feel sorry for the gypsies I would be ousting from the tower."

The equation. Margaret replaced her cup on its saucer and thought of the awful equation. How light Dammerung made of it—how he laughed in the dark! Yet she felt they all three knew how very dark it was.

"I should like to go back to Marenové House," Dammerung said after a silence of indeterminate length.

"So would I like you. You are restless in my quiet halls and make me feel uneasy. And, anyway, it would be nice to trust the neighbour at one's back, as I have not been able to do for years."

Dammerung smiled wistfully into the fire. "How hard it has gone with you, coz." There was gentle mockery in his voice again. He looked up searchingly into Skander's face. "Well I am sorry that I left you all in the middle of the game. Your smile has a little of the strain about it, as it never had before. Did you learn to fight with Rupert in my absence?"

"No." To Margaret it seemed her words came from far off. She, too, was staring into the fire, but she saw Dammerung look at her out of the corner of her eye. "We learned to parry and to dig in our heels, but none us were matched to fight him."

There was a soft crackly silence. Something heavy clunked on wood as Skander set it down, then Dammerung asked gently, "*Were* none of you?" And Margaret, suddenly confused, broke off her stare to meet his eye and wonder where she had gone to and what had she meant. He held her a moment, looking into her eyes with a sense of wandering through her and etching her mind on the glassiness of his eyes...then he smiled—or had he been smiling all along?—and the question slid away as he looked away, slid like a handful of sparks back into the fire.

But she kept watching, for though her body was tired and disused to work, she found the chill edge of the room and the sweep of white light, the familiar tang of tea and rustle of the fire, had sharpened her senses. They had sharpened her senses to many things, to the softness of Aikaterine's passing, like some benevolent spirit always in the rear ground of the scene, to the little iron twist at the edge of a smile that ruined the full amiability of Skander's countenance. But more than that they sharpened her senses to Dammerung. In the cellar, as the fox, he had always been a small, wing-shadowed sort of thing, a sad story in a children's book in which the tales were grim, sometimes awful, but always only stories. In the white light of Skander's study, the bare, branching view of Glassdale flung wide across the windows beyond him, Dammerung seemed a bigger, keener thing, less awful than he had seemed in the firelight of last night—there was laughter in him today which had been quenched by the scars of yesteryear last night. As he sat staring into the flames and she sat staring at him, she knew he was thinking this morning, not of Spencer, but of Skander and Centurion and Mark Roy, of men he had known on the other side of the dark, men he had left in the game. He was thinking of the game—a game now, not an equation, which was a more promising thought—and playing with huge things in his head as a child plays with magical worlds.

And are we not, she wondered, *in some kind of magic world?* She frowned a little at him. *Are you the child that dreams of us? And I had always thought the Overlord awful and grim—a man like Rupert. I had not thought the Overlord might laugh. But—God!—what a world it would be that had not a laughing pulse in it anymore!*

Her eyes wandered off the amber-black crown of Dammerung's hair to the view outside the windows. For the first time she saw the splendour of Plenilune and felt it would not kill her. For the first time she felt she would not kill the splendour. It was sitting next to her, freed from a melancholy dark, and in the moment that hung in the balance, it had reached across to her and taken her by the hand to save her. For the first time, as she gazed at that white winter beauty until her eyes swam with light and something more painful, she felt she understood what Skander had said of the women of old and how, in their hardness, in their adamantine glory, they had known the beating blood of love.

"Skander," said Plenilune lightly, glibly, "I think we had better wrestle."

Skander had been looking for something in the piano bench; he dropped the lid shut with a bang.

Dammerung twisted in his sofa at the sound. "I am two years and a body out of play. What a sorry state I am in!"

As if he meant to commence then and there, his cousin dropped the sheaf of papers—they slipped sidewise on the air and fluttered to the edge of a low table—and, putting his hand to his sleeve, shoved it upward, baring the corded arm beneath. That brought Margaret out of her reverie with more of a start than the bang.

"I'll give you no quarter," warned Skander.

"You had better not!"

The blue-jay man, who had replaced Aikaterine, bent forward and saved the papers from floating to the floor. "I suggest to my lords," he said, straightening, "that the garden would be an advantageous place to wrestle. It is cold but the grass has dried, and—" he cleared his throat "—no furniture will be broken."

"It is not too cold for the Lady Margaret?" his master inquired, but his voice had fallen out of her notice. She turned back on Dammerung, puzzled, and not a little uneasy. With a heave he extricated himself from the deep cushions of the couch and, reaching out to help her, caught her quizzical look. He turned his head away, fixing her with a single eye, quizzical in return.

"What," she murmured, "you have not been beaten about enough?"

He flashed a smile at her, a smile all teeth and fighting dare—but in his eyes she saw a faintly veiled wince of remembered pain. "I seem to have grown used and fond of getting my skull kicked in."

"Have you yet learned to duck?"

Skander turned back from talking with the blue-jay man. "All right, coz. The lawn by the patio will do. There is some sun there and Lady Margaret will—I presume—like a little sunshine on her bones."

Dammerung got a hand under her elbow and helped her up. "Bring a chair, Tabby," he called. "She won't want to stand like a referee."

"I am there before you," murmured the blue-jay man, and sailed out of the room.

They went out onto the patio, into a slight breeze and a clean smell of spring; the wind was in the cherry and the plumes of white were tossing about like sea-foam. There was a sweet tang of woodsmoke in the air. She felt wind-starved, and from where she sat in a pool of sunlight she pulled in breath after delicious breath of high fell country air. Oh, to be free at last! and to breathe the air of freedom! Through sun-squinted eyes she watched Dammerung step into the cold, shimmery turf and strip off his braces, tossing them onto the stone kerb of the patio, and pull his shirt out of his trousers. The linen tails fluttered in the wind. He was still thin—as thin as she felt and, if turned to the light, might prove to be transparent—but he set his hands on his hips in a defiant, cocksure pose and seemed to be the very pleasure of life embodied.

"Were you after precision or strength?" asked Skander as he, too, stripped down to his shirtsleeves.

"Both, I imagine."

Seeing his bare feet, Skander added, "Would you rather I take off my boots for this?"

Dammerung swung a foot up on his knee and tested his heel with the hard of his thumb. "Don't give me any quarter! I am of a mind to go barefoot but I think it unlikely anyone else will. You won't crush my beautiful toes. I'll make sure of that."

"P'uh!" laughed Skander, and flung down his belt.

They took up their positions in the grass and Margaret, forgetting the wind and the sunshine, which threatened to blow her off like a golden plover feather, leaned forward to watch them. Even the blue-jay man, who most assuredly had other things to do, lingered in the brown-shadowed doorway. The two men took a few moments to stretch, their shoulders nearly starting out of their shirts with the strain, and then with nodded consent they were ready. There was no pause. Almost at once Skander sprang, beautifully, like a wild cat, blocking and throwing a blow at the same time. But Dammerung seemed to have turned into a top and whirled, bringing his foot up at the same time into the side of his cousin's head. Margaret cried out in surprise: she had never seen a man bring his leg up so high. She could not remember seeing a man bring his knee up above his waist.

Skander reeled and spun back, crouching, aiming a blow at Dammerung's knee. He almost landed the blow, too, but at the last moment Dammerung swung and straddled the outflung arm and seemed to drop at the same time, twisting as he fell, so that Skander's arm was tangled up in his interlocking legs. Skander was pitched over onto his back with a resounding thud, Dammerung's elbow in the hollow of his throat.

Margaret staggered to her feet almost before she knew what she was doing, but Skander was laughing and Dammerung was yelling, "I've still got it! This tiger has still got it!" With a gasp she sank back down into her chair. Unperturbed, the blue-jay man padded past her and went to assist his master off the turf.

"Shao! That smarts!" Skander poked at his temple.

Dammerung had to help himself to his own feet. "Did I break anything?"

"Only my reputation in the lady's eyes, I'm sure, but nothing more."

"Why, did he have that?" Dammerung called up to Margaret.

She leaned forward. The wind had picked up, and she had to shout into it to be heard. " 'Twas not *wrestling*! What do you do?"

"It is a better sort of wrestling than other kinds you might see, for it better suits our purpose." Dammerung cast about under the bare cherry-verge a moment before returning with a thick branch roughly the length of his arm. His cousin watched him warily. "In brief: our business, that is, the business of war, is more like to our kind of wrestling than two bulls pitting their shoulders together and groaning into the earth." As though the branch were a sword he spun it, and spun with it, his bare, agile feet skimming the short turf. It was a strange series of movements and yet Margaret had to admit that they were beautiful, and if the branch were a real sword the blue-jay man would have been dead.

Skander brought up his arm and blocked a blow from the stick. Margaret thought it was a casual block, but he followed it up with two quick jabs at Dammerung's head—one of which Dammerung avoided with a neat dodge, one of which he dodged right in to. She heard the crack of contact and stifled another gasp. Dammerung spun with the blow, his back to Skander, and leapt, turning over backward until his legs locked around his cousin's neck.

"Damn!" cried Skander, and the two went down again while the blue-jay man, too close to the scuffle, side-stepped to avoid being pulled in by his master's right hook.

Dammerung rolled off Skander's back, staggering, his head tilted and his hand pressed under his nose. "Oh, that can't be good," he said as blood spurted between his fingers.

"Did I not tell you to learn to duck!" Margaret cried. But she could see Dammerung was enjoying himself—possibly all the more for the sudden blood-letting. His fire was up, the wind rushing round him like a roaring mantle of his own wild aura. "The storm is up!" he cried, shaking himself like a dog and flinging blood left and right, "and all is on the hazard!"

The two went at it anew, giving and taking and avoiding blows with a precision and power which surprised Margaret. And she was suddenly intensely sorry that she was a woman and not a man. It was not until they finished, by common consent or by some rule she was not privy to, and had stepped away, saluting each other with broken laugh and bloodied nose, that she realized she had risen and had watched the whole thing on her feet. As Dammerung came striding wearily back up to her, she felt a crying ache in her body and had to put her hand on the tabletop and lean her weight upon it.

"What do you think?" he asked her mockingly. "Do I fit this body well again?"

She dug into her pocket and pulled out her handkerchief, handing it to him. "You are all manner of full of yourself, Dammerung. You outfit any body."

"There, you have conquered me." Then, more seriously, "Are you hurting?"

She shook her head. "I am tired. I think I pushed myself too far today. No, don't—"

He reached out to her and she was afraid that he would try to take the pain for her. She was sure she could manage, and he was hot and breath-spent and his face was bloodied.

"Nay, do not get your fur awrong." He took her elbow. "We will go to the sitting room and be wealthy and lackadaisical now that I have pummelled my cousin and you have fretted on my account."

Skander buttoned his braces and slid them back over his shoulders. "I will put you to quarter-staves this evening. Margaret should like that."

"What are we for," said Dammerung with a sly and martyrly look, "but to make sport for the ladies."

"Tabby, with me." Skander turned away. "I'll see you two inside. Don't bleed on my couches."

Margaret and Dammerung went back inside; she was not sure which led and supported the other. Dammerung was still stiff and recovering his breath, but he seemed otherwise in good spirits. He put her down on a couch in the sitting room and collapsed beside her, his head leaned back, her handkerchief pressed to his nose. "I wonder if Aikaterine could be prevailed upon," he yawned after a moment of quiet, "to bring us something to drink."

"Something warm would be nice," Margaret agreed sleepily. She rubbed at her eye and was surprised by how cold her knuckle was on her wind-blasted cheeks.

But neither of them made a move to call the girl in. The couch's embrace, half pillows and half sheepskin, was luxuriously sweet. A golden clock with a corona of bright, blurred light was ticking on the mantelpiece and, with each hard tick, shook itself and its little spangles of light across the upswept face of the white marble chimney. Dammerung, his head thrown back on the wooden curve of the sofa, handkerchief clamped over his nose, seemed to be almost asleep. It was not until that moment that she saw how tired he was, languid and in shadow, scarred like the thing in the black marble cave which had set him free, still gathering the strength which had been scattered as with a blow upon the water. She wondered what he would look like when he was quite himself again.

He took the handkerchief away and gingerly ran a finger under his nose: it came away dry. With a sigh he crumpled it up and stuffed it into his trouser pocket and rose, aimlessly, and wandered toward the tall, thin, four-legged instrument set up under the windows. After a moment's inquisitive pause, running his hand along the side of it and patting its arched neck, velvety-smooth like a stallion, he propped up the lid, turned up the cover, and sat down at the keyboard.

It was no good sitting alone. Margaret had taken up a pillow and had been holding it warmly in her lap; with a sigh of her own she put it away and got shakily to her feet to join him. He looked up over the sheet-music he was shuffling through and scooted to the end of the bench to leave her room.

"Can you play?" he asked, holding out a paper for her to see.

The notes were done up oddly—in circles, yes, but circles that were more suggestive of curlicues and Chinese script than of the musical written language she was accustomed to. She stared at it a moment before the sense began to bleed through the unfamiliar style.

"I can play better than my sisters," she admitted, "but then, I applied myself better."

"You strike me as the sort who would." He set the sheet up on the piano. "Handle the accompaniment: it is less difficult. Has Skander tuned this...?"

He crooked his long fingers and set them on the keys. A sweet cord trembled up from the long range of strings in the body of the instrument, but it played weakly, as if its voice were coming from a long way off. Dammerung grimaced but continued. With an inexplicable flutter of panic Margaret hurried to join in.

The sly beast! As she played, catching the rhythm of the notes as she went, she knew he was deliberately getting her mind off her own tiredness. In a way, she realized as she left off to turn his page for him, she saw he had not done putting himself back into shape. He had pitted his body against his cousin's stalwart shoulder. As his fingers moved deftly along the ivory keys she watched his attention fix on the whirl of notes and tiny, indicative dots, fix upon the woven fabric of sound emanating from the bed of strings. He had made Skander pluck his biggest, heaviest string to bring it back into tune: like his fingers on the keys, his mind was playing delicately on his finer nerves, matching them against the tuning fork of so intricate a task as playing a piano. It was but a small thing, a simple thing, but the strength was in the details.

She started when he began to sing.

> I wandered the corridors of Time—
> Those gilt-decked ancient halls of yore
> (far off loomed the future's door);
> Gazed on marvel here, and there still more,
> When a wall rose up on the watch's spine:
> A sudden obelisk rising square,
> Like Babel, but taller, and still more fair,

Bricked with diamonds, sealed with gore.

What is this horror, what this sight–
Which seems to pierce the very night–
Fades pomp of kings to moth-wing grey,
Turns empires into a blank Pompeii;
From light is born and births more light?
I stared and could not say.

He leaned forward a moment and squinted at the page, fingers fudging beautifully on a complicated series of interconnected spirals, circles, and dots.

Pompeii I had passed, and Rome too;
This column topped them and still grew.
Its mortar was blood, its seams were stone–
I thought at times I heard it groan,
As flesh-and-blood is known to do,
As if its bricks were bone.

A mason came around the bend,
All covered with diamond-grit and sand:
Ill-omened guide, but the chance I grasped,
And said, "Hark! what is this mast
With stone sails set–for what land!–
Which all pillars has out-classed?"

"Da da-da da dum da da-da dum... I don't remember the rest."

Margaret finished the accompaniment and put her hands in her lap. "Why, what was it?"

He smiled sheepishly into the page. "Only a little song I was making once when I was on holiday here. By the twelve houses, that was years ago! I must have been only a little lad then, and reading some very fine epic literature, too, by the sound of it. I am mortified that I dug it back out at all. An' sure it is no Shiggaion. My memory of it was better than this."

She took the page from him. "The music was very pretty. You play well for someone who is several years out of practice. The poetry leaves things desired, though I feel—"

She stopped, suddenly, a blush of confusion rushing up her cheeks. A hundred painful memories flooded her mind and she wondered if she dared say the one word which fit in the keyhole, that unlocked the door behind which she strove to hide her unpleasant life.

But Dammerung was probing. "You feel what?"

Her thumb brushed the coarse, heavy paper. "I feel Rupert would not like it."

Dammerung laughed, harshly, soundlessly. He took the paper back. "No? No, he wouldn't. I wrote it about the kingdom of heaven. He would not be so fond of that." With a casual gesture he let it go. The paper slipped on the air, circled, notes spinning, and came to rest on the polished hardwoods in a broken patch of sunshine. Sliding his hands into the back of his trousers to be sure the long tail of his linen shirt had not pulled loose, he said, "What can you do? Do you know anything by heart?"

"Hmm!" Margaret moved to command the centre of the instrument. Dammerung swivelled, straddling the bench, to give her room. "Life has taught me harsher things by heart, but I might be able to remember something." She sat a moment in thought, passing completely over the last few months at Marenové House, past the Leeds railway station, past her mother and the nagging, to single, quiet moments she had stolen in order to make something beautiful out of the tedious task of learning an instrument. Those had been moments of respite for her and their memory touched a tender place, a place which smarted if she pressed too hard—as Spencer, she realized, must smart if Dammerung thought too closely on him. Time did not heal such wounds.

Lest he should somehow catch her thoughts, Margaret chose a song at random and began to play. She found she was rusty and that it did make a difference to be playing in the sitting room of Capys Lookinglass, in Plenilune, where they wrote their notes down in curious script. The European way of music, superimposed in her mind over the piano under her hands, confused her and muddled her notes until she was able to find her balance. She played a few bars of an old Welsh hymn and Dammerung, listening to the way of it, seemed greatly to enjoy it.

"It is different," he said when she had finished, "and yet very like us. So they see our way in music there on Earth as well as our way in literature? That makes for good hearing."

As it was a hymn, Margaret chose not to mention that, where she came from, the Welsh were not much thought of—but she was startled by a sudden bang of the keys as Dammerung got up, palms on the ivories, a look of surprise and worry on his face.

"Skander!"

His cousin stood in the doorway—he winced at the jangle of discordant notes as if they had struck him in the face—and his face, which had been battered but pleasant last Margaret had seen it, was drawn and white with horror. He had a piece of unfolded letter-paper clutched in one hand. He was looking blankly, horrified, at Dammerung, and did not seem able to hear him.

"Skander! What the deuce is it? You look as though you have seen my ghost!"

The joke, half-heartedly made, failed to touch Skander. He looked down at the paper, staring through it, then crossed as if in a trance to put it in Dammerung's waiting hand. Dammerung did not look at it at first. He followed Skander with his eyes as the other went to the window and stood staring out blindly at the garden. Skander put his chin in his hand, covering his lips; his hand was trembling.

With an effort Margaret got up and leaned into Dammerung's shoulder to look at the letter, but Dammerung shied away and read it to himself. She watched his eyes flicker over the lines, then widen and pale; his lips moved a little, but so little that Margaret could not read them. Then, "Shuh!" he gasped, disbelieving. "What—" Sitting back down hard on the bench he handed the letter to Margaret, staring, as Skander stared, blankly, unseeingly.

She turned the letter into the light and began scanning it, expecting a death. But it was worse than that. The beautiful script, etched in atrament and gold, breathing with formality, was an invitation—an invitation to the wedding of Woodbird Swan-neck and some man called Sparling. It struck Margaret like a physical blow. The paper slid; her fingers did not respond. Blankly she watched it drift between two long fingernails painted rose-gold and flutter softly to the floor, a pale, skin-coloured leaf against the dark-stained carpet.

"The cow!" hissed Dammerung.

Skander snapped round. "Dammerung!"

"Not her. Black Malkin." Dammerung got up and stepped away from the piano as if to start pacing, but caught himself at the last moment and stood still, thinking so hard Margaret could see the green sparks snapping in his eyes.

Skander had turned back to the window. He leaned heavily on the sill, his forehead pressed against the cool glass. "Damn," he whispered. Margaret laid her fingers on the warm ivories and shut her eyes—as if contact with the instrument would lend harmony to the world. There was a long, uneasy, creaking silence...then: "*Damn.*"

"Yes, it is," Dammerung snapped back. Margaret's eyes jumped open in time to see him pivot toward Skander. "When you told me about the situation," he asked with merciless deliberation, "did you tell me everything?"

Skander pushed off the window. "Yes!" he cried. His voice was audibly shaking and Margaret realized with horror that he, Skander Rime, was actually on the brink of tears. The man turned away and pressed his fist to his lips, hard, trying to get a hold of himself. It was a moment before he could continue. "We pledged ourselves as children. We were dedicated to each other—she was too," he added defensively. "But when my father died and I inherited Capys, and I brought the matter up formally, there was an enormous outcry. I had known of, but had not agreed with my father siding with Feyfax—and I thought that would count for something! But no," Skander laughed scornfully. "The iniquity of the fathers is revisited to the third and fourth generation!" He was quiet for a while, still staring off across the lawn. Dammerung waited, hands on hips; his brows were hard, his lips narrowed into an uncompromising line, but his flint-pale eyes had softened and bore a look of agony.

"Black Malkin opposed me," Skander went on at last. "Black Malkin opposed me, and of course Grane backed her up.

Well I knew then that I had no chance. Woodbird was the youngest, and though strong-minded she knows what it is like to have one's family torn apart by dissension. She was...persuaded to see me no more."

Suddenly he swung back round, anger clouding his fair face. "She might have let it be! Black Malkin forgets nothing done by friend or foe. She might have let it be, well knowing the grief this would cause me."

"She might not have known you are a man, and prone to pain in these matters," said Dammerung in a dead-level tone. His cousin swore softly and turned away. With a heavy sigh Dammerung swooped down and caught up the letter, crushing it in one hand and, at the same time, extending the other to lift Margaret out of her stupor. "You had better see Aikaterine about looking through Aunt Mairwen's trunks," he told her. "You'll need a serviceable gown."

"What?" barked Skander.

Dammerung ran a hand through his hair and looked about him as if he expected the gown to be produced out of the air. "Well," he mused. "It's a rummy long way to Thwitandrake... Anyone got a horse?"

XIX | BELIEVED ON IN THE WORLD

"You said there was bad blood between the houses. How did that come about?"

Skander was ahead of them in the train, well out of earshot. Margaret and Dammerung rode side by side down the sparsely wooded road among the northern foothills of the fell country, the plain of Thrasymene before them. It was a bright, bitterly cold day, brighter and colder than any thus far in their journey. Margaret was bundled up in a white stallion-skin against the harsh wind, and Dammerung, save for his bare feet slung idly by his stirrups, was dressed in a thick black doublet scored over with blood-coloured patterns which Margaret could never quite make out, and wrapped against the wind in a panther-skin. They were well furnished and well fed; the ride had been easy and the weather, though often overcast, had held fair. But it was still winter, and it was still cold, and Margaret was looking forward to the heated wine and spiced meat that Dammerung told her would be waiting for them at the end of the road.

He dropped the reins on his horse's neck and tucked his hands under his arms. "Do you know the Carmarthen?"

"I have heard of them in passing, yes." Margaret ducked to avoid a low-hanging beech limb.

Dammerung pointed wide, over the far-flung knees of the fells, over the vale and woods, over the rivers blurring in the evening spring light. "The Carmarthen live on the steppes to the northeast. Thrasymene territory abuts their land—if you can call it *their* land, for they are nomadic and own nothing but what travels with them— away north, though you cannot see, where the fells end and those woods begin. Thrasymene, we must all admit, has never been a great Honour. They are great seamen but their land is poorer than that of the other Honours, their resources less, their voice smaller among the voices of the other landed men; so they know not to pick fights if they can possibly help it. Unfortunately the grandfather of the three ravens fell afoul of a nomad band of Carmarthen when his hunting led him over his border across what they believe is 'holy ground.' "

"They are not Christian, I take it."

"Shao! Had they been a little more coherent in their culture they might have invented crucifixion themselves."

He left off a moment as they reached the low sloping edge of a stream and waded through the churning, chilly surf to the other side. Skander was still mutely at the head of their train, head up, eyes ahead. Margaret, following Dammerung's eye to his cousin, felt her heart flinch: the man had spoken little and had not smiled since the day the letter had come. Dammerung had made a bold effort to soothe Skander and had tried, with the other hand, to pull away some of the worry so that Skander would not be burdened with it. But in this the War-wolf had not prevailed. His cousin had remained steadfastly stony, internalizing, nursing a hatch-egg of agony where his heart had been.

"Where was I?"

Margaret came back to their horses with a start. "Some kind of holy place and the grandfather hunting."

"And the grandfather hunting. The Carmarthen killed him without warning—how swift man is to quash all blasphemies!—and gave his body back to the crows of Thrasymene. He had left behind a wife, two sons, and three granddaughters. He had a third son, an elder one, by whom the three ravens were fathered, but he had died some years before along with their mother and had left the girls in the care of the old Lady. Richard de la Mare, my own father, told me once that she was a very great woman, quiet and full of steel, and she might have taken her husband's death well and soldiered on to make something good of Thrasymene for her husband's sake and for the sake of her people. But her two surviving sons fell out over the matter. The second eldest, Feyfax, was a man disused to patience and had fire where blood ought to run. He might have been a great man himself—certainly he was a formidable warrior and ever such a one as men will follow gladly—had his father lived longer and kept a hand upon his reins. Feyfax wanted vengeance. Feyfax wanted remuneration by blood."

Margaret smiled to hide the pain of someone else's memory. "Can you much blame him?"

And Dammerung, too, smiled, as if to hide the same pain. "Not much. But his brother Ring had a point when he opposed him, for their father had worked hard at making something great of Thrasymene, and a wholesale war upon the Carmarthen would have damaged their Honour badly. Poor Ring. He was a quiet young man, promising, as like to Hector as his brother was like Achilles. They were each other's downfall, for Ring would not let Feyfax go on, and Feyfax would go on only over his brother's dead body. In the end, through sheer desperation, Ring gave up the ties of kinship and took his own brother down, himself down too, all to save his precious Honour. And he did save it, though, as you can see, at a bitter, bitter cost."

He seemed to conjure a wind, cold and smelling faintly of salt, which whirled around them and lifted panther and horse-skin alike, black and white like a lapwing's plumage.

Would any of us die, Skander had asked, *to keep what looms before us from happening?*

Odd, thought Margaret, that people were willing to die for what they considered worth living for. How curious a creature man was! how full of light and darkness and paradox, the heart as of a devil and the power in his crafting hands of some sort of god. Level westward sunlight sparked on the gemmed headstall of Dammerung's mount and flung out notes of light on the dun-coloured air. How odd...

"Skander's father, in all other things a worthy man, backed Feyfax once in a kind of desperate council, unofficial, and cobbled together by well-meaning neighbours. I remember that my father went and said nothing and saw all, and came back with a sore heart. Black Malkin, who is the eldest of the three ravens, was old enough then to understand, the three of them shrewd enough to realize, that their family was being torn apart from the inside. They had to watch that, and watch their guardian grandmother break under the strain as her two surviving sons killed each other. They grew up quickly in those harsh, forbidding circumstances, and Black Malkin, whose temper is prone to bitterness, has never forgot that Capys sided with Feyfax and not Ring. Though I sometimes wonder if she would have hated Skander all the same had his father chosen her uncle Ring instead. Women are very fickle."

Margaret almost reminded him that *she* was a woman, but for no clear reason she was glad he had not lumped her in with the rest of her capricious sex. It was an off-hand, almost unconscious thing, but she was glad.

They reached Thwitandrake by sundown and found they were not the first merrymakers to arrive for the wedding which was scheduled for the morrow. In the huge wooden-stockade compound of the house, dark and as implacable as a boar, torches burned in the brown shadows, throwing up great smudges of black smoke against the burnished rose-gold sky of evening. The stables were full and smelled heavily of warm horse bodies. Margaret had a confused impression of people everywhere, everyone chatty and happy, everywhere a purl of wine-dark cloak or jink of yellow light off an earring as someone turned her head to see who the newcomers were. Hid inside her panther-skin, a small purr of courage reverberating under her breastbone, Margaret passed them by, breaking her horse off from the rest of the train to come alongside Skander's and Dammerung's. Skander was so much occupied with his own thoughts that he slung down and went on at once, leaving the two of them behind. Sympathetic, but stung, Margaret frowned after him as he mounted the house steps and was swallowed up in the light coming through the open doorway.

"I dare swear the holy of holies is more accessible than he," grunted Dammerung as he shed his hooves and reached up to lift Margaret down. From under the shadow of his hood his eyes gleamed out like moonstones. "Best let him be for now." He looked for Aikaterine and the blue-jay man and, seeing neither of them, mused, "It appears we must shift for ourselves. I am for supper and a bath and bed. And you?"

She looked over her shoulder at the many people gathered in the dark, torch-shot cold of the yard. "I am not in the mood to be sociable just now. I like your programme."

"Simple pleasures. Canst walk!" he added laughingly as, trying to go with him, her muscles cried out in agony and her knees buckled.

"It has been awhile since I rode so great a distance," she said defensively. "Oh, for a bit of spiced wine!"

They evaded the crowded central hall and were soon directed to the guest quarters at the rear of the complex. When Margaret told the servants that Skander Rime was in their party they were given a suite with a cosy little sitting room between the bedchambers, a fire, and news that a warm supper would be brought in to them as soon as the message could be delivered to the kitchen.

"And as soon as the kitchen can spare time," added Dammerung when the servant had gone and left them alone. "I have grown used to eating regular meals. Lookinglass is quite spoiling me."

He pulled off his cloak and took his things into the adjoining bedroom to unpack. "Spencer!" he called back. "Would you bring a light? It is black as pitch in here."

Hesitating in the dark doorway of her own little room, Margaret looked back: in the shadows of the other room she could see Dammerung moving about—a great distance off, it seemed just then—and suddenly she hurt for him and could not move, for to move would make the pain only worse.

But then, "Nay, never mind. There is a candle here." And a light sprang up with a snap, fanning the room with a thin yellow light so that Margaret could see the pack slung on a little, heavily-carved kist, and two low buckskin beds. Dammerung's shadow arched across the wall. With a shaky sigh she turned away.

"Bring a light in here when you are done," she said, stepping into the dark. "I cannot see my hand in front of my face."

"Can any of us?"

He appeared in her doorway after a moment, breaking up the fire's glow with a black, red-winged figure. By use of her shin she had found the low bed and had put down her own pack on it; straightening, she squinted back into his blurred face. He was quiet and still. Had he caught his mistake? Did he hold still to keep it from hurting too much? But no, without warning he laughed, shortly, and said, "There, I have got it now." He put out his hand toward one corner of the room.

At the same instant a light sprang up high from a candle which, in the dark, Margaret had not been able to see. It had been sitting before a mirror, and the reflection-candle flung back the light with more potency than the real thing.

"Moreover these whom he predestined, them he also glorified. This is a cosy little setting," he added, looking around.

It was true. By the candle and candle's reflection, Margaret looked round on her little chamber. There were two low beds and a cramped bath—but the bath had hot water—a low vanity and stool, a clothes-chest and changing screen, and on the wall next to the door was the portrait of a peacock done up in gold paint. Dammerung studied the peacock with approval.

"We have a stag in ours," he said.

Margaret bent to unpack. "Too bad," she said. "A peacock would have suited you better."

He leaned jauntily against the doorframe, arms folded across his chest, pointedly idle as she worked. "An' sure it would... You could have used a wardrobe," he added as she unpacked the gown she meant to wear tomorrow and shook out its folds.

"The fabric seems hardy enough." She gave the ivory skirt a smack with the flat of her hand. "I'll lay it on the trunk. If it needs pressing tomorrow morning I am sure Aikaterine can take care of it."

"Speak of the devil—" he turned swiftly at the sound of an opening door. Margaret came quickly behind him and saw Aikaterine and the blue-jay man come in, followed by their master. The maid and manservant between them carried the supper—which smelled as if it would do justice to Dammerung's promises..

"Where had you gone?" Dammerung demanded of his cousin. He pulled a chair out from under one of the narrow windows and sat down horsewise on it, his arms draped across the back. "You did not go to see *her*, did you?"

Skander remained standing until Margaret took a seat. His face, angled in firelight and shadow, was less tempestuous and more resigned. "Yes," he admitted, "I did go, but I did not see her. Not for want of courage," he added, looking with a painful clenching of his brows toward the fire, away from the room, "maybe for excess of pride... I could not have persuaded her. I had tried before and failed; should I try now, on the eve of her wedding, and spoil what pleasant feeling she might have?"

"Perhaps not," admitted Margaret. She had found she had been nursing a secret hope that he had gone to see her and had prevailed against her sisters' judgment. "I know it will not make anything better, but the fact is that you are too good."

"And so the world is unfair to you!" Dammerung took a cup of wine from the blue-jay man and held it between his chilly hands. "Be less charitable and upright and life might go more smoothly with you. No matter what the end of the wicked may be."

The mockery touched Skander. Margaret saw him smile faintly, introspectively, and shake his head at his cousin. "*Touché*," he murmured.

"A'come, have a bite to eat. They stuff these beasts with peppercorns, I think."

For an hour a thin film of Dammerung's idle chatter and pleasant mockery lay over the sting of Black Malkin's slight. Margaret watched Skander gamely join in conversation with Dammerung and herself, but she knew—and the other two knew—that as soon as the doors were shut and the candles snuffed out, with nothing but the empty dark between himself and the world, Skander's pain would redouble. He bore it bravely, his smile genuine. If his eyes were distant and preoccupied his conversation was on the mark, his attention given to his companions, and Margaret felt that she could pity him no more than she had let him pity her.

When they finished supper it was late, the early winter dark full upon them, and the fire was a rich roaring tapestry of colour in the hearth that beckoned a melancholy cheer from Margaret's heart. She rose stiffly from her chair, put away her empty cup, and bade good-night to the two gentlemen. Dammerung murmured something in reply—she did not quite catch it—but Skander looked up from out of the ring of dark, his face flashing in the light, a small, sweet, sharing smile on his face. Margaret saw it and it hurt her, as much as her forced smiles had once hurt him, and she went away with the gold memory of it burning in her heart. For some time she lay awake in the strange dark, listening to Aikaterine's quiet breathing in the bed beside hers, listening to the exiled wind howling coldly over the Thrasymene plain outside.

The wedding day dawned wretchedly cheerful. Margaret had only just grown accustomed to waking up in her bright bower at Lookinglass; waking up in a low little room in a narrow doeskin bed, listening to Aikaterine running the bath so that it roared like a train, disoriented her for several moments before she could crawl up out of her confusion and grope for her bearings and her bathrobe. The one little window in their bedroom, which looked out over the knoll of Thwitandrake and the bleak plain below, let in a spread of cold white morning light which fell full across Margaret's bed and the kist between the two bunks, lighting up the gown that was waiting for her. With its interwoven threads of electrum and gems of apricot-coloured topaz and sheer crystals, the gown imaged forth thunderbolts upon her dazzled eyes.

"I have made a mistake," she cried, flinging herself out of her bed into the bare cold of the stark air. She grabbed the gown. It had been an innocent, darkened thing of rough ivory last night in the small, dual light of the candle and the mirror.

Aikaterine turned quickly from the bath. "My lady?"

She turned on the maid, thrusting the dress at her. "I cannot wear this! I cannot wear this—it is too beautiful! What will they think of me? This is Woodbird's wedding day!"

The mousy brown brows drew together. Aikaterine made no move to take the dress away. "Yes, and she is not marrying my lord Skander Rime. We did not bring another dress, my lady. It is the one you must wear—unless you would wear your riding clothes from yesterday, which I have not washed..."

Margaret stared at her, knowing she was defeated and yet caught in an irrational panic, desperate for a way out. Her eyes, startled and wide, dropped from Aikaterine's face to the chancy, beautiful, shapeless thing in her hand. She should drop it. In a moment she would drop it, if only she could unlock her fingers...

Aikaterine moved softly; her hand closed over the gown's folds, extricating it gently from Margaret's strangling grip. "You will start a new fashion with all this goose-bump skin," she fussed quietly. She put her hand under her lady's elbow and moved her toward the steaming bath.

"I should almost rather go naked," said Margaret. "What was I thinking? I am so ashamed!"

"No one," Aikaterine said finally, "will be looking at you."

There was no way out of it. Miserable, knowing that in any other circumstance she should have been glad to wear such a gorgeous outfit, Margaret folded herself up into the bath, her knees rammed up under her chin, while Aikaterine ran hot water down her back. The soap was chicory-coloured and smelled exotic. If she did not look at the dress, if she did not think about it, if she focused on the warmth of the bath and the feeling of coming clean, she could rouse her spirits a little—though she wondered what the point was of anyone having high spirits on a day like this. As Aikaterine had put it so very bluntly, Woodbird was getting married, and it was not to Skander Rime.

When it was time, she put up her chin and let Aikaterine get her into the dress and said no not a word, though her heart seemed to mortify inside her. When they went through her toiletries they found they had brought her jewellery and combs but had neglected to bring any pins. That took Margaret's heart and buried it dead. But Aikaterine, seeming nonplussed, brushed out her long Victorian hair, dried it, and left it as it was. As it dried it sprayed upward in low brown curls in a gypsy way, which worried Margaret. Would nothing go their way today?

For once Aikaterine put on a smock of some other colour than white: she stepped into a simple gown of grey bound in pink ribbon. With her lush blonde hair flowing over it, she looked quite a picture. Margaret smiled mournfully and turned from her bed chamber into the little sitting room.

Skander was up. He was dressed simply in dark earthy colours—for a moment, as he stood against the window with his back in shadow and his face turned from her, she almost mistook him for his cousin.

He turned at the sound of her door.

"I thought you were Dammerung for a moment," she said, offering light conversation. She moved toward the tea. "Was your bed too hard?"

"Not too hard. I've slept on harder. You have not seen Dammerung this morning?"

She paused over the round handleless cups and looked quizzically at him. "No. Should I have? I have only just come out."

He shook his shoulders and set his empty cup down on a little table. "I don't know. He was not in the room when I woke this morning and his cloak is gone from the peg."

Margaret swung round. Her white stallion-skin hung alone on the wall: the panther-skin was missing.

"That worries me," said Skander frankly.

It worried Margaret too, though she did not know why. But Skander was in a bad way, boldly though he faced the proceedings, and she could not worry about Dammerung while it was her task to cheer his cousin. "I am sure he can manage. You know him: he is inscrutable and doesn't like to be pried. Have you eaten? More tea?"

She ate and Skander had seconds just to accompany her, but even when they had finished, touched up, and were ready to leave for the ceremony, Dammerung had still not arrived. Though he did not say a word, Margaret could see Skander was doing worse with each passing minute. His lips were compressed, brows clenched, cheeks ashen. But when they left the guest wing and plunged out into the stinging cold wind of the long yard, heading down the little central road for the church, he did, after a few minutes, put out his arm so that Margaret could take it.

It seemed everyone was headed toward the church, blowing in the wind like pretty pieces of paper and feathers. An instrument was playing somewhere: not a piano or a horn—after a few notes Margaret recognized it as her old haunting spirit the panpipe. Under its notes, burning in the crystal sky, she and Skander walked arm in arm, close together for the wind was strong and cold. But once, at the mouth of an alley, her companion stopped short and turned.

Margaret looked beyond him up the alley. A door had opened in the side of a building. In the shadow of a low overhang there was a flutter of white, a rush as of swan's feathers, and from a distance she realized she was looking at the bride. There was a flock of people around her but she stood out, even in that cramped, narrow space alongside the church. Skander stiffened and seemed to draw breath as if a knife had been riven in him. It was too far away for anyone to hear—Margaret barely heard it—but the swan-white figure turned, cast about wildly as if thrown into a sudden confusion, and saw him. Everything hung still a moment. Margaret did not dare to break it; they, it seemed, did not dare to break it. Skander looked as though he wanted to turn away, conscious that he was ruining a moment he had wanted Woodbird to enjoy, but he could not do it.

The crowd did it for them. Someone called the lady's name and she had to go, pulled away, drowned in a sea of attendants. The alleyway was empty. A door banged shut in the wind.

Without a word Margaret pulled Skander gently along. There was nothing she could say. Words cheapened sentiment. She knew his agony, an upturned hourglass mirror of her own, and knew pity was galling. She could only be there to propel him when, of a sudden, like a stallion spooking at a strange object, he balked at the door and almost turned back. She gritted her teeth and went forward so that he, as her escort, had to go too, and they sat together in mute commiseration in the gold light of the church, listening to the wild panpipe playing a hymn that only the wind outside knew the words to.

There was still no sign of Dammerung. The church was filling up—Margaret had to crush to one side against Skander to make room for a lord and lady beside her. She recognized a few faces: Mark Roy and Romage and their two sons, Lord Gro FitzDraco, sketched in grey clothing and black riding boots. Centurion had made it, which surprised Margaret, and she wondered how the falling out of the Overlord ceremony had been met among the lords and land-owners of the Honours. Once, to her horror, she thought she spotted Dammerung on the far side of the church, only to realize, with all the blood shocking back to her heart, that it was Rupert. She stiffed and almost grasped for Skander's hand. Panic crushed her brain. She could not meet that devil's gaze. Did he know she was here? Her ribs ached suddenly, as if the breaks were still there. She looked away, breathing shortly, chin shaking.

I must pull myself together. I mustn't cry. I musn't leave. I am safe where I am. Skander will not let anything happen to me. He can't get at me. Where—where is Dammerung!

She began to dread that Rupert had found his brother and done him harm. Almost she got up then and there to look, but an instinctive better sense rooted her to the bench. She looked at Skander's face. It was grey but calm.

How can he bear this?

The next quarter hour was agony for both of them. Margaret dared not look up from her tiny sphere lest she catch Rupert's eye. She was dying to know where Dammerung was and if he was all right—that thought, that he might be in danger or in need, perhaps more than the thought of meeting Rupert's eye, terrified her. When she chanced to look at him she saw Skander sitting rigidly, fists clenched on his knees, his head turned to watch like a hawk the steady flow of people filling the church benches. But when the ceremony began in a painful blur of candlesmoke and a rush of pentacostal winter wind, it seemed unreal to Margaret. She saw a man at the front of the church standing by the shepherd: a young, well-formed man, not unhandsome nor coarse, but rather plain, she considered, when compared to an image like Dammerung or Aikin Ironside. She had forgot his name. He did not seem important, not until—Skander's hand whitened and slowly relaxed as with a conscious effort—Woodbird appeared in the dove-shadowed church doorway and was led in a long, beautiful flutter of swan feathers to the man's side. The panpipe had been joined at some point by a harp and they sang out an eerie, elemental combination of stark and transient images. It hurt, and Margaret was almost glad when it stopped and the shepherd began to speak.

For all that she had wanted to sit under a church service, she now barely paid notice to the man's words. *You are making a horrible mistake!* she wanted to cry out—but cold good breeding made the words stick in her throat. *You have all the power you could want, all the autonomy a woman could need! How can you willingly marry a man you do not love!*

The homily was concluded. If their ceremonies were anything like those she knew, they would move on to the dedication and the vows now. The groom held out his hand to the bride; the bride lifted her hand, seemed almost to waver, if Margaret's imagination did not get the better of her, and finally placed her fingers delicately atop the man's.

"We will now proceed to join this man and woman before the witness of the congregation." The shepherd turned and looked beyond them to the people sitting on the benches. His simple grey outfit, looking more like a farmer's visiting clothes than a clergyman's wear, was smothered in the sweeping splendour of Woodbird's exotic gown. It was hard to see him between the bride and groom. "Has anyone a claim against either by which this joining should not proceed?"

"I do!"

A gasp of surprise shocked through the room. Woodbird turned in a flutter of feathers. Margaret, as if struck by a whip, whirled toward the door. It was Dammerung—but she had known from his high, triumphant shout, half-laughing, that it was Dammerung—in black and blowing black, throwing down a stark shadow on the threshold as if he stood on the brink between the living and the dead and was on the verge of crossing over.

Someone in the congregation screamed. Someone nearby—it was a man—swore violently and started up.

"Peace!" cried the shepherd. He put his hands on the shoulders of the bride and groom and thrust them unceremoniously apart, coming down off his little dais a step. There was a tense quiet. Margaret could not hear a single soul breathing. Beside her Skander was tense, his hand flat on the bench as if he were in the act of rising but had somehow, irreparably, checked himself. He sat immobile. His face was angry white.

The shepherd and the young war-lord regarded each other in silence for some time. Margaret could see the latter was faintly amused, the light and the dark of laughter jinking from eye to eye; the former's face, at first contorted by a horror of disbelief, then recognition, then quiet acceptance, had a grim kind of humour about it too.

"Well, apparition," he said lightly. "And what is your grievance?"

"Mine, nothing! Or it is not pertinent now what *mine* may be... But I speak of a grievance on another's behalf and protest that, in all honesty, this wedding cannot go forward."

From the front of the church Black Malkin rose, looking beautiful in a gown of thunder-purple slashed with gold. Her face was terrible. "I do not know where you are come from," she said, "from pandemonium or perdition, but you have no right to come in here and arrest the wedding of so high a lady and honourable a gentle—"

"Oh, go saddle your broomstick!" Dammerung cut her off.

Another gasp cracked through the room. Black Malkin stood in rigid indignation; but she did not meet the blow, though she did not sit back down. The shepherd warred in vain to crush a smile.

Seeing that the woman was put in her place, Dammerung turned back to the minister. "Sir, I have but two questions."

"And we have but hundreds," the shepherd replied wryly. "Ask away."

With an acknowledging upward quirk of his lips Dammerung turned to Woodbird. "Madam—" his voice dripped with condescension "—what were your exact words to Skander Rime concerning your separation?"

Woodbird Swan-neck, put more on the spot than ever before, looked rather pale—though whether from anger or anxiety, Margaret could not tell. The woman took her time to remember, then replied in a carefully measured voice, "I believe I said, 'Skander, I must not see you again.' "

"Ah?" Dammerung shot back. "You didn't say anything like, 'Skander dear, I've got to break off this engagement with you'?"

One of Woodbird's eyelids twitched, as if daring Dammerung to mock her too far. "No."

"And Skander—where are—oh, there you are. Skander Rime of Capys, etc.," Dammerung waved a hand. "Did you ever, wittingly or unwittingly, say such words as to break the contract you had with your Ladybird?"

Skander seemed to miss the light mockery altogether. He rose stiffly, faced the shepherd, and said in a husky voice, "As God is my witness, I never did."

Dammerung cocked a meaningful brow at the shepherd.

But the shepherd had lost his laughter for the moment. He seemed to be deeply considering the matter, and looking from one stark white face before him to the other. But in the horrible quiet full of the dry-leaf scuttling of voices from the far corners of the church, the man who had been meant to be the groom placed his other hand over Woodbird's, very gently, and held it a moment, then took both his hands away.

Margaret's throat tightened.

The shepherd saw the gesture. "Well," he said quietly, "it seems you have a sound case. I must, or go contrary with my conscience, forswear binding this man and woman together." Then he lifted his head, cleared his throat, and seemed to recover a little of his glibness. "There is no procedure in the books for dispersing a wedding that has not gone through, so I must simply say—I think there is a good dinner waiting for us. We mustn't let it go to waste."

Dammerung laughed deprecatingly and, blowing about, vanished from the doorway. The bewildered crowd, as if let loose from an enchantment, began murmuring incessantly until the whole room was throbbing with the soft, worried noise. In the confusion Margaret managed to see Woodbird passed off onto her relatives— Black Malkin was white with fury, but Grane seemed to take it coolly—then she had to attend to Skander, who seemed lost inside himself and took several moments to respond to her insistent calling.

"This does not mean anything," he said pessimistically as she got him to his feet. "She still went away, and there is still Black Malkin."

"It means everyone acknowledges your engagement—even Black Malkin must, now!" Margaret took his arm and pulled him through the press, conscious of people looking their way. She hid her hot red cheeks and hoped they would not recognize *her*. There were so many unfamiliar faces... "Man enough to take the challenge?"

They had plunged out into the light and wind. Skander stopped abruptly, roused by her thrust, and a little roughly rearranged her arm in his until it was more comfortable. "Not for want of courage!" he assured her. "Only I did not want to trespass upon her happiness."

"It seems your cousin has no such qualms. And I think he did it as much for her happiness as for yours."

"I doubt he cares much a penny for her," Capys snorted. "But anyway, he is the Overlor—"

He stopped himself, realizing his nearly unconscious mistake. Margaret had been watching a bit of birch twig, still clung about with wrinkled leaves, scuttling down the cobbles. She was careful not to look away from it.

"I would find the devil," Skander finished.

They found him, after some searching, in the sitting room of their guest quarters, feet flung up on the grate, warming at a deep-set fire. He looked up as they entered with the angry laughter of victory in his eyes.

"You sneaking knave," said Skander huskily, throwing down his cloak haphazardly. Margaret took it back up to hang it properly. "Miscreant and little meddling boy! Why I ever picked you up off my courtyard cobbles is beyond me."

Dammerung's smile twisted and seemed to withdraw. "You did not think I was so cruel as to drag you up here in the cold of early spring to show you the promise of a cold, empty life of a cold, empty bed, did you?"

Skander was silent. He leaned upon the back of a chair, grasping it tightly. His big, firm frame seemed spent.

"You are angry with me."

"No!" Skander laughed gustily, mirthlessly, and looked away, dragging a hand over his face. "I was terrified, and you are as good a thing as any to vent on."

"Yes, people seem to feel that about me..." Dammerung took his feet off the grate and, reaching over, pulled close a chair for Margaret. She sat down beside him in the warmth of the fire where she could see both their faces. "I thought Woodbird took it well,"

Dammerung went on. "She did not seem too keen on the match herself. Black Malkin took it rather badly, though, I think."

Skander nodded, but after a moment he shook, suppressed it, and shook again. He had to turn away completely to hide his loss of countenance. "I am not a vindictive man by nature," he said, laughter breaking out through the chinks in his words, "but ever since Black Malkin sent me off without a warm meal or a warm bed, I've wanted somewhat to happen to her. You struck her down most cruelly, coz—most cruelly!"

" 'Twas aught she deserved!" Dammerung laughed back. "She asked for it when she put her oar in. No one puts his oar in my business."

Skander lifted a brow. "And I am your business?"

"You are all my business."

A heavy quiet hung between them; Skander, poised large and solid just inside the closed doorway, Dammerung flung back in his chair, casual, a half-mirthful smile playing at being real on his lips. *Anyway*, Skander had said, and Margaret heard his words clearly in the silence, *he is the Overlord*. It broke upon her—she stirred, looking away toward the white light coming from the windows—that Dammerung had done a great and awful thing, and yet so simple, so simple as casting aside a cloak on a chair... He had squared off before Black Malkin and Grane, the leaders of Thrasymene, before the leaders of other Honours, held his own, and they had followed his word. They had followed him as gladly as she reckoned men had been wont to follow the fireband Feyfax years before, and in that simple gesture as of turning a row of chessmen on the board, they had let him be the Overlord. It had been small, but it had been great, and as if he were thinking of the little huge victory himself, Dammerung smiled up into his cousin's face.

He did care a penny about Woodbird, too.

"I hate to rain on your parade, Skander." Margaret's voice felt disused from fast and breathless thought. Dammerung turned toward her. "Rupert is here."

He merely nodded. "I know. I caught the whiff of him, and he of me, but the stars are not aligned and the silver in our blood is not afire. The time is not right. He won't make a move, not now, not on Thrasymene soil."

"So—he will make a move," said Skander practically.

"Oh, surely—softly! gently!" The War-wolf settled more comfortably in his chair and curled his lean pale toes around the warm iron of the grate. "There is the devil to pay and he is a veritable lord of cunning. He won't come out of the windbreak and the thunderstorm. If anything, he will come surging up through the watertable, insidiously white-livered in that dastardly way no man can ever discount, and he will do it masterfully. And if we are not careful, the man may win."

Margaret looked at him sharply. His face, downthrust in thought, chin against his chest, brows shadowing his eyes until they were hard to see, caught the light only upon the cheekbones and make it leaner, hungrier—again she saw the furious power of Marenové that was a house of fire, devouring all before it.

"Dammerung," she said gently, urgently, "we cannot afford to let him win."

"What of Margaret!" asked Skander hotly.

Dammerung flung up his head, throwing a sharpened look like a dagger at his cousin. "What of—" he began, then broke off and swung back round on her. "Cannot we? What are we, Margaret, in the scheme of the world, in the scheme of time? A little nation under the devil's heel does not sway God's inexorable pen. It is God's own ink the devil writes."

"But *we* cannot afford it," she said doggedly. Her body seemed to clench inside her skin. "Don't think I ever counted myself much, or much worthy of God's notice. He knows full well what a wanderer I am and what thin milk I was fed on. But it matters to *us*. If anything they say is true, how could I—how could you—if we don't put up as stiff a fight against Rupert as we can, I should be ashamed of heaven and ashamed of my soul and cringe to hear anyone speak my name after I am gone."

The purl of quiet rippled loudly in the wake of her words. The half-moon smile on Dammerung's lips was oddly gentle, oddly bright. "O, for a muse of fire!" he breathed passionately "—that I might light a generation with it in the heart-place. Don't fret, Lady." His tone, dropping its richness of emotion, turned flashing upon a blade of mockery. "I am of a purpose now and I know what I am doing. He will have to climb over my dead and untwitching corpse to reach you and the Honours back of you, and he will not get at me so easily this time."

He was certain, and unquestioningly she trusted him, but her own heart-place was ashen cold and for a few moments she had to keep still lest, with a sudden movement, the pain of fear would catch her under the breastbone. When she could she said, "They are still having the dinner. Woodbird will be there. Skander, are you going?"

Skander had already taken up his cloak again. "I will go. I am now almost sorry for the man Sparling and I want to shake his hand in friendship. It was a noble thing he did, giving her up like that." He paused a moment at the door, smiling back at her softly—as if he, too, had a pain under the breastbone that might hurt him if he moved too quickly. "I know it is not easy to give that woman up for anything."

"Go on and see your Ladybird—win her back."

"You are not coming?" Skander took a step toward his cousin.

Dammerung shook his head and turned in the chair, away from Skander, toward Margaret. "Not this time. I don't relish being coddled as a souvenir from Hades, as they suppose me to be, nor do I relish meeting Rupert in the crowd; though I think that unlikely, I don't trust my temper to weigh circumstance against score and grievance. I should lose it, as perhaps should he, and that might be more than poor ruffled Black Malkin could bear."

"Keep your head low, then," said Skander. He set his hand on the latch. "If anyone asks, I'll tell them Margaret is a great witch and conjured you from the dead."

"You tell them that."

He left in a flurry of spirits, passing Aikaterine in the hall on his way out; Margaret could hear him telling her where he was going and that he was taking the blue-jay man, but that he would prefer her to stay with Dammerung and see to his needs. Aikaterine answered—her voice was indistinct—but no one came in. The hallway fell quiet, the quiet rippled through and touched the room, shining in the light, gleaming in the silver.

Driven by a sudden impulse, Margaret admitted, "You gave me quite a scare, you know."

He appeared apologetic. "I was sure I was, especially when I realized Rupert was about, but there was nothing for it and you had Skander's arm to hang on."

"I find I did manage."

"Of course you did," he said frankly.

She tucked her legs up on the chair cushion, shivering in the thin chill. "What now? Do we slink about in here until it is time to go home, or won't you give Woodbird a decent salute before you go? You will be family, after a fashion."

"After a fashion..." His voice grew musing, his eyes distant. She saw him go to that place within, to the huge dreams with which he dreamed of Plenilune; the sharpness of cunning and the tenderness of a master craftsman touched the corners of his mouth. "For now I will lie quietly and be little more than a rumour. Quite apart from getting Woodbird out of her own folly and securing some happiness for Skander, my intention was to startle a flame of hope among them as they have not had, oh, for many years now. Hope is a powerful thing; where it reigns men of even the lowest stature cannot be crushed, and where it has withered into dust whole ships of state run aground and break up on the rocks of corruption and consequence. For now I will be a rumour, a spark of hope, and that will grow to be a stronger thing than Babel in their hearts. Later they will see my face. For now I will go away—and blessed are those who, not seeing, yet believe."

His words were like rods of iron heated in the furnace: hard and glowing they barred across Margaret's heart, and though they shut out the flashing, feathered world, she felt safe behind them. "Half of us is legend," she said, "and the rest is pain."

He smiled mirthlessly and nodded.

"And Woodbird?"

He roused a little. "I will have Skander bring her by and give her a peck on the cheek, if she will let me. Sooth, I would like to see if the maid has become something worth fighting for, as my cousin seems to think."

"I like her," Margaret confessed, "though I little know her. I cannot say she was so very kind to me, but she was like a challenge that I could rise to. I was glad for that."

"You and I," laughed Dammerung; "we do better with a beating: it gets our blood up."

"We look less pretty, though."

"Prettiness is imperative."

They spent the morning lounging in the thin yellow sunshine under the windows, reading what books they could scrounge from the rooms; Margaret took out her diary and jotted down the journey of the past few days and the events of the morning. They were briefly interrupted a little after noon by Aikaterine bringing in a luncheon of spiced apples, maple-cured ham, and wine. They ate and settled back into a sleepy daze of sunshine and warm food. Dammerung turned his book upside down on his thigh and slung back in his chair, eyes shut against the sun, his chest rising and falling steadily in a shallow doze while Margaret, feeling she should continue writing, sat perfectly still for a long time, too contented and too tired to do anything.

Dammerung stirred suddenly with a jolt, startling her; a moment later there was a metallic rattle at the door and Skander swung it open, stepping aside to let another figure come in before him. It was Woodbird, still decked in her wedding finery, a little more at peace in every line of her body—though there was a fulgurant gleam in her eye when, looking beyond Margaret, she saw the War-wolf sweeping up from his chair to receive her.

"So!" she said, stopping just inside the door. She looked him over, from his bare feet to his sly, drooping eyelids. "It is you."

"If you cut me," he said quietly, "I will bleed."

"That is good to know," she replied archly. Then, as archly, though more gently, she added, "I think I must owe you a debt."

But Dammerung shook his head. "The lady owes me nothing. I prefer to not be holden to any man—or woman. It is only cumbersome."

Skander shut the door. Moving further into the room, Woodbird, with her eyes owlish and golden in the striking shafts of light, turned her head so that, no matter where she went, she was always looking at Dammerung's face. "You won't take this receipt of debt even in accord with the dues of honour?"

"Oh, honour be hanged! That, too, is cumbersome. Wilt name a child after me? It will only confuse the annals of history if you do. Let us say, if it will soothe your feathers, that I did it for Skander alone—or, to soothe you both, that I did it as my own whimsy led me. Try to pay back a debt to heaven and see how well you do. Heaven does not care."

She seemed to think a moment, seriously, then, with so small a gesture of her head as was almost imperceptible—save that Margaret saw a spark of light come suddenly off her earring—she seemed to let the matter go. Imperiously, she sat down.

"You have eaten; do you care for a little wine? It tastes of Darkling and is quite good."

Margaret's eye fell on Woodbird's hands draped languidly over the arms of her chair. They were long, beautiful hands, but about the hard knuckles and spread of the fingers she read that they were accustomed to harsh things—to horse-reins and sword-hilts, perhaps—as well as the handle of a mother-of-pearl looking-glass and the polished bannister of a lord's staircase.

"We add our own spices, but Darkling, I will admit, makes the best wine. A glass, please, Skander..."

Two new glasses were filled. Margaret's was filled a second time. Dammerung got up, as if it was his own room, and played host with softly padding care and suppressed delight. Fishscale light scattered across the face of the dark-wood table they drew up between them.

Margaret turned to Skander, who was seated around the table on her right. "Did anyone ask about Dammerung?"

"Did anyone!" He laughed. "I have never seen people hedge so beautifully trying to ask a question while not seeming to mean anything. For some I was too busy to reply, with others I had to say—though I feel I said it too candidly—that you were a witch and had raised Dammerung from the dead. To be honest," he added with a quick flare of suspicion, "even I do not fully know how you came back. You were most cryptic about it."

Woodbird frowned at Dammerung. "Yes. Skander could not tell me adequately. We all assumed you dead, sir. What *did* happen?"

Dammerung, caught between them, seemed to hesitate between a blithe lie and the heavy truth. But his eye wandered to Margaret's and hovered there, and he came down on truth. "My brother Rupert de la Mare tried to kill me to remove me from the running as Overlord." Woodbird's face, careful and still, grew white. "Only he was not skilled enough to kill me, so he locked me in our cellar—where I have been for the past two years—and studied the old arts to murder me. But Margaret went to the Great Blind Dragon, got a spell-breaking spell, and set me free. I have been living at Lookinglass with Skander Rime since. That was a little over a month ago."

Both Skander and Woodbird fixed their surprised and appraising gazes on Margaret. She felt her cheeks burn, suddenly the centre of their attention, but there was nowhere to hide and nothing to say.

"You went to the Dragon?" breathed Skander. He shifted as if he meant to rise, but caught himself. An appreciative curse, which somehow warmed Margaret further, broke through his lips. "There are many things of wood and water and air that I should face, but at heaven and hell I should balk. And you went, lady, just like that?"

She lifted one shoulder. "There was nothing else to be done," she said simply.

"By heaven!" Woodbird exploded. "The man a murderer, a sneak-thief and a rogue? How is it that we countenance his presence among us? I wonder!"

"Because the man is more than a match for any of you," Dammerung said levelly. "I have already said as much to the Lady Margaret: would you say *nay* to the man?"

The woman's eyes sparked, but a touch as of remembered pain greyed the hollows of her cheeks and she said nothing. When she could speak, it was in a low whisper. "I have always hated him and never known quite why. Now I have a reason to hate, but no means. If anything galls me, it is that."

Dammerung flicked a supercilious brow at her which spoke volumes to Margaret, but thankfully Woodbird was intent upon some thought in the middle distance and did not see. But he did say, after he had drained his glass and let her think a moment in silence, "I would be grateful if you would keep that knowledge to yourself until such time as I give you leave to disclose it."

She turned upon him, eyes flashing scorn. "You may find me a paragon of discretion. If anyone asks, that Lady Margaret is a witch seems sound enough. She is largely unknown, and what is known is that she has cause to hold a grudge against de la Mare. Your secret is safe with me."

Dammerung took her words between his teeth and bit them with a smile.

Drawing back from his countenance, Woodbird turned to her beau. "And now, sir?" Her voice was still sharp; her eye, inexorably drawn, flicked back to Dammerung before darting away again. "And now? Do you not mean to expose him?"

"As soon kick over a hornets' nest when you wear no shoes," Skander replied levelly. He avoided his cousin's gaze and looked steadily upon the carpet between their feet, brows furrowed. "The devil is pre-eminently a gentleman: it would not do to strike him in cold blood."

Woodbird looked hard at Dammerung, her lips pressed into a thin line. He sat with his elbow on the arm of his chair, chin in his palm, and smiled back at her coyly, playfully, as if he knew what was warring behind her uncanny eyes. She sucked in her breath. "I see what you mean by honour being cumbersome."

"Don't you?" His head jigged with the movement of his jaw. "But Capys is right: I won't trod on the bastard's head, for sure he should bite my heel. We are gentlemen, he and I—"

"Ha!" Margaret pressed her hand to her lips a moment too late.

"—and play a bloody and delicate game." He slid a smile at her out of the corner of his mouth, though his eyes did not move from Woodbird's face. "Surely you realize what is at stake is more than my life and my honour, a matter more than a criminal brought to justice. This is for Plenilune, and dear God in heaven I should sooner do this gently than upstir the lives of so many innocents and bury them under good Plenilune dirt—as *would* happen," he added, "if I were to step out of that door right now and point my finger at Rupert and let slip to all what he did to me. You see that, Ladybird? You see how all in a moment the hot blood is churned and how quickly a man's sense is blinked out by airlessness? Man has blood enough to power his brain or his brawn, not often both at once."

Margaret watched the colour spring to Woodbird's cheek, angry but quiet. "I, of all people," she said softly, "should know that lesson well."

There was a pause—then Dammerung leaned across the distance and set his hand over Woodbird's a moment before drawing away again. She was still, looking at the hand he had touched...then she closed it, drew in a breath, and seemed to wake from a distant, uneasy sleep.

"I still have guests," she said, "for whatever it is worth. I should not leave them unattended long."

Since Aikaterine had gone away Margaret leaned forward to collect the glasses. "Oh yes," she said blithely. "You mustn't deny them the honour of not knowing whether to congratulate you or offer sympathy. The awkwardness makes one so superior."

Woodbird flung round her head with a sharp, genuine laugh, shedding a cluster of soft candid feathers from her headdress. They fluttered after her as she rose and went out on Skander's arm, settling like late snow on the dark braided carpet.

Margaret stooped and picked them up. The room was quiet; presently Aikaterine would come back to replenish the fire, but for now she and Dammerung stood silently, listening to the words they had said. Her fingers ran over the feathers: she did not know what sort of bird they had come from, only that they were white and one had a suggestion of grey, and that the course of the day had broken open some of their barbs.

"Odd," she murmured, half to herself. "I had thought they would be red."

"Shuh!" Dammerung rocked with his mirthless laugh. He pushed up the hem of his tunic and thrust his hands into his pockets. "Fie for a sceptic! She turned out bonny." He cocked a smile at her. "I dare swear the lady is worth fighting for, after all."

Margaret shook her head with wry disapproval. "You *are* one to gamble before you have tested the mint."

"It is only what I should want someone to do for me," he protested. "*You* did."

She had not thought of it that way. To be frank with herself, she had to admit that she had not thought of it at all. When she had stood before the Dragon, empty of thought and full of determination, she had counted no cost but gambled upon a single life—his own—with a single life—her own—and she had not known the mint of either. Of a sudden she shied, embarrassed by the attention. "Tush! I should break my tooth trying to bite into your metal."

His eyes danced. "Am I that hard to swallow?"

"Sooth!" she retorted, "and taste of fire and iron!"

Her words fluffed up his fur and he purred to himself. But he, too, seemed to have had enough attention. He returned to his book and was quiet, thoughtful, and had a pleasant spirit for the rest of the afternoon. In the morning they would begin the trip back to Lookinglass, but until then Dammerung did not want to stir out of their suite. He and Margaret sat out the afternoon in companionable silence, each at their own work—and yet Margaret could not help feeling that they were both talking to each other in their silence.

That night, in the small, crocus-coloured light of the candleflame, Margaret stayed up a moment after Aikaterine, seated at the little table with her diary open under her hand. She checked the face of the sleeping maid once more to be sure she was asleep, then put her pen to the page for one last line:

"*I ask myself: do you know what pain sounds like? It sounds like the looks in their eyes.*"

XX | TRINITY

Margaret had expected something sudden, like a clap of thunder or a thief in the night, or something inexplicable like poison; but when Rupert, as they all knew he would, undertook to make his move, it was the last move she had anticipated.

The winter had whiled out quietly in Lookinglass. On returning from Thwitandrake, the weather had closed in bitterly cold and had kept them cooped up worse than before. Dammerung had borne it quietly for a spell, then he had paced, vainly trying to amuse himself with books, games, and philosophy. Philosophy had held him best—to hear him and his cousin talk had been as much a diversion and a source of interest for Margaret as for Dammerung—but Skander could not always be on hand for his cousin to sharpen his wits on as iron against iron, and Dammerung, at the end of his patience, stood for long spells at the window willing the weather to let up so that he might stretch his legs.

At last the weather had turned. March, which Dammerung had called the Alder Moon, had raged in more like a dragon than a lion, roaring in the empty woods like the passage of a train, and then torn away at the end of the month into a soft ragged streamer of white clouds in a sky as pale as Dammerung's eyes, teased by high winds that the fell country could barely feel. Even Margaret felt the blood stir inside her as the world took on a fresh yellow colour of sunlight and the woods, full of rising red sap and tawny buds, swelled with renewed birdsong. At the first bunting's cry of "devil! devil! dinna touch me-e!" Dammerung had flung himself out of the house and gone off no one knew where at a running pace, and Margaret could not blame him.

The piano had been tuned. For the whole of the morning Margaret had occupied herself with burnishing her skills at it and she had begun to be pleased with herself. She had chosen a light tune from among the dishevelled sheet music, learning the bars of it, and, when Skander had finally gone away and left her to her own amusement, she had begun to sing.

> *There was a storm in Glassdale-mouth*
> *Only the other day:*
> *The wolf-wind and the torrent rain*
> *Have closed the roads today.*
> *It had been open and bonny*
> *With dap'ling light and shade:*
> *You could almost want to tarry*
> *Where the ford at the water played—*
> *But there was a storm in Glassdale-mouth,*
> *So come by another way.*

It reminded her of Skander and the studious letters he wrote to Woodbird, often more than two letters in a week, which never seemed to take time away from his busy schedule and yet seemed like tiny sabbaths for the young man whenever he could break away to write them.

> *Come in at the garret window—*
> *Left a'latch for you—*
> *Where the curtains billow and bluster*
> *In the last of the evening glow.*
> *I'll leave them open and bonny,*
> *With candlelight for show:*
> *Sure your heart could never tarry*
> *When I sit in the twilight for you.*
> *So there was a storm in Glassdale-mouth?*

Come by the dreaming-way!

As if called the door swung open, startling Margaret's notes into an abbreviated silence, and Aikaterine stepped in. The look on the maid's face was familiar, and sent the blood in Margaret's veins shocking cold back to her heart.

"I have misplaced our lords," said Aikaterine through tight-set lips, "and Rhea has come to call."

Margaret sat in complete stillness at the piano, her fingers resting on the silent ivory keys. She could feel her heart beating interminably—*thud-dump,   thud-dump,   thud-dump*—numberlessly counting out the straining moment. The room seemed to have gone dark, clouded at the edges and sharpened by some hard feeling behind her breastbone. But then it cleared, and she said aloud— though she did not realize until later that she had said it aloud—

"Does the chit want to *die?*"

Aikaterine gestured to the door. "I do not want to leave her long alone and I cannot find either my Lord Skander Rime or the War-wolf."

Margaret awoke. Rising, she said imperiously, "I will go. It seems there is no one else."

They went down through the clear sunlight and the breeze that was blowing through the open windows and doorways, Aikaterine after Margaret, until they came out on the passageway above the round sun-room—an open room full of granite slabs and sunlight—and Margaret saw the little figure of the witching-maid waiting for them below. At the sight of her the scarlet rose in Margaret's blood again: she was not sure she hated even Rupert so desperately as she hated Rhea.

She went down to the landing of the staircase in full view. With a grey flutter Rhea turned at her step; even at that distance Margaret could see the other's cheeks flame as brightly as her blood.

"The War-wolf is not in seat at present," Margaret said coldly. "I will speak for him."

Rhea had to look up—she always had to look up—to see Margaret's face: there was a momentary flash of something cruel, something pained, but it was over in a moment and the maid seemed to choose wisely not to mock as she had nearly done. The lesson had been bitterly learned.

"I have word for either Capys or the War-wolf alone," she insisted. "I am not to give it to anyone else."

"Do you think I am just 'anyone else'?" Margaret demanded. Her hand upon the balustrade tightened until it was white. "Do me a courtesy, if you even know how: I am not so daft as to turn you over alone to anyone."

"You think very highly of yourself!" Rhea replied before she could stop herself.

Aikaterine stiffened, white with rage. Before Margaret could do or say anything—she would have liked to have gone down and given the maid a slap in the face—Skander appeared from the inner hallways of the house and stood a moment, frozen in shock, his eyes fixed on Rhea. The maid swung and locked her gaze on the man; her red lips parted a moment, teeth showing, but whether she meant to speak or to sneer Margaret did not know.

"What," said Skander bluntly. His hand moved to his side as if in search of something sharp.

Margaret came down in a hurry to cut the two apart. "She says she comes with word from Rupert for you or for your cousin. She will not give it to *me*."

Aikaterine followed and, raising herself up, whispered something in her master's ear. Skander's face turned an angry white and his eye, levelled like a blade at Rhea, grew colder and paler amber by the moment. Margaret did not like having her back to the maid; she looked over her shoulder to find the girl had not moved but stood quietly, rigidly, her hands clenched at her sides and her chin downthrust in a bullish, defiant gesture.

"Thank you, Aikaterine," Skander said abruptly. He broke away and went forward, but not close, to meet Rhea. "I am not used to employing condescending tones to my people so I'll tell you frankly: I am surprised you dare come here and I give bare a fig for what you have to say to me or to my cousin. You come bold-facedly, wench, and give little deference to a lady and no honour at all to your betters!" He took another step forward. Something flashed a warning in Margaret's mind—a sick taste of panic surged in her throat:

He's going to do her damage!

At that moment there was a movement in the sun-room doorway, a flood of light and shadow, and all turned as if a harsh note had been struck in the air—Margaret, too, turned, but not before her gaze chanced to pass across Rhea's face and saw the hateful whiteness there.

It was Dammerung who stood in the doorway, his head up, his eyes narrowed, his chest expanding and falling from his recent exertions. He saw them all, of that Margaret was sure, but she had the feeling of being swept away by him, of them all being swept away by him save Rhea alone. To her his gaze went, on her his pale blue eyes were fixed.

"Rhea," he purred at last, a panther-smile curling on his face. "Mine own familiar Rhea, who starved me and took all the light out of my world, what does she here? She knows her cunning and beauty. What need has she of a looking-glass?"

The jest whistled by the maid and Rhea, whose countenance had after that first instant regained its colour, turned her head in scornful deference. "I am come on an errand of words."

The young lord's nostrils flared with a horrible mirth. "Sooth!" he exclaimed. "On an errand of words? Does your lord not know in what esteem I hold you, and does he not fear never seeing your comely face again?"

The witching lashes curled upward; the gaze was piercing. "You would kill a woman?"

"I might," said Dammerung coldly.

She had known him to be mysterious, she had known him to be furious, but never had Margaret heard the blade in Dammerung's words as she did then, nor the perfect honesty which was like final judgment and lent terrible gravity to his voice. The silence that lingered in the room was awful more than it was awkward.

At last Dammerung spoke again, his tone once more civil, if only barely so. Never for a moment did they all, Margaret was sure, lose the feeling that they were held like shining balls in his hands, to be tossed and caught at will.

"Give to me the words of your errand."

Rhea shuddered visibly, as if she had been struck, or as if she were resisting against some better judgment. With a red flash her eyes lanced up into his, with no gesture of obedience did she turn her gypsy-queen head. "The words are of my lord Rupert, Prince of the Mares, and the words are this: that he desires a moot of the men of the Honour-lands, and that they assemble here in Capys Lookinglass, for a naïve man—" her gaze now darted to Skander, and became biting like acid "—and guileless is Skander Rime his cousin."

Skander's face was heavy and mirthless but there was no flicker of desire to parry her thrust.

Dammerung's voice came between them, strangely lazy and almost laughing. "Your lord Rupert would do well to mind his cousin better. He is mistaking him for another man. He is mistaking a falcon on my wrist for a robin in the hedgerow." He turned his head and smiled wistfully. "Does his eyesight fail him so early in life?"

Rhea's eyes flashed a challenge, but she did not speak.

"No?" Dammerung's lips jerked upward. "Then go, having said your piece. Go and wait our pleasure—and don't give anyone the Evil Eye."

Aikaterine made a small movement forward to take Rhea away, but Skander, almost imperceptibly—but Margaret caught it, standing just between and behind him and his cousin—gestured her to remain. After a cold, awkward silence, Rhea unpinned herself from under their gazes and swept away softly on silent feet, like a foreboding shadow passing through the room and enfolding itself among the shadows of the passage.

Margaret jerked her head away to hide her flushed cheeks. The impudent wench! She ought to have taken leave of her betters, had better bowed or curtsied if she could not have found anything polite to say. The impudent, sly, murderous wench—

Skander swung round and broke up Margaret's hot, rushing thoughts. "Dammerung!" he said accusingly. "What cloven pine are you sprung from?"

The fight seemed to blow away from Dammerung like washing off a line in a sunny summer gale. "Nay, not pine—'twas oak, and that mostly scrub. The devil—take—" In a single fluid motion he had set his hand on Margaret's shoulder, throwing much of his weight on it, and turned up one foot to squint at the pad of it. "—thistles," he concluded growlingly, "and one particular furze bush."

Skander looked unsympathetic. For a brief moment he let Dammerung pinch and prod his sole and seemed to take the time to recover some of his temper before saying levelly, "Rupert's maid, who smells of black magic and whose sight curdles my belly, is under my roof, and I would not have it so. What do you intend to do?"

Dammerung looked up from under his brows. "Would you have me kill her?"

His cousin's face did not change, neither did he say anything. Margaret felt her blood run from hot to arctic cold...but then the heavy weight on the bareness of her shoulder, which felt hot in contrast to her crawling skin, lightened and the fingers brushed her neck in passing. Somewhere in himself Dammerung was laughing at her, and she knew there would be no killing.

He let her go and trailed gingerly away into the study. Skander, after an expressive, defeatist gesture, indicated that Margaret should go first. So she trailed after Dammerung and found him sunk down into a chair and the golden gloom, stretched and spread like a heron in flight, with his eyes shut as if she had just come upon him in the middle of a cat-nap.

"Shoo," he whistled gustily without opening his eyes. "I am as limp and disagreeable as a wetling."

"This is no great change in things," his cousin spoke up dryly, having come in after Margaret and taken up residence by the astrolabe.

Dammerung quirked a saucy brow. "Feed me and water me and I shall find my mood again."

"And I shall not." Skander broke his stance long enough to allow Margaret to squeeze by to the sideboard. "Neither shall I let you until Rupert's girl is gone."

"Mm, la, how flatteringly you put it."

Margaret, a tumbler of cut crystal in one hand, looked over her shoulder and caught the white dog-teeth showing through Dammerung's smile. He was playing with Skander—and Skander knew it—as a child plays with golden balls. And as quickly as a child forgets the golden balls, Dammerung's eyes came open, two shards of flint in his foxy face, and remarked coolly, "Margaret is with us in this also, I think—are you not, Lady Spitcat?" He flung his charming smile up at her as she leaned down to give him the drink, but his voice became gentle. "You had quite the tiff, the two of you, just after Christmastide. If I remember rightly."

"You remember rightly," said Margaret softly, and remembered herself somewhat uncomfortably that ringing thrill of red and the world shrunk down into Rhea's face and the desire to blot it out.

Skander's tone was mild but peeved. "I do not remember just after Christmastide. I seem to recall I was fighting for my life... So, cousin? What do you plan to do?"

Dammerung put away the drink and heaved himself forward onto the edge of his armchair, elbows on his knees, chin on his interlocked fists. The paleness of his eyes seemed far away as he stared off mutely into the middle distance. Taking pity on Skander, Margaret found a seat close by where she could see the tell-tale changeableness of Dammerung's face. Skander did not seem to notice: he remained standing, gaze fixed on his cousin's profile. The room was quiet, save for the sounds of light in the crystal on the sideboard—and somewhere in the nearby spur of the woods a mockingbird was imitating a hare's scream. Margaret barely suppressed the shiver that ran up her spine as someone, somewhere, trod on her grave.

At last Dammerung came back to them, pulling in a long, loud breath through his nose as he leaned into the armchair's comfortable embraces. "I say: let them come."

"I would say so also," replied Skander, "but I am concerned that this may be a trap."

The War-wolf looked sidewise and askance. "A trap? Here? In Lookinglass, with perhaps some dozen loyal men at my beck and call? Rupert would be mad to try it. But no—I've thought of the trap, and mad or not, I would trust any room Rupert takes me into to be a trap. It would be a pleasant surprise to be found wrong."

"Why a meeting at all?" asked Margaret, for the question had been bothering her since Rhea had delivered her message. "Rupert knows the vote is in your favour. When word gets out—if it hasn't already—of his treatment of you, how many people does he really think would not be willing to stone him on the spot?"

Dammerung's mouth was grim, but his eyes were dancing when he looked at her. "Not many; and you may lay their cloaks at my feet... But she is right." He twisted and regarded his cousin frankly. "The thing occurred to me, too, that in terms of election Rupert is unlikely to stand any chance against me. So why all this argle-bargle? It smells of a trap."

"Perhaps he intends to turn you all into mice," Skander suggested glibly.

"Mm, perhaps." With a surge and a wiggle, like a child on Christmas morning, Dammerung readjusted himself in his chair. "But now my blood is up! I ache to know what it is Rupert is playing at. So I say: let them come. Make it as official as you like. Invoke all the sacred laws of the moot: even Rupert is bound by those, and you will be unlikely to be turned into a mouse."

Skander's smile reasserted its dominion over his face. They left the cut crystal and the astrolabe and waited in the sun-room while Aikaterine was sent off to bring Rhea back. They had not long to wait: it seemed Rhea had hung about close by to wait for their answer. If they loathed her presence, it appeared to Margaret that she hated being in Lookinglass still more keenly.

She had good reason to. Despite the excitement which he had shown in the study, despite his own glib words and attitude of a child playing at a game, an awfulness swept up darkly round Dammerung as Rhea was brought back into the room. Before she was even to the centre of the room, Dammerung had crossed the distance in a single rush and caught her by the wrist. There was a gasp—of pain or fear, or even rage, Margaret did not know—and looks locked like stags' antlers.

"Mine own familiar Rhea," purred the War-wolf. He put forward a foot alongside hers so that he was forcing her back at a precarious angle. "Would that you could dance with me, Rhea. I would put you through your steps quick enough. I heard tell once of a queen, a wicked witch, who was given shoes of red-hot iron and made to dance and dance until she fell down dead." His lips pulled away from his dog-teeth: Margaret wondered if Death's smile looked so hungry and charming at once. "Would that I were hot iron shoes. Would that you could dance."

Rhea held that gaze unflinchingly, lips compressed in a thin, red line, contrasting sharply with the bloodless transparency of her cheeks. Her breathing was loud in the quiet room. Finally her lips broke apart, slowly; her tongue touched their dryness before she spoke. "What word do you have for my lord de la Mare?"

"Tell him we expect him for tea under the first Hare gibbous moon. I would say there's a good girl—" Dammerung released her somewhat violently "—but then I would be lying."

Like a falcon returning to roost Rhea found her countenance again, smoothed and soothed with her hands unfolded at her sides. Her head was up, her eyes two cold black pools of horrible infinite depth. What ugliness lay in those depths, what plotting of revenge and painful triumph did those eyes dream about within? Margaret shivered again and cursed herself wordlessly for it.

"I go," said Rhea at last in a faintly strained voice. She drew back but seemed to get caught in Dammerung's basilisk stare and hung a moment, frozen, until he laughed harshly and turned away.

What became of Rhea, Margaret never saw. She hesitated, caught between Skander and Dammerung, then followed after Dammerung who had gone up to the study. She had some difficulty with her heavy skirts—for the days were still chilly—on the stairway; when she finally pushed the study doors ajar she found Dammerung standing at the fire, working at the logs with the poker while flames spurted up in unchancy places, a piece of sheet-music in his other hand. He must have felt her enter—she came in silently—for he half-turned, saw her, and smiled, shaking the paper at her.

"Applying yourself?"

The terrible man who had come close and dangled death before a maid was gone: the lazy, latent mockery that was his way with her had returned. With a little effort, moving to one side as if the movement would unsnag her from her rage and discomfort and confusion, Margaret found her centre.

"It was going well—until she came. I liked the song very much."

There was a rushing noise and a bang among the logs; sparks swirled around Dammerung like fireflies on a rich summer night.

Margaret's heart caught, but he seemed unperturbed. Throwing the poker into its bin, he waved the errant flames back into the fireplace—was it her imagination, or did they seem attracted to him, and reluctant to be shut back inside the grate? The corner of the sheet-music caught fire, but he quickly plucked the flame off, as if it were a bug, and tossed the bright thing back in amongst its fellows.

"A melancholy song," he mused, running an eye over its lines as he came back to her. "A gates-of-horn song..."

"You'll find paper, pen, and ink in the desk."

Skander had come up behind them, drying his hands on the flanks of his trousers as if he had just washed them. For some time afterward Margaret noticed him making the same unconscious motion, sometimes idly, sometimes fretfully. It was only when she noticed his fretful gestures, as if in vain to wash off the shadow Rhea had cast on them, that she noticed the evanescence of the darkness which had filled *her*: it had become a shadow for awhile, tempered into form again with the sudden reappearance of de la Mare in Thwitandrake, but now her love and her hatred was a mingled flame of its own on the heart-shaped altar of her life. No darkness now, no shadow: only a pale, moonstone flame that had air with which to breathe.

Dammerung sat on the corner of the desk and swivelled over, dropping to the back of it, and began rummaging among the drawers for the ink-jar, a fresh pen, and presently a sheaf of clean stationary, each page impressed upon the top in gold with the falcon seal of Capys.

"Hoity toity!" he said gaily, sitting down in his cousin's chair. He wet his pen and stopped a moment, forehead cradled in the saddle of his thumb and forefinger. His lips pursed and a few bars of the melancholy, gates-of-horn song came out.

On an impulse of whim, Margaret asked, "Will they come when you whistle?"

Dammerung's head came out of his hand, his eyes, a sudden bright blue, shimmering in a patch of sunlight. Something uncertain was at the corner of his mouth—uncertain, not of *them*, she thought, but of her temper. She smiled reassuringly—a spasm of laughter jerked inside her—and he smiled back.

"They'll come. I'd be lief to see them keep away!"

"Mark Roy first," she prompted. "He is furthest afield. Indeed," she added, throwing up in her mind a dim memory of a cartographer's view of the Honours, "he should be on his horse the moment he receives the letter."

The War-wolf's hand came down and his brain cast a spider-thin shadow, swirl by loop by dash, across the crisp paper. "My lord Mark Roy of Orzelon-gang," he quoted aloud, "and my brothers Aikin Ironside and Brand—"

"—The Hammer," Skander spoke up.

"Brand the Hammer?" Dammerung looked around with stark amusement. "So he got a title in the two years I was out of commission. This bodes something ominous."

Skander ran his palms down the length of his thighs, caught his own movement, and folded his arms deliberately over his chest, annoyed with himself. "He is a good fellow, quite loyal, but he has a short temper and does not rely so on main wit."

"Living in the shadow of his brother," mused Dammerung. It was an uncomfortable, pregnant comment, and Skander wisely did not meet it. After a moment, Dammerung continued. This time he kept quiet until he had nearly finished it, then he handed it up to her while he began on a new letter. Skander pivoted in his chair toward her; catching his movement, in a quiet voice, she read aloud:

"And sure you were expecting this letter, sirs: now it has come. I dare not say as yet how the weather-cock turns, but if you would come see for yourselves be on your horses a full three hours before you have taken this missive into your hands and be on your swift way to Lookinglass, Capys. Rupert de la Mare has asked leave of a moot of the Honours, whose grace it is our cousin Skander Rime's to host, to be held at the first Hare gibbous moon. Of the subject you can have no doubt. If ever I had need of your metal-piece and the Golden Dragon at my back, this is the hour. You know my hand: speed you quickly to us. God rest you and yours."

He had signed it, simply, –D.

When she took her eyes off the page she found Skander seated sideways in his chair, his elbow on the arm of it, chin in the crook of his thumb, frowning thoughtfully at his cousin. But whatever was troubling him he did not say, only, after a moment, he thrust his chin out of his hand and said,

"Give my regards to Woodbird for me."

Dammerung looked up beneath his brows, pen hovering over the paper. Then, recounting the words aloud as he wrote them, he finished with, "*Post script:* Skander Rime sends his affection to his Ladybird. This duty being discharged, and some faith placed that you will join us upon the date, you may, with good conscience, burn this letter to your heart's content."

"You wrote that," said Skander reproachfully.

From her vantage point, Margaret could make out the letters, very cleanly scripted. "He wrote it."

Dammerung thrust back from the table. "I'm afraid you can't escape it now. It is done in ink."

"God forbid," said his cousin crisply, "he should ever elect you scribe of the Book of Life."

"It should make for rummy reading if he did," Dammerung admitted, and moved on to the next letter.

Afterward, Margaret thought *Things must come in threes*, as if the trinity had stamped itself creatively over both nature and happenstance. The letters were written and sent out, the weather had held, and Dammerung had got the fidgets well out of his feet when the blue-jay man found them one afternoon a few days later in the garden, announcing the arrival of a curious individual.

The garden was warm that day, sweetly scented with flaming banks of jonquil and ramson, the faint breeze stirring the barred shadows cast by the single old tamarisk tree that, in its younger days, had done well, but growing older had so encroached on some of the patio stones as to uproot them and cause havoc whenever Skander went to push his chair back across the paving. It was a beautiful day. They had managed to forget, a little, the dark uncertainty that was looming before them. Margaret could feel herself coming out of the close dungeon in which Rupert had shut her: Dammerung's flung sky overhead, vast and blue and full of tempestuous winds, and Skander's steady kindness, were mediums in which her heart thrived. The hardness was soothed out of her—but not, she realized, turning her head and watching a robin skittering across a few decorative boulders—but not the memories. Those she would always remember, those lessons she would always bear like scars. She knew that, and yet, as Dammerung laughed of a sudden at some wit of his cousin's and a bit of discoloured skin showed for a moment, silver and puckered, at the base of his jaw, she knew she did not mind. One could live with scars.

"Ho, Tabby." Skander flung himself back in his chair, catching on the uneven stones—but his wit had put him in an even greater humour and the sudden upsetting made him laugh again. He righted himself and turned to his manservant. "Yes?"

"There is a man here to see you," said the blue-jay man reservedly. His eyebrows fluttered askance; a swift, barely-checked smile of curious amusement started and vanished from the corner of his mouth. "A grand little man, something styled as a gentleman of abiding roots, I fancy. I told him I would bring you at once."

Skander got up. Dammerung, rising, helped Margaret to her feet. "Have you taken him into the receiving room?" the master asked, perplexed. "It is a little early that anyone should come..."

"Oh no," the blue-jay man assured him. "He is quite a lord of the courtyard and would not stir until I had brought you."

"Is he, and will he not?" Skander sounded amused. "We will come along now, I think."

"Very good, sir." The blue-jay man fluttered aside and waited for them to pass, Skander first and then Margaret on Dammerung's arm, but he caught Margaret's eye in passing and looked down on her in that faintly mocking, smiling way he had, as if he were sharing some secret with her.

They went round the end of the house and down the short stair between the stunted wayfaring trees to the courtyard. There was always a bit of flurried activity in the background. Margaret noticed it mechanically: a boy with two dogs, a servant sweeping the spring's shedding from the trees that kept their leaves on through winter. A grackle purled on the curtain wall, etched against the blue-bottle sky, but it was the foreground she noticed most, putting up her hand to thrust her blowing hair out of her face while her skirts whirled in the wind: the lonely, shaggy, ancient pony, the small, bent figure on its back, the bundled length of something wolfish and grey in its arms...

"Why, it is old Hobden!" she cried. She had not thought of him since the autumn day on the earthworks. "Of all people!"

It was old Hobden, of all people, wizened and crumpled on the back of the old odd-job pony, with something long and wolfskin-bound clasped in his arms. He must have come the whole journey on the ancient pony—which might have been born dun-coloured or was dirty beyond washing—and seemed unable to get off it, for he sat it like some forlorn knight-errant whose hope of honour and life has been lost. But when he looked round at them and saw them through the sloe-berry sharpness of his eyes, his old walnut face creased into an easy smile.

Dammerung slipped out of Margaret's grasp and strode forward, jaunty black sleeves fluttering, the dancing lightness in his feet. "Hobden, you old reprobate!" he cried heartily. "What—not dead? I gave you up a year since! Well met—*well* met, old friend."

The odd-job pony ruckled and swung its head around angrily at the tone of Dammerung's voice, but old Hobden, unruffled as ever, shifted sidewise in the saddle and put out a hand toward his old master. Dammerung took it without a second thought and pressed it firmly, light and laughter and a boyish joy breaking up and chasing each other on his face.

"Na, not dead," said old Hobden in his slow, pleasant drawl. "I come up from Marenové 'Ouse on ye's count, for seemed to me the 'Ouse told me ye was among t'living still."

"Did it so?" said Dammerung. His voice had turned soft. "It would, rum thing. It would. And you have come up on my account and left Marenové House without its gate-ward?"

But there was no real reproach in Dammerung's voice, and old Hobden wagged his walnut head. "I come up to give ye summat. 'Twas given away, I think, in spite, and I took it upon my soul to reclaim it. So I come up from Marenové 'Ouse to give it back t'ye."

As he said it he held out the thing in his hands to Dammerung, very tenderly and a little shakingly, for his hands, Margaret realized, were freckled with sun-spots and old, with the veins standing out sharply and blue where the skin had sunk in around them. With an air of ceremony the War-wolf took the long wolfskin-bound thing into his own hands and looked long at it, long and quietly, without the piercing in his eyes. Skander was there, standing back with his manservant just behind them, giving his cousin room, and it seemed Margaret and old Hobden himself were removed for a few moments from the oddly frantic, quiet look that was in Dammerung's face...

At last he said, "The road up from Marenové is a long one—a longer one still from where I think—I *think*—this thing has lain. So come you in, good dog," he tossed a once more laughing look into the servant's face, "and wash the road-dust out of your throat."

There was a gesture from Skander and the blue-jay man was suddenly foremost, one arm under old Hobden's shoulders, helping the walnut-shrivelled figure down from the odd-job pony's back. Margaret, stepping aside, caught the eye of a passing stable-hand and clicked her fingers for him to come care for the dusty beast, which would, itself, have many miles of road-dust in its throat. Then they were turning back into the house, an odd and motley group, with big fair Skander leading them and the heron-striding blue-jay man with the little walnut groundsman, Dammerung in darkness and white mystery, holding the wolfskin-bound thing as closely as ever old Hobden had, and Margaret following slowly after, watching them, feeling inexplicably the fierce pang of being an outsider which she thought had gone away. But it came again, without warning, striking hard and upward under her breastbone, hard enough to knock the breath from her, and it hurt as it always hurt, throat-catchingly, leaving behind it a long cold wave of desolation.

They disturbed Aikaterine in Skander's study. She had been tidying, assuming they would be out for at least an hour yet; she rose from the hearth where she had been sweeping, a dust-pan and a brush in her hands, a smudge of soot on her chin, and looked faintly surprised at the gathering that was filing in. Skander shook his head at her as if to say, "It is nothing. You may stay." And she knelt again on the hearth-stone, her brush moving quietly, her eyes upturned to Dammerung.

Dammerung pulled himself apart from them. The blue-jay man got a glass of yellow wine for old Hobden—the glass glowed as if it held southern sunshine—but it was not until the old man had drunk and they had all fallen silent, waiting, that the War-wolf stirred out of whatever memories were making his cheeks pale and his eyes burn. He looked round at them like someone just waking, displaced and confused, but when his eyes passed over Margaret's face they hung there a moment in recognition. She smiled helpfully, coaxingly—though it hurt her chest to do it—and something in his eyes called to her as surely as if he had spoken.

She crossed the room to his side, standing in a pool of drenching sunlight—the wind whirled the shadows of bare branches over them—and put her hands on the tough leather knotwork of the cord that bound up the wolfskin. Dammerung tipped the thing toward her, holding it as she worked, until finally she had tugged the last length of cord free from the cold furry object and stood back, the roughness of the leather in her palm, the light and shadows dancing, the stark, unfamiliar look on her companion's face.

He held it a moment longer, then gently began to turn back the folds of wolfskin as if he were unwrapping a babe. The grey ticked skin fell back: as it came loose the thing seemed, suddenly, half-living in his hands. Margaret's heart began to quicken and the blood-rush of it helped the pain in her chest.

Why did this hurt so much?

At last the thing was freed entirely, naked and splendid-shining and half-living in Dammerung's hands. It was a sword. She had always known, without thinking about it, that it was a sword, but staring down at the bared thing she felt a new pang—of fear this time, for the thing was fierce and bright and made for war. It had been quenched and quiet, though still soaked with potency, while wrapped in its smothering wolfskin. Bare in Dammerung's hands, the genius of the thing was almost overpowering.

She suffered that for a moment, though it seemed a long moment, and then she looked beyond the clear shining to the thing itself, the thing which weighed so much and was so long, the physical weapon in Dammerung's hands. To her surprise it was unlovely, a serviceable but battered thing, the sheath plain hard leather casing, its chape and locket of half-heartedly decorated metal; the cross-guard was plain, the pommel sported a mere unimaginative sunburst which seemed mockingly incongruous for a man who might have been Overlord of Plenilune. But the potency had been there—was still there—and the shining of it which Margaret could not see but could feel was glinting on it yet. The thing half-lived, whether by Dammerung's will or the life-blood it had drunk, she did not know. She felt the genius of it, and almost imagined it felt her own, and in some way that she did not understand she felt akin to it.

Skander had come closer, though none of them, perhaps Skander included, had been aware of it. He looked down with Dammerung on the sword in his cousin's hands, laughter and high surprise warring with each other at the corners of his mouth. "Widowmaker!" he said at last, softly, huskily. "I had not thought—"

"I had," said Dammerung, not lifting his eyes from the blade. "I had thought, long and bitterly, but no word did I have until today."

Old Hobden's voice, cracked and wrinkled and like a walnut after the full-blooded, husky tones of the two young men, came from behind them. "Aye, 'twas in our hearts, the 'Ouse's and mine, that ye'd want word after we'd had word o' ye."

"*You* old *reprobate!*" said Skander, rounding happily on the old man. "What bee-skeps have you kicked up to fetch this for your master!"

The old man smiled bashfully, but Skander did not wait for an answer. He crossed to the fireplace, set his foot on the grate over Aikaterine's back as she knelt to dislodge a bit of burnt stick from underneath it, and, reaching up, swung down the sword that had hung over the mantelpiece. It was as long as Widowmaker, but perhaps even more battered, sheathed in a hard leather casing and decorated in bronze, its grip wrapped in black sharkskin. He drew it out and tossed the sheath away onto a sofa.

"A fine hour it is," he said gustily, "that my Gram should have your Widowmaker beside her once more."

Dammerung, too, jerked his sheath off and flung it down, baring the grim steel that had earned him his title. Seeing it gleaming fitfully in the sunlight, Margaret knew she had been wrong: it was beautiful. "There now, my pretty!" he told it warmly, running his finger down the blood-groove. He added thoughtfully, "I haven't put this in someone for almost three years. Why, it's practically virgin."

"There will be occasion for that later, no doubt. An' sure I will want you on the Capys border helping me when the tribes take to harrying my folk."

But Dammerung shook his head and kept his thoughts to himself.

Margaret stooped and picked up the discarded sheath. It was cold and hard under her palm. "The sheath could do with new lacquer," she remarked. Her thumbnail found a place where the wooden casing had been split. *It had been given away in spite.* She heard the thump and crack of Rupert's boot against the fox's ribs. Her stomach clenched. "It has seen better days."

"And darker nights." Dammerung held out his hand for the sheath. "The blade needs a burnishing too. Where do you keep such stuff, Skander?"

The blue-jay man was sent off for oil and a rag. Ely Jacland, Skander said, was a good hand at woodwork and could probably be persuaded to touch up the scabbard.

"Who kept it? He kept it in a moist kind of place, the fool."

" 'Twas Malbrey o' Talus Perey," old Hobden spoke up. He had been quiet on the outskirts. "An' aye, he kept it in a dampish place. Tha' too, I reckon, was o' spitely thinking."

"Hmm!" Dammerung's tone was derisive. "It is too lean a grip for Malbrey. He will never have used it. Not a superstitious man, not like Rupert—who would not use this for fear it would turn against him—very practical man, Malbrey: he won't have used it."

Skander turned from murmuring something about coffee to Aikaterine. "Please, have a seat," he told old Hobden. "You must be tired."

Old Hobden tugged respectfully at his forelock. "Nay, sir, not tired. A bit stiff in the limbs is all, from t'pony. Ift is not presumptuous—" he made many syllables out of the word "—I'll put myself to a bit o' work in t'yard. Tha'll suit me fine."

"Good man. I won't stop a fellow who wants to work decently. Tabby will show you the way."

When the blue-jay man returned with the oil and cloth he was sent off again at once to escort old Hobden to the yard and show him about. Dammerung displaced Gram's sheath, sat down on the sofa, and began cheerily to burnish his sword, lean hands running down and down the milky blade, his teeth fashioning an idle whistling tune as he worked. Margaret watched him putting his life back together, piece by piece, and felt the sting of lonesomeness again.

The third thing came five days later. With nothing better to do Margaret had been helping Aikaterine oversee preparation of the guest rooms for the Green Table. She stood in the doorway to one of the rooms, a pile of folded linen in her arms. She had been working hard, harder than a woman of her standing probably should, but she did not want to admit to herself that she was doing it to stave off the ache in her chest so she pushed herself even harder, running from the pain, running from the knowledge of the pain.

"If there is anything blooming in the gardens," she told Aikaterine, "we can put the flowers in vases. But only one vase to a room: it is only April."

"I'll be sure to leave some blooms for the gardens," replied Aikaterine. She disappeared behind the bedstead to thrust a fold of sheet beneath the mattress.

"Margaret!" Dammerung's voice came up from below. "*She-e-e!* Margaret! You got a package!"

I got a package? Bewildered, she started back along the passageway toward the nave. She dropped a pillowcase and had to fetch it, so that by the time she arrived on the walkway over the nave she was looking down to see Dammerung crouched on his heels, inquisitively poking at a large trunk. The preconceived vision of something small—a bundle of brown paper and string, perhaps the size of some books—vanished at a glance: the trunk looked big enough to stuff a body in to, with some delicate folding.

"What is it?" she asked as she trotted down the stair. "I didn't buy anything. Who is it from?"

"Damned if *I* know," replied Dammerung. He thrust the heels of his hands against the lip of the trunk and rocked it over so that he could see the bottom. "The messenger didn't say and I didn't know him. What are you carrying about? Grave-clothes?"

"They're bed linens. Is there a lock?"

"No." Dammerung dropped the trunk on the floor again. "Should I give it a spring?"

"I suppose you had better." Margaret worried irrationally that it might be something nasty, and worried even more that it might be something pleasant. Who had sent it? Perhaps Lord Gro, who respected her? Or Centurion, who was unmarried and had a pleasant disposition toward women?

Dammerung drew his knife and knocked the butt of it against the latches until they sprang open. Then, planting his foot on the floor and his fingers underneath the lip of the old trunk, he pried the top off. A heavy scent of lavender rushed up in a cloud. Waving it off, he stepped back beside her, looking down at the trunk's contents.

Framed in the casing was the chinaberry dress.

"By all the improbable stars," hissed Dammerung. Then, admiringly, "The bastard!" and thrust his hands into his pockets. "This beats all."

Margaret dropped the linens in an unceremonious heap and bent down, fingers hesitant, to touch the dress's crisply-folded skirt. It was as beautiful as she remembered—more so now that she did not have to wear it to Rupert's coronation. The pearly silk shone with clusters of rich golden bead-work and, covering an underskirt of taffeta, rustled like a wind in an autumn wood with the slightest movement.

"How I hate him," she murmured. "Yet he is strangely great."

Dammerung smiled ruefully. "Isn't he? A noble salute to a noble lady. You must wear it to the Green Table."

"If I do, and I think I will, my salute will have something of mockery in it. He does not take mockery well."

"So much the pity for him. What lies beneath...?"

He stooped to peer among the folds of her other dresses neatly packed beneath, but at that moment Skander came in off the yard, caught sight of them at once, and called, "Dammerung! Whose horse?"

"Whose horse?" Dammerung straightened, dropping the lid of the trunk shut. "Whose *what* horse?"

"The big brown agouti that is driving my Blue-bottle mad. Did someone come? What is *that?*" he added, seeing the trunk.

"No!" cried Dammerung. "By all the—no! It can't be! Oh, what a week this has been!" And he took off toward the stables. Margaret took one look at the trunk and linens, picked up her skirts, and ran after him. Askance, Skander followed her.

After the bluster of March it had been a dry spring. Margaret emerged into blazing sunlight, losing sight of Dammerung in the glare for a moment. Cupping her hand over her eyes she spotted him, ducking into the darkness of the stable. With Skander behind her she ran across and slipped into the coolness behind him, smelling an air thick with the scent of horses and hay, and full of little points of light that filtered in through the open eaves. There was a horse turned loose at the other end of the aisle: a dark body with the wizened figure of old Hobden going round and round it. At the sound of Dammerung's footstep the horse put up its head and snorted, pulling to the end of its lead as the young man approached.

"Sure it is me, cousin!" cried Dammerung. His voice had gone thick. "*Shee, shee,* all's better now. We're better now." He folded the bronze-and-black muzzle into his hands. "I thought for sure he had given *you* away, or done for you. He tried to do for me. See? It's me. It's me. *Swef,* my heart, my Rubico. It is only Margaret. You know Margaret, surely..."

He crooned to the great leggy beast like a girl. Margaret stole closer and saw the flush of red-gold come out in the animal's coat as it shivered with delight, its dark hide skipping under its master's hand. A ruckling like a cat's purr began in its chest. Closer, so close she could almost touch it, she saw bars of silver in the brown where it had taken blows and healed over.

Another piece of his life put back into place.

She almost turned to go—it was a horse: of what great interest was a horse?—when Dammerung, slipping under Rubico's neck, caught her hand and raised it to the horse's muzzle. "There, see?" he said triumphantly to it. "You know Margaret. She's got a softer hand than I. You like that?" The enormous black lashes fluttered over the eyes. Rhea had eyes like that, Margaret thought. She cringed, but Dammerung's hand was firm on her own and the soft peach-fuzz skin beneath her palm was warm and questing and she did not have the heart to pull away. "You are getting soft, you brute. You will be having naught to do with me now that you have Margaret. Hmm?"

"He come wi'is tack," said old Hobden. "I put it by in the saddle 'ouse."

"Better and better. We shall be presentable, you and I," added Dammerung, looking to Margaret. "We'll put our heels on their necks."

"Yes." A flutter of happiness betrayed her melancholy. "But I don't think the horse will fit at the Green Table."

"We will bust out a wall."

"You will not." Skander slapped the horse's neck appreciatively. "How old is he?"

Dammerung ran his palm across his lips thoughtfully. After a moment's silent calculation, he said, "I would say about nine, if not exactly. He looks well for nine, don't you think?"

"Considering what you have put him to in those nine years, I should say so."

"Ah, well." The War-wolf put his hands in his pockets and gazed lovingly up at the horse's raw, handsome face. "We've had our enforced sabbatical. Widowmaker and Rubico and I will be ready for you when your borders start heaving like maggoty cheese."

"Yes, I—"

Before Skander could say anything more the blue-jay man was calling him away to rearrange the horses to make room when the guests arrived—they were due any day now—and old Hobden had taken himself off a few yards to toss hay into Rubico's stall.

"Are you put back together now?" asked Margaret.

Dammerung reached up and began pleating Rubico's ears through his fingers as he had pleated the strands of fire. "I—I am not sure," he admitted. Surprised, Margaret stepped to one side to see better into his face. He saw her motion and smiled wryly, looking away as if to hide. "You saw."

"I saw you when you got Widowmaker back. I saw you just now when you found your horse. You don't hide yourself as Rupert does. His face is inscrutable."

"I did not lie," he replied, "when I called myself a Fool."

"Honesty is the greatest of our misfortunes, and caring second greatest." She looked into the horse's unfathomable eye and sorted out thoughts, thoughts which were only partly her own, thoughts which were mostly Dammerung's. "There aren't words for your face or what happened to you. You were put back together, that is all I know how to say. You were put back together and it hurt you."

His head jerked round, blue eyes almost blackened in the gloom. Was it startlement or fear? She met his gaze levelly, smilingly, confused by the pain and happiness playing a harpist's duel with her heartstrings. "It did hurt," he said at last. "It hurt because to get back one piece—two pieces—was to show the empty holes that all the other pieces left behind. I do not feel quite put together. I feel...like a fire roaring for the chimney, trying to fill a hollow place, burning and insubstantial..."

Clairvoyantly she saw the image of the autumn sky alight with the sun's last furnace glory and said, "The hollow place, I think, is Plenilune."

He looked away and nodded wordlessly, a bit of the fox showing through in his face.

XXI | IN LITTLE ROOM CONFINING MIGHTY MEN

Margaret could not find Dammerung anywhere. She had looked in his room, looked in Skander's study, in the sunroom—it was a cool, sunny morning—she had even cornered the blue-jay man and asked if Rubico had been taken out. Of course he had not. The Green Table was to be convened in an hour, and the men of the Honours were gathered in one of the withdrawing rooms finishing a quiet breakfast. Margaret had not had breakfast; she had felt too sick to eat, and consequently the tight-fitting chinaberry dress had wrapped easily around her belly and settled, sleekly, over her hips. She had meant to show Dammerung beforehand so that he would not say anything during the Green Table—one could not gamble on him holding his tongue—but he seemed to have vanished.

Damn him! She stomped her foot petulantly in the middle of the intersection of two hallways. They were empty, full of sunlight, quiet...

"And can you blame me?"

Her heart jerked to a stop. She knew that voice, rich and purring like a cat that is nettled and is about to revenge itself.

"...talk to me alone—" Dammerung's lazy voice answered, and Margaret breathed again "—presumably because we have both grown accustomed to things being that way—only you cannot put your toe between my ribs, so I do not know what you will find to say."

Well, I want to know. Margaret stole down the hallway in search of their voices. She did not like the thought of meeting Rupert again ever, but she liked less the idea of leaving Dammerung alone with him—though what she might do to help Dammerung, she honestly could not say. *Here, then—as you are merciful, don't let them fly at each other's throats.*

It was a poor prayer—she leaned against the wall and slid her eye to the crack in the door—but she felt it would have been poorer still to have left God out of it and presumed the two men could handle things on their own merit.

They stood in a small conference room, longer than it was wide, with a table in the middle and an empty fireplace on the opposite side. There was a mirror over the fireplace, which Margaret thought providential: she could see both Rupert's face as he stood before the grate and his brother facing him on the near side of the table, his back to the door. There was a familiar sense of darkness in the air; Rupert's face had eclipsed the light and Margaret felt again the slow, powerful, black surge of his anger, like a rip-tide under a full moon.

"I wanted to make sure you were appreciative of the circumstances." Rupert flicked a hand dismissively. "They are blind, petty, little people, and they cannot see, as you and I can see, what lies beneath the surface of this, nor can they see what is truly at stake."

The fingers of Dammerung's right hand moved a little, as if almost to touch something... "No, you are right. In this one thing you are right. Some of them have an instinctive understanding that you and I are tossing more than a coin of power in the air, but that is only because their souls are of the very bone and marrow of Plenilune. They know it as in the shapes of dreams. But you and I know. We are not a Great World, but we matter, and we know that we matter—as war can turn upon the charge of one small flanking band of Horse, we matter." He was silent for a moment, withdrawing into his own thoughts. Finally, with a little, angry sigh, he went on. "There was a time when I would have let you come fore."

The angry light leapt in Rupert's eyes, quick, disbelieving, lashing across the bridge-bone of Dammerung's nose. Margaret felt her spirit clench within her. "That is a pretty thing to say in retrospect," de la Mare replied cuttingly. "Why did you not say so before?"

"You might have told me what you were about a bit sooner, but of course with your clap-jaw you never did." Dammerung's voice rose a pitch. "I *would* have helped you, Rupert. The vote rests with the Body Elect, not me, you know that—but I would have helped you. There was no need for this vomit-trail of blood. I would have helped you get the Overlordship."

"Why?" growled Rupert.

Dammerung had taken two impulsive steps forward and was leaning hard into the table so that the edge of it was digging into his hip. He brought his hand down on the table with a bang—Margaret suppressed a jolt. "Because family comes first! Not the Mares, not Plenilune, not anyone—family comes first. But you never comprehended that, did you? You were terrified of Mother, you chafed under Father. ...What you did to me still lies between us and hardly needs mentioning."

Rupert had stepped from the table at Dammerung's advance, but now he came back, leaning across it with the dark light in his face. "You know why I would not lief come to you?" he asked. "Because you would have done it. You would have made a key with sweet words for the keyholes of men's hearts—as you always do—and it would have been *your* work! it would have been *you* who had done it, not me."

For a long moment Dammerung said nothing. He stood still as if cast in stone, his eyes pale and unblinking, lips drawn into a thin line. Margaret's soul cried out in rage and helplessness; she knew that stillness. Rupert had found a chink in his armour and had cut him badly: to move now would be to redouble the pain. She could feel his soul bleeding, and she could see from the look on his brother's face that Rupert did not care.

Finally long habit won Dammerung through. He smiled, dog-teeth showing, his head shaking slightly as if to shake off the pain. "What a rummy sense of honour you have got."

"I wish I hadn't," Rupert said acidly.

"Oh, if only wishes were horses! Well, now, what a fool you have been! You could have had it all, with some breed of honour, with a considerable lack of blood—" his voice snagged as if on pain and memory and he savagely tore himself loose. "If you had but unbent a little and asked, instead of wadding your own pride down your own throat, I would have got you what you wanted."

Rupert brought his own hand down on the table. "You are the very devil of a liar!"

"You would not know truth if it struck you in the face!" cried Dammerung. "And it is feeling a good deal like doing so!"

"You are but talk," Rupert mocked.

The War-wolf thrust his finger at the other's face. "You say it, but you'll rue the day you believe it."

Rupert dropped his gaze to their reflections in the tabletop. Somewhere in the quiet a clock ticked incessantly. Margaret realized she had been clutching the doorframe with white knuckles. Slowly she let it go.

Finally Rupert said, "We both know how this will be."

"By the twelve houses, we all know."

Rupert sighed and turned away. Margaret watched him in the long, ancient, mercury-glass mirror: the face was oddly calm, but in the eyes there was a keen discontent that plucked anxiously at her nerves. He put his foot upon the fire-grate; it was empty, swept clean, cold. "Where is she?"

Her heart stopped again. Dammerung did not move but was quiet for a long time, seeming to weigh how to answer. "She is here."

Quickly—too quickly—Rupert turned. "May I see her?"

Dammerung's shoulder twitched; his coat of brown corduroy flicked back, revealing Widowmaker's hilt beneath. "You're gammoning me."

Rupert's face was motionless.

Pushing back from the table, the War-wolf laughed once, soundlessly, incredulously, and it was the laughter of pure fury.

"You really think I am that much of a fool? Of course you may not see her! You will see her at the Green Table, that is all. Sheer heaven knows you've had enough time alone with her. Good—" He bit back a curse and clenched his hands as if to hold his words in check.

Rupert's voice slashed out angrily with a shapeless hurt that was almost human. "At the Green Table? That is all?"

"Yes! That is all! You have done enough damage."

"What so galls you!"

"What galls—what *galls* me—" The words choked in Dammerung's throat. He strode forward, hands half-lifted, catching himself only at the last minute from putting his hands around the other's neck. "*What galls me!*" he cried. "The thought of *you* between *her* legs!"

Rupert's face turned white like a sea-storm. "You watch your mouth!"

Dammerung flung the words and his own better sense aside. "Do not 'you watch your mouth' at me! Tell me it has not crossed your mind!"

"Whose mind hasn't it crossed?" Rupert hurled back at him.

Dammerung spun away and slung himself into a chair. His foxy face was drawn in white fury; his put his forehead in his hand and looked up at his brother out of the side of one eye, always watching him, but for the moment too angry to know what to say. Margaret knew she ought to feel mortified—she knew she ought to leave—but the blue angry flame where her heart was supposed to be was riding high and hot and she knew she could not leave Dammerung. She did not know if it was a woman's sense of loyalty or a man's, but she knew she could not leave him.

But it seemed to be over. Rupert seemed spent. The great black grimness of his countenance was turned away, turned down, as if seeing all his glass-coloured dreams shattered under his brother's bare foot. "We had better go," he said through his teeth.

Dammerung rallied his breath. "Yes," he replied, setting his hands on the arms of the chair. He laughed, bitterly, for no apparent reason. "They will be waiting."

Damn the taffeta! Margaret tiptoed away as carefully as possible but she could not reach the end of the hall before they emerged from the little council room. She whirled and walked toward them as if she had always been coming. She stopped, however, at the sight of Rupert. There had been a door and Dammerung between them before: she had not realized what a difference that had made. He came out first and saw her alone in the hallway, alone in a swirl of sunlight and gold chinaberry, and she saw the pain clench in his face. Something betrayed her where her heart was supposed to be and she almost turned back. She did not try to speak but she could feel her voice give way.

Then Dammerung came, two paces behind, and saw the thing that happened between them. He did not hesitate. Brushing past Rupert, he strode up the hallway for her as if there was no one else about. Somehow she wrenched her eyes off the necromancy of Rupert's face and latched onto Dammerung's as if grasping a lifeline. Did it show? She hoped it did not show.

"What, did you get lost? I was just looking for you." He slipped her arm in his and pulled her round back the way she had come. "The narrow wicket gate is this way."

She knew Rupert would not be watching them go. He did not look as though he could much stand seeing her alone in the hallway of Lookinglass, let alone walking arm in arm with Dammerung. He would be gone...but his shadow was still there.

"I was looking for *you*," she admitted. "I had wanted to show you the dress without anyone else around so that you would not like it too much and carry on in front of strangers."

"I never carry on in front of strangers," he protested absentmindedly. He twisted as they walked, watching the billow of the skirt and the way the light played on the chinaberries. "And you made all this?"

"Mostly." A glimmer of pride nestled ember-like at the bottom-most corner of her soul.

"Tush, sirrah! It looks better on you than folded up in a trunk, that is for certain. And listen to that racket!"

"Yes, that is the taffeta underskirt. I worried it would give me away."

His brow lifted—the very image of a dog's brow when it hears someone it does not like coming up the walk. Her blood chilled. His eyes pried at her face and she let them: there were not words in any language known to man with which to explain herself. His mouth drew taught like an archer's string, but they loosed no words. If he thought less of her, he did not say it. He let the knowledge that she had been there and seen and heard lie and did not mention it. Margaret hoped, but did not believe, that he was not angry with her.

The men were waiting when she and Dammerung arrived. Seeing them—Mark Roy, Aikin Ironside and Brand, Lord Gro FitzDraco, even Sparling with Black Malkin and the other two Thrasymene women, Skander Rime and his friends Ely Jacland and Periot Survance—Margaret confused herself for a moment with the feeling that she was once again a pawn to be fought over until she remembered that it was Plenilune this time that everyone was thinking about, not her.

Except, perhaps, Rupert and Dammerung.

Rupert had got there a moment before, following Centurion to a place at the table. Dammerung stalked in, his head up, flinging a glance round on everyone until each face had suffered his bright, feverish eye. With a deft twist he pulled out a chair and stood aside for Margaret to take it. With all eyes on her—except Rupert's—she sat down, soothed the angry taffeta, and folded her hands in her lap like a good girl who had not just wilfully eavesdropped on the two most important men in the Honours.

Dammerung seated himself beside her and flung one knee over the other. "Good morning, everyone," he said jauntily, a smile coming out of one side of his mouth.

Centurion put his elbows on the table and leaned forward, looking hard at Dammerung as if he could not quite believe his eyes. "I'll be damned. It is you. I did not disbelieve," he amended, leaning back, "but you have to admit, the news that you were alive was hard to swallow."

The smile froze, but seemed to dance like a gypsy's knife in the eyes. "It was, wasn't it? A good joke on you. But what did or did not happen yesterday is not to the point. We've come for Plenilune."

Skander Rime and Lord Gro—as if Lord Gro knew what foul play had been afoot—looked grim. Woodbird's head was up, brows arched, and was studiously gazing at the centre of the table so that she would not have to meet anyone's eye. Margaret's gaze slid to Brand and she smiled sympathetically: it seemed the young man was under strict orders not to speak, for he was staring hotly but fixedly at his clasped fists on the tabletop before him.

"Well, Rupert?" Dammerung gave his brother the floor. "You called us and we have come."

Rupert drew in a deep, contemplative breath and leaned back from the fist he had been holding against his closed lips. "It is very simple. Great things often are, I find... Which of us is to be Overlord? For no one else," he spread his hand, "has stepped in to take the office."

There was an uneasy silence. Dammerung's eyes went round from face to face, that awful, fixed smile playing softly on his lips. "In Rupert's defence," he put in presently, "you *did* have his inauguration scheduled. Or so I was told. Of course I wasn't there myself."

Margaret touched his leg smartly with the back of her hand.

Aikin Ironside frowned, and his mouth shaped *Where*, but Woodbird flew into the silence to save it. "We did, in lieu of *you*, sir. I hate to say it, but Rupert de la Mare was our second horse."

"And I your dark one," laughed Dammerung.

Mark Roy put his elbows on the table and folded his hands together. "If I were to be frank," he began quietly, as if searching for his words as he went, "I think the decision of the Electoral Body is pre-eminently clear even without taking a vote. But we are not all gathered—I see Bloodburn, at least, was unable to make it, as well as two of my foremost border lords—and the vote would not be fair in that regard, nor in light of the fact that, as the War-wolf has pointed out, we *did* admit de la Mare to be our Overlord."

In lieu of his brother, thought Margaret spitefully.

Sparling spoke up. He had a pleasant, assured voice, perfectly polite, though it had none of the personality she had come to know in Dammerung. "If de la Mare and my lords will forgive me for saying so—" Rupert's eyes, cutting across the gathering, narrowed onto the Thrasymene lord's face with a pointedness that could kill "—we did admit it, but we did not slip on the ring."

Dammerung's jaw came open, but Lord Gro beat him to the mark. "Does that really matter?" the man asked gently, the ghost of a smile on his lips. "To what part of the law do we adhere, the letter or the spirit?"

But when the spirit is Rupert's—! Margaret looked to Dammerung, hoping he would protest, but to her dismay she found him looking sadly at the hand he draped across his knee, his head moving with a faint nod of agreement.

"And your proposition?" asked Rupert coldly, stiffly. "For I am come for your propositions," he added with a spasm of painful mockery.

His brother's head came up and back, teeth showing through a smile. "Oh, how like heaven you deign to ask us what *we* think."

Rupert's face turned white and Margaret felt the air grow thin. Had he been any other man, he might have brushed the mockery off—had it been any other mockery, he would have. But one thing that Margaret could say for Rupert was that he took his love and hatred seriously and did not cover them in laughter. She could almost hear the sheath of his patience clatter to the floor as he removed it.

"By his Infernal Majesty and my Lord Adam," he breathed— the glass pane behind him splintered with a hundred spider-fine cracks— "take back your words or I'll *put* them back."

Dammerung's eyes began to dance, lightly, daringly, like the sunlight on a knife blade as a man spins its point on a tabletop.

"You are a step away from a step too far," Rupert warned him.

The War-wolf's eye dropped a moment to Rupert's hand, then back to Rupert's face. "Oh? I am insatiably curious. What comes after the next step?"

"Clearly you have never known sanity."

"I do not know perdition as *you* do."

The step beyond the next step was taken. Margaret was aware of Lord Gro quietly and deliberately moving his chair back from the table. She could not see anyone else's face. As in a dream they were all distorted, grey, present but unimportant. She saw only Rupert's face, white with fury and what might have been fear. He, too, put back his chair, but he rose, folded back his coat, and, removing a leather glove from an inner pocket, flung it down onto the table.

"Then I will teach it to you."

In the back of her mind Margaret heard a distinct click, so clearly she thought for a moment that it was real, as though someone had put a puzzle-piece in place, interlocked with the others. In the beautiful, terrible scene caught frozen before her—she felt detached from it, like a ghost—with the sunlight breaking up in the glass behind Rupert's upflung head and Dammerung, beside her, his head up too, gazing down smilingly on the gage, she was aware—as if she were in a dream—of Brand unfolding quietly, lifting his head and looking around with a satisfied smile on his face. The moment was broken for Margaret gently when Periot Survance, seeing Brand's reaction, happened to look her way and shared a laughing, half-checked smile with her at the young man's expense.

With a liquid movement Dammerung put back his chair and got up, raising darkness with him; the air seemed to crackle and shimmer around him. "Your hands are bigger than mine," he said lightly: "consider the glove taken."

"The duel is formally accepted," said Skander. He, too, got to his feet, looking remarkably less grim and rather more worried. "We will all gather tomorrow morning at dawn on the bowling lawn. Six o'clock should do it. You're neither to meet nor talk until that time," he added, thrusting a finger from man to man.

Dammerung cheekily pressed his hands together and offered his cousin a bow. Rupert nodded curtly. Margaret lifted a brow archly at the private thought: *I wonder if Skander could have given them a stricture they would have been more willing to obey.* Then, as he was closest to the door, Dammerung was giving her his hand, the coolness quite gone from him toward her, and she was able to put her back on the room at last. Her taffeta purred with her movement. It had all been done cleanly, she thought: the hammer and tongs had been got out beforehand. The two had only to place the puzzle-pieces, to move their chessmen, and the thing had been done. Tomorrow would settle it.

At the door Margaret felt Dammerung's hand pull. She paused: he had turned back a moment. A pool of concentration gathering darkness at the corner of his mouth, he put up his free hand, passing it through a shimmer of air, and the cracks in the pane disappeared. That was all. Transferring her hand to his arm, he took her out into the passage.

"You baited him," she said matter-of-factly when they had holed up in Skander's study. No one would disturb them there.

"It did look that way, didn't it..."

"An' sure it did," Margaret protested. "That was not feigned anger on Rupert's part. I know his anger."

Dammerung smiled sympathetically. "Oh yes, that was real. Perhaps it was rude of me to touch him in that tender spot, but then I wanted it to be convincing." He twisted like a cat on the couch, watching his cousin, who was stealing a few minutes away from his guests, come in and stalk toward his desk. "We both of us knew there was no good in summoning the Electoral Body. Oh, we needed them. Before them the Overlord will stand or fall—and stand he will! But it is between the two of us to decide which will be Overlord. Plenilune is not large enough for the two of us."

There was a long moment of complete silence in the study. Even the fire seemed to have fallen quiet. No one moved. Margaret stared into the fire, stared blindly into Dammerung's words. For a minute or so she was full of a fierce gladness over the bruise he had given Rupert—it had been awful to see the pane of glass break and to hear the man swear on his anger, but she had been glad to see Dammerung dig his toe between Rupert's ribs. But the gladness was soon checked. Without moving them herself, the little puzzle-pieces of Dammerung's words shifted, colourfully, and fell into their proper place...and seemed to fall suddenly away into a pit of emptiness. *Plenilune is not large enough to the two of us... The duel is formally accepted... Some breed of honour... You're gammoning me... We both know how this will be...*

Would any of us die to keep what looms before us from happening?

One of them was going to die.

"Oh, God," she groaned under her breath, and crushed her hand over her mouth so that no one would hear.

Skander leaned on the back of the sofa over his cousin's shoulder. "Well, bully for you, you've done it," he said bluntly. "And leave us to pick up the bloody pieces in the end. Fie upon it! It was a noble gesture, and very smartly acted. I've been pawing through my brains this past half-hour hunting for a better way out, but heaven knows I've thought of none. Still," his cool brown eyes darkened—his fingers, clutching the wooden spine of the sofa, turned telltale white, "when you stand down there tomorrow, you and your brother, who will mediate between you? What man—what woman? You are too much for us and none of us are your match."

Dammerung had had his fingers in his hair and it was pushed wildly awry. Looking up through a shock of hair that was like a horse's forelock, he caught Margaret's eye a moment, seemed to plumb her cold, acute pain, and touched it with a tender, knowing smile. "No, Skander," he admitted, "none of you is a match for us, and no man is man enough to lay his hands upon our shoulders. It is for that very reason that either of us would be Overlord at all."

Skander was quiet a minute, watching his cousin's words fall into place as Margaret had; then—"True"—and he dropped his hand momentarily on Dammerung's lean shoulder before leaving them to return to his hospitable duties.

It was a companionable silence that fell on Margaret and Dammerung afterward, but for Margaret the silence ached. She tasted iron in her mouth and wondered if she had bit down on her cheek. She could not tell. Her hands were immobile in her lap: she could not reach up to check. What was Dammerung thinking? His reflection in a piece of glass was far away, thin and pensive, muted in a cloudy darkness.

What did she want? she asked herself with a sudden unkind fierceness. To tidy the place like a nursery, free of any sharp objects that might hurt someone, to be sure of a happy outcome like a little girl reading a fairytale? Was it not the naked-sabre danger of them that had at first repulsed her from these people, and what had eventually drawn her? With their thin skins, quick to take offence and to defend their bantam plumage, these were men who lived among danger and swords and blood and put a great price on honour. They had not turned their world into a nursery. They loved their world fiercely and their world loved them still more fiercely back...

The high winds of the fells rushed at that moment around Lookinglass, thrumming ominously in the walls.

Margaret looked at the reflection again, keenly. She wanted him to live, for all their sakes, but was it doing him justice to wish him safety? She remembered how restless he had been, like Blue-bottle Glass, when spring had been creeping into the world, how he had bolted out into the huge rushy danger of it at the merest sliver of a chance. He throve on challenge. He met the headwinds and the high waters of life and seemed to laugh at them even as he plunged shoulders-foremost into their jaws. As though someone had thrust a sword into the ground the sharp-edged shadow of the duel lay long between them, ill-omened and uncertain, but she knew Dammerung's blood was happy for it.

A faint, forced smile crawled at the corner of her mouth.

"Won't you play something?" he broke the silence. "It is, perhaps, too quiet."

To play? Doe-startled she looked toward the instrument. To smile was a trial; to play a tune was asking much just now. "The notes are all broken," she protested, but even as she protested she got to her feet.

"I know, but behold, I have seen a son of Jesse the Bethlehemite who is a skilful musician... I'll come turn the pages for you."

With some effort Margaret squeezed her skirts between the bench and the instrument. With some effort, Dammerung found enough bench to sit on without crushing her skirts.

"If I were less skilful," she pointed out, "I might annoy him with my playing and send him away."

He shuffled through sheet-music. "Do you think so? But I'm afraid this is a problem that will not go away with the shooing of it."

She took "The Riven Knight" out of his hand and set it on the piano. "Sometimes it is annoying how right you always are."

His teeth flashed in a kill-devil smile and he leaned his elbow forward, chin in his palm, waiting for the turn as she played. She had not finished the second sheet, when there was a movement over the top of the paper in the study doorway and she was aware through the notes—which seemed suddenly to break again—of a dark-shrouded, feathery figure waiting for her to stop. She reached the best place and broke off, looking up.

It was Woodbird. Her head was tilted like a blackbird's, her golden eyes on some distant place where the notes were making shapes and colours for her. But when the music stopped she seemed to return.

Dammerung got to his feet. "Hullo! Skander is not about. I should have thought him with you, to be honest."

"Oh, no," replied Woodbird. "I have just come from him. Black Malkin sent me to tell you, among other things, that she had better be referee between you and Rupert de la Mare tomorrow, if no one objected."

"I cannot think of a less partial judge," said Dammerung, the cool laughter sparking in his eyes. "Tell her it is a good plan and she shall have the marshal position—and that there will be no foul play for we shall both be quaking in our boots."

Woodbird said archly, "I'm sure she'll like the sound of that. Pardon me for the interruption."

Margaret shook her head and murmured something appropriate—those sorts of things always seemed inconsequential and she could never remember them afterward. Woodbird vanished, trailing bits of gold-leaf and black feather behind her, and Dammerung sat down again on the chinaberries, turning the page with an idle pass of his hand through the air.

"And still I like her better! She has none of Black Malkin's bitterness—though perhaps the good woman cannot be wholly blamed for that—and she has a sense of wit. I like a sense of wit."

"I wonder that you like me, then." Margaret looked at her long fingers resting on the ivories.

He did not miss a beat. "You give occasion for my sense of wit to be employed. I like that in you."

"You like that in *you*," she amended, and took up the song more vigorously than the music demanded.

"Heaven hath been found out!" he cried, and banged the keys in accompaniment.

They played for the better part of an hour, until Margaret's fingers were tired and Dammerung said he was hungry and had best improve his mind a little with some reading. Aikaterine brought them lunch and news that Skander had taken advantage of the fine day, and the mention of the bowling lawn, and was playing bocce with their lordships Aikin Ironside and Brand the Hammer while Mark Roy and Lord Gro looked placidly on. The others she could not wholly account for, save that Centurion of Darkling and Lord Sparling had gone off for a ride. Of Rupert de la Mare she had no news, save that he had not brought Rhea.

"I feel like a little boy grounded for some misdeed," complained Dammerung when the maid had gone again. "I should like to play bocce. Do you play?"

"I might, if someone took the trouble of teaching me." It did not escape her that, had things gone according to her mother's plan, she might be in Italy at this moment, poised beside some swarthy, moustachioed native, listening to the incessant warble of the peninsular language while he tried to teach her the game. "Is it hard?"

"No. Have you got a strong arm?"

She looked askance at him.

"Ah," he said, chastened. "Well, it isn't hard, so long as you have a decent sense of aim. I think you have that—you got Rhea square in the eye, if I remember."

"Yes, I think I have a decent sense of aim."

"It eats at me that I was not there. What I missed when I was stuck in that damnable cellar!"

They ate lunch alone, and for the few hours that they were not wholly stir-crazy Dammerung read aloud from a biographical piece not unlike Caesar's *Gallic Wars*. It was colourfully and engagingly written, full of foreign names and a bright sense of loyalty juxtaposed to lawless tribes from places that did not stick in her mind. Someone—an Auxoris, who seemed to be a famous general from somewhere in the south—had pushed the borders of the Honours farther north than ever before, held the line, and set up steady garrisons and government there. When his time came to leave the military, the province was annexed to him and became what lay under Mark Roy's foot as Orzelon-gang.

"Hmm!" said Margaret, when she learned that.

Dammerung looked up. "*Hmm* what?"

"What nothing, only that it interested me to learn how Orzelon-gang came to be. She seems less foreign now. She has history. And I know a little of it."

She felt she was rambling and silly, and faltered, wishing he would get back to his reading, but he smiled comprehendingly. "You've touched upon an old notion, that to know the secret name of something is to know and hold power over it. Now you know a little more about our neighbour Orzelon-gang, and you can put your hand on her and she seems tame to you."

Tame is not the word I should have used. He went on, picking up with a recount of a battle in some place called Ampersand and how the ground had been confining and difficult and that it had been a nasty, wet spring that year, but she was not attending. She was watching his face, brows rampant as the words formed in his mind and his mouth, his eyes alight with pleasant interest. *You say it so idly, as if it were a silly, ancient fairytale, but you know the secret names of things, don't you?*

I wonder: what is mine?

XXII | THE RED KING

The War-wolf appeared the next morning, not in grim costume to reflect the fate of Plenilune laid out of the blade of a sword, but in a jacket of sparkling white, pristine, supple, comfortable, and stitched with bravado. The smell that came from him—or was it a sense?—was of mingled thunderstorm and spice which made the senses and smells and colours around him pale in comparison. Margaret had gamely eaten breakfast but it had been tasteless to her. Skander, otherwise unruffled, looked up from his toast to see his cousin standing with the early sun aflame around him in the doorway.

" 'Morning. You look game."

Dammerung strode in, Widowmaker flickering like a metal tail behind him. "What—" he stopped by her side and looked down at her, his long hand resting on the back of her chair. "Chinaberries again?"

"It seemed fitting," she explained. Why did her throat feel so lumpy and grey? Her chest inside the constricting silk and whalebone seemed not to have enough room to move. Her arms and chest were cold and seemed abnormally pale; the three freckles beneath her left collar-bone stood out more starkly than ever.

"It does. I was only worried I had smushed them." He turned back to his cousin. "The game's afoot!" he replied as if he had not interrupted. "I can feel all their thoughts like veins, and they are all on fire as if with wine. Quarter to the hour, coz. It grows golden by the minute. Have you seen Rupert?"

"I've been down to the lawn and back. Yes, I saw him: sitting on the patio looking out over Glassdale without seeming to see anything at all. He looked angry and regretful, but when he saw me he smiled."

"I kn-know that smile." Margaret shivered.

"What, the All Hallows smile? Oh yes, we're famous for it. Well, angry and regretful, is he? He is always angry. God knows he will have cause to eat regret for ages to come."

"A cold, unsettling last meal," murmured Skander.

Dammerung said nothing. His hand moved to Margaret's shoulder. She put up her own and took it, and he lifted her out of her chair. Skander left the breakfast dishes to be forgotten and followed after them down to the garden and out through a narrow path onto the bowling lawn.

The sun was coming up, lancing in high, angled beams across the lowlands beyond Glassfell, whose names Margaret did not know. The air was red and golden; someone had set up a tent on the east side of the lawn and the light was picking out its metal pieces with such bright precision that Margaret could not look at it without thinking, ominously, of the coiled brilliance of the Dragon. And such a crowd! Wine-dark like stones in the *mare nostrum*, clustered round an oval of beaten grass, she saw people from as near as Ryland and as far flung as Darkling. Passing down the line on Dammerung's arm, the dawn wind rushing and whirling in her pearl-silk skirts, she happened to look aside and see a lean young man, hardly more than a boy, with large, girlish eyes the colour of verdigris copper looking at her out of the shadow of the horse he held, an expression of stark horror and wonder in his face. Her heart hurt keenly through the careful dullness: through no more than existing she had broke the poor boy's heart.

Dammerung stopped by Skander to leave Margaret in his care and to limber up. He wore no cloak. Twisting, white fabric purling on his shoulder, he looked back at Rupert who stood on the opposite side of the rutted green, the blaze of sunrise behind him, alone, foreboding. Dammerung set his teeth and whistled softly.

Margaret shifted his sword-belt buckle to dead centre. Her hands shook, the pit of her stomach was cold, but she did not feel afraid. Or was this a new kind of fear that was so primal it had no name? "Don't lose your head," she warned Dammerung.

He met her eyes, stark and glassy and feverish, and a bright smile swept up on his face like the swift uprush of a bird. "Too late," he whispered. And, setting his hand hard upon her shoulder, shaking it like a man's, he broke off, swinging out into the open lawn, Plenilune tipping on its axis under his feet.

Into the level grassy space he stepped, easily, head up and eyes flashing like a falcon's, his naked sabre lying lightly in his hands. With more grimness, but just as magnificently—if not more so in appearance—Rupert stepped in from the opposing side, his own sabre throwing back the light from its bare blade. The two swords shook with sky-fire: great beams and swells and halos of golden light broke off the blades as if they were cutting through the secret nature of energy itself. The air was turning golden; the red was draining away.

Somewhere far away Margaret's heart began to beat dully, sickeningly. Her head felt cold.

How alike they looked, she thought. Rupert was the taller, but Dammerung by far the taller seeming. The cool pride was in their faces, the sharp-featured faces of the Marenové line. They bore themselves almost identically: easy, sure, a curious, serious sable-sense edging all their faintly mocking gestures. Old Hobden, who knew what he knew, had once said they were as different as the dark and light sides of the moon, and Margaret had always felt that difference keenly. Yet now, as their similarities seemed to mingle between them in their stark countenances and determination, the differences seemed to stand out in even clearer relief. The light ran up and down the swords.

Black Malkin—who seemed to have little love for either—in her black lace gown, her gold-leaf cloak billowing and snapping angrily around her, stationed herself between the two young men and raised both arms.

"I will here reiterate the terms agreed upon by both parties," she began in her husky, regal tones. "The facts are these: that Plenilune must have an Overlord, and that she, as is customary, seeks an Overlord from Marenové. Marenové has put forward both Rupert de la Mare and Dammerung War-wolf. The contest is this: that one of them must best the other in single combat to attain the position of Overlord of Plenilune. The stakes: all the lands of Marenové, its Honour, its manors, its cantrefs, etc., as well as federal headship over all the united Honours of Plenilune. Ladies and gentlemen, combatants—" here she turned a slow, withering look on both young men "—this contest is in all seriousness and will be carried out to the death."

Margaret clenched her fists until the nails dug into her palm. Beside her, she saw Skander's profile close its eyes and press them painfully shut.

With unhurried step Black Malkin returned to the sidelines, positioning herself like a Valkyrie on the between-edge of everything, watching the two young men like a hawk. As was everyone else. A hush fell over the grassy tableland; only the wind, and the sounding of the wind through numerous articles of fabric, made a noise among them—and it was a dismal noise. The silence was so complete, the air so crackling with tension, that Margaret could feel all her insides coiling up in agony.

With long, unhurried strides the two men met in the middle of the ring. Light broke out jaggedly from their sabres as they gave each other a bitterly proper salute. Then they retired a little space, to give themselves room to manoeuvre, and suddenly the life of the fight came into the panther and the fox. The tension in the air, as though withdrawn by a black star, swallowed itself up into the bodies of the two men, poised, prepared to become kinetic. Their bodies were perfectly situated, at one with their weapons, etched in brilliant, masculine splendour against the blurred backdrop. Rupert stood like a warhorse; Dammerung's sword was circling slightly, counter-clockwise—Margaret could tell by the way the sunlight was coming off the point in little bursts.

If she had blinked she would have missed it, the thing happened so quickly. One moment the two were standing at slightly bent and painfully alert attention, the next there was a growling crack that seemed to split the air overhead in two and Dammerung was catapulting backward across the grass, his sword flung from his hand, his hands round his collar-bones as if to wrench something's grip from his throat. A single collective cry of confused rage lanced through the crowd. Margaret was in midstep before she felt the sharp backward jerk of Skander's restraining hand.

If looks could kill she would have stabbed him mortally with her glance.

When she looked back Dammerung was rolling off his shoulders, gaining a purchase on the ground with his knees, rising all the while and yanking at the air around his throat. He was white, white like a ghost, but at last, as though tearing open the jaws of Leviathan, his hands wrenched apart, sending serpentine coils of red-and-white light away, hurling them back across the grass. Snatching a glance at Rupert, Margaret saw his face was ashen grey, as if the backwash of his own magic made him ill. All the same, she noted—perhaps she alone noted, with all eyes on the War-wolf— there was no hint of remorse in that pitiless face.

It took Dammerung a moment to recover. He had turned away so that she could no longer see his face, but she saw that his hands were scored, the nape of his neck pierced as though by teeth. He stood, if possible, more grandly than ever, legs a little apart as if to show that the turf beneath him was his. The tilt and whirl of Plenilune had steadied. He looked to his opponent; the wind was in his face, and his face in profile was terrible.

It was strange and unnerving and uncanny: Margaret could have sworn she had seen him so before. Somewhere in a book, a long time ago...

How long that horrible moment lasted, she could not have said. No one dared move. No one dared speak a word. Even Black Malkin, hands pressed together before her, stood her ground and would not enter this fray. But at last that terrible countenance on the face of the young man whose mocking white-feather jacket was turning red in the back became almost tender, and still more mocking, and the light went in and out of his eyes again. He put out a hand, much as a man might who meant to dance, and said,

"Come to me."

There was no sound, only the eerie flicker of light along the sabre's blade as it dislodged itself from the grass and spun end over end through the crackling air. The only sound was the soft leather kiss it made as it clapped into Dammerung's palm. He raised it defiantly before his face, eyes on Rupert, and with a fanciful jerk thrust it aside in salute. Rupert raised his arms like an orchestral conductor, head poised half askance, but Dammerung only nodded. Something was spoken between them in the windy quiet, something awful and shining and red-coloured like the War-wolf's back, and the atmosphere took on a more severe and thunder-powered feel.

They opened in a blaze of glory. There was a crack and a shock and an arc of light—from which, Margaret could not tell—and the two were at it with a passion, hurling spells and casting spells aside to left and right, filling the air with windblown sparks. The grassy space in which they battled swelled with a shimmering feeling, and the swelling kept pushing outward until Margaret's skin felt uncomfortably hot and the little hairs on her arms kept sizzling with magic. But it was better this way—she wrenched out of Skander's iron grip and stood her ground, staring fixedly at the match—it was better that the two should fight this way for Plenilune. Plenilune deserved it. Maybe Rupert himself had known that: she realized that he had not meant to kill Dammerung with his first blow. He had thrown down a gauntlet Dammerung could not now refuse. In a gesture of the rightness of things perhaps more characteristic of his family's heritage than his own soul, Rupert de la Mare had forced Dammerung's hand into a high and mighty duel the likes of which Margaret wondered if Plenilune had ever seen.

They were fantastic and terrible, and not altogether safe, to watch. The elements and the full fire of wrath whirled from their hands with the deftness of a juggler whirling his golden balls, but the backwash could be blinding and sometimes blows were cast wide. Once, like Jove, Rupert sent a jagged tail of lightning at his brother's head, which would have blown the fine-boned skull to bits had Dammerung not caught it at the last second on a bank of energy and sent it skyward and over into an innocent pine. Oddly fitting, thought Margaret as the sound of shivered timber was drowned in the crack of magic.

And indeed, there was hardly anything else that could be heard above the whip-crack and thunder-clap of spells being loosed off and breaking up on other spells. Margaret's ears were ringing with the noise. Rupert and Dammerung fought almost wordlessly, though once Rupert gave a grinding cry of exertion as he cast off a dark, heavy spell, and once, vengefully, Dammerung shouted "*Spencer!*" as he hurled a blood-coloured spell that hit Rupert and broke open his shoulder to the bone.

There was a flicker of blue movement behind and beside Margaret that compromised her attention. Exasperated, half-paranoid, she glanced around in time to see the blue-jay man worm through the crowd—she could not remember seeing him leave—and arrest Skander's ear. A word was given; Margaret watched Skander's face draw tight and his lips formed a silent invective. He turned back with his manservant and the two plunged back into the crowd, out of sight. She followed them as long as she could, snatching glances at the fight, divided: did she follow, or did she stay? But then she lost them, and she felt rooted in her place.

The bowling green was a wreck. With his fist to the shivered earth, Rupert cracked open the ground at Dammerung's feet, nearly pitching his brother into a grave. Dirt flew in a storm. The air had drained of red and gold; it was blue now, bright, heavenly blue with the sun cutting it evenly in argent slivers. Dammerung put out his hands and stopped the reeling earth, lit it with Chinese fire, and drew it back toward him; at the same time the blue was closing around him, a whirlwind of silver and pale chicory colour, faster and faster with tawny streaks of earth thrown in. He was being lost in it. It was taking shape, taking a lifelikeness of its own, poised in contiguous motion around the young man with his uplifted, imperious arms.

Was it just her, or did it look like a dragon?

Rupert cried out. His words were lost in the overwhelming thunder of the magic Dammerung was pooling to himself, but the sound of it frightened Margaret. To her sizzling ears it was as though some deep dark thing to which the man held allegiance was calling across to Dammerung, defiant and terrible, ancient, powerful: a roar of primeval rage that took the world in its hands and stood to tear it in two. The blue-whirling thing and the man inside it braced. The darkened, devilish figure sparked with red and put up one hand, ready to strike.

The blows never fell. At that moment, through a crack in the miasma of colour and fear, Margaret saw Skander break away at that moment from Black Malkin's ear. It was too great a distance to see the woman's face, but the set of the chin was unmistakable and Margaret almost loved her for what she did. Taking a spear from a nearby retainer she strode out unflinchingly into the battle, her head up, her cloak rushing like wings around her body, stone-stern like Athena, shrouded in black and gold. She whirled the spear above her head, savagely, gracefully, shouting a single, wordless cry.

The blue dragon whirled into the air and vanished like a blade dropped into the sheath. The horrible black spell sank back like hackles soothed on a dog's neck.

Black Malkin put her spear butt-down into the earth and looked levelly from one man to the other. "Ordinarily," she said acidly, "I would not have interfered, but our host Skander Rime informs me that urgent news has come and he demands the War-wolf's presence in the tent. In case you have need to know there is no foul play," she lifted her lip at Rupert, "you may come too."

But Rupert only slid in his sword at his side and folded his arms, content to stand and wait. With a jerk of his chin he told his brother off. Dammerung seemed to shrug and, raising his hand to Black Malkin, swept past her toward the tent's awning.

"Oh!" Margaret said, as if she had been stung. As if loosed from an enchantment she pushed her way through the crowd; some recognized her and gave way; some took one look at her face and recoiled from her path. In a few minutes she had circumnavigated the bowling green and was bending, thrusting back the heavy tent-flap, to straighten in the intense gloom within.

It took a moment for her eyes to adjust. There was a flicker of silver light as Dammerung, hearing her enter, turned toward her. His eyes seemed to glow blue. "There you are," he said frankly. Then, turning back toward someone else, "Well?"

Margaret saw a strange figure gather at the imperious voice. As the darkness swam in her eyes and settled into a rosy grey with little drifting sparks of orange on her vision, she saw him more clearly: a dusty, sweating figure, ashen-faced, out of place between the trim, clean bulk of Capys and the rich, red-lashed form that was the War-wolf.

"News, my lords," the panting messenger said shortly. "The border lords of Darkling send an appeal: Hol-land has attacked without provocation. Master has fallen; Castel-arreiol is besieged: de Montfort holds it yet, and he swears to hold it until his lord Darkling can come to him." The man looked from one face to the other. Something spasmed in his own; he swallowed as if about to be ill. "My lords...it is war."

Margaret put out her hand and found something—a chair, perhaps—on which to lean for support. The world felt ragged and sharp at the edges, and coming apart in fraying pieces. She could not see Skander's face—he was turned from her—but she could see Dammerung's, downturned, thoughtful, but not, she realized, very surprised.

"So this is his game," he mused at length. "Well played, Rupert. Well played." Then, to the messenger, "Your lord Darkling is among the crowd. Fetch him in and give him news. And stamp it with my name at the end of it."

A flicker of hope, even a sort of loving smile, wavered for a moment on the man's face. He saluted Dammerung and Skander and slipped out into the blaze of morning. For a moment, save for the blue-jay man in the shadows, the three of them were alone.

Skander let out a long, careful breath. "I could take his head between my hands and crush his skull," he said quietly, matter-of-factly.

"I had not looked for *this*," Dammerung admitted. "I had looked for a knife in my back, not a knife in Plenilune." Suddenly his face darkened, pained, and his hand spread as if he were about to fall and meant to catch himself. "War! He would unravel us, just to spite me! I never knew—I knew he hated me, but I never knew—good God, my Plenilune..." And he put up the hand over his face.

He was close. He had seemed far away and now, as he covered his terrible face, Margaret realized how close he stood to her in the interior of the tent. She put out her other hand—a long pianist's hand that had held him once when he was small—and clutched his shoulder, hard, shaking it a little...until she felt the purpose gather in the muscles under her palm, gather like a horse's flanks as it prepares to make the jump. He put down his hand a moment later, the angry brightness in his eyes as he met her gaze. But he seemed to see her for only a second or two, then to see something beyond her, through her, and gently he took himself out of her grip and pressed by her through the wind-shivered tent-flap. Inexorably pulled after him, Margaret stood at his shoulder in the opening, looking out on the scene of uneasy, murmuring folk and the distant blue haze of Seescarfell. She saw Rupert turn as if someone had called his name; across the distance she felt the two brothers lock eyes a moment, then Dammerung pointed, viciously, and slid his first two fingers down before his eyes in a morbid gesture.

You're dead.

Centurion came swiftly, never quite running, but eating up the ground with long strides; the crowd gave hurried way before him.

"What is this?" he demanded as he came up to Dammerung. "I am told Bloodburn has invaded Darkling."

"It's true," said Dammerung lightly. "Would someone—Tabby, would you inform Black Malkin that the duel is over, and why, and tell anyone who is anyone to come, if they have the stomach for it, to Capys and myself, for we mean to stand by Darkling."

Centurion set his hand on the blue-jay man's shoulder before he could go. The blue-jay man took one look at the lord's face, his own face darkened and disapproving, and deftly extricated himself from the beautiful hand. "Listen to me, Dammerung," said Centurion. "For your alliance and aid I am grateful, but I can handle my own. Let you handle this here. If this be left unfinished, what I do in Darkling will have no weight."

"You don't understand," said Skander flatly. "This *is* Rupert."

The fair face of Darkling's lord grew still, for a moment disbelieving, and then a black light of rage overswept it. He opened his mouth once as if to speak, and shut it again, teeth clicking, biting off his thoughts. It was a moment before he could say, quietly in lieu of the rage he could not vent,

"Then it is I who should lay my head at your feet and offer you my sword."

Dammerung shook his head slightly. "If in your hearts I am the Overlord—as I believe I must be—then Widowmaker and I are at your service and at the service of the lords of the Honours. Get you home and save your general. We will come to you shortly."

Centurion flew to the salute, the wind in his reddened sleeves, and was gone from them like a hawk from the hand. The wind felt cold on Margaret's bare skin; she tucked her arms around herself in an effort to keep warm, but it was a coldness, she realized, too deep for a superficial remedy.

"To think," said Skander in the quiet, "the Honours were once hailed as the fatherland of peace."

Dammerung smiled mirthlessly at his cousin, and in so doing his gaze fell on Margaret shivering with the taste of fear in her mouth. "I am sweaty and bloody and in no fit state to receive anyone," he said. "Give me a moment for a plunge and splash about and time to slip into a new set of clothing. I will see you all again—"

"The study will do."

"—In the study. Margaret?"

She gathered up her whirling skirts. "I am coming."

They walked back toward the garden. Margaret could feel the eyes of scores of people on the back of her neck and she felt the overwhelming urge to run, to run and hide. An inexplicable pall fell across her. Like a little girl she felt the need to cry and she hated herself for that. Dammerung's face beside her was oddly serene—unhappy, but serene. *Why can I not face this that way?* she asked herself angrily. *How many are there of us against Rupert? He cannot hope to win. This is foolishness.*

But he is so serious about it. Perhaps it is not foolishness. What do I know? My world was beginning to be something clear, something steady. I had air and I could burn brightly. Why did providence have to come and kick my embers? Is that kind? Is that merciful? Is that just?

I should not say such things. What do I know?

God, I just want to crawl into a small place and hide.

It was the cowardice of the notion that she hated so much. It was the slip of white feather, silent and softly blown, that had settled where her heart ought to be, that she hated so much. She had once despised a little fox for that same notion. Even with Rupert, she realized, looking back, life had been certain: dismal, but certain. Now the brightness of her life lay scattered and sizzling out, and the dark loomed fathomless before her. There was only Dammerung, and even he—she looked at him, and a sudden panic prompted her to say,

"The wind has blown me. I will go up and tidy while you wash."

The sound of her voice seemed to recall him from his thoughts. He turned toward her at the foot of the sunroom stairs. She had not got a clear glimpse of the right of his face until now: the brow had been broken open and a great winging of blood swept back into his hair and pooled in the contours of his ear. It was a ghastly visage and sent a shudder through her nerves.

"Oh, of course," he said, unaware of how horrible he looked. "Your hair looks as if something has tried to nest in it. Keep the dress?"

"I—" She hesitated. "It seems a little garish for the occasion now, don't you think?"

"Well, if you can find anyone to help you out of it, the more power to you. A bit of sun, however, would not go amiss in this hour, is my opinion."

It would be easier to let it lie—and to look like Black Malkin in all her funereal black would be to wear her heart upon her sleeve. The English in her refused to be so transparent. She left him, not realizing until later that she had not said another word. She heard his single step, as if to come after her, but that was all. She found her room and slipped inside, lost in the eastern blow of wind and light and shadow, feeling the wind and light and shadow blow about inside of her. Staring at the neatly arranged bedstead and prim white dressing table washed in a delicate rose light, the core of her hardened bitterly.

I was wrong. We are more than half pain and the legends die so quickly.

Knowing she was succumbing to a nihilistic attitude, knowing she ought to be happy Dammerung was alive, she moved numbly through the motions of combing her hair and putting it to rights. Aikaterine was absent; after a tussle with pins, which would not obey, and the wind that was coming through the open lattice-work window, she finally gave up and left her hair was it was, curled and flowing and a richer brown than it had been before. It would do. She did not like it, but it would do.

With a sigh she fixed a string of golden pearls about her neck, wondering if perhaps she had left the space too open before, and matched it with earrings. Small-seeming and dark-hearted, but unable to keep away, she left her room and went in search of Dammerung.

She found him alone in the study. She had meant to join him—when was she herself with anyone else?—but when she stepped into the doorway and saw him, she was struck by a paralyzing uncertainty. He was seated at the desk, the light falling on his back, working studiously at a letter. He seemed oblivious to the world. He seemed, in that brief instant, normal; and that normality slapped her in the face like mockery. For the first time she felt shy of him, and after the shyness came a powerful wave of fear. She remembered that he had been a fox, a talking fox—*that* had turned her world on end—and she remembered the unexpectedness of it, the horror she had felt, completely unprepared, when she had discovered he had turned into a wolf. He had turned into a man again and that, too, had startled her. Vividly over the present picture she saw him stripped for a duel, shining white, hurtling the blades of his heart and soul like sky-fire through the air. What might he do next, she wondered, and might there come a time when he so changed that she would no longer know him at all?

With a cold shock of blood she realized he had turned and was looking at her, and had been for at least a full minute. She did not want to meet that pale, worried gaze, those eyes which had seen her unguarded fear, but she found she could not look away.

"Why, Margaret," he said softly after an uneasy quiet, "I am still not dead. You need not look at me as if I were a ghost."

"Oh," she groaned, almost inaudibly. She could look away then, and she dropped her gaze to the floor. She felt trapped and she wanted to run, but she did not know where to go—to whom would she go?—and she wanted him to do the impossible: to tell her nothing had happened and that the world was all the same.

His voice touched her gently. Was that a trick of his too, that he could turn his voice as if it were his hand, and touch hard or lightly as he chose?

"Tell me what is troubling you."

The thoughts bunched and clotted in her throat, all of them struggling to come out at once, none of them coming at all. Her hands had clenched into fists: she could feel the nails biting into her palms which were still sore from the tension of the duel. Finally she said, desperately, the smallest, truest thing she felt:

"I am afraid of you."

His hand dropped the pen and pushed the paper aside—it smeared, but he did not notice. His chair turned toward her. He was on the edge of it, poised as if to rise, but he stayed where he was, hanging in the balance. His hand moved as if to take something from her. She was afraid of him, but more than that she was afraid she had made him angry. A part of her mind warred with her, telling her that it was stupid to be afraid of *him*: when had he ever given her cause to fear him? Yet beneath the sun-browned skin, behind those wall-pale eyes, she had seen a power that seemed able to crack Plenilune itself in two.

There was no anger in his voice when he finally spoke. She had expected him to protest at once, but for a long while he sat in complete silence. When he spoke his voice was gentle but firm, as if he were arranging some small, precious object toward which he was tender, something which, once it was set, no power could remove.

"There is no spell or word of power in the smallest crevice of my soul," he said, "that could do you any harm."

She shuddered; her eyes crushed out a single tear, and as she felt it slide down her cheek she whispered, "*Damn*," because she wished it had not got out.

His thumb brushed roughly across her cheek. Startled, she opened her eyes to find he had crossed the room and, frowning, was flicking the bead-bright tear off his finger. "Do not you fall apart now," he admonished. "They are due here any minute."

"I am not falling apart," she protested. "I feel sick, that is all."

"Don't we all."

Sniffing, brushing her hand across her face, she noticed for the first time that his face was clean and the bust in the brow was noticeably missing. "What happened to you? Your face was all over blood a moment ago."

He evaded deftly. "I told you I heal quickly. Hark! their tread in the hall."

Turning quickly, Margaret could hear the hard step of boots on the stair and the tile pavers of the hallway. She smoothed her cheeks and her skirts and ran back to Dammerung's side as he stole Skander's seat at the desk. He laughed at her, briefly, then settled back into the chair like a raja.

Except for Aikin Ironside, who looked unruffled and almost pleasant, the faces of the men who came in behind Skander were grim to a fault. Surely even Rupert, thought Margaret, if he could have seen them so, would have balked at the thought of meeting them head on in a pitched battle. But, looking past Aikin Ironside's face to his father's, she heard the man's words ring black in her ears: *"De la Mare is a man who will dare all things."*

"This is not as you had expected," said Mark Roy's eldest son. He slipped off his heavily embroidered cloak and let it fall on the back of a chair.

Dammerung rose instinctively as the three Thrasymene ladies—Woodbird drifting close to Skander's side—came into view. "No," he said, "not quite. Have you all been brought abreast of the events?"

"That Hol-land has unfairly invaded a brother Honour while that lord was away from home? We have been brought abreast of that." Mark Roy folded himself up in a sense of thunder and spice like the dragons threaded into his cloak. "It has been three generations and one since the Honours were in the habit of warring among themselves. The scars of those years are silvered almost to nothing. And Rupert? Is he behind this? I would have taken it on intuition had you not stopped the duel altogether."

"Are you very surprised?" Dammerung smiled.

The dragon-lord shook his head. "Nay, not so."

His eldest son interrupted him gently. Smiling sidelong and tenderly at his sire, he added, "Not so. An' you would stand—just so—over the balcony, over Orzelon-gang bathed in sunset, and wonder aloud, half to yourself, half, perhaps, to heaven, how long would the scars have to lie silver before they were opened red again?"

Mark Roy's brow flickered. "I had hoped they would lie silvered beyond my lifetime."

"But you did not really believe it," prompted the War-wolf.

"But I did not really believe it."

Margaret, speaking impulsively, added, "They have been red, I think, for awhile now."

They all looked at her save Dammerung, who had his hand flat upon the desk and was looking at the paleness of the knuckles—but even he, with his mind, was looking at her: she felt it. She felt with sudden keenness her foreign birth and her stomach clenched, willing them to accept her, to not look at her as they were looking, with the shadow of Rupert's attention fallen across her face.

It was Dammerung who saved her. Without raising his head he said, clearly, "So they have... Did any of you really think, when I appeared in Thwitandrake, that I had sprung back from the grave?" He lifted his head and looked them each in the eye, hard, with eyes like bared and snarling teeth. "I am whole. I bleed: I am no ghost. It was a great and bitter lie you were made to swallow when the world was told I died the day I was going to fetch young Brand the Hammer to hunt. I did not die. It was the day Rupert cut open the first of Plenilune's old scars."

There was a terrible stillness and silence among them. They were all listening to his words and to the fanciful illusions of horror in their minds. But Lord Gro—who seemed, of them all, to have least to do with illusions—said presently, "What did he do, and where did you go?"

"He made to kill me with a spell, and I made to live with another one," said Dammerung simply. Interest and indignation, but no real shock, Margaret noted, kindled in their faces. "These past two years and more I have whiled away in my own wine-cellar, bound by Rupert's variously compiled enchantments—while he studied to kill me good and soundly—until Lady Margaret came and sprang me free." He looked round on her with a smile, a smile with a touch of bitterness and remembered pain at the edges that she knew only she would understand. "Seems fitting, don't you think, that he and I should lie at the centre of all these newly-opened wounds?"

Margaret looked down at the tabletop. "Yes, Dammerung. I hope that warms his heart at night, knowing that."

"Shuh!" he laughed. "And now you know," he told the rest, "what is really going on at the heart of all this, and why I called off the duel when I did, and why it is so serious a thing that we should rally to our brother Honour's aid. Against Hol-land, Darkling will have need of you. Against Rupert," he spread his hands, "you will have need of me."

"I foresee this being an unruly war," said Mark Roy, staring off into the middle distance. Margaret glanced at him: whatever he saw there seemed to disturb him.

Skander moved toward the desk as if he meant to displace his cousin. "I will call together my lords and arms. We should be assembled at Ryland within three days—two, perhaps, for I think I should leave someone on the border in case the Carmarthen choose to poke a finger in my defences. Dammerung, do you have any insight into getting us all to Darkling? Rupert and the greater bulk of Hol stands squarely in our way."

"By main force and ride-by-night," replied the War-wolf. "It is indeed an unruly position. But if we meet Black Malkin—madam—at Wossen and push from there into Hol, I think we will do passably. Centurion was right: he can handle Bloodburn, though it will be a messy, dragged-out business I should as lief avoid. If we can hard press Bloodburn's northern defences so that he must relieve them with troops from his invading army, we may even the balance in Centurion's favour."

"And Rupert?" asked Skander.

Dammerung looked at the sheet of paper under his hand. "Rupert will be wherever I am: a strange, dualistic fate we share, he and I..."

"And Margaret?"

Me? She looked up from the fine, flecked hand on the desk. With a pang of fear she realized for the first time what she should have always known: as a woman she was not expected to go, but to wait patiently at Lookinglass until news came back from the lines. Good or ill, she would have to wait for it, and the terror of being left behind—of Dammerung leaving her behind—dried her mouth to cotton.

But Dammerung suddenly pushed off from the desk and stood aside for his cousin. "What, Lady Spitcat? She is my shoulder-to-shoulder man." He whirled, wing-sleeves fluttering, and strode toward the door as if all were over, calling back as he did so, "She comes with me."

He disappeared. The bare padding faded away and Margaret was left blushing furiously, still sick from fear, under the awkward scrutiny of the assembly. For a long while it was quiet, then someone shifted and Mark Roy, clearing his throat, said graciously,

"Capys, we should see to a horse and mule for Lady—Margaret."

Skander smiled apologetically at her. "Tabby, see to Mausoleum's tack and ask Jacland if I cannot have the loan of his mule. His is pretty well tempered, isn't it?"

"Yes, sir."

Aikin Ironside spoke up. "I mean no disrespect to her ladyship," he said in a level, lazy voice, "but I don't consider a battle-field a suitable place for a woman with no military training, on various accounts. Furthermore—" his warm, half-laughing eyes fixed on hers with a stark, shared memory "—ought she to be roughing it?"

Before Margaret could form an equally respectful defence—because the young man was right in all his objections—Skander cut into the gap with a mirthless laugh that was characteristic of his family and retorted,

"*She* has been roughing it with de la Mare this past autumn. She is old hat at this."

Like one saluting, graciously admitting defeat, Aikin Ironside put up his brows and bent his head to her. "Yes, I see that, when you put it that way. Your pardon, Lady Margaret. You are a veteran among us. And for whatever it is worth—for you have the War-wolf as your guardian shadow—please accept my allegiance. It may be I am good for more than boar-hunting—it may be not."

The others smiled approvingly, as if they, too, were offering her the same words. The sweetness of it, the open-handed acceptance they were offering her without a backward glance or sting of misgiving—for which, if they had any, she would not have blamed them—touched her heart so sharply she felt it bleed. Dammerung was not here to laugh her out of it. Swallowing, she took hold of her skirts and bent her knee until it was brushing the carpet. She could not meet their gazes.

"These are your Honours and your war, my lords. If anyone is to offer allegiance, I should offer you mine—for what it is worth. I only hope to be worthy of your approval."

In the quiet she could hear Dammerung down below—walking, by the sound of it—singing a Te Deum as he went, and singing it remarkably well.

XXIII | AMPERSAND

Rain was going to break. The rolling hill country and valley-land of Ampersand, which wedged itself between Hol-land and Thrasymene at the pinch-point of the fells and sea, was overshadowed by a furious tiger sky, brindled and heavy with fire and clouds. There was salt in the air, but the sea, which Margaret had not seen, lay beyond the next range of hills. What must it look like, she wondered, under the wings of this seraphic sky? Her mind wandered back to the summers of Aylesward when the sky at night was a long twilight, and the ocean a rolling expanse of living mercury-glass. How much more beautiful would it look here!

She shivered with the cool breeze that was coming on with evening and comfortably folded her arms around herself, achy in body but glad to be off her horse at last and pitching a more permanent tent. That tomorrow the Honour-lords meant to wet their swords on Bloodburn's first northern defence did not yet concern her. In the little wood on the western side of the valley a nightingale was tuning up, and the cooking-fires of the whole camp sent up a blue haze of warmth and thin tranquillity over the roaring sky.

Without warning Dammerung tore past her in a flutter of massive black cloak and intent face, soundless on his bare feet but for the soft, muffled booming of thrown-about fabric. She watched him sprint across the grass for Rubico: in one fluid bound he was astride the horse, and the horse must have seen him coming for it was in motion almost before Dammerung left the ground. The effect was a confused, dark, water-smooth image of kinetic bodies that was both beautiful and oddly awful. Dammerung bolted from the makeshift green and disappeared among the pine-gloom and gold blaze of sunset. A moment or two longer the splutter of hoofbeats came back to Margaret, then the pine-wood hush fell in again as though it had never been disturbed.

"Three riders there are in all Plenilune none other man born of woman can match..."

Margaret turned and ducked into the tent, but paused in the entryway. Skander was there at the table, his broad frame fitted gingerly into a camp chair which was long past its prime. A lamp was burning at his elbow, but it was not quite dark enough for it.

"Where has Dammerung gone?" she asked.

"He has gone scouting."

She frowned. "Do you not have Scouting Masters for that kind of thing?"

"Yes," admitted Skander absentmindedly. He searched among the papers for something. "And Dammerung has colourful words for them." He left off searching, somewhat exasperatedly, and met her eye. "He's a man who likes to see things with his own eyes."

A dreadful moodiness settled over her, partly because she felt out of place without Dammerung and partly because—though she hated to admit it—she wished she had gone too. So, petulantly, she refrained from pointing out to Skander that Dammerung was a man who seemed able to see things without his eyes. She watched for some time in silence as he continued to paw among the littered table until, unable to bear it any longer, she strode across, snatched a wax-stick from the inside of a tumbler, and handed it to him.

"Ah." He took it from her. "Much obliged."

Dinner that evening was roast venison and roast potatoes and roast onions, and a sweet yellow wine—which Margaret liked and Skander did not—and Dammerung did not come back until after it. There was a soft splutter of hooves in the distance—which was nothing unusual, as horses and horsemen had been going about ever since they had set up camp—and silence. A moment later Dammerung came flying through the tent flap, shedding his muddied cloak as he came, and flung himself down in a chair. It rocked violently onto its hind legs before thumping back to ground again. Margaret was sharpening a knife, because it was something useful to do and because the *si-i-ing si-i-ing* of the blade gave her a fierce, blood-coloured feeling, but she looked up as Dammerung's poor chair creaked to stillness. There was mud splattered on Dammerung's cheek and a streak up the back of his head, and his feet were black with pine-muck. He looked as though he had ridden far and hard, but he seemed cheerful enough.

"Have you eaten?" she asked.

Sing! sing! sing! said the knife.

"Eh?" He turned a languid, rampant brow her way.

"I wondered if you had broke your fast."

"Shoo!" He heaved himself upright by his elbows and the arms of his chair. "No. Is there aught else to eat? I smell the ghost of supper gone but see no apparition of it."

She said "Hm!" and put aside the knife and whetstone. She had enjoined the blue-jay man to set aside some roast against Dammerung's return and she fetched it from the board. He smiled beatifically at her and the plate as she set it down before him—but she saw in the eyes behind the smile that he was tired.

"Do you want red wine or white?"

"Red! Naturally."

As she fetched and poured the wine, she wondered what he would think of her for liking the sweet yellow vintage. She poured herself her own glass of red—it was an awkward business, she thought, sitting and watching someone eat without anything to eat for oneself—and joined him with the glasses. He raised his to her, then for a long time the only sounds in the tent were the tinselly crackle of the apple-wood fire—more for light and the comfort of the thing than for necessary warmth—and the clink of glass and silverware. A horse screamed angrily on the fellside: the sharp sound echoed in the hollow of the night. A horn sang out and Margaret jumped, but Dammerung said,

" 'Tis only the change of watch."

He finished his supper and they finished their wine. The dishes they left for the blue-jay man to see to, and while Dammerung retired to one side of the tent to wash the flying muck off his face, Margaret moved her chair to the tent opening and sat on the rim of the firelight, looking out on the night from the golden, feathery comfort of the enclosure.

Night had fallen low over the land. It seemed to have heaped up so heavily in the sky, rolling in off the sea, that it was sinking under its own weight, groaning lower and lower over the fells. She sat wrapped in a fine surcoat of doeskin and ermine, for the summer night was growing chill and the hushing rush of wind in the rowan-wood bore portents of rain, and watched the dark moth-wing dusk gather about them and the firefly-lights spring out of the black. The nightingale was still calling across the camp, sweetly and bewilderedly, and in the southwest there was a lingering primrose-glow of earthlight which would soon burn away to black with the turn of the world.

My world, thought Margaret, and she dug her toes in her boots as if to grip the grass under foot.

There was a soft step beside her and Dammerung was there, clean, cast in gold and black, looking out, as she did, over the firelit dalescape. His hand dropped on her shoulder, heavy and still, sinking down through the ermine collar to rest against the soft warmth of her skin: his fingers felt cold. She looked up into his face once, but he was looking in a far-off way over all, far off enough to see into tomorrow—had she not meant to tell Skander such?—so she settled in under his hand and continued to watch the way the lights lay scattered like kicked embers down the valley. The sounds of shadows blew fitfully around them. The southwest was quenched: the mounting storm clouds lay black and close above them.

"There is rain in the wind tonight," said Margaret presently.

"Yes."

She turned her head toward him but did not look up. From where she sat she could see down the Prime Horse picket-line, long faces and warm bodies all in a row, ruddy and alabaster in the torchlight. "Will there be rain in the morning?"

He stirred, then, and sighed, as if wherever his thoughts had taken him had too little air. "No; we'll have a storm-song tonight and a sword-song tomorrow. This should be fair blown over by dawn."

"It seems fair big to me," Margaret replied with an involuntary shiver.

His thumb and middle finger tightened their grip. "They are all monsters, our fell country storms, but this is only a mad cat which will yowl and spit and run away soon." He was quiet for a moment and in the silence the wind swelled with silvery noise.

"Keep your chin up, leman. Not long now."

He did not say it condescendingly: he meant it, and somehow it was more comforting than even her soft doeskin surcoat. But she felt compelled to say, honestly, "I am not afraid, Dammerung."

"Have you come past that, then?"

His voice was suddenly sharp with bitterness. She started at the sudden change of tone—but then he changed his tone faster than a woman changed her mind: it would be gone in a moment. "Are *you* afraid?" she countered.

He turned to her, eyebrows flyaway as if with surprise. The bitterness was gone again and the firelight was turning his eyes silver-pale. "Afraid? Of pain?"

"I suppose that is what I mean. What is death? It is pain, not death, that we have to live with."

His mouth quirked. "Nay, then, I am not afraid. It takes a braver man than I to fear pain. *I* am just a fool."

There was the bitterness again, the veil parting slightly to let past grievances peep through. How these men were defined by their glories and their insults! She looked away and sighed as a pigeon sighs at the start of a long wet evening. "Dammerung, sometimes you laugh and there is no laughter in it."

His hand upon her shoulder had been heavy and companionable, as it might lie on Skander's, but unexpectedly it left and took hold of her chin, turning her to face him. The pale eyes, so pale as almost to be clear, gazed hard and laughingly, mockingly, into her own. She had learned to meet that gaze lightly and even tried to read what was in his face.

"Yes," he said at last, and gently let her go. "I see why he chose you."

He did not wait for her answer: he went back into the tent and she rose, puzzled, turning away from the flickering vision of the north where the lightning was beginning to break up in the clouds to see what Dammerung was about to do. One always knew when he was about to do something: he gathered a brooding aura about himself like a cloak—and in it there was always a bit of fierce laughter that was like mockery—and she felt that aura about him now.

He got down on one knee before a trunk and flung back the lid of it. There was little light in that corner of the tent and he rummaged for some time seemingly by feel, until at last he unearthed what looked, in the light, to be a bodice made of moulded leather, quite hard and plain, which he held out to her. "Of your courtesy," he said, "I would be obliged if you would wear this tomorrow."

"You do not expect me to fight," she said, staring at the thing with a real thrill of horror that, for some bizarre reason, he did.

"No; on my honour, I would not have you fight. 'Twould not be sporting fair not to give the foe an even chance." He hefted the bodice closer toward her. "Yet I have some notion that you ought to wear it, and I have learned not to deny my intuitions."

She put her arm through both arm-holes and felt it drag, though not as much as she had expected it would. Meeting his eyes, she wondered what he saw, or whether it was the mere whim of feeling which prompted him to offer the armour to her. But something held her back from asking.

"You will wear it?"

She pulled it close. "Of course I will wear it. And thank you," she added, hoping it did not sound so much like the afterthought that it was.

He turned away, smiling as if to himself. "And sure you would have done the same for me. To bed with you, Lady Spitcat. Tomorrow brings many awful and new things for you."

"And for you?"

He turned at her question, slowly, and there was not a trace of laughter or mockery in his eyes as they met hers. He knew what she was thinking: they were both thinking it. Tomorrow, more awfully than when they had faced off for their duel, Rupert and Dammerung would pit themselves against each other. It had been dreadful before, for it had been kin-blood and, in a sense, an inner quarrel with Plenilune looking on. Now it was war, with Plenilune blood laid on the line, Plenilune lives taking Plenilune lives. And all because of Dammerung. All because of Rupert.

It must be awful, thought Margaret, to carry that weight.

He reached out and gripped her upper arm, again as he might grip Skander, and shook it a little, hard. "Good hunting, Margaret."

She smiled wanly for him. "Good hunting."

He let her go and returned to his chair where he sat, broodingly, looking off goodness alone knew where. She watched him a moment longer before breaking away, and ducked between the heavy hangings into the rear part of the tent which was her chamber. She pulled the hangings to, propped the leather bodice against her trunk, and, disrobing, crawled into her bed. It was stuffy in the tiny room; the lamp-smoke made a fine blue haze on a blurred backdrop of gold and ruddy shadow, and though the storm-wind buffeted the sides of the tent, little draught leaked in to disturb the heavy atmosphere. Her heart began to quicken in spite of herself. Rolling over, settling into the pillows, she did her best not to think about tomorrow nor Dammerung's awful, distant face.

Three quarters of an hour later the storm had broken over the fellside. It roared and gusted and brought down hasty, light sprays of rain, and Margaret dozed to the sound of it. It was more sound than rain, and it was pleasant to be cosy and dry while, on the other side of thick canvas, the fell country cat howled dismally, unable to touch her. She did not know afterward if she dreamed it or not—she was so close to being asleep—but she fancied once that the hangings parted and a figure that she though was familiar, but had darkness where its face should have been, stood in the opening, looking down at her. It was only a confused image. She did not remember when it came or when it passed, or if it was real or not. When she woke in the morning the nightingale was singing and the sound of the storm had ceased.

Aikaterine had been and gone. The chamber was arranged, her gown from yesterday folded and stowed, her gown for today draped over the trunk. As she sat up, rubbing absently at her eyes, Margaret saw her articles laid out in a perfect row on the little table that served as her vanity: cosmetics, brushes, hairpins, jewels, as if she were, not at camp, but at Lookinglass. She thought she was meant to be comforted, but the juxtaposition of the articles with their surroundings made the camp world only starker.

What time was it? She had slept through any sound of watch change. The hangings were so dark that they let no light through; her lamp was so low that it cast only a thin light over the room. Deliberately she swung out of bed, flinging back the rugs that served as her blankets. The air was not of a nighttime cold, but there was still a chilliness lingering underfoot. It must be dawn, or past it. With swift strides Margaret crossed to the vanity and sat down, pulling the brush through her hair and, giving it a twist as Aikaterine had taught her, secured it in place with the heavy ornamental comb. The matched garnets of her earrings and heavy tiered necklace winked back in the glowering light at the red-moon curve of the comb.

Still in her shift she rose and, with a feeling of dark foreboding, fitted herself into the leather bodice. Her shift kept it from sticking and chafing on her skin; it was a little too tight, but that was better, she thought, than it being too large and unwieldy. She ran a quick, appraising eye over it in the little mirror and thought it looked ghastly plain next to the lavish sparkle of her jewels. Hastily she flung overtop of it the silk gown of scarlet and gold stamp-work that gathered and flowed and purred in the lamplight, and with that the picture was perfect But oh! the silk was cold, and it was odd to feel the weight of leather—unlike whale-bone, to which she was accustomed—pressing her body in all over. With some delicate manoeuvring she managed to put on her boots; it did not help that she was hurrying, hoping that Dammerung would have woken her if things had begun already. Finally she got the last loop of cord through the last loop of metal, tied off the cords and, though she had told Dammerung last night that she was not afraid, she could not deny the horrid clenching of her chest—which had nothing to do with the bodice—as she thrust back the hangings and stepped into the fore part of the tent.

There she stopped, hesitating with her arm still out to hold back the curtain, on the outskirts looking on.

Skander was up and had joined them; he was bent over the scarred table looking at a topographic map, his brows furrowed, a piece of bacon sheeny with grease in one hand. He had not noticed her—or, at any rate, he had not yet acknowledged her—and she got a good impression of his likeness in that moment. He was dressed in the rich earthy colours of red and brown, rather simply, with a quilted leather jerkin and leather reinforcements over the most stressed part of his clothing. She marked that his current gear suited him better than his New Ivy finery: his frame was more at home and looked far more fetching in bullhide and broadcloth than in silks and silver thread. But though he was dressed simply, he was heavily armed. An ornately acid-etched battleaxe hung like a gibbous moon over one shoulder, gleaming milky and dark-iron in the dim morning light. A two-handed sword hung with it, and the long cavalry sword Gram swung at his hip. He had a crop and knife on his opposite side, and pouches and daggers and what looked like small cattle-trops hanging from his belt. Every way he turned light caught fire on hilt and buckle and worn silvered wolf-skin. She shivered with cold apprehension and turned away.

Dammerung was nearly finished: he was just fastening the last toggle of his tunic at his shoulder. He did not wear white today. He wore a light tunic of silk with a complicated tea-green and tea-brown pattern over a quilted leather jerkin like Skander's. His breeches, too, were backed with leather where a long day in the saddle was liable to chafe. He turned—bits of gold thread woven into the tunic sparked in the mirror—and picked up from a table a claymore like Skander's, which he fitted over one shoulder and under the other arm at his back. To the claymore he added, not one, but two short swords; he settled Widowmaker in an honourable place at his left side and checked over a number of knives on his person.

He examined the entirety in the mirror and seemed satisfied, then he caught sight of her watching him. He turned sharply round. For a moment he looked her over. His eyes dropped for a fraction of a second below what, had he been anyone else, Margaret would have considered couth: he marked that she wore the leather bodice. A smile jerked at his mouth and the bitter, half-laughing wing-lines flashed round his eyes as they jumped back to her face. "Good morrow."

"You are wearing a lot of weapons," she replied. "Is it not very heavy?"

"He has a tendency to break things," said Skander without looking up.

Margaret looked from him to Dammerung again.

The War-wolf touched his trunk smartly with one toe: the lid crashed down and the latch clicked to. "True an' I hit hard: you could fill an armoury with the blades I have broken. Only Widowmaker has survived me."

Margaret surveyed his arms but there was not much to see for the long, loose silk sheaves that were his sleeves. He was not big and muscular like his cousin, but she did not doubt the image of him breaking an axe in two while shearing through buckler and bone.

Skander's voice cut aptly through her thoughts. "Dammerung, must I insist?"

Dammerung only smiled and did not let his gaze waver from her. "Nay, Lady Spitcat is all one for this, isn't she? Not a blanch on that cheek, coz—look at it!"

"I am not inclined to look at ladies' cheeks," muttered his cousin.

The grey-blue eyes danced. "After all, what is death?"

What is death? Last night she had not been afraid, not of death nor really of pain. This morning she was worried about pain and, had it not been for that single stark moment just before bed last night in which she and Dammerung had looked into each other's eyes and seen the shared horror in them of what was happening in Plenilune, she might still flick death a careless hand. Now it was different. Now it meant something: not for her, not for him, but for what was left behind.

"It is a damned inconvenience to the rest of us," she said. The words came so quick out of her mouth they surprised even herself.

Like a falcon bating, his brows flickered upward. "Yes," he mused. "I thought so too at the time."

Skander opened his mouth as if to speak, seemed to think better of it, and smoothed his own feathers. "I go to rally before the mists lift," he said, rolling up the map and stepping toward the tent opening. "If you have need of me you'll find me where the ravens thicken."

"I'll look for you among the spears," Dammerung said with a click and a flash of one ringed hand in salute. When Skander was gone he turned to Margaret. "You have not eaten. Are you hungry?"

"No," she replied truthfully. She could not dream of eating. All her insides, she found, had gone wrong and felt more like cold lumps inside her skin against which her heart pounded with a sickening heat.

She was grateful that he did not look sympathetic. "You will be," he told her uncompromisingly. "I give it five minutes before Mark Roy and Lord Gro come up. There are nuts and fruit on the table there: best scarf while you have time and before we have to be on our best behaviour. I'll join you."

They sat in comparative silence and ate the strawberries and blueberries and nuts that Aikaterine had brought up. The bacon was gone, but the heady scent lingered heavily on the air and made Margaret nauseated. She ate gamely and numbly. She would have liked to have asked Dammerung questions about how he thought the day would go forward, but she found that not only did she not know enough about war to ask, she did not want to pester him. He seemed lost in thought, eating mechanically, fetching her on occasion a brief glance, and at another moment twisting suddenly to look out the tent-flap. But he did not seem concerned, and that comforted her.

It was precisely five minutes, and just when Margaret felt she could not safely swallow another bite, when the entryway darkened and Mark Roy's short, broad figure cast a watery shadow on the ground. He stepped in and Lord Gro ducked in behind him.

"You've come," said Dammerung frankly, and gestured to Skander's vacant chair and a battered stool.

"We've come," Mark Roy replied lightly. The two men bowed to Margaret and took their seats. "The mists are still lying low," the king went on. "What do you make of the lie of our foe?"

Dammerung's lip curled upward in a playful smile. "I think it a pretty lie, but an old one. Nay, what—the lie? He holds the dalemouth like a boar and backs up the fellsides so that he has height and downward speed for his ally. We have that here, but we must stretch ourselves to meet in the middle." He turned again and peered outside. There was not much to see: from their height they had a view over the picket-line and the top of the next tent down, and then nothing but a beautiful steel-blue swimming of dawn air and the huge blurred bulk of the next hill over. "You are right about the mists. The war-dogs will have sport today."

Margaret shivered.

Mark Roy said, "Gro wants especially to pair with Lifoy. There is some matter between them, it seems, that needs finishing."

"Oh?"

Put on the spot, with Dammerung's inquisitive eye lying lightly upon him, Gro clenched his lips in a thin line and looked, for a moment, as if he meant to politely bow out of explaining. Margaret liked him and she felt sore on his account for Mark Roy singling him out. But a moment later he lifted one hand, as if the explanation lay in the palm of it, and said frankly, "There was some quarrel between him and my lady, and the wound has never closed."

"So you choose rather to make it mortal," said Dammerung without any tone of disapproval. "They say hell hath no fury like a woman scorned but I find sending flowers to a man scorned lacks any potency. Still," he smiled, "I think she made a good choice, your lady. You may have the field before Lifoy. And God help his soul."

Lord Gro nodded wordlessly and Dammerung turned to Mark Roy. "I hope you have no especial place to be because I need you to take Aikin and Brand under your wings. Aikin—I don't mind where he be, but Brand has the makings of Achilles and I would rather him bang about where you can keep an eye on him."

Mark Roy looked troubled. "He had hoped to run among your pack, my lord."

"Well I know it," said Dammerung gently, "but when last I was to let him run among my pack I had a man have his guts torn out at ten yards by the Man of Blood down yonder. Brand is fierce—

too fierce as yet: Plenilune has more need of him than of his corpse."

"On that score, my lord, we are well agreed."

Margaret carefully tucked her arms up close, for her skin was beginning to be cold and she did not want Dammerung to know. He knew, though: she caught his sidewise glance at her face and downward over her arms, but he looked almost faster than thought and no one caught it but herself.

"Is that all?"

"Unless you have more for us, that is all. I think we know our places."

Dammerung rose and clasped Mark Roy by the forearm. "God's grace to you, my lord," he said warmly. "I trust my back to you."

"I will be at your shoulder. Gro—"

The two went away again, ducking out into the thin yellow light, and it struck Margaret that it was almost time.

"Yes," said Dammerung, as if she had spoken her thought. "Very soon now, before the day is old. We must have time to tidy up before supper."

She shut her eyes and smiled. "Always you are so glib."

"Life is war," he replied lightly. "When you have grasped that you learn to hold life loosely between your fingers, ready to drain away like sand upon the shore. You have long since counted the cost. You are always ready to give up your life, always ready to give a defence. The glibness," he added introspectively, "is a soldier's kind of courage."

"I know. I have been at this war awhile now: which is what I meant when I told the men in Lookinglass that Plenilune's old scars have been red for some time. But the glibness does not come to me: I grow afraid, and then angry—"

"Because you are afraid?" he asked clairvoyantly.

"Yes, I think so. Because I am afraid. And then the anger sharpens my tongue and I say things so beautifully and I nearly...get myself killed..."

"Hmm!" He felt about his person, clinking and throwing off sparks of green and yellow light. "You and I are alike in that also. We will bury ourselves in our own mouths." He slipped out a knife and passed it to her. It lay flesh-warm in her palm, shaped like part of a shark's tail, and slick with silver light. "I have to go now," he said, "and this time I can't take you with me."

She gripped the hilt and hung it at her side. "Don't worry about me," she said flatly. "When you are down there between death and the next man's blade, don't spare a thought for me. You won't have time for it. I will handle myself if there needs to be any handling."

"I believe it!" He rapped his knuckles on her shoulder where the hardened leather lay, giving off a sweet, nutty sound, and with a jink of light and metal he ducked out without a look back. She was glad for that. She followed him to the tent entryway and watched him fling himself astride Rubico and trot away, dark plumed tail adrift in the mist.

"Hmm, hmm, hmm... Hmm, hm-hm, hmm..." she began idly. A pheasant rocketed from the hillside and scolded as it banked hard and disappeared toward the south. The sleek form of the agouti warhorse and its glib master the War-wolf slipped through the blue haze of mist and camp-fires. Soft, spluttering thunder seemed to well out from him as he made his way through the soldiers to the division of Horse which he would command. A smile bloomed impulsively on her lips. "Beneath the skies of hueless make—" she began huskily.

> Through tigery midsummer's brake,
> Wi' hoofbeats and the thunder-quake,
> Through swimming heat, the air a-shake,
> Rode down the Hawthorn Moon.
> Beneath the skies the dales a-teem
> Wi' horses and the trumpet's scream;
> And on his fell brow an argent gleam:
> The Lord of Plenilune.

She could see Aikin and Brand riding out together, Brand looking like a shard of sunlight and Aikin with his dark hair spiked and dyed red at the ends. She lifted her hand to salute them, as she had once almost done for Centurion, and, as before, caught herself—but she laughed impulsively and turned, leaving the tent to walk across the hillside to an open place where she could watch what went on below. Where the pine-wood thinned she found a bit of flat earth with a convenient tumble of rocks to sit on. Cold, bare seeming under the blank blue sky, she settled on a rock speckled with lichen like a peewit's egg, pulled her knees up to her chest, and rested her chin on her knees.

She found she had not given much forethought to the elements of battle, but it unfolded not unlike the way she had been expecting. She vaguely remembered hearing—like glimpsing things in a dream—of the distant conquests of what had once been her Imperial Britain. But those had all been so far off and confused even at the time, things she only heard in passing as one man told another, and had never been shapes clear enough to her for her to see. She had never thought about dry-mouthed, cold-skinned, sweating men all in lines with bayonets, smelling smartly of gun powder and fear. Those things had been kept at a great distance by hangings of silk and the breakers of waves. But the only silk here was the silk she wore and the silk that fluttered colourfully over the numerous regiments; the only breakers were the rolling grasses that heaved up the sides of the hills and broke in swells and little points of pimpernel-red at her feet. The images called out to her in a strangely familiar way, far more familiar than the burn of powder or the dark Indian face: high Teutonic sentiment, pale as electrum, and the awful blare of war-horns, seemed to gleam in a long stark glare over the valley.

Under the glare was a riot of medieval colour, flecked and fierce as a grouse's wing: silvers and golds and the warm ruddy colour of the common sorrel horse, guards in scarlet livery, a mounted archery brigade in slashed greens, the blue of a rolled cloak on someone's arm, saffron-bloom amid a field of sable Foot... Over the orderly mess flew the Colours, coiling through mist and sunlight like living things, living things all the hues imaginable in a world where colours were proud of their stark richness. The sight of them struck a fire under Margaret's breastbone. There were yellows like honey, running in the gloom and looking for the light, yellows like falcon-eyes looking this way and that over the men that rallied to them; blues like periwinkle that seemed to laugh and blues of indigo that seemed like foreboding; among the reds were every colour that blood could be; among the greens was one checked with white so that it looked like a field of clover.

There were animals, too: she saw the Falcon of Capys and the Falcon of Thrasymene, she saw the Boar of Gemeren and the Golden Dragon of Orzelon-gang. Only she did not see the Hound of the Mares beside the Boar. A rough bit of blue silk fluttered at the end of an ash-shaft, that was all: the proper banner was at the other end of the valley. But Margaret thought that the men who followed the ragged bit of blue had better cause and will to fight than did the men under the crisp and formal Hound.

Margaret shifted on the rock: the stone bit into her pelvis and she wished, belatedly, that she had brought a pillow, but she did not dare run back for one. The chilly morning hour dragged on. The sun was now well up, casting the western half of the valley in a fierce yellow light and sending her shadow streaming away down the hillside. Regiments moved through burning mist and blue shadow; the soft thrum of men's feet and horses' hooves moved the air even as high as where Margaret stood. Horns called briefly, sharply, scoldingly. There were always people moving independently about between the ranks, messengers riding at full tilt between captain and captain with the sod flying roughly from their mounts' feet. She watched as the Foot were moved into place in a great wedge-shape at the centre, an enormous black spear-head with a mounted archer troop of Mark Roy's on either forward-facing flank. Someone with a black, gold-flecked banner was held in reserve behind Dammerung's Horse on the left wing; Sparling at the head of the Thrasymene Horse formed a dense square behind the colourful ranks of Horse under Aikin and Brand on the right wing.

With a shock Margaret realized that she could no longer see the mingled blue and gold of the Capys banner. She searched the ranks until her eyes smarted but nowhere among all those Colours could she find the familiar Falcon. It had vanished. She could just make out Dammerung's figure at the head of the left cavalry wing: he did not look concerned. Did he know? Surely—

There was nothing she could do about it, and what did *she* know of war? Like a spectator of some foreign drama she could only watch and hope the actors knew their lines. Her heart began to quicken again with a new and formless terror.

At last, though the messengers were still flying to and fro like dark martlets over the turf, everything seemed ready. One horn called out from high up on the western fell where Aikin Ironside stood. Dammerung's cornet began to call back, but broke off suddenly as if it had been choked, and then it began again, this time in the tell-tale *trou trou tro-o-u-u-u* that was meant, in the chase, to call huntsmen together.

It was like Dammerung to take so cavalier a view of things.

There was another pause for about a quarter of an hour—Margaret's legs began to ache but she could not bring herself to get up and walk about—then, with a ghostly silence, the Foot began to move forward. It was uncanny to watch them from her height, to see the black mass moving at a lope across the uneven valley floor like a deathly tide. No horn called. There was a soft splutter of thunder from the flanking Horse... Then, from the neck of the valley, a trumpet screamed its scarlet call and the enemy Foot began to move as well, with two lines of Horse sweeping down on either side to hedge the middle grounded fight in from any mounted aid. Arrows were loosed: the air between was thick with black splinters, looking to Margaret, at her distance, like a cloud of windswept pine-needles. It did good work: the friendly Horse dropped the first few ranks of the mounted enemy and caused momentary havoc among the following lines. Another volley followed, mingling in the air with the first answering volley of the enemy, and then the lines closed. It looked like two waves meeting, sable and white, crashing and mingling and grinding almost to a halt while the Horse battled it out fiercely on either side.

Another horn! Margaret yanked her attention away from the middle of the field to see the enemy's left wing sweeping up in full career, line after line of beautiful, deadly bodies with the sun making a glory of their naked swords. They crossed the shallow stream and gained the old dike, then came on up the level turf with the birchwood on one side of them and the mess of engaged Horse and Foot on the other. It was a squeeze for them. There was no getting by that dense crowd: Aikin and Brand would have to cut their way through.

She did not get to see Mark Roy's sons come down to meet that charge. Even as the enemy Left made the open ground, the familiar note of Dammerung's cornet shivered in the air, close and clear and thrilling. The red Rose of Hol and the plum-coloured banner of Lifoy were stirring, poised on the brink of charging, and already Dammerung's Horse was flowing into the wide ground between. They had plenty of elbow-room: the turf and hillsides were treeless and, unlike the western side of the dale, there was no watercourse they had to watch for underhoof. Rank after rank, rider knee to knee with the next rider, Dammerung took his troops at a steady trot down the gently sloping turf. They were near enough that the thunder of their movement made Margaret's heart shake. Each successive line was staggered from the one before it so that, if one escaped the pounding of the first row, one was sure to be crushed under the next. She was not breathing: she watched fixedly as the first three hundred or so mounted troopers broke off from the reserves and moved out well into the open. A moment later Lord Gro had started, making a checked pattern with his block of horses and Dammerung's, side by side, two compact regiments of Horse moving at a gentle but deadly swing down the valley.

Bloodburn and Lifoy were in motion. In one wall they moved together, compact but confusing at that distance. Margaret was glad she was not among the soldiers: she was not sure she had courage enough—or glibness enough—to meet such an onslaught. They came swiftly to meet Dammerung, swift as the enemy's left wing had charged up to meet Aikin and Brand. She winced. They would shatter the friendly Left at that speed.

But they were the ones who shattered. They hit at a gallop the stubbornly trotting Left and seemed to spray to right and left like blood from an opened artery. There was only a brief waver in Dammerung's lines, barely a check, and the dense line of trotting horses ground on, driving home the charge through several confused ranks of Bloodburn's Horse. By now Gro had met Lifoy and the two were fighting bitterly. Lifoy was doing his best to arrest Gro's progress and Gro, his whole troop showing grim determination, ploughed desperately onward to keep pace with the War-wolf. They hesitated once, nearly lost their footing—then seemed to find a break and take it. Lifoy broke, split, lost some of his riders among the Horse of the fight that was raging round the central Foot, and had to break off. They fell back in order, regathering and clumping into a rough square-shape that drew off, turned to beat down Gro's pursuit, and turned to withdraw again. Lifoy was broken. He was out of the game.

Horns were yelling at each other across the valley. By now the Right was too much of a mess for Margaret to make out what was happening. Something had happened on the right side of the Foot which did not look good—there was too much white among the black and too much black among the green turf—but now Dammerung was drawing off. His initial impetus was spent and, like Lifoy, he was steadily recalling his troops, only not so desperately, with rapid bursts and wheeling turns, but at the nonchalant trot. They fell into a thin long line against the mounted archers of the middle, with a volley or two of arrows to cover for them, and left the field to the Harlequin banner which was already swinging down the slope to drive home the new charge before the Hol-land Horse had fully recovered.

At last Margaret caught sight of the dread Hound. On a low narrow knoll that turned the stream out of its course, the blue banner of the Mares fluttered high and free of the press. She did not know how long it had been there: already it was moving, coming down with a terribly large body of Horse, to drive diagonally across their right wing and deep into the heart of the Foot. Brand was drawing off. Sparling was coming to the fore alongside Aikin Ironside. The atmosphere on the far side of the battle seemed to be growing desperate. Mark Roy—she could still see him among the Foot, gallantly bearing the brunt of the renewed attack—was in sore need of his sons' flanking protection, but the birchwood and stream were making footwork hard for Aikin, Sparling was having difficulty fitting his fresh troops into the narrow strip of turf, and Brand was still pulling back to catch his breath. It would put up a wretched, bitter fight until the end, but the Right was giving ground.

The Foot was nearly finished. The mounted archers had left off with the bows and had pulled into a tight knot around the lozenge-shaped mass of soldiers with their swords and horses' bodies put to the gruelling work of giving the Foot a little breathing space to recover. But though they were still a goodly-sized force, the ground was so strewn with bodies that they could hardly gain purchase, and with the enemy Horse crushing them on either side they were being squeezed like a wet pebble between the fingers back up the valley, back over ground that they had won, back over the bodies of their comrades who had died to win it for them. They were a pin-drop away from being shattered under the hammer of Rupert's attack.

Ta-a-an tan-tan-tan-tan! ta-a-an tan-tan-tan-tan! Dammerung's Horse had recalled and regrouped, and with the familiar hunting call to rally ringing in the air they swept down upon the Foot, driving hard into the white so that, like a shield, they held off the enemy wave from drenching the sable Foot in red. The shock of their drive took them nearly to the forefront of the enemy Horse; the blue banners wavered over the heads of the riders, pitching at each other, struggling to reach each other. Hands cupped over her eyes to shield them from the glare, Margaret painstakingly made out Dammerung in the whirling mass, and Rupert to one side, under the Hound, cutting his way through the press to meet his brother. The swords flickered in red defiance. The horses wheeled and churned and plunged and dove. It seemed everything was crushing in toward the middle of the field, driving the two together like a black star pulling in denser and denser upon itself.

Light arced between the two swords, blue and white like lightning. At the same instant came the thunder that seemed to split the air and the hills and Margaret's head. The backwash was so powerful that it flung her several yards away, face down into the turf. Ears ringing, head splitting, bones jarred from the fall, she could feel the blue shimmer of magic crawling up every hair on her body. With the world reeling in amazement she struggled up, staggered, and smacked the magic out of her arms as though it were fire. She looked round against the light that spangled her vision, but the shock had thrown her so far that she could no longer see over the lip of the hill into the valley below. Her feet fought the ground as if it were a pitching deck, but she ran back to see how the battle went forward. Every second counted.

She never got to see how that battle ended.

The soldiers under the Red Rose were a wreck, lost among Lifoy, flogged mercilessly by Lord Gro on their heels. Margaret looked down at a rout and, after a moment of numbness, taking it in, a surge of panic filled her mouth: some ten riders or more, clumped together for safety, were tearing out of the mess, the scarlet banner wrapped and stowed among them, and eating up the hillside as they ran. To her left, but too far away, Gro was swinging round, checked a moment, looking back to see what was afoot. He saw, and, cornet shrilling to gather and follow, plunged after the Holland soldiers to cut them off. But he was too far away. He would not get to her in time. That she knew clearly, perfectly clearly. Her blood and her brain felt cold, but she did the most sensible thing which came to her in the split second she had.

She ran. She whirled and ran, her knife in her hand, toward the thick pine-woods which would offer her some shelter and foil the panicking horses. If she could gain them she would be safe: she was encumbered by skirts, but the Hol horses would surely be flagging after an hour in the field and, with Gro hard on their heels, who would stop for her?

Hooves drummed behind her, louder and closer. The sweetness of life sang in her ears as she dodged a rock, a swift, upward rush of crow startled from its hiding, and ducked under the overhang of the first lone standing pine. She would make it—

A horse's knee flashed beside her; something struck her hard in the small of her back and sent her flying, tumbling like a thrown stone across the littered earth. Pain splintered in her back. She tried at once to rise, but the tiger had got its claws in her back and seemed to be tearing her ribs out one by one. *I've broken!* she thought despairingly. She looked up through her torn, bedraggled hair, through the sob of pain. Four horses were bearing down on her; someone was stooping, stooping to grab her; in the distance, his grim, stony face contorted by fury and determination, Gro bore across the level hilltop toward her, the flicker of his cornet making a halo of light behind him. A hand snagged her leather bodice—it made a good handle—and lifted her off the ground. The sound of her pain tore out of her mouth. The world turned a vivid vermilion—

—and erupted in a landslide of earth and thunder. She was tumbling again, running and stumbling on a four-legged thing; trees were whirling like matchsticks around her, earth was caving in and rising up. Gro was lost. She struggled with her knife, with her vision which was being caught in pain like a fly in amber. Somehow her hand opened and the knife fell, slowly, shiningly, lost in a soft float of stone-shards the colour of a child's marbles. It fell into a black place that had no bottom. With a jerk and a lurch, the world spinning suddenly with a feverish speed, Margaret lost her hold on herself and followed her knife into the dark.

XXIV | BLOODBURN

"If you manhandle me, or mistreat me in any way, he will wench you."

Bloodburn looked down passively into her face—a somewhat less lovely face than it had been before, after bruising and roughing in the dirt, a private cry that had completely ruined the last of her make-up, and now the pallor of light that was shimmering behind Caesar's impressive bulk at the casement of an eastern window. Her heart thumped hard with fear for she did not know the man nor what he was capable of, but what stung her most in that moment was Bloodburn's apparently total lack of interest: that was an insult almost beyond bearing.

"You had much better have run and let me be," she went on coldly. How she wanted to call him a coward—he *had* run; it had been a rout—but she did not dare touch that word. Life was yet sweet to her. "Much better you had died at Ampersand. You are meddling with the wrong man."

"Spare me." His tone was dull, emotionless. "I am a man more than twice your age and have been around the countryside a time or two. Furthermore, I have long had dealings with Rupert de la Mare. I do not think I need a little girl to lecture me on whom I choose to meddle with and whom I choose to let be."

The man was a stone. She looked up into his face, into his washed-out old eyes, past his words: the veil of rage parted a moment and she could see that it was no use to argue with him or even to warn him of the tempest he was pulling down on his own head. She let out a long breath through her nose until something unknotted in her middle. Perhaps it was sleeplessness. Perhaps it was the dull throb of pain in her back which had sunk down but never gone out. She stared for a few minutes at Bloodburn's knees, thinking ranging, disconnected thoughts about medical attention and Rupert and whether Lord Gro had survived the landslide, about the battle and about Plenilune herself.

"So you are using me as a bargaining chip?" She tilted her head back with some effort, squinting up into the lord's face. A smile spasmed across her mouth. "I want to be here to see this. I *should* be here to see this. You have the two most powerful men in Plenilune on either side of me, both of them for me and each of them against the other, and you think to pluck me out from between them and expect to get something out of it. Who will thank you?" An uneasy laugh turned over and fluttered like a caged and angry bird in her mouth. "The War-wolf, who will laugh at you as he takes you between his teeth and grinds you into small stone pieces—art made of stone, I think? Or de la Mare, who trusts no one and is slow to give anyone thanks, is jealous of the least attention another man gives me and would not let me have a friend, much less a lover, save himself? You think—" she got out of her chair, balling her fists to keep herself from falling "—you think to bargain with the likes of these? I thought you a grim, impressive fellow before. Now I think you are only a fool dreaming of his prime."

She was expecting the blow, and she took it manfully across the face, crashing back down into the chair with her head backflung, teeth on edge as the blood pooled in her mouth where her teeth had cut the inside of her cheek. *Softly, softly. You are losing your head.* "Did the little girl touch close to the sore spot?" she asked quietly, mockingly.

But he said, "You appear to be of that old style of woman: too independently-minded and free of tongue. There is an easy remedy for spirits like yours."

"I am sure," she replied spitefully. "You do but break them: a very easy remedy, though inconvenient for the spirit." She got back out of her chair—the world swam in darkness a moment, then shredded with blinding light as the morning sun pried away the black again. "You would have found me a more temperate guest," she went on, "had you been less heavy-handed. The fault of the oppressed is often that of the oppressor." *What am I going on about?* She pressed her hand to her head, careful not to shake it for fear everything would shake loose. *Margaret, you need to sit down. You need to—damn, there is the floor.*

The drop shocked up through her legs and into her back as her knees struck the ground. A grunt of pain, which was all she would allow herself as she knelt before Caesar, ground between her teeth.

"If my honourable host—" somehow her mouth kept moving, filling with a reckless sense of glibness that she did not feel was quite her own "—if my honourable host has not immediate need of me—and I think it would be better if he had not—I would like to be taken to my room now."

"Perhaps it should be one with bars on the windows."

"An' sure it will, but if you want me to outlast your pitiful little scheme, it had better have a good bed too. Ah—ah!" she added as someone put an arm around her and dragged her to her feet. Her feet tangled with someone else's. Bloodburn was speaking, his voice dwindling away—it was being lost in a mounting roar of noises which Margaret recognized as the imminence of the dark. In a moment it would overwhelm her and for a little while she would be free of this confusing world of stone passages and tapestries and sudden banks of hot silver light. They took a corner; she stumbled on an uneven stone and blacked out.

I was hoping the guard would be Dammerung, she thought resignedly when she woke in her new bed. The door had just shut and the lock had clicked, leaving her alone in a lush little chamber with a bed and chairs full of cushions, a rich window seat, curtains to hide the stonework of the walls, and a carpet so thick—she rolled gingerly over and peered over the side of the bed—that she could sink her feet into it. *Not a bad prison, but it loses none of its odiousness for being so plush.*

She tried to sit up, but only made it to an awkward seal position before she had to stop and gulp back a heave. Slowly, like an injured dog, she inched her legs under her and got onto all fours. *I must have a fever. Everything is swimming. Where am I? How far am I from Ampersand? Will Bloodburn send Dammerung news of me, or does he mean to return me to Rupert? Oh, I should be terrified of that thought but I must have a fever—I am going to laugh. I am going to—I should not laugh. This is really too serious to laugh at. These sheets are silk—!*

Her knee lost purchase and nearly flung her to the ground as the slippery bedclothes shunted off the mattress onto the floor. For a minute she knelt on the floor, her face pressed into the mattress, and laughed until she cried, and she cried for awhile dismally without any shade of humour. When that was spent she lifted her pounding head from the rakish sheets, stared into the light splintering through the barred windows, and tried to sort out her kitten-skitterish thoughts.

I should have some sort of horehound tea, was her first clear thought. *And then perhaps a boiled egg. What did I eat last...? That is too far back to remember.* With care, touching and gripping the floor firmly with each foot, she got up and made her way slowly through the mess of chairs and tables and sudden inexplicably placed ottomans toward the little dressing table on the opposite side of the room. *It would be on the opposite side of the room. A lamp. Are there any matches to go with it?* She pressed her hand on the cold marble lip of the table and bent down to open one of the drawers, rooting past a jumble of brushes and pins until she discovered a little shut tin that rattled woodenly and with the sound of promise. She produced a match, struck it lit, and shakily set it to the wick in the lamp. It was appalling how badly she was trembling—from latent fear or hunger or sickness, she was not sure—but she screwed up her lip in her teeth and steadied herself as best she could until the fire took, then she flung out the match and set the shade back down.

"Oh!" she cried, startled by the ghastly apparition that glared back at her out of the mirror. Laughter warbled up her weak spine. *Small wonder Bloodburn was so disinterested. I should be disinterested!* She settled her torn, scarlet-and-gold flaming gown into the backless chair—she did not realize at first there was no back and nearly lost her balance over the side. Her feverish mind could almost feel

Dammerung's hands on her shoulders pushing her upright, could almost hear his sharp, mocking laughter as Lady Spitcat nearly tumbled on the floor. Patiently, finding her centre in the golden, gloomy chamber, she drew a comb through her dishevelled hair. She was too tired to put it up: a combing would do, taming the unruly locks until they fluffed into an aurora of ruddy gold about her worn face. They were soft, comforting, purring with sparks as the light ran up and down each strand.

Better now? she asked Lady Spitcat. *He will be here soon, and when he comes he will bring the fire. Not long. He won't leave me. Unless*– Her eyes travelled to the casement, barred and backlit with midmorning light. More surely than she knew anything, she knew he would not leave her, but it had been a desperate fight at Ampersand. While the Red Rose had been routed, had the Right won ground against Rupert? How had the day gone? Would he come quickly, or would he be tied up digging his heels into Ampersand and making sure of victory? She did not even know if it had been victory.

She put down the brush and made her way to the window. Through the bars she looked out on a little lonely patio, sunwarmed and ringed with potted cypress trees and old, pot-bound roses. One rose was growing right up against the wall beneath the window. Margaret could reach it if she wanted to; small beads of dew, swelling with silver and the closeness of the thing, shone on a Lancaster-red petal. Her fingers ran against the wooden sill. Living with Skander and Dammerung had given her balance and better spirit; two weeks on the march had given her strength. She could pry the wood away if she had to, if she wanted to. She could put her elbow through the glass and twist her shoulders through the iron-work. She could do it...

But not yet. She turned from the window and looked over her prison. Give it a day, maybe a little more. She needed to eat and bring down her fever, and she needed to know where she was. *Patience.* Her lips twisted in a wry smile. *I'll find a break in the wall. For now I'll run beside it.*

"Art taking over for me? I just arrived."

A man's voice came muffled through the door.

"Nay, just sitting," said another man. There was a pause. "So...hast seen her, then?"

"I should hope: I brought her in. Maddish, I think: she was laughing and crying a moment ago."

The second man scoffed. "Dost not have a woman? They are all like that, laughing one moment and crying the next, and somehow or other 'tis all thy fault. So hast seen her?"

"Surely! Tall, young, not so badly endowed, too. If ye gave her a bit of a wash and some clothing, she would look fetching. But we're not allowed in. Anyway, chit has the look of a biter."

The second man, who probably had a woman, grumbled indistinctly for a moment. Margaret tilted her head to hear better. "Well endowed or nay, I shouldn't go in there. Biter besides, I heard she was a powerful witch and raised the War-wolf from the dead."

"Th'art gammoning me."

"An' sure I'm not, sirrah! However it did happen, the War-wolf is flesh-and-blood alive and *she* had something to do with it. So!" he added defensively.

"Fwoosh," murmured Margaret, and swept her hand toward the lamp. *A powerful witch. Perhaps some part of us is legend after all.*

"Say, oh! is that for us?"

A new voice spoke up beyond the door: a brisk voice belonging to a woman who seemed to know their type. "Gish on wi'ye! 'Tis like to spill and burn the flowers out of ye laps—and shouldn't I howl of laughter to watch ye dance. Give way—and do ye unbolt the postern, as my hands are muckle filled!"

There was a metallic clatter as someone untangled his sword from his stool, and a rattle as the bolt was pulled back. Margaret, conscious that she had been spoiled by Aikaterine's careful attention and pleasant demeanour, steeled herself against the rough nature of the serving woman bustling through the doorway. She caught a blurred glimpse in the gloom of the hallway of the two guards: they peered round at her and she looked back at them with fever-flushed eyes and cheeks, her head up, her torn and fiery gown hanging about her squared shoulders and thin, weary body. The two heads ducked back round the doorframe and the serving woman, short of stature and nearly as round as she was tall, kicked the door shut with her ankle.

Wordlessly she bustled to one of the many little tables and plunked down a tray full of broth and bread, an egg in a cup, something in a glass, and a bowl of cut fruit. It was a fully decent breakfast—Margaret was pleasantly surprised—but the serving woman straightened immediately, unceremoniously, and turned at once to go. A swift rush of hot rage flooded into Margaret's cheeks, but she bit her tongue; the woman was not *her* servant, nor did she have any particular desire to suffer the sight of her for long.

The woman swung toward the door but stopped halfway, her attention snagged on Margaret's stance, and looked at her as if just seeing her standing backlit in the light coming through the window. "Well!" The woman put her hands where her hips should have been. "I see tha' thinkest very highly of thaself!"

Lady Spitcat's lips pressed tight together. After a count of ten she said quietly, "You speak very freely to a lady."

The serving woman's face, which years of standing before a hot oven had done no justice to, reddened further. On a sudden impulse Margaret wanted to laugh, for the rotund, unlovely creature, fluffing like a grouse, was no match for Rhea's sleek, witching beauty. The other opened her mouth to speak, and some kind of preambling sound came out, but Margaret did not wait to hear what the sharp-tongued creature had to say. Moving quickly to keep herself from losing her balance, silks rustling angrily among the cushions and her legs, she crossed the room and swept past the serving woman to the door. Her hand on the latch, she jerked it open.

"Look! If any man desires to be first, he shall be the servant of all. Have you read that? I read that once, years ago. I can't remember where. Give my regards to Bloodburn: I hope he didn't put poison in the soup, because I know a cure for that." Her eyes followed the waddling, puffing woman to the doorway. "And furthermore," she added—the woman turned back, her tongue bit, her eyes alight with insult. "I recommend a bit of cold cream and snitching less of your lord's victuals; then perhaps you, too, might bear yourself like a lady and think highly of yourself."

With a smart shove she swung the door to and listened with a heady flush of satisfaction as it crashed into the frame. There was a splutter of confused voices and then the serving woman's, raised angrily over them all, pushing through to get away. A laugh startled out of Margaret's mouth before she could repress it.

The bolt sliding to on the other side of the door helped to steady her. She eased herself into a chair, her back still throbbing—but not as sharply as before—and, picking up a spoon, began to test the broth. It was thin and full of little green flakes of onions, and smelled strongly of chicken. Pulling the scent of it in through her nose, Margaret felt healthier on the instant.

If it kills me, she thought, *at least I will die healthy.*

But it did not kill her. She wet the bread in the broth and ate that—it seemed to settle decently—drank the broth, and tentatively dug into the egg. The egg needed salt so that it was tasteless and uncomfortable, but she found she could not complain. She washed it down with the spiced wine that made the sweat stand out on her skin, and after that she was overcome by a profound lethargy; after a brief and fruitless struggle to stay awake, she drifted off to sleep in the chair.

She woke later to the thump of the door shutting again. Starting out of sleep, she found the tray had been replaced with a fresh one containing the same foods so that Margaret had the curious feeling that she had gone to sleep and dreamed about eating, and had not eaten at all. But her head was noticeably clearer and, save for a crick in her back and neck, she felt almost herself again.

"The lady be sound asleep," said one of her guards. There was a rattle of metal against wood. "I say as thou and I fetch ourselves a bite to eat; guarding women is petty work."

"Even if she is a witch," said the other, "she makes poor sport of guarding. I almost wish she would give a show of trouble and put our arms to better use. Still, she sleepeth, and my hunger does not. After thee..."

They tiptoed away so quietly Margaret could not be sure they had gone. She waited a moment, still, listening for the least sound that would prove they had only been fooling her. No sound came. When she was nearly certain she was alone, she moved at once: she drained the bowl of broth so quickly she hiccupped once and followed it with the fruit downed in three bites. The bread and the egg she wrapped in a napkin to be eaten as she went along; the wine she did not touch for she was sure it would put her to sleep again. For a cloak she dragged a heavy, dark rug off the bed and wrapped it round one fist. Going to the window she looked out, craning round to see as much as possible, but the landscape was empty.

How I wish I could use the Dragon's spell. She pulled back her arm. *But I do not know where I am going, and how do I know where it would drop me, or if it should accidentally pull me apart?*

Her fist struck the pane. The glass broke in several large shards, singing out in reproof, and crashed to the stonework at the base of the window. *Everyone heard that!* Without hesitation she tore off the rug and laid it over the ragged glass, then began gingerly to thread her way through the rough square of opening like a camel trying to coax his way through the eye of a needle. She miscalculated her design and ended up rolling headfirst out the window into the rose-pot—which wrapped its thorny arms around her shoulders and held her for several precious seconds in painful check before she could delicately extricate herself. Panting, stinging, trying to suppress the urge to run, she got to her feet and threaded the rug out the window and rolled it up in her arms.

Which way? She looked to the right and left. The sun was nearly directly overhead, affording her little sense of direction; she could see a low range of hills and a wood beyond the house meads, but were they the piedmont of the fell country or were they foreign hills of Hol-land that she had never seen before? She sniffed: there was no smell of salt in the air.

Well, I must move anyway, she determined, *and if I go amiss, they will not look for me deep in enemy territory. I may even meet Centurion's folk if I go far enough. Now, for it—*

She dashed across the patio, down a little stair onto a circle of lawn, and bent close to the perimeter of box-woods so that she could not be seen from the house. For a few yards the world was quiet and full of small shadows and the blaze of summer light, then she found herself slipping down a gentle swell of turf, coming dangerously into view from some of the windows before slipping back into the box-wood lee. The sound of falling water began to ripple in the quiet. People were talking somewhere, too, quietly, tentatively; their voices pattered on the stonework and mingled with the echo of the falling water.

She stopped at a break in the box-woods and looked into a water-garden, with a pond only a stone's throw away and, up a rise and under the shade of the house, another patio with a wrought-iron table and chairs where Bloodburn and his lady sat. Bloodburn was attending to some papers and did not look up; the lady was speaking, quietly, determinedly, as if the knowledge that her husband was not listening gave her just enough spark of indignation to give some courage to her voice. They would not look her way. The gap was barely two people wide: Margaret could make it easily.

A stir of motion in the foreground drew her attention. The little man-cub, which she had seen only once before clearly, came waddling on all fours through the grass and low shrubs, padding inexorably toward the side of the pool. Margaret's stomach tightened. *Someone will come fetch him. His nurse must be close about.* The child crawled on, unsteadily but determinedly, his noble, round, babyish face screwed up in acute concentration. *Surely someone must come. Where is his nurse? The devil and his unholy angels take that nurse!*

The child stumbled out of the grass, recovered, and padded across the slate border of the pool. There was no sign of the nurse.

"Damnation!" hissed Margaret. She vaulted to her feet and rushed across the distance, propelled by panic and the rage of being disappointed. She caught the child just as his paw wavered out into space and he began to tip wildly over the edge. With a groan she swung the heavy child into her arms and reeled back from the pool, panting, out of breath. He looked at her with surprise and she looked back at him with despair. He was obviously puzzled by her rushing out of nowhere and swooping him from earth like a goddess snatching up a poor mortal; his brows thickened and clenched, forming two perfect imprints of shadow over his nose. Not an unhandsome face, she thought, as babies' faces went. If he smiled he might avoid looking like his father.

"I hope you know you have ruined all for me," she told him severely. Hefting him onto her hip—which made the leather of her bodice rub hard into her skin—she marched up the walk between the shrubs and pencil cypress trees to the patio. Neither parent saw her coming until she was nearly on top of them, her short shadow falling across them, her voice stinging with a sense of insult which she could not justify but keenly felt.

"Here is your son. You had better keep a closer eye on him. He nearly pitched himself into the pool and drowned."

And she put him down on his back on the tabletop.

The crushed sapphires of the woman's eyes leapt from the baby to Margaret; the pale, disused hands snapped out instinctively and wrapped the child up into them. Margaret's heart twisted for the poor woman. There was an awful dread, not merely of what had almost happened, but of Margaret herself: she met those eyes only a moment—that was all the time she could afford—but in Kinloss's face she saw a pang of regret and a sweep of horror at the instantaneous recognition. Margaret's mouth jerked wryly but that was all. She had Bloodburn to attend to.

"Perhaps you adhere to pedobaptism?" she suggested.

He was not amused. For a full minute he sat motionless in his chair, turned a little with his hand on the arm of it, his eyes squinted into the sunlight to look up at her face. The warm summer wind pattered quietly at their clothing and stirred the loose ends of Margaret's hair. A new, quieter rage swelled inside her: she wanted, very simply, to strike his face with the crown of her knuckles and see if that made him any prettier in her mind. The silence arched and bristled like a cat's back, but curiously Margaret found she did not care. Perhaps the fever lingered still in her brain. She wondered: if she reached out, could she stroke the silence down as one might soothe a tom? But she was too angry to speak. If Bloodburn, to whom she left it to break the silence, said anything she did not like, she could always hit him and see where things went from there.

What he said surprised her. A frown twitched his craggy brow: "You were on your way out, no one knew, and you came back for a wetling."

She felt the hair rise on the back of her neck, the blood drain with the rage from her face. "We are a reckoning folk and warlike, but we are not Sparta," she said coldly. "We turn back—even for the wetlings."

"At your own cost?"

"They depend upon the currency of our charity," she retorted. "They have no other wealth."

The bolt flew, but in Bloodburn it seemed to be swallowed up in a fathomless carelessness, though in Kinloss it struck a nerve; the woman turned her cheek into the child's crown of hair and hid her face from Margaret.

"Why did you try to go," he asked after a moment, "if you are so sure of his coming?"

Here it comes. Her fist closed; blood sang in her ears. "Do you know duty—and, if not, how could you understand?"

He got up; he was taller even than she. She had the impression of some Egyptian obelisk—a totem of a death religion—being raised in her face, its cold cultic shadow making her pupils jump wide open in her eyes. She saw his hand draw back, but she had the time to note—there seemed to be an awful lot of time in that single moment—that he did it without rage, without even a sense of pleasure. The whole lack of personality in the cruel will put the blood back in her face.

She caught the hand before it struck her. The blow shocked through her and it was all she could do to stay on her heels, but she stopped the blow before it could strike her and something sang golden and bloodily in her heart. The big fist under her hand clenched, hard as stone; she could feel the old stark veins pulsing under her fingers.

"Do not you ever strike at me again," she murmured.

Bloodburn looked down into her eyes, his eyes passionless, fixed, his heavy face a mask for whatever grinding will was moving beneath. Whatever he thought of her, whether of scorn or respect, she could not see, only after a moment he took his hand out of hers and put it back at his side.

"Get into the house," he told Kinloss, "and take Lady Margaret with you."

He left deliberately, following the garden path back the way Margaret had come. In silence she and Kinloss watched him go. She knew she could make a break for it then, Kinloss would not stop her, but by now Bloodburn was on the alert and she knew the chances of her reaching the nearby wood and some measure of cover were slim. She turned in beside Kinloss.

They did not speak of the cub nor of Margaret's capture, nor even of what Bloodburn meant to do with her. On silent feet, with a little swishing of her skirts, Kinloss led the way back into the darkened halls of the house—a house not unlike Rupert's, Margaret noted now that she was not mazed with sleeplessness and pain. The lady of the house led the way into a little bower not unlike Margaret's. Hesitant at the door, Margaret watched Kinloss cross to a low crib and lay the child down: the beautiful lean figure, crowned with light and golden hair, caught in a mirror-shard of one of those most tender moments, touched her sympathetically. Unlike Margaret, Kinloss had known no respite, no brief breath of companionship, let alone love. She knew at once the woman would not accept pity; Margaret felt she no longer had it in herself to offer that. She did not like strangers, as a rule, but she stepped outside of herself and into the room, shutting the door behind her.

"He was angry with me when I grabbed at him. What a little prince!" She strode to the mother's side and looked down at the bloom of baby face. "I was not great enough to touch him, in his mind."

Kinloss smiled. "He shows signs of pride even now."

"A congenital trait of humanity," said Margaret, goaded by a spasm of philosophy.

Kinloss stood away from the crib, motioning for Margaret to follow. "He will not go to sleep if he can see us. Will you take a change of clothing? You are much alike to me in size and stature."

Margaret watched the woman cross the room through bars of sunlight and pause, hesitant, waiting for an answer. An enormous wardrobe loomed in the background—full, no doubt, of gowns fit for a lady, a lady fit to be queen. Without looking at herself she was conscious of her own wild appearance, of tattered reds and golds hanging about her like the plumage of a bird of paradise when it has been blown by unchancy winds out of next world over: her leather bodice showed through, her hair was tousled from her tumble in the rosebush, and her jewellery—which had not been taken from her—shone out fiercely against a skin darkened by dirt.

"For a little while," she replied, "until the War-wolf comes."

The crushed sapphires betrayed the longing of the caged bird before they were quenched in the shadow of the downturned head. Kinloss strode to the wardrobe and flung back the door panels; a scent of lavender wafted across the room.

"Come, you are d-darker than I am," said Kinloss with a telltale stutter. "Will purple do, do you think?"

Margaret murmured something discreet and polite—she could not afterward recall what—but with some surprise she watched the woman pull out a linen gown the colour of a cyclamen's blood, which could, if Dammerung had been arguing it, have been called a sort of purple, but it was not the purple she had been expecting. A second later she put her well bred shoulder to the surprise and shoved it out of the way.

"This robe has seen better days." She tugged hard at the cord toggles of her rags and flung it off her; a cool breeze swept through her thin underdress. "I am sorry to see it go—it was a handsome thing, once. I will give this back," she added as Kinloss passed her the rouge gown, "as soon as the War-wolf comes with my things."

But Kinloss put out her delicate chin and shook her head. "It is a small thing," she admitted in a little, hard voice, "but I do what I can. Keep the dress and do not bother yourself if you cannot return it to me."

Who would remember you, that is what you must be thinking. Not as tall as her husband, Margaret was still taller than Lady Kinloss and could look a little downward into the cold, proud, crushed blue eyes and see into the face of a woman who had once been a great lady. Her hands slowed on the open neck of the dress. She had raised her foot to slip it through the hole—she put it down again, gently. She put out one hand and found the other's shoulder: it was an aged, thin shoulder, and the hollow of the other's collar-bone seemed to empty into her back.

"You have seen hardship," she said boldly, "and, I think, some tears. Do not speak to me of doing me a little thing. All the great men of the Honours are turned out in full regalia to do a great thing for the likes of *you*. You owe us nothing. We lay our heads at your feet."

One pale shard of eye, watery and swimming in the colour of a chicory-blossom, hung fixed on Margaret's gaze; she saw distinctly the pupil swell open with emotion—anger, perhaps, or was it the terror of a hope kindled in the distance? The pale lips, lips that caught suddenly on the sharp corners of words and stumbled, opened in a pink curl, a sudden glint of teeth...

Curse it! There was a harsh knock at the door. Impulsively Margaret thrust her feet into the dress and hauled it up over her shoulders. *Dost eat? Dost eat a thing?* she wondered vehemently as the fabric skimmed over her knees and stuck, obstinately, at her thighs. *To put a little healthy fat on your bones would be to do a little thing for me, and no mistake!* With brute force and coaxing that would have warmed Dammerung's wily heart, she got the gown on and stood with her back to the wall as Kinloss crossed to the door and fiddled with the bolt.

The gap at her back where the buttons had been left undone was very chilly.

A stranger at the door said clearly, "My lordship sends for the Lady Margaret without dawdle, madam."

"She will be right out." Kinloss shut the door. Her face was white again. Margaret saw one of her hands—the other was lost in the folds of her gown—was shaking badly. Her own stomach clenched.

Shore up. A little longer and it will be over. "I heard," she said aloud, lifting her chin. "Do up my buttons and I will go at once. And—thank you."

The woman went round and stood at her back, her cold fingers tugging and wrestling with the little pearl buttons. There seemed to be a lot, or else her hands were slipping at every twist. Margaret could feel the tension thrumming in Kinloss and listened in the silence to an ominous, dark music that the other's soul was singing like a dirge.

"I can guess," her voice was limned and hard with steel, "by your silence that these summons bode no good."

Kinloss could not speak, and in her silence Margaret felt her first pang of terror. *Shore up. No panic; panic will blind you from a way out. Shore up your defences.* She grasped the lower edge of her bodice under the linen and gave it a tug and a twist to get it back into position. She did not say good-bye—to say good-bye was to admit defeat—but went quietly to the door with her heart's blood hot in her neck and went out without a look back.

The corridor was dark and lit with only a little sunlight at the far end.

What have I to do with the wicked? What good am I among them, that I should walk with them or perish with them? I scorn them. I would crush them under my heel—if my heel were big enough. As the Lord lives, she took a deep breath and did not let it out until it had rearranged into their proper positions all the organs in her middle, *I will detest their lies and habits forever. Get me from them. They have nothing to do with you or your ways, and so they have nothing to do with me. In your rough and ready compassion, pluck me from among them like a brand from the fire.*

Her lips curled; her eyelids fluttered hard in a sudden impulse to shut against the bitter irony.

I am standing a little too close to the wicked. I will smell of smoke when you smite them. I hope you do not mind the scent of it.

She was taken to what appeared to be a study, lined with bookshelves, with the windows facing advantageously south. There were no lamps lit. In the half-light and gloom Margaret stopped in the doorway and looked warily around, first for Bloodburn and then for a way out.

There was no way out. The servant stood directly behind her and she stood in the only doorway that opened on the room. Bloodburn was standing at one end of the desk with his arms at his sides; facing him was a man between them in age—he could not be much more or much less than forty—with black, white-grizzled hair and a tough, homeless face. He looked sullenly round as Margaret stepped into view. For a moment their eyes met: she saw an answering flicker of surprise in the man's face before the eyes were dropped again toward the floor.

"Get in here," said Bloodburn.

She took one more step inside the room, her hand put surreptitiously back with a finger in the doorframe lest the servant should choose to jerk the door shut, and looked with a faint air of offence from one man to the other. "Why, what is this? A tea party?"

"Do you know this man?" Hol demanded. "Look at me, for I will know if you lie: *do you know this man?* Was he in with you on your ill-planned attempt at escape?"

To tell the truth was easy. "He was not in with me for anything. I have never seen the man before in my life."

The man winced, his brow clenching. With the movement the sunlight showed up a conspicuous discolouration of the flesh between his brows in the shape of a T. Anxiety shivered through her flesh.

Did I say the wrong thing?

"Have you not? Perhaps you have not. Huw Daggerman is not a man easy to miss in the crowd."

"A pretty name." She recovered herself as quickly as possible. "What has this to do with me? I am come from Capys and the Mares: I do not know your people. What is the meaning of this?"

"When my men went to repair the glass you broke they found him in the chamber rifling through my possessions. It is not the first time he has been caught thieving." The man Huw Daggerman's eyes flickered upward, still sullen, but certain of his fate—it made his countenance awful. "Mayhap it will be his last."

"One job I have left," the man said, taking the time to toy with a little smile, "and that is to cheat you of my scream when I die. I never scream."

Caesar's face cracked, like white marble, into sardonic pleasure. "Man is a creating god when it comes to ways of making other men suffer."

"I would not punish him for a thief," Margaret broke in. Her stomach was betraying her with a sick, uneasy feeling. Bloodburn swung his head toward her, grey, bullish brows lowered. Huw Daggerman did not take his eyes from Bloodburn. "Rather punish him for a fool. Who comes to a broken window—itself already conspicuous—and says, 'Oh yes, it would be a good idea to plunder here.' What rot! Do you make that mark on his brow for thieving? Give him a smart one on the hand and a slap on the back of his head—there are no brains in the latter, it would seem: it will do him no harm."

Bloodburn's hand moved to a walking stick that lay across his desk. His face, gone suddenly too like Rupert's, spoke murder. "No one," he breathed, "least of all a woman, tells me what I will and will not do, nor councils me in aught."

Margaret saw Huw Daggerman shift his shoulder toward her out of the corner of her eye, but her gaze was on the walking stick, swinging slowly in the air, a moment from pulling back to strike her.

"I warned you not to strike at me again." It was with an effort that she kept her voice level. Those old shoulders did not appear to have lost any of their sureness: it would not take long to beat her to death.

"There are worse ways to go," said Bloodburn.

"See here—" Daggerman blurted, quite out of his station.

Bloodburn turned and struck the man a cruel blow to the jaw. With a grunt he went over and down across a chair, breaking one of the chair's legs, and landed hard on his side as his hands were tied at his back. Impulsively Margaret started forward but stopped, conscious of the walking stick wavering between them.

"*You*," Bloodburn told Margaret, "I should not like to beat. Damaged goods fetch lower prices."

"No? Not because you lack the skill of it?" she retorted recklessly.

Daggerman rolled over and pulled himself up by clenching his stomach muscles. Hearing her, he shook his head warningly, eyes alight with worry. *A little late for you to come into an inheritance of caution!* she thought angrily. She opened her mouth at Bloodburn, her teeth bared like a vixen, but whatever she meant to say—she could never remember afterward—she never had the chance. She was interrupted by a boom and a shock like a cannon shot that made the floor tiles ripple and flow like water. She was thrown around, her hand wildly reaching for the doorframe for support— somehow she snagged it and managed to hold on while the floor ran in two directions at once under her feet.

"Oh!" she cried as Bloodburn, recovering himself before her, pushed past her through the door. She reeled after him, but a second thunderclap nearly reeled her back into the room. She staggered, fought the treacherous floor, and ran after him toward the great reception hall.

Kra-KOW! The door to the hall wrenched like a broken picture frame to one side as she stood in it, sending the world askew. But her heart, suddenly uncaged, sang like a canary as she stood behind Bloodburn and watched the thunder get its fingers into the huge front doors of the house. They splintered, letting in shards of light, and finally blasted away altogether into a fine shower of wood. A grey, wind-whirling figure mounted resolutely over the debris and came striding in, followed by several others at a hesitant distance.

XXV | THE CEDARS OF LEBANON

Dammerung emerged from the dust rather more furious than Margaret had been expecting. *"On your knees!"* he roared, sweeping his arm through the air as if to cut them in all two. The startled servants and retainers seemed to have their feet knocked from under them, and they crashed to the ground on their hands and knees. Bloodburn he left standing, but even Bloodburn looked apprehensive for the brief moment it took Margaret to break her gaze from Dammerung and look at the lord's face.

The look there left her satisfied.

"By heaven and thunder—" Dammerung was still roaring as he came "—by flood and fire, by all the improbable stars, by the shoe my horse cast to get me here, you have meddled with the wrong man!" And he stopped dead in front of Bloodburn, his finger thrust under Bloodburn's nose.

There was a soft tinselly sound of falling dust and the heavy breathing of the War-wolf; all else was silence. On the background outskirts of the scene Margaret looked on, oddly quiet now in her heart, and oddly aflame beneath the quiet. None of the servants had dared to rise yet. Beyond Dammerung Margaret was aware of a bright knot of fellows, bare-headed and on the alert: Brand the Hammer and Sparling were among them; and Aikaterine too, she noticed with faint surprise, clad in light armour that would have shone gold had it not been so covered in dust. The high light fell softly on her and made her look gentle and terrible at once.

"Lady Spitcat got your tongue?" asked Dammerung quietly.

"For a woman," Bloodburn replied, "she has been most unusually candid."

An angry doggish smile slashed the War-wolf's face. "A unique quality in a woman—I prize it most highly." He was silent again for a moment, then thrust like the thrust of a dagger: "Why?"

Bloodburn must have felt the game was up, for he shrugged philosophically and said, "It is an old chess move, to take and to hold the queen. I meant to get a costly ransom out of you for the lady."

Dammerung's eyebrows flickered playfully. "Is that so...? But in your heart is Rupert de la Mare not rightful heir of Marenové, and would your ransoming not be robbing him?"

"What do you know of where de la Mare lies in my heart?" It was Bloodburn's turn for the deadly lightness to lie upon his voice. "I might have given the money to de la Mare...then again, I might not. Only I know that I despise you—and it please you—and would lief see you ruined to right and left."

"Then better you had broken the lady, which would have been a death-blow to my soul," said Dammerung softly, seriously. Margaret's skin crawled cold.

Caesar merely shrugged; his face was impassive.

Dammerung took in a deep breath and drew back, as though he needed space to think. "I might fain kill you now, you know— and it please you—though killing in cold blood has never set well in my mind."

Bloodburn's voice turned scornful. "With all due respect, that tendency to mercy is what cost you your freedom, and will cost you more yet."

The War-wolf's eyes flashed sidewise at Hol's face, angry and stabbing. "I would not curse mercy just yet, blackguard, for your life yet hangs upon it—heaven so help you."

At that moment someone touched Margaret from behind and she jumped mutely, heart in her throat, to find Aikin Ironside smiling down at her from the shadows of the corridor. She got a confused idea that there were several others in the corridor behind him.

"If you would permit me—" he said in an undertone, simultaneously pushing her gently aside.

Dammerung caught sight of him stepping out into the hall and his face lightened briefly. "Have you got them?"

"Aye." Aikin Ironside held up a ring of keys with a heavy chunk. "The old brute gave fight and tongue, but he quieted quick enough with friend Huw's fist in his mouth."

The thief stood free beside and behind him, looking, quietly and casually, for a way out.

"You have not killed my steward?" asked Bloodburn hastily.

But the question, which made Bloodburn a touch human for a moment, only enraged Dammerung. "What wonder is it to you? What of your wife and cub? You do not ask after them. Nay, we have not killed the grizzled brute, for we are not swift to kill." He turned to Brand. "Rout out the dame and dog-pup. Bring them to us."

Brand took a detail of men and crashed away, their nailed boots echoing on the stone flags.

Dammerung turned back to Bloodburn. "I like it when the punishment fits the crime. It gives one a pleasant, assured feeling that God is in his heaven and all is right with the world, and all that. So since you, you dog of an Amalekite, took *her* face from me—" he beckoned up Margaret, though she did not move "—which is a wandering home to me, I will, rather than pay you ransom, take her back and burn the roof-tree of your hall."

"I did not burn your...wandering home," Bloodburn argued rhetorically. "It does not seem to my mind that the crime deserves such punishment."

"Hy my!" cried Dammerung, flinging himself back and walking round Bloodburn, looking him up and down. "What, thee of little faith! I said burn the roof-tree of your hall and I meant the roof-tree of your hall, no more, no less."

Caesar's colourless eyes swept the gathering; Margaret could see his head move ever so slightly as he counted them off. "Even with thirteen of you—an unlucky number too, I think—you would be hard-pressed to keep a blaze particular to this hall."

The War-wolf smiled scornfully. "How sceptical hell breeds its men," he remarked. Bloodburn frowned but did not contradict him. "I know the high arts and the Golden Tongue which men of old spoke to shape the world, but I use them but rarely since men now are often low and mealy, and it is not sporting fair to come among them as a god come among worms. So I content myself with blowing to smithers your thrust-jawed door and teaching your servants a little respect—and lighting a blaze under your thatch. Come out," he added imperiously, as if calling the souls up from the grave. "Come out and see the handiwork of your own folly."

Aikin Ironside and an Orzelon-gang man who was often not far from the prince's side stepped forward, flanking the Lord of Hol. Dammerung swung aside, his head up, his gaze a little detached as if he were seeing into Bloodburn, not roving over his face. Bloodburn went, silently, regally, passing down through the mute ranks of his servants and retainers; one dared to move as if to draw a sword, but Aikin Ironside turned and fixed the man with a flash of a look like a falcon, full of blood-lust and the mockery of a man taunting, and the little movement died before it came to anything.

Dammerung watched them to the pile of rubble before he turned to Margaret. For the first time a smile began on his face, then he saw her gown. The smile crumpled into a look of startlement. "What—"

"I know. It is a terrible colour. But my other dress was done to rags. Have you brought my things?"

"Hello to you too," he said, recovering. His eyes peeled away from the bright rouge fabric. "I have brought them. I will toss the dress on the pyre too, if you like."

She took his arm. " 'Tisn't mine, 'tis Kinloss'. I promised to give it back."

He passed his hand over his lips thoughtfully, leaving behind a smudge. "I could make it look like an accident. I *am* here to rid the world of evil and suchlike. Are—all well?" he added softly.

She smiled. "My head is still unwell. I think I must have been out in the elements too long. And I took a blow to the face. But they fed me and clothed me, after a fashion." Her eyes travelled ahead to the back of Bloodburn's doublet. "I wonder if he was not kinder to me than he was to his wife."

"He was," said Dammerung coldly. "He was, but I will soon put those things to rights."

"O-oh..!" she protested as they stepped out into the stark afternoon light. She was momentarily blinded. He set his hand in the small of her back to steady her; between the high swimming light and the loud crunch of gravel underfoot, she noticed the dull jangle of pain in her back had gone. A blast of warm air hit them in the face; looking round, shoving her hair out of her face, Margaret saw Dammerung watching Bloodburn out of the corner of one bright, narrowed eye, like a cat watching a dog which has not yet got its scent. But aloud he said, "Why, friend Huw—" and turned, flinging a look over his shoulder.

Huw Daggerman stopped in the act of slipping away down the line of ornamental hedges that made up the front garden. The brand on his forehead, a ghastly reddish colour in the full light, showed up in plain view of them all, but Dammerung, Margaret was sure, could have seen the brand in the dark.

"Where do you go?"

Daggerman put his foot down. "Just—over the next hill to see whatever is on the other side. My lord," he added, watching the way the wind was blowing Dammerung's cloak about like death's wings. Was it the heat or the harsh bruise forming on his face, or Dammerung's heel on his tail, that made him look so white? *Poor chap.* Margaret's hand tightened on Dammerung's supporting arm.

The War-wolf jerked his head northward. "Why not that hill, if any hill will do?"

Daggerman's eyes slid past the War-wolf to the north, hung there a moment warily, then returned to Dammerung's face. "What lies beyond *that* hill, sir?"

"A war." The war-lord's lips curled.

Still the thief hesitated. Margaret could see him staring at some place on the ground between them; the thumb and forefinger of his left hand were rubbing methodically together. "Do I have a choice, sir?"

"Yes."

Huw Daggerman nodded, first as if to himself, and then as if to Dammerung. "Then I would as lief go over that hill than any other. Best earn a little decent bread—as decent a bread as war can buy."

"You have a sir's way about your speech. Art handy with a weapon?"

Daggerman smiled. "Oh, fair to middling, my lord, but I can take a blow."

Dammerung laughed shortly. "I can see that. It takes training to learn to give a blow, but gut to take one, and I put a higher price on gut."

"I had heard you were just and I thought I would find you so, for your reputation precedes you." Bloodburn spoke up from where he stood not far off, Aikin Ironside's fist clamped round his arm. "I wonder if they are all wrong."

Dammerung swung round on him. "Reputation is like quicksilver in the hand and, like a rumour, a wind in the grass. Rumour had it I was dead. Rumour has it I am just. How true is one or the other, do you think, and by what solid measurement can you weigh me, not having known me?"

"I know that you have a reputation for being a brutal captain," replied Bloodburn—fixing, Margaret thought, on the one attribute he could understand. "You are a hard taskmaster, implacable if somewhat inscrutable, and I have heard that you are ruthless with disobedient soldiers: I hear you flog them sometimes, and hang them often."

"It's a hobby of mine," smiled Dammerung wolfishly. "But I have always found it hard to flog a man after I have hanged him... And you!" he added, coming back out of his own morbid humour. "Who are you to talk—and to talk to me! for I hold you in the hollow of my hand. Out of one side of your mouth you knock me for being merciful, out of the other you besmirch my justice. If I were to let you place your heel on my neck you would blaspheme God for giving man a humble heart."

"Do it and have done," Hol replied, jerking his head toward his hall.

But Dammerung said awfully, "You are in no position now to give an order to the meanest man, much less his prince. Come, Lady—" he beckoned to the golden-haired woman who had appeared with Brand the Hammer on the steps of the house. "Come! I am about to tear the universe in twain."

Lady Kinloss, with her sleeping man-cub in her arms, came down the front steps and walked with practiced tread toward them as if she were always walking on glass and had learned long ago not to cut herself. Her eyes jumped from Dammerung's face to her husband's, warring with hope, warring against despair.

Margaret held out her free hand. "Don't worry," she said. "I told you he would come. It is better now."

Dammerung slipped her arm from his and stood apart. "The hurt and the heartache has gone on long enough. There will be an end to it. My Lady Kinloss," there was no mockery in his voice—he spoke very gently— "Bloodburn of Hol has long since broken his pact with you and the bond between you is dissolved. I strip you of him. Of his house and his honour others will strip him: I can leave that work undone for now. For now I bid you: of all this, be free."

As the words were coming from his lips, full-blooded and final and curiously tender, Kinloss had been staring at Bloodburn's face. There was no surprise in her countenance, no regret, but there was not much relief either. When she spoke her voice was thin and grey.

"I know. I have known for a long time now. You did not think I knew, but I always knew. Once I was sorry, for you had been a fool, but then you were a fool who wanted no enlightenment and I was not sorry for you anymore. For these past few years I have quietly, desperately hated you. My only regret was that I had not courage enough to get free."

"Few of us do," Margaret observed. "We must, many of us, have someone come to get us."

"Hmm!" murmured Dammerung. "That is my gift to *you*, my lady. I only regret I could not have given it sooner. And now for *your* gift, sirrah! A lord and gentleman must keep his promise." He stepped out toward the house, interlocking his fingers and swinging them back behind his head until the muscles across his chest crackled. Then he put out his hands as if to grasp something, braced his knees, and cried, "Splinter the cedars of Lebanon!" —and jerked his elbows down.

The ridge-pole of the hall cracked like the spine of a sacrificial bull. With a groan of timber it reared and buckled, blazing with a corona of sunlight—and struck fire, flames licking pure-white in sheets and swirls and serpentine banks of heat down the support beams and across the shingles. A serving maid somewhere gave a shriek of dismay but no one took a step toward the house. Dammerung passed a hand through the air—the fire leapt skyward at the gesture—then he fitted the saddles of his thumbs into the lean curve of his hips and watched the blaze at work.

"You bastard!" Huw Daggerman cried of a sudden. Margaret jerked round toward him, but that was her mistake; she did not see that Bloodburn had wrenched out of Aikin's grasp and had made a lunge, not for Kinloss, but for her. She swung away and had her back exposed to him for a split second. She saw Daggerman sprinting back up the hedges toward her and felt the jolt as Bloodburn swung her up in his arms—the world was a whirl of sky-fire and gravel—and begin to run. She screamed incoherently with rage and fought him like a cat, kicking and clawing, hitting with all the sharpest bones of her body, but the whipcorded old man ran doggedly on, down the hedgerow, through a low arbour—she knocked the back of her head on the wood—and turned in through an alae of trees before she found mind enough to see.

Daggerman was still hot after them, dodging bushes with the agility of a man half his age, but Dammerung was already matching him with speed—overtaking him—leaving him behind. Through the wrecked streamers of her hair and the jolting of Bloodburn's gait she could see the rage on the War-wolf's face.

You fool! She kicked with her knees at Bloodburn's stomach. *You fool! You are done for!*

Dammerung flung out his hand, fingers spread and stiffened. Bloodburn's body seemed to come dispossessed of his spirit: he came to an abrupt stop on wrenched knees, his arms locked, his head flung back and the veins in his neck standing out as if he were being throttled. Margaret was hurled to the ground and rolled over and over until a low hawthorn stopped her with a leafy crash. She staggered to her knees and looked back.

Dammerung came abreast of Bloodburn and wrenched him round by the shoulder. The man's eyes were bloodshot, filled with an inner agony, but Dammerung was beyond pity. He pressed his fingertips into the man's shoulder and drove him to his knees.

"Did you think you could play this game with us?" he rasped, the breath growling in his lungs. "You are no match for my family or the quarrels that may arise among us. If you should die before we meet again, I'll know you on the Last Day and testify against the blood on your hands. If we should meet again here—" he snapped out a knife and slashed it, two strokes, down each of Bloodburn's cheeks. The man shuddered but made no sound. "You'll bear that mark and I will know you, and I promise I will be your death should fate bring us to the battlefield together. Now get you gone," he roared, jerking the man to his feet, "before I forget myself and braid up your guts in your belly!"

He flung the man away. Bloodburn stumbled, blinded by blood and sweat, and was lost down the curve of trees. That was the last Margaret ever saw of him.

"No—ow!—I am fine." She shrank away from Huw Daggerman's attempts to help her up. But then Dammerung was there, reaching down and grabbing her by the forearm to haul her to her feet. His palm was searing hot. "Why is everyone doing that to me?" she demanded irrationally. "I only want to be left in peace!"

"For some it was a war over Helen, for some it was a war over shipping rights to the Black Sea—" green sparks glinted from between the War-wolf's teeth as he growled "—and for some there was no difference and God help us all."

He stood a moment in silence, watching the blaze of the roof over the tops of the hawthorns; in the distance a mockingbird screamed. Over the building the sky was shivering with heat until the blue seemed to run like water and the clouds flickered like wings. The fire was still white-hot: a quick, consuming fire that did not deign to curl the shattered ends of wood into petals of orange flame, but sent the wood up in flashes of light, gone in an instant, too hot to chew before it swallowed. Her head cold from exhaustion and dizziness, Margaret wished she had the knack of reaching into that fire so that it might warm her.

"It is good to have you back."

She took her eyes off the fire and fixed them on Dammerung's face; it wavered under a film of weariness before it came into focus again. "I said you would come," she insisted. She put out her hand for his shoulder, uncertain on her feet. "I said you would come and that you would bring the fire."

His fingers locked around her wrist. His eyes, serious and half-laughing at once, flickered like his witching flames across her face. He beckoned Huw Daggerman to go on ahead of them and made to gently lead her back along the alae, but as soon as the thief was out of sight he stopped her, took her jaw in the saddles of his thumbs, and turned her head from one side to the other, a frown gathering between his brows.

"Bloodburn did this, I take it."

The tip of his forefinger touched a bruise and made it smart. A little reproving grunt spasmed in her throat. "Mm, yes. I lost my head—for once." Briefly, as he caught his tongue between his teeth and worked at the broken skin, she told him what had happened to her since she had come to Bloodburn's hall. Every now and then his eyes would jump off his work and fix on hers, and there was a high light of laughter in them that made her feel happy.

"Better?" he asked at length, stepping back.

She prodded her face. "Yes, I think so. Quite."

"And your back?"

"As good as it was before."

They walked side by side up the row of trees, through the mockingbird's shrieking and the dappling, eastward-streaming shadows that fell across their path.

"What happened?" Margaret asked. "Did we win the field?"

Dammerung appeared grave. "We won, but perhaps only because Gro and I shattered their Right Wing and Skander was admirably swift to come in from the rear. The Foot was a mess and the losses on either side comparable."

So, that was where Skander had gone. "And the Left Wing?" She hoped, but did not believe, that any good word would be had concerning Rupert.

Dammerung shook his head. "We gave and sustained heavy losses, but in the end we took the field. Rupert—he and I did not meet. I was...busy with other things."

The explosion. The explosion and the landslide. "That was you! I thought Vesuvius had gone off. I don't know *what* I thought. I blacked out before anything could make sense."

"Of course that was me," he said, slight offence in his tone. "You told me not to spare a thought for you, but I did and you had better be bloody thankful for it. I nearly killed Gro, though," he added, with a ruckle in his throat like a horse's laugh. "I saw only the Red Rose, nothing else, and there was not time to think! In cool, meditative retrospect it would have been better had I not blown the top of the hill out of itself and collapsed a whole side of it, but then I had a battle-axe scratching between my shoulder-blades and a shock of lightning in my face, and I was not thinking very clearly."

"Well, I forgive you," she said placidly.

"*Avaunt!*" he called to the others as they came in view, the humour of her simmering at the edges of his voice. "*Avaunt! Sa cy avaunt!* There are still acres of daylight hours left. Art done here? Oh, enough!" he added, and swept his hand at the house. With an inhaling roar the fire swept into itself, shook in a circle of crystal light so fierce Margaret could barely look at it, and like the angel of death called abruptly home it rocketed wholesale into the mellow summer sky.

A soft haze of smoke lay over the building.

Dammerung turned on Lady Kinloss. "Is there aught I can take you, madam, or would you rather stay here?"

Kinloss did not turn from watching the empty sky and the film of smoke that lay like the soft murmuring pall of sorrow over something that has died. "No, my lord," she said at last. "No, I think I will stay."

He went to her side; his hand moved as if he meant to place it on her shoulder, companionably, but before the crucial moment he dropped it back by his side. After a quick glance at her face he, too, watched the sky and the images the smoke was sketching on it, and Margaret knew he was saying something gentle with his silence to the shell of Kinloss's heart.

Kinloss looked at him finally and something like hope bloomed on her lips. "Good-bye. And thank you."

But he shook his head. "Not good-bye, my lady. I never leave my people, though I may go away from them for awhile. Until next time." And he saluted her.

She watched them as they went across the lawn to their horses and sorted out their mounts. There was none for Huw Daggerman; he swung up behind Aikaterine—which Aikaterine did not appear to like—and contrived to get the reins from her.

Rubico bounded from the press. "Send the cub to me when he is of age," Dammerung called to Kinloss. Digging into his tunic, he withdrew the house key and tossed it underhanded toward her; it fell in the gravel at her feet with a ping of metal light. "I will teach him what it is to be a man."

Kinloss raised her hand.

"I forgot to give her back her dress," Margaret noted when they had reached the high road and were going at a smart lope through the open pastureland.

"We will package it and mail it post," said Dammerung, "just as soon as we rejoin Skander."

"Where did you leave him? And where are we?"

Dammerung stooped to avoid a low-growing branch and murmured something about highway maintenance. "I left him on the bank of the Besor. Mark Roy has gone on ahead to Orzelon-gang: it seems, while we were speeding to Centurion's aid, Rupert had already taken Bloodburn's fleet and stationed an army on the coast of Orzelon-gang. Word of the invasion came last night."

Margaret's eye travelled over the pastoral country. It looked a little like Seescardale, but longer, wider, and more green; in the distance she could see a red barn and a herd of white milk-cows huddled under the awning of a long milking bothie. She wanted to curse Rupert—for he deserved it—but she was too tired of cursing. Cursing did no good.

"You are quiet."

The horses' shoes rang out on the metalled causeway.

"I am always quiet," Margaret protested.

"Yes—" One silvered eye flickered her way. "But it is not your raging silence anymore. It is more like the silence at the eye of a storm."

"This is no small wonder." She twisted her shoulders as if to let the notion slide from her back. "The eye of the storm is where you are."

He seemed to smile and, setting his teeth on edge, began whistling very prettily as they went along.

They rode until sunset at a smart pace, but Dammerung told her that they would not reach the camp until tomorrow morning at the earliest. "We came like the whirlwind," he admitted quietly, lowering his voice so that the others behind would not hear, "in case Bloodburn should have hurt you. But better now we let the horses have a breath. We will need them in Orzelon-gang later."

The lights in the countryside were coming out; in the groves whole swarms of fireflies lit up the gloom, and across the swells of pastureland Margaret could see candles set in the windows of the houses, calling the menfolk home to supper. Woodsmoke hung in the air. It did not look like a war-ravaged landscape. Not yet.

The rattle of their hooves and the jink of their accoutrements sang out silver and telltale menacing in the dark.

They did not meet anyone until they swept down the low brow of a wooded hill, passed a turn-off for a ford, and moved to continue up the other side of the depression. Of a sudden Rubico shied and leapt into Mausoleum, who put back his ears and grumbled, halting, bumping against the next horse behind.

"Come on out!" There was sing of metal as Dammerung drew Widowmaker; a pale tongue of silver fire gleamed in the dark. "We all smell you—and my horse is like to rustle you out with his hooves. Stand forth and show yourself like a man."

"I do not hide," came a thin voice withered like an apple-leaf.

The hair rose on the back of Margaret's neck.

Widowmaker lowered. "I see you now," said Dammerung softly. "Come on out. Come out into the circle of our light."

The mean, gnarled little figure of a woman limped into the ring of lanternlight; two translucent eyes, paled with age, turned up against the light and looked back into Dammerung's face. Margaret saw his lips come apart with a faint, confused surprise, as if he knew her from some place but could not quite place her.

"Do you wander by habit alone in the dark, old mother?" he asked. "All lands are not safe now, even for you, at night."

"I be not far from habitation," she replied. Then, putting out a knobbly, vein-laced hand, she touched his knee. "Yea, 'tis thee, after all. I thought I heard thy voice at last among the voices of the living. The dark star hast given up its secret at last."

For a moment Dammerung was very quiet. They were all very quiet; even the soft chuffing of the horses' breathing had withdrawn to the outskirts of all sound, leaving their little stretch of road in silence, limned with the thin trickle of the stream. Dammerung's hand stole forward and touched the old, cold knuckles on his knee. There was a soft spark of light, blue light—if the gloom and the lanternlight had not been so uncanny Margaret could have sworn a blue light echoed in the old woman's eyes.

"So," whispered Dammerung. "It is you. Well, old mother—" humour tinged his voice "—what oracles do you have for me?"

"Dost not mock me, young man," the old apple-leaf woman replied, withdrawing her hand from the War-wolf's touch. "Thou knowest the council of the twelve houses."

His countenance softened; his smile ran and hid in the corner of his mouth. "There be but one house-door of heaven at which I would peep in."

And she, still more gently, murmured, " 'Tis left ajar for thee."

Margaret felt Dammerung go very still, still as a stone, the sensation of his presence withdrawn into his smallest inner self. Then, roughly, he put the back of his sleeve across his face as if to scrub something away and said, "Can I prevail upon your hospitality for us? For we are without house-beam and without fire in a foreign land."

"With a willing heart at a good hour," she replied, and turned to slip back into the way to lead them on. Dammerung hastily flung his cloak off his shoulders and, bending down, wrapped it around hers; her smile, seeming oddly far away, shone back at them in the lanternlight the way Margaret's dreams of the sickle moon would shine. Rubico shuffled after her. Reaching across the distance, Dammerung grasped Mausoleum's reins and pulled Margaret along after him as they left the stone road and turned in pressed knee to knee down a narrow deer-track in the wood.

With her free hand Margaret reached round to soothed down the hair that was prickling with electric feeling up the back of her head. It would not be soothed.

At the end of the track, up a long, winding rise, was a huntsman's hut set squat into the narrow of the wood like a cornered boar; firelight shone out from its open doorway and a blue smudge of smoke muted the flame and the cobalt of the evening sky overhead.

There was no shelter for the horses, but as it was such a fine night Dammerung had them slip off their saddles and hitch the animals to the low-stooping branches of the surrounding trees. Margaret, too, heaved the rough travelling saddle from Mausoleum's back and staggered under its weight after Dammerung to the doorway of the house. He pushed in, foxy bold, and stood just inside, looking round on the old apple-leaf woman's little domain. Gathering courage, Margaret pressed in after him through the thin screen of faience-beads—they whispered and clinked together behind her—and stepped to his side to look too.

There was not much to speak of. There was a low central hearth, shaped in a circle and made completely of brick, with a dozen low wicker stools littering the floor around it. The walls were crowded with wooden shelves, each shelf crushing shoulders against the next shelf, and each full to bursting with pottery, oddments for cooking, and the sort of unchancy, ominous stuff Margaret would expect to find in an alchemist's shop.

Dammerung slung his saddle down inside the door and reached for Margaret's to consign it to the same treatment.

"Would it do any good," he asked the bent figure by the hearth, "to offer help in making supper?"

The old eyes looked up at him, an inexplicable look of wonder in them. "Nay, 'tis my place to serve thee. Wouldst not take from me my place?"

"Of course not. Only—"

"Thou feelest the oddness of it, and thou laughest in thy heart."

The thin, imperious face lengthened with a toothy smile. "Oddities I am no stranger to. Margaret—" He steered her to a stool and pushed her down onto it. He folded up on one beside her, elbows on his knees, and she was vindicated by seeing how close to his ears his knees came, for the stools were fit for children and not much else.

The others crowded in around them, fetching a stool out of corner there, budging up shoulder to shoulder with the next man. Margaret found the sharp scent of spice lingering in her nose and turned to find her next elbow neighbour was Aikin Ironside, folded much like she was—with elbows misplaced and knees where his chin should be—on a stool, his eyes like a cat's eyes reflecting the light of the fire. Huw Daggerman sat next to Dammerung on his other side and quietly began pulling knives off his person, laying them on the edge of the hearth. When they were all assembled and stools had all been found for them, there was hardly any room for the apple-leaf woman at the fire.

" 'Tis not such fare as my lords are accustomed, but—you see—I have put forward my best."

Dammerung leaned forward, pulling in the scent of fresh barley cake and a gardener's stew. "Ah! But we have food which ye know not of... The mortal flesh, which the Greeks declaim but gives forth a mighty argument for importance when the stomach goes empty, is passing happy with this, old mother. You have outdone yourself on our account."

The old woman cracked open a clove of garlic and began patiently to shave it into the iron pot hung over the flame. Sparling pulled a hawking glove out of his coat and, donning it, swung the pot on its hook until the flames were licking evenly round its full-moon curves.

A warm sense of camaraderie enveloped Margaret. Dammerung had leaned back against the nearest shelf and flung his arm round her shoulders in a rough possessive gesture; the men were chatting sleepily together over their bowls of stew; Huw Daggerman was edging his way into their life, testing the waters as he went: she saw him make a pass at Aikaterine and be rebuffed deftly and finally, and it made her smile.

As the talk grew louder and more comfortable and the perry cider which the old apple-leaf woman gave them to drink soothed their aching limbs, Dammerung turned and whispered into Margaret's ear,

"What do you think of our worthy host?"

Margaret's eye jumped beyond the ring of rough, tousled heads to the red shadows on the outskirts where the old woman dutifully worked making a powdered concoction of dried herbs. The figure, so innocuous, so small and shrunken as if she had slipped into a crack in the world and it would take only a breath of mortality to blow her clear through, made the hairs simmer on the back of Margaret's neck. Nothing the old woman had done for her had ever made her feel comfortable or safe. She remembered the defiance in Skander's hall, the reckless laughter she had thrown in Rupert's face, the slyness of Periot's stolen book, the riddle...

...the riddle...

"I have seen her a few times before." The words came surging out of her mouth as if she were sleepy, as if she were talking at random about the deepest things in her heart, and yet the world was clear-cut to her, very small and sharp as if she were holding it in her hand. "Yet I have that uncanny feeling that I have *known* her before. You know, that feeling you get when you *know* you have never met a soul before in your life, and yet that sense of having touched them before comes to you, inexplicably, powerfully. That is how I feel."

"I know the feeling," he murmured.

"And...and...I would trust her into a hellmouth," she tore her gaze from the old woman and looked at Dammerung's safe, familiar face, "but I would never want to be left alone with her."

Dammerung's lips were smiling mockingly, but there was a cool, patient understanding in his eye. "Wouldn't you? I think you would do passably..."

"What does she mean?" Margaret demanded in a suppressed, hard whisper. She bent her head; her hair, sliding down over her ear, hid her face from all in the room except Dammerung.

"How do you mean 'what does she mean'?"

"She is like the fairy godmother in the stories, that is always popping up at the most inconvenient times to save the day."

His nostrils flared with laughter. "What, you think she is a fairy godmother? Shall I tell her that?" He stirred as if to rise.

"Of course you shan't!" With a little flutter of panic she put her elbow on his knee. "She has never once said who she is or where she comes from, and she seems the sort of person who will tell you or not tell you as she pleases. I wouldn't press her, not for the world. I would trust her to be good, but I would not trust her to not be terrible."

"A little old woman who blows about like the wind and barely weighs much more than a feather?"

She opened her mouth to answer, and even as the words were swelling with formation on her tongue she thought very clearly, *There. You have cornered me into what you wanted me to think. Good job.* "Aren't so all who are born of the Spirit?"

With a worming movement he pushed her elbow off his knee and put up his bare feet on the warm bricks of the hearth, spreading and closing his toes so that the firelight shone through and was cut off by turns. "I always thought souls were a bit heavier than feathers," he mused. "Especially when they begin to wake. Oh, speaking of waking—" he put down his feet again. "Are you done there? We are starting out at the crack of dawn—"

"No preamble? Plunging me back into life on the march wholesale?" Her limbs felt hopelessly tired already anticipating the cold early morning.

"—and you need a decent night of sleep, which you have not had for the past two nights."

"I slept decently the night before last. I think. I remember dreaming..." Was it a dream of someone on the edge of reality, on the edge of her dreams throwing back the curtain to show her reality, someone looking in on her from some other world? Had that been only a dream, or had that really happened? She could not remember, and Dammerung was suddenly busy spreading the word to sleep around the fire and giving the old apple-leaf woman a series of sound compliments that would have made a girl blush.

They bedded down on the floor, rolled up in their blankets with saddle-pads for pillows, some men shoulder to shoulder and others stretched out like chessmen packed in their case, head to foot, head to foot. The room darkened as the fire went down, sullen red, casting up a volcanic glow on the ceiling. Margaret lay in a corner, Dammerung's feet stretched by her cheek, his pack, which formed the barrier between his sleeping place and hers, digging peculiarly sharply into her bent knees. With the soft swelling of even breathing filling the place, the night-noises of insects and a badger murmuring on the other side of the wall, she turned over like a dog on her belly, cradled her head in her arms, and plunged without a backward glance into a deep and much-needed sleep.

XXVI | GEMEREN

Glad as she had been to put the ship behind her and stagger on dry land again, after the first two days of straight rain riding across the hilly south country of Orzelon-gang, always damp, always stiff, always smelling of horse, Margaret pointed out as amiably as she could that passage on shipboard was faster and, even if the water was all around, it was considerably dryer.

"One of the many mocking paradoxes man has contrived to thread into his world," remarked Dammerung from beneath the dripping crest of his hood. "Give yourself until evening," he added, "and we will be in Hannibal—where we will, by God's grace, light such a candle as shall dry our shifts a bit."

By midafternoon, to Margaret's relief, the rain slacked off, and by the time they threaded their way between a post rider and a merchant's train in the mucky churning bottom of a ford and were clipping, sodden and hungry, up the stone road into the wide swell of Tarnjewel dale, the high winds were shredding the clouds in banners of white glory and the sun was splintering across the western sky. Dammerung's cloak was beaded with gold raindrops; throwing back her hood, shaking her hair loose into the wind, Margaret felt her dampened spirits unfurl and dry into cheerful equanimity. In two conjoining fields and across a wood-enclosed brook she saw signs of recent warfare—fire-scars, an enormous, freshly-turned mound of earth, shreds of stained clothing—but the slant of the evening summer light and the fresh rain cast a brilliance of slumber over the farmlands so that, were it not for the clink of Widowmaker and the way it would fling off a shard of light every time Rubico rebounded from his trot, Margaret could almost believe the world was at peace.

"I cannot help feeling," said Margaret as Hannibal came in sight, "that it would be less pretty in less flattering lighting."

"Why do you think I kept only a lamp in the cellar?" Dammerung asked without skipping a beat.

She recalled something evasive about being afraid of the dark, but that moment, rushing back on her with no tinges of humour to soften it, was too deep and secret to mention between them in the presence of other people. She managed a half-hearted laugh and said vaguely, "If you are fishing for compliments, I may just bite."

He looked pleasantly surprised. "Why, because I deserve it, or because you are so kind?"

"Let us say both: it casts us in the best lighting too."

They took the eastern bridge of the old shallow cirque with the sun in their faces and the wind singing a coming-home song in their ears; riding under the ancient earthworks of the town, the sharp scents of spices and the evening's hundreds of suppers cooking over the evening's hundreds of fires swelled to meet them and brought the warm sweet water to Margaret's mouth.

Dammerung twisted in the saddle. "Aikin, I was—where are you? Oh. Aikin, I was going to drop in on your honourable High Sheriff to get the local news. You know these folk. Would you care to join us?"

"Us" meaning...?

Aikin squeezed out from among the others and shouldered in alongside Dammerung. "Certainly!" He squinted into the blade of sunlight and pointed up the street. "At the other end—of course—and where this road corners with the dyers' shop—you cannot miss it, it sports always a viciously red bolt of cloth—is a decent sort of way-house if the others care to wait out from underfoot. The evening traffic is thick with everyone coming back in from the fields."

"Oh, so?" said Dammerung. "Towns and peoples are not so unlike the whole world over. I will make note of the way-house. Hallo!" he called back over his shoulder. "You're to go on to the way-house by the dyers' shop: it sports a red cloth so that the Hebrews will not miss you."

"The sheriff's building is just here," murmured Aikin, gesturing to a tall wooden building set off the sidewalk.

They parted; Margaret watched Aikaterine go with obvious misgivings on the maid's part, though Huw Daggerman, since the evening with the old apple-leaf woman, had been nothing but respectfully courteous. She watched them mingle with the street traffic from where she stood on the sidewalk, then turned to follow Dammerung—only to nearly run into him, for he, too, had stopped, and was laughing silently after Aikaterine's prim, metal-plated back. He caught Margaret's eye, shared the humour, and then neatly dodged a mother and child, crossed the sidewalk, and was halfway up the wooden staircase of the High Sheriff's building in two bounds. Aikin beckoned an "after you;" hauling on her rough aubergine-coloured skirts, running fast to avoid the thick sidewalk traffic, Margaret shimmied up after Dammerung as he reached the top and landed two hard thumps on the worn shell-coloured door.

There was a pause. Aikin pushed off his hood and ran his fingers through his hair to reawaken its natural liveliness; after another moment, he took the time to scrape his boots off on the edge of the top stair riser.

"Should we—" began Margaret, peering at the two-story window on a level with them and thinking the place looked like a public building.

"Hark! the host advances!" Dammerung interrupted: the sound of boots on a wooden floor echoed in the room beyond. The latch rattled and the door swung inward.

"Better late than never," said a man's voice, "but if you expect me to boil a lamb-shank at this time of—oh." A middle-aged, sandy-haired fellow who could have gone shoulder to shoulder with Skander and have given Capys a run for his money stopped in the middle of his sentence and his doorway and looked, obviously surprised, on the three of them. Only for a moment, then he regathered himself. "That boy is very late."

"What, the groceries?" Dammerung chimed. "Quite."

The Sheriff's gaze fixed on Aikin with a light of recognition. "Hallo! Good evening! Never mind the lamb-shank—please, come in." He stood back, pushing aside a long bench on which, Margaret was sure, many errant bottoms had sat, and motioned them in. "This was unexpected, my Lord Aikin. Word through the grape vine was that you were in Darkling."

Aikin slung off his cloak and reached to take Margaret's. "Not so far as that, good sir. We were but in Hol-land easing the tension on Darkling's borders. Word came that our father was in some need of assistance here; we saw signs of battle on the way."

The Sheriff nodded gravely. "That was a week ago. Rupert de la Mare landed west of us and pushed eastward, very nearly into Tarnjewel, when my Lord Gro returned: he and Capys managed to shove the bulk of de la Mare's force northwestward, out of our hair."

"And your pasturelands," mused Dammerung. He had strolled to the window and was looking down into the street.

The Sheriff turned at the sound of his voice. "Forgive me for a man's shot in the dark. You must be the War-wolf."

"Today I must." The pale blue eyes swung and glinted in the level light. "Tomorrow too, perhaps. Later I will be someone else."

The Sheriff's brow said, "What?" and his eyes cut across to Aikin with a look that said clearly, "Dost deal with a mad man, my lord?"

But Dammerung pushed off from the window sill and came back into the middle of the room, his head back, his eyes coursing over the Sheriff's face. "You must forgive me, though I never shoot in the dark. I think you fall on my side of the fence."

"Summerlin is a good man and true," Aikin vouched.

"But perhaps," the Sheriff added, "the War-wolf should be the judge of that."

A brief, genuine smile thrust up from Margaret's heart-place onto her face; she turned her head to hide it, for as soundly as she was liking the Sheriff, she saw the man was in earnest.

"I am usually my own judge, but what I hear and smell of you rings fair about the metal Aikin Ironside has staked for you. A clean toss. Now for the news, for I am a cat for news: can you give me FitzDraco's and Capys' whereabouts?"

The Sheriff had been pleased at first with Dammerung's obvious approval—Margaret knew that feeling, of being swept up into a rich warm inside place that was at once still as a wood and crackling with latent energy—but upon Dammerung's prying the rough tawny smile stiffened and Margaret saw the fair eyes flash, for an instant, for a way out. Her heart leapt forward in her chest like a tomcat on the defence.

"Well—" He began by turning up the hem of his official tunic and digging his hands into the pockets of his corduroys. "Last I knew for certain, which was three nights ago, Capys engaged in a full-out battle with Locklear on Helming Side."

"That's good down country," Aikin interjected.

Dammerung noted it with a twitch of his brow.

"I think Capys had the better of it and put the flower of de la Mare's army to by. I heard he chased the remnants clear to Oaksgate and they fought in the streets from house to house until they cornered the stiffest of the foe in the forum. Nigh burnt the place down, too, I hear, and it dates back some hundred years, but I am told Capys managed to stamp out the fire and the foe at once."

"The Capys come of big-footed stock," said the famous All Hallows' smile.

Summerlin laughed shortly, awkwardly, as if he felt a jest in Dammerung's words but could not be privy to it. "That was the upshot of it, but as is a matter of course handfuls of men got shaved off the dark on the way to Oaksgate and are making nuisances of themselves in the countryside. I have many of my men out on Long Patrol sweeping for errant soldiers and my Lord Gro—" he hesitated again. "My Lord Gro has gone back to Gemeren where he is in state now, overseeing his domestic affairs."

He got the last out in a dead-level voice, looking Dammerung squarely in the eye, but Margaret felt him bracing for impact. But whatever it was he expected Dammerung to give him, Dammerung did not play into his hand. The War-wolf seemed to think a moment, pinning up thoughts between Summerlin's eyebrows, looking at them, taking them back down and exchanging them for others. He took hardly a minute before he said,

"I expect Capys would be in Aloisse-gang, then, or very near it: perhaps south of it in that rather bonny bit of glen."

"Oh, you have been to Aloisse-gang?" Aikin turned to Dammerung, pleasantly surprised.

"Once, about four years ago."

Aikin smiled regretfully. "Then you had only ravens, I think, for company. I have been meaning to overhaul the place and make it habitable again as soon as I find a skirt-train that strikes my abiding fancy."

A knock at the door called them up short. Instinctively Margaret took a step toward the door before she remembered it was not her house. In an attempt to recover her dignity she stepped in behind Dammerung as if that had always been her intent.

Her movement caught Summerlin's eye. "Excuse my lack of manners!" he exclaimed, making a few strides at the same time for the door. "My lady, we have not been introduced. I do not have the pleasure of knowing whose fair presence I am in."

She cursed pleasantly inside as she coloured under the buttering of his compliments. Saving her, Dammerung said, as if it were an idle thing, "This is the Lady Margaret—I see you have heard of her—and that must be your lamb-shank. From dust we came and to dust we shall return, but the sweet aroma of lamb-shank shall endure forever. We had better leave you to your supper and get on to ours."

They took a warm leave of Summerlin—very mocking on Dammerung's part, Margaret thought, and very respectful and perplexed on the Sheriff's—jostled with the grocery boy—who gawked at Aikin Ironside and gawked still more at Dammerung, and seemed to wholly forget himself when Margaret, sucking in her breath, squeezed past him in the narrow doorway—and finally plunged back out into the swimming golden light of the evening street.

"Why," asked Margaret when the door was safely shut behind them and the crash of the street damped any threat of being overheard, "was the Sheriff so worried about Lord Gro? For a moment I was really quite worried myself that something bad had become of him, or that he had done something bad himself."

Aikin's face was closed; he looked very studiously for his stirrup and jammed his foot into it. But Dammerung turned at

Mausoleum's side, fingers linked to give Margaret a boost, and admitted roundly, "He had a right to be worried! A man doesn't pack up and trot home in the middle of a war. They have a fine and bitter word for that."

Desertion. The word moved like a little cold worm in her stomach. *But not Lord Gro, surely—!*

"Only, as much as Bloodburn likes to knock it—hoo-oof! up you get! put on some weight, woman?—I take a draft of mercy with my tonic of justice. We fight for Plenilune's right to live: what Gro does today is fighting for her life itself." Dammerung fetched up her reins. "He knows as well as I that the ploughing and crops must be seen to or we'll have naught to go back to when once we've laid down our swords."

When once we have laid down our swords. That seemed a long, dark time off to Margaret. With the heavy sense of a realist she jabbed at her stirrups and put her feet in.

"Aikin," said Dammerung, "I think you and Brand and Margaret and I ought to trot down to Gemeren and collect Gro while the rest go on ahead. I would be remiss to be in the neighbourhood and not pay my respects to Herluin."

Hannibal lay close under the Westphell overlooks and as it was growing late in the swimming, gold-shot evening, much of the street was plunged in shadow, topped by the timber houses and the metallic clang of electrum sky. Everything was a moving confusion of deep brown shadow, blue steam, and a high brilliant light. On horseback, high above the press, the three of them occasionally passed through shards of sunlight which were still streaming over the felltop and down the lanes between the buildings. When they passed into the light it was like being caught up in some other world entirely, a world in which the air was gold and every drifting speck of dirt or feather was made of glass and silver and the manes of the horses were made of thin-pulled copper. Margaret felt tired and sore and not at all beautiful, but looking at her companions in the light her heart lifted, for the light made them very fair and terrible, as if they wore all normal lights and shadows as cloaks over their splendour, and the late witching light of evening, level and strong, cut through their disguises and showed them up proud and powerful, their brown hair cast copper like the horses' manes, their angular faces sharpened and yet strangely distant. Their eyes were hard to see, for they narrowed them against the glare; it was only that, Margaret thought, which kept them from being overwhelming in appearance.

The red length of cloth at the dyers' shop called out to them over the milling crowd. They were almost under the sign of the way-house before Margaret could pick it out from the urban backdrop. With a duck and a twist in the saddle Dammerung turned in to the way-house yard, under the low stockade lintel of the yard doors, and gave Rubico his head. Margaret felt her horse pick up its feet a little as the scent of hay and oats sang out with a kind of candle-colour in the gloom. Margaret had hope of a little supper before pushing on; earnest as he could be in order and battle among his men, Dammerung was very particular about food—though she did not know if that was wholly for the sake of his men or if two years starvation in the wine-cellar had given him an involuntary flinch at the thought of going forcibly without a meal.

He helped her down onto the way-house porch and untangled Mausoleum's reins from her fingers. "I'll mind him," he said, the shadow of the building on his face and the sharp-cut slice of gold that was the side of Westphell shimmering like a kind of moon behind his head. "Tell the others, if they haven't already, to order a bowl to go round."

"Stew or punch?" she mocked.

Dammerung hauled Mausoleum away. "Both, if we could spare the money, which we can't."

"I'll rout out their cook for a bite, then," she called, and, turning, pushed open the heavy-lidded old door of the establishment. It took a moment for her eyes to adjust, then she saw the familiar figure of Brand rising from the settle by the fire, tall and barley-crested with the fire at his back casting his face in shadow as he came toward her. Several of the others looked round as he passed and saw her in the doorway. How familiar they all were! she thought with a sudden, inexplicable pain. How blunt and unlovely and covered in flying muck and stubble—and *familiar!* The image of the room seemed so close and tangible that she felt she could reach out and hold its warm red roundness in her hands, as Dammerung held them all like fine golden balls. Was that what he felt? she wondered. Was everything to him small and round and fragile, cupped in one hand to be broken like an egg or treasured as he willed?

Brand the Hammer loomed over her. "Have we our marching orders?"

She blinked and came back to him. "Yes. You and Aikin and Dammerung and I are pushing on for Gemeren where we are to collect Lord Gro. The rest go on to Eastphell to rejoin Capys."

Brand's face opened with a boyish pleasure. "I had hoped that might be the way of it... Come have a drink with us before we leave. Are you hungry? Capys' maid Aikaterine took the liberty of ordering some supper."

She went, and they set her down between Aikaterine and Huw on the settle—it was a narrow seat, and she had to ram her feet against the floorboards to keep from slipping off—and handed her a horn cup of perry that was light and chilled but made the blood run hummingly warm in her veins afterward. They relaxed back into their meal and went on talking quietly among themselves while she sat in warm silence with her own bowl of chicken and dumplings steaming and smelling and slowly filling her stomach with a luxurious sense of delight. It was moments like these, she reflected, which made the war seem less ominous, though without it she knew they would not be where they were nor have fallen in together, and Huw ruined the fragile, happy feeling by singing softly to himself—

> Pipe clean away the azure blood,
> Pipe away the fame;
> Pipe away the laddie's youth
> And the beauty of the dame.
> Pipe to the old macabre dance—
> It's all a-one to me.
> Birth is had with a hefty price
> But death we have for free.

Dammerung and Aikin Ironside stamped in, throwing a greeting to the innkeeper, and came over, pulling up chairs to join the circle. Huw began to get up to relinquish his place on the settle to Dammerung, but Dammerung waved him down.

"Lady Margaret told us the way of it," said Brand. "The four of us bound for Gemeren, and the rest to rejoin Capys at Eastphell."

"That is the way of it." Dammerung leaned across the low table and pulled a cup of stout into his grasp. He slung his right ankle over his left knee and leaned back comfortably into the embraces of the rough arrow-backed chair. "We'll stay the night and take Gro with us in the morning." He took a stray fork, speared several hunks of chicken and dumplings from Margaret's bowl with a single thrust, and put them away in his middle. "Are we nearly finished here?"

Everyone murmured assent and hastily drained his cup to prove it. Margaret gamely put away the perry and, lowering the cup, saw Dammerung flash her a laugh over his stout. Huw went away to pay the innkeeper for the meal—which, Margaret could not help thinking, was a test of faith on all their accounts—and the rest of them plunged back out into the warm summer evening to collect their horses from their own brief supper.

They all parted at the gate, Aikin, Brand, Dammerung and herself swinging right and Sparling with the rest swinging left; no other words passed between them. Riding in the rear, she looked back apprehensively over her shoulder to watch them go. Huw Daggerman, however, all roguish and at once courteous, bouncing to his rock-legged horse's gait, twisted, too, in the saddle, and caught her eye. He lifted his knuckle to his forehead in salute, then a bend in the road cut them off from view of each other. Dammerung set his teeth on edge and began a skirling tune.

> ...Birth is had with a hefty price,
> But death we have for free...

Achy in her limbs, with the beginnings of a headache where the sun was slicing level into her eyes, Margaret urged Mausolem alongside the lean warhorse with the consolation of a full stomach and a warm wash at the end of the road. As reconciled as she could be to plunges in mountain springs and the awkward communal washrooms of way-houses, the manor of a land-owner with its promise of wealth and decent, quiet, domestic familiarities continued to have an almost alarmingly powerful sway over her. But as they went out through the west gate, over the little low thunder-humming bridge onto the road, her interest was tempered by the sudden clear signs of war in the landscape.

The low eastern parts of Tarnjewel had had only a few telltale signs that she could ignore if she looked away. Here in the west she saw whole farms burnt down, woodcutters' lodges around damp coppices broken down and empty—in a field by the way the turf was pocked and discoloured and she could make out a number of grotesque, twisted figures in the middle ground, heaped into a pile and attended by only the ravens. She looked at them stone-facedly, but her stomach still spasmed with nausea and her heart still ached with a formless, awful pain.

> ...Birth is had at a hefty price,
> But death we have for free...

The sun had gone down and the land was blackened, the sky a swirling disc of pearl-gold and old pearl-grey, when the four of them, riding abreast on the lonely road, passed the stone wayside statue of what might have once been a fox but looked to Margaret more like a badger and entered the outlying meads of Gemeren. As the fireflies began to seep out of some other world into the intense gloom they took the road through the spacious park, down into a little watery dell and out again onto a swell of ground with the house, a shuttered lantern full of lit coals, standing high above them. Brand made some contented sound that Margaret could not quite hear but could sympathize with.

It was Rubico who announced their arrival. They shuffled into the cobbled yard, hooves ringing on the stones; catching the scent of another horse that annoyed him, the warhorse tucked up his chin and squealed angrily.

"A picky, womanish, high-maintenance kind of fellow," observed Dammerung as he swung out of the saddle, his feet saying "pa-pat!" on the ground as he landed. He reached to help Margaret down.

The door from the house banged open. Her hands on Dammerung's shoulders, ready to slip off of the saddle, Margaret turned to see a familiar bulk of silhouette in the doorway, the body of a huge dog pressed against its thigh. The figure carried a sword in one hand.

"Good evening, uncle!" said Aikin pacifically. "We've come to crash the night with you." And he strode forward, breaking the tension, to give Lord Gro a kiss on each cheek.

"A pleasant surprise," Gro said. "Is that you, Brand? I thought you might have stayed in Hol-land a little longer."

Murmuring something to a stable-boy who had materialized from the shadows, Dammerung took Margaret's arm and pulled her into the light spilling from the doorway. "No, sir, we left the conflict there in the capable hands of Darkling. Word was that we were needed more sorely here, and so we came."

"And so you came, as you are always wont to come, when you are most needed."

Dammerung smiled.

Gro turned to Aikin, who had mounted the step beside him. "Do you have luggage?"

"Only a little. We came lightly—but it rained this morning and we rode through the thick of it, and we are in need of warm baths."

"Of course," said Gro, as if all this went without saying and, had anyone save Aikin mentioned it, he might have been offended at the inference that he would not have offered those services without prompting. Much as she liked him, Margaret found herself beginning to be a little afraid of him again, for here he was on his own turf and his own man, and not the drifting, mercurial grey figure he had been at Lookinglass. But then Dammerung was handing her up the step and pushing her on down the little passage ahead of him, and, as she fell under Gro's eye—and met it inexorably—she saw the cool, unhurried pleasure shift in his eye like the idle shifting of the sea.

"Good evening, Lady Margaret," he bade her.

"Good evening," she murmured back, flattered and abashed and flushing angrily at herself for being so unnerved. She slipped past him and followed after Aikin.

"Mind the rise," Aikin said, gesturing to an old threshold of brick in the floor.

Dammerung's voice came drifting from behind her. "You have a pleasant place here, sir. I am sorry I could not come before."

"She gets better with age," Gro replied. "Better you see her now than two years ago, or better yet two years hence."

And Dammerung, with a fresh ache in his words, added musingly, "To have this business done, and to see to my own meads again...!"

Margaret passed out of earshot and did not see Dammerung until after her bath. Aikin led her into the kitchen and passed her off on the nearest manservant—a man called Tunner, she gathered—who happily led her to a spare chamber in the guest wing by way of the servants' stair—she said the shortest way was better and she did not mind which stair she took. Tunner lit a handful of candles, rummaged in the linen chest for fresh towels, and ran the water until she was afraid it would boil her.

"There you are, madam," he said, standing in the doorway and looking over the tidy, spartan little room. The water in the pipes roared from the narrow washroom. His head nodded like a cat's when it is taking the calculation of a leap, and he seemed satisfied. His unhandsome face bloomed with a smile in the candlelight. "If you have need of assistance but ring the bell. One of the maids will run up from below."

"Thank you." Margaret set her pack on the rough wooden trunk at the end of the bed. "Has the family dined or are we expected to join them, and should I hurry?"

"No, no. No hurry whatsoever, madam." Tunner's face appeared almost frightened at the thought that she should hustle. "The family has taken supper already. I am sure a little late repast will be provided, but that can linger until you and the young lords are ready for it."

She smiled sympathetically. "You are too kind. Thank you."

He bowed and swung out, setting the door firmly shut behind himself.

You are not the same woman now, Margaret told herself, her thoughts ranging from the similarities between the tempers of masters and servants, to the places she had been, to the places she had come from, as she stood in the washroom and looked at herself in the single tiny mirror. *You are a most unfashionable nut colour, you are most unfashionably at war, and your language*—the reflection jerked with a smile—*has become most unfashionably to the point.* My poor mother, she added magnanimously, aware that her attitude had turned from bitter and spiteful to gently condescending; *you would so very willingly give me up to some other family just to disconnect me from the Coventry clan. There, I have disgraced you all. I hope you will not take it too much to heart.*

In a pleasant state of mind she washed and groomed, taking her time, and finally stepped from the room in a glow of cleanliness and health and a gown of soft brown moleskin.

Dammerung was waiting for her in the hall. In an alcove someone had set a little plush couch, framed in heavy curtains; in the reddish pall of two sconce-lights she saw him stretched out, asleep, one arm flung over his face. He had already washed and had put off his rough mucky travelling clothes for a tunic the colour of red wine. She hated to wake him. For a minute or two she stood beside him, making up her mind to do it, and finally touched his shoulder gingerly in the hollow of it with two stiffened fingers.

He came awake at once, sniffing sharply, and dragged his arm off his warm, sleepy face. He blinked up at her, first both eyes, then each eye at a time, until she seemed to come into focus. "Mmm," he grunted discontentedly, and rolled over with his back to her.

"I'm sorry," she said bluntly. "We wouldn't want to sleep through bedtime. Isn't Lord Gro waiting for us? The couch is too short," she added practically. "You look very uncomfortable."

"I am very comfortable," he protested, his voice muffled by the cushions. He shifted his long legs for a better position while the lower back half of him teetered dangerously on the edge of the couch. "I have been making a study of cats. They have all the best notions for sleeping in unorthodox places."

"Oh, I see." She sat down where the crook in his legs made room. "So, Gro is *not* waiting for us?"

"Mmer-mer-gerd," he protested with more vehemence; he slapped his hand over his face to hide it.

"I know, I'm tired too." She sat and stared blindly into space; an enjoyable, creeping sense of sleep was stealing over her and she found she did not mind if it was either genuine weariness or the determined aura of Dammerung to fall back asleep. "Personally, I would as soon fall in myself. I am a little hungry again, but less hungry than I am weary. I have not yet got quite used to this never-ending dashing about the Honours. I think it is often your own indomitable sense of energy that keeps me going when I am too worn out to think beyond anything more sensible than how pretty the candlelight looks." On a whim she added, quietly, "But even your energy has a limit."

He turned his head, his hand sliding off, his eyes shining out silver in the weak light. He was very still and silent for a minute. She could feel him probing among thoughts, both his and hers.

"Do you regret coming?"

Startlement awakened her with a rush of adrenaline. "No! Never for an instant! I think I might feel awkward if it were not for Woodbird and her sisters, who are also in the field—even Aikaterine is here. But no, never for an instant. I should hate to have been left behind."

He smiled, wriggling more deeply into the embraces of the couch. "I should hate to have left you. I could never be sure you were safe, and who would I have to mock? Life would be empty and dull indeed."

"There would be Skander," she pointed out, exhibiting her hand, palm upward, as if Skander were in it.

"Mm, well, true," he conceded; "but you have to catch my cousin in a rare spirit to get him to mock as well back the way you do. No one has the guts to give me back as good as I give forth except you."

"I think that is because they are a little afraid of you. You can be very terrible."

The image of Bloodburn, his body twisted in agony, flashed like an icon of judgment between them.

"So, you have learned not to be afraid?"

The image was exchanged for that of Skander's study, backlit in morning light, tinged like a drinking glass with a rim of bitter salt. "You told me I never had to be," she explained simply. "Also, I have the privilege of seeing you thus, worn out and jealous of sleep, and quite ambivalent about the fate of the world, as others do not see. You are less human to them than you are to me."

Instead of becoming melancholy, Dammerung pulled up his legs and swung himself to a sitting position, arms folded against the stony chill of the hallway, a little musing smile on his face. "Yes, even the Son of Man wearied in the way. People *will* forget that."

"Except that even the foxes of the field had wine-cellars in which to sleep, but *he* had nowhere to lay his head."

"I am conquered!" he laughed. "Indeed, I am quite overthrown. What a pair of Fools we make, you and I. Oh..." He ran his hands through his hair and yawned. "I feel Calliope is coming back to me. I think we had better go down now before she leaves again."

Margaret put her hand under Dammerung's arm and pulled him up, and did not let go, lest he fall and for the mere comfort of the thing, as they walked together down the passage.

"Is Lord Gro really Aikin's uncle?" she asked.

"Hmm? No. The houses are quite separate. But Gro and Mark Roy are such intimates and—if you could believe it—the very best of friends, that I dare swear Aikin and Brand have spent as much time around Gro as they have around their father."

"I can imagine Gro being a good friend—really the best sort of friend," Margaret admitted, "but it is sometimes hard to conceive of him as being *friendly*."

"I don't think he often tries, but then I have never considered that the measure of a friendship."

"I think he tried for me, and whether or not he succeeded in it I cannot say, but the gesture meant something. He still frightens me a little with his grimness, but I remember that he tried to be friendly, and he cared, and that means something."

Dammerung put out his arm and thrust back a curtain from a doorway, holding it aside for her to slip through. "Some people have the knack of friendliness but are not quick to be friends. I am that way: I suppose it is a failing of mine. Others, like Gro, make no pretence except to what they truly feel. And, indeed, I fear the man has very few friends."

Margaret felt surprise and, in the wake of the surprise, defence. "What, why? Are all men blockheads?"

Like spice thrown on the fire, her words brought out a flash of laughter from him. "Hy my! I would not be a man's reputation for the world once it got under *your* heel... But no, there is some cause, if you are inclined to call it a cause. The material fact is that the lady of the house, whom we are going down to meet, never stood by the altar with Gro."

As blunt and calloused as she had become, as used to roughing it with Dammerung and his pack, Margaret felt a flush of embarrassment limn her cheeks and she was glad for her own sake—and a little, curiously enough, for Gro's—that it was dark and that Dammerung could not see it.

"Not a peep out of you," he remarked admiringly.

"Well," she pointed out, "there must be a story. And Gro himself is a very admirable sort of man. There must be something to explain it."

"As a matter of fact, there is." They emerged from the maze of hallways on the first floor and began the long descent by way of a stair to the ground floor below. A red carpet rustled underfoot, thick about the edges and well worn where countless feet had gone countless times up and down. "And for the very gallantry of it," Dammerung went on, "I could lay my head at his feet. He found the Lady Herluin—who was not then a lady of anything save decency and virtue—one winter while he was out on one of his days-long rambles. He had only Snati—worthy pup—and together the two of them stumbled on the caved remains of a woodcutter's hut. There had been a heavy snow that year and the roof, it appears, had not been built to withstand the extra weight. One side of it collapsed, smothering two people, the roof-beam pinned and crushed a third, and the poor Lady Herluin, quite alone in a vast, cold world with her only relatives dead around her, was found in that state by first Snati's nose and then Gro's rare tenderness."

"It sounds like a fairytale," Margaret noted.

Dammerung's nostrils flared with a horsy laugh. "Oh yes, fairytales have a way of being bittersweet. At all events, the fact on whose bell-pull people yank most is that, as they were too far from civilization to set out that day, Gro spent the night alone with her, in very close proximity, I imagine, for the night was very cold and the wood quite wet with snow. Whatever they thought of each other and whatever they talked of, I can only guess it was agreeable, for the next day Gro brought the lady home to Gemeren in quietude and decency and they have been together ever since."

"And the lady was all very willing?"

"Only too, I imagine. I have not met *her*, but I gather she shares her lord's sense of propriety and all-things-done-in-orderliness."

He stopped to ask the way of a servant, who informed them that everyone had gone down to the wine-cellar. Margaret, glancing quickly aside, saw the little flinch in Dammerung's face, but it was gone again too fast for the servant to have taken note; he gave his words of gratitude and hauled her off toward the cellar.

To divert him, she remarked, "I can see how it would be a tale to inspire your sense of chivalry."

"Yes," he said a little flatly, "but my fairytale was all over on its head: the lady saved *me*."

"Let us not be accused," she told him firmly, "of ever being cliché."

They went down a narrow stair with the cold scent of earth mingling with the warm scent of vintage. Dammerung slid his fingers along the wall on the descent as if, through his skin, he could feel the coolness and warmth and sleepiness of the world around him seeping through into his arm; his fingers left, for a blink of a moment, little trails of greenish light behind them in the dark, an eerie and beautiful phosphorescence that Margaret wished, girlishly, she could take and spin as he spun the fire and wear about her like a dress.

Unlike Rupert's cellar, which was utilitarian and dark, Gro's wine-cellar was well-lit and furnished, faced in stone, and "As comfortable a bolt-hole as you could wish," Margaret said as she stepped through into the room.

"You like it, then?" Gro rose up from his chair—behind him she was aware of Aikin and Brand, also, rising—and gestured to a woman in gold who was seated beside him. "Lord Dammerung, Lady Margaret, my wife—Herluin."

She was not a very lovely woman, not as Romage or even Kinloss were lovely: she had vibrant golden hair, very demurely plaited, a decent gown of grey stuff that shimmered with a touch of pearl-gold, and a working woman's face: honest, open, sensible. As she turned in her chair and got up beside her husband to greet her guests, Margaret saw, somehow, beneath that pleasant, unlovely face, something like worry shift for a moment and then disappear, and she summoned her own charity about her—*For here*, she thought, *is a woman who knows she is not much to crow about and is conscious of a true lady's face. Hers, I think, is the greater heart.*

"My Lady Herluin," she murmured, and sank down on one knee.

Herluin did not appear surprised, but her husband actually smiled. Then Dammerung stepped forward, his cloak of mockery thrown off, more like a boy coming before his mother than a young man with a birthright to power condescending to slip the hand of a commoner between his fingers. "My lady," he whispered, and kissed her cheek. "We are honoured by your hospitality."

Somehow the staunch, blushing woman found her voice. "Truly, sir, you honour us. I think that you did not have to tarry and turn aside out of your way. Your way, I think, lies to the north among the warlords and the lands at war."

She had a soft, nutty, mousy kind of voice that was very pleasant to listen to. Margaret saw Dammerung rise to the occasion, nostrils trembling on the scent of her voice, a light of daring in his eye. "Maybe my friend your lord does not speak much of war to you—and should he? It is a man's business." He gestured to the chairs and remained standing while Margaret sat down and Herluin, a little bemused, sat beside her husband. "But it would be poor sport to come so close to so great a house and not pay respects to its lord and lady. And—hullo! what is this mouse I spy in the corner? I mistook it for the mirror of my lady!"

Gro turned in his chair and beckoned to the slight, golden-haired, blue-eyed creature that stood in the shadows between Aikin's and Brand's chairs. "Come here, Ella," he bade. She came, followed by Snati, and she really looked the image of Herluin, so much so that Margaret thought it uncanny. But where the girl had her mother's face, she had her father's grimness about her mouth. She could not be over ten, certainly not twelve, but she stood up straight before Dammerung, her head held high, and looked him back in the face. Gro murmured something about Ella being their daughter and only child.

"Well!" breathed Dammerung. He thrust his hands onto his hips. "By the twelve houses, they smile upon this one! We had but one fair woman—this house has two! Happy me!" And he sat down, hard, in a chair, and beckoned her onto his knee. She came with stately grace, hefted herself up with the agility of one accustomed to riding a pony, and settled back into the crook of Dammerung's arm. He linked his arms around her and peered hard into her face. "Oh, no, hold hard, friend Gro. This one has the look of a mischief-maker. You had better keep a sharp eye on this one."

"Which," asked Gro in a dry, level tone: "you, or she? For you are both thickened like thieves and together pose us all great threat."

"Oh—ha!" cried Dammerung, and Margaret was glad that her own sudden shock of laughter was drowned in Ella's. Blushing, but much amused and glad that he had been roused out of his near depression by the little blonde-headed girl, she took her glass of wine from Gro and hid her reddened cheek behind her hand. "She has Mercury's laugh, too, Gro," said Dammerung. He began jigging her on his knee and fetched out one hand to take his own wine-glass. "She has the sure makings of a charmer."

"I think you smell like horses," she spoke up for the first time. She had a surer voice than her mother, more like her father's. "I like that."

He kissed her cheek and told her he was flattered.

"We've got to take your papa away again in the morning," he told her. "The king needs him in the north. He is quite irreplaceable."

"I am glad you think so now," said Gro with what were the stirrings of humour.

Dammerung looked round sharply, a wolfish smile shining off his teeth. "Oh ho! Am I not forgiven? And here her ladyship had been so kind as to offer *her* justification by faith."

Herluin said bluntly, "Oh, are we speaking of that? Yes, Gro told me you had nearly sent him home to me on a bier. Small thanks we get for our pains."

Dammerung looked cornered. "Here I am come to a friend's house with all intentions of friendliness and good-will, to be hounded by a simple mistaken made—*in the heat of battle*, I might add...!"

Margaret put in sleepily, "I do not assume responsibility for any of this." But to herself she thought, marvelling, *They make me laugh—me!—these grim folk and these warlords. They make me laugh. Perhaps that is the greatest wonder of Plenilune, that I, of all people, can look on them and that they can make me laugh.*

Dammerung fashioned some kind of mock defence, which was as beautiful as it was ramshackle, with the lamplight from the wall casting a flare of yellow light across the dark, upreared crown of his hair like the sharpened halo from ancient iconic paintings. "You'll stand by me, won't you, sweetheart?" he asked Ella at last, jigging her closer to the hollow of his shoulder. "You and Lady Margaret will witness I would never blow your father to the kingdom-come on purpose—although I cannot say that is such a bad place to be blown to. An' sure I can think of worse."

"Lady Margaret might," said Herluin, getting up in a rustle of fabric, "but Ella must go to bed."

Ella's head erupted from Dammerung's shoulder in startlement and protest. "But Mama—"

"We'll be sitting on no buts," her mother retorted. "I told you, you were to stay up in time to see Aikin and Brand, and Lord Dammerung and Lady Margaret, but it is now far past your bedtime and I will have no protests after such a privilege."

Dammerung rose, Ella still in his arms. "I cry you mercy—I was not aware we were causing such a stir in your routine. Be a good girl then, Ella, and pack yourself off to bed. Goodness knows I shan't be up much longer either, for I have an early and a busy day tomorrow." He set her in her mother's sturdy arms.

Gro cast an enormous shadow on the wall as he got up. Turning to Margaret, he bent forward deferentially and explained, "I must go tuck Ella in and say her prayers with her. I will return presently."

"Oh, no," she murmured, waving him on. "Please, do not hurry on *our* account."

In her imperious voice, as her mother was carrying her to the door, Ella called out, "Aikin and Brand promised me they would read Snati's story to me!"

Her father's face darkened. "How did you come to contrive that?"

Aikin, spreading his hands and appearing himself all deference and sly smoothness, protested, "She said please, and marked that we did not know when we would be next in Gemeren."

In a cool tone of triumph Dammerung said, "I did tell you, Gro: you must needs keep an eye on that one."

Gro seemed to hesitate, but Margaret, seated and twisted in her chair to see the grey, grim lord's face, saw his greyness and his grimness crumble before his daughter. *Hast conquered him!* she thought grandly. *There is great kindliness and heart beneath that mask, after all.*

"Very well," he relented. "But make it quick, and no deliberating over the voices of the characters. Whatever comes first will do." He turned to Dammerung. "Please excuse me. I will not be long."

"Nonsense, sir. We are trespassing into your world. Take all the time you need with no thought to us. We can shift very well for ourselves."

He meant it, and Gro saw that he meant it. With his brief, straight-lipped smile he left them, turning to duck out after Brand, who was the next last to go; the clatter of their shoes came back to Margaret for a few moments before the heavy weight of stone swallowed it up.

Dammerung sat back down and refilled his glass and hers in a companionable silence. For awhile Margaret sat with the cool cut glass held suspended between her fingers, the light of it playing red on the long curve of her hand, the warmth and richness like the sweetness of life itself singing through her veins as the blood chased the wine through her body. There was a little clock-face shining at them from the top of a tall wine-rack; the high penny-tick of it echoed against the stone.

"You seem much taken with the little girl Ella," she ventured.

Dammerung seemed to wake from distant thoughts. A smile flickered like a gull on his face. "Do I? And you, in your way of reservation, I think."

"A little. But I've never had fond memories of little girls—not even of myself as a little girl. Ella doesn't seem like such a bad young lady, though."

Dammerung appeared surprised. "All children are mischievous, girls and boys alike."

"True, but I know from personal experience that little girls can be wicked creatures, all politeness on the outside and dressed in clean frocks—you would not guess that the same creature had just put her heel through the porcelain face of your best doll not five minutes ago in the nursery."

"And that tidy, brushed boy was only a moment ago rubbing the face of the next tidy, brushed boy in the mud."

She looked levelly across at him, the bitterness of that porcelain doll pulling down one corner of her mouth, the light of remembered victory on his face turning the other corner of her mouth upward. "Poor Rupert."

"Yes, well, at the time I don't suppose he deserved it. He has grown into the gift now."

"Children are such prophets, dolling out justice long before the crime is conceived."

"The Psalmist, I think—" he passed the flat of his hand across the back of his neck, "—wrote a thing or two about that."

"Which one?"

"I—och, I don't remember!"

There was a single thump at the door. Dammerung looked up, puzzled, but as she was closest Margaret pushed back her chair with a sigh and climbed wearily to her feet. "I am coming," she called, and hauled back the door-latch.

She felt the blow in her chest before he landed it. In a physical state of shock she found herself staring up into the brute, bloodied, hounded face of an armed stranger. A sound came out of her mouth, a kind of sharp, scared scream—Dammerung's chair went over—and the man made a dive for her, arms around her hourglass, before she could dodge him. The air was knocked out of her and the room swept up past her in a blur. The man took three running steps and flung her on the top of the drinks-cabinet—she felt something tear on the inside of her thigh and saw sickening sparks as her head collided with the stone wall. She could not see him, only smell the closeness of blood and unwashed body; she kicked out wildly, angrily, feeling her leg scream in a blood-coloured agony, and felt the pressure of a knife dig into the soft small area of her pelvis.

It all happened in a moment, a bare moment of horror, then Dammerung was there with a bound, his foot catching purchase on the man's belt, himself mounted on the man's back like an angry polecat; he twisted his hands to get around the man's skull and jaw. He almost managed to make the jerk that would snap the man's neck, but, realizing what was happening, the man pitched himself backward, stumbling into the narrow of the open door. Dammerung dropped from the man and sprang back, hands before him, fingers tight together, his bare feet clenching and unclenching the stone flags beneath. The man made a jab; Dammerung wiggled away of range. The man, half-blind with blood and weariness, lurched forward, hands open to grab Dammerung, and Dammerung impishly slapped him away, batting at the rough, clawing hands and giving the grimy face a stinging blow with the flat back of his hand. The man staggered back in surprise and Dammerung swung up his leg: the crack of his bare heel hitting the man's temple sounded loud in the room.

"Guh!" the man grunted, stumbling back, recovering, and blinking through his own surprise and pain.

Dammerung put his foot down, balled his fists, and trembled all through with pain. "Damn."

The knife flashed in the man's hand. Dammerung's hand flashed with his ring. The man came down heavy with the knife; before he could recover Dammerung put his elbow hard in the man's neck, which buckled him and set him to one knee. Dammerung brought up his own knee into the man's face, doubling him over backward—the knife went skittering across the flags under the table—and Dammerung brought the heel of his left hand down, hard, a high, fierce look on his face and his lips pulled back in a snarl, into the man's nose. There was a sudden liquid grunt and the man's body spasmed, flexed, and fell limp.

Dammerung dropped the body and stumbled over it toward her. She had been in pain before but the pain had not reached her through the muffling shock and stunned appraisal of Dammerung's fighting. Now, as his hand closed over hers and he tried to pull her off the cabinet, angry flame-coloured streaks of pain flashed up her leg and into her stomach, clenching it so that she heaved.

"Ah—Dammerung—my leg!" she cried, throwing her weight away and supporting herself on his shoulders.

He swore beautifully. He was in a hurry, she could see the hurry in his eyes, but with a certain deliberation he flung her hands on his left shoulder, giving himself room to work, and shoved up the heavy moleskin of her skirt to the thigh. He got a hand under her left leg, gripped it where the cabinet had bruised it, and felt the tear in the muscle. Margaret bit down hard on her lip as the pain became a constant pulsing sea that threatened to blot out her vision. She was not aware of digging her nails into his shoulder.

And then suddenly it was over. There was one last pinch where his ring snagged on the fabric and then the last red wave of pain coiled away into she did not know where, and it was over. She could feel the rightness of the leg and gingerly brought her thighs together, half expecting the pain to reawaken, but felt only a cool soundness that she could not recall feeling before.

"Come along, moon-face," said Dammerung, lifting her off the cabinet. "And keep beside me."

She took two steps after him, a hand in his, and stopped again as a slimy warmth rubbed against her skin. "Wait, Dammerung! I think I am bleeding."

He took a firmer hold on her. "Nay, it is his, not yours. It came off my hand. Now *come*, for heaven's sake, woman, or there will be nothing left to go to."

"I *come!* But let me have a piece of steel for I left mine behind."

He pulled her through the wine-cellar doorway, raging thickly under his breath a curse upon all wine-cellars the whole world over until a shimmer of reddish heat was wavering around him. He passed a dirk into her hand—it was still warm and stained on the pocked wooden handle with old blood—yanked out the silver pinion of Widowmaker and dashed up the stairs toward the muffled sounds of a fight.

Margaret was a few strides behind him, hampered by her skirt and something that was either extreme fear or extreme anger—she was never afterward sure—so when she came out into the low back hall off the kitchen wing she was able to get a clear view of what went on. The invaders, rough, country soldiers that had been demoralized and shaved off in the dark on the run to Oaksgate, ran amok through Gemeren, crazed with survival, cornered like wild animals.

And if anyone knew the danger of a cornered wild animal, Margaret thought, it would be herself.

Brand came through a near doorway swinging a warhammer. It sang close to Margaret's head and crashed through the unlucky head of a rage-blind White infantryman. The blood and brains of him splattered in a wide arc across the floor.

"Yo-o!" Dammerung howled like a hunting dog. "Cover for me!" And together he and Brand plunged into the unorganized mess of armed servants and infantrymen.

Between the intent, reeling bodies, on the other side of the hall, Margaret saw the white, gold-crowned figure of Ella FitzDraco appear in a doorway, startled but erect, lured out by the sounds of turmoil. *This is my first taste of a fight,* thought Margaret, and she plunged under the metallic spray of a broken sword and wormed her way toward the girl.

But it was not a fair fight. The White soldiers, most of them infantrymen, a few of them cavalry officers who had lost their horses and their honour in their hunted run through enemy territory, were fighting like blind, rabid things, out of strength but charged with rage; and Dammerung, cheated out of half a night's sleep, was angry. Someone broke glass—the sound sang sharp and sweetly over the din—and with a sweep of his hand he had turned it into a silver storm, wracked by lightning, and was cutting an uneven swath with it through the faces and exposed arms of the surprised soldiers. Lord Gro, Aikin and Brand, and many of Gro's menservants, were excellent fighters, but Dammerung fought with the full abandon of his power and the slight pettiness of a man who had been banking on sleep and has been robbed of it.

Margaret dodged a parabola of fire, feeling the closeness of the thing draw up the hairs and sweat on her forehead, and flung herself at Ella's side. She came so quickly, she had only a brief image of the girl's face, white with wide eyes, looking up into her own face, before recognition snagged in the grey eyes and her arms had closed around the lean little body. There was no wisdom in running, still less in staying out in the open. With a whirl Margaret flung aside a curtain and dropped with Ella on her lap into the little chair she found in the alcove there. The darkness enclosed them like bats' wings. The noise of the fight, disembodied, horrible, full of the sounds of the agonized dying, beat at Margaret's heart until she could feel it bleeding, running like a shot hare through a wire fence in an attempt to simply escape the hellish screams. She clapped her hands to Ella's ears and hid the child's face in her chest.

Then the silence came. It dropped like darkness over Egypt, sudden, deafening, profound. Not a body stirred, not a soul breathed—if there were any left to breathe, and Margaret, stirring forward with her fingers twisted in the fabric of the curtain, did not know. Her hand closed on the curtain.

It jerked out of her grip. A huge silhouetted body loomed over her, hands reaching for Ella.

"Nay!" Margaret cried reflexively, spasming backward into the wall. "An' sure I have got her!"

"There they are! I thought I saw a light in the dark." Dammerung was there, pressing in beside Gro, reaching for Margaret as Gro took Ella. Dammerung's face was white, but he seemed unscathed. "Fast work," he noted, gesturing toward the chair.

Her head reeled a moment longer before she began to recover her wits. She pressed her hand to her forehead and breathed until the hammer of her heart had stopped dinting her ribs. Everyone was making much of Ella; for the moment she and Dammerung were a little apart and alone. She looked at him through the spread of her fingers, saw his white face, felt the whiteness of her own, and laughed suddenly, softly, very unsteadily, and admitted,

"I said you were like angels in church windows. What a fool I was not to realize angels all come with swords."

His smile twisted apologetically. "Yes, you look a bit peaky. Sit a moment—there—and put your head between your knees. It will pass shortly."

She sat down again in the darkness, Dammerung's outstretched hand resting lightly on her shoulder; she did not stick her head between her knees—for, one, she wore skirts, and two, it seemed beyond ladylike. Dammerung's closeness, his hand on her shoulder, and his two commending words "*Fast work!*" would do well enough, presently, to sort out the appalling sickness in her middle.

By thunder, I wish I were a man! she thought angrily, and shoved the back of her sleeve across her damp eyelids.

Someone asked sharply, "How many—and did any get away?"

"I counted two dozen," Dammerung spoke up, his voice echoing grandly in the little stone alcove. "But sure there are more—the ground is throbbing with them. They will have gone on and left their dead fellows. Gro, are your folk all armed?"

"And told to kill," said FitzDraco bluntly.

"Good show! And here I was afraid the past decade of peace had made some of us soft... I want to go to Hannibal." His hand flexed; he moved inward a little until his palm touched her shoulder reassuringly. "Your man Summerlin should have the soonest word of this, and my horse makes good speed."

"Sir—"

The War-wolf pivoted, picking Brand out of the press. "Your bay beast has a pretty pair of heels, I think. Wouldst ride with me?"

Brand's young, serious face lit up for a moment but, having learned the knack of silence, he merely nodded.

"Then get our mounts ready. I will be at the mounting block in three."

Yanking a cloak off his brother's shoulders, Brand turned and thrust his way to the outskirts of the gathering; a door banged behind him.

Dammerung turned back to Margaret; as if they were some kind of puppet, she reflected, her head came up to meet his face as he turned toward her. She knew what was coming and she steeled herself adequately against it.

"I cannot take you this time, Lady Spitcat," he said. "Will you be well enough here?"

She got up. "I must be. And anyway," she added, meeting his eye with equanimity, "I will get a little sleep, which you will not be able to do."

"Depend upon it," he replied with grave resentfulness.

"Well, I shan't lose any sleep over you. I dare swear you can manage on your own."

"And you! When men are not hurling you over drinks-cabinets, you put up a pretty fight. I should not want to kidnap *you.*"

But she was aware, even as they made light of it and even as they were both truthful—why should one fear for the life of a man who could take the world at both ends and wring it dry?—that the ugly bloodiness of war, the seriousness of it, the grotesqueness of it, lay conspicuous between them. And it was nice to know, she thought, that even after all these years a man like Dammerung could look so white and feel something regretful in his heart after he had had to kill.

For Plenilune, I suppose, and all the families left behind with an empty place at the table, and the schism and the blood and the heartache. He feels that keenly—more keenly than most, I imagine.

He went off with Brand without a backward glance; Margaret found a window at the front of the house and listened as the horses' hooves rumbled in the quiet night and faded, at last, into the thick mothy silence.

XXVII | THESE WRETCHED EMINENT THINGS

In the cobweb-grey of dawn, seated in the same bow-window, her nerves put back together after a few hours of sleep, Margaret listened to the frank, weary voice of the War-wolf as he told the land-owner of Gemeren what had become of his High Sheriff.

"As the report has it, he went out with his night time Long Patrol and met what must have been an off-shoot of our deserter band by the river Tanjou. I regret to inform you that he was killed. In the dark a man must have ducked to avoid a patrolman's sword and the blade caught Summerlin in the throat. I am told it was a clean blow and death was swift. For what it is worth," the War-wolf's mouth, stiffened, speaking almost mechanically, jerked with a wry smile, "the patrolman missed his footing in the dark along the bank and fell, splitting his skull open on a rock. So that is settled as heaven settles."

Brand dragged his fingers over his blind-weary eyes. "I should not have wanted to have been that patrolman and lived, with that weighing on me."

"Sha!" Dammerung said half-laughingly through his teeth. "We left the High Sheriff with his people. They will bury him soon. But we must take you, Gro," he added, a single vein of apology warming his cool imperious voice. "Your king—and I—have need of you."

"And I am willing to go," said Gro. He set his hand over his wife's, which was laid across his shoulder.

"Then give me the better part of an hour and we will be gone. My health to you, my lady." The War-wolf bowed to Herluin.

Herluin curtsied in reply but Margaret got up then to intervene, for Dammerung, making the forward movement, betrayed a slight check in his body and she knew that she must get him out at once to relieve him of the strain. *He would manage.* She slipped her arm in his and turned him to the door. *But why torment him?*

When they were out of earshot he laughed gustily at her, once, without explanation, and let her drag him up to her room where he sat down hard on the bed and stared at a crack in the floorboards.

"Have you eaten?" she asked.

He nodded. "Brand and I got a bite from a street-side stand on our way out of town. We did not know if anything else might come up to delay us so—"

"Better to have taken the chance at some food while you could."

He nodded again. He leaned to the side, his elbow slipping on his knee, and placed the side of his face in his hand. "Have you?" he asked, squinting up at her.

"Yes, and probably better fare than you had."

"Pssht." He waved a dismissive hand. "My stomach isn't a lady's purse. It can handle the oddest of meals. The farmer's sausage was genuine and fine, if a little spicy. It seems to be settling well." He ground his teeth on a yawn.

She passed an eye over his clothing. He was rumpled and dogged by sleep, and had very much the look of a man who has passed a night without a bed, but, save for his bare feet, he was remarkably clean and warmly clad. As the day warmed he would need to shed some layers; if she could contrive it, she would persuade him to exchange his unpressed clothing for something fresh from his bag. She mentioned it, and he murmured something into his palm about it being a sensible idea, but he made no move to fetch his pack.

"I'll ring," she said, striding to the bell. "No need to bestir yourself."

"Mm."

Tunner appeared in the doorway as she was bending to her own pack to remove her riding gear. He, too, was pale and looked ill-used—his left hand was in a bandage—but his brows spoke an eagerness to serve.

"Madam called?"

"Would you be so good as to fetch the War-wolf's bag from his room?"

"I am already there." The man's figure disappeared around the doorframe and his voice came back to her from halfway down the hallway.

She left the door to the room ajar and slipped into the narrow washroom. With some difficulty—her skirts were voluminous and the room was confining—she put off her surcoat and nightgown and put on a dress of some white, transparent light stuff with the moleskin dress, its sleeves detached, overtop. She put on her boots, folded up her discarded clothing, and knelt to cram the unwieldy fabric back into the oblong canvas bulk that was her bag. To her surprise and satisfaction she was not wholly out of breath when she was finished.

Tunner had been and gone when she emerged, fighting in the washroom doorway to get both herself and the bag through the frame. Dammerung's pack had been left on the floor at the head of the bed; Dammerung himself, unceremoniously, had pitched over the length of the mattress and appeared to be sound asleep.

Either that, or he's a damn good faker. She dropped the bag on the floor with a thump. Dammerung did not stir. She had been in the washroom, dressing and preening and putting things away—and making the room look as nearly as it had when she found it—for nearly fifteen minutes. Fifteen minutes would have to do. She poked him, got no response, prodded him to no avail, and felt a sudden pang of terror at the blankness of his face. Gripping the front of his tunic in both hands, steeling the muscles of her back, she jerked him upright, calling his name.

He came awake with a quick movement of his hands, wrenching free her grip and thrusting her back a step, and jerked, instinctively, to the side so that he smacked his head into the wall. "Oh!" he grunted, and sat a moment in perfect stillness with his head in his hand.

"You wouldn't wake," Margaret said accusingly. "I was really quite worried about you."

"I was waking up," he protested. "I had a dream inside my dream. When you called me I woke out of the one dream into the next and you were angry with me for some reason." He swung his legs over the side of the bed. "You said I had tracked blood all over the place and oughtn't I to be ashamed of myself and who was going to mop it up but yourself?"

"Don't be silly." She stooped and hauled at the resisting strap of his bag. Did he keep bricks in it...? "Tunner would clean it up. Now change or iron yourself, one or the other. We should be going soon."

With a languid, fluid motion he slipped the bag onto his lap and began unbuttoning it, teeth on edge, a whistle fluttering between them.

> ...Birth is had at a hefty price,
> But death we have for free...

"The blue one, do you think?" His hands twisted free a bit of sky-blue silk and the wing-tip of a gold embroidered peacock. "I think I mended the tear under the arm."

"No, I mended it, but you were there. Do wear it—it makes your eyes less pale and unchancy—but be sure not to sling into it so violently as you did before. By the twelve houses," she added, turning away. "You would think you were wrestling Rupert to the ground the way you haul the jackets on."

"He is less easily torn," Dammerung remarked, rising and passing on into the washroom.

But Margaret was left standing, stunned, in the middle of the floor; in that unguarded remark she found herself facing the vivid scene of her last night in Marenové with its whirl of lanternlight and Rupert's face, forever fixed before her in a kind of wretched, golden horror, looking back at her with the expression of one riven to the heart.

How sorely I hurt him, she thought without any trace of fury. *I did not even know the choice I was making, to run with the War-wolf or to live as the submissive shadow of de la Mare. He knew, and he knew I did not know, which could only make it the more bitter to him. He lost me. He lost me good and soundly, and I think—I think, in his way, he actually did love me.*

But then she remembered what way that was, that stark, cruel, selfish way, and the blood rushed bolstering into her cheek. Very busily she repacked the bags and had them by the door, waiting for Dammerung to shoulder them, when he emerged from the washroom. The fifteen minutes of sleep seemed to have revived him; there was a brighter spark in his eye, a yearning in the twitch of his nose for the scent of the road and blood and glory, and with the wrinkled, mud-splattered clothing exchanged for clean broadcloth and silk, he looked,

"Quite the war-lord," Margaret noted. "That is the idea, I think."

"If I can fool you, I can fool anyone." He stooped, silk rustling, to swing the bags under his arms.

"Oh, I don't know..." Leaning into the movement, Margaret stepped after him into the hallway and swung the door shut—shut and finished—behind them. "Do we lie when we are only human, and not gods, and bear ourselves up on a thrill of greatness? And what are humans, after all? Should we consider ourselves thoroughly cheated if we happen to find a little of the fool among the gold?"

Dammerung laughed under his breath and a strain of longing edged his voice. "To have time to answer all those questions with you—well, it has taken the life-span of more than one great man for men to work at an answer for each of those questions, and the answers, I think, are not complete."

"I know. And death, for all of them, is the last and hardest question mark."

"So it is. So it is..."

In a blaze of golden hour Margaret rode out alongside the man who had come out of the barrow and brought death upon many of them, toward the northeastern horizon and the myriad of question marks that waited for them there. She thought of that, for a mere moment, then the level yellow rays of the sun—which was drawing on close to Midsummer—and the flash of gossamer in the breeze swept the grimness of war away and she jigged gaily to the jig of her horse while someone among Gro's few retainers sang— jauntily and raggedly, for they were all going at a smart trot—a hymn that he must have learned in church. The gardens around Gemeren were lost in a bend of the road; over two hills and a long stretch of pastureland, the upper ramparts of the house were swallowed up from view.

"Gro," said Dammerung, breaking out of a conversation with Margaret the way a kingfisher breaks out of the woodshore, "the land around here is something half park, half pastureland. This is not like the Mares."

Riding behind and between them, Gro replied, "You are not often in Orzelon-gang?"

"Not for two or three years, certainly, and Orzelon-gang is a peaceful, quiet Honour. I am not needed here very often."

Gro went on as if there had been no interrupting question. "South Tarnjewel is wholly agrarian, but here in the midlands we fly our hawks and run our hounds, and my friend the king spends time here, when he can spare the time, on long weekends hunting. So you see a little pasture and tended parkland, for my people both tend the soil and attend to the upkeep of our lord's deer."

"Oh, you are a hartman for Mark Roy?" asked Margaret. She checked on Dammerung's face to be sure she was not stepping out of bounds. "I did not realize land-owners held that position."

"An' sure," said Dammerung. "To be a steward of the king's land and of the meat of his board is one of the greatest honours a man can bear. After all—what is man?" he added in a sidelong murmur to her. "What...what is man..." And his voice trailed off, his eyes, narrowed suddenly, fixed on something ahead and beside her.

Mausoleum ruckled anxiously as her hand tightened on the reins. They were coming to the convergence of two roads in a wood; through the tangled undergrowth, on the other side of the way, Margaret could see a movement of horses' legs and a long low trail of dust.

Rubico bounded ahead of her, head tucked in, legs flashing out and coming in with exaggerated show. Dammerung had flung back his black cloak so that it purled and billowed away from the hilt of his sword, and in magnificent state he reached the crossroads before the conjoining caravan and halted, horse's legs spread wide. Coming up behind him, Margaret's heart spasmed like a hare in a wire when she saw why.

In a slant of sunlight, poised uncertain at the sudden appearance of another stallion, the familiar sheeny figure of Witching Hour stood in the way, the armed, helmed figure of his master in the saddle.

Dammerung set his fist on his hip and twisted askance in the saddle, one brow cocked. After a pause, Rupert reached up and jerked the chin-strap free on his helm and slung it off to rest it on his knee; his face, now bared, was at once grim and handsome; his brow was silvered and sanguine where the rim of his helm had left a weal and the sweat had pooled in the depression.

"And you are?" he asked.

Dammerung jerked up his chin defiantly. "Numbering some eight, if you count the lady—and she has proven nigh as good a man at this game."

"I am not surprised."

"And you?"

"Sixteen."

"Oh! Should be fair even, then."

"Something like that... What are you about?"

Dammerung thrust a thumb over his shoulder in a vague way. Rubico, feeling his master's movement, snuffled and sidled and appeared uneasy. "These are the king's parks. We have found some curious game in these thickets."

The emotive brow—as famous, Margaret thought, as the All Hallows' smile—slashed upward in a sudden daring humour. "You don't say? I, too, have been about a hunting business: a few hounds, it seems, had gone white about the mouth and needed tending to. But here is a pretty quarry: two war-lords and a war-lord's cubs, some hounds-at-leash and a woman who is almost as good—" his tone turned iron "—as a man."

Dammerung's voice, too, sang softly like drawn steel. "Best not kick over this bee-skep, sirrah."

"And do else what?" the other demanded. He put his helm down more firmly on his knee in a gesture both mocking and askance. " 'Tis either that, or gang on together—and we know we cannot do *that*."

Dammerung was silent for a moment, thinking. Margaret knew he was thinking very seriously along the thin, magical, almost imperceptible lines of cause and effect, chance and circumstance, that this small, important moment could produce; over against that, she could not help thinking simply what an unhappy piece of providence it was.

At last Dammerung seemed to rouse and gestured to the open road. "Oh, go you onward. We will come quietly on behind and go, when the parting of the roads comes, on our own bloody way. Unless," he added, turning his head in a way reminiscent of his ruddy familiar, "you suspect me of duplicity."

De la Mare's nostrils flared with contempt. "There is a simple code of honour in the little mind of a fool. Of duplicity, it is the lady I would suspect."

Margaret heard and felt the tear and gash of bitterness rake through the man's words, but it came to her as a relief, out of the simmering danger of the moment, that she did not even feel the need to suppress a flinch. His words flew wide of her, but they hit Dammerung square. She felt the War-wolf's anger, which had been half-mocking and almost mere annoyance before, become an awesome, terrible thing—she felt it, not in his look or in his aura, but in the little fox-coloured search-light that had fallen down inside of her months before and had burned steadily there; she felt it flare in a burst of angry light, bare its teeth in an airless roar, and almost—almost—pull back to strike.

To stave them off she interposed bluntly, "I have often found, sir, that it takes one to know one."

Rupert struggled mightily—it could not be seen, but she could feel it—and overwon his worse sense; after a moment, he lifted his helm off his knee in a kind of salutary gesture, the black horse-tail plume of it spraying in the wind. "Perhaps I speak out of place in the presence of two who know me so well."

There was an embittered truthfulness in his tone, but there was an acid regret in his eye and a hardness, a fierceness like fangs, that shaped his lips. Margaret took the green branch of his honesty and tossed it aside. "What do we know of each other, save that, for good or ill, by heaven and hell, we will always, the three of us, be set at odds with each other? That is enough to know. That is enough to judge by."

"I would give but this one piece of advice," he retorted.

She arched her brow. "Advice? For us? Why?"

His haggard face darkened like a sun eclipsed. "Because I am honest, and it can do me no harm."

The soft breeze purled and thumped in Dammerung's cloak; out of the movement of it Margaret heard the many times it had been said the War-wolf had died, innocently, on a boar-hunt, and felt the gall of the lie in her belly. But aloud she said only, "Honesty is the greatest of our misfortunes, and caring second greatest. Think a moment longer: you may regret your advice."

They had gone beyond swords now. The flare of search-light had been the true measure of the soul at war, and Margaret watched the dark heart of the war-lord clench and harden, muscles rolling with power, sick with bitterness, hungry for revenge. In another moment he would decide against it and hold his tongue. *Hold it,* she willed him furiously. *Hold it! I want neither praise nor censure from you, only silence. Only silence.*

But the moment did not come. Before it could be too late he said, quickly and angrily, "This is my advice to you: to know that I have the one advantage that I know the human heart, for I am a master of it. It is full of power and cruelty, and will dominate, for that is the destiny of man. You speak of goodness and of heaven, but in that you only cheat yourselves. There is a heaven—surely I know! for it ever lives to make life hard for me and mine—but who are you to think there is not a chink in your pretty armour, a chink of human will and self and blind ambition for power that I will not find, that I will not use to get a hold of you and bend you or break you? You are born of the stuff of my lords, like clay in their hands, and I will always—I will *always* rule you, for you are of the same spirit and flesh and blood, and when the time comes for the last reckoning and war you will roll your dice with me and lie buried under my fields."

"Rupert?" Dammerung called softly, questioningly. Rupert turned his head, an apocalyptic shining in his eye. "Is Plenilune a hollow cup for you, with which to hold your wine?"

"Which vine shall we plant here, you and I," Rupert flashed back, "and whose vintage shall we drink?"

"As the Lord lives, not yours!" said Dammerung. "An' sure it tastes of vinegar and blood."

"You would know that."

Margaret was afraid the fight would break out afresh, and she was not sure what she would do to overset the balance of the chessboard in their favour again—was it ever in their favour, or did God's little soldiers go singing in the dark to their deaths, she wondered?—when Dammerung did a sudden, awful thing. He flicked his hand through the air, turned a swift little gust of wind that sang with light on its razor-sharp edges, and said in a low voice that rumbled in the stones at their feet—

"Go."

It could have been Plenilune herself which spoke—it could have been the Dragon. It was so small a word, so simply spoken, but even Margaret felt the weight of it—*A word of power*—and Rupert, with his head uplifted, though she knew his spirit bowed, gave his jewelled spurs a jink against his horse's flanks and shouldered on, wordless, the dark light of murder flashing sidelong in the corner of his eye.

When at last he was gone, and the bend in the road had hidden the last horse-tail in his train, she shuddered as if someone had trod on her grave.

He actually did love me.

Staring after them, Gro said, "I feel in my bones that great history is made between you in our midst."

But Dammerung's lips curled in a foxy, feral snarl. "Aye, and with great history comes always great losses. Step up, Rubico!"

They rode into a hectic camp in the midst of a thick scarlet dusk. They had left Rupert somewhere along the road and had never seen him, save for his tracks, until a parting of the ways; then they had climbed northeast into the hill country until the ruddy, shadowed bulk of empty Aloisse-gang was the only thing etched against the golden twilight and the haze of the campfires hung low in the sudden drops and glens of the land.

"It seems we have come in the wake of a battle," remarked Dammerung, sniffing at the blood in the air. Margaret smelled only wood-smoke and horse-sweat—most of the latter came from Mausoleum and drenched her gown. But despite whatever had gone forward that afternoon among the steep runs of the glens and the rolling scrub-and-turf around the ancient castle, a weary cheer went up on all sides as they rode in. Men stood up, leaning on their swords, to salute them; war-hounds bayed and signed greetings in the air with their forepaws as they reared up against the strain of their leads. Jewelled fires winked out of the dusk; the scent of roasting meat brought the warm sweet water to Margaret's mouth and she realized that all day she had lost her appetite and was only just now getting it back with a ravenous ferocity.

"Heigh-o, here we are—"

Rubico swung to the right, cutting Mausoleum off, and trotted the last uneven bit of turf to the bald patch before the conspicuous blue tent of Capys. Skander was out front, limned with blood and tattered, a weariness about his shoulders; he was just taking a letter from a post-rider when the shadow of Dammerung's horse loomed over him. With a little sickened start Margaret watched him look up: his face was haggard and grey and his upper and lower lip, in a perfect diagonal, had been slashed and then stitched together again.

"Whoa!" cried Dammerung, to his horse and his cousin at once. "That's a pretty piece of work. Rum luck for Woodbird."

"Joo you know," said Skander through ground teeth, "I shot the very shame t'ing when Lock'ear gave it to 'e."

"I hope you gave him back as good as he gave you." Dammerung swung his leg over Rubico's neck and jumped to the ground; he passed the horse off and Margaret twisted as he reached for her, his hands closing about her waist to lift her off. "I'll have a look at it before supper. It is all sort of unfun trying to eat with two busted lips." His eyes fell on the letter. "News?"

Skander broke the seal, opened it, and ran a hasty eye over the contents. His hand wavered inconsequentially. "Shurvance. Jus' an update: all'sh well at home." The *h* seemed to have given him pain, for his cheek convulsed and he folded the letter away. "You?"

Margaret looked over her shoulder to find Lord Gro and Mark Roy's sons had drifted silently away, falling in among the other lords and land-owners. The cousins and she herself—whatever she was—were left alone.

We walk alone.

"Among other things," murmured Dammerung, slipping her arm in his and turning to the back-flung tent-flap of the blue booth, "we met with Rupert on the road today."

Skander's head turned a fraction, too quickly, and he stopped it before he could meet Dammerung's eye. He said nothing. At the entryway to the tent Dammerung pushed Margaret forward and she went in ahead of them, ducking into the familiar lamp-washed interior of the war-lord's war-room. Gold pricked out from every surface and where the gold was not growling, the deep purr of dark-stained wood was thrumming. On an impulse she smiled; the heart-thing in her chest unwound and relaxed.

Dammerung put his cousin in a chair, turned him into the light, and stood with his knees bent a little before him, thumbs and forefingers playing with the gashes and stitching on Skander's lips. Skander took it gamely; he watched out of the corners of his eyes as Margaret helped them all to glasses of wine; she did not feel quite up to watching Dammerung at his work.

While he worked, Dammerung sketched a brief overview of the past twenty-four hours. She thought he played up his annoyance over the intrusion at Gemeren rather much, and downplayed his encounter with Rupert significantly. Leaving a chalice of wine in Skander's hand, Margaret's eyes met his and they shared a little understanding between them while Dammerung went on, soothing angry red skin and slipping loose cat-gut. *You and I,* thought Margaret, *know him too well to miss when he is hurt and nettled.*

"You can talk now," said Dammerung, giving Skander's rough, unshaven cheek a smart clap with the flat of his hand. "Now is your turn. Thank you—" He took his own glass from Margaret.

"We saw Rupert too—the man gets about." Skander tested his lips. They still sported angry red lines, which would turn later into silver scars, but the skin had closed. Cutting her eyes aside to Dammerung's lean, lithe figure thrown casually against a battered table, the sparking red-speaking wine-glass clasped lightly in the long fingers, Margaret wondered how much of the War-wolf was good flesh and how much was, like Plenilune's own scars, silvered tissue from past wounds.

The foxy head twisted at Skander's words; a brow arched.

"We had the better part of Locklear's forces against us—quite the flower of Rupert's army, I reckon from experience. I swear no sooner did I get here, coming up from Helming Side, then I was entrenched in a glen-war. Locklear better knows glens than I. I think, providence aside, that it was sheer determination on our part that saw us through. I did give the man back as good as he gave me, and more, I imagine." He gestured out toward the limned night where the Tarnjewel sky was lighting the tapers in honour of the dying day. "Five glens down, between a nasty burl, a few rocks, and a drop into a stream, he cut me across the face—a masterful stroke, too, though it wasn't enough to kill me, which is what he wanted—and of a sudden I saw red. I gave him a neat, clean clip across the waist-band, enough to sever his leather and trousers and even felt a bit of bone come too. I nearly wenched him, and the blow sent him into the water. I was too busy to go after him. I don't know what became of him, but I doubt he met his end there."

"You said you saw Rupert," Margaret reminded him.

He shifted in his chair toward her. "Only at the end. He came up by way of the post-road and went west along the outskirts of us. The battle was over thirty minutes after that. That was all I saw of him."

Dammerung, too, looked toward the twilight glory of the west, and though he did not speak, Margaret could hear his thoughts move in the narrow seaway of his eyes:

You are out there, watching me.

Aloud he said, presently, "I wish this were over."

And Skander murmured, "Not for awhile yet, coz."

Margaret put down the little silver tureen full, not of soup, but of meat pasties. What fickle things appetites were: she had lost hers again. "Not to sound callous and cold-hearted," she broke in: "is there a place where I might bathe?"

Dammerung came off the table. Skander leaned forward and took a pasty and eased it into his mouth. "There is a secluded bit of glen with a fall and pool just down the slope back of the house—tent," he amended. Grimly, stiffly, he shouldered out of his chair and moved toward the tent opening. "I am going on the rounds. I lost my lieutenant Scilay a week ago and until I can replace him the rounds are mine to do alone. Do you come?" he asked hopefully, turning back to his cousin.

But Dammerung smiled wearily, foxily. "God rest his soul. No, sorry. A lonely, introspective walk it is for you."

The man murmured something under his breath about Woodbird, something which Margaret could not quite catch, and then he was gone.

Dammerung leaned back against the table, one foot crossed beside the other.

"He called it a house," she remarked, looking over the tent.

There was a mirror on the far side of the interior; in it, she could see Dammerung nod once. "Months of campaign will do that to you. But tell me you did not feel a little stirring as of feathers in a nest when you came in here."

She nodded her admittance, found her pack, and dug in it for a clean shift. Beside her, upreared in shadow at odd angles with everything, Dammerung looked down and watched her. A pent-up feeling simmered under the form of him; when she had found her comb and had gone looking further into her bag for her second pair of earrings—which always fell to the bottom corner and seemed to get lost—she said,

"Whatever it is, you had better say it or your hair will catch fire."

He laughed gustily and small sparks crackled around his dog-teeth. "I wanted to ask if you would be bull-set against me accompanying you."

Sitting back on her heels, she frowned up at him. His head was bent into shadow, but his eyes were oddly illumined. *What a truly callous, thoughtless creature I have become!* she half-laughed to herself. "Truth to tell," she admitted aloud, "I had always counted on you coming. It isn't safe, anyway, for me to go alone."

"Had you?" He put out his hand and shoved it through the crest of her hair, hard, as one might rough the head of a favourite hound. She unbalanced and landed on her buttocks. "My main thought was that you had assumed—but God help a man who assumes upon a lady's favour!"

"Tush!" she said, and grasped after his hand to haul her to her feet. "*You* could use a rinse too."

He went to a trunk and rummaged for some clothing. "I know," his muffled voice came back. "The grit and grime and shadow of Rupert is loathsome even to me. I come. *Après vous...*"

There was still a little light on the horizon when they went out but not enough to light the way. Dammerung, canny in the dark, stepped up beside her and together they wound their way down the little half-worn path to the sound of running water. Presently Margaret found herself on the sloping drop of a rocky bank looking down into a rocky pool with a fall a little more than a man high. With care she crouched, steadied herself with her hands, and extended her legs onto the narrow shore below. Dammerung stepped down beside her.

"You could really believe," he murmured, glancing round, "that a place like this was magic. It has a warm and pleasant genius."

"The water is cold," said Margaret, testing it.

With a flick of his wrist Dammerung found a stag's-crown of branchwork that had got caught in the rocky wall of the tiny glen; a few dozen points of light sprang out of the dark from each twig-tip, casting a yellow pall of light over them and sending down little waving flecks of light to play in the deep dimension of the water. Margaret felt them dance inside her.

Her companion sat down on a low stone and began rolling up the hem of his trousers. Crouching, she untied her moleskin overdress—which the water would have ruined—and slid, one leg first and then the other, sucking in a startled breath as she did so, into the frothing water.

"O-o-oh...!" she cried.

Dammerung looked up from a blind fiddling with his shirt buttons. "Very cold?"

She swept up to her shoulders in the black water. "The air was warm and this is cold!"

"Sets the blood tingling!"

He knelt like a dog at the water's edge and thrust his head into the stream. With steady scrubbing he pulled and tousled the pliant ends of his hair through his fingers. Doing the same, Margaret noted that he would need a pair of scissors presently and wondered if the blue-jay man was also good at that sort of thing.

"I forget how hair grows," he said into his knees. "I never had this problem when I was a fox..."

Her own hair had grown in the past nine months: a mermaid's net of darkness spread across the surface of the water all around her, flickering gold with firelight, flickering white where the crescent of the earth shot down a few spare rays of light and lit the wet dark around her. The ends were caught in the bubbling torrent; her feet, rolling and catching at rounded stones below, were buffeted in a forceful, watery dance. She felt submerged in Plenilune and the warm loam-scent of dusk swelled in the light and the dark into her nostrils. She shut her eyes and breathed.

She was half done, and Dammerung all finished, when suddenly he said, "What does Lord Gro do here?" and he rose, spinning on one heel. Margaret looked up, surprised and a little blushing; against the heirloom-blue of nightfall moved the staid figure of the Gemeren land-owner, the silk-moving grey figure of his dog at his side.

"Capys said I would find you here," he said, stopping on the rocky overhang of the bank.

"And so you do," replied Dammerung levelly. She felt him reaching, feeling, testing the air. "What is amiss?"

But Gro put up his chin indicatively toward Skander's tent and said, "He asks that you come."

"Then I come." The War-wolf stooped and swept up his fresh shirt, white and shining in the dark, and pulled it on. "Of your courtesy, would you leave Snati with Margaret?"

Gro said nothing, but clapped his hands once and pointed to a bit of level ground on the bank. Obedient, Snati dropped onto his hindquarters and gazed down brightly, knowingly, at Margaret. She sank a little deeper into the water.

Dammerung cast her one last assuring glance before going back up the hillside with Gro, but Margaret did not feel assured. She finished her bath and climbed out under the golden gaze of the big wolf-thing who, with the jerky canine movements of its eyes, watched her kneel over the water to wring out her hair and bend, grimacing, to peel off her soaked underdress to exchange it for a fresh one. Worn and breathless, but clean and newly clothed, she stood pantingly, looking back at Snati's inscrutable face.

"You are but a dog," she told him. "What do *you* care?"

He seemed not to; his face, though intelligent, was not the fox's: he seemed only to understand and care that she was not in danger.

Margaret bent, cupping her hand, and scooping up a handful of water to fling on the flaming branches. The water hissed and burst into steam, but the flames, cowed a moment, rose again. Pursing her lips, she flung another handful of water and hit the greater part of the flames; they would not go out.

Very well, be that way! she thought petulantly. But as she stooped to wrap up her bundle of soiled clothing she was touched by a cold sense of being watched, as if by eyes, by all those points of flame.

But she had other things to think about as she toiled, limbs chilled and gently aching, up the slope toward the tent. Two sentries stood at hand, faces to the southwest, and they watched her intently as she and the dog walked up to them. They saluted promptly—which was nothing out of the ordinary: the men were always quick and eager to show her deference; but there was something curious in the way the two moved aside for her and the one said,

"I trust thou hast not gone far, my lady."

She stopped, surprised by his forwardness in speech. "No," she said slowly. "Only to the little glen. I had the War-wolf's permission," she added, though she could not fathom why she should be defending herself to a soldier.

One tentatively patted Snati's brow. "Thou hast a fair watchdog to heel. That is well."

She went on, prickling with disturbance and curiosity; she could feel the two soldiers watching her as she went.

It was when she reached the level of Skander's knoll that she became aware of the tension in the air. It was like moving through a band of dark electricity. Her hair, heavy with the damp, rose even so with the surge of power all around her. Bristling like a witch's familiar, tensed, wary, she stepped up to the down-flung tent-flap and pushed it aside.

The energy struck her in the face.

Almost upon the instant she stepped in, though few heads turned, all eyes were on her. Skander and Brand and Aikin Ironside were there, grim-faced, standing in a little ring about Dammerung where he sat in a low-slung chair. He had not put on any more than his mud-spattered trousers and his clean starched shirt, but he was wrapped in a sense of fire and spice and danger so thick Margaret feared that if she stepped in any more she might prick the bubble and let loose a hurricane. They all looked at her, sharply—the same looks the soldiers had given her; Margaret had the sense of being pulled into some protective ring by their glances as Dammerung might pull her clear of physical danger with an arm around her hourglass. Frightened now, she looked to the figure they had under guard in their midst.

The man stood between Huw and Gro, arms bound at his back. He had the familiar look of a soldier who has just come through a day-long fight and has had time only to put up his horse and drag his mucky harness over his head. He had several days' growth of beard on his dirty face, and one cheek had been laid open raggedly, as though by a blow from someone's signet-ring. He was stripped of armour; his rough shirt had been dragged back on his shoulders so that the collar rose high and uncomfortably under his chin, baring his shoulder-blades at the back. He was a brute-handsome devil, and as the chill night wind blew in past her he, too, looked round, catching her eye with a searching glance unlike that of the others'. She coloured and felt her stomach cringe.

Swiftly, smoothly, Skander stepped out of the ring and raised his naked sword to rest the point on the man's unbroken cheek. "Put down your eyes, dog," he said, "or I'll put them down for you."

The man switched his eyes from Margaret to Skander; the lips twitched with a sour, involuntary tic, and then the eyes obediently dropped. At the same time Dammerung's hand, which had been resting stiff and white on the arm of his chair, turned over, beckoning for Margaret with a single sharp gesture.

She could move then. Head uplifted, the hot blood coursing in her throat, she swept past them. Brand stepped back to make a place for her behind and beside Dammerung. Skander, satisfied, left the soldier to be pinned under the War-wolf's eye and went out of the ring of war-lords to fetch Margaret's surcoat from her trunk. She did not look round but she felt the comfortable warmth of it drop about her shoulders and the man's familiar, big, rough hand settle a moment reassuringly on the curve of her upper arm.

An awful silence, which she had disturbed, fell over the tent again. The soldier and the War-wolf regarded each other in a hot-blooded quiet. Whatever the soldier was thinking it was angry, sullen, but forcibly self-assured; the War-wolf seemed to be listening at once to his own thoughts and to the thoughts of the man he held under the silvered point of his gaze.

As last the latter tipped up his chin, rousing from his silence. "Lord Gro, what has been done with the woman's body?"

The lord deftly turned his head, deferring to Huw—who, mimicking the War-wolf's upward thrust of the head, said, "No one claimed her, sir. She was given burial alongside the soldiers of the day."

Gro added, "A little inquiry revealed she came from a small village whose orchards border the land which was fought over today."

"All alone," said the War-world with a sudden savagery.

In a more careful voice Huw continued as if on report. "I think she must have got caught in a sortie, sir. I was coming down to collect the dead and saw her lying dead, too, among the apple trees; and saw him," he nodded his head toward the prisoner, "just stepping up to take a dance with her."

Dammerung put up one heel on the rung of his chair and draped his forearm across his knee. For now Margaret chose not too look at the prisoner's face, but watched Dammerung's from a high angle—and saw, not the fox this time, but the wolfishness of him staring out from under the sharp-edged, dark brows of the de la Mare face as a wolf peers out from under its native bush. She saw the lips part a little and reveal the hungry dog-teeth. He leaned a little forward to meet the motion of his leg, chin upthrust to look into the prisoner's face.

What must it be like for the prisoner, she wondered with a shudder, to have to stare back into that violent disapproval?

"What is your name?"

"Púka," the man said stiffly. His lip did not appear to work very well on one side. "Bazel Púka."

"You are native to Orzelon-gang, then."

The man did not speak, but his face affirmed.

The hand lifted, tightening into a fist; Dammerung rested his chin on his knuckle. "It appears that you have an appetite for corpses."

Púka twisted one imprisoned shoulder carelessly. "It could be worse."

"Truly?" the War-wolf's throat growled. "Truly, I am not so sure. The living have a say and might strike back—hast got a woman's claws across your cheek before?—but the dead are silent and motionless, and depend wholly on Christian charity for decency."

With a little look round, Púka asked back, "Hast *thou* ever, sir?"

Every body in the tent chamber stiffened except Dammerung's. Huw made a visible movement which looked like a flinch away from the prisoner, as though expecting Dammerung's lightning to strike the man at any moment and he did not want to be too close. Margaret flushed with angry surprise and wondered if the man Púka knew to whom and to what he was speaking.

His eye momentarily straying among the heavily-clad feet of the men, the War-wolf murmured rhythmically, "How happy is the blameless vestal's lot! The world forgetting, by the world forgot... Do you know—" he seemed to come back out of himself "—what I do with men like you?"

The breath of mortality chilled the soldier's cheek. His throat involuntarily clenched as if it could already feel the noose about it.

"I was answered that once, by a man who thought I was altogether such a one as himself." The War-wolf got up, tall-seeming and cloaked in dread. The reflection of him glinted back out of the sudden swell of black in Púka's eye. "You will hang, and you will hang high, and you will hang long, and the crows will come and pick your flesh—and you, like all the dead, will not be able to stop them."

The eyes, blackened by the promise of a swift drop into death, tore off the War-wolf's face and found Margaret's. She felt him call across to her, proudly, stiffly, yet desperately. But if he thought to find some solace and womanly compassion in her, he was sorely mistaken. Dammerung's words had laid hot bars across her heart and she was impenetrable.

"Nay, sirrah," she spoke lowly, huskily. "Do not look to *us* for mercy. Our hearts are iron-clad."

"Nor have you any right to ask a lady for her kerchief," said Dammerung acidly. He thrust his hand, fingers spread, toward the tent opening. "Get him out of my sight and bind him: let him be, but bind him." He stepped away, dragging his dark aura after him, but swung back at the last moment. "You wanted a cold companion," he said. Púka's cheeks paled. "You'll find death's kiss very cold indeed."

"Hie with you," snapped Huw, and jerked the man about. They went, with a little more prodding from Huw than was strictly necessary, Margaret thought, but then the ex-thief was probably glad for the excuse to strut a little.

Skander said something level and appreciative to the others and they, too, left—Margaret heard Aikin say in passing to Brand that he had better follow along after Huw and be of help. Finally they were all gone—Gro, unlike himself, doubled back and bade them good-night at the tent-flap—and it was only Skander and Dammerung and herself in the soft haze of lamp-smoke and the feeling that her bath had been in vain.

Dammerung was staring at things he could not look away from, though she could see from the whiteness of his eyes that he wished to. His shadow seemed to move of its own accord and sang a little along the edges with a brief marshlight flame.

"Dammerung," she called quietly. "Come back out of the cellar now."

"A moment..." he said without moving. Then, with a deep breath, he seemed to break out of the spell of his own thoughts.

Her brows quirked with a spasm of sympathy. "Is it very hard being you?"

"Sometimes."

"Aikaterine," said Skander as the maid stepped in out of the dark, "I would rather you slept in here tonight. You can bed by Lady Margaret—if she does not herself object."

"Of course not." Margaret met the maid's surprised, questioning eye. "I should not feel easy myself if she were elsewhere. Oh, Dammerung," she added as the blue-jay man followed hard on Aikaterine's heels, "you need a haircut. Would Skander's man do?"

But Dammerung had oozed onto a couch and had rolled over, his shoulder to her, and she knew in a moment she would lose him. "One must look one's best for a hanging... In the morning. Could you find me some sort of blanket, Spencer?"

Skander turned, surprised, from digging among the litter on his table. But before he could say anything Margaret swept her hands harshly through the air, shutting his half opened mouth, and she dragged a rug off the back of a nearby chair. Dammerung's introverted form, ruddy in the lamplight, was easily engulfed by the blanket. She bent into the shadow as she pulled it over his shoulders; his eyes were open, staring into the further dark, his lips set in a thin angry line.

"You look green," she whispered.

He rustled his shoulders but did not look up. "I am angry," he confessed. "Can you blame me?"

She opened her mouth to assure him she was just as angry as he, but he went on in spite of her.

"I am angry that it happened. I was hoping we might make it through a whole season without..." His voice trailed off and presently he began again. "I am angry that I have to hang a man—not for the man's sake, for he made his own choice, but for the simple selfish fact that my own gut crawls at the thought of the drop and the snap. But most of all I am angry that you had to know."

The fox in him flashed out so keenly she half expected the backward curl of his lips to reveal all pointed teeth. She sat down on the edge of the couch and crossed one knee over the other. In the background Skander was talking to the blue-jay man, quietly, comfortably, and Aikaterine was making up a bed for herself and Margaret. Dammerung, like a mature fire, smouldered inside himself and only she, Margaret felt, could reach out and touch him and not be burned.

"I'm a big girl," she told him. "I was not lying when I said we have guts of steel."

"I have seen human guts," he said coldly. "I know they are not metal made."

So, he had caught his own mistake and that, too, was gnawing at him. A sudden desperation, which felt a lot like anger, to rid him of his dark mood rose up in her. In that same husky tone, like one of the Thrasymene women, she said levelly, "It will be over and we will get through it, and—God help us—it will be done. And we are the high, strong people of Plenilune who will not let on that we bleed and that we feel and that we ache and that we grow weary in the middle of the battlefield. We will not let on that there is a little of the fool among the gold." She got up. "Go to sleep, War-wolf, and bloody your teeth tomorrow."

He rolled over and looked up at her, squinting through the lamplight. "Your heel is sharp," he laughed. "Why—*why*—was he such a fool as to pick *you?*"

It was a backhanded compliment, but it was the familiar stuff of his soul and she smiled back, content that he was better, and left him, musing on the torment of a great genius, to curl up in her own doeskins and stare out at the breathing dark, her back to Aikaterine's. She had spoken colourfully, bluntly, because that was what had been needful, but in her heart she nursed a wretched sickness—just as she was sure Dammerung did too—and she wondered to herself, *Why do I feel what little is left standing of the world is about to crumble?*

She was not surprised the next morning when the news came that no trace of Bazel Púka was to be found.

XXVIII | THE WITCHING THING

Margaret stepped back with a sharp, angry cry into the tent opening as a whirlwind of fire, dislodging from the chaos, passed across her cheek. Her vision sang with white light, then cleared away again in fragmented, floating petals of brilliance, torn up by the black bulk of the panther and the crack of spells.

In a lithe arc Dammerung sailed by her and turned back on one hind paw, raising a column of dirt and turf, parting the ground as the hand of God had parted the Red Sea. He was huge, as big as the panther that now faced him, tail lashing. His face was a singing hot-iron white, his body shifting in and out of being flame and scarlet fur; he had nearly a dozen tails—they moved too quickly for Margaret to count them—and they stroked up the wind into a tempest behind him. The eyes gleamed; one paw lifted a fraction—it had been white; it was red now. He was still for just long enough for Margaret to get a clear view of his face, as she had not been able to do since the moment he had flung himself through the tent opening into the jaws of the panther. He was angry, she could see, yet oddly happy. As the wind of his own fury swept the soft white hair on his brow it parted just enough in that moment to reveal a single bar of gold running down his forehead—nothing more, and yet the sight of it chilled Margaret in the heart-place. She did not need to have seen that mark before to hear it speaking its name to her.

Resurrection.

The two war-lords came together. The panther reared, shrieking until her bones rattled; it swung one massive paw at the fox's head. At the last second the fox ducked, hindquarters clenching, and sprang in under the panther's elbow, snapping his teeth for the flesh along the ribs. Neither struck. The panther's blow fell wide and cut into the ground. The empty clack of the fox's teeth—like a gun going off at close quarters—shocked out a ring of endless light that sheared off a heavy portion of turf and dismantled a tree that stood behind the tent. Margaret half turned at the sound of crashing limbs but did not dare look away for long.

Rupert knocked Dammerung down. There was a shearing of cloth as the body—flickering between a man and a fox—crashed through the side of a tent, skidded into a pile of Capys blue, and then erupted again, cloth sailing round the lean, twisting shoulders. Rupert sprang, the muscles beneath his shimmering night-coloured coat clenching and stretching; the hair along his spine rose higher and higher, catching fire and shining phosphorescent blue. Margaret looked for a thing to throw but there was nothing sizeable to hand. She opened her mouth to shout but at the same moment, by some wicked sense of genius, it seemed the black side of the moon had sensed her cry: her stomach shifted forward, straining against her skin. Pain screamed in her middle and she fell back, gasping, clutching her stomach before it was torn out of her the way it had been torn out of Spencer.

You horrible, God-forsaken, spit-hearted blackguard. I despise you! She swallowed, struggled, and tried again.

All that came out was a gurgling croak and the intense feeling that she was going to vomit. Through her parted strands of hair she saw the enormous panther come down, like a little hunting cat, on the place where, a second before, Dammerung had been wresting himself out of the wreckage of the tent. Dammerung himself was nowhere to be seen, but as the paws touched the ground and the shock-wave of weight nearly flung Margaret to her face, there was a great crash of noise and light and, from somewhere down the hillside, Skander's voice roaring through the chaos—

"*Hell damn it, you bastards—we can't see!*"

Rupert's teeth let out a surprised yowling scream and he rocketed sideways, landing on his feet. With the side of his face in ribbons and his arm hanging at a grotesque angle, Dammerung emerged in a swell of blue thunder, staggering a little, but very angry and determined to have done.

Suddenly Skander was there, Blue-bottle Glass a king of fury and triumphant movement against the evening sky, with his lashing forehooves dancing dangerously near Dammerung's head. "We're going into Holywood," he shouted, leaning down so that his cousin could hear him. "Do well enough here?"

"Fine. Put your hand a moment here."

Skander dropped off his horse's back while the panther looked on hungrily, courtesy galling him. With a firm grip Skander took Dammerung's shoulder in hand, braced himself, and held still while his cousin twisted himself violently into the embrace. There was the sound of a little click, muffled by the distance: Margaret's wounded stomach crawled. But Dammerung staggered out of Skander's hold—and suddenly there was no bloody, sweating young man in a tattered sable tunic but the fox again—a huge humming, many-splendoured thing—rushing without check into the panther's jaws.

Before they met Skander was already in the saddle, Blue-bottle Glass already wheeling to run; Rupert's counterblast singed the hocks of the animal as it tore screaming down the hillside. There was a sound like a hammer hitting a gong, a whirling planet of light, a ring in singing motion, a spray of stars—to Margaret it seemed the whole cosmos had met in the teeth and claws and angry, defiant wills of the two men slashing and biting on the uneven green before her. She winced and tensed and strained for Dammerung's sake, as though by so doing she might lend him a little energy where he might most need it.

At the sound of rending cloth she sprang round like a loosed bowstring. Between an intruding bough and a metal upright in the tent's side a soldier's cavalry sword was cutting a way in. She stepped back into the opening of the tent; magic raised the hairs on the back of her neck and sent the wildest sensations of thrones and dominions singing into her skin.

With a twist and a thrust the soldier got in and stumbled a little over a bit of rug. He wore the familiar black scarf of Friend about his upper arm, but as he raised his head and got a look at her, and she of him, she recognized him at once.

The rack of Standards went over outside, crashing and clattered with a chill foreboding of disaster.

"The humour in it is," said Bazel Púka, "that he thinks I'm fetching you for *him*."

"You *bastards*," she said with the tone of one putting one's foot down.

He sprang for her and she sprang to the side, hands reaching for the nearest serviceable object. She had never been so little frightened in her life: the emotions she felt chiefly were annoyance at being torn away from Dammerung's snarling fight and anger at the unwelcome demotion of Lady Spitcat to a mouse.

The first thing she found was a metal map-case, half as long as she was tall, and she swung it as soon as her hands closed over it. Púka, surprised, was taken off guard and in the right temple with a satisfying clang. The shock ground up into Margaret's arms and the metal tube bent over on itself from the impact. She dropped it and ran for the next weapon while he stumbled after her, cursing, strong as a warhorse and as lithe as a racing hound. She went over a table and dropped to the ground underneath it; he grasped the edge and heaved it over, like a boy kicking over the top of an ants' nest, but she had already gathered, cursing her skirts, and was leaping for a nearby couch. There was nothing on it but a rug, but she snatching it up anyway, whirled—there was nowhere else to go—and flung it over the quickly-moving bulk of the soldier bearing down on her. Half of it he shaved off, cutting her arm, but the rest, with a little cry of determination, she got wrapped round his head somehow and then it was her turn, with a sense of exultant power, to dig in her heels and heave over on him, driving him backward while he shook and writhed and swore and growled under her grasp like ten tomcats in a weakening sack.

"A pawn!" she screamed, too angry to care how hennish she sounded. "A pawn, do you think? to be snatched up at will by any comer? You fool! You fool—who could not even court a corpse!"

He cried something damnably about all women, dropped down onto one knee, the rug slipping sideways, and grabbed her with one alarmingly large hand under her breast—the ribs that Rupert had broken. A sudden shock of memory, of pain and torment, lanced through her brain. She knew her defence was going down and was too blind with nauseating fear to stop it. The next moment she was going over, the ground rising up to meet her back, the man Púka had a knee on her sternum and was stooping to gather her up.

"Io-o-o-o!" the air roared. "Io! io! io!" Something—a man and a fox and a dragon all at once—seemed to explode between her and the man Púka and to thrust them from each other, and then, by the same force, riding on the manic wave of movement, she and the confusion of man were tumbling clear, out of the tent, out of the ragged blue fabric, across a lawn and into a crashing tomb of scrub trees and undergrowth.

"Hoc habet!" cried Dammerung, getting up on his knees. But he was not looking at her. Out of the ringing of sensations Margaret rolled onto her bruised elbow; through the parting of the grasses which a tempest from the War-wolf was flattening she saw the hulking shoulders of the panther tearing down the tent, heard the crack of wood and the snap of metal, and watched, without feeling anything—that frightened her most—as Rupert caught the errant ex-soldier and began to play with him, skilfully, furiously, all his claws extended, just as a cat plays with his dinner before he eats it. A swipe—a part of Púka went flying, bloodily, with a piercing scream; two swipes and a batter of teeth made several living pieces of the man. Dammerung got up, his fists clenched, a ring of blackened gold around the crest of him; taking her eyes off the wreck of Bazel Púka, Margaret saw, for a moment, a kinship between him and his brother which had never been before, which would never be again.

"To have done that myself—" he growled, then seemed to remember her as Púka's last scream was cut short by a clawed blow across the mouth. The pale eye focused out of the bloody face that framed it. It was curiously like a touch, and out of the shimmering welter of thunderbolt and counterblast she felt his mind again. He reached out—

—She swung up her hand and grasped his forearm. With a jerk he pulled her to her feet. "Go on!" she panted. With a violent shove she pushed up the cloth on her arm and squinted dispassionately at the gory laceration. "I'll be fine. Go on!"

Instead Dammerung took hold of her arm again, thrust his fingers between his lips, and blew a shrill whistle.

There was a stirring along the thinned picket-line. The panther jerked his head up, muzzle stained purple, scarlet dripping from bared teeth. He was looking hard at Dammerung, questioning, daring, but Dammerung did not look back. Trailing his lead Rubico rounded the end of the picket-line and came at a swallow's gallop up the hillside. Margaret watched the bloodlust move in the panther's eyes. The warhorse's path would have to cross Rupert's. In a moment, a few more strides, the panther would have it. Still the horse came on, never swerving to the right or the left.

Without realizing what she was doing Margaret spread her hands, tensed, as if she were going to gather up the ground in them and fold them over the horse herself—she, who had not a flicker of power in her entire being.

The panther was not watching Dammerung now. In a chink of time he had been put aside, smothered in a blinding spitefulness—the spitefulness that had killed Spencer—and with a white laughter Dammerung took his chance. The panther gathered to spring, paw rising to crush the horse in two; the War-wolf stepped forward, flickered, and seemed to disappear. Margaret could never afterward describe it adequately: he seemed to go away into the ether, or to wrap the ether around him, to pull the frontiers of numinous air and airlessness around him as a cloak, passing through the midst of things unseen...

An arc of light encircled the horse, blue and white-cut like the atmosphere of earth. At the same moment a pillar of fire—with the sense about it of being human—cracked the air and sheared it apart. The air was burning. It was beyond burning. With a force that ripped her breath away Dammerung shivered the air into the netherworld without passing it through the grave. The panther was hurtled backward, opening up darkness and closing it again, beginning to make and to unmake things like stars, to tear up earth and sky and human passion as it went; and still the pillar, eating up the hillside, roared upon the brink of everything now and the everlasting after, a guardian in the gap, a titan at the threshold. Under her feet Margaret felt Plenilune tremble—with fury and with colossal ecstasy—and all the elements flew.

The panther skin tore away. For a moment she saw Rupert, crouched, braced against the blast, then Rubico was on top of her and she had to swing round, reaching desperately for the black-lightning flicker of the reins, and save herself from being run down.

"Heel, boy!" she cried. Power seared her flesh until it felt red and raw. Blindly, she reached into the swirl of blue as it engulfed her and, with her heart in her throat, she felt her hand snag and close on the worn leather reins. The next moment her arm was nearly wrenched out of its socket as the stallion plunged and turned on the face of coin, hooves lashing round her head. She felt an iron-hot shoe sing down over her brow; her head yanked back in time to save her cheekbone from a splitting. "Heel! Get down! Whoa-ah!"

"Be still."

The blink of a dragon's face dashed round them, huge, unreal. Then Dammerung was there in his proper body, foot raised and jammed in the stirrup. His face was thoroughly bloodied but his smile was the same, half-mad, all teeth. He took the reins from her and grabbed a handful of mane; with a spring he was in the saddle and pulling her up after him.

She grabbed onto his belt as the horse surged beneath them. She glanced back—no sign of Rupert, only a sidewise drift of smoke and the wreckage of a tent. Rubico jerked her back around with a sudden headlong stumble, a twist to the side, and a check and bound that somehow kept them upright.

"Where are you going?" Margaret shouted in Dammerung's ear. "What about Rupert?"

"Centurion needs me!" was the cryptic reply.

She could say no more; the horse's pace, gathering into a reckless speed, jarred her words off her tongue between her teeth, her rattling teeth crushed them before she could get them round her tongue again. Faces flew by, faces white and bloodied and blackened by smoke. She saw the sable armbands of the Friends and in amongst them the Whites too, grappling back and forth from tent-line to tent-line. Once, looking over her shoulder again, she caught the nightmarish sight of a pale Standard upraised over the tents, snapping in the high wind, sporting a scarlet flower. The sight of it tasted foul in her mouth but she could not remember why.

The ground opened up into a low, long depression, interrupted here and there by the knees of the hills, furred a little with woodscrub on the edges, but mostly open, Margaret saw, as Rubico flung himself onto the outskirts of the camp and clear of the last tent. They were facing west: the sun was in her eyes. She saw a confusion of battle-mass locked and grinding in the tiny valley—and upreared against the halo of sunlight, shining like a beacon, the eagle-Standard of Darkling, the tattered black cloth in a riot of wind hanging from its talons.

"*Io! io! io!*" cried Dammerung.

Widowmaker sang out of the sheath.

The first wave of soldiers fell back before the war-lord like men giving way before a loosed bull. The next few moments were like living the ring of struck metal. Margaret caught the faces of people around her, never really taking them in but recognizing some of them: she saw Malbrey, encased in leather up to the chin, swinging a claymore at Brand. They were close enough that she heard the drumming whoop of Brand's war-hammer as he whirled it over his head. Holyoke of Hol—in a spray of yellow cloak—she saw for a moment between Rubico's forehooves. What became of him she never saw; her world was mostly holding on and keeping out of Dammerung's way, for he seemed to have forgotten her. He plied about him with Widowmaker, spraying blood in his face—spraying some into hers—shouting, cat-calling, rallying, until the air thrummed with his voice. Once she twisted to avoid his elbow, twisted so far she was at right angles with Rubico's body, holding onto Dammerung's belt with one hand, the other strained out for balance, and looking under the War-wolf's rein-arm she watched the head of someone whose face she did not know, whose name was unknown to her, slide cleanly off his head and spill everything it had been keeping inside down the slumping front of the body. She was too charged with fire in the blood to feel any sickness at the sight.

A shield-ring. A wall of shields giving back, cracking open to let them through. In the centre of them rose the eagle and beside it astride an angry sorrel horse was Centurion himself, chin-strap askew and darkened with blood, sword in a white-knuckle hand. He jerked the hilt of his sword up to his forehead in salute as Rubico came down with a bang beside him.

"You must needs watch your flank!" he roared over the din at Dammerung.

"Well I am glad of your sanguine face today," the War-wolf retorted. "All our flanks needed watching, and lacked it."

"Poor scouts?"

"Man from the inside!"

She could not hear what the other said—a new wave was coming against the shield-ring and the noise was overwhelming—but she saw his lips shape the angry invective. He leaned in close. "I saw Capys head southeast into the wood. Who holds the high ground?"

"The Harlequin is holding Olympus. We have to get you out of this mess and secure the north face. But Rupert is here."

Centurion's head came up, looking toward the high ground, eyes narrowed against a stream of blood. "Well—" He jammed his heels downward in the stirrups. "To dare is to do—isn't that what your father used to say?"

"Then let us dare!"

"Mm!" cried Margaret as the warhorse came around and planted itself hard by the sorrel beast. Her own expletive was lost—which made her angry, because she wanted the comfort of hearing it coming soundly out of her own mouth—in Centurion's roar of orders.

"Up shields—together—a-a-and—FORWARD!"

Shank! clank! Shield-rim kissed shield-rim. At a steady pace, half-running, the ring began to move forward across the uneven ground; Rubico high-stepped between the antsy brown horse and the Standard-bearer. Margaret caught a glimpse of the Standard-bearer's face: a grim, upraised, stone-wrought thing that might be pleasant at other times; with the shadow across his face he looked like a sentinel of the dead.

They had rejoined those who had not made it into the ranks of the shield-ring. The ranks suddenly opened out, every man moving as one with his neighbour—chills ran up and down Margaret's veins to watch them—into a star-burst pattern with half a dozen White soldiers caught in the wedges between. A horn blared a warning; a pack of horsemen, swinging through the low scrub, hit them in the south flank. A wave of desperation flowed in on Margaret from the hard-pressed Darkling soldiers around her. Centurion looked back over his shoulder, looked her way: she saw the tension in his jaw-line.

But Dammerung, wheeling round, cried, "The back door is going! You—you—you three, come by and run at my flanks. Hie! hie, cousin! *Yah!*"

And Rubico, with another of his flying leads, was off again, the star-pattern making way for him and the men running at his heels, all of them yelling for courage and anger—which were easy to mistake one for the other, she thought.

They fanned out at the last moment and took the onslaught of horsemen in the chest. One man went down almost instantly, but he was good enough to fall with a twist and, with the horseman's lance in his chest, wrench the rider out of the saddle under the hooves of his horse. The rider got one accidental blow to the head, that was all—the horse sprang clear and trotted off in bewilderment—but that was enough: the White horseman was dead on impact.

Margaret looped her arms through Dammerung's belt, clung on for all she was worth, and kept her head down.

A shield flung down among the knees of the horses rang in the tumult. A snatch of Psalm, shouted at the top of someone's lungs, broke clear like a hawk banking on a breast of air. Dammerung was half-laughing, half-crying in an agony of exertion; the whirl of the War-wolf's sword cast bars of sunsetting light on the bloodied turf.

Why not blow them all to Kingdom come? she wondered as the War-wolf's muscles screamed in her ears. *Why all this bloodshed?*

Why all this trouble when you could only speak a word and crush them out of life forever?

She began to hear Dammerung's battle-name being yelled from man to man. Four horsemen among the White riders were left still in their seats; they checked at Dammerung's approach, checked at the sight of the sword and a face Margaret could not see from her position. She saw their jarring forms waver, their horses wheel at the bit, but they stood their ground. With an angry wrench her heart went out to them, for it took a man of iron will to stand firm against the kiss of the War-wolf's steel.

The first blow severed the head of the horse and stuck in the breastbone of the rider. With a cry Dammerung twisted in the saddle, dragged back by the pull—the blade sang in Margaret's ear as it was hauled reluctantly out of the bone. But she did not have time to think about it. The next rider had passed by and swung at her, raising the heat of terror in her ear as she ducked and felt the wind of the sword go whistling by. He swung again; she ducked to the other side.

"I don't have a sword!" she yelled in Dammerung's ear, hoping—but not really believing—that she would reach him in the red place to which he had gone.

Something must have got through to him, for he turned his head toward her voice. His eye, in a face of brown, dried blood, was luminescent silver.

Like the moon.

He dropped the reins. Rubico ascended on his hind legs, slowly, inexorably. Before she could begin to slide, the War-wolf reached back with his free hand and grabbed her hard by the shoulder and wrenched her down to the side; her cheek was pressed against his thigh. Like a man wielding a hammer he spun Widowmaker over his head, and from her angle—feeling the powerful muscles in the leg clench and jump with strain—she watched the blue-star point of the sword break open the face of the rider behind.

Rubico pushed Plenilune out of orbit, back into the frontier realm of Earth. With a bound he shoved the ground away seemed to dislodge from gravitation and all the laws that governed the world. Waiting for the world to reawaken and reclaim them,

Margaret put her arm around Dammerung's waist and held on tightly.

The horse's body hit another's. Metal sang. The sun had gone down and the valley was awash of brown and scarlet shadows with sudden points of flame on swords and buckler-rims. Something warm and running hit Margaret's face; she smelled iron. The familiar sound of Widowmaker finding home in someone's body tore open her little envelope of the world; the familiar sound of a surprised, pained grunt, which was the end of a man's life, clawed gratingly at her ears. Then—

"S'all, sir! They've had it!"

The warhorse was standing still, head lowered, flanks heaving. The sound of battle still rang from woodshore to distant clearing, but it was breaking up, growing fainter. A bell was banging somewhere, for what reason Margaret did not know.

"Take the lady," said Dammerung quietly.

He let go and she slid, rolling, into the arms of a soldier she could not quite see in the gloom. She stumbled on the ground and felt surprised to find it there.

"Oh, my lady! What—nay, take thee my arm. What dost about in battle?"

Plenilune's buckling subsided at last. Feverishly, she pushed out of the soldier's arms. "No, I'm fine, thank you," she insisted, making a concerted effort to sound friendly though her instinct was telling her to strike the man's hands away and to shout at him to leave her be. "I'm *fine*. I can walk."

With a groan Dammerung's leg spun against the gold-hammered sky and he dropped, like a rock, out of the saddle. "There, my heart." His hand sounded smartly against Rubico's neck. "Let us not, you and I, do that again. We get too old for such things."

Margaret forgot the soldier from Darkling. The horse was already walking off—he knew the routine—and as if he were on the lead-line and Rubico was pulling him, Dammerung began to walk beside the horse. Margaret lengthened her stride to fall in step with him. She almost put her arm in his, for his sake, but for his sake she stayed her movement and walked with her hands at her sides.

He did not speak to her, but then she found she did not expect him to. They passed round fallen bodies, Friend and foe alike, passed the cluster under the eagle where Centurion stood with his lieutenants setting up a camp, getting the watch-fires going, burying the dead, picketing the horses, starting a supper...

As if anyone could have stomach to eat.

Dammerung called to a man she did not know. "I saw you! Very neatly done."

She could hear the blush in the dark. "Sooth, sir, and thank you!"

They went on.

"I saw you get thrown out of the saddle and thought you were lost. Lived to fight another day, eh?"

"Oh, aye, Lord Dammerung. Bit of a bump, 'tis all."

"Best have it looked at."

"There be men that need the surgeon's attention more than me, my lord."

"A fine weapon, sir. An heirloom?"

"My Lord Dammerung! I—yes, sir. 'Twas of my family's line, my father's and his father's before him."

"You bear it proudly."

"Trouble thee about thy horse, my lord. I'm going to fetch fodder. May I bring thee a pitchfork-full?"

"No small thanks to your courtesy, captain, but Rubico has an iron stomach. He will pass for now with a mouthful of grass and a handful of grain. There are others need your pitchfork-full of hay more."

"Good-night, Lord Dammerung!"

"Good-night, sir! Good-night, lady!"

The voices called across the darkness as the light went out of the sky and the last brazen clang of sword-work finally vanished from the woods. Margaret walked wordlessly along the incline beside Dammerung, tired beyond reckoning, her eyes wandering from new-sprung fire to new-sprung fire.

I wonder where the enemy goes when we defeat them. Do they slink back to their own camp? How strange that it is so quiet now, like every night in camp before this, like this morning, before...

Out of the surf-sound of the rising wind she heard in memory the noise that raised the bile in her throat: the sound of panic, the sound of a battle in the heart of the camp, so sudden, so unexpected, upon them before anyone could think. It had been some moments, not until the war-lords of the camp had sunk their teeth into the threat and stayed its rampage, before she had felt anything but terror. And then she had been angry.

"Oh."

Dammerung had stopped. She had come blindly up a bit of earthy, shelving ground, across a burnt patch of grass, and stood beside him before what had been his tent. Her bottle of perfume must have been broken: she could smell it distinctly.

"I don't care," she said wearily, not sure if she meant the bottle or the tent.

Dammerung, putting one arm over the horse's neck to support himself, waved his other hand unceremoniously through the air. The fabric of the tent hissed and snapped; the bones of the tent came together, bone to bone. With awkward, jerky movements, like a camel getting to its feet, the thing came back together and stood, shivering in the wind, the flap over the entryway burnt and shredded, but beckoning half-heartedly.

"Why didn't you do that before?"

Dammerung went in, pulling Rubico after him. Candles—it did not seem to matter where they were, on the ground or on tables or chairs—lit up at once. Margaret blinked and staggered back in the sudden light.

Dammerung picked up a chair from the mess—there were still a few charred bits of Púka lying about—and sat down heavily in it. His first two fingers flickered wordlessly and she went to him. "Put your left hand against my right shoulder," he told her, "and take hold of my shoulder with your right hand."

"Oh, this game?" She felt her stomach clenching already.

There was a brief flicker of laughter in his upturned eyes. "This game. Have you got it?"

She took hold and felt the limb out of joint beneath her palm. Distaste pulled at her mouth.

"Ready? Brace yourself."

He yanked away to the side. She nearly went with him, but at the last moment she dug in her heels—*I am good at that sort of thing*—and held back while the joint whined into place and snapped between her fingers. Dammerung let out a gusty sigh and fell back in the chair, his elbow on the arm of it, his face in his hand. Rubico approached and butted in gently, snuffling along his master's neck for a bit of something to eat. Margaret, seeming to wake out of a curious numbness, said absently,

"I'd better take off his tack and rub him down." Then, casting about for a brush, she added, "I suppose a handkerchief will have to do."

"Get on with your bad self!" The War-wolf jerked away from the horse's fingery lips. "Margaret, may I have a kerchief for Widowmaker as well?"

Out of the rubble she found his clothes chest and rummaged about inside. She found two linen handkerchiefs, both of which would be ruined in a moment, passed one off on Dammerung—whose face, though bloody, was looking less torn—and began rhythmically rubbing the steaming warhorse down. A soft silence, full of the tinsely rustle of fabric and candle-flame, fell about them. In the distance Margaret could hear the splutter of horsehooves and calls in the night, but in their tent there was a snatched moment of quiet in which her own soul, at least, stooped and ached and found time to rest.

"Why didn't I do what before?"

She turned at the sound of his voice. He was still burnishing his sword, leaning down over the blade with the soiled cloth running with the grain of the metal.

"I beg your pardon?"

He looked up. "As we came in you asked me why I didn't do something before."

Memory jarred her. "Oh yes, that. I meant the magic. I've seen what you can do—tear down things and build them up—but I couldn't understand why you didn't do it out there with Centurion when he was in such a hard place. Wouldn't it have been easier?"

He continued burnishing, his movements slower now. "Would easier have made it better?" he asked presently.

She was silent for a moment, thinking. "No," she admitted. "Not necessarily. But what about the lives of your men? If you had a chance to save them, shouldn't you?"

He leaned forward, shifted, and tucked his ankles one over the other under the chair. He was quiet, looking up at her with the feeling of a smile on his face—when she looked hard at his lips she could see there was no smile—a kindness, a wistfulness in his eyes. She waited for him, but as the silence drew out she realized he was not going to speak.

If they love her, isn't it their right to die for her?

"I think you see now," he said.

She nodded and continued rubbing down the horse. Once she glanced back, thinking perhaps to say something more, but he had gone back to his own work and something in her self forbade her from speaking. But she noticed for the first time, in glancing back, that Dammerung had a fine feathering of silvered hairs at his temples, mingling with the tousled brown.

She thought he had marked her staring for, without warning, he flung up his head; but he was poised tense listening, and in a moment Margaret, too, heard the quick half-run of steps along the rough walking-path. A moment later Brand came ducking into the tent, carrying urgency with him, and blurted out,

"It's Skander Rime, sir. Best come quick."

Margaret had the distinct sensation of leaving her stomach behind and her heart falling down where her stomach had been. Dammerung was in the entryway almost before she had flung down her handkerchief. She stumbled after him through the light-shot dark, through the hanging smoke and thick night—which was becoming lightning-flicked—along the narrow walk-path down from the hill toward the long tent that belonged to Skander. She did not think: she did not have time to think. Already she expected the worst, Brand's drawn, white face etched with nausea's clarity on her mind. Its pale illumination seemed to light her way.

Ahead of her was the sharp splash of light coming from the open entryway of the tent. Someone was standing outside, pacing, but Margaret never got a clear look at his face. She went in, blinking in the stab of lamplight, skipping the low, damp depression that had been trod in the middle of the entryway, and suddenly hung back, struck in the face by the surgeon atmosphere that hung about the room. The whimper of nightmare struggled in her throat.

Everyone—Aikin Ironside, the blue-jay man, Woodbird, Lord Gro, Centurion—looked round as Brand and Dammerung came whirling in. Brand joined his brother and at once everyone gave back, save the blue-jay man, from the body that lay stretched in gory wrath on the low couch. Margaret felt her stomach clench. All over blood, Skander still clutched Gram, his arm dropped off the side of the couch almost listlessly, but she could see the veins standing out like cords in his arm, and his knuckles were stark-white. It was his leg that was the trouble. His right leg was a mess of blood and splinters, some of which were as long, though half as thin, as Margaret's forearm. It looked past repair.

"It was a supplies cart," Woodbird said in a strained, carefully schooled voice. Her owlish eyes were quieted; everything about her face was careful and reserved. "A runaway team took him and his horse down a ravine; everything fell on top of him. His leg is smashed, at least, if not other things."

"I dare say other things have come out serviceable, don't worry," said Dammerung with a grim kind of humour.

The blue-jay man looked up from where he squatted at his master's head, his blond forelock hanging low and damp between his eyes. They were hard, daring, soulful eyes, stabbing straight up into Dammerung's face. "Well, lord?" he asked quietly, challengingly.

Dammerung's face, too, was hard, and carefully turned away from all eyes, fixed on Skander's leg. He moved forward, putting out one hand upon the blue-jay man's shoulder, and said softly, "Well done, Tabby-dog. I will take the matter from here."

"Can you do the witching-thing?" Aikin's voice cut down hard and bright.

With a fierce, mirthless jerk of a smile Dammerung flung a warning look at him. "The witching-thing? Would that I could! But I must have the devil's teeth out, and that by finer skill." He tapped his thumb and forefinger together. "I must be at it the hard way. Now look you all—" he gestured markedly at Woodbird and the blue-jay man "—can a man breathe in such close quarters? Get about your business."

The blue-jay man's face looked to be disagreeing but Dammerung's tone, though quiet, was firm. No one dared cross him, and with an eerie silence they went out. Aikin took Woodbird's arm to help her, though she did not look as though she welcomed any help, and the blue-jay man hunkered down dismally just outside the tentflap, his head craned round to listen within.

It was then that Margaret realized she had not gone out. Inexplicably she felt that she alone was allowed to stay, not because she was anyone special or could be of any service, but because Dammerung had put her in the back of his mind as one might put down and temporarily leave a glass on a table, and she was, for the present, no bother. She felt no offence: she felt ill and not at all as though she *wanted* to stay, but she thought she would find it worse to be away. She could not go back up that dark path to Dammerung's tent with no one but a horse for company, leaving this business behind her and having to wait for hours not knowing how the task went ahead, not knowing whether Skander, who seemed to be hanging in the agonized balance, would make it. Gingerly, shakily, she sank down into a chair.

Dammerung shoved his torn sleeves up above his elbows and crossed to the low battered washstand at the head of the couch. Deliberately, and with an eye on his patient's face, he washed his hands, rinsing off his own blood before he got mussed up in the blood of his cousin. "Look at that brute," he said conversationally to Skander. Skander seemed to be just beneath unconsciousness; at the sound of his cousin's voice something flickered in his face. "You never do things by halves, do you? You and I both. It must run in the family. I did tell you, you would end up under my knife one day." He smiled gamely, lowering himself onto a milking-stool by Skander's leg. "You stay with me now. I hear Acheron is bloody cold this time of year, and we can't let that black cat have her vaunting-day. You and I, let's see to this hedgepig that has got in your leg."

He fell silent for awhile. Margaret shuddered and bit her lip as his long, lean, powerful hands began to deliberately work in the long wound. Skander's frame jumped and shivered with a quick convulsion of pain, then lay rigid again, held under the surface of consciousness by the sheer weight of agony; sweat began to run down his standing veins and drip off his knuckles. Dammerung worked on, unhurried, his lips set hard but his fingers gentle. The wind kicked up, blowing the canvas sides of the tent so that the backdrop of this gory play shuddered like Margaret's own stomach and made things hard to see clearly. The wind buffeted the sides of the tent but the air within seemed oppressive.

A quarter of an hour went by. Dammerung paused once, flung back his head and arched his back until his spine crackled. His hands were now thoroughly bloodied and the splinters, as he drew them out and dropped them on the ground, were beginning to slip in his grasp. He swung aside to wash them again, saying as he did so,

"Spencer, bring the light. My eyes cross and darken at this closeness."

Margaret hesitated, then, putting aside the confusion, she pushed herself out of the chair and took the lamp off the table. It flickered under the movement, doubling back on itself and fanning out into a fragile, perfect petal of flame. It was warm and beautiful and seemed to Margaret just then to be the very preciousness of the living soul.

"Where do you want it?"

Dammerung looked up, visibly startled by her voice. "There," he gestured, recovering. "At the end of his couch. Nay, never mind that. Come across from me and hold it. That will do better."

She had been afraid he would ask her that and had prepared herself, her stomach kept in tight rein, her jaw pulled back and set hard. She knelt on the other side of the couch across from Dammerung, sinking into the rich, throat-catching scent of blood and open flesh, her elbows raised on the side of the couch to steady her hands, the lamplight shining full upon the operation. Dammerung reached up once and shifted her wrist, leaving a bloody print there, then wordlessly returned to his work.

For a few minutes the smell became almost unbearable. Her stomach was a continual mess of sickness rising and falling, twisting, threatening her with a dishonourable upheaval, but at last she seemed to acclimate. A bit of wind came in through the tent-flap, stirring a coolness over her face. She hitched up her heels and got more comfortable, leaning over Skander's leg so that Dammerung would have as much light as possible.

That's not so bad, she thought when she got a level-headed look at the wound. *A bit of broken bone and torn muscle, but Dammerung can mend that. It is the splinters that are the trouble. And the time lost.*

Dammerung sniffed and put up one hand to rub the crook of his wrist against his nose—that was all: he went back to work, digging his long fingers into the running mess, fiddling for every last splinter. Margaret glanced up, half expecting him to speak, and when he went back to work her gaze lingered a moment on his blood-streaked face. She realized for the first time that he had freckles, myriads of tiny, dark freckles all over his face; but one was so captivated by the clear, fierce eyes, darkened now with concentration, that one did not notice the freckles at first, if at all. Her mind wandered off, wondering if Skander had noticed, if Skander had known.

Or Rupert...

"Who-o-o..." With a gusty sigh Dammerung dropped his forehead against his cousin's thigh.

Margaret sat up. With the sudden movement her back and legs cried out in cramped agony. "Oh—is that it? Is that all?"

He drew back. His face was as bloody as before. "I think so. I don't think we have to worry about ill humours—I think he has bled them out by now. I may or may not have picked a bit of bone out with the splinters. *C'est la vie.* We'll make good shift of a bad job. Oh, I'm done with the light."

Too readily she dropped the light on the floor. It rocked and nearly upturned into the carpet, but righted itself at the last moment and the wick, after fumbling with the flame, caught it again and held it tight. She did not care. She hefted herself up by the edge of the couch and looked into Skander's face for any sign of relief. It was deathly still but death had not yet stolen over it. Dammerung was speaking softly, and ever afterward she was not sure what language he was using.

"We're not out of the woods yet, sir, but we've come to a clearing. The halloo is quiet for a moment. There is a fountain. A unicorn. Softly—don't startle the animal spirit. It is stirring the water and there is scarlet coming from its horn. The halloo again—"

His hands lay flat against the wound, flat, then clenching, drawing the lips of skin together.

"—The summons to go on. We're going upward, sir. *Swef*, my heart, my bold, my brave. The arbour is behind. The sphere of Mars is calling..."

It was the simplest thing. She had never been one on the outside looking in. She had been the one under the knife, under the questing, healing hand. This time she paused, half-stooped over Skander's brow, and looked back to see the War-wolf, master of death, pass his hands over destruction's handiwork and bind the severed flesh together again. The simplest thing.

Dammerung smiled.

Margaret laid her hand on Skander's brow. It was damp and warm, but still. The eyelids were motionless.

"Poor brute," she murmured. "A third time will do him for sure."

"Nay, not him." Dammerung twisted back and forth to get the kinks out of his spine. "Fortune favours the bold. *Sa cy avaunt*." He waved toward the tent-flap.

Out of the darkness the blue-jay man rose, ducking back in with eyes curiously bright in a pale, drawn face. Neither he nor Dammerung spoke; one look between them seemed sufficient. Margaret was almost pathetically glad to get out of the manservant's way and follow after Dammerung into the windy dark. The air on her face was cool, but the horror of the whole day, which she had not realized she had been holding in check, whelmed up at her out of the blackness. She went doggedly after the sound of Dammerung's feet, but she knew the game was up. The warm water welled in her mouth; her stomach, punching round against her diaphragm, stopped her breath and clogged up her throat. She made it nearly to the entryway of Dammerung's tent before, with a little cry of warning, she doubled over and vomited. She did not know what was coming out of her mouth, only that it tasted like shame.

He was there with an arm round her hourglass, one hand bunching back her hair out of her face. He was saying something softly, soothingly, which made her cheeks burn hotter with shame, but she could not hear him until the last heave subsided and she was bent panting, empty, shaking—and by then he had fallen silent.

"I'm sorry," she gasped.

"Come in-by," was all he said. "You need some wine. You're all peaky."

The stuff in her mouth screwed her lips into a grimace. Looking up through the lamplight at his face, with his hand still hauling back the tangled mass of her hair, she saw the same sort of twist to his own mouth and wondered if *he* was going to be ill.

"What about you?" she blurted.

He let down her hair and held out his hand. In the light she could see it was shaking.

A laugh stuttered out of her throat.

XXIX | THE PALE PORTS O' THE MOON

"Well, if that doesn't take the salt out of you..."

The War-wolf folded up the missive and tossed it aside, but he did not try to stop Skander Rime from hefting himself up on the couch and reaching, stiffly, for his boots.

"Not a moment's peace," Skander went on grumblingly. "Not a bit of land but he has to rouse the Wild Hunt on it."

Dammerung got up and whistled shortly, shrilly, and the blue-jay man was gone at once, ducking out into the grey-and-gold welter of an overcast dawn—to see to Skander's horse, Margaret presumed.

Dammerung turned back and put a hand under his cousin's elbow to help him up. "Well, not that, else *I* should be going in your stead. You had better take Woodbird with you, if her sisters will spare her."

Skander spoke through clenched teeth as he wrenched his harness of leather over his head: "They had *better* spare her..."

Moving aside, Margaret's curious, questing fingers picked up the letter. It was only a little weather-stained: the letter-head bore a date antepenultimate to the day. She recognized Periot Survance's hand from the notes he had made in Songmartin's book.

"*The border defences are falling,*" she read, mouthing the words, feeling again the quickness of the blood roiling in the cauldron of her heart. "*Rupert has raised the Carmathen against us. The border defences are falling. Come, lord—come soon.*"

Sha-ang! Gram sang home into the sheath. Margaret looked over the crumpled edge of the letter to see Skander, leaning to the side to get his weight off his weakened leg, standing in the doorway of the tent, Dammerung beside him, the pre-storm tempest of the morning winging them with a shadowy glory.

"I can't come," Dammerung was saying frankly. "I can't come—not yet."

"No," mused his cousin. "Your way lies through the plains of Orzelon-gang."

A brief silence.

"There is a storm coming."

"I can hear the ravens on the wind of it."

Skander looked to Dammerung. Withdrawn on the outskirts, Margaret watched his face become a strange thing, a foreign thing, grimly carved and pale. "You hear them too?"

Dammerung stared out across the landscape, his face to the lifting wind. "The names they are calling? Yes, I hear them."

She, too, listened, but she heard only the rushing of the wind and the growing drum of hoofbeats drawing nearer. The two men moved apart as a flea-bitten mare charged into the entryway and Woodbird's voice, imperious, called down,

"I came as soon as I heard. Skander, I am coming with you. Also Ewing and Aelfhorn and their men come."

"Nay, now I am jealous." The mockery had warmed the embers of Dammerung's voice. "You will not miss me!"

Within half an hour the columns were assembled and on the move, salutes flung across the intervening spaces, and Margaret, who had long ago grown used to how quickly camps were packed and unpacked, stood beside Dammerung watching Skander's blue banner dwindle into the purple thunder of the air on the shore of Holywood, a small panic under her heart which she was trying desperately to crush as one crushes out the life of a small broken bird for whom death is the only mercy.

"It is Orzelon-gang for us," said the War-wolf, "and the relief of the Dragon-lord of the North. And do not tell anyone," he added, "but there is not a worse hour for me to lose Skander Rime, the Fighting Dog of Plenilune."

She set her hand on his shoulder and pressed hard with her fingers until his leather harness cut her; his face gashed sideways with a smile. That was all: they turned together to pack their own things and fill their faces with the familiar dust of the open road and the ominous glare of summer thunder on the horizon which was the colour of hard crimson, the colour of the hour.

Out from under her foreboding rose the latent curiosity, born in her months ago, to see Orzelon-gang's mighty palace. The storm did not break. It hung in a heavy tabby-skin of purple and gold and scarlet overhead, racing across the sky with gale winds but never dispersed, and under its rich gloom, having crossed nearly every Honour in Plenilune, Margaret saw Mark Roy's palace.

It was a city in itself, settled in a little lift of a valley at the bend of a wide, navigable river. With the angry golden sunset-sky behind it, it was a dream-silhouette of black spires and shadowed towers, gilt-edged banners and sable walls: a piece of imagery that had got lost and wandered from the old medieval poetry Margaret had once known on the other side of many bright, black turnings in life. For a moment, on the lift of the track where there were no trees and only wind and the sudden, stinging glory of the landscape, she caught Plenilune off guard—or did it catch her?—and she saw the life that beat beneath all small, mundane things sketched for that instant in the indomitable blackness of Orzelon-gang's walls—awful, half-checked, unreckoned, unreal.

"*He* stands directly in our way."

Aikin's bitter voice broke through her swimming agony. She tore her gaze from the city and saw the haze of many cooking-fires lying over the valley; between them and the stronghold, all across the way, were Rupert's forces. On the riverbank she could just make out the glint of the Standards all in array: the tent nearest them would be Rupert's.

"He has been busy," she said coldly, "in the time that Skander has been mending."

"A week and a half, little more," said Dammerung. "In war, time is of the very essence of victory."

Aikin Ironside's face was hammered out of bronze in the late light. "Do we go down now, sir?"

"At once. Margaret, keep by me—you have your steel? That is good—"

He spoke something more to Aikin and the others behind him; with a great show of heels and sun-shot spear-points, flowing crests and rush of muscle they dispersed along the line. But Margaret did not notice them. She felt them move as she felt Mausoleum shift and clench beneath her, but she did not see them. She was listening in shame to the singing in her ears and wishing she felt angry at Rupert and not so white and cold. Dammerung caught her eye.

"Me?" she asked, for that was all she needed to ask.

He smiled sympathetically. "There is not a safer place in Plenilune. I daren't leave you behind. And look—Grane and Black Malkin go out in battle-array. Come along, renegade heart. Fly under my shadow and you'll do fine today.

"Huw," he added to the man on his left, "give me a loud halloo on the horn to wake them."

The moon-curve of the horn went up; the man drew in a powerful breath. In that thick twilight Margaret could almost see the sound swelling, an enormous golden belling, brazen, turning scarlet; the ripples of it went out and came back to them over the land.

A momentary silence. Then, from the lower lands, another sound went up in answer: a yelping in defiance, once, twice. The challenge had been accepted.

Dammerung snapped his fingers. The horn was dropped and the swords sang out. Margaret felt clammy inside her own leather harness, but she gamely rolled back the folds of her teal-stained cloak and laid her own sword bare in her hand. It was not much more than a short sword, and not very effective for cavalry work, but it would be heavy by the time she was done wielding it and it would be enough, she hoped, to poke a hole in the life of anyone who came near her.

The War-wolf, barefoot, bareheaded, put his gauntleted hands over his mouth and screamed like a falcon in the dive so that even Margaret felt the blood rush into her face and the hair on her neck stand on end...

...Dammerung struck her cheek with the flat of his hand, jolting her upright. His eyes were dancing in a bloodied face. "Are you still with me?"

She caught the words by watching his lips. Beside them a horse was going down in a welter of blood and muck, screaming like a child. She staggered forward and yanked her messy blade out of a dead soldier's body where she had put it a minute, two minutes before.

Three war-lords, two of whom she vaguely recognized—the rank of the last she knew only from the sight of his spurs—broke at them from the rest of the press. Her shoulder collided with Dammerung's. Side by side, blades pulled back at full, they careened recklessly into the steel embrace waiting for them. Margaret felt the shock and bone-tingle as her sword sheared along metal. The war-lord's sword sketched a martyr's ring above her, bisected briefly, in a streak of black blood, by the flying head of the next war-lord as Dammerung cut it cleanly from the neck. With a wrenching twist she got her sword free of the other's hilt and ran it up into the craggy, concentrated face. Something bit her in the shoulder—not bad, not enough to sway her, but enough to make her curious—but at that moment her foot was slipping on a patch of blood, and she had to fling herself mightily forward into the plunge and she bore the body over without any grace, her sword pulling out of her hands as it fell.

A hand—Dammerung's hand—collared her and flung her to the ground nearly up to her elbows in the muck. *Not a safer place in Plenilune?* she thought with irony. With one mucky hand she pushed back her hair and looked up through a haze of glorying sunset as Dammerung and Aikin—where had he come from?— cleared a space around them. They were nearly under the doors of the palace. Looking over her shoulder, Margaret could see them rising above her, doors fist to fist, the squared shoulders of the rampart towers set firmly against the besieging army.

Yanking her skirt out of her way she rocked to her feet, impatiently grabbed her sword out of the dead war-lord's face, and flung her back against Dammerung's.

"Arrow," he shouted into her ear.

"Rummy way to go," she yelled back—in the heat of things, it seemed to take too long to tell him how grateful she was for him flinging her on her face before it could be split open by a stray bolt.

Aikin made a roundabout gesture with one hand. "Here comes my father!" he bawled.

She stood in the eye of the storm, the sky the colour of an elfhorn's bugle above her. The gate-doors shrugged apart as Dammerung's people surged around it, closed around it, shield to shield, horse-flank to horse-flank. The first horse to come through the doors wore a head-piece full of blazing antlers, a cloak of scarlet billowing over its hindquarters. Soldier after soldier poured after him, mingled with the friendly relief: the two forces became one.

In all that noise and tumult she was sure she had not heard a voice. Yet she *had* heard a voice. She ripped her gaze off the beauty of Mark Roy in full war regalia and turned, mud-stained, panting, herself a wreck of wrathful blood and terror. Two things she had learned: that she was not much good with a sword, and that a man is alone in the press of a battle-field. She looked out alone after the voice which had called with a sense more like feeling.

If she had not recognized the voice she would not have recognized him. A stone's throw away a torn, ragged, mud-clotted, bloodied man stood, on the brink of turning away, but staying a moment, hoping to catch her eye. The face was blackened by blood and mud and smoke—the eyes were too far away to see clearly.

The figure raised its hand and almost beckoned.

Something inside her screamed in an angry, torn confusion, a sudden profound weariness, a smallness, a helplessness—when out of the cloud-wrack, above the dark furring of woods that bordered the river, she saw the argent bow of earth. It meant nothing to her, she felt nothing akin at the sight of it, but it was like the eye of a dragon in appearance, a majestic, ever-gazing thing hung above her, watching her, and on a quick swell of wind she turned from the man of blood and ran with the wind at her heels to rejoin Dammerung.

The War-wolf shone in the growing gloom. He had reclaimed his horse, and leaned over holding the reins of hers so that it would not bolt. She jammed her foot in the stirrup and leapt into the saddle: an old, familiar movement now.

"One more charge, sir," he was telling Mark Roy. "Once more and we'll have them into the river."

And all Mark Roy said was, "We are ready."

They were the flower of Plenilune, Margaret saw. Looking along the line of the land-owners and war-lords of the Honours, save for Skander Rime and Woodbird Swan-neck, who were conspicuously missing, the grim, high faces of the blue-bloods shone with a soft red light in the shadows: Mark Roy, Aikin Ironside, Brand the Hammer, Grane and Lord Gro, each black-crowned and terrible, Centurion of Darkling with his horse a-dance beneath him with excitement, Black Malkin robed like death, and others, others which were the pillars of the world.

The old pain came back, the old pain of unbelonging, and Margaret withdrew a little into herself to keep the pain at bay.

The flurry of the second charge was diminished by the memory of the first one. The pain in her chest rooted her to her body and, after that first crazed ride into the closing ranks of Rupert's soldiers, which had been like the shredded black banners of a nightmare, the second charge—upswept thunder of horses into the riverscrub and rolling bank country, skirting sudden rocky walls, plunging headlong over fallen timber and wet water-soaked trees—seemed clear and sharp to Margaret. The land was darkened, the sky a heavy panel of hammered bronze—like the lid of a pot clamped down over the war seething below.

The rich, throaty call of a horn blared nearby her. Mausoleum put down his head and shuddered after Dammerung, but at that moment Rubico turned on his heel, cutting Mausoleum off, and Margaret saw a figure rush out of the sound of the horn, battle-axe raised, to meet the man on the warhorse. It was a huge, dark figure, bearded like a badger, roaring an incoherent hatred that she had come to know of war.

How strange. The man had always been so soft of speech.

The weapons sang together, rang and crashed, and flew away like spitting, shooting stars. The three bodies, men and horse, blurred in the shadows and seemed born of them. Margaret felt the genius of the moment overwhelm her with urgency: this was the moment of mastery, the moment from which there was no turning back. With death like a cloak about his shoulders, the old Master of Marenové raised up his infamous sword against the disloyal lord—vengeance glittered on the blade—and shaved down beneath the uplifted axe, beneath the badger's beard, cutting the head from the shoulders. The mighty body heaved to one knee and then flat on its front—and Talus Perey was without lord or master or warm hearth.

Aikin's eerie war-cry, like the ecstatic scream of a peacock, split the dusk air and soared, for a moment, over the heavy din of battle. She did not see him; she heard him, and the sound of him lifted up her heart like a torch on fire. It was like a cheer for paradise—a paradise unwon without bloodshed.

She was on the front lines with Dammerung when the first wave of enemy soldiers were pushed into the river. There was a desperate struggle—her blade got messy—a bitter grapple on the water's edge, then a splash and a cry choked off by a sword's bite, a rending of the heavens by a friendly horn, and the enemy ranks gave way.

Pipe to the old macabre dance—
It's all a-one to me.

Mausoleum fetched up violently against a bit of brush-furze and gave a startled scream, kicking out against the pain. A bolt flickered by her ear and made her wince and the world turn dark a moment. With the suddenness of a plug being pulled, the blaze of the moment passed her and she clung to her horse's mane, breathless, cold, out of place like a hare caught in a dual of falcons. Where had her sword gone? Had she lost it in the bush? Where was Dammerung? He seemed to have been spirited away.

Alone for a moment in the swirl of battle, Margaret tried to regain her bearings. Squinting against the sky's glare off the water she peered ahead into the gloom. There were men in the water, but none of them answered to Dammerung's figure. The land around her was a mess of shadows and moving bodies. The anger of panic twisted her lip between her teeth until it stung in the place where it had once been split.

Move! said an imperious voice. *Move, thou blockhead!—move before he finds you!*

"She-e-e ha!" she cried, digging her heels into her horse's sweating flanks. With a piteous squeal the horse lumbered forward over the dark, uneven ground. There were sounds of a concentrated fight going on upstream; she steered toward it.

"Is the lady lost?" said a voice at her elbow.

"Oh!" she cried, flinching before she placed the voice as Dammerung's. Then, ashamed of her fear, she retorted, "Where were you? I lost you by the river."

She could not see his face clearly in the dusk. "I—don't know," he admitted, his tone apologetic. "Here and there. On the threshold of life and death. Nowhere new. I'm here now," he added.

She put the back of her muddy hand against her cold, sweating brow. "It's too dark to see friend from foe now. Are we finished, can you tell?"

And the voice of the War-wolf, rumbling out of the dark, rumbling out of that place between life and death, said, "For now. It is not finished, but we hold the field. For now."

They had come to a little rise of land covered in short clover-turf. Turning back, Margaret saw the last of the evening's glow fading from the water. The cold fear was still upon her—she hoped it would go soon—and when she tried to lift her lip in a smile her chin trembled and the smile failed her and she felt how lonely it was to be on the brink of mortality.

"Did you meet him?" she asked, only half aware of her own words.

A momentary silence, then— "Our dice did not roll together in the cup today."

Wearily, stiff-legged, and caked in muck and blood, they dismounted and she struggled along beside him across the last bit of grass and the churned, damp soil to the gates of the palace which, having shut behind their lord, were being opened again to receive them in.

They were met in the gate-breach by Romage. Unlike Black Malkin and Grane—and herself, Margaret realized, though she did not think she had done much in the way of good for the fight—the queen of Orzelon-gang had not gone out among the soldiers, but she stood as Margaret remembered her, regal and erect with a plume of torchlight around her, her ruddy crown piled atop her head and decked with peacocks' feathers; a train of some shimmering black stuff flowed from her shoulders over her body, and in her hand she bore, like Victory, a spear with a collar of red junglefowl feathers.

Oh God—Margaret balked in horror of herself. *I can't—I simply—*

"Good evening, your grace," said the War-wolf, never perturbed by his appearance for an instant.

The amber-coloured eyes, darkened in the shadows, turned slowly and without surprise to Dammerung.

To thee the reed is as the oak.

"My lord." That soft, certain, honey-running voice. "You are most welcome here."

Dammerung was quiet for a moment and the sounds of the soldiers putting to rest the battle behind them lingered softly on the outskirts. Margaret looked from face to face, reading in the silence a curious similarity between the young war-lord and the woman who was mother of two great war-lords and the wife of a war-lord among men.

It seemed the recognition was what had run between them, for Dammerung's mouth jumped into a wry smile and he said, "I think that I salute another of my kind."

Romage smiled—a distant, secret smile. "We are but children playing marbles with the pebbles your mighty foot upstirs."

"False modesty does not become the gracious woman. Why else is Venus so bright a star?"

The crisp dark brows flickered upward in a momentarily startled amusement; Romage glanced for a second to Margaret—it was only a moment, a heartbeat, but she felt the touch of those eyes like a warm pressure on her cheek. Before she could say anything more—and others were coming up to join them—Dammerung added in a swift undertone,

"The look is unmistakeable, my dear. When you have seen *it*, it shows."

She was looking on beyond them, head upraised, to watch her husband approaching, but her smile was as much for Dammerung's words as for the man labouring up the slight slope toward her.

"My hearts!" cried the king breathlessly. "My hounds. Oh, you, too, my lady?" He landed his hand on Dammerung's shoulder and turned to Margaret, surprised.

The fear wavered at the back of her throat, shaking her words, but she pushed them to the forefront gamely. "I, too, my lord. Not a one to sit idle while Plenilune is in danger."

Mark Roy nodded appreciatively and Dammerung, looking at her across the king's shoulders, threw her a wink and a smile that twisted her in her middle with a sudden unchecked joy.

"Are you all unscathed?" asked Romage as her two sons and Centurion approached. Huw, hesitant, trailed behind them with a pretty gash over one brow and an arm that he seemed to be favouring.

Her eldest son made to lean in to kiss her, then, realizing what a mess he was, stopped short of the gesture. "Mostly, I think."

"It is in my mind," said Dammerung, pursuing his original subject, "that her grace had little doubt of that."

Mark Roy pushed through them all and took his wife's hand—though which supported the other, Margaret, looking carefully, could not say. "All things are laid bare before him with whom we have to do. Come in, all of you. My men will see to the field. Tonight I will toast to the victory on the field and show you— my lady, did I not say that you ought to come and dine with us here in Orzelon-gang?" As they walked into the forecourt he half turned, catching Margaret's eye.

But her gaze was already being drawn off into the golden lights and thick red shadows around them. Was that a dragon she saw at the top of that pillar—was the pillar itself a dragon holding up the colonnade roof? "Yes, you had," she answered absent-mindedly. "And it quite surpasses your description."

"Come along in," came back Romage's jewelled voice. "I will take her ladyship. Will Black Malkin and Grane join us?"

"They are seeing to their own people," said Brand, "and then I think they were of a mind to join us for supper."

At the inner gate, which was made of bronze and decorated with the sweeping bodies and tails of two enormous metal peacocks, Romage slipped out of her husband's grasp and held out her hand—a long, fine, beautiful hand—and beckoned for Margaret. A swift, powerful loathing to detach herself from Dammerung stopped her for a moment, but then she made herself go, one foot in front of the other though her legs seemed like unlovely lead. The queen slid an arm in hers and took her through the doors.

They passed into the fabled room of the black pools and golden fish. At first, disoriented by the sudden dark and peeps of red light and draped red linen from the upper corners of the atrium, Margaret thought the golden flickers in the water were reflections of hidden light until, passing on the edge of one long pool, she saw the light turn slowly, hugely, and drift to the surface. A red-and-white mottled face appeared out of the shifting black, wet and whiskered like a water-drake, and then slipped under again with a kiss of closing water.

"You like them?" Romage did not turn her head.

Had her legs been more serviceable, Margaret thought she might have stopped and knelt on the water's edge to get a better look at the creatures, and perhaps even—her flesh tingled—have touched one. In the dark she could get no clear image of them—they never moved quickly, but seemed to be always shifting out of the light into the dark again—but they looked enormous: huge, half-spirit things made of light and blood and bodies living in a strange, powerful medium. They seemed, in those disjointed, dark moments, to be akin to her.

It was not until later that she realized she had never answered Romage's question.

The queen took her down a dark hallway, up a flight of stairs, and all the while Margaret was aware of those sentinel dragon-pillars rising on either hand, holding up the sky, holding down the earth. She felt akin to those, too. They went through another wide atrium, with a lower roof this time and mobile panels of red honeycombed wood, over acres of rich carpet, to a gold-painted door that slid in the wall. Romage put her hand inside the little indentation that was the handle and said,

"This is your suite... My lord, you are not allowed in."

Out of the dark behind her Dammerung's voice, softly laughing, said, "Oh, I know. Surely the smell of holiness grows stronger here. You will find me, if you have need of me, behind the next door. I'll come back for her ladyship when we have washed."

She and Romage watched him go, swallowed up over-quickly in the heavy darkness that seemed to fill every corridor of the palace. He was still there—he seemed to be everywhere—and yet he had withdrawn, hiding behind the dark as God hid his face behind the vault of heaven: watching, ever-present, and unseen.

Romage said, "I have seen it only once. That man, I think, has its face ever before his and walks in its white shadow."

"You know," murmured Margaret, "I think you may be right."

The queen's face was a bright flash of almond and fire-colour in the dark, laughing at her soundlessly. She slid back the gold panel and ushered Margaret into a well of black room lit only at the far end by a long narrow of rectangle and the slit of green night sky that showed through.

Beside her there was a sound of thin metal being shifted and a red coal-light sprang up against Romage's bent face. In the gloom Margaret saw her dip a taper into a little bin of lit coals. Lifting the flaming taper, the queen passed quickly into the dark, moving from place to place with her light outstretched until she had found a few dozen candles and the room was coming reluctantly out of the dark.

Fishing in the wall gap, Margaret slid the door shut again behind her. Her fingers left a smudge of blood behind on the gold.

"Never mind." The queen came back, hands outstretched for Margaret's surcoat. With gestures and glances, and very few words—*Just as if she were handling a wild animal*—Romage got Margaret out of her soiled clothing and had her kneel on a square setup of travertine tiles in one corner of the room. There was a drain to one side and several bowls of scented water. Shivering in the air, a great length of cloth heavily played over with spangled grouse gathered around her waist and over her legs, Margaret let the queen systematically wipe the grime from her skin. She never used the same cloth twice once she had got it dirty, but presently, as her skin was coming clean, Romage settled on a piece of soft linen and dabbled rose-water over Margaret's skin until the room was full of the scent of rich gardens and candle-smoke.

"Bend forward now," said Romage, twisting to pick up one of the largest bowls which she had not used yet, "and put your hair in this."

The powerful smell of lemons and honey hit Margaret in the face as she crouched over her knees, her back screaming in protest; but Romage, pulling the hair through her fingers, gently plied out the worst of the tangles and began to soothe the warm smelly mixture down the sorry hair.

Silent, too tired to make conversation, Margaret glanced aside across the room toward the door. Romage's handling was relaxing: it occurred to her that the fear had gone now. She was careful not to think about the battle that had just passed. *I wonder what Dammerung is up to. Does he get honey run through his hair? Or is he, perhaps, miles away in his mind, dreaming and scheming about what Skander is doing? If he is not rattling the ear off any poor servant assigned to him, he probably is miles away. He is probably miles away regardless. He can rattle and travel at the same time. I wish*—her heart clenched in her chest—*I wish he wouldn't go without me.*

"Oh!" she said of a sudden as a chill ran up her spine.

Romage's warm hand, slick with honey, ran down her back like a man soothing the neck of a horse. "Ah, someone tread on your grave? There, that is the last of it." With a deft movement of her hands she had wrapped the hair up in a twist, piled it on Margaret's head, and thrust a pin of blue amber into it. "Now come to the bath."

Still bent over, Margaret looked up, startled.

The queen rose and looked down from her height, laughter in her eyes. "That is not all! When we get very dirty we take baths, but we do not get into them completely filthy. We do not bathe in such grime. You are just clean enough to come really clean, I think. This way..."

Margaret hitched the damp silk up from her hips to her shoulders, got laboriously to her feet, and padded after Romage to an upright tub of travertine set in a little alcove along the west wall.

It was lit by several squat plum-coloured candles; the light skipped off the surface of a white liquid and shone off a number of lemon-slices and several handfuls of rose-petals.

How far I've come from the dirty girl who knelt in a cellar and cried.

She flung the silk down and stepped into the tub.

As the milk closed over her body, Romage sat down on a little three-legged stool, unscrewed the cap of a squat glass jar, and scooped out a handful of sweet-smelling stuff into her palm. With it she began to rhythmically massage Margaret's hands.

"Was this your first battle?" she asked conversationally, but always in that careful, low tone.

Again, as if I were a wild animal. Her skin threatened to shiver again at the thought of the fight and how close she had been to death, but she clamped down on the feeling before it could break. "Yes... And no." She forced a smile. "I have been at this war for awhile now."

"So you have. So have we all. Rinse that."

Margaret stuck her hands in the milk and shook them while Romage, without asking permission, suddenly craned her head back and began the same plaiting movements with her hair until much of the honey had been washed out.

Presently she did not have to force the smile. Lying back against the cool edge of the stone, the milk soft against her sun-scorched flesh, a smile untwisted with her muscles. A perfect circle of lemon, alight with the reflection of candle-flame, drifted across the surface of the milk and settled on her freckled shoulder. Her voice came out of her as if conjured by magic, and she did not wholly realize what she was saying.

"You are a people fond of battle and glory, but I think you know gentleness and comfort too."

Romage rose and washed her hands. "Man is the student of many things. When you are finished soaking I will rinse you again on the tiles. Meanwhile, I will lay out your clothing for you so that you may see."

Hope, a strange and girlish hope, turned Margaret's head like a shot. She said nothing, but her eyes followed Romage like a hawk following a hare. The woman moved a panel in the wall aside, revealing what looked from across the room in the circle of candlelight to be a great well of darkness. Out of the dark Romage lifted several dark, shimmering gowns, and from a drawer in the well she took a number of items which fit roughly in one of her hands. The items she put on a table, out of sight for the moment, then she laid the clothing on a chair and began to shake them out.

"Your underdress," she announced, and held up a gown purple like thunder, cut wide and low with fantastic sleeves. She held it up so that the light could play a drum-beat on its folds, then she put it aside and reached for the next part of the gown. "Your overdress."

Margaret put her hands on the sides of the tub and hefted herself forward.

The gown was made of a blue-black fabric—it seemed to play at being one or the other, depending on the light, and sometimes both at once—and was picked out all over, unevenly, in clear jewels that shone white even under the harsh glare of the candles. This, too, fell in many folds about, but never quite on, the shoulders, and was cut like a robe to be wrapped round the body and tied with the enormous black-and-silver slashed ribbons that Romage produced from the pile on the table.

"There is jewellery to match," said Romage, "and I will put up your hair with a heron's feather. I think that will look best, don't you?"

Margaret knew without asking that these things were meant for her to keep, as a kind of grace-gift from one mighty woman of Plenilune to another. Pain jangled at the back of her throat. "I—I will look as though I wear the universe," she stammered.

Romage put the clothing down. "That will be no great change in things," she noted. "Come, or you will wrinkle like an old damson."

Once more Margaret knelt on the travertine tiles with the grouse-silk wrapped around her waist, but this time it seemed Romage could not work fast enough. Rhythmically, as if rubbing down a horse that has had a hard run, the queen swept the linen over and over, down and down Margaret's softened limbs, and while she knew the work was meant for good, she was impatient to try on her new gown. She would never admit it, she would never complain, but she had not known until now what a relief it was to slough off the months of half-pressed, burn-washed clothing for something truly glamorous.

If I could stand in the middle of a battle like this, she considered as she rose and stood while Romage wrapped the purple folds about her body and laid on her the airy lightness of the silk sky-cloth, *there would be no battle, there would be no war. I should do what Helen should have done—gone out and thrown down their shields and spears with a single glance. I am some kind of cause of all this, am I not? Why shouldn't I— why shouldn't I...*

Bending her fiery crown, Romage fixed a little row of buttons on the sky-gown to be sure it would not slide open unadvisedly, then round and round she passed the wide ribbons about Margaret's body, pulling them tight until her hourglass was more pronounced than usual.

"Kneel again, and I will do your hair."

The dark brown folds, which boasted none of Romage's tiger-striped beauty, were nevertheless closely attended to. While she could not see what the woman was doing, Margaret felt the heavy lengths go up strand by strand, curled and twisted and tweaked and coaxed, sweet-scented, pinned, piled, slung about with a heaping trail of clear gems and encircled as with a cloud with the single white plume of heron's feather. Romage slid two strands of diamonds through the hole in either ear, then laid a simple short ribbon of three diamonds about her throat and tied it off.

"Am I all ready?" Margaret's fingers touched the precious diamonds in a shiver of wonder scarcely suppressed. Was there a woman in Plenilune as richly blessed as she? From the pit into which she had been thrown, to have climbed so high, to be so free— to wear the heavens on her shoulders!

"I will do your eyes—" from the mess of things on the table she took a little pot of black stuff "—for the eyes are the window of the soul, and then, I think, you will do."

Margaret held still, although instinct told her to jerk away from the tiny paint-brush Romage dragged across her eyelids. It seemed an elaborate process, but at last it was done, Romage had put a little scent on her hands and smacked Margaret's cheeks smartly once or twice, and then, no less in awe of her, but less in fear, Margaret went out with her into the gloom of the red-panelled atrium to discover Rupert waiting for them.

Margaret's heart stopped in her chest, but then the man in black swung round into the faint light and she saw his flash of a kill-devil smile in the familiar, freckled face. He was not all in black: on the breast of his heavy, smouldering tunic was a dragon etched in pearl-coloured thread.

"I forgot," Dammerung remarked in an amused, superior tone, "how long it takes women to prepare."

"Perfection takes time," retorted Romage. "Even our Lord tarries over his kingdom yet."

"*Touché*," said the War-wolf, but his attention was elsewhere. "Nay, but I had come to wait on the little merlin-bird that I entrusted to your care. Do you not remember? That fierce little falcon-barred thing I carried into battle with me. This is a swan to rival the one they keep in Thrasymene!"

Romage's voice was warm honey. "Do you like what I've done with it? I am sorry to let it go: my temper was relieved to find an outlet on someone other than myself."

"Such is the artistic fire man shares with God! that he is never content to make something good merely for himself. The merlin was all well and good, but I'll take the swan. You won't hear me complain."

"When you two are done," said Margaret, "isn't supper waiting?"

"Indubitably." Dammerung slid an arm from each of them in his. "But we will make a better entrance if we come in last."

Margaret could not help agreeing, and she blushed with surprise at her own forwardness.

The dinner, when they arrived, proved to be a simple affair. The table was laid in a long low atrium like the one of the red honeycombed panels—it was encircled by the dark and laid across with bars of golden lamplight—and a number of couches and chairs had been drawn up round the table's perimeter. Upon seeing them enter, Mark Roy got up from his chair and Centurion, who was still seated, leaned away and flung an arm around the back of his chair.

"The body count," he said, raising a piece of paper between two fingers.

"Indeed?" Dammerung put Romage off on her husband's arm and indicated a couch for Margaret. She sat on it, reclining as she saw Grane was doing on a similar couch across from her. "Let us have it, then."

"Grace first," said the lord of the house.

The gesture was familiar now: Dammerung, seated in his chair, held out a hand, palm upward, and Margaret laid hers in it, head bowed. Her smallest finger lay across Dammerung's wrist: she felt the vein of it swell as the lord of the house began the invocation.

"For the grace of life, we thank you. For another day of freedom from oppression, we offer our most heartfelt gratitude. We remember the dead who have suffered for the sake of a kingdom that is passing, and we remember together the kingdom to come. Come, Lord—"

The pain, unexpected and swift, closed her throat.

"—come soon. We commit ourselves to your hand."

Mark Roy seated himself and the dishes of fruits and white meats began to pass. There were no servants, Margaret noticed, looking round: every man served himself and passed the dish on to his neighbour.

Dammerung crossed one knee over the other and twisted imperiously in his chair, elbow on the table, a fluted glass of red wine in his hand. "Well, Centurion?" he prompted. "Whom all have we sent out of life today?"

Centurion hurriedly spooned summer fruits into the little bronze bowl before him and shoved the cut crystal dish off on Aikin. "Among ourselves," he said, clearing his throat, "we have lost Sparling—" he glanced up at Black Malkin, but the lady only shook her head sadly and said nothing "—Zealon of Tarnjewel, the border lords and brothers Mirran and Kahmeny of Orzelon-gang, I believe; Howl of the Wastes I saw go down with my own eyes in a blaze of glory and many enemy dead. You would have been proud to have seen him, my Lord Dammerung."

The War-wolf's face wore an appreciative smile, but to Margaret's eye it seemed distant and she felt his deeper darkness move restlessly beneath them.

Many names followed she did not know. Theran of Darkling. De Montfort of Darkling. Hama of Thrasymene. Birch of the Wastes. The steppe-lords from Drakeskar in the north. Jermaine, Lady of the Tribute. Bri Hearthstone. Chevalier of Darkling. Spyridon of Capys...

Lord Gro spoke up after awhile. "It makes the food tasteless, do you not think so?"

"Sometimes it makes it taste even better," said Dammerung—or the body of Dammerung that his thoughts had left behind. "At least *you* may still eat."

Margaret swallowed the soft, seasoned turkey meat and felt callous for how sweet and warm it tasted. "I am sorry for Spyridon. We must needs send a letter to Skander and let him know."

Dammerung finished his wine and made short work of his turkey. Twisting the cap off a huge red strawberry, he prompted Centurion again. "What of the enemy? How many of them did we encairn?"

"*In toto* I do not know—I left the count at three hundred and it was still going."

Mark Roy's knife scraped against his plate. "We were close on one hundred seventy-five, I believe, as far as our counts went."

"*Shee!*" whistled Dammerung under his breath. "A red day."

Centurion had attended to his list again. "Among those of note of the enemy dead are Malbrey of Talus Perey, Sebastian Leswey, Charles Fin—an ironic last name—and Hector of the Academy, the Fabii men of Ethandune—"

"All of them?" asked Mark Roy with some surprise.

Centurion's head nodded in a circle as he tipped the paper toward the light. "All six of them."

Out of the corner of her eye Margaret watched Lord Gro carefully pick up his napkin, use it, and replace it on his knee. *You sly thing. I warrant you did it single-handed, too.* But she chose, for his sake, not to call him out on his achievement.

"Forswear!" laughed the War-wolf. He refilled his own glass. "We run the risk of shorting Plenilune of her men."

Centurion said, "Well, we can always institute polygamy... Hugh, Baron of Hemmin-law—"

"For a moment I thought you meant *me*," interjected Daggerman.

"Tist! no, sirrah." Darkling shook out the paper.

Dammerung remarked without looking up from his plate, "You may have Hemmin-law if this all pans out the way we should like it to."

Huw's face in the half-gloom was a brindled moon of surprise, but then he smiled and said, "Well, if your lordship cannot find a better man to take it..."

"By the time Darkling reaches the end of his list, I will probably need to restock all the manors and great houses of the Mares. You're welcome to it."

The ex-thief and thorough rogue stumbled over a few words, discarded each one of them, and finally gave up altogether. Ducking his head, he touched his knuckle to his brow in salute.

It was a simple meal. Finished, Margaret laid down her fork and knife and set her elbows on the edge of the table, one hand over the other, and settled her lips against the curve of her forefinger. Out of the corners of both eyes, constantly, she caught the elusive glint of her jewels moving as she did.

"One thing I cannot fathom," Dammerung went on, half-humoured, half-puzzled, "I could have sworn I spotted Hol's banner among the spears, yet when I looked for it with my sword, it was not there. Sure I know he is a fool, but I was hoping he was less the dastard."

Centurion looked up from his letter. "Speak well of the dead!" he laughed. "It was Brand the Hammer who fished out Hol's guts with a battleaxe. You won't see the Rose among the Colours anymore." Then his face went all wrong when he saw Dammerung's countenance. Jerking her head around, Margaret saw Dammerung was staring at him as if he would eat the other alive, face so cold white with fury that, in the lull of her arrested heart, she expected Centurion to crack like ice and die. Then the great man turned his head ever so slightly and found Brand. No words passed between them, but she felt that she and Aikin, who was looking intently into the depths of his glass, were the only ones who understood what Dammerung was saying. She saw Brand's jaw move, as if he was going to swallow and had decided not to.

"I dare swear." The War-wolf's voice was carefully light. "How late it grows. Thank you for the supper, my lord. I will see you in the morning."

He rose, pushing back his chair, bowed stiffly to Romage, and turned into the shadows. Margaret did not wait. She knew that if she waited the awkwardness would grow unbearable and she would not be able to move. She flung her napkin onto her soiled plate and swung after Dammerung, jewels rioting white light; she wondered, as she ran on soft feet through the dark, how long the others at the table could see the winking fire of her gown until the dark and the turn of the hall finally swallowed it up.

"Dammerung!" she hissed.

There was no answer. She could feel him, a dark tide ebbing away in front of her, and she knew that he heard her call after him, but he did not stop and he did not speak. Angrily, she clenched up her skirts and ran faster through the dark, bumping into a doorway here, tripping down a flight of stairs somewhere else, losing all sense of direction until she came out into a breath of air and the fabric her gown had been cut from blazed above her.

A silhouette of shoulders broke up the sky.

"Dammerung, by the twelve houses—" She ran forward to stand beside him. She opened her mouth to say more, but words failed her and she shut her jaws with a clack she knew he heard. He did not turn. He stood with his shoulders set square against the world, arms folded, staring out across the dark and other things that were just as dark as the night, and the rawness of his wounds were tangible even to her.

Finally she found her breath. "You ought not have done that to Brand. He did not know, Dammerung. *He did not know!* He was a man doing his duty. You can't pick and choose men on the battlefield to kill like children picking and choosing dolls to play with! He did what he had to do. It was not providence's design that you should have killed Bloodburn."

"I promised." The voice was low, like the voice of the ground. "I swore before Heaven and Plenilune that his death would be mine. It was against me that he lifted his hand, and by me he should have been destroyed."

"I know. I *know.* But you could not have killed him then. It would not have been a fair thing. Bloodburn was guilty of being a foolish man, old of life and withered within. He had cut himself off from all that might have done him good. The fault was not yours for giving him that mercy, in letting him live a little longer to see another red dawn. The fault was not Brand's for killing him in battle."

"I *promised*."

"Thou stubborn old thing!" she cried, and grasped him by the shoulder. The hardened muscles resisted her pressure. "I hear you! But you must hear me now. We swear, and we swear meaningfully, but what are we before the might of Heaven's oath? What are our words but little things when God speaks? It was not to be. Don't begrudge the boy a little honour, thou proud, proud son of the Mares!"

He turned and there was a sudden light—from where she did not know—and she could see his face. He appeared startled, taken aback, but he had whipped the anger behind his back as if ashamed of it.

"Old?" he parroted. "Boy? What are you, Artemis—ageless?"

"*It is an ill thing for me that you look so like the Huntress—unless I be Orion.*"

A cold wave of premonition stopped her full-blooded heat. "I do not mean old. I borrowed the agelessness from you. But compared to some of you, Brand is just a boy. He was only going to come out, after all, two years ago when this all began."

"I do not know... How easily one forgets age when one is all of Plenilune at once."

Without realizing what she was saying, Margaret murmured, "Even Plenilune must come to an end some day."

Dammerung was quiet.

"I think I should go to Skander tomorrow," he said presently. "My gut says to go home."

A single fleck of light skittered across the sky and vanished on the horizon.

"Are things coming to an end, then?" she asked.

She heard the wry smile in his voice. "Am I a prophet, that I should know such a thing? But yes. One way or another, I feel, the end is coming."

XXX | OUROBOROS

"You are looking rather better. Where is Woodbird?" Margaret twisted her head so that Skander, bending, could kiss her cheek.

"You have just missed her!" he said remorsefully. "She and my huntsman just left to rejoin the border troops."

Dammerung did not turn from surveying his men, hands on hips, as they moved like shuttles through each other, weaving a camp on the slopes below Lookinglass. "And you?"

Skander Rime hitched at the thick belt about his waist from which hung the ominous hunk of metal that was Gram. "There has been a shadow growing in my mind," he admitted. "The Carmarthen are a threat, a seen threat. Yet ever I have that sense of eyes on the back of my neck whenever I turn to face the steppes. I do not trust de la Mare. I do not like to turn my back to him."

"No, I know what you mean..."

The day was hot. Nothing could be seen for a great distance; the horizon swam with gold. But Margaret cupped her hand over her brow and squinted south and southwest toward the lower knees of Seescarfell. News among Skander's scouts was that Rupert had swept through in the night like an angel of death, soundless, leaving nothing alive behind him that had put up a fight, and had entrenched himself in Marenové House—following, skirting, Dammerung's own movements.

I wonder if they are not a little afraid of each other. Or, if not afraid, wary of what they will awake in the other. If they are not careful, they might split Plenilune in half between them and destroy everything they sought to hold.

"Will he come?" Skander asked bluntly.

Dammerung's head turned—but he was only following the progress of the picket-lines. "What, out of Egypt? He would do well to stay within the stronghold for a little while. I have drowned his mighty men in a sea of blood."

"Will others come to him, do you think?" asked Margaret.

"There are not many left. From a realm beneath the Earth, perhaps—we have kept the gateways open for the past few months, always feeding souls through to the dark: who knows what archon he might invite home to bolster his ranks?"

Skander shivered and shifted as if to hide it. "Don't talk as such! The man is flesh and blood, same as you, no matter what else he can do."

The War-wolf's brow cocked back at his cousin. "Yes...but what *else* we can do!"

There was something wrong with Skander's face, Margaret thought, as the two looked at each other wordlessly for a moment, but she could not place the errancy. No one spoke a word—that seemed beyond any of them for the moment—when it grew on Margaret's awareness that a clinking of metal accoutrements was coming toward them. Turning, she saw the blue-jay man coming up a flight of stone steps set into the slope, ducking under a spray of pine-scrub. He had something in his hand.

"News, sir," he said, drawing up before the two war-lords. "From Orzelon-gang, I believe."

Dammerung waved a hand and Skander took the letter. With a snapping sound he broke the wax seal, sending a shower of scarlet shards to the ground, and pried open the thick writing-paper. Grimly he scanned the words inside.

"It is in Aikin Ironside's hand. *'The news will spread quick enough, but I would rather be the first to tell you. Brand of Orzelon-gang, surnamed the Hammer, second son of his majesty Mark Roy my father, is dead.'* "

It was quiet for a long time. A curlew called on the hillside. A warm wind puttered in the blue-jay man's long sleeves.

Skander folded back the note. "That is all."

Without a word, Dammerung turned and left them, crossed the courtyard without looking right or left, and disappeared inside the house.

A kind of horror of everything nearly choked Margaret out of words. The world seemed to have shrunk, as if she were looking at it out of the wrong end of a telescope. "What—what do you mean, that is all?" she demanded of Skander. "How did he die? Doesn't it say?"

"Truly, Margaret," he protested, abashed by the news, by Dammerung's response, and by her vehemence, "it says no more. Look—see for yourself!"

He tried to hand her the letter, but to her mind it came at her like the mouth of a viper. She recoiled, saying something that she could not hear in her own ears about going to see Dammerung, and retreated blindly toward the house, deaf to any sound but the pounding of her heart, insensible to anything but the chill that was coursing up and down her limbs.

Dead. Brand—dead.

How many more? How many more until it is over?

How many, Rupert?

How many!

She ran to her room, never stopping to look for Dammerung. For the first time in months—long, half-happy, golden months—she flung herself across the length of her bed and cried. She clutched the bedsheets and screamed into them—for Brand, for Dammerung's broken heart, for the broken heart of Plenilune. Like hot gold poured into the crucible they fell into her, filled her up, and shattered her clay frame.

How much longer can we stand this! We are all dying. There will be none left!

The immanence, the inevitability, of extinction fell like a shadow over her.

What if Gro died? She began a macabre spiral of thoughts. *Who would be there for Herluin and Ella? What if Skander died? What would Woodbird have to live for?* What would happen to Julius and Julianna if Centurion were killed?

Julius and Julianna!

She sat up, blinded by a gold welter of tears and sunlight. There, in white and uncanny purple eyes, was the small, soft, beating heart of Plenilune. All things precious were like them. And if the iron armour of Plenilune were smashed in, if the mighty men went down, it would not take much to squeeze the soft liveliness of Plenilune to death.

How fiercely we fight, she thought with an odd calm in the wake of her torment, *for that which must die one day.*

She pushed away from her bed, suddenly loathing herself, and sat in her chair in the sunlight where the breeze could reach her. The summer birds sang in a riot; the tree insects rattled incessantly, swelling to the breaking point, dropping away again, swelling, dropping away... The light wind teased her swollen eyes until they felt stiff and dried, and, in a detached way, she knew they had ceased to look puffy and telltale.

But the pain was still there.

I am losing hope, she realized quietly. She watched the wind move the hem of her skirt about the floor. *God, we have tried. But I fear that, like Arthur, we must die with our foe and become nothing more than legend after all.*

The faces of the dead and the old morbid hopelessness of Arthur—what good was there in the legend that the man would come back, when he had not?—passed in colourful panels before her mind's eye, as if they were playing cards that she slid one after the other on a tabletop before her. She played with them and lost, and a soft knock at the door some hours later found her entertaining the thought of burning them in a candle, one after the other.

She did not turn her head. "Come in."

Aikaterine put her head in. "Supper is ready, my lady. My Lord Skander waits for you and my Lord Dammerung on the portico out back."

This news roused her a little; turning, frowning, feeling as if she were just waking, she asked the maid, "Oh—where is Lord Dammerung?"

"My Lord Skander told me he had gone to his room and that you were likely to go wake him. We thought it best if you did it."

It was comforting to know that she was not the only one who had felt fear of the War-wolf.

"I come," she said, getting stiffly out of her chair. How empty she felt! She went on light indoor slippers after Aikaterine with the feeling of being made out of thistledown. And still the long shadow of mortality came after her.

Aikaterine left her at Dammerung's hall. There was no one else about, only a long curve of hallway and light and the softness of the carpet underfoot. The door to his room was shut when she came to it. Her knock, sharp and light, clacked down the hall and back again, but seemed to lose itself beyond the door and did not return. She waited a moment, listening to the silence. As it dragged on unbroken, the image of the dragon's hall crept into her mind, huge and black, and—in her imagination—inexplicably empty. Her hand clutched the knob and twisted: it turned.

The room was dark within. The curtains had been pulled tight; only a few fish-scaled shards of light slipped through the chinks, twinkling to the floor, running up and down her skirt as she passed through them. In the gloom she could see Dammerung stretched out on his couch, stripped down to his shirt-sleeves, asleep. But it was an uneasy sleep she caught him in. Before she had quite reached his side she could feel the angry heat emanating from him, and in the thin slivers of light she could see, through his open collar, the sheen of sweat pooled in the hollow of his throat. He was shivering in his sleep like a horse that smells fire. The fear raging behind his eyelids was so strong that even Margaret could taste it in the back of her throat. Holding back the taste, holding back the sudden lurch in her middle, she reached out and gripped his arm, hard, and called his name.

He snapped out sleep as if he were a glass mirror and her hand, her voice, were a fist she had put through him. With a surfacing gasp like a sob, he reached across and grabbed her ribs under her left breast, fingers grinding until the pain turned the gloom red.

"Dammerung!" She struggled to keep the pain out of her voice. "Dammerung, wert dreaming."

He stared up at her with sleep-blind eyes. They worked her face, dazed at first, then with a mounting panic as he struggled to place her in his memory. Then suddenly he seemed to remember, and just as suddenly, though he did not let go, the pain went out of her side.

"Sha...!" He gasped and fell back off his elbow. He let her go and dragged his hand over his damp face. While he tried to swallow the pounding of his heart, Margaret took a handkerchief off a nearby table and pressed it to his throat; the sweat seeped into the fabric and made her fingers slippery. His skin was cold, his eyes, when he looked at her, were distant and glassy and seemed to call across a gulf of pain to her. She knew what he had been dreaming.

"You startled me."

She arched a brow. "You were already startled. Truth to tell, I expected you to try harder when you woke. It would have taken nothing to overpower me."

A grey smile pulled at Dammerung's mouth. She had handed him the opening move to his favourite game—flattering and making jokes at her expense in turn—and he grasped the first piece as naturally as a fish grasps the water. "Oh, really, Lady Spitcat? Whose face makes Helen of Troy look like Bardolph? Who steps on Honourmen like a child walking across daisies?" He frowned. "That was the one that broke."

She looked down and touched her side gingerly. "One of them... It is sound now. No harm done."

But he knew how easily he could have done damage, and he pushed himself up—his shirt stuck to him at all points, heavy with sweat—bare feet flat on the cold stone flags. "What did you wake me for?" he asked, rubbing the heel of his hand into his eye.

"It is time to go down to supper." She followed him with her eyes as he rose, blindly, still scrubbing the nasty clinging sleep from his face. With his other hand out before him he found his way to his clothes chest and flung back the lid, digging in the black interior for a fresh shirt. He tugged at the slippery buttons of his soiled garment, but she was distracted by the dampness on the cushion under her own hand. She had expected it to be blood: it was only sweat. The cushion was soaked with it. Dammerung's shirt was soaked with it. This whole house was soaked with it. Glassdale, Ampersand, Tarnjewel... They were all soaked with Dammerung's sweat. If she looked in his eyes she knew she would see them, spread out in rolling blue-green splendour, but melancholy under the grey haze of war. They were drowning under the sheer strain of his labour. They were not going to make it. The balance was too keen, too perfect. They would drown in their own sweat before victory was struck.

Dammerung thrust his shirt-tails into his trousers and turned, hauling his braces over each shoulder. With a heavy sigh he ran his fingers roughly through his hair; still thick with sweat, the effect was wild and rakish and desperate. It was almost chilling how easily the idea came to her then, quietly, smoothly, full-formed like Athena. The slyness of it was almost galling, but the idea itself, once it had sunk in, froze the marrow in her bones.

"Margaret?"

She looked up at his face—she had been staring at the button of his right brace—and yanked the curtain closed behind her eyes in the same moment.

He looked concerned. "Are you sure it is sound? I will have a look..."

"It is sound," she assured him, "but you may look if you like."

"No..." He frowned at her and grew still like an animal, watching her, eye flickering to eye, crisscrossing her face. Breathing was beginning to grow difficult. If he should see—but she could not afford to let him see, of that she was perfectly certain. So she held her ground, knowing that everything depended on it. She held her ground, and at length he said, "No, I trust you. But tell me if it hurts again. They are so little and brittle." His hands curved in the air, then flung wide, dissipating the image.

"I know you trust me, Dammerung." The words tasted like ash in her mouth. With a great effort she rose, shoving down her own shivering fear, crushing it beneath his own, beneath the harlequin images of war-ravaged landscapes, hunger, blood, and death.

It is time we put an end to all this. It is time we laid down our swords.

He sensed her anxiety. She could feel him reaching out with his mind, touching it, running, as it were, his hand over it to get the feel and shape and texture of it. But he did not question her. She put her hand in the palm he held out for her and felt the lean, strong fingers interlock with hers: the simple gesture sent the blood shocking back to her heart, and she had to swallow back the sudden sharp sweetness of life before it could prick the tears out at the corners of her eyes.

They met Skander on the portico overlooking the garden. Dusk was only just falling; the earth hung huge and wide like an eagle's feather in the Harvest Moon sky and round it burned, like the aftermath of the summer, the rich red clouds of evening dissipating in enormous columns until they faded into the deep, pale blue. The blue was so deep, the red so rich, Margaret could almost feel them whispering over her skin. She breathed them in, feeling them flicker like fire in her veins. The woods, burning with the backwash of evening light, were the colour of damsons, and somewhere, clearly, like the white soul of falling water, a thrush was singing.

Skander looked up as they approached. For the first time Margaret noted how haggard he looked. He seemed to have aged years in the past few months; there was a tell-tale darkness around his eyes which was only lost when he looked directly level with the sun's evening rays, and even then the spark which had always been in his eye did not kindle to fire again. His broad, strong frame seemed weary in its chair; his hand, big and scarred, clutched his goblet in a hold that was too tense, as if he were waiting for the alarm to blare in the lower terraces at any moment.

Not here. Not here at Lookinglass.

"There you are." He let go of the goblet and rose as Margaret came to her seat.

Dammerung pushed her chair in. "I was asleep. She had to knock me about the head to wake me."

Skander looked up quizzically under his brows as he sat back down. "I am sorry. Were you sleeping deeply?"

Dammerung, too, sat down. "When you plumb sleep and gradate it for me, I'll be able to tell you how deeply I was sleeping."

As they bent their heads to say grace, Margaret stole a look at Skander's face and saw that his cousin's evasion had not worked: Skander knew how lightly and uneasily he had been sleeping and it made the harsh, worried lines on his face gouge deeper with concern.

"Any word from Centurion?" Dammerung asked when they had begun eating.

"No, none yet." Skander's knife flashed in the light, peeling back the soft, white sides of his fish. "But word came down from the Marches that the borders are holding."

Swallowing fish and something even harder, something that stuck worse than bone, Margaret said, "You beat them hard. They will remember that, for a while."

Skander smiled at her wistfully. It struck her that he was oddly flattered by her remark, and listening to her own words and the words that lay unspoken between the lines, she felt the last tie to England snap loose and drift away.

"Have you got any word from Woodbird?" she asked.

Dammerung looked up from reaching for a fig, a brief smile flashing up on his face. "None for *us*... How does she?"

"Well. She sent a note this evening saying they had reached Mucklestrath in one piece. Black Malkin even unbent enough to send a greeting herself from Holywood and to ask how I was doing. She did not ask about you."

"What a wet cat. It will be a long time before she forgives me."

"If she ever forgives you. I am thinking it would be a sorry thing and tempting fate to have you lead her behind us down the aisle."

Something passed across Dammerung's face, something shadowed and pained, as if Spencer had been mentioned. "I don't think you will have that problem," he said quietly, ominously. Margaret looked to Skander, but Skander was suddenly interested in his plate.

After a pause Skander went on. "Anyway, I do not much care either way and I confess I have very little warm, familial sentiment in my heart toward her, but if she is going to be kin you might try rubbing her hair the wrong way less. I do not want her...casting hexes on my children or giving them the Evil Eye."

Margaret looked beside his chair and tried to imagine a smaller version of him clinging to his braces and digging a pudgy fist into his pocket for a sweet. He would do well as a father, she thought sadly. This whole place needed youngsters running over it, upsetting the firm routine of Aikaterine's and the blue-jay man's lives. And Woodbird, too, would like it here—she followed the upward flight of a pair of barn swallows, black and arrow-shaped in the golden air, until they disappeared under the stable eaves—here where the world was small and brightly coloured at their feet, here where the winds were cleanest and sharpest. She would live well at Lookinglass.

The thought of it stabbed like a knife under her breastbone.

They ate quietly, talking in fits and spurts; was it just her, or did the shadow of her resolution lie across them all, and what if they could make out the shape of it? Margaret had trouble meeting their eyes. Skander did not seem to notice her evasions: the tired melancholy ached in all his lines. Dammerung seemed preoccupied with his own thoughts. When supper was over and the blue-jay man brought out the chessboard at Skander's behest, Dammerung played a reckless, terrible game with seemingly only half his mind, and at the end only won because he seemed to wake to the realization that, if he lost, Skander would know for certain something was wrong. Margaret tried to read one of Skander's books but she could not keep her mind on the words. Her eyes skimmed the lines, blindly, until she realized she had failed to read them and she had to start afresh.

"Margaret." She started at her name. Dammerung was twisted round in his chair, one of Skander's red pieces in his hand. "You have not turned a page in half an hour."

With an angry sigh she shut the book. "*Je ne sais quois.* I do not know where my mind is this evening. I cannot seem to focus on what he is saying."

"Who is it?" asked Skander, frowning in concentration over the board.

She squinted at the spine. It was growing dark and the light was thinning into a rose-grey. "Marlitos."

"He will do that do you."

Dammerung set the piece down on the tabletop with a click. "We are almost finished here. Then perhaps you had better go to bed."

Go to bed early! Margaret carefully did not meet his gaze, but made another attempt to read. If she could gamble on Skander's face and Dammerung's dream-ravaged mind, she could hope they would both be asleep as soon as they hit their beds. She, curiously, did not feel tired. Every nerve was stretched until she felt Dammerung, in a moment of playfulness, could reach out and pluck one like a harp-string if he cared to.

Skander sucked in a breath and put his elbows on the table, dropping his head into his hands and running his fingers through his hair. "I see it, I see it. There is nothing I can do."

"Checkmate." Dammerung gave an abbreviated salute and leaned back in his chair. "Checkmate, and what was that little ruse you were trying with your queen? I could see right through that."

Margaret's blood ran cold.

Skander swept the red into the tray and rose, setting back his chair from the table. "I had no great hope, but it was all I had." Then, voice sharpened with melancholy, he added, "Passing strange that we sit here playing at chess, who have been playing it in greater scenes the past few months."

"Passing strange." Dammerung, too, rose. "But I am glad for the game. I know I do not lose my life if I should lose my ivory crown." His finger, hard upon the crest of the king, knocked it into the tray. "Good-night."

"Good-night. Good-night, Margaret. Rest well."

"Thank you—and you." She got up in the dark, moving with the heavy weight of shadows on her shoulders.

Skander picked up his empty goblet and turned on his cousin. "I will be up for awhile reading, if you have need of anything."

Dammerung's brows flinched as if a wound had been touched. "I will be wrapped in linen like a dead man and asleep in my bed, if you have need of anything from me—which you are unlike to get if you do."

A horse called up from the stables. In the gloam, the last rim of late sunlight catching at his hair and signet-ring, Skander dropped his hand heavily, briefly, on his cousin's shoulder. They stood a moment so, still, sharing some weight between them that was more hopeless than what Margaret herself bore. It cut at her again; she felt herself bleeding inside and knew that not even Dammerung could fix this wound. It was his wound, Skander's wound, the great mortal gash plunged into Plenilune's heart, that she was going to fix herself.

"Come, you," she said softly. A moth puttered by, brushing against Dammerung's face as he turned to her. "You need your sleep."

For once he came without any pretence of mockery or playfulness. His feet skimmed the floor wearily; his strong, lean shoulders were bowed beneath the weight Skander had dropped on them. Looking back over her own shoulder, Margaret saw Skander watching them go, his hand moved to the back of his chair as if to support himself.

It cut her again. And again.

They went up wordlessly to Margaret's room. She walked beside Dammerung with a mingled sense of dread and cold excitement that made her feel faint. At every step she wished he would break off, bid her good-night in the way he always did—lightly, carelessly, knowing that tomorrow he would have cause to cheer and tease and worry her again—but she knew he would not do it. He was too keen a man, too honest even in the midst of his little charades, to lie like that. She was more afraid than anything that he would ask her bluntly what was on her mind. He wanted to know, and if he asked she knew she could not deny him. That would be breaking a faith too dear. That would be ruining all.

Finally they reached her door. She wanted to slip in and bolt the door at once, but she did not dare. She waited with the pretence of normality, a faint smile on her lips, looking through the grim grey agony in his eyes. She smiled, but her soul was bleeding badly now, and he seemed to be watching it bleed, eyes blindly fixed on hers, watching, as it were, some nightmare from which he could not break. She opened her mouth to say good-night, to release him gently and hope her voice went with him into sleep, to charm away the horror of the past few months, but the movement seemed to break him violently from the nightmare. He started, the reckless anger that had driven his chess game leapt into his eyes like fire, and she stiffened with a sudden unreasoning fear. Rupert had hid it from her until the last moment and he had bit her lip, hard, at once angry and triumphant over her. She saw it in Dammerung's eyes. She had the warning, she had the narrow slip of time in which to turn her head away. But she did not turn her head away. She felt his hands, hard and trembling, entwine in her hair and pull her forward. Her heart was in her throat: could he taste it? His lips were firm against hers, but trembled: did he smell her fear? She tasted salt and did not know from which of them it came. Instinctively she had shut her eyes—had he shut his?—but she could feel no tears tracking down her face. She could feel only the rage of her heart and the rage of fear, and the warm touch on her lips of something that might have been but would never be.

He drew away; his forehead brushed hers, his fingers still tangled in her hair. She did not remember opening her eyes, but she found herself looking into his, closer than she had ever been before, clearer and bluer and fiercer than they had ever been before. They seemed to stab into her, to probe into the wounds her own resolve had left on her soul. She did not know how long he held her, searching her eyes, gently but relentlessly; all the while the little finger of his left hand moved counter-clockwise, idly, combing the hair at the base of her neck. She held her ground, though it hurt worse than anything she had ever endured before, though she wanted to crumble into his arms and give him what he wanted: the awful thing that was in her mind to do. But she could not give it to him and she had to endure it, and finally his thumb brushed over her lips and he let her go as a man lets go a wild thing he hopes might come back some day.

"Good-night, Lady Spitcat," he murmured. There was no reproach in his voice.

Her hand went out of its own accord and touched the back of his. "Good-night, Dammerung."

His hand turned, as if he meant to grasp her hand in his, but he checked himself and drew away. His face plunged into shadow. Already he felt a world away and the shadow that lay between them was the shadow of death. She could feel the warmth of his hands on her neck, the pressure of his lips against hers...

Swiftly, smoothly, she turned to her door and went in, shutting it behind her—and shutting out, too, the thing that had happened and could not be. Her room was dark; earth-light fell like petals through the thin patterned curtains, and through its light she moved mechanically, pulling at the tie of her gown, flinging it carelessly away as a man, baring for a fight, flings down his hampering gloves and strips for war. Dammerung had made her hair a wreck. Bending in the thin silver light before the mirror she thrust it back up, pinning it in place, then went to her wardrobe and pulled out a heavy travelling gown. She pulled it on with ruthless vigour, careful not to think, careful only to do what needed to be done. She would need a bath, but she could do that later. She put on her boots and paced the next half-hour away, walking the length of her room over and over, careful not to think, careful not to think...

When she was sure Aikaterine would have gone to bed she stole out of her room, fingers brushing against the wall to guide her—she dared not light a lamp—until the many winding hallways and staircases of Lookinglass finally brought her to the kitchen. There was a little red light coming from the banked coals of the stove. She found a candle on the huge central table and, kneeling, eased back the door of the stove until she was staring into a phoenix-nest of embers. With the heat beating on her dry face she thrust the candle in among them until the wick caught, then she bore it to the pantry.

Trusting to her instincts and common sense, she went straight to the back and began hunting among the jars and cans and dusty paraphernalia. She was not disappointed. Though it seemed to take many long minutes, the flame of her candle finally flashed up on the ominous lettering of the can she was looking for. She took it down—it left a telltale dustless mark on the shelf—and tiptoed back to the kitchen sink. Easing the spigot open she refilled the can with water, put the lid back on, and shook it until the powder was sloshing all around inside. Then she blew out her candle and stood, heart hammering, in the red hollow dark.

"Determinas loco—" she whispered "—come home to me! Determinas loco—far from the sea! O hunter, come home from the hill!"

She was hit in the chest by the boom of a drum-wind. Lookinglass tore away behind her. Somehow she kept her feet. Somehow, fists clenched, teeth ground, eyes tight shut against the shriek and roar of the fabric of everything, she stood her ground until the ground stood still. The wind stopped. The roar died to a soft summery calm. Opening her eyes she found herself looking up at the grim, stalwart front doors of Marenové House.

The great doors were imposing and uninviting, especially under the pallid glow of earth-light. Shadows huge and full of form stood guard on either side, their curves and jagged edges made of a kind of otherworldly iron. Margaret felt the blades of them slide across her skin as she mounted the steps and stood small under those doors. But she did not hesitate. If anything, the long empty lawn and lane behind her made her feel more naked than those doors. She pressed down the latch, surprised and relieved to find that it had not been bolted for the night, and she slipped out of sight into the vaulted entryway.

It was dark inside, and had an almost deserted air. She felt at once that something hung over the place. Around a corner, within the dining room, she thought she could see a single light. On the ground floor no light nor form stirred. She stood alone by the doors, her breath loud in the silence.

A latch clicked. She jerked her head around to see Rupert's big black man Livy step out of the north wing of the house. He saw her upon the instant and he, too, froze, his white eyes uncannily gold in the light of the candle he carried.

She was the first to make a move. "Good evening, Livy," she said coolly.

"Lady Margaret," he replied in a wary tone. Somehow he shifted the candle so that his eyes were lost in the shadows thrust up by his cheekbones, but she could feel him searching her, noting her travelling attire.

"Livy, is your master at home?"

His eyes sprang out again. She hated how wide and white they were. "Ye-es," he said slowly. Then he shifted toward the stairs. "He is upstairs in the astrolabe chamber. Come—I'll put you through."

Margaret stepped up after him. After the spell she knew she ought to have been bone-weary, but if her bones had been cast of spring steel she could not have felt lighter. She swept after the manservant; her skirts filled the quiet—for Livy's feet made no noise—with an urgent rustle. Against the steel cage of her ribs her heart jostled and thumped.

From the first floor landing they took an immediate left into a long wood-floored corridor of the north wing. At the end of it they began mounting a long spiralling staircase, and Margaret knew they were going up to the curious tower that presided over the whole length of the house as a watchtower over a garrison. The foreign, forbidden chamber to which she climbed did not help to calm the shaking in her breast, and she was glad for the thickness of her coat lest the movement be visible. She would have reached into her own chest and crushed her heart to stillness if she could.

There was a single door at the head of the stair, shut and barred with hinges of iron scroll-work. A wide beam of saffron light leaked out beneath the door and brushed up the front of Margaret's gown.

Livy knocked. "Sir," he called, fetching a glance over his shoulder at Margaret. "There's someone here to see you."

There was a long pause behind the door, then, muffled through the wood, came Rupert's weary voice: "Show him through."

The old latch squealed in protest as the manservant opened the door for her. The light of dozens of candles dazzled her vision. She stepped through into a profound sense of thick darkness that was not the darkness of mere shadows. She heard the door shut and latch to behind her.

It was a wide octagonal chamber that she stood in, rather larger than she had expected, but cluttered profusely with tables, chairs, bookcases, candelabras, cabinets, and countless smaller objects that she did not have leisure to observe. In the centre of the room stood the largest of the tables, a great pale oak thing with dragons for legs, and by it stood Rupert—Rupert, who stared back at her like a stag caught on a woodshore scene, staring as if he were looking at a ghost.

"Good evening, Rupert."

Her words fell from a great height, dissipating into the silence.

He stirred at last, slowly, as if afraid his movement might cause her to vanish. "Fiends of Hell," he murmured, and he took a hesitant step closer. "Margaret."

She laughed airily. "You once chastised Skander Rime for pressuring you into entertaining here at Marenové. I can see why you were so reluctant."

The old spark flashed into his face. "You come upon a man in the dead of night like a vision, and expect a cool reply? You might let a man collect his wits once you have dashed them out of his hands." Then, after he had fallen quiet, he began again in a quieter tone, "Am I to believe you...*have* come back?"

"You are to believe it."

All the while Rupert had been bent a little over the table, supporting himself on his splayed fingers. Now he seemed to come alive again and he pulled away, coming upright. The darkness seemed to thin a little. She had never seen his pale eyes so softened, nor, strangely, so afraid. He was still expecting her to vanish. Suddenly he laughed, softly, self-deprecatingly.

"I've had this dream before," he said. "But even if it is just a dream, I'll follow through with it. It is pleasant enough while it lasts."

Margaret cracked a smile. "Well, I'm not a dream."

At that moment the clock chimed its introductory tune, high and gaily, and then struck off the time: it was an hour and a half past midnight. A momentary wave of weariness broke over her, but ebbed away at once. At the last chime Rupert pulled his eyes away to look at the face of the clock, and he seemed to hear the time as the echoes died away into the stony distance below them. "One-thirty."

"A batty time of night," said Margaret encouragingly. "You look tired."

"Not at all." He left the table and came to her, hand outstretched, a smile on his face. *Their smiles,* she thought; *their smiles are the same.* "You will want to freshen up. Would you like a drink?"

"I was hoping you would ask." They turned and ducked through the little doorway again and began to descend the stairs. It was like walking down the throat of some animal. Rupert went ahead so as not to tread on Margaret's skirts. "You have a bottle of pinot noir—"

"The bottle from Thrasymene?" His tone was incredulous. "That is a one-of-a-kind."

"All the better to open it now," purred Margaret.

They passed through the long wooden corridor and paused at the head of the stairs. Rupert turned, folding up her hand in his own. In the uncertain earth-light that filtered through the glass-domed top of the atrium his face was pale, but sharply featured, and she could see him clearly. "An extraordinary wine for an extraordinary woman. There is not a more appropriate bottle in my cellars."

"I'll fetch the wine and glasses."

Wordlessly he leaned over, through a shaft of light, and kissed her, warm and slowly and searchingly, as if to assure himself that it was not just a dream that was about to vanish. One hand closed over her forearm; she felt the other grip her above the thighs. She had his upper arms in her own hands, and even through the sleeves of the tunic she could feel the powerful muscles clenching and relaxing like the sinews of a racehorse. They sent wild shivers playing up and down her spine.

He let her go reluctantly, wordlessly, and backstepped a few paces along the hallway, pulling his eyes from her with some effort. She listened to his fading footsteps and stood for some time at the head of the stairs, alone, a small shaking going all through her body. Then with a deep, harsh breath she turned and descended the stairs for the dining room.

There was a candelabra set up in the dining room and all its five candles were lit, burning down at regular intervals as a way to mark off the passing of time. The glass front of the drinks cabinet, the glass panes of the windows and pictures, caught the light and cast it back, filling the room with a warm subtle glow. She moved through the familiar yellow, smoky air, feeling as one in a dream, each footstep put to the tune of a heartbeat. She opened up the drinks cabinet, but the cold bodies of the bottles and glasses arrayed on their long narrow shelves could not quench the warm cast that flushed her skin.

The Thrasymene pinot noir, encased in its flame-red bottle, was a creature of dark foreboding: velvet, rich: if she could only strain her ears enough, she imagined she might hear the low cat-hum of it. She set the bottle down on the board and put her hand into her pocket, feeling for what she had stashed there.

"Rupert," she called into the entryway. "Rupert, which sort of glass did you want?"

Her fingers found the knob of a drawer. Sliding it open, she fished out the syringe meant for soda.

It took a moment for the voice to filter back down to her. "The burgundy glasses will do. You will find them behind the port—tall with the wide bowl."

Her fingernails nearly breaking, she unstopped the little can and bent, hand iron-firm, to fill the syringe. With the sense of plunging a knife into herself, she pushed the syringe through the cork of the bottle, depressed it, and removed it, smoothing the cork back into place.

She searched the shelves and found glasses. With her fingers through their stems she lifted two off, retrieved a whale-tusk corkscrew from a drawer, and returned to the entryway with the precious bottle tucked firmly under one arm. It took some fighting to climb the stairs with her hands so occupied. Her feet fought her hem grimly, but she made it to the top without tripping.

Rupert met her at the doorway of his chamber and took the articles from her. He had changed. He had stood up in his astrolabe chamber in trousers of corduroy and a thick tunic the colour of the pinot noir itself, but now he stood up in black trousers and a simple white shirt, the collar of which had been carelessly left undone. She noted it but did not look at it.

"I'll pour out the wine," he said. "Don't be too long."

He moved, but she coyly avoided him, shooting him such a smile that turned his brows rampant. She almost expected him to snatch her back around, but if he had wanted to his hands were full, so he let her go, and she toyed with him by sweeping off and not looking back, even as she passed into her old room and shut the door after her.

It was dark within. Someone, most likely by Rupert's order, had lit a candle or two within the washroom, but all else was drenched in darkness, lit only in the most metallic places with the thin yellow light that worked through the sky and through the heavy curtains. She moved through the velvet dark like a ghost, shrugging off her jacket and working the buttons of her skirt as she did so. She had some surface understanding that the room, so long deserted, was cold as ashes, but she could not feel the cold for the burning in her skin. She entered the washroom and tossed down her rumpled clothing with pointed carelessness, and plunged at once into the long closet.

The cold began to fight with the warmth as she stood before the long racks of articles, fingers pressed against her thighs, her right leg jigging slightly with faint irritation as her eyes roved over the clothes. Colours vivid and muted, pastel and dark, white and black, silver and gold, jostled against her vision. But there was an extraordinary wine in a wine-glass waiting for her, this was an extraordinary night at one-thirty in the morning, and they needed an extraordinary gown.

She stepped up to the rack as one might step up to one's dance partner, and took down with deliberation a long gown of fierce, rich purple velvet. It was simple—not like the heavy, sky-like thing that Romage had given her—stitched of pure midsummer's night, and she ran it through her fingers with satisfaction. It was perfect. It was tailored for this night.

She laid it down on the vanity chair and callously pushed the hot handle of the faucet, opening up the water until it roared through the pipes. The sweet scent of hot water filled the room.

She got into the tub as it filled with water and leaned her head back against the rim. She watched the candlelight play in watery shivers on the ceiling; if she looked down, she could see the thumping of her heart. Mechanically, after a few minutes, she picked up the container of soap, scooped out a handful, and began rubbing it over herself. The memories of nearly a year ago splintered through the thin partitioning dark, vivid under her mind's eye, full of the scent of that soap, the sight of the billowing steam. She rinsed, feeling as if she were a dream—

—A dream shattered, suddenly, by the quick gasp of fury from the doorway.

Margaret looked up like a raven on the battlefield, teeth bared, heart set against life. Rhea hung with one hand on the doorframe, the other hand clenched into a fist, the light of murder in her eyes.

With a rush and cascade of water Margaret lunged to her feet and sprang out onto the rug. At the same moment Rhea came forward, feet planted firmly—she seemed to know her business—hand pulled back for the blow. But the maid, canny and small as she was, had not reckoned on the sheer iron hardness of Margaret's resolve. Like dead Brand's war-hammer she caught Rhea's wrist in one hand and slammed the other into Rhea's face. Bone broke—she felt it go, shocking away upward into the spaces where no bone belonged. With her left hand she grasped Rhea's hair, yanking her head down; with a jerk she brought her right elbow down onto the bared neck and felt the sickening wave of exaltation as it broke and the body sagged limp at her feet.

So much for the bath. Reaching for her towel, Margaret stepped over the body and stood before the mirror, insensibly watching the eyes of her reflection as she dried off.

How quiet the house was.

XXXI | THE RED QUEEN

Dried, she flung the towel over Rhea's body and plunged forcibly into her gown. It was a tight fit, but then she had wanted it to be. She wrenched first one arm and then the other into the sleeves and fought with the décolletage until the cold night air played on her breasts and in the opening at the back between her shoulders. Despite the chill, it looked well. The velvet took the light and seemed to come aflame with it: lines of fire-orange encased her breasts and hips and fanned with the train behind her. She turned and turned, and bit her bottom lip to crush a smile.

It is just as well that I am so tall. Now, Helen: we will see which of us stands better in history for the fame of our beauty.

Two steps forward, she peered strongly into the mirror, fetching a look over her skin. The summer had brought out several fine freckles on her cheeks and chest, and the open wind had teased a glorious lustre into her hair. If she had not been quite pretty before, the high wilds of Plenilune had infused into her a goddess-light that shone out now.

She left Rhea dead on the bath-mat and went to join Rupert in his room. She knocked for the sake of the thing and let herself in.

She had never been in his room before. It was shaped not unlike hers, but more cluttered, with every inch of the walls taken up by full bookcases, and the floors covered in rugs and sofas, tables, and, in one place, a large globe of Plenilune that she seemed to take in more clearly than anything else. The lamps had been lit; on a low sheeny wood table before Rupert's couch, a little plate of black stone lay, and across it smoked two sticks of scented wood.

He rose, setting down the bottle which he had just been using to fill the glasses. He looked at her for a long time, taken but quizzical. "How insensible life is," he murmured, "and all the people in it, that one mistakes it for a dream sometimes."

"Do you still?" she asked.

The hard laughter glinted in his eye. "I am standing here, wondering if this be an ivory dream or a dream of horn."

"If you put out your hand and touch it, it may or may not vanish, and then you will know."

He sucked in a half-laughing, uneasy breath. "I do not know if I want to risk it." His voice hardened. "Come—come here."

She went of her own accord and sat beside him, falling back into the deep embraces of the couch. He, too, leaned back, sliding his arms around her and settling his chin on her shoulder so that, whenever he breathed out, she felt the heat of it on her neck.

"What were you doing," she asked mockingly, "in the cloud-capped tower of yours?"

"We have fair weather at present," he protested. And just as mockingly went on: "I was summoning the dark powers and principalities of the air. They are great friends of mine."

"Sooth?" She shifted and the hem of her neckline shifted a fraction too. "Do they have names?"

He sat up, frowning—but she saw the want for a smile lingering behind his eyes. "You do not believe me, you little heathen."

"No, no, no!" she cried pacifically. "Of course I believe you. They were all standing about your door when I went up to you. I wonder they were not a little angry that I got in and they didn't. I rather jumped the line, didn't I...?"

He sank back on one elbow and, twisting, swept the glasses into his hand. "They can wait. They, too, are time-bound as we are, but they have less enjoyment out of life than we do."

Margaret took her glass. It was cold and had sweat a little. "Oh, I don't know about that. Not that I know anything about them, but I wonder if they don't enjoy life more fully than human beings. They have no obstructing conscience."

His teeth flashed like the sword of the conqueror. "I'll drink to that," he said.

The glasses clinked softly against each other. Margaret slid the blood-red liquid across her tongue and reflected that, beneath the taste of that other thing, it was a really good wine indeed.

Rupert drained his glass and set it on the table, then lay back again beside her, head pillowed on his arm, a sigh of contentment escaping his lips. She was propped up on one elbow; his hand, questing, found a length of her hair and began to twirl it round one finger.

Pipe to the old macabre dance—

The eyes which had softened to a mother-of-pearl colour, watching the movement of his fingers, unfocused sleepily—the fingertips brushed her skin—then, without warning, the steel came back into them and he jerked upward to his feet, took two steps forward, and turned back on her, fixing her with cold, disbelieving rage.

She sat still. She did not dare move, lest he make a move for her—not that it would have done any good—and because already the room was growing faded and dark at the edges. There was a curious feeling beginning in her stomach that she did not like.

At last, with a supreme struggle, the man raised one brow, as if in salute. "You must love him a great deal to do what you have done."

With an effort she managed to get up. The scent of the burning sticks was cloying now. "I love Plenilune," she replied harshly—she had to force the words or else they shook on their way out. "And I cannot stand by and watch you tear her open and raise hell in her midst."

The grey eyes were haunted, angry and haunted, but she went on recklessly.

"That was your mistake, Rupert. You never loved Plenilune. You never loved anything. Except me. That was your mistake.

Liking," she parroted mockingly, "is a small, dear door out which you pass in the night unseen."

Resignation stole across his face. "But you saw. By all the gods—!"

"I saw," she cut him off. "You never took me seriously. I was only ever a pawn to you. Well." She lifted her chin against the grey terror encroaching on her vision. "Even a pawn can break a stalemate."

The disappointment hardened and became an expression of intense longing. "Oh, Margaret, I hate—. You are not a pawn." His eyes roved, unfocusing, and he blinked against the grey. "Curse him," he murmured. "*Curse him...* Oh, Margaret, what a queen you would have made."

Blindly, he took a step toward her, though what he meant to do she did not know—the high sense of panic sang in her ears—when of a sudden his head jerked to the side as if the voice of someone he feared had called him without remorse.

Without warning there came a sudden uprush from underneath, as if the vaulted fell-country sky had opened at their feet and they were plunging wrong-way-up through it as the falcon, tucking in its wings, plunges for the kill. If she screamed, Margaret could not hear it. Everything was a whirl of white and grey and sudden thunder-tailed streaks of deafening black. The black came faster and faster, thrashing her vision, quenching it, strangling it, until it engulfed everything in a blood-curdling shriek.

She caught her footing just before she lost her balance completely. She was clutching the stone casement of an immense stone double-doored gate; reeling from the fall, reeling from the shock, her feet slid among what looked like pools of blood that gathered on the wide stone threshold. She thought they were pools of blood until her whirling vision cleared and she saw that they were the petals of wine-dark roses.

With an effort she pushed off from the casement and looked out of the Gate. The doors opened upon a plane of white, dimensionless, endless, fathomless: the three giant stone steps descending from the threshold stopped abruptly and dropped into a nothingness of white, a nothingness filled only with the eerie tendrils of smoke from a fire she could not see. The scent of burning filled the air.

One tendril reached out close to her, brushing against her cheek. Cringing, Margaret turned away.

The sight within was even more appalling than that unbearable nothingness without. There was enough room within the Gate to stand comfortably and not be concerned about falling off the threshold, but within there were no steps. The stone ended with a sharp drop, a drop she could have made but one she felt suddenly loathe to try. Beyond the threshold was a darkness as shifting as the empty white. At times she thought she saw looming shapes, big as the shadowed figures of the fells at night, and at other times it seemed all was a vast floor of obsidian flags, sparking light from fires that she could still not see, catching light and throwing it back in forms like snickering, sneering faces. They were always moving; she snatched only brief, disquieting glances of them.

She stared at the empty dark for some time before she realized it was not empty. On the stone flags near the base of the threshold knelt a figure, a figure distorted out of familiarity and yet all the while horribly familiar. Margaret stood on the edge looking down at it, watching it drag itself up to its hands and knees, bent over in apparent agony. Water was running off it in incessant streams, dripping from its clothing, from its splayed hands, from its brow. Like one remembering a dream, her mind launched across a year to a wet train-carriage and an impudent young man.

"Rupert!" she called. She knelt, peering against the strangely tangible darkness. "Rupert! Can you see me?"

He could hear her. At the sound of her voice he gave a hacking gasp and reared back on his heels, squinting up at her. Pain had dilated his eyes. Staring back at him, even at that distance, she could see the wildness, the terror, the agony in that face. The fingers clawed at the uneven stone floor. With a spasm he bent double again, and with a horrible sound that churned Margaret's own stomach, he began to vomit. He vomited up streams of fire like some kind of sickened dragon. The liquid flames pooled around his hands and knees, sending up sparks that burned his skin, casting a death-pall glow around him. He came to a coughing end and knelt in shuddering silence; with each breath smoke and the sound of sizzling oil came from his mouth.

Margaret got up and stepped away. For a moment she felt as one moving in a dream, moving without a body. The things before her vision shifted, as if they were not really there but puppet-shadows conjured up to frighten a child. She was not frightened, and the knowledge of that steadied the otherworldly scene again. She needed to know two things: where was she, and ought she to go down and help Rupert?

With a despairing gargle, the agonized Rupert began to vomit again.

Wherever they were, they were dead, and a dead Rupert was a Rupert that needed no help. She looked at the torn wreck of the man, alternately doubled in pain and clawing in a kind of animal fury at the floor until his own blood mingled with his bile. Margaret's stomach was clenched tight against the scene, but she did not feel fear until it broke in on her that the two of them were not alone.

A figure stood beside her, wrapped up so dark and close that she had mistaken him for one of the shadows beyond the Gate. As she started involuntarily and looked up, she saw him looking back at her with a gaze so strong it was almost physical. It was a fierce, pale, Scandinavian sort of face into which she looked, a face that turned her blood cold. The beautiful blue eyes seemed to claw across her own face; she could feel them leaving red marks on her skin. And yet she could not quite look away. In that void of darkness, his pale face, his flaxen hair, were a kind of sick candle that shouted out their own sort of light against the black. She could not quite look away...

A distant scream, piercing and blood-curdling, dragged cold nails down her spine.

"What are *you* doing down here?" demanded the tall dark Scandinavian. He took a step closer. He towered over her, swathed in his enfolding darkness, blue eyes stabbing her so that it was with conscious effort that she made herself not flinch. Out of the darkness of his form appeared two hands, unfolding toward her, as if to beckon, almost as if to hold. The movement of them sent cold waves across Margaret's skin. "You have the blood all over you, but you have been Marked Out." His hands withdrew into his darkness and the eyes narrowed, switching back and forth, coolly, like a cat. "It is a shame."

"What—" In that place, Margaret's voice sounded in her own ears like a glassful of warm yellow wine. "What is a shame?"

"The Marks are the most rewarding of quarry," said the Scandinavian. "But my new posting has just come in, and we are not to be."

For one moment, one horrible moment that hung mockingly before her eyes like the dead-moon paleness of his face, she thought he seemed familiar. Was it in Rupert's own face that she had seen him? Was it in a nightmare? Was it—worst thought of all—in the mirror when she had looked back at her own reflection? But with blissful swiftness the moment was past, broken with the distant but perfect clarity of a lazy summer afternoon calling through the Gate:

"Damn it all, it's smoky in here. Someone ought to open a window. Give her up, Erebos! A vine of thorns is a bloody thing to make an engagement ring out of."

"Little fool of a worm," said the Scandinavian, and he shook loose his cloak. Only it was not a cloak, but huge wings—more wings than Margaret in that stunned moment could count—shaking and rattling and hissing on the scorching air. With a brutal gesture he flung them wide and with the elbow of one hit Margaret full in the breastbone. Images of graves, worms, skulls with their skin still clinging on despairingly, the pungent tang of rotting flesh, lashed across all her senses and stabbed into her soul. With a choked cry she fell backward across the threshold, down the steps, rolling—skirts whirling against the white and grey—until she lost them altogether and she was falling into nothing.

The dream-fall gripped her lungs and shoved her heart up into her throat for what seemed like an age until, with a jolt, the spangling white snapped away like a pennon and she was blinking up through the sick blur of her own eyes into Dammerung's face.

Two waves of feeling, confusion and relief, crashed over her so close they were nearly one. A moment later she gave a choked cry—her throat was raw and disused—and propelled by an instinctive panic, she launched up and vomited across the carpet. There was not much in her stomach beside wine and the vomit came out stained with it, and the single powerful heave all but emptied her.

"That's better," a familiar voice was saying in her ear. "Get it all out. Dying is a nasty shock. Don't struggle—! There's nothing to struggle about. I've got you, you idiot. This is a goodly kettle of fish you have fried yourself in..." With one arm and knee behind her to prop her up, Dammerung let her relax into his hold while he wiped her mouth with a handkerchief. "You'll find water in the pitcher over on the wash-stand," he told someone. There was a hurried, half-running tread of boots, a shadow that made her shy, and someone was kneeling across from him handing him a glass. It clinked against her teeth as he held it to her. "Get the taste out of your mouth," he told her. "Nay, it is but water! That's it—that's the way of it."

She had sense enough to know that she was meant to spit the nasty spoiled water out into the porcelain that someone was holding out to her. Later on she dimly remembered doing so. The third party left—a jangling slash of light broke up on her vision and made her wince.

"Shh," said Dammerung, rocking her gently and brushing the hair from her forehead. "Shh, *leman*, it is only the sun. Lie quiet, you brave, blasted fool."

It took her a few attempts at speech before she could make herself understood. "I want—I don't want—can we go?"

He pulled the damp hair off her neck and pushed it away. "Not any great distance. We can't go to Market. Here—" he stripped off his cloak and worked it around her own shoulders. "Tabby, tell your master I've taken the reprobate out of doors. You have the floor?"

"Yes, sir," said a voice from a long way off. "Very good, sir."

He was not quite her height, but he was strong and unusually deft; Dammerung got his arms squarely under her and lifted her in a single fluid motion. Figures seemed to clear from before him to left and right, someone held a door, someone else asked if aught else was needed. He shook his head and said something in sharp jest, something a little unflattering about *her*, but Margaret could not remember what.

It seemed like a long way to out of doors. With each bare foot set gingerly, Dammerung walked gently and she began to doze before they had reached the patio. There the wind woke her cruelly. It was unusually cold for the Harvest Moon—one of those rare, inexplicably chilly days with a biting wind off the fell slopes and not a cloud in the whole beryl-coloured sky. The sun was still low—it had not quite got over Glassfell—its shadow and the half-shadow of Seescar drenched the grounds in a glistening purple quiet. Stepping out into that cold, unbroken morning quiet, Margaret felt curiously as though she were just getting over a long illness—an illness from which she and no one else had ever expected her to recover. The wind caught at her and her skin felt paper-thin. There was no warmth anywhere in her body; her gown and cloak hung heavily about her frame. She might have stopped when Dammerung set her down, or doubled back inside, if his hand had not been under her arm to guide her to an old, wide-branching tamarisk tree.

He put her down with her back against the trunk; with a sigh he sank down beside her and passed a heavy hand across his brow. Seen clearly for the first time in what seemed like a long time in the pale light of the out-of-doors, with the blue of shadow and the silver of the air against his skin, he looked worn and haggard. He looked grey. He looked a little sick.

"Did I give you a scare?" Her voice was still thin and sickly itself.

He nodded. The jesting seemed to have been mere pretence: he could not now even pull his lips off his dog-teeth and give her a wan smile.

She was so used to hearing him laugh about reverent things and fling high matters about like a dog worrying a bit of old cloth that his grimness frightened her. Was he angry? He had never been angry with her before, not like this. He got cross and brooding with other people, but thinking back now she could not remember him being anything other than agreeable with her, as agreeable and comfortable as one would be with one's own shadow. Now suddenly she felt detached from him, as if the long shadow of death had come between them.

How strange that that should be the worst thought on her mind—and yet, it was.

Dammerung shuffled his feet in the tufts of grass and laid his arms over his knees, hands pulling at his hands. Fetching a searching, sidewise glance at her, he said, "You look pale. Do you feel any better or are you still going to be sick?"

"I am not going to be sick again," she replied wearily. She seemed to have lost her backbone and was having difficulty keeping from pitching forward. "It is very cold out here."

"The wind will clean you out. Our fell winds are good for that." He put his elbow on his knee and turned his head, laying it in the flat of his upturned palm. "You—do you have an answer for the question I asked you?"

"The que—oh." There was salt on her lip. Those images came back to her from a very far off place, clear for all their distance—but the clearest thing of all was the sense she had had then of a treasure she could never possess. And now she could. "Yes."

She was not looking at him, she was looking at a shard of black gravel among the pink; but she saw him flutter a moment and look keenly into her face. They were both very quiet for a very long time, listening to their own thoughts—and straining for the thoughts of the other—and the rush of the wind and the hum of bees in the flowers. At last, long past Margaret could take the silence, he prompted, "I think you always knew."

He was ridiculously coy about the obvious. Yes, neither of them had mentioned it, or even thought about it so far as she knew, but she imagined they had always known, and so had everyone else.

He tucked his chilly hands tightly under his arms. "It was difficult waiting and wondering if you already knew. But I did not feel I could tell you until—" his brow contracted in a kind of inner agony "—until yesterday evening when I felt something awful was on your mind. I had hoped you would tell me... But I couldn't say anything. You would have regretted it."

She stared at him in hurt surprise. "I wouldn't have regretted it!"

"Not all the time," he shot back. "But you would have, sometimes, when you were lonely or felt out of place, or Plenilune pinched you like a shoe that is too small." He rucked up his shoulders defensively and shifted away like a ruffled hen. "It wouldn't have been right to ask you. You would have felt as if you had just got out of the frying pan only to be asked to jump into the fire. We—we are not so unlike, Rupert and I."

So. He had thought about it. And here she had taken things for granted and never really thought the situation through. Of course he had always been there for her: he had been there all along the way, a hand under her arm, a smile for her sadness, a figure in the gap to come to her defence. Had she been a complete unfeeling fool to nearly throw it all away? Did he hate her for it, even though he *had* come?

But she knew that if he had asked her before, or if she had thought it through, things would have been even more confused than ever and she would not have been able to go through with her desperate bid to end things. She would never have understood so clearly how much she loved Plenilune, and Dammerung, and all the people they held in their hands and across the green fell folds of their knees. She would not have been able to see that. She would not have been willing to lay down her life for them. And she *had* laid down her life for them. It was strange to be able to look at Dammerung's face, and at the face of the garden and the wood and the fells and tell them she had died for them. Only, she knew she could never say it; and they knew it without her saying so.

He was not really angry at her. Whatever he was angry at, formlessly and blusteringly, it seemed to slip off his shoulders and blow away from them both in a minute. A weak smile began to grow in the shade of his stubble. "I almost feel sorry for Rupert. He had no idea that when he chose a girl of wit, he got a girl of grit as well."

"I was never very witty. I was scared, and I talked with a mouth full of daggers when I was scared, but I was never very witty." She pulled herself deeper into the panther-skin cloak. "Skander told him I was a force to be reckoned with. I think perhaps he was the only one among us who really believed that."

"He did not have the privilege of meeting you in the dead of night in your nightgown with your eyes red from crying and your lip red from bleeding. One forms a different view of a woman when one meets her under such circumstances."

The distinct tone of friendly mockery was coming back into his voice and it made her pathetically comfortable. The sharp scarlet warmth of embarrassment crept up her cheeks. "Had I known who you were I would have gone away at once."

"No, you wouldn't," he laughed at her, and, flinging an arm round her shoulders, switched places with her, his back against the tree, and pulled her back into his lap. "I am just too appealing."

He mocked her—he mocked himself, with a face that was still pinched and pale and blue-veined from his scare—but the truth of the matter was that he was right. She shivered nestlingly into his arms like a cat into a pile of cloth. Though comparatively small to other arms, his were hard and the muscles bunched and gathered under the fine broadcloth of his sleeve. He rubbed vigorously at her arms and put the back of his free hand to her forehead.

"Here is hoping the day warms up. This is hardly the sort of harness for a chilly morning."

She had completely forgot until he mentioned it that she was still in the shockingly inappropriate purple gown. With an involuntary cry that made him howl she pulled the cloak tight over her chest and his arms.

"I cannot believe I have come out in this," she gasped. Several horsemen, whom she did not recognize at that distance, were walking together by the yard and she watched them in horror as if they could see her clearly from where they were.

"In light of recent events," Dammerung protested reasonably, "I don't think it matters much."

"In light of even more recent events," she retorted, "it is becoming increasingly important!"

He set his chin on her shoulder and did not let her go. His hands, she knew, if she tried to pry them, would prove immobile. His warmth began to seep through her back; her resolve began to waver.

"At the risk of being grim again," he said sleepily, jaw jigging on her collar-bone, "I would rather not let you go off again just yet. You—you gave me *quite* a scare."

"I know. I am sorry."

"Not enough to take it back?"

She hesitated. "No...not enough to take it back."

"That is just as well."

They were quiet for awhile, content in each other's silence. A door slammed in the house. A bee, swimming by, blundered into a low-growing patch of clover and got lost. Somewhere a dog began to bark. Margaret shut her eyes.

"Margaret?" said Dammerung sleepily.

She did not open her eyes. "Yes?"

"Did...did he touch you?"

Her eyes opened. She was looking directly at the bumblebee's head as it emerged, laden with pollen, from the grasses. "He kissed me."

Dammerung breathed out heavily, a breath more full of expletives than a scorching desert wind.

She leaned her cheek into his. "What did you expect? I had to do something. By the twelve houses, the man took it almost without a backward glance. I thought he would have been far more suspicious."

The pale eye looked up into hers, askance. "Have you looked at yourself in the mirror, and do you know the heart of man? We don't overthink the matter when the matter is you."

"I would be flattered," she countered, "if I could be certain that was not man's way with any girl he fancied."

"Well, no, it is the way, that's a fact. But you can be flattered all the same. Later. When once I have finished feeling sick over the whole ordeal."

"Me too," she admitted, and huddled back still smaller into his arms.

"Oh, hark! we have company." With a little deft move he grasped the cloak, which was slipping, and pulled it back over her shoulder as Skander came up, boots crunching in the gravel. "This one is mine," said Dammerung, squinting up through the sunlight at his cousin's face. "Go get your own."

"I already have one," said Skander placidly. "*You* look like a fox that got into the henhouse."

"Oh, I haven't got into any henhouse yet."

Skander turned to Margaret. "How are you feeling?"

"Better," she admitted. "Still a little peaky, but better; thank you."

"Yes," said Capys wryly. He thrust back the hem of his tunic and put his hands in his pockets. "I imagine *dying* does that to you... Do you know, Dammerung, we found that bitch of his dead in the washroom? Had her nose broken in and her neck busted in two. It was quite a pretty piece of work."

Margaret smiled wistfully into the clover-patch. "You know, I had forgot..."

It seemed Skander had caught her involuntary expression, for he chuffed and said blithely, "I told you she was a force to be reckoned with," and jerked his chin indicatively at her. "Nay, that was Rupert that I told."

"And *he* is quite dead."

"Oh yes, dead as a doornail. He...looked really very awful once we turned him over. There was a bruise around his neck and his mouth was open—we could look right down it: it was completely burnt out. What did you give him?"

Black, unpleasant dream-pictures shifted across the warm summer landscape. "Only some sort of rat poison."

"These are spirits of a different sort," said Dammerung. Margaret felt him gather, pushing her forward, and get to his feet behind her. He bent back down to lift her up. "O-oh...! Is there no end to your legs?"

The ground shifted, slipped, and steadied again. Skander stepped in and put a hand under her other elbow. "Oh, we grow ourselves tall in England," she explained. "We must, for it is so cloudy, if we want to reach the sun."

"Well, you're closer to the sun now," said Dammerung, taking complete charge of her. They began walking across the gravel, and he added in a thoughtful undertone, "I forget that you are English..."

"Hullo!" said Skander, turning and putting a fist on his hip. "Isn't something—the roses! The roses are in bloom again!"

The heavy trailing plants swarming over the yard walls were dancing in the early morning wind, and each vine was shouting out a spark of scarlet colour: a perfect Lancaster rose.

Dammerung looked askance at the shrubs. "I had not taken you for such a romantic sort, coz."

"No, don't you see?" Margaret protested. "No, of course you wouldn't. Old Hobden told me ever since you died—or disappeared—the roses haven't bloomed. And now they have blossoms again!"

The War-wolf's eyes were dancing as he said, "I can trounce any man in astrology and split a world like a diamond with the old arts, but I am unlearned in the ways of herbology. Come along, Lady Spitcat, before you cause a real scandal."

XXXII | UNDER A DRAGON MOON

Dressed in something less glamorous and more socially acceptable, Margaret sat in the old familiar way with Dammerung and Skander in the library, eating a scratch breakfast that the blue-jay man had ousted from the kitchens below. The eggs were warm and the milk was fresh; she heard no one complain and she ate as heartily as the men. She had not realized death made one so hungry.

"Why do you suppose he said, 'Give her something to eat'?" laughed Dammerung, passing her the bowl of twelve-hour-old biscuits. "Skander, the jam, if you will..."

Skander, his scarred face rejuvenated with a smile, passed the jar of jam across. "Does it feel good to be ordering the breakfast table about in Marenové House again?"

"You would not believe. But I can't stay long. I have letters to write this morning—people will want to know that Rupert is dead—Margaret needs to get her feet back under her, and then we have an old friend to see."

Skander frowned, sceptical.

"And you," Dammerung tactfully ignored his cousin's expression, "have a bride to recall and a wedding to plan. Better make it a double one."

Wiping excess jam off her fingers, Margaret asked, "Where *are* we going?"

"To see your parents," said Dammerung without looking up.

A knife clattered to a plate. Margaret was not sure if it was hers or Skander's. Cold, blank horror swept over her. She wanted to look to Skander, to ask for his help—like a child being dragged away to bed she wanted to grab the nearest thing on Plenilune and hold on tight. But she could not take her eyes off Dammerung's reserved, demure, down-turned face.

I would—I would rather go through the agony of last night than go back to England. I can't go back. I won't!

"If I remember what you said correctly," Dammerung put down his utensils and used his napkin, at the same time pushing his chair away from the table and rising, "your parents will be expecting you back from—what was that place? No matter. They will be anticipating your return within the next few weeks." He crossed the room, soiled napkin thrust into one pocket, and began rummaging among the dusty old articles in a secretary under one window. "There will be a great scandal and waste of money I am sure if you don't show up again and make some account of yourself." He dug something out of a drawer and shut it behind him. "The whole purpose of your being sent away was to get a husband. I never did ask properly. I can't quite seem to do anything the orthodox way."

"Oh, Dammerung—" Her words failed her.

He upended a little fabric sleeve into his hand: out tumbled three old but shining rings, two simple bands of gold, and one other a ring of gold with a clustering crown of pale green gems.

"Would you marry me?"

She swore she would not cry, but the tears came anyway before she could stop them. With a little sob she hid her face behind her hands and nodded—she seemed to have lost all her words.

Hands gently pried her fingers from her face. She watched through a beautiful heartbreak as Dammerung slid the begemmed ring onto her finger, wiggled it over the knuckle, and settled it into place.

"There. You and Mother have the same slender hands." He looked up into her face, smiling. "So you will be Lady of the Mares, after all."

Skander leaned on his elbows across the table. "Let's have a look," he prompted, and Margaret swung round, so happy she could scream, and thrust the beautiful thing out for him to see. The morning light got into the green jewels and glowed like summer. The crystal dishes paled in comparison.

"Isn't it just the loveliest thing?" she demanded. "Oh, Dammerung! And this was your mother's? Oh, Dammerung!"

The blue-jay man, stopping nearby to see, spoke up. "If you could see her now, you would not guess she had just saved all of Plenilune not four hours ago in the most self-sacrificial way."

"Away with you, brute!" said Dammerung laughingly. "Let the poor girl have her hour. God knows she has had enough sorrow as is."

"I'll go," she told him. "I'll go back to England. I want to show Mother—who never believed in me anyway—just what I can do. And won't she bite her tongue for once!"

"If the picture of her I have pieced together is anything like the original, I doubt it."

"Before you go," Skander waved toward the big black oak desk, "you need to check your books. There is an army to pay, and you owe me several new doors and a staircase."

Margaret stopped turning her ring in the light. "Doors and a staircase? What?"

Dammerung dropped the rings back into their bag and replaced them in the secretary. "Oh, chances are I have *two* armies to pay... But the Mares are wealthy. We should be able to manage it. I have letters to write. Drag out the dusty thing and read it to me while I write."

He fetched a pen and paper and sat down next to Margaret. She shoved the breakfast things away to make room for him.

"What staircase?" she repeated. "What doors?"

"Oh, tush!" said Skander. He sat down with the enormous, ragged ledger. "Only he slammed his door and broke the frame, he tore your door off its hinges, broke several marble treads with his heels, and I am not yet sure what he did to my door. It looked like this."

He took one of Dammerung's papers, while Dammerung protested, balled it up in both hands, and tossed it across the room.

"Like that."

"Then that is probably what he did."

"That is in my mind also."

Dammerung unscrewed the cap of his pen and fished out a fresh sheet of paper. "You will remember, I was in something of a state. I felt your dragon's spell when you left, and it may warm you to know it is one of the few I *don't* know, but I knew—I *guessed*—where you had gone, and I knew the amount of time it would take me to get here. I was not fully rational. Who—what? No. I am writing to Mark Roy."

He cleared his head and began to make his letters. Margaret was made to sit quietly while the two men talked over domestic matters and the dissolving of the armies. She wrote addresses for a few letters as Dammerung passed them off on her—she put her left hand on each folded, sealed sheet so that she could watch the sunlight in the jewels—but she tired soon of that. She laid her head down on her arm and listened to their talk until she found she had faded quite out for a little while and Dammerung was lifting her up. He walked across the room with her and laid her down on something cool and soft and spread something warm overtop of her. He said something about being close by, and that was all she needed. She fell asleep directly after that.

"Hullo, sleepyhead," his voice was saying seemingly a few minutes later. "It's time for you to get ready. I've given you a good hour. Will that do?"

Margaret blundered sleepily out of an avalanche of pillows. Squinting at the window, she saw the light appeared late. "But it's almost evening..."

"Of course. We're going to go the way you came."

She scrubbed the sleep from her eyes. Dammerung had already changed: he had put on a clean white shirt and dark trousers, and he was wearing a dark doublet cut as close to a suit coat as one could get in Plenilune. He would look out of the ordinary, but he would not look bizarre.

But then, he always looked out of the ordinary.

Margaret climbed out of bed, brushed out her rumpled clothing, and went back to her own room to find a suitable gown. Dammerung trailed her like a puppy.

"It's a shame I don't have my chinaberry dress," she remarked, thrusting her head into the closet. "Or my sky dress. Even the red one would have looked well, though perhaps too bold for England. White linens will do. It is summer."

She changed and stepped back out for inspection. With a careless air Dammerung turned her about, then, bending her head down, thrust a scarlet rose into her hair.

"There we go, that will do. And now we'll go."

She glanced toward the door. "Now?"

"Now. Before anyone interrupts."

He took her hands in his and nodded to her. For a moment, captivated by his eyes, she lost the words...but then they came back to her. It grew easier every time.

The room rolled up on itself like a scroll. Margaret's candid-coloured skirts flew in the wind. Then the world had snapped back on itself and they were standing on the slope of a hillside that was furry with red fern and turf and tottergrass, a blue evening sky above them, a wood below them thick with foliage and roosting birds which had been empty and silent when Margaret had seen it last.

"And now thou art finished with thy labours," said a familiar voice.

"The labour goes on," Dammerung said; "but I think we are out of the woods at last."

Margaret turned to see the old withered apple-leaf woman standing in the entryway of the mountain. That woman, she thought, was everywhere!

"Hast come to tell me the good news," the woman asked, "or to beg a boon of me?"

"To beg a boon." Dammerung's melting smile slashed across his face. "Dost think, perhaps, that I have earned it?"

The woman tucked her head down and the sunlight around her shimmered white. *Whatever my lord has need of, he has but to ask his servant.*

The wind shrieked again and pulled at the woman's body. It distended into the mountain in a streak of white, paling, translucent, and finally vanished altogether. From within the voice came back to them:

Come here and meet me in my hall.

Once again, but not alone, Margaret went down to the Great Blind Dragon's black-marble lair. She was glad for Dammerung's company: knowing who lay coiled within, she was not sure she could have gone down again. Ignorance, desperation, had made her very bold.

The creature waited for them as she had first seen it, suspended in the air, coil on coil of its white, shining body wrapped in an endless ring above the floor. Its one good eye watched them as they stepped out of the passageway into its light.

Once again the sight of it took her breath away.

Some time I have woven dreams of ye, Lord and Lady of Plenilune: dark dreams full of disaster. I think we have all had such dreams of late.

"But we have all come to waking together," said Dammerung.

The Dragon's jaws moved from its teeth to form an enormous smile. *'Tis good, O Lord, to hear thy voice among the living and to see thy light again.*

"It was some time coming, old friend. But even now I'm afraid we can't stay. We are on an errand—and you can't come."

It lifted its head. *The Cruciform World?*

Dammerung nodded.

To Margaret it actually looked wistful. *Hast my malformed eye to that world. I shall not be able to see ye.*

"That is as it should be. I have need of you to guard the doorposts of Plenilune while I am gone—'twill not be long. My dear old friend, it is not the Nether World! I have been and come from there! You need not look so mournful."

The dragon raised its head and looked into the distance far above it, up to where its light faded and the marble dark closed in. It was very quiet for a very long time, then Dammerung prompted gently,

"A soldier knows his post, old friend."

A sigh ran round the edges of the chamber. *A soldier knows his post.*

"You'll see it one day." Dammerung took a firmer hold of Margaret's hand. "Come! your master has need of you. Blow us into the Cruciform World. Blow us down the universe. And stand by to recall us into Plenilune."

The dragon roused itself. The chamber shook as it unloosed its folded body; the mountain quaked to its roots.

With a ready will, my lord.

The jaw came open, throat fathomless in light. The great horns gouged the air and seemed to tear it open. Margaret felt the entryway behind her crumple in on itself and be thrown away, like the piece of paper Skander had thrown, and felt the leagues of starwoven space come roaring up behind her.

Herald the mighty! A Lord and his Lady have come—

In a blink Margaret found herself on a familiar tract of lawn between the rose garden's brick wall and the glass wall of the hothouse in the back garden of her family's home. She was looking up at the east wing—a disused part of the house—and a few feet from her, at her back, was the door through the garden wall that let out on the road. She could hear the rattle of a cart going by.

"We seem to have come in at the back of it," mused Dammerung. "I suppose I must be on my best behaviour and be a front door sort of person today."

Margaret put her arm in his and they began walking along the path toward the side of the house. "I don't know that it is of any consequence what you chose to do or not do. I don't think they will like you. They never liked *me*."

"You like me."

"I like you."

"Then that is all that matters. It is rather cold underfoot..."

At the front door Dammerung deliberated. Margaret did not remember the doors seeming so small, or so shabby. They had always seemed grim and imposing to her. They seemed pitiful now. "Ought I to knock?" he wondered. "Where *do* we fit in society? It is in my mind that knocking would be most polite, rather than barging in and saying, 'Hullo, Mother, I'm home—and look what a stallion I've got!' "

"I can think of many things more polite than that."

Dammerung knocked dutifully and they stood, awkwardly, on the doorstep, catching each other's eye while they waited and looking away again. Margaret could not help wondering if one of her relatives would come around the opposite corner of the house just then and catch them. Dammerung began whistling a few bars of Huw Daggerman's tune.

"Oh, for the love of charity," she breathed as footsteps came back to her from within the house.

Dammerung muttered, "At least it isn't *raining...*"

The door latch clicked and a maid's face peeped out. With some shuffling of memories, Margaret placed her as Amy.

"Good afternoon," said Dammerung, nodding magnanimously. "Is the master of the house at home?"

"Oh!" cried Amy, catching sight of Margaret. "Oh, miss! Oh, didnae hear? The missus sent letters."

"I did not get any letters." Margaret lifted her skirts over the threshold and moved in past Amy. In her mind's eye the landscape panned out: her relatives in Naples would receive her mother's letters addressed to her; puzzled, they would write back that she had never come to them. Her mother would be frantic and outraged. The whole story—which might have been comfortably ignored under the ruse of her mother's original plans—would come to light and there would be a lot of impossible explaining to do.

"It's the master, miss." Amy looked for a coat or hat or stick to take from Dammerung. Having none, he smiled beatifically at her. In consternation she backed away, spotted his shoeless feet, and uttered a small, demure whimper.

"What *about* the master?" demanded Margaret, although she felt she already knew.

"Good Lord!" a voice echoed down the hallway. Her mother came toward them at a thunderous clip. Margaret had forgot what a sizable woman she was. "Here's a time to be showing up—just in time to be late for the funeral! I suppose all the trains were tied up. You could not even send a letter?"

So. Father is dead. How strange that Brand's death should have hurt me more. "I'm sorry, Mother," she lied gamely. "I didn't get any letters. What happened?"

Her mother hit the air aside with one hand. "I don't know. Fit of apoplexy. Stroke. Brain haemorrhage. Barker found him at his desk on Tuesday simply gone. We hadn't any warning. Lord! how I hate this house. We'll have to sell it, of course. It's a crying shame James Firethorne had to go and die. We might have moved in with him. He was a sentimental soul. Had a lot of faults, but he would have stood up for us."

Margaret's cheeks burned with shame as her mother rattled on like a train—a train that, never in the whole of time, had been late or tied up or run down. "Mother," she said, forcing a smile around each letter as the word came belabouredly out of her mouth, "may I introduce you to Dammerung?"

The woman stopped long enough to get a look at the young war-lord standing tall and barefoot in her foyer. There was a little late sun coming in through the door window which made his eyes very pale and cast his shadow from him across Mrs. Coventry's face. His dogteeth were showing and there was a sly, not altogether pleasant smile slinking across his face.

"Madam. Margaret has spoken to me of you."

"I should suppose she has! What do you mean, 'Margaret'? Here—" With a little viper-like jerk she caught Margaret's left hand and turned it up, revealing the ring. She looked at it critically, then dropped it again. "No wedding ring as yet. It'll be 'Miss Coventry' until then, young man, if you please."

"I don't," said Dammerung ominously.

Mrs. Coventry looked so astonished she could have eaten her own hat. Margaret felt a most horrendous laugh beginning to form in her throat. It was all she could do to hold it back.

"Margaret has led me to believe," the young man went on, "that you have no sons. Is that correct?"

"I don't see what business that is of yours!"

"Only, as your son-in-law, married to your eldest daughter— she is, I gather, your eldest—I am *de facto* sole executor of your late husband's estate." He turned to Margaret. "That is how things are done here?"

She swallowed the laugh with some effort. "I don't know. I never studied law. But it would seem so."

"Do you know if your husband was in the black?"

Margaret watched her mother's innate disposition to dislike everyone war with her dawning realization that this impertinent young man might be a way out of her hole. "So far as I know," she said sullenly.

Dammerung turned and looked up the staircase vault. "It's a goodly house. It needs more open windows, but so long as it is not a drain on the revenue I don't see why you should give it up. I'll have a look over your husband's books just to see where you stand and where you may need help. Is his room upstairs?"

"Yes, but—well!" Mrs. Coventry added as Dammerung began climbing the stairs, making himself at home.

"Margaret," he called back down, "if there is anything you need to take, best pack it up. Oh—hullo! You must be Barker..."

"Well!"

If only she would be reduced to that one word for the next five minutes, I might have a little peace. Skirting past her, Margaret, too, began climbing the stair.

Her mother sprang to life. "Just you wait, young missy! Who is this fellow? Where are you going off to? I hope it's to buy wedding clothes!"

A tread went off underfoot like a shotgun. She had forgot about that. "We're going back to his estate, Mother. We left his cousin in charge—"

"Oh, he's got a cousin, has he? Is *he* married?"

Margaret's mouth opened in a silent scream. "His cousin is engaged to be married. His brother just died—"

"Oh, and so you're going to make it to *that* funeral!"

Come to think of it, I would rather miss that too. "Yes, Mother, in all probability, I will be at that funeral."

Her mother began climbing the stair behind her. "So you can't make it to your father's funeral, but you can go to a complete stranger's. I like that. Young people these days—!"

The blood, the fire. The wrack and ruin. Brand's death. Men's faces twisted in agony. Rupert's face distorted out of recognition. The great winged man who smelled of death. Dammerung. The Great Blind Dragon.

Margaret turned at head of the stair and stood above her mother, fury trembling in every vein. "Be quiet," she said imperiously, "and have a little respect for the dead."

If it had been a dragon-spell, her words could not have stopped up her mother's mouth better. Mrs. Coventry stood mute, her mouth hanging a little open, and without a backward glance

Margaret left her like that and retired to her old, small, creaky-floored room with the single window and the sill that leaked a draft.

She looked condescendingly on the scene and smiled a little. There was nothing, she realized, that she wanted to take. These innocuous articles were the furniture of an old, nasty, tortuous life that lay on the other side of a long death, a long death and a slow, agonized climb to a new life. She went across the room to the window and looked out, looked up.

In the sky she could see the eye of the dragon looking down on her, blind and white. Her fingers brushed the pane.

Stand at the ready. We're coming back soon.

Dammerung's reflection bloomed in the window beside hers. His questing fingers worked round her hourglass; turning, she leaned into his embrace.

"Are they rich as kings?" she asked. "Can we leave them and never look back?"

"Probably not. Barker is getting the books down for me. An admirable sort of fellow—all seriousness and fur about the jaws. It took me some time to convince him that I was really permitted to look at the books. He seemed uncertain of my feet. I almost told him I was uncertain of his name, but then I thought better of it."

"What, Barker? That's an old name. No one thinks twice about it."

"Really! What a rummy place this is."

Down the hall the one tread on the stair went off like a cracker, and presently the sound of hurrying feet came to them. Amy appeared in the doorway, eyes agog as if she had never had a day like this one and was not sure what to make of it, and gasped out,

"Miss Coventry, your muther wants you in the parlour. Tha' cousin of yours, Miss Firethorne, has come home!"

Margaret stared at her insensible. Firethorne—that little white thing that had run away nearly a year ago?

"And, wha's more," Amy added as the climax, "she's got a burly great man of a husband with her!"

"It's a rummy, rummy world," said Dammerung.

ABOUT THE AUTHOR

JENNIFER FREITAG lives with her husband in a house they call Clickitting, with their two cats Minnow and Aquila, and their own fox kit due to be born in early December. Jennifer writes in no particular genre because she never learned how, she is make of sparks like Boys of Blur, and if she could grasp the elements, she would bend them like lightning. Until then, she sets words on fire. Living with her must be excruciating.